MASSIVE VINEGAR JOE PLATFORM

STEPHEN FRANCIS MONTAGNA

Printed in the United States of America
Published by: Stephen Francis Montagna

ISBN: 978-1-970301-12-0 PAPERBACK
ISBN: 978-1-970301-13-7 HARDBACK

PROLOGUE

December 21ˢᵗ, 1996. The war in the Middle East and Northern Africa was ended for well over a month, and the hordes of scientists set to work inside the all but destroyed nations of Israel, Egypt and Jordan in their attempt to try and save lives. These more friendly nations were only partially destroyed by the terrible war that raged there.

The countries making up the United Nations fixed the blame for the war on were all but abandoned for the present time. These nations were the last ones to be offered any form of help from the rest of the world. It was estimated it would take over fifty years before most of the Middle East, and also Northern Africa would finally return to near normal. A third of the world's oil reserves were lost for decades, locked in the nuclear hell released during the brief but devastating war, plunging many struggling small nations into sheer chaos. Many of these lesser nations lost most of their industrial development due to the loss of these much needed oil reserves. This caused the United States to change her opinion on nations classified as a thorn in its side. One such nation was Cuba. After years of anger between the two nations, Cuba was being recognized by the American President who was slowly releasing the stifling sanctions leveled on the tiny Island nation for many years.

President Albert Cole was the first American President ever to visit Cuba in over thirty years. The change in attitude came about when Cuba's aging Leader, Fidel Castro, denounced the actions of Iraq and Libya in their aggression in the Middle East. Another reason for this change of heart was Cuba's economy was in such terrible shape. Inflation was near a hundred percent, and many of Castro's people were slowly being starving to death. Crime ran rampant on the tiny Island, as gangs of criminals and toughs stole from the poor, and Castro's police forces were almost powerless to stop the attacks on his own civilians.

On the American Leader's visit to Cuba, President Cole promised Castro two billion dollars in financial aid, with another two billion in six months. This time frame would assure the United States government Castro was going to live up to his side of the bargain, and hold free elections on the Island. Castro gave in to this demand because of the poor shape his country was in. Despite everything one heard about Castro, there was one fact no one could deny. He loved his people, and was willing to do anything to help them.

Castro's once powerful military machine was about non-existent, and what soldiers he had left on active duty, were reduced to riding bicycles for transportation. Castro still had some ancient Soviet tanks under his power, but they were about useless because he did not have the fuel or ammunition needed to run the aging and defend the rusting war machines, and he was no longer willing to continue his tightfisted military stranglehold on his people. Thousands of Cuban refugees, who once fled to the United States, poured their monies back into Cuba to help their people survive until the stifling sanctions were lifted against the Island and people. Castro used a large chunk of the money to rebuild his depleted police forces, thus bringing some form of stability back to his country.

Some United States companies slowly returned to help rebuild the crumbling infrastructure of the country. Construction companies from all over the world moved in, bringing their workers, especially from the United States, helping with the stimulation of the American economy also.

Other agreeable changes took place throughout the rest of the world. The North American Free Trade Agreement was a disaster and Mexico would still not allow any American ownership of their country in the Bolgin exchange, or American companies to own any Mexico land. The Mexicans hated and discriminated terribly against the American companies. Yet, the American companies continued to drift across the border, to take advantage of the much cheaper wages, and lack of medical coverage needed for the Mexican workers.

Another one of the reasons for the agreement's failure was the automobile companies was infiltrated by drug traffickers. Every nook and cranny in the majority of American cars built in Mexico, were packed with drugs. It was so bad the United States Customs built factories on the United States side of the border; one was built to take apart and examine the cars coming into the United States. After removing the drugs, the car parts went to a second factory that rebuilt it and then sent it on its way to the American public. The joke was the trade agreement created jobs for the United States workers, by having them take the cars built in Mexico apart and then rebuild them. This added over three thousand dollars to the price of the imported vehicles, and caused the car manufacturers to abandon their plants built in Mexico, and head back to the United States so they could bring down their prices again.

Drugs were flooding into the United States from Mexico in about any imported goods they could be stuffed in. Typewriter carriages were hollowed and packed with drugs. Drugs were found in fake bottoms of paint cans and anything was used to flood drugs into the United States. Eventually, all but a few American companies who jumped across the border to Mexico were finally forced by increasing their prices to come back over the border to the United States.

The trade agreement was not a total flop though. The agreement with Canada was working well; it leads to dismantling of most of the border regulations. The Canadian and United States border guards were still in place, but this was a formality. This part of the agreement was working out so well Canada and the United States, worked on plans to align the tax structure to be equal on both sides of the border. Both nations began to pool the taxes of the workers to help both countries expand their interests. Canada even toyed around with the idea of using American money as their nation's currency.

With this new cooperation between the two nations, led Congress to act on the concept of mutual borders not only with Canada, but England also. The idea was a popular one with many citizens of the United States, England and Canada. American citizens were for the idea, because many felt Canada and England always backed the United States, and vice versa. This feeling extended all the way from the First World War, to the recent war with Libya.

One Congressman observed England and Canada deserved some special treatment, because they stood by the United States in her times of need, and they pointed out these were the few countries we could always depend on. He also wanted to include France in his offer, but that request was not so well welcomed. These statements were well received by the people of the United States, England and Canada, and the plan of mutual borders with Canada and England, and possibly France, was sure to pass the vote in Congress that month.

An agreement between the three nations involved, would cause the standard currency to be based on the much strong

American dollar. The demise of the European trade agreement, along with the breakup of the once powerful so called Seven, caused by countless disagreements among the countries involved, and this made the United States the major target for many separate and private agreements and arguments.

America's economy was hurting also, until President Cole gave a jump start to the construction field, by pumping one hundred billion dollars into new construction, rather than to dump another ten billion dollars into the unemployment system again. With this program, jobs were created by the monies spent by the government.

The attempt at taxing the rich to death, and also taxing the economy back to prosperity, was a complete disaster. Taxing the rich only caused the job market to shrink rapidly, because the rich did not invest in creating any new jobs, and the rich also refrained from any further expansion plans. Thus, fewer jobs were created with this trend. Many programs of giving to the poor without them trying to help themselves caused the working people to revolt and drive the past President and certain Democratic members of Congress out of office. There were calls for the former President Bush to come out of retirement, and to take over the country, but President Bush would not budge and answer the call. But when he put his confidence behind President Cole, he took over the office by a land slide, with seventy percent of the popular vote.

President Cole incorporated the help of former President Bush in another way, and had him work on creating jobs, and getting a handle on inflation eating a hole in the country's heart. When the rich realized they were going to hold onto more of their hard earned money, as one tax increase after the other was lifted, they began to invest heavily in their country and her people again. Business picked up as more people found good paying jobs in the construction field, helping to put more people back to work. With so many companies coming back into the United States, more people were suddenly able to find steady and well paying jobs.

While all this was going on, General Edward (Popeye) Campanelli returned home from the war in the Middle East and Northern Africa, and lived in New York for two months. Most of his minor wounds he received when his helicopter was shot down healed. The wound he received to his heart when Captain Renee Mendoza died in the same helicopter crash was far from forgotten though. His merely existed around the house was exactly that, an existence. He no longer loved his wife, and if Mendoza survived the helicopter crash, he knew he would no longer be married to his present wife, and he would have taken Mendoza as his new wife.

They drifted apart over the many years of marriage, particularly because he was working for the government, either protecting some politician's life, or making an attack on a pack of terrorists who had taken American hostages somewhere in the world. He was deeply involved in the Panama situation and the Granada mess also. But the straw that broke the camels back as far as his marriage was concerned, occurred when he went off to war during the Libyan attack on Chad, and then the Sudan.

His son barely took notice of him any longer. So he was going off to the VFW Post more and more lately, or getting involved with anything involving the military. He was sort of retired, the brass knew of his love affair with Captain Renee Mendoza, and the trouble his marriage was in. Yet, the government was not through with the General quite yet, because they had information of trouble heading America's way again, and it was decided to keep the hurting General hanging on until the present danger came to a head one way or the other.

The General was kept in the service by requiring him to report to Camp Smith on the fourth weekend of every month, to have him keep up with the current events. He did not mind the slight inconveniences, because he kept his medical coverage intact, and it gave him something important to do with his life than just existing and bugging his wife.

Everything in his life came to a head one day when he was kind of hanging around the house driving his wife nuts, mainly because he had nothing to do with his life. An argument started over nothing, and it kept running for most of the afternoon. It went on until his wife had enough and she broke down and cried. To see her cry broke his heart, and he pulled her close to him and whispered at her. "Hey honey, this is no good, we're killing each other, and we have to do something before it gets out of hand on us. We can't keep going on driving ourselves crazy like this. It's no good for either of us or the little one."

His wife stopped crying and stared in his eyes for a long moment. She knew she still loved him as she cried. "What do you think we should do about us then, Edward?"

He did not realize his wife still loved him, because he felt he was letting her out of an impossible situation when he smiled, and suggested they try a trial separation for a few months.

His wife cried as she pulled away from him, and ran from the room. She lay on their bed crying when he came in and sat down next to her, and softly stroked her hair as he offered, "C'mon baby, what's this about? You know everything's gone between us baby, and we're only going through the motions. It's been months since we last shared a bed together honey."

His wife stopped crying and rolled over and sat on the edge of the bed, and then she stared at him as she replied, "Maybe it's over for you, but I happen to still love you, you know Edward."

He was stunned as he replied with surprise lacing his voice. "I didn't know you still loved me. How the devil could you after all I put through? Bringing up our son almost single handed while I was off playing soldier somewhere in the world, how the hell could you still love me?"

"Well, I still do love you, and I can't explain why you know when I don't know why myself. I was so lonely all those times when you were called back for active duty by the government, worrying about you every second of the day." his wife replied.

"Gees honey, this really messes things up a might in my mind. The only reason I wanted a separation, was because I thought I was wasting your time. Look honey, I think I'd like to try it again, if you don't mind that is. But I don't think we should try it from here though baby."

She looked at him, and then asked, "What do you mean by not here Edward?"

"I think if we're going to try to save our marriage then I think we should move the hell outta here and start all over in a new place."

"Where do you want to move to Eddy?" Her words allowed an edge of excitement in her tone.

"Well, for a long time now, I've been thinking about moving down to Florida, honey. You know, the fishing and great weather down there and the fun we can have down there."

"Florida! But you hate the warm weather. How are you ever going to get along in Florida?"

"Honey, you have to remember something. The last three projects I was involved in were carried out in warm climates. I guess I become acclimated to the warmer weather now baby."

This surprised his wife; she always wanted to move down south. That's before she came to love where she lived for the past seventeen years. She loved Carmel, in Upstate New York, but she had to admit the idea of moving down to Florida intrigued her, as she offered her husband, "Ed, I think I like the idea honey. When do you want to move to Florida?"

"We're going to have to put this place up for sale first, and then take care of all the damn details pertaining to the sale while we're waiting for the place to sell, baby."

His wife smiled and added, "I can help. A girl at work has been telling me she wanted to move up here. I can tell her our place is up for sale, and see what she thinks of the place."

"Great, you know something; I think this is going to work out pretty well for us, baby."

"Ed, where do you want to move to in Florida? I don't know very much about the state or where the best place to live down there is," she repeated with some concern in her tone.

"I've been doing some reading about Venice. It's just outside of Sarasota, or Clearwater I believe, honey," he replied as he gave his concerned wife his full attention now.

"Gees, I guess you really have been thinking about this for quite a while I see, Edward." She smiled again at him as she added to her words to her husband, "Do you really think we can start over again and make it work Eddy?"

"Sure, why the hell not honey. We've been through tougher times than this together baby."

Suddenly, she became serious as she stared in her husband's eyes for several moments, before getting the strength to ask, "Ed, have you ever cheated on me, when you were away I mean."

General Edward Campanelli gave a quick nervous laugh as he tapped her lightly on the hip and replied in a soft tone to her, "C'mon honey, don't try and start any of that crap again please. Let's not go there for now baby. Let the past die will you please honey."

"I have to know this, for my own peace of mind, Edward," his wife was pressing the issue as she continued to stare him in the eyes and waited his reply.

The General knew his wife was not going to get off this subject, so he finally retorted, "Let me ask you a question if you don't mind first please baby. Honey, have you ever cheated on me while I was away so much from you in our lives?"

His wife slowly lowered her eyes until she was staring down at the floor, but she refused to answer his last question her husband just asked of her.

He got real serious and pressed the issue this time as he told her, "Look at me, look at me I said, dammit. I want to look at you in your eyes when you answer me." He started in his wife's lovely eyes for the moment.

His wife slowly raised her head so she could look at her husband, but she still did not answer his question of her.

"Sonofabitch," He cried as he jumped up and began to pace around the room until he finally mumbled at his wife, "you had a fucking affair!" He suddenly yelled as he rubbed his face as if he was slapped in his face. His wife did not deny it as she just stared back at him.

He let out his breath in a sigh as he got control of his anger, and then he offered kindly, "Hell baby, I guess I can't really blame you any if you had an affair with some guy. I've been a real big bag of shit of a stinking husband to you over the past few years I guess, my love."

His wife gave a slight smile as she stared back at her husband for a moment.

"I guess I better tell you all about my affair then honey. I think you better sit back for this one, because this is going to take a little while to explain to you, honey." He then began to explain about Mendoza and her death.

CHAPTER 1
BEIJING, CHINA

At a specially called for meeting between certain members of the Chinese Ruling Party, plans were being set forward by the chosen few. The subject being discussed was the fate of Hong Kong. Most of the members of this Council were seated as the Chairman, Mao Cheng-yu and his Vice Chairman entered the room, and they quickly took their seats.

The Chinese War Council became quiet as the powerful leader of their nation looked over the gathering faces of the

Ministers, as a smile slowly crossed his cracked and aged lips. His eyes stopped searching when he found the face of the Minister of State Security, Hong Kuo Feng. His smile then widened as the middle aged Minister nodded back at the old and respected Chinese Chairman. He then began to address the council members. The Chairman was well aware that certain members of the committee were conveniently omitted from this private meeting, solely because of their extremely radical views of opening China's shores to the hated western ways. Along with the constant arguments these few ministers always started at any meeting lately.

The few conversations taking place in the meeting room came to an immediate halt when the Chairman rose and remarked, "Good afternoon gentlemen, I guess you're all wondering why I invited you here on such short notice. I'll enjoy explaining why, it has come to my attention the worthless English fools, along with a number of other nations doing business with Hong Kong, are presently involved in removing vast sums of money from our country, in lieu of our retaking control over the Colony in 1999. I want to place an immediate stop to this constant draining of funds from our country. Hong Kong will be worthless to us if these lowly mongrels remove everything of worth from the Colony, our Colony."

The elderly Chairman paused when the Minister of Commerce, Jin Yeh-pin stood, signifying he wished to address the Council members. The Chinese Leader nodded and the Minister bowed and began speaking right off. "Mr. Chairman and Ministers. I don't understand, the money belong to the countries removing it from Hong Kong, sir. I feel they're entitled to it and..."

The Chairman instantly and angrily slammed his fist on the table as he cut the Minister off by screaming savagely at him.

"If the money was made on Chinese soil! Then it belongs to the Chinese people, not to these godless hated lowly mongrels who used the land of China to fill their filthy pockets with the riches of China, at the price of the poor Chinese workers."

The deeply concerned Minister tried to interrupt the raging Chairman, but Cheng-yu ignored him and roared on at everyone attending the meeting. "I omitted some other foolish members of this office from this meeting, for the same exact reasons you're creating here, Minister. I have not called you here for a discussion, I called you here to tell you what is happening in Hong Kong, and I intend to put an immediate stop to this stealing, before the lowly horde of mongrels remove all of Hong Kong's funds. This is currency China desperately needs to survive in these hard times we find ourselves locked in."

The Minister of Commerce tried to interrupt the Chairman a second time, because he did not understand what he was trying to do. The elderly Chairman refused to be interrupted, as he shot a harsh glare at the concerned Minister, and then slammed his fist on the desktop again as he warned. "If you wish to keep your worthless head resting upon your shoulders for the remainder of this day, you'll keep quiet until I'm finished speaking to you and the other Ministers."

The Chairman's glare was more than enough to make the Minister of Commerce to retake his seat. He slowly lowered his eyes and then stared at the table surface, hoping the extremely angry Chairman would not order him killed for his impertinence displayed at the meeting.

"As I said, the worthless English mongrels are removing vast sums of monies from our country, and I'll put a stop to it. This money belongs to the people of China for the years these hordes of mongrels made profits on our soil, with the labor offered by our Chinese peoples."

The Minister of Justice stood and waited to be recognized, so he could address the members.

The Chairman nodded and in return, the Minister bowed to the old man before he spoke. "Mr. Chairman, Ministers, I happen to agree with the Chairman, these monies belong to China. But how are we going to place an end to these fools removing these funds from China's lands?"

"That is a good question Mr. Yu-wei, and I'll answer it. I have a plan; I worked this out with the Vice Chairman, and the Central Military Commission President, Yang So. We intend to make an offer to extend the lease on Hong Kong to the English fools, for another twenty years. We'll make this offer maybe as early as tomorrow morning. We're certain when the English know they're going to have Hong Kong for another twenty years. They shall redeposit their foul stocks, bonds, precious metals, art treasures, and over one trillion dollars in cash, and then cease removing more monies from China. When we're certain the money is redeposited in China's banks, we'll move in with our troops and forcibly remove the hated English and the godless mongrels that take from the Chinese people, and never give anything back to China."

There was a low murmuring between the members, but this came to an immediate end when the old man raised his weathered arms over his balding head and grumbled, "Gentlemen, allow me continue with my plans. There is much more to this, there'll be plenty of time later for any questions. We have come up with an idea to take suspicions off our true intentions. A predator's defense in an attack is camouflage, no? And this is our camouflage. We're going to call for a special meeting of the Security Council. We'll prey on their fears of the nuclear threat constantly coming from North Korea fools. At this meeting, we'll make an offer to invade North Korea alone, to disarm those foul fools of their nuclear weapons and foolish aims.

"Once we invaded North Korea, we'll destroy their population, keeping alive enough of the worthless mongrels as workers for our purposes and needs. All the members of the United Nation's Council will fall over themselves to accept this offer from us, when they realize it'll cost them nothing in money or their cursed soldiers or their military equipment.

"I need not remind everyone attending this meeting, because you know it's a matter of time before the United States decides to do something about North Korea, and we might as well do it before they react. Think of the mileage we could get out of this situation by attacking North Korea. World opinion would be as great towards us, as it was for the United States when they invaded Iraq a few years ago. No members of the free world would dare talk against us, and once England realizes we're trying to eliminate an extremely dangerous and highly unstable situation. They'll be more than pleased to stay in Hong Kong, and bring back their foul money so we can confiscate it on the fools. Once we destroyed North Korea, we'll make peaceful overtones towards South Korea, and we should be able to take over South Korea peacefully, without a shot being fired. If not, they'll receive the same fate that'll befall the North Korea dog eaters. Neither of the Korea's deserves a place in the civilized world. We'll turn the two Korea's into one massive military and civilian seaport that'll serve China well for us.

"When we have the Korean lands, we can mass our troops on the coast looking towards Japan. I doubt even the United States would mind if we attack Japan. We'll offer the United

States a deal she cannot refuse. If she allows us to attack Japan, we'll take Japan and erase the great debt owed by the United States to Japan. We'll regard the debt paid in full. They'd be sheer fools not to accept this wise offer," The wise Chairman stopped speaking for a second, and looked at all the members. He saw many of them shaking their heads in the negative over his remarks.

The Chairman did an immediate about face to try and save face as he offered in a rush. "We can mass our troops on the coast with Japan, and allow the United States talk us out of further threats towards Japan. This way we could build up the United States position, and they'll save face with their Japanese friends, because we'll allow the Americans to think they saved the foul hides of the Japanese people. Let me remind all you gathered here at this meeting of our goals. Our plans consist of taking Hong Kong anyway, when we're certain the hated English monies are returned to the Colony. Then, when we have Hong Kong under our control again, we'll attack that miserable Island of Taiwan."

This time the murmurs almost droned out the old Chairman and he had to stop speaking.

The Minister of Railways, Long Shao-chi and the Minister of Coal Industry, Kang Yao-pang, along with Minister of Nuclear Industry, Zeng Chi-mao rose and the rest quieted.

The Chairman looked at the Minister of Nuclear Industry. He trusted this younger man and he nodded as he took his seat. The Minister bowed to the Chairman, but he was drinking water and did not notice the politeness as the Minister began speaking, "Mr. Chairman, Ministers, we have to move with wise caution in this endeavor. We could be talking about starting another World War, maybe the last one the earth could stand, especially with the war in the Middle East fresh in the minds of the world. I fear they might react quickly to our threats, and cause this plan to blow up in our faces, thus ending in the destruction of our great nation of China."

The old Chinese Chairman and leader of China instantly jumped to his feet and warned the members with surprising strength in his voice, "And who'll stop us you great fool of fools, Russia? Don't be an ass, Comrade. There is no more Russia to take any fear of. Only a shell of that worthless nation lives on, selling off its once mighty military power to the highest bidder. Russia is like an old whore with her legs spread wide for the rest of the world to take advantage of. The United States? I doubt she'd get involved in a war with us. First, the United States would try and bore us to death with endless talk and angry rhetoric, and then they'd resort to threats. By the time the United States takes an active role in this upcoming war, it'd be far too late for her to make any real difference in the final outcome.

"America's children would become mere rifle fodder for our far superior fighting soldiers. Japan? Japan will never send her children to die in a war against China. She'd rather pay some other nation to send their children to their deaths, and it'll not be the Americans this time. Remember, Japan has thrown the Americans out of Japan, America's closest operating military base to China. The United States no longer has any military bases in operation in the Philippines. They too have driven the powerful Americans off their soil. Besides, the United States is still reeling from the great loss of American lives in the Middle East war, the results of America's involvement in the biological and nuclear war there. Now, their closest military base to China is Guam, and that base is far too small an Island to mount any substantial attack against us."

"What about their military bases in South Korea?" the Minister of Nuclear Industry asked.

"Again, I repeat to you. When we attack North Korea, with the blessings of the United States mind you, and also from the other worthless members of the Security Council of that useless establishment, we shall offer peace terms to South Korea. Once they accepted our terms of peace, we'll slowly takeover all of South Korea, until we have enough power to take the entire country over. Then we'll demand the United States close down their military bases in South Korea, and leave the country all together. Thus, we'll have a gateway opened to Japan, or against the Colony of Hong Kong, and then Taiwan. But I promise you this much, once this plan is set in motion, there shall be no turning back. We'll succeed, and we'll own the two Korea's, Japan if we want, with Hong Kong and Taiwan under our control. Then we'll be free to turn our full military attention against the Philippines, Vietnam, and then finally Russia."

Most of the Ministers at the meeting were in shock by the Chairman's so casual talk of world conquest. The Supreme People's Court President, Tseng Chung stood and then he faced the powerful Chairman. All the talk came to an end as one of the most powerful people in China requested permission to address the Chairman and the other Ministers of China.

The Chairman could not help himself and his eyes flashed anger as the Court's President slowly stood. Chairman Cheng-yu felt he could rely on the Court's President to back anything he decided to do for China and her people. Mao Cheng-yu stared at Tseng Chung intensely for a long second before he finally gave him permission to speak.

The powerful President Chung bowed towards Chairman Cheng-yu as he offered in a calm and controlled tone of voice, "Mr. Chairman, with the trends China has bent to over the past few years, I fear China might be torn apart from within. If we were to follow this plan, and allow it to proceed further then what you have suggested to us here today, sir."

The Chairman shot a flash of sheer anger at the old people's President as he hissed savagely at him. "Chung, I fail to see where your concern is based on. What do you mean by China being torn apart from the inside?" he stopped speaking and stared at the President, hoping he would get the message, and stop doubting him and his ideas for the future of China and her people.

The People's Court President Chung did not take the warning as issued; he was suddenly highly insulted the Chairman dared to omit Mister or President before addressing him as he groused at the old man. "Mr. Chairman, we have to remember the civil unrest that plagued China in the past, when the Ruling Party made unfavorable decisions concerning the youth of our country. Look at the terrible blemish we suffered through during the unruly Tiananmen Square movement. Three thousand of our young children were killed when we were forced to bring the soldiers in, and we watched in horror as they fired on our defenseless children. We have to remember the out of control riots when we stayed out of the war in the Middle East.

"No Chairman, I fear what will happen to China from within as well as from without, if we were to place your plan in full operation, sir. How many more of our children will we kill this time, sir? I beg you to reconsider what you have proposed today, sir. We have three years before the English have to be out of Hong Kong, because of the extension we already extended them. I'm certain if we try, we could come up with a far less war like way to take over Hong Kong, and get our hands on the English money at the same time.

Maybe we should even consider selling Hong Kong outright to the foolish United Kingdom for a large sum of money, if we truly need funds as badly as you suggested." The Court President stopped talking and bowed to the leader sitting at the front of the table, and then sat down.

The Chairman decided this speech just cost President Tseng Chung his life, for displaying his weaknesses to him and the other Ministers attending the meeting. He looked to General Jiyun, and gave him a slight nod. General Jiyun put a sneer on his lips as he looked to the Supreme People's Court President Tseng Chung, and then back to the well aged Chairman.

When the message passed to the Chinese General, the Chairman puffed up his chest as he rose and yelled at the other members at the meeting. "I for one am sick and tired of hearing about this Tiananmen Square disaster we allowed to take place against our rule over China and her people in the first place. Some of the great fools in this country blame anything that goes wrong on this cursed riot we crushed under the treads of our main battle tanks. These foolish children of China received exactly what they justly deserved for trying to defy their government's orders and wants. They're the ones who chosen to go against the government, and we had to put a stop to their treason, before it spread to the rest of the country."

Chung stood and spoke before he was recognized, "This is what I was trying to say. If we go along with this plan our youth will surely riot, and then we'll send out the Army again to kil..."

The Chairman screamed over President Chung's last words. "Quiet you worthless mongrel you! I did not give you permission to speak again. I caution you to remember where you are, and to whom you speak, before I have your head removed for your insolence."

Both men stood staring at each other until Tseng Chung decided he had better take his seat.

When he was seated, the Chairman shot a hot glare at the General, and he went in action. The General and two soldiers walked up behind the Supreme People's President before he could sit down. The soldiers took the President's arms and yanked him out of his chair as the General snarled at him. "You follow me!" his spittle sprayed the President's face and suit as he talked.

The soldiers forced Chung's arms behind his back, and then they dragged him out to his death.

The warning had not gone unnoticed by the other members of the meeting, as everyone made up their minds not to challenge the Chairman further with his plans for the future of China. The room remained deathly silent until there was a shot fired outside of the building, causing many to flinch. Then they heard the old man mutter. "Just punishment for all traitors."

It took the Chinese Chairman a few seconds to build himself up to a fever pitch again. He ranted and raved a great show for the weak and scared Ministers. "I had it with the youth of our country. They look too much at the West and their evil ways, thus destroying our country. These ideas of freedom, bah. These foolish children of China don't understand they're already free to do whatever they want to do here in China. I'll not bend a knee under their threat of another Tiananmen Square demonstration. If one takes place again, I'll order our tanks not to stop for anyone who tries to block their path this time. I'll not allow any troublemakers another hero to look up to. I'll make it a law for our soldiers to go in the country, and arrest any troublemakers of the past before they have a chance to make more trouble for this country.

"If trouble comes, I'll order our soldiers to squash any riots before they start. I'll cut off all communications with the outside world, and then I'll deport the hatful news reporters before they can transmit their lies to the rest of the world. I'll select certain reporters who favor China's interests to stay, and tell the world what is truly happening in China, until we put a stop to any rioting. I have the support of the Army, Navy and Air Force. I'll have any Ministers not in full support of my plans, eliminated, just as I had this mongrel Tseng Chung shot." The old man stopped speaking and looked to the Supreme People's Court Vice President, Yao Yuan, sitting with his head down. "Mr. Yuan!" Chairman Cheng-yu called out at him angrily.

Yuan's head snapped up and he looked at Chairman Cheng-yu.

"Mr. Yuan, you're the new acting President of the People's Court, sir."

Yuan rose and bowed towards the old man. A smile crossed his lips, a look informing the wise Chairman he was glad for his life, and he would do anything he asked of him.

The Chairman spoke to the rest of the Ministers at the meeting, "I'm certain everyone knows certain Ministers were not invited to this meeting. This was not a mistake on my part; I did not invite them, because I knew I could not trust them to stay the line. You'll never see these fools alive in China again." Chairman Mao Cheng-yu shot a glance at the Minister of Finance, and Mr. Ling stood and bowed towards the old man to show his support.

The Chinese Chairman Cheng-yu, smiled at the Minister as he offered, "That's much better. I know I have not given you all the conditions of my plan, I intend to give you a complete workup of the plan. But I'm going to start the wheels in motion right now. Mr. Chow, our Ambassador to the United Nations, and our Representative to the Security Council, will be ordered to request a special meeting of that Council to be convened by no later than this Monday. This gives us exactly six days to prepare our plans for immediate employment. At this worthless meeting, we'll inform the members of that foolish Council that China is willing to tackle the problem of North Korea and its nuclear ambitions on our own accord. I have no idea how the great fools will react to our kind offer, but I'm positive the fools will allow us to go after North Korea as long as it does not cost them any money or lives. We know we have to act before the other members of the Council take the lead, and they choose to attack that wasted nation first.

"When Mr. Chow requests this emergency meeting take place, he'll have the liberty to invite the six nations who'll make up the Security Council of the United Nations. I'll order him to invite Japan, India, Italy, Spain, Canada and Sweden. I'll not tolerate any argument about these choices. These nations will have the most to lose if North Korea continues her development of nuclear weapons. You must understand we too have a lot to lose if North Korea develops the nuclear bomb to fit their rockets. We know they have rockets strong enough to reach Japan or Peking, and if they arm them with nuclear tips, we'll have a major problem on our hands."

The elderly Chinese Chairman took a quick drink as his arms shook from the strain his body was under, while he talked about bringing China under a war footing over North Korea, and he took another sip and then he offered, "I see by your eyes you question why I want Japan as an invited nation to the requested Security Council meeting. I'll explain my thought to you further, because of the position they assumed during the Middle East, Northern Africa war. They lost their right of sitting in on any Security Council meetings any further. Plus, there have been bad feelings existing between our two countries for many years now. But I'll now put these ill feelings aside, it's a short distance from North Korea to Japan.

"North Korea is a poor nation of lowly mongrels, and we read the papers last year when the North Korean government actually contacted us concerning a possible invasion of Japan. At that time, North Korea wanted our help in their planned attack to enable them to take over that nation of lowly mongrels. The Korean fools planned to raid the countries' banks and steal Japan's great wealth, much the same way we want to take over Hong Kong, and take the English monies. I have to admit, their plan gave birth to ours. We allowed these secret papers from the North Korean government to fall into the hands of the hated Americans, to show them what the threat North Korea was about. The foolish Americans did not take action because they were on the outs with Japan, over her selling of their fighter planes to the Libyans during the war.

"The worthless leaders of the United States chose to sit on their dom rumps on this information, but Ambassador Chow's job will be to make certain this information surfaces at this requested Security Council meeting. Not in a way it'd hurt the foolish Americans in any way. We'll have need of their future help, if we're to be successful in talking the Security Council into allowing us to attack that mongrel nation of North Korea. This explains why we want Japan to sit in on this special meeting of the next Security Council with us.

"Ambassador Chow is instructed to send over an exact copy of the proposed North Korean, Japanese invasion plans to the Japanese Ambassador himself. In this manner, they'll apply more pressure on the Security Council, and the United Nations. To help Japan fend off any impending invasion by the two Koreas. I hope I explained the plan to your satisfaction at this time. If not, I'll entertain some questions now." Chairman Cheng-yu took his chair, allowing the Vice Chairman to field any questions from the other members at the meeting. The old man was having a little trouble stopping his hands from shaking, and controlling his breathing at the same time. He knew his remaining days were numbered, because his health was rapidly failing him.

The Minister of Petroleum Industry stood, and the Vice Chairman nodded at him.

"Mr. Chao Tso Jen, how soon will you put this plan into operation sir?"

The Vice Chairman smiled, and then he replied in a sharp tone of voice, "Immediately after this meeting is over. I'll be in direct contact with Ambassador Chow, and I'll instruct him to request the special meeting with the United Nations to be convened. It'll be up to the Security Council as to how and when we'll start our operation in motion against North Korea. I believe we could start massing our troops on the Chinese, North Korean border by no earlier than January 18th, 1997, and we should be in full operation by no later than February the first."

The Minister of National Defense, Ting Chung stood and then he waited.

Vice Chairman nodded his head slightly, and then he in turn and bowed to the Chairman.

"Mr. Vice Chairman, how long will it take for us to destroy North Korea and how many of our troops will we employ for this operation against North Korea, sir? How the devil are we going to protect the nation if we have to use so many of our military troops in this mission, sir?"

The Vice Chairman retorted to the concerned minister, "It's good you ask questions of me. It shows me you're thinking. I have a list, we'll commit the 11th Group Army, consisting of One Tank, One Mechanized, and Two full Motorized Divisions backed by Two Infantry Units, the 15th Group Army, consisting of One Airborne and Two Infantry Divisions, One light, One heavy backed by light tanks and many helicopters, the 21st Group Army, consisting of One full Tank, and Three Infantry Divisions. The 5th (Mountain) Group Army, there are Four Infantry Divisions back by Twenty Four helicopters, and the 35th Group Army of One Tank, One Motorized and Two Infantry Divisions. This will leave our nation with Thirteen full Army Groups to protect China from within and without, sir. More than a million soldiers will remain inside our country, more than enough to protect us from any attack, or riot no matter how well organized it might be aimed against us. We feel we should overrun North Korea in thirty five days."

"What do you think our losses will be to us?" the Minister of National Defense asked.

This angered the powerful Vice Chairman, because he did not like being interrupted, and he shot a hot glare at the Minister who immediately put his head down, because of the severe reprimand he received. The younger Vice Chairman had to quickly thumb through a stack of papers sitting in front of him, before he found the requested information.

"Ahhh..., here is the information I was searching for," The Vice Chairman offered with a snap in his voice as he pulled a page from the stack and then continued his words. "we're going to commit over three hundred and thirty thousand ground forces to this operation, and out of this number of soldiers. We're expecting to lose no more than thirty thousand with another fifty thousand wounded. We shall also commit two thousand tanks, and seventy infantry fighting vehicles, one thousand armored personnel carriers, plus a thousand pieces of artillery. Out of this, we expect to lose fifty tanks, ten IFVs and fifty APCs. We're also committing a thousand long range fighter planes, and a thousand heavy bombers. We'll begin our preemptive invasion of North Korea by sending in our advance troops to sabotage airfields and aircraft. We have numerous sympathizers to our cause ready to destroy many of their worthless radar and SAM missile launchers, before we're to begin our attacks on the two Koreas, sir."

The Vice Chairman looked at his watch and announced, "Gentlemen, it's getting late, and I have people I have to get in touch with, to get this operation moving before this day is over."

The Chairman and Vice Chairman left the room. The Ministers bowed as they watched them leave. When they were out of the room, conversations erupted as Ministers paired off and left.

When the old Chairman and his Vice Chairman got back to their offices, the Vice Chairman placed a call to Chow, their Ambassador to the United Nations. Chao Tso Jin explained what was expected from him, and Ambassador Chow let Tso Jen know he understood his instructions.

When the Ambassador hung up with the Vice Chairman of China, he immediately placed a call to the French Ambassador, who was the current Secretary General of the Security Council. When Ambassador Bartlett answered his phone, Ambassador Chow quickly explained about the

North Korean plot the Chinese government uncovered, concerning how North Korea was planning to invade Japan in the near future militarily.

The deeply concerned French Ambassador and acting President of the Security Council, was stunned by this revelation, and quickly informed the Chinese Ambassador he would convene an emergency Security Council meeting on January 9th, 1997.

Ambassador Chow asked the Frenchman if he would allow the nations of Japan, India, Italy, Spain, Canada, and Sweden to be invited nations, and sit in on the meeting as interested parties.

The French Delegate balked at China's want for Japan being invited to sit in on the Security Council meeting, but when the Chinese Delegate explained Japan had the most to lose if North Korea carried out their threat and invaded Japan. He further explained it was absolutely vital for the Japanese to be informed of this threat and to sit on the Council.

The Frenchman relented under Chow's heavy pressure, and he extended the invite to the nation of Japan, but he informed Ambassador Chow he was going to have to get the okay from the United States, before he could give permission for Japan to sit in on the meeting. To Bartlett's pleasant surprise, Ambassador Chow informed him he would be more than pleased to speak with the American Ambassador himself.

The French Delegate jumped on the offer, because he was not pleased to be the one to have to inform the American Ambassador of this new trouble arising from the moves of North Korea. Ambassador Bartlett informed Ambassador Chow he would get in touch with the other members of the

Council, and the invited members to get them to New York by January 9th.

Ambassador Chow then placed a call to the American Ambassador, Mr. Walters the moment he was off the phone with the French Ambassador. His secretary answered, and informed Chow the Ambassador was attending a special White House party. He informed the secretary this request to speak with him was an emergency. The secretary asked the Chinese Ambassador to hold the line. The line was disconnected, and music soon filled his ears.

WHITE HOUSE, WASHINGTON D.C.,
A PRIVATE PARTY IN THE GREAT HALL

In less than a minute, the concerned American Ambassador was on the line with the Chinese representative. Ambassador Chow could still hear the music playing in the background, and knew the Ambassador was still attending the party as he replied, "Yes Ambassador Chow Sir. How are you today sir? I'm quite certain this call must be extremely important, to disturb me while I'm attending this special White House gathering, sir?"

"I'm very well sir, thank you for asking of my health Mr. Walters, and this is of the utmost importance to you and your great nation, and you must forgive me for interrupting you at this gathering, sir." The Chinese Ambassador offered to his American counterpart kindly.

There was a slight pause before the American asked. "Sir, you told my secretary this was an emergency, sir. Can I ask you what form of an emergency this might be? I'm rather busy sir."

Ambassador Chow drew in air, and then let it out quickly in an attempt to calm his nerves and get his breathing under control as he offered, "Mr. Ambassador Sir, my government has in its possession certain documents informing us North Korea is planning to invade the Island of Japan, and possibly China in the near future, sir. We have the papers informing us the North Koreans are planning to explode their first nuclear weapon capable of affixing to the tip of one of their ballistic missiles later this month, and they're using the ruse of further talks with your country to stall for time to complete their tenth complete nuclear test. My government has informed me the United States already has these papers in their possession, about the pending attack by North Korea on South Korea and also Japan, sir. My government has no intention of embarrassing the United States over this matter in any way, shape or form, Mr. Ambassador. I've been instructed by my Chairman to act as if you have no prior information, sir."

The American politician winced, he was aware of the paper's existence as he replied. "I'm sure my government will be pleased to know this. What are you asking in return, Ambassador?"

The Chinese Delegate laughed as he offered back, "Ambassador Walters, I have no ulterior motives. My country wants to preserve the peace, that is all sir. If Korea goes through with their plans to build bombs, their bombs will not only threaten the world, but they'll also threaten the security of China. We'll not stand for this threat for one moment, sir."

"Ambassador Chow, exactly what is it you want my government to do for you sir?"

Again Ambassador Chow laughed as he replied, "Mr. Ambassador, my government doesn't want your country to do a thing about this present situation, sir. All we want of you, and your country Mr. Walters, is to attend a special meeting of the Security Council on January 9th, and I'll explain what China has in her mind, to eliminate this arising problem at this time, sir."

The remark of eliminating this problem with North Korea actually sent a slight shiver up the American politician's back as he replied to the Chinese Ambassador's chilling words, "Ambassador Chow, you peaked my interest, I'll certainly be there sir. It's strange this situation has come to the surface at this time sir. Just last week we held a special meeting with the Chiefs of Staff, Defense Secretary, and the President. We actually discussed this problem of North Korea going after the bomb at length. Many of our Generals requested permission for a special covert strategic attack on North Korea's nuclear facilities, sir. If your government's planning a military action, maybe we can hook up with your operation, and make a joint military venture out of this thing, to do the job completely so to say sir."

The Chinese Delegate immediately cut off the American politician as he replied to his request, "No Ambassador Walters, if we go into North Korea with our Armies, we'd like to go in alone sir. We don't wish to be the cause of America losing any more of her youth to pending war. Ambassador Walters, at this meeting, you'll learn exactly what my government has planned for this attack against North Korea, and you'll either back our plan completely, or you shall reject it if you so choose, sir. My government is extremely angry over this present situation, and feels this is an all Asian problem, better solved by Asian people and their soldiers, sir. That way, no country can say the United States, or any other country is favoring any one nation in this region. It'll save your country the problems it had to deal with over the Middle East war, when the Arab countries complained the United States favored Israel over Arab states, sir."

Ambassador Walters laughed this time as he replied to the Chinese politician, "Yes Sir Ambassador Chow I understand what you're saying sir. I'm quite certain my government will be thanking you for this kind consideration, sir. I'll be attending this meeting, and I'll be looking forward to meeting with you maybe in private then, sir. Maybe we can go out for a drink later after the meeting concluded, sir. I'm going to have to go; I'll inform my President about this situation you brought up to my attention during this phone conversation, and your call for a special Security Council meeting, sir. Thank you and have a good day sir."

"Yes, and you have a good party, and I shall be looking forward to sharing a drink with you after the Security Council meeting has been concluded as you suggested, sir" the Chinese Delegate said, his voice dripping with sarcasm.

The tone of his voice hit home with the American politician, and he snapped in not so friendly a tone of voice at him this time, "I have to go; I'll be talking with the President presently I assure you, Ambassador Chow." With that, Walters hung up on Ambassador Chow.

Ambassador Walters quickly scanned the group looking for the American Leader, spotting him he walked up to the President and stood off to his right, and waited for the American Leader to stop talking with two of the people attending the party. When the President acknowledged his presence, Walters made the quick remark, "My son's so proud; he just caught his first fish sir."

The President's arm sank slowly as he stared at the American Ambassador momentarily. His remark meant there was trouble, and he wanted to speak with him in private immediately as the President replied, "Is your son still on the line, Ambassador Walters?"

"Yes, he's speaking with his mother right now Mr. President Sir."

"Allow me to congratulate him," The President turned to the Senator. "Sir, excuse me."

The Florida Senator smiled, "Yes sir, some things have to be handled in person sir."

The President turned to Ambassador Walters and snapped at the well liked politician, "Follow me please, sir!" President Cole ordered an agent to find the Vice President and National Security Director for him, and inform them to head over to the Oval Office. "Tell them there's a crack in a window. That should get their asses in gear."

The serviceman was gone in a flash, as the President led the way with Ambassador Walters following him closely. When they entered the Office, the President took his seat and then asked the Ambassador who followed him to his office. "What the hell's going on that's so damn important it has forced me to leave this damn party, sir?"

The President nodded to the Nation Security Director Norman P. Griffin as he entered the Oval Office with concern in his eyes, and he quickly headed for his seat.

The Security Director nodded as he followed Norman into the office, and then he sat and looked at Ambassador Walters as he began to speak.

"With all due respect Mr. President Sir, I just received some rather startling information from the Chinese Ambassador, sir. The Chinese Delegate informed me he had certain evidence in his possession that North Korea was planning to fire off their first small nuclear detonation from a system that can be fitted to the tip of a ballistic missile, as early as this month sir. The Chinese government's rather concerned about this upcoming nuclear test Mr. President, and they planned to do something about it, sir. He's requesting, and received permission for an emergency meeting of the Security Council for later on this month, sir. The ninth in fact sir."

The Security Director interrupted as he offered with a smirk on his lips, "I bet the Chinese government's concerned about this upcoming North Korean nuclear test, sir. It's a definite threat to China's security, as well as to the security of the entire Asian region, Mr. Ambassador. Did their Ambassador inform you what they had in mind as their action against North Korea sir?"

Ambassador Walters turned to Norman and offered, "No Director Griffin, he did inform me what they plan, I'll be forced to wait until the Security Meeting to find out what they intended to do about the Korean nuclear test. Ambassador Chow informed me their government was going to introduce the papers about the invasion at this meeting, sir."

The President jumped to his feet and bitched angrily at the Ambassador, "Dammit to hell and back again, the damn Chinese told me they'd never bring those fucking papers up to the damn United Nations, Ambassador Walters. Do you know how bad we're going to look if this mess comes to the surface on us? We knew about those damn papers over a year ago, and we didn't react to them sir. The Japanese are going to scream the United States chose to abandon them, and they're going to be right dammit. It was the last President who was so angry at Japan for selling those damn fighter planes to the Libyan government, and he chose to do nothing about this damn threat until the North Koreans attacked Japan first. He was going to allow Japan to sweat for a while before he intervened, and I couldn't blame him in the least, dammit. Now, those damn Chinese are going to dump those papers in the lap of the United Nations, shit, shit."

Ambassador Walters offered to the extremely upset acting President of the United States, "With all due respect Mr. President, the Chinese Delegate informed me he was going to introduce these papers to the Council, as if he just received them himself, sir. He also informed me his government was going to protect the United States at all costs over this matter sir," the Ambassador tried a wasted smile on the President.

The Security Director piped in, "Uh-oh, when any foreign government wants to protect us, it usually means their country's preparing to stick it up our asses, Mr. President."

The President held up his hand and remarked, "Well gentlemen, I intend to find out, I'll place a call to Chairman Mao Cheng-yu when this meeting's over with. Ambassador Walters, I'll not send you to this Security Council meeting if we're going to be dumped on for not reacting to this threat to South Korea and Japan from North Korea, sir. I'm sick and tired of sending our kids to fight off another sonofabitch who thinks they can take over the damn world.

"Just look at the damn mess still taking place in Yugoslavia. The damn Serbs have all but annihilated the Moslems. I had no other choice but to send in our kids to be killed, because these assholes wanted to sterilize their country of a certain race of people. Another damn Nazi move if you asked me. For the life of me, I can't understand how soldiers can wage a war against children and unarmed civilians, dammit? How the hell can anyone who had a child, lift a gun in anger after seeing the slaughter done to these children of Bosnia? I can't stand by and witness that kind of sinful slaughter. We had to send in fighters then tanks and now troops, and yet the slaughter of children continue for Christ sake. I'm not going to be stuck sending our troops to North Korea again. Not unless we get some help from our damn Allies this time I tell you."

The President saw the look on the Vice President and Ambassador Walters' faces and he offered in a more calm voice, "I don't mean our real Allies of Canada and England. I mean our Allies like Italy, Spain, and the damn Alliance States. I'm tired of these other nations telling us to send in our troops, while they sit on their damn asses and complain our operation changed from what we proposed, to a different operation like that damn Somalia action. Hell, we went from feeding them to open warfare with the insurgents, and becoming targets to be forced out of that nation like we're the ones who done something wrong, and look at what happen when we left that damn nation. Their people are again dying by the hundreds and this time, no other nation is willing to lift a damn hand to help them, and I don't blame them."

Ambassador Walters stood in an attempt to cut off the President's anger by saying, "Mr. President Sir, from what I was able to gather from the Chinese Delegate, it looks like China wants to handle the entire military operation against North Korea for themselves this time, sir. Ambassador Chow informed me he didn't want us sending in any of our children this time, or spending our money defending Asia. He further informed me this was an Asian problem better off being settled by Asian troops this time, Mr. President Sir. Ambassador Chow told me this way, no one could possibly accuse the United States of taking any sides in this situation, sir."

The President suddenly smiled as he asked the American Ambassador with some concern lacing his voice, "Do you really think this politician could smell what he was shoveling?"

Laughter filled the Oval Office as Ambassador Walters answered the President's remark, "Mr. President Sir, I have to believe that the Chinese Delegate was acting in good faith with this offer, sir. What could they possibly be after if not to stop the North Koreans from developing a small enough nuclear weapon that could be mounted on one of their damn ballistic missiles? Invading North Korea for another reason sir? What the hell for sir? The damn country is dying on its own accord, and the North Korean people are starving and are down to eating grass to try and stay alive, and most of their natural resources are used up. Their air is bad, and there's no fish left in the seas surrounding their country.

"China is in some serious trouble herself, and she can ill afford any type of military operation, unless it was either to protect her nation's security. Or it'd bring the country a vast amount of much needed money in a fast hurry, and make it worthwhile to commit their troops to any action she wants to pursue. No, I have to believe China is not up to anything underhanded here, sir."

The Vice President chimed in and offered to the President, "I happen to agree with Mr. Walters on this one Albert. I've been approached by many investors lately, all of who told me they'd gladly invest in China, if her economy was in better shape. I don't think they could possibly sustain a military operation considering the economic conditions of China today, sir."

The Security Director offered as he got back into the conversation this time, "Has anyone heard anything from the Alliance States? They'd be up in arms if China moved any of her troops in the area of North Korea so near their border with the two Asian nations, sir."

Walters answered that question, "The Alliance States will be informed of the situation by the Security Council, because they have to inform the Alliance States of the meeting, and I'm sure..."

The President interrupted the American Ambassador's words by saying, "Look people, we're dealing in suppositions here, and I for one don't like it one bit. I want some damn answers to the questions raised here today. I'm going back to my guests and cut the damn party short. Once everyone's gone, I'll place a call to the Chinese Chairman, and see if I can figure out what the hell's going on around here, dammit. I want everyone back here tomorrow morning by six o'clock sharp. Including the damn Chairman of the Joint Chiefs of Staff," the President directed his attention to Norman and he repeated, "I want Rockjaw here sir."

Director Griffin laughed as he questioned the President, "Are you sure you want him to beat on me instead of you. Why do I get all jobs with life threatening situations, Mr. President Sir?"

Everyone in the Oval Office laughed. Because General William (Rockjaw) Weidenbacher's temper was well known and also well feared throughout all of Washington. He received his nickname of Rockjaw, because one day he was actually kicked in the face by a police horse, and his jaw did not break. The joke floating around the Pentagon, and the rest of the Capital, was the fuming General was so pissed at the horse he walked around the animal and punched the horse in the face, breaking its jaw instead.

The President looked to each of the men and one woman seated in his office and then he announced to them, "Gentlemen, and Lady, let's get back to the damn party, before some nosey ass reporter puts two and two together, and realizes we're missing from the party. The next thing you know, there'll be a trumped up major crisis on our hands saying I turned my back on my guests, dammit. Or they create another national emergency and cursed and blame me for it."

All five of the powerful politicians stood as one and followed the President out of the Oval Office in silence. The President and Ambassador Walters went back to the party, while the female Vice President and Security Director took a second hallway, and reentered the party section from the bathroom area, removing any possible suspicion of a special meeting going on between the politicians. The President mumbled to Ambassador Walters as they reentered the party area, "Well Ambassador Walters, I believe it's time to lick the clit and apologize to some of our guests around here, sir." as the President went over to his wife and asked her if anyone had missed him from the party. She shook her head no to her husband's question as she smiled pleasantly to him at the same time.

The President then whispered she had to cut the party short, and he did not offer her any reason for the want, nor did his wife ask why he wanted to end the party so quickly. His wife went to the head waiter, and told him to serve coffee, indicating the end of the party to him, and all their guests attending the special gathering.

CHAPTER 2

Six o'clock the following morning, General William Weidenbacher sat in the Oval Office along with the President Albert Cole, Vice President Mary Hirshfield, the National Security Director Norman Griffin, and a rather sleepy looking Ambassador Walters. Rockjaw was rather upset at having to be attending this meeting, because he already had his entire day planned out; before he was ordered to attend the President's special meeting. He was pissed off, but when the anxious looking President began to explain what this meeting was about, the General immediately calmed down and listened to the President's words.

The President looked the General dead in the eye, and then he said, "Smile, will you please you old fart you. You could stand to lose some sleep every once in a while, General. Bill look, I need to know what the hell the Chinese might commit to a military operation involving an all out invasion of North Korea, in terms of troops and military equipment and aircraft, sir. Then I need to accomplish a complete overrunning of that country, and I'll need this information by no later than tomorrow morning, General Weidenbacher Sir. I also want to know what the Chinese might commit to this operation they have offered to carry out for the rest of the world."

The General glared as he griped at the American Leader, "Jesus H. Christ and miracles, by tomorrow morning Mr. President Sir! You gotta be shitting me sir. Dammit sir, I'd need a helluva lot more time than that to put this kind of report together sir. Hell sir, I'll have to put half of my damn staff on this report, if I have such a short deadline to gather this information. I..."

The President cut the still angry looking General off by grumbling at the military officer, "I don't remember asking you how you were going to get this report done for me, General Weidenbacher. All I remember saying was I needed this report from you, period General. Next week there's a special Security Council Meeting scheduled. Ambassador Walters needs to be well prepared to answer any and all questions concerning the Chinese military strengths and weaknesses, sir. I don't trust the damn Chinese as far as I can throw them sir, and I want to be well prepared in case their real intention comes out during this damn meeting, General."

General Weidenbacher rubbed his stubble covered chin with a massive paw, and then he responded, "Mr. President, do you have any idea why the damn Chinese want to do us such a favor, as to attack one of her main Allies, sir?"

The President let out a disgusted hiss as he replied, "I don't have any idea what they're truly up to here, sir. That's why I have you, and your expensive staff of military geneses hanging around, mister. If there's another reason China wants to attack North Korea, I want you to find out what the devil it is before they spring it on us, General Weidenbacher."

The Security Director interrupted the conversation as he quickly addressed his question to the President, "Mr. President Sir, I completed a workup last night when I left the party, sir."

"I should've known you would've spent the entire night working, Norman."

Security Director Griffin stayed seated, but he nodded slightly for the kind compliment from the President as he offered, "Sir, if there's another reason for an invasion, it has to be the one we have come up with last night, Mr. President. We feel China wants to attack North Korea, so they can use this action to go through the whole of the Korean Peninsula, and possibly attack Japan from a land base opportunity, sir. Before any one interrupts me, please allow me to finish with my statement before you jump on my ass. We feel China wants to attack Japan to loot their banks to get needed funds to keep her country afloat."

The President was stunned by this summary and he asked in a surprised voice, "Do you truly think this is really possible, Norm?"

"Possible, but unlikely sir. We have two hundred thousand troops currently stationed in South Korea, and two Carrier

Strike Forces in striking distance of Japan's coast. I wish we had active military bases still operating in Japan or the Philippines to make our work easier to carry off, sir."

President Albert Cole raised his hand in the air so he might speak again, without cutting the Director short. The Director stopped speaking and looked at the President.

The President looked to Ambassador Walters, and said, "The Director has brought up a valid point here sir. While you're at this damn Security Council Meeting, I want you to take the Japanese Delegate aside, and see if you can talk him into allowing us to reopen a military base or two in Japan, sir. Explain to him it's to the benefit his country more than it's ours, sir. I want you to also speak to the Philippine Delegate at the same time, and see if he'd allow us to open a military base there, sir. But only on a temporary basis tell him, Ambassador. Inform him of our fear there may be some underlying reasons for the Chinese offer, sir. I'll have Vice President Hirshfield get in touch with the Prime Minister of Japan, and see if she can be of assistance with getting a military base reopened in Japan for our use, Mr. Ambassador."

President Cole next looked at his watch and announced, "Its late morning, and I have other commitments scheduled today. Mr. Walters, good luck next week. I'll be in touch with you later on this week to update you. The rest of you will work on the information I requested, sir."

The President then looked at the General and asked him, "I'll see you tomorrow, right General Weidenbacher Sir?"

Weidenbacher did not reply, he just nodded in the affirmative to the President.

"Now that's settled, I wish to call this meeting to a close." As the President rose, the rest at the meeting stood. He left through the door leading to his private dressing room, followed by the Vice President. The other men were led to their cars by Presidential aides.

JANUARY 9th, 1997.
THE EMERGENCY MEETING OF THE SECURITY COUNCIL IN NEW YORK CITY, NEW YORK

The members of the Security Council were gathered and waiting for the Chinese Delegate to begin speaking to them. Ambassador Robert Chow stood as he looked at the many faces staring at him. He spotted the Japanese Delegate, Ambassador Hugh Lang, and smiled at him. The Chinese Delegate then handed an aide a file folder, and instructed him to give the folder to the Japanese Delegate. He bowed towards Ambassador Chow.

The Chinese Delegate then began to address the other members of the Security Council while the Japanese Delegate quickly read the papers he sent to him. "Gentlemen, ladies, I'm pleased you chose to meet with me today. I come to you armed with certain information of North Korea's attempts to join the nuclear family. I handed the Japanese Delegate certain papers, papers which will prove beyond a shadow of a doubt North Korea intends to not only attack South Korea in the near future, but also Japan." The Chinese Delegate paused for the proper effect, before continuing with his words of warning again.

The Japanese Delegate raised from his seat slowly, a paper clutched in one hand, and the file folder in the other, as he continued to read the papers from Ambassador Chow with a stunned look etched on his face. He was heard saying, "My God sir, how long have you known about this present threat to the security of Japan, sir?"

Ambassador Chow sneered, knowing he had the full attention of the Council, especially the Japanese Delegate, "My government known of the existence of these documents for three weeks. That's why we chose at this time to request this special meeting of the Security Council."

The President of the meeting, French Ambassador, Gene Bartlett remarked, "Perhaps the Chinese Diplomat would be so kind as to share these found papers with the rest of us, sir."

Ambassador Chow bowed to the frail Frenchman as he motioned to another one of his aides.

There was a low murmuring as each member of the Council read the reports handed to them.

The Alliance States Delegate spoke without waiting to be recognized by the Security Council President. "The Alliance States will not allow any military buildup so close to her borders, by either China, or North Korea soldiers. We have to protect our country from all aggressors, no matter who they might be. I shall order a full military alert throughout my entire nation. I'll..."

President Bartlett banged his gavel to speak over the Alliance State's Representative, "Mr. Antich, the Council has not recognized you sir. Please take your seat. Now is not the time to make threats. We know what this situation could mean to the security of Russia, err... excuse me sir. The Alliance States and every member will do everything in their power to protect your country. Please, sit back and see what our esteemed colleague has in mind to put a stop to this situation. Mr. Chow, if you'd be so kind, the floor is yours. Will you please continue sir?"

Ambassador Chow bowed towards the Frenchman controlling the meeting of the Security Council as he added to his words, "My government finds this information most disturbing to the security of China, as well as to the rest of the Asian region, sir. I understand how Ambassador Antich must feel with his country so vulnerable to attack, as it is now."

Ambassador Antich was up on his feet again complaining bitterly, "My country is not as vulnerable as you might think, Ambassador Chow. I'll have you know we have the…"

Bartlett again banged his gavel and called out angrily, "Will the Representative from the Alliance States please take his seat, and refrain from further outbursts," Bartlett turned to Ambassador Chow as he said in a softer voice. "Ambassador Chow, will you please refrain from inciting the Representative from the Alliance States, sir?" Bartlett shot a glare at Ambassador Antich, as a further warning for him not to interrupt the proceedings again.

Ambassador Chow bowed to the French President, and then spoke again to the members, "My government wants me to inform the other members of this Security Council we understand the severe consequences the world will be facing, if we allow North Korea to develop nuclear weapons capable of fitting on the heads of their ballistic missiles. My government wants me to inform the esteem members of this Council we're more than willing to do something about this present situation inside North Korea, by ourselves if needed sir."

The Alliance States Representative sat up and rested his elbows on the table while staring at Ambassador Chow as he continued with his words, "My government is willing to invade North Korea and completely destroy their nuclear capability. We wil…"

The meeting erupted with many conversations while members yelled out, demanding to be heard over the other Delegates at the meeting. The Japanese Delegate was for any plan that would stop the North Koreans in their quest to threaten the Island of Japan. The Spanish and Italian Representatives threatened to walk out of the meeting, if China continued to request permission for their government to be allowed to invade a country.

The India and Sweden Delegates wanted Ambassador Chow to continue his explanation, while the Alliance Delegate threatened to walk out, but not before he warned the Chinese Delegate with death. If his country tried to build up its military presence near the Chinese, Russia border. When Ambassador Walters had enough of the bickering he stood, and the other Delegates looked at him as they quieted, waiting for him to address the Security Council members.

Ambassador Walters cleared his throat as he wiped his face with his handkerchief, and then spoke, "Gentlemen, Ladies, let's allow Ambassador Chow a chance to finish his words. I must admit I'm stunned by this latest information, and we must thank the Chinese government for sharing it with us. If this nuclear buildup is allowed to continue unchecked then we could find ourselves involved in a shooting war, or even possibly a nuclear confrontation. We know we were about to do something about North Korea ourselves. We held meeting months ago about instituting certain sanctions against the North Koreans, if they didn't abandon their interest with nuclear weapons. I say again, let's wait and hear what the Chinese government has in mind, and then we can vote on which course of actions we'll adopt, whether it be from the Chinese government, or a joint military action involving all nations here, or a few of us.

"We're talking, and as long as we continue talking, there's a good possibility we're going to work out something that'll make all members of the United Nations, and even the

North Koreans if we're lucky, happy with our decision," Ambassador Walters turned and looked directly at Ambassador Chow and then he added. "Ambassador Chow Sir, will you please continue outlining your plan for us sir. I, like everyone else attending this meeting are interested in hearing all of what you have to offer us today, sir."

Ambassador Chow did not bow this time, he was tired of being interrupted as he grumbled, "My government is willing to attack North Korea. If necessary with our forces, if we cannot make them see the error in their ways, and to leave the nuclear weapons out of their arsenals."

The Alliance State's Delegate was on his feet and bitching again, "I'm certain no members here would think my country would sit by, and allow the Chinese government to build up its military forces so near to our nation's borders. I, for one, can assure you we'll not stand idly by, while so many armed troops mass near our borders." The fuming Russian Delegate looked to Ambassador Walters, and then to Ambassador Leslie Alexander looking for their backing. He stared at the female Delegate from the United Kingdom, as he waited for a response by them towards the Chinese request, and his counter threat.

Ambassador Alexander looked at the angry Delegate from the Alliance States then responded, "Ambassador Antich, we'll sign a non-aggression pact with your government, including China." She then turned her gaze to Chow and offered, "Ambassador Chow, if your government happens to make a threat on the Alliance's territory, all nations here will step in and put a quick stop to this threat, by all means we deem necessary to accomplish this feat, sir. I hope our threat in this region of the globe, is from North Korea, and not China, sir."

Ambassador Chow smiled at the middle aged woman and spoke, "Ma'am, my country has no claims on Russia's soil. I admit we made a foolish move in 1995, and my government paid dearly for that discretion. We have no intention of making that same mistake twice in one lifetime, Ma'am. All my country wants is put a stop to the nuclear threat from North Korea."

The Indian Representative stood and requested permission to speak to the other Council members. Ambassador John Dutrow stood and questioned the Chinese Delegate, "Ambassador Chow, I'm interested in knowing why China is so suddenly concerned about the threat of nuclear weapons from North Korea, sir. Was it not your country that blocked a recent United Nations resolution condemning North Korea for her nuclear experiments just last year, sir? I find this change of heart rather interesting, and most confusing at the same time, sir."

Ambassador Chow glared harshly at the Indian Delegate, a fact that did not go unnoticed by Ambassador Walters. He made a mental note of the situation as Ambassador Chow drew in a huge breath, and then responded, "My country has a hidden agenda at that, sir. In addition to becoming a threat to South Korea and Japan, North Korea is rapidly becoming an extremely serious threat to China. For years, China has enjoyed being one of the two most powerful nations in this region, who controlled nuclear weapons to deter aggressive acts on her soil, sir. Now, with North Korea fast becoming a nuclear power that'll make three nations with nuclear weapons in this region of the world, sir. If North Korea joins forces with either nation against the other nation with nuclear weapons under their command. It'd certainly change the balance of power in this region of the world at that, and it could also lead to a world confrontation being waged between three nuclear powers, thus ending the world as we know it sir.

"My government for one does not want this possibility to take place, and that's why we're making this kind offer of a preemptive invasion of North Korea, before that nation develops nuclear weapons that can be mounted on the tip of their ballistic missiles. We know North Korea developed a missile platform capable of reaching Beijing or Tokyo, and this is an extreme threat to China's national security, and we'll not stand by under this severe threat, sir."

The Japanese Delegate interrupted then he waited until he received permission to speak.

The Chinese Delegate yielded to the man representing Japan, because he knew Japan's only hope, was for China to go through with her plans to attack, and destroy North Korea. Every nation gathered at this special meeting, knew if China invaded North Korea, she would not stop with Korea's nuclear threat. China would continue with her attack until she destroyed North Korea's entire military machine, much the same way the United States did to Iraq in 1992.

The Japanese Delegate spoke up in an excited voice, "I'm displeased at what I'm hearing said at this meeting of the Security Council. Here, we have a rebel country threatening to disrupt the peace of Asia, with her attempt to develop nuclear weapons. In this time of disarmament, and the state of peace that the world is currently enjoying. There's only one reason to continue to develop nuclear weapons, and that is for world conquest. Any country that disrupts the peace of any region should be shunned by the rest of the civilized world. Have we not learned anything from the nuclear war that took place in the Middle East five months ago? And now, for the nation of Japan to come under a direct threat of a nuclear attack, is most inconceivable.

"Japan will make history as the only country in the world, to come under nuclear attack twice in her existence. I'm appalled at this terrible thought, as I'm certain many here are. We must stop North Korea in her attempt to join the nuclear arms family at all costs. I pray if China is willing to put a stop to this drive. Then we must agree to assist China in this endeavor. I don't like having to ask another country to send their children to war, but Japan has no real Army of her own, mainly because of the treaties we were forced to sign at the close of World War Two. I'm sorry to ask another nation to protect the shores of Japan, but I must in this instance. Japan will send as many troops as she has, to help any nation willing to help Japan protect her country, and Japan will pay for all financing of the military operation needed to make this terrible task a successful one. Japan needs help if she's going to remain a free and democratic nation."

When Lang finished speaking, Ambassador Walters immediately addressed the other Council members, especially Lang from Japan. "Members of this Security Council, the United States signed an agreement with Japan, promising to protect Japanese soil from invasion. I'm renewing this commitment. The United States will send in her youth to protect the sovereignty of Japan, and any nation who proves they're America's friend." Ambassador Walters sat to applause.

Mrs. Alexander announced England would stand with the United States, Japan and China in their quest to keep peace in the region of Asia. The Canadian Delegate, Mr. Francis Farrow announced Canada would stand by America and England to fend off the threat from North Korea.

The rest except for India, pledged to stand behind China in her attempt to stop this latest aggression from the North

Koreans. This pledge was not a declaration of war. It did not even give the clearance for China to use force against North Korea. It was nothing more than a vote of confidence coming, and going to all members who made up the Security Council.

The Secretary General banged his gavel on his desk, and all conversations stopped. He looked at the members then announced he was pleased to see them united in this common cause of protecting the peace of Asia. "I think we have other issues on our menu to discuss at this meeting today. I don't think we should give China permission to invade North Korea this easily though. We should draft a memo, threatening North Korea with a new series of sanctions. Then with military intervention, as well as condemnation by all other nations of the world, if she doesn't abandon her foolish attempt to develop further nuclear weapons."

The Frenchman turned to Ambassador Chow and offered, "Sir, if we authorize your country to attack North Korea. There are a number of questions which need to be asked, and answered first. For instance, what troops would you employ in this operation sir? What military equipment? How long do you think it'd take, before your troops would leave North Korea? How many troops, and from what other nations, would your country need, and who would these troops be commanded by, sir? China or the country the troops are from? We know Japan offered to pay for this operation, but this mission will serve the world, sir. I feel we can't expect Japan to shoulder the full financial burden this action will bring. It's only right the expense be shared equally, by all members of the United Nations. Mr. Chow, there are many questions needing answers, before we consider a reaction to these disturbing papers you brought before us, sir."

Ambassador Chow opened another folder and removed papers then offered, "Gentlemen, my government has given me a complete list of our troops she'd commit to this operation, including the military equipment needed. But first, allow me explain my country intends to shoulder the military burden of this operation. China does not intend to use the children from any other nation to keep Asia free. China wishes to keep this operation an Asian problem, for lack of a better term." Ambassador Chow stopped speaking to allow these words to set in. Many conversations filled the void as hands shot up and members begged permission to speak.

Ambassador Bartlett scanned the hands then offered to the gathered, "I think its far better we allow Ambassador Chow to finish with his country's proposal to us, before we allow any other Delegates to interrupt his words. It's in the interest of time I make this statement to you members. Ambassador Chow Sir, will you please continue with your offer sir."

The Chinese Ambassador Chow went to another paper and read from it. "My government has completed a workup and we came up with this estimate. The operation would take no longer than six weeks to completion. This estimate is from the initial invasion, not the military buildup that will be necessary to mass our invasion forces along the Chinese, North Korean border.   There's only one thing China requests, if the fighting is heavy in North Korea, China must not be stopped once she committed her troops to this operation. By this I mean, if loss of life becomes too great, there must not be calls for China to stop her advance against North Korea. Any calls for peace must be aimed at the

Koreans. China must be backed, or we'll withdraw our offer to put a stop to North Korea's nuclear quest. China does not need a Vietnam type war on her hands.

"We must have the complete backing of all nations involved in this situation, or the Security Council wastes China's time if the nations represented here, cannot agree completely to this request of my country. It'll be China's young men and father's who'll fight this time, and we don't need any other nation who has no youth involved, undermining China's fighting men's will to fight. If every nation cannot agree completely to my government's request. Then I'm instructed to withdraw my offer, and the world will have to contend with this threat of North Korea on their own, without the help of China, sir." Ambassador Chow stopped speaking at this point and scanned the faces of the diplomats, waiting for their answers.

The Delegate from India took this time to speak, "I have giving this offer of China's much thought, and I think it's rather presumptuous of us to write off the country of North Korea. From the way the Chinese Delegate is speaking, it sounds like they intend to wipe North Korea off the face of the earth, and he wants us to agree to standby and allow his country do this. I know there has to be another way in dealing with Korea, other than sending the Chinese military in their country. What happened to precision air attack, to destroy their nuclear development program?"

The Chinese Delegate interrupted Ambassador Dutrow as he grumbled at the other members of the Council, "We all witnessed what happened when we do precision air raids. Remember what happened in Iraq? The United States didn't go far enough during their war campaign, and in less than two year's time, the Iraqi government was once again playing with their nuclear weapons and finally, during the

Middle East war. Iraq started the only nuclear exchange ever waged between other nations, this world has lived through. No, I'm afraid it has to be an all out, or nothing attack from China's point of view. We have to learn something from our previous wars. We learned we have to cut off the head of the snake, if we want the snake to die completely." Ambassador Chow took his seat and then waited for the next speaker to talk.

The French President spoke, "Mr. Chow, can you tell me how many troops you intend to commit to the operation, if you're given permission to attack Korea on our behalf that is sir?"

Ambassador Chow pulled up the paper he needed, and read the list from the sheet.

American Ambassador Walters took a slip of paper from his folder, and checked off the items Ambassador Chow offered to the Security Council members. The paper Ambassador Walters was working from was the one General Weidenbacher drawn up for the President last week. It covered all the Chinese troop strengths, and all known Chinese military hardware and military equipment the United States had on file on the Chinese might of their war machine.

"Yes Mr. President, my government will commit the following military forces and equipment to the engagement with the North Koreans, sir: The complete 11th Group Army, the 15th Group Army, the 21st Group Army, the 5th Mountain Group Army and the 35th Group Army along with the 10th Air Group and the 3rd and 4th Helicopter Groups, sir."

"How many troops is that in all, Ambassador Chow?" Ambassador Alexander asked him.

"Over two hundred thousand forces please." Chow replied proudly and confidently.

Ambassador Walters interrupted him, "Excuse me Ambassador Chow, but I added the troops you offered, and they add up to nearly three hundred and fifty thousand soldiers. That's not including the Air Force and helicopter units you intend to employ in this operation, sir."

The Indian Delegate snarled, "That's a hell of an invasion force that'll be used to attack a few military and nuclear installations throughout certain sections of North Korea, sir. Sir, with an Army this size, I could take over the entire Peninsula of Korea, both North and South, sir."

Ambassador Chow let out an angry breath as he hissed at the Indian Delegate, "This is exactly what I meant before sir. This is what happens every time there's a problem for this esteem Council to preside over. China has offered to eliminate an upcoming nuclear threat to the world, and here we have another nation crying we intend to employ too many troops to get the job done properly. Maybe India would like to eliminate the nuclear problem threatening the peace of Asia, and use her children to fight in the jungles of North Korea, sir. Mr. President, my patience is thin. I offer the world a way out of a terrible developing situation, and other nations with nothing to lose, pick our offer apart, sir. China's offer stands, but I'll withdraw the offer within twenty four hours, unless statements are put forth to my government by the members here, sir."

The Japanese Delegate jumped to his feet and spoke in an excited voice to the other Delegates attending this emergency meeting of the Council, "We have to allow China to attack North Korea. They are the only country in the entire region, with enough forces in Asia to do the job."

The irate Indian Delegate cut Ambassador Lang off crudely by saying, "We know why Japan wants China to go through with her offer, sir. Because Japan is under the threat of an invasion from North Korea. Japan is allowing her foolish fears, to rule her mind in this situation sir."

The Japanese politician stood again, but before he responded to the Indian's remarks, he was gaveled back down to his seat as Bartlett snapped at the Chinese and Indian politicians, "We understand the serious threat Japan's under with this situation, and we'll band together to protect Japan from attack from any nation. North Korea or China."

Ambassador Walters growled angrily this time, "Look, I had enough of this constant bickering from the Delegates at this meeting. We have a world threatening nuclear situation developing here, and we need a solution, and we need it quickly. On one hand, China put forth the noble offer of shouldering the entire burden of putting an end to this situation, by using enough ground forces and military equipment to get the job done as it should be. If I were to send in United States forces, I'd want to commit more than enough ground forces to get the job done, as quickly and as safely as possible, with little lose of life as possible. Any solution we come up with here will not be satisfactory to all members involved in this situation. However, I have a proposition to offer the Security Council members, but first I have a few questions I must ask."

Bartlett nodded to Walters's request. He turned to Chow and both men bowed to each other, "Mr. Chow. How long would it take for your troops to be placed in position for the attack?"

Ambassador Chow replied sharply to the President, "Our troops could be set in position in as short a time as two weeks, fully equipped and ready to attack on a moments notice, sir."

Ambassador Walters could not help it as he let out a slight whistle at the short amount of time Chinese Delegate just suggested they would need to move so many troops around, and be ready to open their attack against North Korea as he added, "One more question I have to ask, sir. Do you have a time frame as to how long it'll take your troops to get the job done?"

"As I already stated today, sir. Six weeks at the earliest, and up to twelve weeks at the longest, barring complications we didn't take notice of, Ambassador Walters."

"Complications?" Ambassador Walters asked his eyebrows arched slightly in concern.

"Complications sir. Like unforeseen complications, such as a much stronger resistance from the North Korean soldiers than expected. Perhaps underestimating the enemy's troop strengths and armor, sir. There could be trouble with our rail system, and trouble with our attack aircraft and artillery. The list could be endless as you should well understand, sir."

The United States Ambassador Walters laughed as he offered calmly, "Ah yes, I know of these complications you speak of only too well I assure you, Ambassador Chow. Very good, you answered my questions to my complete satisfaction, and I thank you for that. Sir, other members of this Council, I ask you to consider my next offer please. I beg the patience of the Chinese government for a month, before I shall vote to allow China to go through with her offer to attack North Korea, sir. I suggest we send out a special mandate to the North Korean government, demanding they pull out of all further nuclear weapons development. If the North Koreans choose to continue with this foolish quest then I suggest we try a month's worth of stifling trade sanctions, and if this fails to get their attention.

"Then we should give the Chinese government the okay to attack North Korea. Before anyone gets upset with my words, allow me explain a little more clearly for you. I suggest we send a letter out this Monday. What is it, January 16th? We'll give the North Koreans two weeks to reply to our latest requests. If no reply comes in that length of time then we shall try a month worth of stronger sanctions. That'll push any actions against North Korea off to March 4th, a Friday. On that day, China should be given the final okay to start her military buildup, and when she's ready to begin this invasion for a lack of a better word, she should attack. No further communications with North Korea should be used or offered after this time limit has expired. I know we're going to override some of the other members of this Security Council."

Ambassador Walters turned to the Russian Nicholas Antich and added, "Ambassador Antich, I understand your government isn't going to like Chinese troops massed in force by your borders, but I beg you to bear with this present situation to see if we can workout this problem peacefully. I'm quite certain China will not pose a threat to your country, sir."

Ambassador Antich gave a slight nod as he spoke, "My government will request permission to activate our border troops, and I'll suggest we increase our border patrols. Just in case the unexpected happens to become a reality." Ambassador Antich turned to the Chinese Delegate and glared at him. Even though Russia was no longer in existence, there were many Russian politicians who remained in office, and trusted neither the United States, nor China.

Ambassador Walters spoke again, "I'm quite certain China will have no problem with the strengthening of your country's borders, as long as your troops stay on the Russian side, sir."

All eyes went to the Chinese politician, and he merely shook his head in the affirmative.

Antich snapped at Walters. "Our patrols always stay on the Russian side of the border."

The President of the Council stood and announced, "The Ambassador from the United States has just put forth a proposition for vote. I feel it's a good solution to a bad situation for the moment. I'm calling for a vote. Will everyone sit down and prepare to give their vote please."

When everyone was seated, Bartlett made the roll call. He started with the United Kingdom.

"Ambassador Alexander, how do you vote on this subject please Ma'am?"

"The United Kingdom votes for the American proposition as offered sir."

"Ambassador Chow. How do you vote here please sir?"

"Sir, China votes in favor of the American proposition as offered at this meeting sir."

"Ambassador Antich. How do you vote for the American plan just offered sir?"

"The Alliance States votes for acceptance of the American proposition with objection sir."

"Very well sir. Your objection is noted sir." President Bartlett replied to him in a flat tone.

He turned his attention to the Japanese Delegate and asked. "Mr. Lang. How do you vote?"

"Sir, Japan votes in favor of the United States proposition as it was offered sir."

"India, Ambassador Dutrow Sir. How do you vote for the American proposition sir?"

"India votes no on the proposition as offered by the United States, sir."

"Very well sir. Italy, Ambassador Caporelli Sir. How do you vote today sir?" The Secretary General asked the Italian politician.

"It's with regret Italy has to vote in the affirmative for the American proposition, sir."

"Ambassador Evangelista, the Council members heard very little from you throughout this conversation, sir. How does Spain vote to the proposition up for vote, sir?" The French Delegate asked the Spanish Ambassador how he was going to vote on this subject.

"Sir, Spain votes for the proposition, and Spain will offer any help China may need to make this a successful military operation, sir. Whether that help comes in the form of money or troops, sir. It's important to Spain no other nation joins the dreaded nuclear weapons family, sirs."

"Canada. How does Mr. Farrow vote on the American proposition before the Council, sir?"

"Sir, Canada is only interested in peace and security of the rest of the world, sir. Therefore, Canada has no choice but to vote in the positive for the American proposition at this time, sir. Once again, Canada is proud and will to stand at the side of America, and the other nations who have committed to safeguard the security of the rest of the world at this meeting, sir."

Ambassador Bartlett then turned to the last member of the Security Council. Ambassador Ackerman and asked for his vote. "How do you vote on the proposition before the Council?"

Ambassador Ackerman did not stand and offered, "Sweden votes for the American proposition and will help any country who takes up arms to block the expansion of nuclear weapons."

"Ambassador Walters, its plain how you're voting on this offer, sir. But I'm bound to ask you for your vote, sir." The Secretary General asked of the American ambassador at this time.

"Mr. Secretary General, the United States votes for the proposition before the Council, and furthermore, the United States is willing to commit troops, and financial aid to China, if she's forced to attack North Korea. I do have one question to ask the members of the Council." American Ambassador Walter offered as he stared at the Secretary General for a moment.

"Very well Ambassador Walters. You may ask your question." Bartlett replied to his request.

"Mr. President, I have to demand we refrain from informing the North Korean government she might be on the verge of being attacked by China, if she doesn't dismantle her nuclear weapons. If North Korea finds out what was discussed today, she'll be prepared for China's attack, and this knowledge will cost many needless lives in the Chinese attack, sir."

Chow bowed to the Ambassador as he thanked him for his concerns for China's fighting men.

Ambassador Bartlett responded also, "Yes Ambassador Walters, we have to keep what was discussed here today a secret until, and if China is forced to invade North Korea. That was a good point to bring out. I'm pleased you brought it up before our fellow Ambassadors left the meeting sir," Bartlett turned to the Indian Delegate and warned. "Ambassador Dutrow, your country was the only one who voted against this proposition. Therefore, I must warn you against informing the North Korean Delegate of what was discussed here today, sir. Under the threat of expulsion from the United Nations, if your country betrays the trust of this Council, sir."

The Ambassador from India was angry at the harsh reprimand from the French President and he snapped, "I don't remember hearing of France's vote over the American proposition, sir."

Bartlett smiled, "France votes in the positive for the proposition before the Council."

The Indian Ambassador nodded to the Frenchman as he took his seat again. His mind worked on how he was going to regain the trust of the other members. Suddenly, he had an idea and raised his hand and requested to address the members again. He was given permission to speak.

"After further consideration, I come to the conclusion it's in the best interest of India, for me to go along with the other members of this Council at this time, and I wish to amend my vote to the affirmative on the offered proposition before the Council. Ambassador Bartlett Sir, if you could see your way to change my vote please, sir."

"Hmm, this is rather unusual Ambassador Dutrow. But if no other members of the Security Council have objections to your request to change your vote. I'll be pleased to change your vote to a yea vote. I was hoping we could have a unanimous vote on this issue at the meeting." Ambassador Bartlett looked around the room, and when he noticed no objection to his request, he added to his words to the Indian Ambassador. "Very well Ambassador Dutrow, I'll change your negative vote, to a positive one sir. I'll send the results of the vote over to the United Nations. I decided to change one item myself though. Instead of sending a messenger to North Korea, I'd like to convene a special meeting in the United Nations. At this meeting, I'll have North Korea informed of our warning for them to get out of the nuclear arms business, or risk severe sanctions, and possibly worse actions taken against them and their nation in the future. I'll convene this meeting for next week on Wednesday, January 14th, 1997. Do all the members here agree to this latest proposal please?"

All members of the Security Council answered in the affirmative to the last question.

"Then I guess we completed the scheduled business of this current Security Council Meeting, and I suggest we call this latest meeting to a close. It's getting late, and we're all hungry. We have worked through lunch." The Secretary General offered to the other members.

Ambassador Walters headed for his private office in the United Nations building, so he could place a call to the President, and report on exactly what had transpired at the Security Council Meeting. Something was eating at him about the Chinese offer to invade North Korea though. The funny look and the ease at with which Ambassador Chow changed his plans. Something he could not place his finger on. The Ambassador decided to ask the President to secretly place the bulk of United States troops on a war time full alert, just in case things turned sour in Asia.

The President's phone was answered on the third ring by one of his aides. Seconds later, the American Leader was on the line and he offered. "Ahhh... Ambassador Walters, Pete. How the hell did it go at the Security Council Meeting today, sir?"

"Very well I like to offer Mr. President." Walters reported on everything that had transpired at the meeting. When he finished, he informed the President about his concerns over the way the Chinese Delegate responded, and how he reacted to some of the questions asked of him.

"Well Pete, what do you suggest we do about these damn concerns you brought up to my attention, sir?" The President asked, allowing a touch of concern to enter his tone of voice.

"Mr. President Sir, I think we should send some of our Carrier Strike Forces into the Asian area, or at least have them prepared to ship out on a moment's notice, sir." The American Ambassador offered in no uncertain terms to his Commander in Chief over the phone.

President Cole laughed as he replied, "Ambassador Walters, are you overreacting a little to these fears? How in the heck could I possibly clear a level three alert based on just your say so? Next, you'll be wanting to drag up Three, Three, Seven again, Ambassador Walters."

"With all due respect Mr. President Sir. That was going to be my next suggestion sir, to start up Three, Three, Seven and get that project back up and going, Mr. President. Sir, if all hell breaks out in the Asia region, you have to remember we no longer have any active military bases stationed in Japan or in the Philippines, sir. We could get ourselves romped until we're finally able to fight for a foothold in the area, if war breaks out in the region, sir."

"Will you Ambassador Walters? I can't possibly call for Three, Three, Seven to be reinstated. Think of the enormous cost to the American people, if I request that system started up again sir."

Walters dared to cut the President off. His friendship gave him the power to speak his mind, no matter how angry the Commander in Chief was going to get over what they were presently discussing as he added to his words, "Mr. President Sir, I am thinking about the enormous cost to the American people. But I'm also thinking about the cost if we don't have an operational military base in this area, and all hell does break out. The cost in American lives alone sir."

There was silence on the phone for several long seconds. Pete knew the President was still on the line, because he could hear his breathing, and then the American Leader moaned at him, "Gees Pete, you sure do know how to fuck up someone's day. I want you to get down here right away. I want to speak to you personally about these sudden fears you have, and how we're going to respond to them. I'll have Mr. Griffin and Mr. Levenhagen here when you arrive, sir."

"Al, I think I'd really like to have the Secretary of State attend the meeting as well if you don't mind that is, Mr. President." Ambassador Walters offered to the President with a little concern lacing his tone this time.

"Jesus Christ Almighty Pete! Why the hell do you want her at the damn meeting for, dammit? This is just a preliminary meeting at best sir. If things get going then we can always drag her in on the situation. She's a real pain in the lower end lately, sir. Always blocking you when you want to get something done man."

"Sir, she's a smart one or she wouldn't be in your Cabinet, Mr. President Sir. She can read between the lines, and she'll deduce what if anything, the Chinese are truly up to with their offer to attack North Korea to end their nuclear aims, sir. Besides Mr. President, she does the work of three people, and she never needs any help while doing it sir."

"Very well Pete, you win, she'll be here. How long will it take for you to get down here, sir?"

"Five hours at the most Mr. President Sir." Ambassador Walters replied to his boss.

"Good, I'll see you then Ambassador Walters. I'll have everyone waiting for when you arrive. I'll have the cook get you something to eat when you finally get down here, sir."

Pete knew this remark was a warning he was to get to the White House A-SAP.

CHAPTER 3
THE WHITE HOUSE, WASHINGTON D.C.

Upon his arrival, Ambassador Peter Walters was immediately led to the Oval Office, where President Cole, the Secretary of State Mrs. Hernandez, the Security Director Griffin and Secretary Levenhagen were already waiting for his arrival. The President nodded to his aides, and a pile of sandwiches were brought into the office for anyone who was hungry. After they had something to eat, Ambassador Walters started speaking.

"Sir, something about the Chinese proposal has rubbed me the wrong way, I'm worried Mr. President. I can't place my finger on it, but its there, and it's screaming like hell at me, sir." Ambassador Walters stopped speaking and looked at the group and waited for someone to speak.

"Jesus H. Christ Pete, and you expect me to set Directive Three, Three, Seven back in motion, just because you have a fucking itch between your damn balls, sir?" The Security Director bellowed, and he instantly turned his attention to Mrs. Hernandez, and then he apologized to her for his poor use of curse words and crude remark.

She smiled pleasantly as she remarked kindly to the Security Director, "Mr. Griffin, this is a meeting, and everyone is expected to say whatever's on their mind, and express themselves in the manner they're used to speaking, sir. Don't treat me any differently because I'm a woman, or I'll cut your damn balls off, and use them for a paper weight on my desk, sir."

"Point well taken Ma'am. I'll treat you like everyone else here. Sorry for my oversight."

Ambassador Walters began again, "Mr. Griffin Sir, I'm afraid it's more than just an itch that has me upset, sir. I saw the jackrabbit's eyes and they were hiding something in them sir. If it wasn't for the Japanese Delegate, I think I would've voted down the Chinese proposal at the meeting, sir. Mr. President," The Ambassador turned his attention to the American Leader and then went on. "we better call for a Joint Chief of Staff meeting, and allow the military minds pick who they want to run this operation if one's needed, sir. I repeat a request we start in motion Three, Three, Seven and also go to a Level Two Ready Alert immediately, Mr. President. This way, our troops will be ready to move out on a twenty four hour notice, sir. We have to be prepared to stop China in case she veers off course, and we had better be ready for it, sir."

"Dammit to hell Mr. Walters, what the devil do you think the Chinese might be up to? We already decided if North Korea does have nuclear weapons developed for their damn missile systems, she becomes a serious threat to China, and China's right to react to this information the way she's reacting. What has you so upset sir?" the President asked his Ambassador.

"I have no idea what they could be up to at this point. But the more I think about it, the more I feel to almost certainly they're up to something, other than what they're trying to sell us here sir. Maybe they're going to attack South Korea also. I don't really know as yet, Mr. President."

"No great loss there I'm afraid." The National Security Director, Norman Griffin remarked. His remark brought an instant harsh glare from the President.

There was a slight commotion as an aide knocked on the door, and he waited to be summoned in the office by the President. He handed a memo to the President and then left the room as quickly. President Cole unfolded the paper and read it. He then looked at Ambassador Walters and offered, "Pete, suddenly, I think you might be right. Here, take a look at this crap sir."

Walters read the five lines of print and then he looked at the President as he refolded the paper.

There was silence in the office until the Secretary of Defense, Jerry Levenhagen suddenly bellowed at him, "Damn, I guess we're going to have to ask then, what the hell's this note sir?"

The President replied with a snap in his voice, "We just received word China offered England a twenty year lease on Hong Kong, and the offer came with a request for the

United Kingdom to buy Hong Kong outright from them. This scares me to death sir. The Chinese are never this nice, they have to be up to something around here. Pete, I'm going to listen to your thoughts, you never disappointed me before, sir. I'll also call General Weidenbacher in, and inform him of what we got and have him call a Staff meeting so they can pick a leader and get some wheels in motion. I'm going to hold off on Three, Three, Seven for the time being though. I'll have the Officer picked and briefed on Three, Three, Seven, but we're going to hold off on it until the last possible moment, Ambassador Walters Sir.

"If I remember correctly sir, Three, Three, Seven will end up costing us almost fifty billion dollars to get completed, Ambassador. I hope what was started in preparation for the war in the Middle East was left intact, and no one disassembled the damn thing on us sir. Maybe we can save some of the taxpayer's money that way. I'm going to go to a Class Three Alert for now. This will get the most important military troops set in place, and also get the Officers on the move. I hope you're not seeing damn ghosts hiding behind trees on this one, Pete? It'd be most embarrassing to my ass if all this is for nothing, sir."

"Sir, what can I say? I can only react to my gut instincts, but after reading that last report Mr. President Sir. I'm certain the Chinese are up to something and I want to be prepared for whatever the hell they're doing sir," the Ambassador offered the President a reassuring smile.

"I'll set the wheels in motion then. Thank you for getting here so quickly Ambassador Walters Sir," the President stopped speaking as he popped a small candy in his mouth, he was having difficulty swallowing, then added, "Does anyone have anything to add to this damn mess?"

President Cole looked to Secretary of State Hernandez, but she shook her head no. Now, he was really worried, because if Hernandez was agreeing with the rest of the Cabinet. Then there was serious trouble heading their way.

"I'm going to place a call to the General when you leave. Thank you for your time and patience today sir." The President announced as he dismissed the rest of his staff.

Everyone stood at the same time and began to leave. When the President was alone, he leaned back in his chair and let out his breath in a deep sigh as he stared up at the ceiling. A concerned young White House aide came in with cup of coffee for the American Leader.

"Ah, that's great young man. How the hell did you know I needed a cup of coffee at this moment?" he moaned as he smiled at the aide.

The aide smiled pleasantly at the American Leader and placed the cup down on the desk and then left. President Albert Cole leaned forward and took a sip. He swill the cup, causing the coffee to roll, he stared at it as if trying to find an answer in the liquid. He leaned back in his chair and sipped his coffee. He could smell the faint odor of exhaust fumes coming from the snow blower outside his office, as the workers labored to keep the walk ways surrounding the White House free of any snow. The President decided he was going to close the window he had just cracked open for a little fresh air, but he made no move to close it. Washington was expecting three more inches of snow by morning. The exhausted President looked at his watch, it was eleven p.m. He finished off the rest of his coffee, and then he leaned forward and reached for his rolodex. All the military officers would be gone by this time of the day. So he decided to try General Weidenbacher at his home.

Two rings later, the President had the well respected and powerful General on the line and he was bitching at the President, "Jesus H. Christ Mr. President Sir. Don't you ever do anything during regular working hours around here for Pete's sake, sir?"

This comment made the President smile as he began speaking to his military officer, "I'm truly sorry for the hour General Weidenbacher Sir. But one of my people has an itch in his jockies, and I'm afraid you're going to have to scratch it for him, sir."

"Gees sir, tell him to take a damn bath will ya please, I'm no stinking baby sitter sir."

"I think you better hear me out first, before you give me any grief over my call to you General, it's that important, sir. I want a Class Three Alert broadcast."

This got the General's attention as he sat up and swung his legs out of bed to the floor while looking at his clock. His wife was already busy making coffee for him, she had that sixth sense which told her he would be leaving their home to meet with the President shortly.

"Mr. President, I'll be heading for the Pentagon within the next five minutes, sir. I'll call you the first moment when I'm set in place sir. Err... Mr. President, I'm sorry for the smart ass remarks before, sir. You kind of caught me a little off guard with this call sir."

It took the upset General fifteen minutes to get over to the Pentagon, he was stuck behind a snowplow most of the way. When he was in his office, he placed calls to the Chief of Staff of the Army, General Vincent W. Palmieri, Chief of Naval Operations, Admiral Thomas (Woody) Standlund, the Chief of Staff of the Air Force, General Luther Claiborne and Commandant of the Marine Corps, General Marianne G Matteoni. Everyone but 'Nails', General Claiborne was at home, but his aide said he would get him and have him report to the Pentagon.

Once General Weidenbacher placed his calls out, he returned his call to the President. "Sir, what the hell's the reason for the alert increase? Are we going to war Mr. President Sir?"

"No General Weidenbacher, but I decided to raise the alert status because of the developing Chinese and North Korea situation, sir. I fear things are going to happen in a hell of a hurry, and I don't want to be caught flat footed if it does, sir. General, I want you to put together a number of Marine Expeditionary Forces. At least three for a start at this time sir."

"For now, how the hell many troops do you think we're going to need all together for whatever the hell got you going here, Mr. President?" The concerned General asked.

"I have no idea at this time General Weidenbacher, I truly hope we're not going to need any troops over this situation, sir. I want three forces, with preparations for another three forces if needed. Wake up the Army too, I want at least nine groups from them gearing up also."

General William Weidenbacher gave out a low whistle, but the President ignored it as he continued with his orders, "I also want six Air Wings armed, fueled and ready to go at a moment's notice, General. I want the attack submarines on the prowl off the coast of China, and Carrier Strike Groups placed on ready alert as well, sir. I want one man controlling this entire operation like we had during the Middle East war. That worked out well for us before, that guy had balls. I'm clearing the way for you to get things set in motion. Pick your leader out carefully General, and brief him on Directive Three, Three, Seven. Give him the file on that operation."

"Three, Three, Seven? I thought that operation was placed on the dead pile, Mr. President?"

"I as well believed that General Weidenbacher, but I'm pulling it out of the mothball pile as of this moment, sir. I hope we'd never need the damn thing. Never liked the plan in the first place though, sir. But Congress liked it, and it was passed. I'm of the understanding that there's plenty of money put aside for the damn thing as well, General. I'm damn glad I didn't dip into it for any reason, sir." President Cole griped as he flashed a quick smile on the phone.

There was some noise and the President stopped speaking. General Weidenbacher placed his hand over the receiver and then he was back. "Mr. President, my people are beginning to show up at my office, sir. I'd like to talk to brief them on what we're talking about, sir."

"Very well General Weidenbacher, stay in contact with me and let me know what you're doing at all times, sir. Open the lines up to the Situation Room from the Pentagon, and leave them open until this current threat's over with, General Weidenbacher Sir." The President ordered as he broke off the communication with is General.

The General hung up then ordered coffee brought in as General Palmieri retorted, "It looks like we're going to be here for a while I see. The General's ordering coffee for us." He lit up a cigar and then offered one to the General, "No thanks sir, I'm trying to quit the damn things."

"That's the same thing my wife says when I want some." The General offered with a smirk.

This remark brought some laughter, before General Weidenbacher growled at General Palmieri, "You bet your stinking ass we're going to be here for a quite while, mister."

It took the better part of an hour for the powerful General to brief the rest of his command staff over the situation between North Korea and China. Once done, General Matteoni wanted to know what the next step was, being the alert was going up to level three for now.

General William Weidenbacher leaned on his desk with his arm and then sat down on the edge of it as he added to his words, "I've been ordered to pick out a leader to run this entire stinking operation for our Commander in Chief. I want you to check out all the Two, Oh, One file, if we have to go up to Alert One, sir. The President wants one man, or woman to command this mess," General Weidenbacher said as he looked to the lone woman on his staff then added, "to run this damn operation like the Middle East mess was ran. Any suggestions on who people?"

General Palmieri started the ball rolling by offering. "I have the man who served under the Colonel in charge of the Middle East war in my Command, sir. He's Colonel John White. In fact I just spoke with the man a few days ago, and I cut him a furlough, sir. He's scheduled to be gone for two weeks, sir. He went down to Florida, it seems one of his friend's in a little bit of trouble, and he wanted to help the guy out some, General. I can get in touch with him, and have his lazy ass back here in Washington by no later than tomorrow, sir."

"Do you think this guy's qualified to run an operation of the size we're speaking of, General? If we have to go that is. You know the President ordered me to give the man we pick the Three, Three, Seven file, and I don't want this guy overwhelmed by the damn thing, General Palmieri. By the way everyone, I branded this new operation 'Wine Press'."

All the members of the command staff stared at General Weidenbacher, as the Senior Military Officer remarked. "Sir, I thought we shelved that damn thing a few years ago. This has to be big if the President's thinking about authorizing

Three, Three, Seven by having it pulled out of the closet. I think we better check the personnel files a little closer, and see if we can find anyone else more suited for Command. I'd like to have a few officers to pick from sir. A Colonel isn't going to get the job done for us, our pick has to be a combat and bloodied General."

The rest of the command staff agreed, and General Weidenbacher ordered each of them to search his or her personnel files, and pick out at least two officers each, and submit them so they could evaluate each of the officers. Then he turned back to General Palmieri and snapped at the officer, "General, in the mean time I want you to call this Colonel you brought up to my attention, and order his ass back here toot sweet, sir. We might as well start off picking his brains to see if he'd fulfill our needs for this possible operation, sir."

General Palmieri announced he was going to place the call to the Colonel, "I'll order a fighter aircraft there and pick him up, sir. He can be picked up at the Homestead Air Force base stationed in southern Florida, General Weidenbacher."

"Get it done for me mister. We'll go on coffee until you get back and let me know how you made out with this damn Colonel White fella, sir."

General Palmieri walked over to the phones and placed the call after he checked the phone book he carried with him. The phone rang four times before someone answered it. It was a woman. "Err... excuse me Ma'am, I'm General Palmieri, and I'm looking for Colonel John White, please. He gave me this number if I needed to get in touch with him while he was on leave, and I must locate him immediately, Ma'am."

"Oh hello General Palmieri, how are you today sir. This is Cathy Campanelli, Eddie's wife."

"Well how the hell are you making out Cathy, and how's that old sourpuss of a husband of yours doing, Ma'am?" General Palmieri offered, surprised by who he was speaking to.

"He's being a real pain in the ass as always, General Palmieri. Always hanging around the house and getting in my way and bitching about everything, sir."

General Palmieri wanted to speak more to her, but he was pressed for time at the moment and he offered to the lady, "Look Cathy, it's been real pleasure speaking with you, but I have to speak to John on the double quick please. Is he there Ma'am?"

"Yes General Palmieri. Please hold on while I get him for you sir."

A second later. "Yeah General Palmieri, what's up sir?" The out of breath Colonel said.

"John, you have to get your ass back up here to Washington A-SAP, sir. Make your way over to the Homestead Air Force Base, sir. I'll have a two seat fighter aircraft waiting there for you sir. We're currently on a Stage Three Alert up here sir."

"A Stage Three Alert General Palmieri Sir? What the hell happened in so short a time sir?"

"Nothing yet, but I need you back here in Washington PDQ. Get on your horse and get going."

"On my way now sir." John said as he hung up the phone and turned around, only to come face to face with a rather worried looking Popeye, General Edward Campanelli.

"Trouble John?" General Campanelli asked his old friend with some concern lacing his tone.

"Yeah Eddy. I gotta get going sir. Can you give me a ride over to Homestead AFB?"

"You got it." The two officers piled into Campanelli's Buick Regal, and were off like a shot. It took them three hours to get to the airbase from Venice, Florida. There was an idling F-15 G two seat Eagle resting on the runway. When John was out of the General's car, an armed guard escorted him over to the aircraft. He was pushed up the ladder, strapped in and in the air in less than five minutes from the time he arrived on the airbase.

Eddie watched the sleek aircraft streak off into the heavens. His heart was breaking, he was longing to be on active service again, instead of attending all the terribly boring dinners with all the stuffed shirts, or talking to young, gun ho recruits. He walked back to his car, and then he started his long drive home.

Colonel White was plastered in his seat as the sleek two seater fighter aircraft shot in the air. It was going to take him an hour and a half to touch down at Langley Air Force Base in Washington D.C. It took another half an hour for the Colonel to reach the Pentagon building. The snow had finally come to an end and the accumulation was less than three inches, and the going was slow for the Army staff car sent out to retrieve the Colonel from the airport. It was past two in the morning, when John entered the National Military Command Center, the largest room which was the Pentagon's main communications center and heart of the Pentagon.

This communication and command center was hooked up directly to the Situation Room constructed some sixty feet below the White House building. This way, the President could sit in on every meeting being held in the Pentagon if he was needed, without having to go to the building himself. From this command center and the Situation Room, the mind thrust of the American government and military command could be in direct communication with any in field military unit commander, aircraft, whether on a bombing run or just a recon mission over some hostile land. Any foreign government or embassy head, and all the commanders could receive their real time data on the progress of any operation currently underway. The entire military operation of Desert Storm, and the Middle East war, was controlled from the Command Center and the Situation Room at the same time.

Colonel John White headed down the long walkway leading to the seated officers. General Weidenbacher nodded at him as he reached the table. Rockjaw motioned to a seat and waited for John to be seated before he began speaking, "John, good to see ya. How have you been?"

"Fine sir." John replied and then shut up and waited to be briefed on the pending operation he was called back to Washington for.

General Weidenbacher let out his breath in a sigh and then began explaining, "John, I sent for you because we have a problem possibly cropping up on us, sir. It's not clear what sort of problem we're expecting quite yet, but we've been placed on a Class Three Alert by the President. We have to move a number of ground forces and military equipment around in a hurry it up, Colonel. I've been ordered to pick a Field Commander to oversee all land, Sea and Air Forces, like we did in the Middle East bullshit. You've been offered up as such a Commander we need by your boss, General Palmieri."   The General stopped speaking while John glanced over at Palmieri, who in return nodded to John.

After the pleasantries were concluded, General Weidenbacher continued with his thoughts, "You're the man so far, sir. I ordered the rest of the Generals to offer up two men or women from their ranks, and we'll pick the best possible Commander from the personnel offered. A Field

Commission of two rates will come with the Command, as it usually does. No other General offered anyone else so far, sir. John, do you have anything to say to what I informed you of sir? Or better yet, do you have someone you might want to offer up here instead of you, sir?"

A grin quickly spread across John's face as he replied to his Commanding Officer, "Why the hell would anyone want to nominate me for Commander of this possible operation? After all the gray hair I gave General Palmieri over the past years, all I figure him picking me for was a firing squad, General Weidenbacher Sir. This shit's new to me, sir. Don't get me wrong sirs. It's a great honor for you guys to pick me and I'm deeply honored by it. But I don't think I'd want to be in Command of a joint forces operation like you Generals are speaking of."

General Matteoni interrupted Colonel White's remarks by offering, "You seem to forget one thing around here, Colonel White. I don't remember any of us giving you another choice in the matter, mister. You're laboring under a false illusion here mister. If we pick you, you're the leader, period Colonel. This isn't a Democracy here, sir. It's what we say that goes sir."

Colonel White bowed to the Senior and he realized how she got the nickname Dragon Lady.

General Weidenbacher started as he announced, "Colonel White Sir, would you like a breath mint to suck on, sir?" This remark caused everyone to laugh as John shot back.

"No, but I'd like a chance to change my skivvies if you don't mind sir."

"Seriously sir, I'd like to know if you have anyone else in mind to lead this operation."

John thought for a moment and then he offered confidently,   "You gotta be kidding me, General

Weidenbacher. There's only one man in the forces who's qualified to run a military operation of this size, he's General Edward Campanelli, Sir."

The Senior Military Officer growled in an angry tone at the Colonel's offer, "Jesus H. Christ and miracles, you have got to be shitting me Colonel White. Why in the name of the good Christ Child would you ever offer us that sack of shit up to run a military operation of this size, sir? The only reason that waste of a Military Officer is still in the service, is because someone felt sorry for the damn ass, and assigned him some talking shits to keep him occupied. So the damn fool could make his thirty then get out, and not soon enough for my liking, sir."

John glared at her as he snapped, "Ma'am, you're the one who asked me if I knew of anyone else more qualified to run the operation, and I gave you my answer, take it or leave it for what it's worth, Ma'am. But I'll not stand here and allow you rip apart a damn good man, just because you have a finger up your ass for the man, Ma'am."

"You better watch your damn step with me around here mister, or I'll have your ass for..."

Rockjaw cut in and placed a quick end to the slight confrontation going on between the two military officers, "Enough! John, I like it when my Officers speak their mind, just as long as they speak the truth. But I'm forced to agree with General Matteoni on this one sir. This man was politically put out to pasture, sir. He's all washed up, John. Is he still moping around and crying over that bitch he was screwing in the Sudan during the war, sir?"

John was really pissed off as his fists tightened up, and he openly glared at the General.

The General easily read the harsh look and fired off at Colonel, "I think I might have over stepped my bounds a might here sir. I apologize sir. I know General Campanelli's a close friend or yours sir, and I appreciate you sticking up for him like you are, sir."

John took in a quick breath and let it out slowly as he fought to control his temper and then offered, "General Weidenbacher Sir, putting my friendship for the General aside, he's the one best qualified to run this possible operation. He's well respected by his Commanders who'll be in the field carrying out staff orders. He has great command of the ideas of warfare, combining Army, Marines, Airforce and Navy operations to make a complete attacking force, with the least loss of life to all military forces. I can't tell you how his forces reacted to every command issued by the now General sir, during the Middle East conflict. There wasn't one unit that wouldn't have followed Campanelli to hell and back if he ordered them, and that's all anyone can expect from a Commander, sir. But that's not the half of it sir. I can't explain it, no soldier can sir. But, you'd have to be in the field under fire, to know what I'm trying to say here, sir."

General Weidenbacher interrupted the Colonel's words again, "Colonel White, I was in the field as every other soldier at this table has been, and we understand what you're trying to say to us, sir. You gave me something to think about though, mister. One question I have to ask you is, what's General Campanelli's state of mind, sir? Is he over Captain Mendoza's death? I know how much she meant to him and I can sympathize with the Officer, but will he be able to take command again, and what's the status with his wife, sir?"

"General Weidenbacher Sir, I went down to visit him, and I can tell you that he's..." The Colonel's reply was cut off when a question was thrown out at him.

"Hold it right there for a moment Colonel White Sir. General Palmieri informed us Officers you requested emergency leave to be with a friend in need. Is General Campanelli this friend in need, and if so, what's his need, mister? This is extremely important to all gathered here this morning sir. We can't possibly have a General in Command of this massive an operation, if he's unstable, sir." The Senior Military Officer snapped at the Colonel.

"Whoa, I didn't request any damn emergency leave time, General Matteoni. Let me straighten this here mess out before it goes any further, Ma'am. I requested leave time to visit a dear friend who was having a little trouble in his marriage. That's all Ma'am."

"Trouble in his marriage is trouble in his life Colonel White, and I don't want any Officer in Command of an operation like this one, Colonel. If he's having any damn trouble in his marriage or personal life, sir."

General Weidenbacher held up his hand to silence General Matteoni's gripe as he offered in a calm tone, "C'mon John, as I said before, I respect your sticking up for this fucking friend of yours, but I have to know what the hell's going on in General Campanelli's life and mind, sir. Before I can dare offer him up as Supreme Commander of this operation to the President, sir. Give me the true low down on this fucker, or you'll be cleaning out a mind field using your damn foot as a fucking mine detector, mister."

John deflated a bit and then grumbled, "General Weidenbacher Sir, General Campanelli's getting a divorce. Part of his problem is his not having anything to do, so he spends all his time driving his wife nuts. If he's placed in Command of this project, it'll be the best thing to happened to him, and I feel we owe him this much for all he did in the Middle East." John looked at Matteoni then added. "Ma'am no matter what state his private life's in, I know it wouldn't cloud his decisions or military actions, or cause him to make a mistake. He's all soldier and he worries about his troops. I'll always say Campanelli's the best man for the job."

She was angry over the way Colonel White spoke to her in front of the other Generals attending the meeting. But General Matteoni also respected him, and his commander for the spirit he had instilled in this black officer. She rose as she openly glared angrily at him, and then she leaned her hands flat on the desk.

General Weidenbacher kept an eye on Matteoni. He wanted to see if the Colonel was able to get her goat with his last remarks about General Campanelli which were obviously aimed at her.

General Matteoni glared at White as she barked at him angrily, "Mister, I changed my mind about General Campanelli. If he could get you to challenge me in this manner, he must be one hell of an Officer. But I'll warn you in no uncertain terms Mr. White, if we give this General the nod, and he fucks up in any way, shape or form, buster. I'll personally have your ugly black ass hanging from my door, and I'll spend my time throwing darts at it, sir. Do I make myself perfectly clear to you? It's your ass on the line if he falls apart if we use him sir."

Laughter instantly filled the room until General Weidenbacher stood. He too, was glaring at Colonel White, and then he turned to Matteoni and snapped at her, "General Matteoni Ma'am, I'm pleased this insubordinate piece of shit here wasn't able to get your goat. Of course, I wouldn't have blamed you if you tore him a new asshole, Ma'am. He would've deserved it Ma'am. I surrounded myself with all top notch Officers who can control themselves." After saying this, the powerful General turned back Colonel White and addressed him again, "You better watch how you address my Officers around here if you know what's good for your ass, mister. The only reason I tolerated your insolence is because when any Officer, no matter what his grade is allowed to speak his mind when he comes before the Staff. You almost stepped over the line in your damn defense of your Commander, it's a good defense might I add, Colonel White. I feel this Officer deserves a closer look at, sir.

"I want you to get your ass back over to Langley Air Force Base. I'll have a Navy EA-6B Prowler four seater being used for a trainer waiting on standby for you, mister. I want you to go back down to Florida. You can have the pilot land at the Venice Airport this time, and pick up that sorry ass sonofabitch, and get his ass up here so we can talk with him, and see how bad a shape he's really in, Colonel White. If he doesn't want to come, you're to leave him behind to rot, and then get back here yourself without him, sir.

"I'm gonna send the Generals home for the rest of the day, they're well beat out, mister. I want you back here by no later than tomorrow morning by Seven Hundred Hours. Don't be surprised at what you might see resting on the tarmac at Langley when you leave for that pain in the ass friend of yours, sir. The pain in the ass Navy League has been busting my balls about the forced retirement of the A-6 Intruders. We held out enough of these aircraft to give each of the eleven active Carrier groups six each of these aircraft. The damn Navy League have been a strong enough force to have three Carriers put into limited use as trainer ships. Now, get your ass out of here before I have it shot off for ya, so I can go home and get some sleep sir."

General Matteoni requested to speak before the Colonel was allowed to leave the room. She stared at Colonel White for a long moment and then said, "Colonel White Sir, I assure you General Campanelli's not out of the woods quite yet, sir. I can't wait until he sees whose going to be sitting in on the meeting he's going to be attending, mister. You can tell him for me Raymond P. Manning is going to be here waiting for the pleasure of seeing him again, sir."

The Colonel's face betrayed his anger as he openly glared at General Matteoni.

General Weidenbacher saw the harsh look and remarked angrily, "Is there something wrong with Mr. Manning meeting General Campanelli, Colonel?"

"General Weidenbacher Sir, I don't think so but just in case, I can't be held responsible for the welfare of Manning once General Campanelli lays eyes on his sorry ass again, sir. You see General Weidenbacher, General Campanelli and Manning had numerous run ins throughout the years sir, and the last time they met, I think General Campanelli at the time, threatened to frag the pain in the ass civilian, sir."

The General rolled his eyes and then moaned at his officer, "Colonel White, I think it'll be a wise idea for you to warn General Campanelli in advance that Mr. Manning will be attending the meeting, and he'll treat this civilian with the utmost of respect, sir. You better warn him I'm going to have armed guards at the meeting, and they'll have orders to stop him if he makes a move on this civilian. His personal feelings will have to be left outside this door, you got it sir?" The General warned as he pointed at the two wide oak doors which led to the meeting room.

General Weidenbacher got up and continued speaking to his command staff. "Why don't you people all go home for the day. We'll meet at Oh, Six Hundred Hours tomorrow morning, have some coffee and wait for these two to show up. Good day Generals." Weidenbacher was the first to leave the room, but he didn't head home. He reported to the President on their pick. He found himself asking the President if he could eliminate the civilian from the meeting.

President Albert Cole refused General Weidenbacher's request without asking why. However, he did inform the General he was going to be an active participate in the meeting from the Situation Room, and the Secretary of State, along with the Secretaries of Defense, Navy, Army, and Airforce, along with the Director of the CIA John Raincloud, and the Deputy Secretary of Defense, were all going to be present with him at the meeting. That meant the hated civilian was going to be at the Command Center itself also.

General Weidenbacher did not like having this civilian attending his meeting. It was one thing to have him sitting in on the meeting from the Situation Room, but it was quite another to have him actually sitting in at the Pentagon. All of a sudden, he could understand why General Campanelli disliked this civilian so much, and he never even met the man. He bid his good-byes to the President and then hung up, feeling weary as he reached into the breast pocket and removed a sliver flask with the crest of the First Air Cav., and took a stiff belt of warm Rye. The almost hot liquid made his body shiver. "What a hell of a fucking world we live in." He growled as he started for the parking lot and his vehicle. He wanted to get home, have a steak and make love to his wife. Then he was going to turn in for the day.

CHAPTER 4

Colonel John White found himself sitting in the cockpit of the refurbished Prowler aircraft, as it taxied down the runway. He glanced at the other A-6 Intruders lining one end of the rarely used runway, and wondered how many more of the aircraft there were not sitting in plain sight. He knew if the General said they had sixty six of the planes set aside for the Carrier Strike Force. Then there had to be at least twice that many kept in the ready, hidden out of sight. Which would explain why the Airforce base would have a Navy aircraft sitting on the ground? Evidently, the Navy was using the Prowler to train pilots for the A-6 Intruders. The planes were identical, except for the second cockpit behind the first one to allow four pilots to sit in the aircraft.

The Colonel shook his head sadly as he thought how far behind militarily the United States had become lately. With the deep cuts in military spending, and the forced retirements of many good officers and military equipment, only served to severely weakened the United States, although it remained superior to all others militaries of the rest of the world. Couple this with the two recent police actions carried out in Somalia and Haiti by the military, had drained off much of the money reserves of the Armed Forces, causing even more in the ways of cut backs on maintenance of military equipment and aircraft, until many tanks and other military vehicles became undependable. It was a real shame the Armed Forces had to resort to hiding aircraft and sneaking around to keep the retired Aircraft Carriers ready for active duty.

He was so deep in thought that he did not realize his plane was given the final clearance to takeoff. Seconds later he was on his way for Florida again. After a rather bumpy flight, the pilot called out to the green looking Colonel. "Well, there it is Colonel White Sir. Venice Airport, off to our left side sir. We should be landing in less than ten minutes now sir. It sure is a great day to be in Florida sir. The weather's warn and the chicks will be out in force, sir."

He listened in as the pilot contacted the Venice Airport Tower Air Traffic Controller as he fought to keep his stomach down.

"Venice Tower, this is Flight R, One, One, Eight out of Washington. Am requesting permission to land at this time sir. Over." The pilot reported over his radio.

"Flight R, One, One, Eight, this is Venice Tower. You're cleared to land on Runway Three, sir. I repeat, Runway Three, sir. You're to make your final approach from the southwest. Winds are at three miles an hour from the northeast with gusts of up to ten miles an hour. Temperature is seventy four degrees, sir. You're cleared to drop down to one thousand feet. I have a baby Cessna landing then you're up Flight R, One, One, Eight. Stand by please. Over."

The pilot looked at John. "We should be on the ground in a few minutes now Colonel."

"Thank Christ for that much, mister. I gotta take a damn piss so bad my fucking eye balls are floating in my skull, sir."

The pilot laughed at the Colonel's remark as he replied, "I hear that loud and clear sir."

"Flight R, One, One, Eight. You're cleared to land sir. How do you wish to land your aircraft sir? Do you want us to control it for you, or do you wish to control your own landing, sir. We know how you fighter pilots like to use the instruments whenever landing, sir. Over."

"Tower, I'll take that option. I'll make this an instrument landing. Starting my approach now."

"Very well then Flight R, One, One, Eight, you control your own aircraft sir. Over."

The pilot landed as smooth as silk. John hopped out and he actually ran for the bathroom. When he came out he asked the lady behind the information desk where he could catch a cab.

She pointed to a man sitting by a window and said, "He'll take you where you want to go sir."

John hurried over to the sleeping man and snapped at him, "Hey buddy, I need a fucking ride. You up to taking me where I gotta go, buddy?"

The guy got up and asked John where he wanted to go. In ten minutes, he was standing in front of General Edward 'Popeye' Campanelli's house. The Colonel checked his watch, it was after eight in the morning, and he spotted Ed doing something in the backyard. John walked over to him and Ed did not see him coming so John called out. "Hey shithead, is that all you gots ta do around here, old man. Fucking around with a stinking fishing pole all day long my friend."

Campanelli spun around, only to see his old friend coming at him, and he immediately bitched at him, "For Christ sake, don't tell me you saved the damn world already John. I thought I just got rid of your stinking black ass around here, old buddy. Did you eat yet man?"

"Hell no, since when does the government feed its hired help man." John turned serious. "Say Eddie we gotta talk some. Something's come up, and I think we're going to need you again sir."

The General's shoulders sagged, he always hoped he saw his last action, but yet, his heart was beating faster at the news he might be need again. "C'mon in John. We'll eat and then talk."

Cathy was messing around in the house and when she saw John, she kissed his cheek.

"Honey, John's hungry I believe doll."

His wife fixed up some ham and eggs. She was a soldier's wife long enough to know when something was up, and the two officers needed to talk privately. She made a lame excuse she had some shopping to do, and then she dressed her son and she was gone that quick.

Both men did not speak until they were certain she left then Campanelli looked at John.

John smiled as he said with a mouthful of eggs, "Hey Campey, I hope I didn't open my big mouth again, and get you into a heap of trouble with your pretty lady, my friend."

"Why is that man?" he replied as he stared back at his life long friend.

"Well, as you know Eddie, I was called up to the Pentagon, because we're on a Class Three Alert. And the Big Brass informed me they looking for someone to place in Command of a possible major invasion force this time around, sir. General Palmieri decided to place me in Command of this possible invasion force, can you imagine that shit for a stinking minute, man?" the rather large black Colonel replied to General Campanelli as he sort of stared at him.

"Jesus Christ, we must be in trouble if they want you in Command." Eddie laughed at John.

"Shit, I felt the same way Eddy. Anyway, I told them I didn't want the stinking job Ed. Rockjaw asked me who I felt should be placed in command, and I told him you Eddy."

The General did not say anything, instead he rose and began to pace the kitchen as John cleaned his plate. "Shit, shit, shit." he said as he walked back and forth before the kitchen sink.

John looked at the pacing and obviously troubled man and mumbled at him, "Ed, they sent me back here to ask you if you'd take the fucking Commanding position, sir. Nothing sure yet mind you, Eddy. We might be overreacting a bit here, but this new Republican President wants to take nothing for granted, sir. He wants us ready for any event, just in case Ed."

"What's it all about John?" Campanelli asked with some concern as he retook his seat again.

"Dunno yet man, when I told them I wasn't interested in taking over the Command, I was immediately dropped from the loop, sir. They stopped talking about the operation, Eddy. They were more interested in who was going to run the damn operation, rather than tell me anything more about the possible mission. One thing I do know though Ed, is this thing is big sir."

"Shit, shit, shit. I can't believe this damn shit for a fucking minute, dammit." the General grumbled as he stood and began to paced the kitchen again.

John interrupted Campanelli's thoughts, "Campey, they're concerned about your home life, my friend. If you decide to head this one, they're going to really bust your horns about it, sir."

He turned to his friend and offered. "Cathy and I are going to get a divorce, John. We decided that just today. So this is no longer a problem they should be concerned about, sir."

"Shit, I'm sorry to hear that crap, old buddy," John replied sadly and shook his head.

"No big thing. It's been over for a long time. We were just too stubborn to realize it John."

John poured himself a glass of orange juice as he added, "One thing I have to warn you about though. Your old friend is gonna be at the stinking meeting, if you choose to come to it that is."

"Oh yeah, who is that?" General Campanelli asked as he poured himself some orange juice.

"Ray!" Colonel White replied, and then he braced for the flood of curses he knew was coming.

"What the hell's that cocksucker going to be doing at a military meeting for crap sake?"

John laughed as he quickly added to his words to the General, "Calm down a little my old friend. He has a job advising the President on saving money, and where to make further cuts. The man's a personal friend of the President's, so you better watch your Ps and Qs with him. I have a warning from General Weidenbacher. He told me to warn you he'll have an armed guard in the room, ready to deal with you if you aggravate the stinking shitbird. I know he's kidding about the guard, but he was serious about how you treat the lousy dude, so go easy on him will ya sir."

"Shit, I didn't give you my answer yet, and you're already giving me warnings from the damn General on how I should act." Campanelli smirked as he grinned at the Colonel.

"Eddy, I know you better than you know your fucking self I believe, and when your country calls, you're going to fricking jump my friend and come a running, man. And your country's a calling ya ass loud and clear, and from the looks of things here, if you don't mind my saying so, Eddy. You have nothing holding you back here any longer, sir."

He glared at his friend, mainly because he was right about leaving nothing behind him. He looked to a snapshot of his son, the son who all but ignored him. "Right. What's our next step?"

"Ed, I have a Prowler aircraft at my disposal waiting for us at that tiny thing you people call the Venice Airport down here, sir. We don't have to report to Washington until Oh, Six Hundred Hours tomorrow morning, sir. You have plenty of time to pack your shit, and also say your good-byes to Cathy and your son. I'm going to try my hand at some fishing while I'm down here man. That's the real reason why I came down here in the first place, Ed."

"Don't hand me that shit you fucker you. You thought I needed your stinking help, and that's why you dragged your black ass down here," the General laughed at his friend.

John laughed as well, partly because he could see life quickly returning to his old friend's eyes and body, now he knew his government needed him again.

He was off like a shot, as he stuffed his clothes in a old sea bag. Soon, the General was whistling as he rummaged through his drawers, looking for what he wanted to take with him.

John knew the whistling would stop real soon, because it could cause a soldier his life to absentmindedly let out with a whistle on any battlefield. General Campanelli was ready to leave within an hour later, but the Colonel had a hook in the water, and he already caught himself two red snappers.

He laughed at the sight of this big man with his son's tiny fishing pole locked in his massive hands as he grumbled at him, "Hey John, I hate to tell you this shit man, but red snapper's are out of season right now man. If the game warden spots you with those damn fish, he's going to fine your dumb ass big time for each one of the damn things you caught there, mister."

He looked from Campanelli to the fish, "Well Christ, you picked a fine time to tell me these fucking fish are illegal." John picked up the fish and made a move to throw them in the canal.

"Whoa, hold on there for a minute big man. Don't throw them damn things away now buddy. They're dead, we might as well leave them for Cathy, she loves to eat fish, John."

"What about the stinking fish cops?" John asked as he looked at Ed then back to the fish.

"They rarely come in here, so don't worry about the damn things will ya. Fish cops, gees John damn." General Campanelli grumbled at his lifelong friend as he smiled at him now.

Both men laughed as John quickly wrapped up the small pole, "Aren't you going to wait until Cathy returns, so you can tell her where you're going, and when you might be back old buddy?"

"Naw, she doesn't care and neither do I. Its better this way for me to just get the hell out of her life before she returns. It'll be much easier for the both of us this way, John. I left her a note explaining most of it along with the bank books, and I also signed the house over to her and told her where to send the divorce papers. It's really over my friend."

"Shit." John said as he followed his friend out of the front gate. A cab instantly pulled up and he looked at the General as if this was some kind of Omen.

"Put your fucking eyes back in your head will ya. I called the guy before I left the house, asshole. No one here has ESP." They piled into the cab, John soon found himself at the airport.

The Prowler was in the process of being refueled by a DEA fuel truck. Where it came from was a mystery to John. The pilot waved them over to his plane when he noticed the two officers.

"Major, how soon until you're ready to be airborne sir?" he asked the pilot.

"Shit Colonel White Sir, I was kind of hoping to get something for myself to eat, and to check out some of the night life around here before we left for Washington, sir. I heard some wild stories about Florida women, sir. Can't you wait until a little later on before returning to the cold, snow covered Washington area, Colonel White? After all Colonel, we don't have to be back until tomorrow morning at the latest, sir." The pilot complained to the military officer.

He snapped at the over excited young pilot, "Naw, General Campanelli wants to get the hell outta here toot sweet so he doesn't have to face his wife, so we're going right now sir." he pointed at Campanelli with a slight movement of his head.

The Colonel and Edward followed the pilot over to the aircraft. They took the rear seats so they could talk. The General's nerves were tightening up already. He hated flying with a passion, especially since his helicopter crash when he lost Captain Mendoza. He tightened his grip on the arms of his chair as the pilot fired up the engines to full takeoff power.

The Colonel immediately noticed his friend's predicament and smiled to himself. He did not mind flying and could not understand Eddie's fear. The two were plastered in their seats as the sleek aircraft shot up in the air. The pilot climbed to twenty five thousand feet before leveling off. The flight was over water this time, because the weather calmed down some. The pilot contacted the Control Tower at Langley when he was in range on the special coded channel.

The General listened in as the pilot reported their present position, speed, direction and height. At the end of the communication the pilot remarked. "Flight's feet are wet sir. Over."

General Edward Campanelli looked to Colonel John White who was also listening to the pilot's communication with a confused look on his face. The Colonel realized he was looking for an explanation of the pilot's last remark.

"Christ Ed, don't you know shit about pilot jargon sir? Wet feet means the flight's over water. It's no big deal sir," Colonel White offered to the General with a huge grin on his lips this time and then he glanced out the side window to make sure he was right about what he offered to Ed.

General Campanelli smiled as he looked out of the window. His death grip he had on the handles of his seat lessened a little, as he became a little preoccupied with the unusual cloud formations moving over the Ocean.

The Army Colonel laughed for no reason this time. Colonel White looked at his friend as if he was losing his mind. The General kept laughing as he rummaged through his sea bag and then mumbled at John, "You gotta see this stinking shit man." He kept searching until he found what he wanted and offered, "Ah, here it is." the General said as he fastened a button on his shirt.

John had to lean forward to read the words on the button. "Don't blame me, I voted for Bush."

A smile spread across the Colonel's face as he busted out laughing himself. After a few minutes, he grinned and offered at the other officer, "Shit, I hope you don't intend to wear that damn thing to the fucking meeting my friend. It'll drive dear old Manning nuts if he sees that shit on your ass, man. He really hated President Bush with a passion you know."

The General continued to laugh as he moaned between his laughing at the Colonel, "I know, and I intend to shove the damn pin right down his damn throat if he says one fucking word to me over it, man. I hate that lousy little cocksucker that much I tell you man."

"C'mon Eddie, you're really not going to start any trouble with the little prick at the damn meeting are you? It's gonna be my stinking ass if you do start something, sir."

"Only if he picks a fucking fight with my stinking ass first, John." General Campanelli laughed again, knowing as soon as Manning and the General saw each other, the shit was going to be hair in the air and blood on the ground at the meeting.

As the aircraft got closer to Washington, the sky started showing some signs of snow in the air. The General looked to John who snorted at him, "It was snowing before I left, they're expecting three inches of the crap. I want you to spend the day with my wife and I when we land. That way, we can head for the Pentagon together tomorrow morning, Ed. I'll take you out for supper, this way you won't have to go to a damn hotel, and you can enjoy some good eating man."

"Sure thing." The General retorted as he glanced out the canopy and saw more clouds.

The last fifteen minutes of the flight was completed in silence as the General prepared for the landing. He figured out it was not the flying that bothered him so much, but the landing and taking off that bugged him. His hands tightened on the handles of his seat again as the plane swung left to align itself with the runway properly. The pilot leveled off as he began his descent, keeping in constant contact with the tower because of the icy weather conditions below. Seconds later, they were down and the General was standing on the ice covered tarmac stretching his arms and legs. A staff car immediately made its way over to the two military officers, stopping right in front of them, and a young Sergeant instantly jumped out of the vehicle and opened the door.

"Sirs, my name's Sergeant Thomas Donaldson, sirs. I'm assigned to be your personal driver all the while you're visiting Washington, sirs. I've taken the liberty to register you two Officers at the Washington Hilton Hotel, so you'll both be near everything in the city, sirs. I made certain you can see all the monuments and stuff from the rooms as well, sirs."

The General cut the smiling Sergeant off by saying to him, "Son, I'm going to be spending some extra time with Colonel

White here, he so graciously offered to put me up at his home while I'm stuck visiting here…"

"I'll cancel all of your reservation then, General," the Sergeant said, not missing a stride.

"Good recovery there Sarge." The General laughed as he got into the waiting car.

"Seems like old fucking times again, huh Eddie? Damn, I really hate meeting like this Ed. One of these fucking days, we're going to meet under much more pleasant circumstances than always preparing for another possible fucking war, sir," John offered with a grin.

"Yeah, it sure does man. I just hope no one has to die in this upcoming possible operation though John," General Campanelli replied and then he thought what a stupid remark that was. When soldiers of different Armies come together, kids are going to die.

"Forget it, they wouldn't be calling on us if they didn't want someone to die in this possible mess Eddy," John snapped back as he turned his head and looked out the window.

No matter what the General did, he just could not get warm as he complained at the Colonel, "I didn't miss this fucking shit, not for a stinking moment I tell ya man."

"I hear you there Ed," John pulled his collar closed and shivered. He called out the roads to his house. His wife rushed out and when Popeye got out of the car, she kissed him and shivered.

"Get back in the house before you freeze to death Beth. You're freezing standing out here like that honey," John snapped at his lovely wife as she immediately ran back inside the home with her arms folded across her chest. She looked at Ed, and then complained at him, "Poor man, you must be freezing also, Edward. You have to be nuts to come back up here from Florida, Eddy."

"Fraid so Beth," General Edward Campanelli smiled at his best fiend's wife warmly.

When John entered his home, he announced he wanted the children dressed for supper, and he was going to take everyone out on this night for a good meal.

His wife balked at the offer as she complained at her husband, "There's no way you're going to take me out to dinner on a day like this. First off honey, its 2:30 and miserable outside, and besides, I've been slaving over a hot stove all day. Ever since you called and told me you were going to drag this poor soul back up here in all this mess, my love. You men are going to go upstairs and wash your hands for supper. Then I'm going to serve you a meal that'll make you guys never want to leave home again. Edward, it's so good to see you one again," She kissed him as he gave her a gentle hug. When he let her go, she asked him how Cathy was.

The General lowered his gaze and he then offered her in a low and shaky voice. "Not too good, I'm afraid we're in the middle of getting a divorce."

Beth frowned as she ran her hand down his arm, "Ohhhh, I'm so sorry to hear that Edward."

John cut her off before she said too much, "Enough hon. will ya please. C'mon Eddy." The two military officers went upstairs to wash for supper as they were ordered. Half an hour later, they returned to discover the table set, and Beth was sitting in the living room watching her children playing Nintendo on the television. She stood as they came in.

"Oh boy, I love the WWF Royal Rumble man. C'mon man, I'll take you on Johnny. I'm pretty good with this damn game you know, kid." General Campanelli challenged John Jr. as he stepped over John's daughter lying on the floor, and she handed him her controller to use against her brother who was already beating her in the game.

John looked at his wife and she said to him with a smile on her lips, "I'm afraid he'll never really grow up honey. Look at the big fool enjoying himself with John Jr."

"And you love it and you wouldn't be happy if he wasn't acting like this, my love," John replied as he watched his friend play with his son and the game.

John's wife Beth smiled again as she headed off to the kitchen, followed by her husband. He helped her in the kitchen as Ed and John Jr. argued with each other, as they beat each other silly on the screen with the game they were playing.

John smiled at his wife as he gently cupped her breasts from behind her and then he offered in his sexy voice. "He really loves John Jr. my lady."

"He also loves you too you know hon. I think he'd die if he ever lost your friendship, my dear," She shot back as she enjoyed what he was doing to her body.

Listening to the two of them playing the game together, John had to admit to his smiling wife "Yeah, you're right honey. He's having some fun with our son, baby."

Supper was a great success, and Beth had to actually stop serving food to get the two men away from the table, so she could start cleaning up the dishes. The children received the silent message from their father, and they immediately announced they were going off to bed.

General Campanelli looked at his watch, it was seven thirty and he asked, "How the hell did you get them to go to bed so early and easily, John?"

"It's easy, all you have to do is give them one of John's looks, and the kids will leave the room in a heartbeat,

Edward," Beth offered to the General as she smiled warmly at him.

"I know what you mean Beth. I was on the receiving end of a few of those looks myself, and I wanted to leave the room as fast as I possibly could too, Beth," he said to John's wife as he turned and looked at John and grinned at him.

The three close friends talked half the night away, before finally turning in for the night for their bodies need for some sleep. The General was awakened by Colonel White at exactly three thirty in the morning, as White announced in a rather warm tone of voice to Campanelli, "Hey Eddy, I'm afraid it's time to get up and get going, buddy. Beth insists on making us some breakfast before we leave for the stinking office this morning, Ed."

After they ate, Beth gave both John and Campanelli a kiss before they left.

The staff car was already waiting outside John's home for the two officers.

Most of the heavy snow was cleared away from the main roads already. But it was still dark out, and with a heavily overcast sky with snowflakes still lightly falling, no light came from the hidden stars or moon on this night. The street lights gave off an eerie and low glow to the streets below, and when a town truck suddenly appeared roaring down the road. It looked like a metal monster coming out of the murkiness while breathing fire and sparks, as the metal snow plow dragged on the road surface, in an attempt to remove all the snow as possible from the surface.

The two military officers watched the massive snow plow truck as it slowly passed them. The Sergeant held open the door to the staff car and announced, "Ready to go sirs?"

The young driver of the staff car gunned the motor a few times, and then the car bucked and then skidded and spun its tires along the slush covered roadway leading to the Pentagon building, before finally catching traction and driving correctly. The two officers knew they were going to be early for the scheduled meeting. But it did not matter much to them, because they knew sure as hell, General William Weidenbacher would already be at his office at the Pentagon, and he would be waiting for them to show up, no matter what time they arrived at the building, or what the weather conditions were like outside.

The staff car stopped at the guard shack, and the Gate Sergeant and an armed Army security guard checked their military ID's. The driver then pulled over to his designated slot, and from out of nowhere, another Army Corporal security guard instantly appeared, and he growled hotly at the two officers for them to follow him. The two soldiers followed the guard as he entered the heated foyer, and then they headed for the elevator.

"Get in, General Weidenbacher is waiting for you two Officers in his office already," the security guard grumbled as he held the elevator door from closing on them.

"For Christ sake Corporal, what the hell's wrong with your stinking ass anyway, did you get up on the wrong side of the fucking bed this morning, and bump into a damn wall or something, buster? Lighten up some will ya mister. You're young and you have your whole life ahead of your ass, mister!" John snarled extremely angrily at the young and rude acting military security guard, as he stared at the non commissioned officer.

The Corporal completely ignored the angry remark from the officer in the elevator cab with him, as he continued to stare straight ahead at the highly polished brass doors before him, waiting to be relieved of the two officers already. All the while, the Corporal was cursing the two officers under his breath for making him leave a nice warm bed, with a hot young broad he picked up at the local bar last night waiting for his return. Just his luck to get stuck pulling this special guard duty at the building on such a shitty day.

The military security guard watched the floor designator as it quickly marked off the levels of floors they were passing. F3 clearly showed up in the small window, and the elevator cab slowed down, and then the still angry Corporal announced in a dry and hot tone of voice to the officers. "You're on your own from here on in sirs," the security guard spat out at the two officers still in a rather angry tone.

This time it was General Campanelli who shot a harsh glare at the angry sounding Corporal, as he warned him in no uncertain words, "Why the fuck don't you go home and get yourself fucking laid or something, mister. Maybe it'll help improve your god damn disposition a might for you, you little fucker you."

The Corporal snapped back at the pair of officers without missing a beat, "Sirs, that was exactly what I was doing when I pulled this shit duty for the damn day, sirs."

General Campanelli looked at Colonel White with a smirk on his lips, and then they both laughed as they left the elevator with John complaining at the General, "Now I know why the little fucker was in such a shitty mood this morning, Eddy. I'd sure as hell be snapping at anyone and everyone I came across, if I had to leave a good looking young hen lying in bed for this shit duty, man. The poor kid, he's probably going to end up fighting with his lady when he gets back home to her today. But the damn jerk knew what he was doing when he first enlisted in the service. So fuck him where he breaths from, man. Let's get going, I'm certain General Weidenbacher's already busy checking his fucking watch, and he's probably cursing the living shit out of us by now my friend. The old man has no god damn sense of humor any longer, Ed."

Page 97

CHAPTER 5
CENTRAL COMMAND CENTER
THE PENTAGON, WASHINGTON DC
JANUARY 13th, 1997 WEDNESDAY 0430 A.M.

When General Edward Campanelli and Colonel John White turned the corner in the hallway of the Pentagon, they immediately spotted General William Weidenbacher stuffing a Danish in his mouth, while sitting on the edge of a table with three coffee pots perking. General Weidenbacher saw the two of them coming, and he nearly choked on the dry cake, and then he put his huge paw out and General

Campanelli shook it. He was sorry, because he felt like he stuck his hand in a vice as the General pumped his hand and said in an excited voice, "Well how the hell are they hanging sir, it's good to see ya again Ed. How's life treating you lately my boy?"

General Campanelli pulled his hand free and shook it to get his circulation back as he replied, "Not too bad, I'm hanging in there sir."

"Don't give me any of that shit, mister. Life sucks the big one and you had your fair share of shit sandwiches to gnaw on, General." The Chairman suddenly turned serious as he warned the lesser General, "Look Ed, I have to warn you about something, it's not going to be a fucking cakewalk in there my friend. I don't want anyone slamming his dick down on the damn table. But we have to make certain you're okay sir, before we put you in Command of a force twice the size you Commanded in the Middle East war games, sir." He looked Campanelli over for a moment, he was tall, six foot three or better, with large shoulders and a waist which was just starting to spread a little. His once brown hair was showing some streaks of gray. But the General knew he would not want to have to mix it up with Campanelli in a hand to hand fight.

"Christ sake Ed, you're getting a little thick around the fucking middle I see there, mister," The powerful Chairman of the Joint Chiefs of Staff rarely if ever used his nickname to General Campanelli's face, out of respect for the man and the soldier.

General Campanelli laughed as he retorted, "It ain't from my wife's cooking I can assure you General," He then patted his belly and added, "It's from sitting on my fucking duff while you guys figured out what the hell you were going to do with my sagging ass, sir. General Weidenbacher Sir, I never figured I'd be leading another invasion force in my life, sir."

"Who the hell told you this was going to be a damn invasion force, buster? All we're talking about at this time is a possible defensive operation needed to stop a possible invasion of one of our Allies. The actor, (The Enemy) isn't defined so far in this damn drama, sir. It could be one of three different countries. China, North Korea or the damn Alliance States, sir."

"The god damn Alliance States, sir?" Campanelli questioned Weidenbacher.

"Look bud, I assure you General, you know all you need to know for the time being. You'll learn the rest, if and when we pick your ass to head this upcoming operation. Why don't you have a cup of coffee and a chunk of cake. It's going to be a long fucking morning for us, and I don't intend calling for any breaks until we picked your brains clean, mister."

While Edward and John stood with the General, other members of the Command Staff came in. Generals Palmieri and Claiborne came in together. Palmieri walked over to John and slapped him on his broad back and remarked at the officer, "I see you got the lazy sonofabitch up here safe and sound for us, sir." General Palmieri then shook hands with Campanelli.

General Luther Claiborne chimed in a booming, deep baritone voice as he grabbed General Campanelli's hand and offered in an excited tone, "How the hell you doing my boy? It's damn good to see ya lilly white ass again, mister. When this shit's over with, you have to come down, and I'll have Martha cook you up a mess of crawdads and grits. There's some damn good looking snappers moving into the area lately, sir. Are you still nuts I hope, my boy?"

"Yes sir, still nuts after all this time sir," he retorted with a grin to the General.

General Claiborne added as if in a warning, "Good, good. Say General, you know that fucking asshole Manning's gonna be attending this here little meeting of ours, and I gots to warn you son. He's the biggest pain in the ass on the entire White House Staff, sir."

"Thanks for the warning General Claiborne. But I have the proper thing to take care of that guy right here, sir," he retorted as he grabbed his balls and then went on. "I'll stick these here babies right down his damn throat if he tries to bust my horns at the meeting, sir."

General Weidenbacher immediately stiffened as he groused at Campanelli in an angry tone of voice, "Look here mister, if you try any of that bullshit against this fucking guy at the damn meeting, I'll cut those little babies off on ya and feed them to my damn dogs. Respect Ed. He's a close friend of the President, and we need the President on our side on this one, if we're going to get the proper military equipment and troops we need for this operation to be a success, sir."

General Campanelli shrugged and then mumbled at the other powerful officer, "I'll give the lousy little turd respect, as long as he respects me, sir. I'm no hand puppet and no one's gonna have his hand rammed up my damn ass to the elbow and pulling my strings, General."

General Weidenbacher put down his cup and offered as he angrily eyed the lesser General, "Except for me mister. I have the feeling you and this civilian is going to give me a shitty day, sir." He ran his hand across his chin and then added to his bitch at the other General, "Look here Ed, I may be a tough audience, but if I'm on your side, I'm on your side, period."

Colonel Mary Locker came down the hall next. She immediately locked onto Campanelli, and headed right for him. She like the man, though she would never tell him so. She respected the way he handled the Marines during the Middle East war as she announced as she put out her hand to shake his, "Well well, General Campanelli as I live and breathe sir. It's amazing who you run into when you're unarmed, sir. I guess the Army will never put you out to pasture I see? If it makes any difference to you sir, my Corps is always looking forward to working with you, sir. You have my vote, and I don't give a shit what's happening in your personal life either, sir. A soldier's a soldier first, and a family man second, sir." She declared as she grabbed his ass and gave a good squeeze. Then she walked away and entered the meeting room laughing.

General Weidenbacher laughed as he feigned shock at her gesture at grabbing Campanelli's ass, and he quickly offered his General, "She's some shit there sir. The service could use a helluva lot more soldier's like that one, sir. I'd give my left nut for one more like her, sir. Ed, if she's on your side then you have nothing to worry about here, son."

"Yeah, and I wish she'd grab my ass once in a while sir," General Claiborne complained.

General Palmieri smirked at the large black General as he offered with a smirk, "Now why the hell would she ever want to grab your black ass for sir."

General William Weidenbacher suddenly looked at his watch, it was already five twenty. He shoved himself off the table and then announced sharply to the other military officers gathered with him, "It's getting late people. So I suggest we go in and sit down and start this damn meeting off. Ed, I want you to come in after I send for you sir. We might have some things we want to discuss without you in our presence, sir. Sort of talking behind your back if you will, mister. John will sit in the meeting with us, and I'll send him out to fetch you if and when we have any need of your ass in there, sir. Is this okay with you General Campanelli Sir? I have to make certain everyone is working off the same sheet of music for this damn meeting before we drag your ass in there, and then we start tearing you apart for some sport, sir."

General Campanelli shook his head in the affirmative as he took a sallow of his coffee.

General Weidenbacher led the way with the rest of the officers gathered in the hallway following him into the Pentagon Command Center. As he entered, he noticed Manning was already seated. Weidenbacher shook his head, because he hated having a civilian sitting in on a major military briefing. The General nodded towards Manning who nodded back at him.

It took a few moments for the rest of the military officers to take their seats and end their own conversations. When they were all seated, the three television screens came on. Sitting in the larger middle screen was the President of the United States. On the screens to either side of the President sat other members of his White House Council. President Cole nodded politely to General Weidenbacher as he spoke, "Good morning General Weidenbacher Sir, I think everyone on both sides of the screens knows each other, so I won't waste time with any introductions. I'd like to set some guidelines for this meeting before we begin though, sir. General Weidenbacher Sir, I know you like to have your Officers say what's on their minds in their own fashion sir, but I must ask anyone responding to a question, to try to keep a civil tongue in their mouths during this entire meeting, sir. There are a number of women on the board today, and I don't like any unnecessary cursing going on myself. Is this clear to everyone, sir?"

Weidenbacher remained seated and he replied to his Commander in Chief, "Yes sir, but on the other hand Mr. President, I can't have certain members of this meeting trying to goad on my Officers, or I can't guarantee anything, sir. Especially if they don't belong here Mr. President."

All eyes immediately went over to the only civilian attending the meeting Manning, and before he could reply the obvious dig at him, the President snapped at his powerful military officer, "That's exactly what I mean General Weidenbacher Sir. Let me set you straight right here and now sir. Everyone attending this meeting belongs here sir, and I'll not stand for any bull about it sir. I know where and at whom that last remark was directed General, and I assure you sir. Mr. Manning's important to the outcome of this meeting, sir. And I'm as quite certain he'll not goad any of your Officers on, and if he does sir, your Officers can respond accordingly, sir. Everyone here has to speak his or her mind, or this Council won't work, General.

"General Weidenbacher Sir, I didn't go to a higher state of alert because of the offer China made to the United Kingdom, sir. I went to a higher state of alert, because I don't know what might happen in this damn region when, and if China enters North Korea. I don't trust any country in that entire region of the world, sir. I don't know if North Korea will resort to the use of nuclear weapons to try and stop China's invasion of their nation. I don't know what direction China might go in if she has so many troops in this area. Will she choose to attack the Alliance States? Will China stop at the North and South Korean borders, or will she continue and attack South Korea, and if she does, what next? Will she be so bold as to dare attack Japan?

"I don't know, but I'll tell you this much, General Weidenbacher Sir. I intend to have enough troops and military equipment staged in the area, in case China oversteps her offer. I dislike not having any operating ground bases in the Asian region, and that's why I'm considering Operation Three, Three, Eight be implemented. You have the file with you General Weidenbacher, in case we settle on this wild card of yours to Command any operation we decide to employ here, sir?"

The General shook his head in the positive to the seated President.

"Good. You'll give General Campanelli the file if I tell you to do so sir. Well, that's all I have to say. But I'll stop anyone from disturbing this meeting, no matter who he or she is, General," The President shot a glance at Manning, who put his head down over the obvious reprimand.

General Weidenbacher turned to Colonel White, and told him to bring in General Campanelli. He went out the double oak doors to fine General Campanelli enjoying a second cup of coffee and grumbled at him, "C'mon Eddie, they want you inside buddy. Keep your head in there, I'm warning you General, the President's in a shit mood already sir."

Campanelli followed John in the room, his eyes settling on Manning who glared at him.

General Weidenbacher easily picked up the harsh look that passed between the two men, and he shook his head again as he let out his breath, and he realized there was going to be some fireworks going off at the meeting soon.

General Campanelli remained standing as he saluted the President first then the rest of the members of the meeting. General Weidenbacher told him to be seated when he was done. No one spoke, it was up to the President to start things rolling at the meeting for them.

"General Campanelli Sir, I must say it's a pleasure to meet you at long last, sir. I heard much about you, both good and bad I'm afraid I must offer you sir," The President announced firmly and then went on with his words. "Let me introduce you to the other members of my Council, sir. To my right is Secretary of State, Maria Hernandez. To her right is National Security Director, Norman Griffin, and on his right is Secretary of Defense, Jerry Levenhagen, and next is Secretary of the Navy, Admiral Dennis Richardson, sir. On my left side is Secretary of the Army, General Dominick Tomasello, and to his left is someone you know already I'm lead to believe, sir. The current Director of the CIA, John Raincloud, sir. You had one of his sons with you in the Middle East mess I was told, General Campanelli Sir."

He nodded politely at the huge Indian, who immediately smiled back at him.

"Sitting at the end of the table is my Deputy Secretary of Defense, Harold B. Clifford. A very dear friend of mine, sir. Well, shall we get down to some brass tacks here." The President said as he clasped his hands together, and then he turned his attention to General Weidenbacher.

General Weidenbacher started as soon as the President gave him the nod, "I believe General Campanelli has already been briefed about the present situation we're facing in Asia. But I'm certain he'll have some questions for us. Colonel John White offered General Campanelli as Supreme Commander over all United States forces to be employed in Operation Wine Press."

"Sure, and why the hell not," Manning mumbled in his microphone and then added to his angry words. "the two of you are joined at the hip."

General Campanelli instantly jumped to his feet to respond to the slanderous remark aimed at him and General

Weidenbacher by the civilian observer, but he was immediately cut off by the suddenly angry President. "Apparently, you didn't understand when I warned everyone to keep a civil tongue in their heads, mister. That'll be quite enough of these inciting remarks from you Mr. Manning, if you wish to continue sitting in on their military briefing, sir."

General Campanelli was still on his feet, his hands clenched tight in balled up fists as he continued to stare at Manning. His body was actually shaking he was so angry at this man. General Weidenbacher turned to Campanelli and ordered his lesser officer, "General Campanelli, take your seat sir. I must apologize for the last remark aimed at you, General."

Campanelli turned to the General, who made a motion with his hand for him to sit down again.

Manning smiled as he watched the General struggle desperately to regain control of his temper again. With one comment, Manning had Campanelli off stride, and right where he wanted him.

"General Campanelli Sir, a question of your state of mind has been brought up to our attention, sir. Everyone here knows of your terrible loss in the Middle East war, and we sympathize greatly with you and your grief, sir. It has also come to our attention your family life's kind of up in the air as well right now, sir. Do you care to make a comment on any of these concerns of ours that I have just brought up to your attention, General Campanelli Sir?"

"Sure thing, I got a handle on my grief of losing a close Officer, and a good friend in that war."

"Lover you mean." Manning snapped nastily back at the large General.

The fuming General was on his feet again, and this time he wasn't to be stopped as he snarled savagely at the smug looking civilian. "Why you lousy little sorry ass sack of shit you! I have a good mind to rip your god damn lungs out through your stinking nose on ya rotten ass."

"General Campanelli, remember where you are sir," General Weidenbacher warned him.

Manning got on his feet also, and then made a threatening stand against the General.

General Campanelli immediately assumed a linebackers stance against Manning, a sign he was digging in for a fight as he warned the civilian in no uncertain terms, "You want to fuck with me, you little paper pushing sack of shit you? Take your best shot at my ass, and I'll stomp a damn mud puddle in your fucking face for you and walk it dry, you little pussy bastard."

Manning hissed, "I don't have to take this shit from a god damn barbarian of a General."

"Why don't you try something then, you piece of shit if you got the balls that is, buster."

General Weidenbacher was on his feet now, and so was the President at the Situation Room of the White House. The extremely concerned General tried to get control over the meeting, glad to see the fires of hell burning bright in the officer before him as he roared, "Gentlemen, and I use this term loosely might I add, you'll take your seats and be quiet, now!"

Both men ignored the General, with their eyes were locked in a stare down of pure hatred.

The President yelled out this time at the two, "You two knock this shit off right this minute! Or I'll have the both of you hog tied and gagged and forced to be seated." The President looked to the Master at Arms standing by the oak doors at the Pentagon.

"Master At Arms, take control of this meeting at once, before someone gets hurt sir."

The good looking Staff Sergeant snapped to attention, and then he turned and opened the double doors. Four rifle carrying Army security guards rushed in and took up position between the two angry men. The guards did not aim their weapons at either person. Instead, they just stood between the two men and waited further orders.

When General Campanelli noticed the security guards enter and take up positions between them, he immediately became calm and took his seat. But Manning had not finished his complaint yet. He looked to the screen and President and cried, "Mr. President Sir, I have never been spoken to by a Military Officer in this manner in my life, sir. I demand you do something about this vile man. I suggest we throw this bum out of the service, sir." Manning turned to General Campanelli and glared as he added just as angrily at him this time. "I'll have your ass busted, and then drummed out of the service for speaking to me like this, mister."

General Claiborne suddenly piped up this time, because he also did not like having this civilian advisor sitting in on the military briefing, and having him jumping all over one of his officers, and pulling his weight like he was important to the meeting. He stood up to emphasize his anger and he glared at the civilian for a long second, and then growled at the man, "Mr. Manning Sir! You're not going to have anyone's ass busted and driven out of the service, mister. I don't know where you think you got this god damn power from sonny. But I aim to tell you buster, you don't command that kind of power here, buster."

The General took a quick breath and then continued with his angry words, "Sir, there's an old saying 'If you go poking a Hornets nest with a sharp stick then you're going to get stung.' And sir, in case you don't realize it yet, you have just been stung, mister. I suggest you sit your skinny little ass down and keep your mouth shut, and stop trying to showing us how stupid you are. Challenging one of our Military Officers to a fight is rather stupid on your part, Mr. Manning. General Campanelli would tear you a new asshole given half a chance and enjoying it, sir."

Manning was furious as hell as he turned his glare towards the other General and hollowed at him this time, "How dare you speak to me like that, you old goat you."

Claiborne smiled and remarked, "Mr. Manning Sir, I thought you could do much better than that, a man of your learning, and me being a dumb black man from the hills of Tennessee. I hope I'm not reading you're challenging me to a fight now sir. Because I don't have to be as polite as General Campanelli here, sir. I have my job secured. A job you can't do anything about, and I'll be damn pleased to rip your fucking head off your shoulders and shit down your neck, you little fucker you." He roared, sending spittle flying everywhere as he grew angrier.

There was a audible click on a handheld radio, and two more security guards ran in the room, and they took up position in front of General Claiborne this time, as he glared at the civilian.

The President was banging his paperweight on the desk and screaming at the same time, "If you men can't act like the professionals you are, I'll have all of you removed from this meeting and you'll be replaced. And I have the power to do so General, and I will." The President glared at the two then turned to the sitting Campanelli and bitched at him now, "You know mister, I heard you can bring out the best, and the worst in men, and I see that statement was correct, sir."

General Campanelli remarked. "Sir, this man started it, and I'm not going to let him get..."

"Don't debate with me mister. You'll come out on the short end of the stick every time I assure you, General Campanelli," the President warned him in no uncertain terms.

Once quiet was restored to the meeting, the Master at Arms nodded at his guards, and they quickly disappeared out of the room. Most of the Generals laughed to themselves as they listened to General Campanelli burn the civilian down to the ground. Most women present were just as pleased at the way General Campanelli handled himself with the civilian.

President Cole plopped down in his chair and let out a disgusted sigh, and then he complained to the other members of the meeting, "I hope that'll be the last of these childish outbursts we'll have to endure at this meeting, if you still have the presence to Command an Army, General Campanelli Sir. I'd have to answer yes to that one. However, respect and command's not based on your powers of presence, sir. I'm sorry for the terrible remark of Mr. Manning, and I'll straighten him out after this meeting has been concluded I assure you, sir. Mr. Manning, I want to see you at my office at four o'clock this afternoon sir."

Manning nodded to the extremely angry looking President of the United States.

The Secretary of State raised a pencil, informing the President she had something to ask, and she got the nod to speak. "General Campanelli Sir, I hate to be the one to ask you this question sir. But I will before someone else does sir. I'd like to know what's happening in your home life sir, and please excuse me for having to ask you this terribly personal question of you sir."

General Campanelli smiled as he nodded at her and then replied to one of his favorite politicians. "Ma'am, I talked to my wife, and we're getting a divorce. We no longer love each other, but we respect one another, Ma'am. It'll be an amicable split, and we'll remain friends for the sake of the children."

"Is this split because you had an affair with, err... excuse me please sir, another woman sir?" The Secretary of the Army asked his subordinate. He did not want to mention Mendoza's name.

"I don't understand the last question sir." Campanelli exploded as he looked at the Secretary.

"It's not that complicated a question I just asked of you, General Campanelli."

"I don't see what the hell that has to do with my taking over Command of the troops, sir."

"Take my word for it sir, it does General Campanelli. Please answer the question General," General Palmieri remarked as he took over questioning the general from the Secretary of State.

"Very well then sir, no. If you must know, my wife also had an affair, even though this wasn't an excuse for my having one, sir. But it happened, and every soldier knows why it had happened, it was because I was never home with her, General Palmieri."

"You're okay? You have no guilt feelings, no reason to go off the deep end?" Palmieri asked.

"No Sir General Palmieri Sir," Campanelli offered back proudly to the other General.

"If you're picked to Command this possible operation, I'm going to recommend you be examined by a Doc for a psyche workup sir, and if he says you're okay, I'll have no problem with you taking over Command of the operation, sir. I looked over your service file, and it's rather impressive, General Campanelli. I can't understand why it took you so long to get a raise in rate sir, but the thing I can tell you sir, is I'd trusted you with my son in battle. And I don't make that statement lightly, sir. It's one hell of a compliment I offer you General. With you at the helm then many mother's children will have a much better chance of coming home, if war breaks out sir." The Secretary of State offered as she resumed her remarks to the concerned military officer.

The rest of the council members realized what a compliment the Secretary was paying to this fine military officer, and most of them had already made up their minds to place General Campanelli in complete Command of Operation Wine Press.

President Cole stared at the Secretary because of her last comment. His usual spitfire who rarely agreed with anything or one, was obviously in love with this officer. The President turned his attention from the Secretary back to General Campanelli. As he studied the stern looking face, he easily picked up the strength emitting from his person, and he too made up his mind to allow General Campanelli have Command of the operation without further debate. His thoughts were suddenly interrupted by Manning, who requested permission to speak by standing.

General Weidenbacher tried to block his request by moving in front of him as he complained at the civilian advisor, "Mr. Manning Sir, you're a civilian, and I don't believe you should have anything to say about a military operation, sir. Besides sir, anything you have to say will only serve to upset my Officer, and the other members this Council, sir."

Manning nodded to the President as he overlooked the angry General and received permission to ask questions. He looked over the angry faces locked on him. He could feel hands tightening around his neck, and it sent a chill down his spine. But he hated this man so much he was willing to risk the wrath of the President to keep him from taking over command of this future operation. He looked at General Campanelli to show him he did not fear him in the least as he snarled angrily at the officer, "General Campanelli, after the war in the Middle East, or should I say when your helicopter crashed. Did you not threaten to kill one of the rescue workers, sir? Didn't you lose control under the pressure of combat and the Fog of War, sir?"

President Cole let out an audible groan over Manning's question as he shook his head.

"I take offense to that remark, you rotten shithead." General Campanelli growled as he stared back at the smug looking civilian advisor. Wanting to take his head off of his shoulders for him.

The word shithead was ignored by Manning as he pressed on with his angry words. "Ahhhh, I'm sorry you're so sensitive I see, General Campanelli. But will you please answer the last question I just put forth to you General Campanelli Sir? Why did you lose your temper with one of the rescue workers helping with the injured on the crashed helicopter, sir"

General Edward Campanelli let out his breath in a sort of sigh as he forced himself to think about the crash that killed Captain Renee Mendoza. His shoulders sagged with the weight of the world, as he tried to get his thoughts together and he responded, "I didn't lose anything under the pressure of combat, sir. The event you're speaking about took place after my helicopter was shot down, and the United States launched missiles on Egypt and Libya. I guess I did lose my temper a little, and I growled at a rescue worker. But he threw my Captain's body inside the helicopter, and I told him I'd kill him if he wasn't more careful and respectful with her body, sir."

"Her body? Do you mean the body of the woman, err, Officer you were having an affair with while you were still married to your present wife, sir?" Manning spat at the officer.

"Mr. Manning, I don't believe you for one moment mister. How dare you force this fine soldier to relive that horrible crash. It doesn't matter whether the dead soldier was his lover or friend. If he thought the body was treated without the proper respect, he was within his limits to growl at the rescue workers. I'm certain the General wouldn't have killed that worker. I think you asked enough questions at this meeting sir. Now you have me angry with you, and I don't like General Campanelli." The Senior Military Officer, General Marianne Matteoni snapped.

Manning gave up as he angrily took his seat again. He glanced at General Campanelli, only to see him wearing the biggest, shit eating grin on his face as he stared back at the civilian. He felt the heat from his anger as he stared back at him.

President Cole looked at General Weidenbacher, and then remarked to his powerful military officer. "General Weidenbacher Sir, please make certain that Mr. Manning's given every possible courtesy while he's within your presence, sir. I'm a little concerned for him over the terrible questions he was just asking, sir." What the President was saying, was he was ordering the General personally, to make certain no harm came to Manning.

General Weidenbacher nodded to the angry looking President.

The President turned to Campanelli and griped at him, "General, you're one pain in my ass."

The room erupted in laughter, breaking the tension that filled the room for so long.

"General Campanelli Sir, it's getting late, sir. I'd like you and Colonel White to leave this meeting, while we have further discussion over the situation facing us at this time, sir. I'm ordering you not to leave the building though, sir. We'll debate today, tomorrow, you'll be invited back in because the United Nations will be convening at the same time as we'll be meeting, General Campanelli. They're going to give North Korea two weeks before sanctions will be imposed, if they fail to get out of nuclear arms development, sir. We'll settle you while we listen in on the damn meeting, sir. We're all getting tired and short tempered here I see. There'll be a two hour break, get something to eat and we'll meet again at two o'clock, sir.

"General Campanelli, I wish to apologize for some of the comments directed at you. I didn't think some of us would be so vicious at this meeting, sir. The Master At Arms will lead you to the waiting area. There's a television and bar, and sleeping quarters nearby if you choose to turn in, sir." The President stood and quickly left the Situation Room. The center screen went dead as the Generals rose and began speaking to each other. No one spoke to Manning. They all headed for the coffee surrounded by trays of sandwiches and cakes. The soldiers descended like locusts, not realizing just how hungry they were, until they started to eat.

A number of the powerful military officers quickly gathered around General Campanelli and Colonel White. Everyone wanted to talk to him at once, making it rather difficult to understand any of the conversations going on between the gathered officers.

John quickly ushered Ed down the hallway leading to the bathrooms, where they happened to run into Manning washing his hands. The two officers walked towards Manning who stopped washing his hands, and then he looked at them like he was searching for someplace to run and hide in fear they were going to attacking him. The General thought to himself, 'Yeah, that's it little sucker you. Scream like the scared pussy you are, you little piece of shit you'.

Campanelli stepped close to the scared looking civilian, near enough to the his face to be extremely intimidating, without verbally threatening or hitting him. He suddenly reached out and grabbed Manning's arm and gave it a hard squeeze. When Manning had enough he pulled his arm free, but the silent message was delivered loud and clear. 'Stay off of my ass and out of my way if you know what's good for you'. The officers stepped aside and allowed Manning pass. Manning practically ran down the hallway, scared to death and looking back over his shoulder.

John slapped Ed on the back and then grumbled at him at the same time, "Shit man, you sure do have a way with fucking words I see, Eddy."

Both men smiled because he did not have to utter a word to Manning to scare him to death.

"I bet the little scumbag went Code Brown and he has to change his damn pants, John." Campanelli offered to his friend as he continued to grin at his friend.

Again, they both laughed as they entered the bathroom area. It was filled with smoke, the bathrooms were the last place in the entire building where anyone could grab a quick smoke for themselves, but if caught by any of the pentagon security guards. The offender would be fined twenty five dollars donated to the Cancer Society at the end of the month.

General Campanelli opened a window in order to let out the smoke as John offered, "Shit man, they really dragged you over the stinking coals in there, sir. I'm really sorry I got you into this fucking mess in the first place, my old friend."

"What the hell are you so damn sorry about, John? I was just wasting away in Florida, sitting with my fricking thumbs stuffed up my damn ass all day long every day I was down there for Christ sake, sir. I really need this, or I was going to die watching the stinking grass grow, sir. You did me a big favor here John, even though it might not look like one now sir."

"Nevertheless Ed, I can't believe what they just put you through in there man, the lousy fuckers they are, sir. That damn Manning's a real stinking little prick, sir. I'd like to put my foot up his stinking ass all the way up to my knee for him, the lousy little bastard he is sir."

"Jesus John, could you believe General Claiborne in there? I thought he was going to wring Manning's neck for him, sir. I didn't think Claiborne liked me that much, to come to my aid like he did at the damn meeting, John." Campanelli offered his old friend.

"You really don't remember him do you, Eddy?" John asked his friend of many years.

Ed looked at the smiling Colonel while cocking his head to the side and shook his head no.

"Ha, you don't do you? Remember that wild party we went to, oh I think it was about five years ago. The one that had the all nude female band at it? It was a Halloween party I think sir."

"Yeah, yeah I remember it, so what man. Was he there John?" The General asked his friend.

"Sure, he was the fucking guy who had one of the strippers sit on his face and sing the Star Spangled Banner. Hell, he must have banged every bitch attending the damn party, Eddy. He even went after a few of the wives too if I remember right, and I believe he was caught with, hell, I think it was Colonel Locker with her private parts stuffed right in his fucking mush, the dirty old bastard."

"Christ sake, I remember the fucking guy now, dammit. Are you really certain General Claiborne was that guy, John? We had a helluva time with him, sir. Didn't we level a stinking bar after the party if I remember right that is?"

"Yep, and we all ended up spending the night in the can for it. It was his wife who bailed us all out of jail, and then we went to his house to sober up some, and you threw up all over his living room rug. Man was he pissed off when you did that mess in his house I, well ya Eddy."

"Ohhh shit, please don't tell me it was his stinking house I messed up so bad in, sir. I don't believe it John. Why the hell does the man like me after the way I messed up his damn house on him like that, sir?" General Campanelli asked John.

"Dunno for certain man, but we had one helluva fucking good time with the bastard, and I guess he didn't forget it either, sir. C'mon Eddy, I could sure use something to eat, I'm starving. I think they're going to bring in some hot food this afternoon, sir."

By the time they got to the food, everyone was gone and so was the food. A guard stood at attention by the doors. John walked over to the Corporal, "Hey buddy, where did everyone go."

"Colonel Sir, they went to the bar and TV room sir. The food was moved in with them sir."

"Where's this TV room mister?" White asked the young and good looking man.

"Colonel Sir, if you go down Hallway Three, and then at the first intersection you turn left sir, and then you go down to Hallway Seven, sir. Until you come to another intersection sir, and then you have to go left and head down to the..."

"Whoa, this is worse than finding your way to the local whore house," John complained.

"Sir, I can call for someone to bring you down to the bar room if you'd like, Colonel Sir?"

"I think that's going to be the only way we're going to ever find the damn place, son."

"Very good sir, hold on a second, Colonel Sir." The guard keyed a portable radio. He informed the listener that he had two officers lost in the building, and they were looking for the bar area. He stopped talking, and then turned to the Colonel and announced proudly to the officer. "Colonel Sir, they're sending someone up to take you there sir."

As an Army guard came over to the officers, Campanelli smiled. It was the same guard who was in such a bad mood earlier in the day. The General slapped him on the back and smirked at him, "Didja ever get back to that little piece of ass you had waiting for you this morning?"

"Yes sir. While they were roasting your stinking balls at the meeting, I was in bed tearing me off another slice of Heaven, sir." The Corporal bragged to the General.

John added, "Sure he went back to her. Look at the sonofabitches eyes, they're still crossed."

Campanelli looked in the guard's eyes then all three laughed, and they were joined by the guard standing his post outside the meeting room as the other guard offered, "Let's go sirs. I could be home doing her again. Instead, I'm playing wet nurse to a pair of Officers, sir."

The two officers laughed as John replied to the young Corporal, "That's much better mister, come on, let's get going, I'm fucking starving."

When they entered the bar area, John yelled out in a booming voice, "Two Michelob's here."

"Hold on John, I don't drink anymore," General Campanelli offered with a grin on his lips.

John stared him in the eyes for a second and then replied with astonishment in his voice, "What the hell kinda shit are you trying to hand me now, buster? Whaddaya fucking mean you don't drink anymore man? Don't tell me you went and got some religion on my ass, sir."

"I don't smoke anymore either," Campanelli added to show he wasn't fooling his friend.

"Zat fricking so. Whaddaya do after screwing your wife, blow fucking snot bubbles and farts or something, General?" the confused Colonel offered his old friend.

"Cute numbnuts, real cute wiseass. Where the hell do you think I got this here shit from, man?" General Campanelli lightly patted his expanding belly.

"What the fuck ever happened to your ass man? You're no more fucking fun to be around if you gave up smoking and drinking, Popeye. How are we going to get in trouble now, Ed?"

"Cathy didn't like me smoking and drinking so much, so to try and keep the peace between us, I gave them both up, buddy. At the time, we were trying to make another go of it with our marriage, sir. I hate to admit it, but I do feel much better for it though."

"You might feel a little bit better for it, but you don't have as much fun anymore, Eddy."

Colonel Locker noticed John and Campanelli looking at the hot dishes and headed for them. She snuck up behind the unsuspecting General and she grabbed his ass again as she purred at him in his ear, "You have the nicest can I have ever seen on any man, mister."

General Campanelli jumped and then turned and retorted with a grin on his lips at the female Colonel. "You keep grabbing my ass like that young lady, and you're gonna have to take me out for supper before you bed me. I ain't easy you know and I come with a price, Locker."

Mary looked at him as she snapped back with a smirk. "Your place or mine General."

Campanelli stared at her for a second, he did not know if she was serious or not. But he decided he would not mind taking her to bed as he replied, "Your place Locker."

"You got yourself a deal mister, tonight then. Wait here until I get out of the meeting. We'll go home where I can show you what I learned when I was stationed in Germany, mister."

"Are you serious?" General Campanelli asked the female officer with a grin.

"You bet I am mister. I'll see you later on tonight, mister. You better rest up some, and make damn sure your life insurance policies are all in order while you're at it, Mr. Campanelli."

"I'll be there," Campanelli replied as he returned to the food and thinking of his good luck.

"Now you done it asshole. The last guy she bedded is just getting out of the hospital."

The room was filled with some of the other officers from the meeting. Soon, they filed out. General Campanelli looked at John stuffing a chunk of steak in his mouth. He stopped chewing and looked at Ed and then he grumbled at him, "What's up man?"

"What the hell are you still doing hanging around out here with me, buddy. Don't you have to go back to the damn meeting too, buddy?" Campanelli asked White.

"Hell no man, I no longer count in this damn drama, it's you they're interested in now, buddy. I'm going to hang around with you for the rest of the day until their damn meetings over with, sir. Then I'll go home and enjoy my lady and then I'm going to show back up here tomorrow morning and see how they all voted on your sagging ass, and see if you're still alive from your date with Colonel Locker, buster. It's that simple man."

"Great. That's just fucking dandy John. You really got me in one helluva stinking pickle here, buster. I'm going to have a little talk with Beth and have her get on your ass for getting me involved in this mess, asshole," The General offered as he nibbled at his steak.

CHAPTER 6

The two officers sat in the bar for over three hours, when General Campanelli finally got a little nervous and he took a quick walk. Minutes later, he found himself standing outside the Command Center looking at the Army guard standing his post by the double doors. He could hear an occasional argument, and someone yelling inside. The security guard noticed what he was doing, and he brought his rifle to porter arms as a warning against him.

General Campanelli tried a smiled, but the guard did not react, so he shoved off before he got in trouble. He went back to the bar where John was enjoying another Michelob. He tipped the bottle to Campanelli when he spotted him walk in and he asked the General, "Are you sure you don't wanna enjoy a beer with me man? It'll help take the edge off for ya, sir."

"Naw, I'm gonna grab a fucking Pepsi though," Campanelli offered as he went to get the soda.

"A fucking Pepsi. What the hell ever happened to you man? She really ruined you man." The concerned Colonel offered to his lifelong friend and fellow officer.

"Aw, I got hooked on the shit when I quit the beer and booze. Now, I can't get enuf of the crap, sir. I even stuck by them when they had that little tampering scare, sir. I was straining the stuff through a damn tea strainer to be sure, sir. I wasn't going to give up the stuff, John."

Colonel White laughed as he looked at his friend, "Shit, you really got caught didn't you sir?"

"What the fuck are you talking about now?" Edward asked his old friend.

"You went over to the meeting room to see if you could hear what they were saying from the outside, didn't ya, you shithead you?" John laughed as he took another sip of his beer.

"What the hell's this crap? Do I have guilty written all over my damn puss or something, man?" he snapped as he looked at his hands.

"I know you, and that's what you did, didn't you sucker? Gees man I can't fucking believe you for a stinking second lately, sir." John smirked as he stared at Ed.

"Yeah. So what!" he admitted as he grinned and then he lowered his head.

"I knew it man. I knew it asshole." John giggled as he took another pull from his beer, "What happened? Did the security guard threaten to stick his weapon up your ass for ya, stupid?"

The meeting lasted for three hours before all the Generals filtered back in the bar. General Campanelli waited for one of them to come over to him, and let him know what went on. But the officers totally ignored him as they had a drink and then they talked amongst themselves. Finally, Colonel Mary Locker came over to him.

"You ready to leave now General Campanelli?" she asked with the devil shinning in her eyes.

The General didn't say a word, he just followed her out the bar to the tune of taps, which the Generals whistled. Locker laughed at their action as she flipped the bird to the officers in the bar.

General Campanelli crawled into Colonel Locker's car and within ten minutes he was in her apartment. She had a drink and offered him one.

"Do you have a Pepsi?" Edward asked the fine looking female officer.

"A fucking soda you want mister? I was kind of hoping you had some stamina, soldier. This is a new one on me I'm afraid. A General drinking soda before he has the fuck of his ever loving life. I'm stunned, I have to sit down," Colonel Locker turned on her heals and went to the bathroom. A second later, Campanelli heard the water running in the shower. Moments later, she came out dressed in a short bathrobe and she announced, "The shower's all yours General."

General Campanelli took a quick shower, and then wrapped himself in a towel and went out in the living room where Colonel Locker sat on the light blue crushed velour couch in a stunning deep blue, low cut short chemise. The

General drew in his breath, because he never realized a woman of fifty plus could look as hot as Locker was looking.

Colonel Locker rose, reading the message he was sending her with his eyes and she slowly pulled the slip over her head.

The General stood with his mouth hanging open. Locker had great legs, tight, no wrinkles. As the slip rose, he stared at her. Locker's waist was flat and he could see the muscle tone in her belly. Her breasts were large for a short woman, but they pointed up with little sag. Her nipples were large, and her chest was streaked with strong, tight muscles. The slip slid over her head and then fell to the floor. She undid her hair and allowed it to fall free and came to rest on her shoulders. She placed her hands on her hips and for a second, she reminded him so much of the way Mendoza always stood, because this was Captain Renee Mendoza's favorite stance.

Colonel Locker moved over to him, she grabbed his towel and pulled it free from his body in one swift motion. Then she swung it over her head much like a trophy, and let it go flying across the room. The female Colonel smiled when she saw the effect she had on him. She knelt before him and took him in her mouth. They made love right on the floor. An hour later, they made love in her bed. Then they had something to eat at nine o'clock, and then made love to each other again. They turned in for the night, but the General was woke twice by Locker, who was getting him ready with her mouth, and they made love twice more on that night. They got up at six, and Colonel Locker tried to get General Campanelli interested again, but he could not rise to the occasion. She finally gave up and took a quick shower. They had breakfast together, knowing they had to be back at the Pentagon by nine o'clock.

"Would you like to walk over to the Pentagon? It'll take us twenty five minutes to get there walking though, General Campanelli Sir. Unless you'd like to have sex again?" Colonel Locker asked as she reminded him they had plenty of time left to kill.

"No thanks. I don't think I could raise a hard on if my life depended on it now, young lady."

"It does General Campanelli Sir!" Locker shot back as she opened the top of her robe.

"In that case I think I'd like to walk over to the Pentagon building, Mary."

"That's how I stay in shape mister." When they both were dressed, they came out of the apartment house and Campanelli immediately realized he made a bad decision. It was freezing and more snow fell overnight. All he had in clothes, were the items he left Florida in, and they were not very warm. By the time they reached the Pentagon, they were almost jogging and frozen to death. The entrance was heated by a metal grate from below. Both General Campanelli and Colonel Locker allowed the heat to penetrate their bodies from below. When they were warm, they went through the doors where an Army security guard checked their identification.

As they entered the coffee room, General Claiborne, Colonel White, and Generals Palmieri and Weidenbacher stood trying to hide something behind their backs. Each of them were wearing a stupid grin as they watched the two. As Campanelli entered the mess area, the officers whistled taps again at him. General Weidenbacher smirked as he offered to his female military officer. "Hey Locker, you must be slipping a might there girl. He's still walking and in one piece." The officers stepped aside and Campanelli and

Locker joined them in laughter as they saw what they were hiding, a wheelchair. General Claiborne spoke up.

"Gees Mary, I thought we were going to have to wheel his sagging ass over to the Command Center for the meeting. I guess you're getting a little old there, girl."

"Anytime you think I'm getting old, you old goat you. Try climbing in bed with me, and I'll show you who's getting old. You old fart you." Locker snapped with a smile on her face.

Campanelli warned the General with a grin, "General Claiborne Sir, I don't think you should take her up on her offer sir. I ain't going to be walking right for at least a week or more sir."

This remark made Colonel Locker feel real good as she took it as a compliment. She was battling over the fear of getting old and ugly, and worried no one would be interested in her any longer. Whenever she bedded a younger man, and he remarked in the positive about her love making abilities or body, she felt young and happy again. She smiled at the General as she gave his ass another good squeeze, making him jump forward a few steps.

General Weidenbacher stared at Colonel Locker and then remarked at her, "I trust the confidence of the meeting's still intact, Colonel Locker Ma'am?"

"By all means General Weidenbacher Sir, General Campanelli was the perfect gentlemen with me all night, sir. He never once asked me what was said at the meeting about him, General Weidenbacher Sir," she smiled at the staring back at and rather large General.

"Good, I was afraid about that shit when you two birds went off like you did last night, Colonel. But I know you, and I know what anyone would have to do to you, to try and get any information out of you, Colonel Ma'am. Thanks for not compromising my Officer, General Campanelli," General

Weidenbacher offered as he turned his attention to the other General.

General Weidenbacher stared at General Campanelli as he remarked, "General, we're going back to the meeting room and you're ordered to wait outside until we send for you, sir. Someone might have thought of something else they might want to add without you present at the meeting, and we have to give them that right to speak freely about you, sir. This won't take long General, most decisions were already settled last night, and all this will be just a formality I believe, sir. The President might want to address us without you present. Stay here with Colonel White and enjoy another cup of coffee. Has anyone seen Woody hanging around anywhere?"

"Yes Sir General Weidenbacher Sir, the last time I saw him, he was making a phone call, sir. I believe I heard him tell the security guard he was going to be in the Command Room, he had some paperwork to get caught up on, and he was dog ass tired at that sir." The guard turned server replied as he filled another cup of coffee for the General.

"I know what you mean by being dog ass tired around here, General Campanelli," The well respected General replied as he turned to his other Generals and stifled a yawn.

General Claiborne laughed as he added to the conversation this time, "Yeah, when we're done here, our fearless General has to see the President, and let him chew on his stinking ass for a little while, and he does some chewing might I add, sir. I had to have my wife check, and make sure I had some ass left after he finished up with me, sir."

"I think I better get going myself, sir. It's getting late, and I don't want to keep the President waiting long. I don't need him in a bad mood even before the stinking meeting starts for cripe sake. I'm a little worried there'll be words, because I'm certain someone's going to want to ask General Campanelli a few more questions, sir." General Weidenbacher was going to talk sense to Campanelli before the meeting, and he turned to his General and stated, "I don't mind telling you pissed my ass off real bad in there yesterday afternoon, mister."

General Edward Campanelli was in a good mood, and he decided to try some levity on the older and powerful General himself, "You know what they always say sir. It's better to be pissed off than pissed on, General Weidenbacher Sir."

"Who said that!" the General demanded as he glared back at General Campanelli.

"I did, didn't you recognized my voice sir?" Campanelli smirked back at the military officer.

"Funny smartass, you're a real fucking Jerk Benny you know, General Campanelli. You just watch your damn Ps and Qs in there this time, or I'll take a giant piss on ya face, sir. Relax, it's going your way, so don't be thin skinned, and don't allow anyone upset you in there sir."

The Generals hustled over to the Command Center, and after about twenty minutes, Popeye was finally sent for. No one said a word to him until General Campanelli was set in his place.

President Albert Cole spoke up first at the meeting, "I hope we're not going to have a repeat of yesterday's little fiasco at this meeting, are we mister? I expect you to hold your temper in check at all times, General Campanelli. Now let's get down to business. Before we make our recommendation, I'd like to know if anyone wants to ask General Campanelli any further questions. Now is the time to get it done people."

Manning raised his hand, and the President sighed before he gave him the nod to speak at the meeting. But before he spoke, the President warned him in no uncertain terms, "Mr. Manning, I expect you to pick out your questions extremely carefully today, sir. You do remember what we discussed last night when you reported to the White House, sir?"

Manning ignored the warning from the President as he started, "General Campanelli, I'd like to know how you felt when you sent so many young men to their deaths in the Middle East war."

General Weidenbacher started to protest Manning's first question of his military officer, but General Campanelli was already on his feet and storming at the civilian advisor. The General decided to allow his General to carry the ball this time, and see where he went with it. After all, it was Manning's poor choice of questions that was going to get him eaten alive again. He sat back down and then watched General Campanelli go to work on the stupid civilian.

Campanelli was beside himself as he jumped on Manning, "Now you look here Manning..."

"It's Mr. Manning to you sir. I demand respect from you, General Campanelli Sir."

General Campanelli ignored him as he continued his assault on the civilian advisor. "Look here Manning, you don't know what the fuck happened on the damn battlefield. All of what I lost, all the kids I had to send to their deaths. You weren't there mister. You pencil pushing sleazbags never are, dammit. Your type stay well behind safe and sound, shuffling your fucking papers around to make yourselves look so damn important while staying well out of the line of fire, and letting someone else pick up the tab for your stinking ass, mister. Only so you can do all the medal pinning, and reports which you fucking birds always seem able to twist around to suit whatever circumstances you need, to make yourselves look good, and so fucking important to everyone. While we, the damn foot soldiers do the fucking fighting and dying in the mud, paying the price for your damn follies with our blood, you fucking shithead you."

The angry General was steaming as he continue to lock horns with Manning, he hated him so much, "I wish for just once in my life, I could get you out on the damn battlefield, allow you to witness the damn dying. Smell the death, see the miserable death, see the suffering of a dying soldier. Let you get scared to death as the enemy you picked out, is attacking you from all sides. Let you shit your damn pants, and lose your fucking water on the battlefield. Mister, war's hell, and until we get you bastards who hide behind a stinking desk out in the damn field, we're going to continue to have these fucking wars, until there are no more children left to fight with, or you bastards finally find a god damn way to stop the fighting once..."

General Weidenbacher cut off General Campanelli just as the President began to stand, anger was etched on his face, "General Campanelli. Please, let's not get a little over melodramatic here now sir. Either keep to the damn subject or back down some, sir."

Manning took this break in the attack by General Campanelli to continue with his stinging words. He stood as he shot a harsh glare at each General, especially Campanelli, before he locked eyes with General Weidenbacher, and he snarled at him with as much anger in his voice as General Campanelli used on him moments before. "General Weidenbacher Sir, one thing I detected while attending this meeting is, there's a serious lack of discipline from all your

Military Officer's, sir. It makes one wonder how they're receiving their training, sir."

There was a rumbling from the other officers attending the meeting, General Weidenbacher even heard some curses being aimed at the civilian.

Manning paid little if any attention to the grumbling as he continued to rip the officers apart, "Ever since this meeting began, I've been verbally and physically assaulted. I've been treated like a bag of shit by you arrogant, snot nosed, hot shot Military Officers, and I resent it deeply, and something better be done about it in order to correct this dangerous situation, mister."

General Weidenbacher got hot this time and he hissed back at the angry civilian, "One thing I don't need around here, is some fucking civilian asshole coming in my fricking territory, and degrading my Military Officers in front of me, mister. Let me tell you something Manning. The only reason you're still alive, is because you're a personal friend of the President and..."

The extremely upset General Campanelli cut the General off as he jumped in on the attack against the civilian trying to back down the general against him, "You piece of rotten garbage you. I don't give two shits and a fart what you feel or think around here, mister. You don't belong here, dammit. No stinking civilian does, buster. I have a mind to disassemble you..."

The President interrupted the two angry men as he growled at the both of them, "This is the last outburst I'll tolerate from you so called Officers and gentlemen." He glared at Manning and aimed his next words at him "Mr. Manning, you'll remove yourself from this meeting at once. Then, you'll get your ass back to the White House immediately. I want to talk to you again mister." The

President turned back to General Weidenbacher and snarled at him, "General Weidenbacher Sir, you'll control yourself, and your people, or I'll have your ass hanging on the Oval Office door. I warn you General, I'll find out what Mr. Manning meant by he was physically assaulted, and if any of your soldiers laid a finger on him, I'll have his, and your job, mister. I suggest everyone get a handle on themselves before we continue with this meeting."

Manning quickly gathered up his papers and then he stormed out of the room to the muttering and curses from the soldiers who the nation's security relied so heavily on. When he was out of the meeting room, the President let out his breath in a rush as he looked at General Campanelli and said to the officer, "General Campanelli, you're not going to be as big a pain in the ass to me, as you're being here today, are you sir? When you finally take over Command of Operation Wine Press, sir. Are you, General Campanelli Sir?"

Laughter filled the Situation Room under the White House. The President of the United States allowed the laughter to continue until he felt all the hard feelings disappeared from his officers. He smiled as he watched the military officers calm down and relax.

General Campanelli smiled as he searched the room for Colonel John White, to share this moment with him. The excited General realized he was going to be in command of an Army again. He found Colonel White's eyes and gave him a wide grin.

"General Campanelli, I asked you a question sir? And I expect an answer to that question sir." The President allowed what looked like an expressions of anger to cross his lips and eyes.

"I'll try not to be a pain in your ass, Mr. President Sir."

More laughter, but the President put a quick stop to it as he said, "General Campanelli Sir, I don't have much more to add to this conversation, sir. I know you're going to be a might busy for many weeks to come, sir. But I'll leave you with this thought, sir. General Campanelli, I trust the fate and the children of the United States to your hands. Don't waste them needlessly sir, good luck General, and may God be with you, sir. I fear you're going to need them both on this one, sir. General Weidenbacher, I suggest you call a break and allow your Officers to get something to eat. Have your meeting in the concession room, sir. Tell General Campanelli what and who he'll need, and give him the file marked Three, Three, Seven for me, sir."

President Albert Cole stood up behind his desk, but he immediately waived his officers in both rooms back to their seats as he added as if an afterthought for them, "I want to say one more thing while I still have all your attention here, sir. I want to thank all you Officers for your time and great wisdom, and especially for your patience over this present situation we're currently facing here, General Weidenbacher Sir. I also feel I must apologize to each and every one of you Military Officers for Mr. Manning terrible behavior and equally as terrible questions he asked of my Officers at this meeting, and I promise you from now on, I'll keep him well out of your hair, sir. Good day gentlemen, ladies, and I thank you all once again for coming here today to attend this here meeting, sirs." President Cole then left the room in a rush, followed closely by the rest of his cabinet members and closest advisors.

When the President was gone, and the screen once again displayed the maps of the world that the President was using to attend the meeting with the officers. General Weidenbacher called the meeting to an end for his people.

Both General William Weidenbacher and General Luther Claiborne walked General Edward Campanelli over to the concession room. General Campanelli ordered a Pepsi, while the other officers ordered hard drinks.

General Weidenbacher stopped what he was doing and then he stared confusingly at his General as he drank his soda, and then asked him with some concern lacing his voice, "What the hell do ya call this shit you're fucking drinking there, mister?"

"I stopped drinking alcohol a while ago sir," Campanelli offered in his own defense.

"Well, if that don't beat all to hell and back again, mister. You know Edward, you did us all a great service in there today sir. You got that fucking Manning little prick the hell out of the damn meeting, and that was good for us, mister. I never believed a stinking civilian puke should ever be allowed to attend a military briefing no matter the reason, sir."

JANUARY 14th, 1997. 11:30 A.M.

The meeting at the United Nations had been taking place for over two hours, during which a select number of nations of the world were trying to force North Korea, out of their nuclear development and aims.

The concerned General William Weidenbacher gave a quick thought to the meeting, and he smiled as he thought of the fireworks that must be going off there. He just finished his lunch when a Pentagon security guard rushed in the room looking for him.

General Weidenbacher glanced at the guard then growled at him. "Yes, what is it mister?"

"General Weidenbacher Sir, I just received a report in from New York City, sir. You're wanted at the Command Center immediately, General."

"Trouble son?" the unconcerned sounding General asked the messenger.

"General Weidenbacher Sir, I have no idea what it's all about sir. I was only ordered to find you, and inform you about the present situation, sir."

"You delivered your stinking message to me, beat it now so I can collect my thoughts for a moment mister" he barked at the guard.

General Weidenbacher cleared his throat. Immediately, all conversations ended as he began to address the few officers sharing lunch with him. "Gentlemen, we have to get back to the Command Center. It seems there's been a problem at the United Nations Meeting."

General Luther Claiborne bellowed at Campanelli as he stood and prepared to leave the lunchroom. "Hey Edward, I'm giving you a warning, sonny. You better invite me to the party I know you're going to have celebrating your new Command position, sir. I have one hell of a stain on my living room rug caused by you, white boy. So it's only fair I return the favor and puke on your damn rug, mister. Then we can gets down to some serious drinking boy, I gots to get even with you sir." He giggled in a heavy southern drawl, mixed with a black accent.

The officers fell in line with General Weidenbacher leading the way and as they quickly filed into the room just as the center screen came on. Ambassador Walters was on and when he saw the General enter his field of view he spoke right off, "General Weidenbacher Sir, I just finished briefing the President about what took place at the Security

Meeting, sir."   He stopped speaking and waited for the General to get comfortable before continuing.

"General Weidenbacher Sir, when General Secretary Bartlett, suggested North Korea refrain from trying to make any further nuclear weapons that might be affixed to the head of a ballistic missile, Ambassador Kim Sun-neh became rather obstinate, sir. He demanded to know why the outside world was poking their noses into the internal affairs of North Korea. An argument erupted, and then when peace was again restored to the meeting, Ambassador Alexander from the United Kingdom demanded North Korea explain her intention. The reasons why North Korea wants to develop such offensive nuclear weapons. She even accused the North Koreans of threatening world peace for personal gains and even blackmail. There was no talking to the extremely upset North Korean Delegate, until China finally spoke up at the meeting, sir.

"Chinese Ambassador Chow warned the North Korean Delegate that China was keeping a close eye on all of North Korean's nuclear activities. This seemed to make a slight difference to Ambassador Kim Sun-neh. I guess the North Korean Ambassador didn't want to upset their closest ally. As the meeting continued, I offered to send in workers who could help the North Koreans dismantle their nuclear research factories, sir. This seemed to hit a raw nerve, and Ambassador Sun-neh went off the plantation again at the meeting. It was at this point Secretary Bartlett threatened North Korea with a bushel basket of new sanctions.

"The North Korean Delegate announced North Korea would consider any new sanctions leveled against their nation to be an act of war, and they'd react accordingly against them. The Ambassador further warned North Korea would no longer pay attention to what the United Nations had to say about what they did within the borders of their nation. He further warned only North Korea governs North Korean activities. Then the Ambassador stormed out of the meeting chamber. Later today, we're going to vote on the new sanctions against North Korea. All trade with North Korea will cease at twelve o'clock midnight tomorrow, January 15th, 1997.

"We also plan to confiscate all their nation's assets spread out here in the United States, and then offer two weeks of new sanctions, if no reaction comes from them by that time limit, we'll give China permission to start her military buildup at her border with North Korea, sir. Thirty days later, China will be given the green light to invade North Korea, and her troops will destroy the North Korean nuclear weapons factories and research buildings in and around the Yongbyon nuclear complex, General Weidenbacher Sir."

General Weidenbacher piped up the first chance he had to get a word in edgewise with the politician, "Ambassador Walters Sir, do you really think the North Koreans will come around?"

Ambassador Walters slowly rubbed his chin as he thought for a moment, and then replied, "No, I seriously doubt North Korea will ever come around, sir. I fear we'll be in a shooting war within the next two months, General. But at least we have an ally in this one sir, China."

"Yeah sure," the General growled as he stared at the American Ambassador on the screen.

This response startled Ambassador Walters as he asked, "General Weidenbacher Sir, is there a problem I don't know about here, sir. Did you discover something I should know abo..."

"Hold on there a moment please Ambassador Walters. I'm only reacting to what you just informed me of, Mr.

Ambassador Sir. You're the one who pushed the damn panic button here, not I sir. I never trusted the damn Chinese for anything in the first place sir."

"Sorry General Weidenbacher, but for now I'm forced to react to China as an ally of the United States, sir. Until she does something to change my mind that is sir. Are you going to have your forces ready by the time China invades North Korea, General Weidenbacher?"

"Don't worry about my military forces for one moment Mr. Ambassador. You see if you can get this damn mess settled before I have to commit any of my soldiers to action, sir. I feel this one will be bad if we're forced to go active over this rapidly developing shit filled situation, sir. I'll have my Command Structure well set in position by later on this afternoon, or tomorrow morning at the very latest, sir. I might even petition the President, to see if I can talk him in to going up to an Alert Two Situation Status, sir. That way I can get everything in motion much faster, sir. Six weeks is a rather short time for me to move all my people and military equipment into their vital positions, sir. I have to activate Marine Battalions and Army Divisions, as well as pull my warships and aircraft out of moth balls, Mr. Ambassador."

There was a slight commotion as Ambassador Walters was suddenly interrupted. He spoke to an aide off the screen and then quickly he got back to the General, "General Weidenbacher Sir, it seems I'm needed back at the meeting immediately sir, I have to go. If anything further comes up sir. I'll get back to you at once, and I'll inform you of any possible changes, sir. You'll be at the Pentagon from now on, right General Weidenbacher Sir?"

"Absolutely sir. I'll be here until I know what the hell's going on around me, Mr. Ambassador Sir," General Weidenbacher offered the American politician.

"General Weidenbacher Sir, I have to go now I believe sir. Good luck sir."

Once the Ambassador was off the screen, the General addressed his Officers. "The actors performed as was expected," He looked at Ed and then added, "General Campanelli, I'm going to put you in the soup right off the bat, sorry you didn't get much time to enjoy Washington before you had to go to work, sir. You're gonna hit the ground running on this I'm afraid, General. I want you to put together the list of Units, Divisions and Marine Battalions you're gonna need for this possible major operation, sir.

"I'll need to be informed about what possible Army Groups, Air Force Wings and support groups you'll need. Also, what Naval Vessels, Carrier Strike Forces, Submarines, Amphibious Assault ships and support ships you'll require to make this operation a successful one, sir. I'll have General Palmieri and Colonel Locker work closely with you, General Campanelli.   I'll need this information by tomorrow afternoon at the very latest, so I can submit any requests to the President, and get him working on them pronto. Any questions sir?"

"No sir, not at this time General Weidenbacher Sir," General Campanelli replied.

"Good. I'll have a number of aides placed at your disposal at all times who know what the hell will be expected of them. General Campanelli, why don't you take your Colonel White along with you for ballast, sir? After all, he's the one who got you involved with this Command in the first place, sir," General Weidenbacher suggested with a smirk on his face.

General Campanelli turned to Colonel White, standing directly behind the General and replied, "Yes Sir General

Weidenbacher, I was thinking about a way of getting back at that SOB, sir."

"Oh, I forgot something, I have a file for you to review, General Campanelli Sir. I'm interested to see if you'd like to place this weapon in service for this possible operation sir," General Weidenbacher reached in his briefcase and removed a yellow folder, and then he handed it over to General Campanelli as he offered, "I think you'll find this information to your liking, General Campanelli. I gave preliminary orders to get this operation underway, sir. So it'll be well in motion, if and when we need it, sir. It's going to cost the taxpayers a helluva bundle. But I'm sure they'd rather pay it than have to learn Chinese or Russian, sir."

General Campanelli took the folder and glanced at the cover sheet, it read. 'TOP SECRET', in parentheses then went on, 'OPERATION THREE, THREE, SEVEN, VINEGAR JOE'. His head cocked as he tried to figure out what type of operation would be named Vinegar Joe.

General Weidenbacher offered with a smirk a second time, "I think you better be on your way sir. You have a helluva lot of work ahead of you tonight, sir. Get going General Campanelli."

The General took off, followed by Colonel White, Colonel Locker and General Palmieri. They headed for room 117, given to Campanelli and his Command Staff to work from until he worked out the Units he needed. The General took a desk for his own as Colonel Locker took the desk right next to his. Her fingers danced with the speed of light across the IBM keyboard, pulling up the Marine Battalions and troop strengths. Before he was settled, the Chief of Naval Operations stormed in the room and informed him he would have the list of Carrier Groups, support ships and manpower on his desk within the hour. The Command General nodded as he laid out the file 'Vinegar Joe' on his desk. He was dying to know what it was about.

The Chief of Naval Operations ducked out of the room as Colonel White directed the other officers in the room on what was needed of them by General Campanelli. The concerned General curiously opened his file and began to read the information.

'The Operation Vinegar Joe Platform was ordered placed in operation in the event all Ally forces were driven off dry land in the Sudan and Ethiopia, during the Middle East, Northern Africa war of 1996. It was devised as an alternative if the United States no longer had a viable military land base to operate its military from in that region. Three, Three, Seven was designed to take the place of a massive military land base in an active war zone. The Vinegar Joe Platform would take thirty days to assemble, once the ships were set in place. The support ships assigned to protect the Vinegar Joe Platform would trail the commandeered once super oil tanker ships to position. Once the Vinegar Joe Platform was fully assembled and fully operational, computers would control the pitch and yaw of the massive floating Platform by flooding and draining a series of ballast tanks spread throughout the ships.

'Once the massive Vinegar Joe Platform is fully assembled, she would become in essence, an independent floating Island, and airbase with the fighter aircraft receiving fuel from within the tankers supporting the Platform. The attacking Marine and Army Units, would also be housed inside the once huge tanker ships below the Platform decks. Armament for fighter aircraft and troops would also be stored within the tankers supporting the Platform. The Vinegar Joe Platform comes equipped with a number of reverse osmosis water purifying plants, ten in all. More than enough to desalinate and purify enough water for one million troops a day. It will also be equipped with generation plants, and enough stores below decks to feed her troops and support for three months with ready to eat meals.

'The Vinegar Joe Platform comes complete with its own docking facilities, in order to enable any Strike Forces, and all supply ships to moor up to the Platform. Thus making the Platform a completely independent floating island in its own right. The only war aircraft which could not possibly use the landing deck, would be the massive B-52 bombers, and also the huge C-5 B Galaxy, along with the C-141 Starlifter transport aircraft. The smaller C-17 transport aircraft would be capable of employing the Platform successfully, but with extreme caution exhibited by the pilot landing this larger aircraft on the Platform deck.

'The Vinegar Joe Platform would be more than capable of supplying the United States with a fully working Platform from which she could conduct a very successful war against any aggressors within striking distance of the platform. It effectively gives the United States a fully operational airbase, deportation base for all troops, and a supply base for both ground, Naval and airforce operations, where a military base would not have existed before. Example, this Platform would replace many military bases once in operation on land in the Philippines and were lost to government changes in that region, or the Platform would also replace the military land bases lost in Japan due to political decisions and civilian pressures.

'This massive operational Military and Naval Platform could supply military bases operating within the Central American zone, where a permanent United States Military Base would be hard pressed to be establish or easily maintain, or it could also serve as a strong Military Base stationed in the Middle East waters, where the United States would not have to further rely on any Middle Eastern countries for an active Military land base. The movable floating Platform would further give the United States a fully operational Military and Naval land base in the middle of any Ocean, any where in the world, if we so chose to place the Platform in any possible troubled region'.

General Campanelli let out with a low whistle as he slowly leaned back in his chair, while trying to absorb all of what he just read of the specialized Vinegar Joe Platform system. He closed his tired burning eyes for a brief second. Seeing his chance to speak to the General, John asked him if he wanted a cup of coffee in a low voice, in hopes of not disturbing him very much.

The extremely exhausted General opened his eyes and smiled at his lifelong friend as he replied to his question of him, "How well you know me, mister. Yes, I'd love a damn cup. Seems to me like we just did this shit yesterday John."

"You got that right Campey, at least we're back together on this one sir," John offered with a smirk plastered on his lips.

General Edward Campanelli went back to the report while John headed out for the coffee.

'The massive Vinegar Joe Platform will incorporate the entire United States Fleet of twenty seven super oil tanker ships, with each super tanker measuring nine hundred and ninety feet long, and one hundred and eighty feet across. These tankers were fitted with the specially and heavy magnesium planking system measuring thirty feet by thirty feet, with an extra plank off on each side of the massive ships. Extra planking can be added where needed on the flight deck to increase the flight deck to accommodate other special aircraft. When these planks are lifted and set in place, it will supply the ship with another sixty feet of landing flight deck. Each of the heavy planks are six inches thick, and every sixty feet there's a specialized expansion control joint. Each ship would be positioned, so that when the side planks were raised in place, each ship would be easily bolted together. Other plates could be added to increase the size of the landing deck for future operations and larger aircraft as already suggested.

'The super tanker fleet would have one thousand fighter and bomber aircraft stored below their decks, and two elevators on each of the tankers containing these aircraft, in order to bring the fighter aircraft up to the flight deck as they are needed for military operations. There will be six aircraft carrying tankers, giving the Platform five thousand aircraft stored below her deck. Add this to the eleven operational Aircraft Carrier Strike Force compliment of aircraft supporting the Platform, and possible land military operations. The United States would have an air supremacy wherever the Platform was employed. Five of the massive tanker ships would also hold weapons for the fighter and bomber aircraft, and also for the ground forces employed in any military operations the Platform is dispatched to. Four of the super tankers would have fuel storage supplies for the aircraft, tanks and helicopters stored below decks.

'There would be five more tanker ships that would house the foot soldiers. Each ship should house over twenty five thousand ground forces if need at its maximum need. Another three ships would be used for food storage: One for processing of human and food waste before it's released into the Ocean, the three remaining ships are to be classified as miscellaneous ships which could be adapted for anything needed to support the Platform or troop, or naval operations.

'The Vinegar Joe Platform system would also be supported by a fleet of Naval support ships, along with a number of protective ships, and weapon systems for defense planted right on the flight deck of the Platform. Four nuclear fast attack submarines would also be attached to the Platform security, three attack and one ballistic missile submarines, and a system of steel walled barges. These special barges would have a wall reaching one hundred feet high constructed out of heavy reinforcement rods. This specialized wall would serve to force any cruise wave skipper missiles fired at the Platform, to raise one hundred feet in the air, which would make the missile susceptible to all defensive weapons employed by the Platform. A ready air cap of ten attack aircraft would fly over the Platform during any deployment.

'Once all twenty seven of the super tanker ships are joined together, there would be a landing surface for the fighter and support aircraft measuring over two thousand one hundred and sixty feet wide, by over six thousand eight hundred and forty five feet in length. The size of a .... The report ended here with the last paragraph to the report.

'Other specifications employed on the Vinegar Joe Platform System, are to be found stored in the file 339 under section 552 in the Security Department that is stored in the White House. These secured and restricted files are for the private use of the seated President of the United States only, unless the President gives written special permission submitted to Congress and ordered released by Congress. This is the only way to gain special access to the private file system for the President of the United States only.
'END OF REPORT'.

CHAPTER 7

"Jesus Christ Almighty I can't believe what I'm fucking reading here, dammit," General Edward Campanelli mumbled to himself as he closed the folder then vigorously rubbed his eyes with the palms of his hands. Then he placed the detailed file in the metal drawer of his desk. He locked the drawer and placed the key in his pocket.

John saw him finish up with the report and he came over to his lifelong friend. He noticed he had not touched his coffee, and it was now cold and he asked, "You want another cup of coffee Ed? One you can enjoy this time sir."

"Naw, I'm done with coffee for the day, how's everyone doing with picking out the damn units and military equipment we're going to need for this possible fucking operation, John?"

"Good, very good in fact General Campanelli, we successfully singled out many units we'll be employing, and a number of them are going to have to be activated. While you were reading that report, Woody dropped off the papers you requested from him on the ships and Carriers, sir."

"Woody?" General Campanelli asked as he let out his breath in a deep sigh.

"Sorry sir. Woody's Chief of Naval Ops, Admiral Thomas Woody Standlund's nickname. You better get use to it Ed, because he usually signs many reports with his nickname only sir."

"No nicknames yet please John. I'm having enough trouble remembering everyone's real names, without trying to remember their damn nicknames already, sir."

"You got it man. No more nicknames for the time being sir," John laughed as he stepped back when General Campanelli went to stand and then offered, "C'mon buddy, let's see what you got so going far for me." The General followed John over to Colonel Locker's desk.

"Whatdaya have for me so far Colonel Locker?" the General asked her as he sat down on the edge of her desk and then he waited for her reply.

"General Campanelli Sir, we have available seven ready for immediate active duty Marine Expeditionary Forces (MEF). That gives us four hundred and thirty four thousand Marines if we use all seven MEFs, and they come equipped with three thousand tanks, and two thousand helicopters. Their numbers are the 1st, 2nd, and 3rd Expeditionary Forces. The 5th, 7th, 8th and the 17th Expeditionary Forces, sir. I also have the Wasp and Nassau, along with the Mount Whitney Amphibious Assault Ships standing at the ready, and the Shreveport Landing Dock Platform's getting equipped and fitted out as we speak, sir. These Congressional cut backs kicked the crap out of our preparedness ability, maintenance is down the sewer, General Campanelli Sir.

"The rest of the Marine Units will be airlifted out to the possible war zones once the advance Marine Units were successful with creating a beachhead landing area, sir. I also have a Wing of C-5 B Galaxy transport aircraft available, with ninety five aircraft in all from the 456th Military Airlift Wing out of Dover AFB (Air Force Base). I'm also working on getting a few more Marine Units up and running for us, sir. I'm asking you to suggest to General Weidenbacher to reactivate the 21st and 27th MEF as well, that'll giving us another hundred and twenty thousand fighting troops if needed, General Campanelli Sir."

General Campanelli was thoroughly amazed Colonel Locker was able to pull up so much information on troop and aircraft preparedness in such a short period of time as he replied, "Outstanding work there Colonel, keep it up, Ma'am." the General and John left her desk and walked over to General Palmieri and Campanelli asked the General, "How you doing sir?"

"Good, I didn't realize I had so many military forces still intact General Campanelli. I ordered the 7th Infantry Division out of Fort Lewis in Washington, originally stationed at Fort Ord in California, but Ord was closed during the base closing rave, to an active status. I also have the 25th Infantry Division from Schofield Barracks in Hawaii; the 29th National Guard Division from Fort Belvior VA; the 10th Mountain Division from Fort Drum New York; with the 6th Snow Mountain Division from Fair Banks Alaska standing by on ready alert, sir. Their commanders are calling in their officers and strips (Sergeants) as we speak, sir. I ordered on alert the entire 1st Cavalry Division, along with the 5th and 7th Air Cavalry, and the 12th Cavalry Division.

"I also have the 82nd, and 101st Airborne Divisions up and ready to go on a moment's notice if their Unites are needed, sir. This gives us an active force of over four hundred and ten thousand troops ready for the field within a ten day notice, sir. That doesn't mean I could have them out in the field at this time stated, General. It merely means the troops will be on their prospective bases at this time suggested, sir. I have a tank force with these units of three thousand five hundred machines. This will give us a ready reserve of five thousand tanks in the States and throughout the rest of the world, sir. I have three Wings of seven hundred Apache Fast Attack Helicopters, and three thousand pieces of artillery. Add this to the Marine's four thousand pieces of artillery systems, General Campanelli."

"Good report General Palmieri, I'll need this shit written up on paper, so I can give the damn list to General Weidenbacher, sir. Then he can get the rest of what we need in operation on the move, General." Campanelli replied to the report General Palmieri just offered to him.

General Palmieri interrupted General Campanelli as he added to his report, "General Campanelli Sir, I could sure use the 101st Airborne Air Assault Division stationed at Fort Campbell in Kentucky on this one, sir. Along with the 24th Infantry Division Mechanized, and the 1st Cavalry 2nd Armored Division out of Fort Hood, and I could also use the 197th Infantry Brigades Third Armored Regiment if I had a wish list capabilities, sir."

General Campanelli laughed, though he thought the remark was removed from the Military vernacular years ago as he offered, "I'll see what I can do about filling out your wish list, General Palmieri. John, let's see what the Chief of Naval Operations has put together for us."

John led General Campanelli back to his desk and then said to him, "Here you go sir." As he handed him the report from the powerful Admiral.

The concerned General sat down and quickly read the list of Naval ships available to him.

Nuclear powered Carriers:

CVN-68 the Chester A. Nimitz, Bremerton Wa. CVN-69 the Dwight D. Eisenhower, Norfolk Va. CVN-70 Carl Vinson, Alameda, Ca. CVN-71 Theodore Roosevelt, Norfolk Va. CVN-72 Abraham Lincoln, Alameda, Ca. CVN-73 George Washington, Norfolk Va. CVN-74 Stennis, Bremerton Wa. CVN-75 United States, Alameda, Ca. CVN-76 Frank B. Kelso, Norfolk Va.
Conventional Power:
CV-67 the John F. Kennedy, Norfolk Va. CV-66 the America, Norfolk, Va.

All Carrier Strike Forces consists of Three Guided Missile Cruisers, Two Guided Missile Destroyers, Three Guided Missile Frigates, One Amphibious Warfare Ship, a Mine Warfare Ship, a Combat Stores Ship and a Oiler and Two Conventional Destroyers, One Nuclear Ballistic Missile Submarine and Two Nuclear Fast Attack Submarines. Other ships available as of this time are two hospital ships, five USNS Sea Lift Vessels, Three Replenishment Oilers and Nine Food Stores Ships. Any ships may be ordered to duty as needed whether they be mothballed or on the Ocean at the present time.

General Campanelli quickly scanned over the lists connected with the Carrier Groups, the list was endless. About every ship the Navy employed was available to him for this still possible upcoming military operation. He smiled as he yelled out to everyone working in his sector, "Anything come in from damn Air Force yet, dammit?"

"I just received a number of preliminary requests for Airforce Command, they were dropped off along with a stack of Navy reports, General Campanelli." Colonel White reported to his Commanding Officer while speaking over his shoulder at him.

"John, you slipping up a little on me I believe, mister? I should've had this damn report in my hands as soon as it became available to us sir," General Campanelli warned his Second in Command as he stared at him over the rim of the report held in his hand.

Colonel White smirked at his lifelong friend as he began to read the report General Claiborne put together for them "General Campanelli Sir, General Claiborne states here this report's incomplete as yet, sir. He further states he'll have the complete list prepared for us by tomorrow morning's scheduled meeting. Here's what he put together for us so far, sir."

"The General reports he has the entire compliment of the 37th Tactical Wing, that's including the 57th F-17 Blackhawk Stealth Fighters, and the forty Bluelight Stealth Fighters. The 1st Wing F-16 Fighting Falcons, a hundred and fifty aircraft, and the Tactical Air Lift section. I activated the 41st Air Refueling Squadron of fifty five KC-135 Rs. The 1st Tactical Wing consisting of seven hundred F/A 18-D Hornets, and the 71st Tactical Fighter Wing Squadron. The F-16 Wing from Langley AFB, the 3rd and Seventh Tactical Air Lift Wing out of Pope Airforce Base, sir. I also put the

Three Hundred and Sixty Third Tactical Fight Wing, and the F-111 Fighter Bombers from Shaw Airforce Base on full alert, sir.

"The General further reports he ordered up the Four Hundred and Thirty Third Military Air Lift Wing from Kelly Field, and the Forth Tactical Fighter Wing from Seymour Johnson Airforce Base, in North Carolina on full alert. He placed the 6th Military Air Lift Wing consisting of forty C-5A Galaxies from Travis Airforce Base, and their hundred C-141 Starlifters, with the 456th Military Air Lift Wing consisting of another fifty C-5B Galaxies, and ninety five C-141s from Dover Airforce Base on alert. This move makes up ninety percent of our C-5 A and B Galaxies, and eighty five percent of the C-141 Starlifters in reserves. He has the entire Air Lift Wing of C-17s consisting of a hundred and thirty five aircraft, from the 17th Air Wing reporting in.

"The entire 27th Support Wing from Washington is reporting in too. This Air Wing consists of ninety CV-22 Osprey Tilt Wing Troop Transport Aircraft, and a number of CA 22 Osprey Water landing Tilt Winged Aircraft on guard. The General has assigned all Air Wings currently stationed in Germany, England and Spain, along with the two Tactical Wings stationed in Italy checking in also sir. He states here that he doesn't know their total strength though. He grips we can blame that on the damn cut backs, General. This is my assumption, if you were to add this to the air strength of the Carrier Strike Forces, you should have enough aircraft at your disposal, to fend off any attack, or to air in any invasion force. I'm not supposed to inform you of this shit, but I have ninety A-6 Intruders at my disposal as well, sir.

"General Claiborne further reports this is the best he can do for the time being sir, and offers to search the other reports to see if he has access to any other fighters, or bombers or support Air Wings. He then thanks you sir, and offers you to feel free to call on him for any help you might need. He signs the report, Sincerely, General Luther 'Nails' Claiborne.

General Campanelli smiled to himself, because this was one of the first times that he saw a report from General Claiborne worded so politely.

An Army security guard knocked on the door then entered the room and saluted the officers. Then he turned to the Commanding General and waited.

"Well?" General Campanelli grunted at the young security guard Sergeant hotly.

The security guard instantly snapped to full attention as he replied, "General Campanelli Sir, the time's getting a little late sir, and I've taken the liberty to have the cook prepare something special for you and the rest of your staff to enjoy, sir."

General Campanelli suddenly realized how hungry he was as he complained to the rest of his officers, "Gees, it's seven thirty, I don't believe it. Everyone listen up, it's late, and we have a shit load of reports I'll need for tomorrow's meeting. What do you say? We've done enough work, let's call it quits. We'll meet here tomorrow morning at Oh Eight Hundred Hours."

The military officers stared back at him as he waited for their response.

"Christ Almighty, go home already for Pete's sake will you people, this is a fucking order dammit." General Campanelli suddenly snapped at his support officers as he stood and said to the security guard, "I guess we'll have something to eat before we leave for the stinking day. Thanks for all the concern for my people, Sergeant."

Colonel Mary Locker quickly caught up to exhausted General Campanelli and she grabbed his can again and asked him with a smile. "You're coming home with me again tonight, right soldier?" She offered as she leaned up against him.

"God, I don't think I could live through another night like last night. Give me a break huh?"

"No way in hell mister. I've been waiting too long to get you in my bed, to let you go so easily now. I'll take it easier on you tonight though, you big cry baby. I promise Edward."

"Okay, okay you win. You driving, Colonel Ma'am?" Campanelli gave in with a slight sigh.

"We didn't take a car over to the Pentagon this morning, if you remember right mister? We walked over to the building this morning sir," the female Colonel replied with a smile.

"Shit, you're right Locker. I'm too damn tired to walk back to your apartment tonight though, Colonel. Maybe we should call for a cab to take us over to your apartment, Mary."

"Have no fear General. I'll order up a staff car to take us home," Locker offered with a wink.

In an hour they were back at Mary's apartment. There was a fresh inch of snow on the ground already, and the temperature was dropping fast for the night. It was ten degrees out, and it was predicted to be one of the coldest night of the year so far in Washington.

General Campanelli started a fire as Mary made a hot toddy for herself to enjoy, and she poured a Pepsi for him. They made love just once that night in front of the fireplace, and at six A.M., her phone rang. It was the front desk, Mary left a wake up call.

As he dressed there was a knock on the door. A waiter barged in pushing a food cart when the General opened the door and he offered, "Good morning sir, breakfast is ready for you General."

Mary came out of the bathroom with just a robe on. She sat down and started to eat. As they ate, her robe opened as she reached for some food. Soon, she was almost topless.

General Campanelli enjoyed the view and they ate mostly in silence, with some small talk.

Mary finished and watched him read the paper she smiled, "You in the mood for a quickie?"

The General grinned as he replied to her question, "Sure, why the hell not Locker."

They made love again, and then they dressed. Mary went for the car, and picked the General up in front of the building. They reached the Pentagon twenty minutes before eight.

JANUARY 15th, 1997 ;
O800 HOURS, COMMAND CENTER
MEETING, PENTAGON, WASHINGTON D.C.

General Edward Campanelli took a seat as he handed the stack of reports he held over to General William Weidenbacher. The concerned Commander quickly read over the requested units and military equipment, and then he drew in his breath and bitched at General Campanelli, "Jesus H. Christ Ed, I could fight World War fucking Three with less military equipment and soldiers than you're requesting here, mister."

General Campanelli cut the General off and bitched back at his Commanding Officer, "Fine, then you fight the fucking war if it starts, sir. I'm telling you what I need to protect my damn forces, and the United States and all her Allies, sir. If I can't have everything I requested then you might as well have me fucking replaced, because there's one thing I'll not do under any circumstances General Weidenbacher Sir. And that's enter into a war with less troops and equipment then I'll need to win the damn battle, sir. No soldier would attack without enough troops, if he intended to win, unless he was on a suicide mission which I assure you I ain't sir."

General Weidenbacher smiled at the steamed military officer and then replied to his gripe, "Pardon me sir, I stand corrected General Campanelli. If you feel you need all this shit then I'll request them for your use sir. Mind me General, I'm not guaranteeing you'll get everything you requested on this fucking list, but I'll try my best to get most if not all the troops and equipment you're requesting, sir. The final word as always, rests with the President, Ed."

"Very well General Weidenbacher Sir, but I'd request you tell the Boss if I don't get all the god damn units I'm requesting. Then he might as well stay the fuck home, sir. Because my fucking troops will not be strong enough to win this possible war, and we might as well not even try it sir," General Campanelli complained at his Commander.

Weidenbacher laughed as he fired back at his military officer, "You're a fucking livewire mister! Are you not attempting to tell the President of the United States what he might and might not do, mister? Why don't you run for his damn office so you can make all the decisions?"

He was getting angrier and growled at his Commanding Officer this time, before he could stop himself from firing off, "I have to protect my fucking troops out in the field as well as win this fucking possible war General Weidenbacher, and if I'm expected to win this damn war. Then I'll need all of what I have requested, sir!"

"You better mind your tone with me mister, or I'll have your damn ass for fucking coffee, buster!" General

Weidenbacher made note of General Campanelli's omission of 'sir' at the beginning and end of his spouting off and he resented it. But the General would have resented it more if this young military officer did not fight tooth and nail for the safety of his troops.

"Okay buster you win, I'll ask the President not to shave off any troops and equipment you requested on this dream list of yours, sir. I'll request even more troops and equipment then you originally asked for, mister. Boy, I could just see Manning's fucking puss when he reads this damn request list of yours, General. I spoke with the President at length about Three, Three, Seven, and my gut feelings is, he's calling for the damn Platform to be put in full operation for this situation, sir. He didn't like the fact much though, not with the present state of the economy. But he bit the bullet, and I expect to hear from him later today that Three, Three, Seven's a go.

"I put aside for you General Campanelli an Osprey to use as a command and control aircraft, and to get you back and forth with, sir. It's equipped like your helicopter was, but this Osprey's skinned with a special titanium and Kevlar mixed armor plating, sir. You shouldn't be knocked out of the air by an enemy fighter plane, unless he has plenty of time to play with your ass, sir. This CV-22 will have an air cover escort of three YF-27s at all times while she's in the air. No mistakes this time around sir, I need you too much for this one, General Campanelli."

The lesser General nodded slowly, because every time he remembered the crash in the Middle East War and what he lost there, he would vow again never to take another command of troops, and never fly again as well. But the call of the colors were too strong, and it made him change his mind, and here he was once more, responding to his country's call again.

"General Campanelli Sir, I don't see the damn list of command officers you'll need for this possible mission included in this request of yours sir. Have you picked them out yet sir?"

"Sorry General Weidenbacher Sir, I have the list of officers I'll need, and I'm certain all the officers I picked will in turn, pick the other officers who'll best serve them during any battlefield situation they engage in, General Weidenbacher Sir."

"Give me the damn list of names you have put together so far for me General Campanelli, and I'll get on with ordering them to report to you by communications, before reporting for duty, sir. I just hope none of the officers are retired, sir. It'll take a god damn act of Congress to get them back to active duty status if they are, General Campanelli."

"I'm quite certain that the officers I have requested are still on the active duty list, General Weidenbacher Sir," General Campanelli handed another report to the General.

"Hmmm... not a very long list at that I see General Campanelli. I expected to see a helluva lot more names here, sir. Colonel White, well how the hell did I know his name was going to head the damn list here sir," General Weidenbacher said as he turned to the Colonel sitting next to Locker and then announced. "Colonel John C. Salsiccia, I don't know this Officer sir, but if you want him, you have him sir. Commander Robert 'Bear' Owens, good pick there, but he's no longer a Commander, sir. He's now Admiral sir, and is floating around on the Roosevelt. Am I to take it the Roosevelt's going to be the Command ship for the Strike Forces, General?"

"Yes, and I picked Admiral Owens because he served me very well in the last war, and I know he'll do the same if there's another war, sir."

General Weidenbacher handed the list over to a security guard standing to his right and he growled at the young man, "Corporal, see to it these Officers are notified they're needed, and they're ordered to get in touch with General Campanelli here, A-SAP mister. Be sure to include the General's phone number at the Pentagon on the order."

The security guard stiffened as he took the paper and then left the office in a rush.

"General Campanelli, I have a question for you if you don't mind, are you going to keep the office I gave you here in the Pentagon, sir? Or do you want to move closer to any of the ships or military base soon under your command sir?" General Weidenbacher asked the General.

"I'd like to stay where I am until I know what's really happening with this damn mess, General. Though I'll need transportation when I have to get around, sir."

"Of course you do, I'll have that CV-22 Osprey turned over to you right away, General Campanelli. It'll use Langley Airforce Base for its temporary home base, sir. I'll also have a staff car and driver released to you on a twenty four hour a day basis, Ed. One call, and the driver will be waiting for you in the downstairs parking lot. I can't impress on you how important it is you have all the transportation you need at your disposal at all times, sir. Hell, I'll even have cars assigned to Colonel White and this Colonel Salsiccia officer you requested, sir. Admiral Owens has his own staff car and private driver already setup, so he's okay. I'll have you issued your new uniforms and a heavy overcoat to guard you against this damn cold ass weather we're having lately sir,"

General Weidenbacher offered to Campanelli as he shot him a quick smile.

"General Weidenbacher Sir, I have my old uniforms still, and they're good enough for me to use sir. I can have them sent for sir."

General Weidenbacher started to laugh with the rest of the officers in the meeting room as he stared at General Campanelli for a moment.

"Okay, what's the big fucking joke around here General Weidenbacher? I don't trust you fucking guys as far as I can throw the lot of ya," Edward bitched at his commander.

General Weidenbacher tried to control his laughing as he replied to his concerned looking military officer, "Sorry Ed, but you're going to need all new uniforms, sir. I guess I neglected to inform you a rate bump of two lifts comes along with this new Command. Sir, you're now a Three Star General at this time, and as a Three Star General, you're entitled to new uniforms compliments of your government, mister. I'll have a tailor up here tomorrow morning and all your uniforms will be ready for you no later than the day after tomorrow, sir. What do you have to say about that mister? You're never at a loss for fucking words, huh?"

He laughed as he looked around, until he found John beaming back at him. Then he turned to the General who quickly regained his composure and he offered, "Sir, what can I say to this but thank you, General Weidenbacher Sir. Although I do have a added request, now that I'm a Three Star General that is, sir."

"Uh-oh, I don't think I like the sound of this next request, mister. I knew you were letting me off the hook to damn easily mister," General Weidenbacher snapped at General Campanelli.

"General Weidenbacher Sir, I was wondering, now I've been given a rate lift because of this operation. Is it at all possible to have Colonel White lifted up in rank along with me, sir? He's going to be my Second in Command in this upcoming mess, and I can't have a mere Colonel yelling out my fucking orders to the rest of my Command Structure, General Weidenbacher Sir."

General Weidenbacher looked hard and long at the younger General sitting three seats away from him for a moment. He wiped at his brow before he spoke to his General again, "What the hell, I guess you have a good point there General Campanelli, and if not a point, you have me bent over a fucking barrel, mister. And I don't like being dumped over a damn barrel, so this is what I'm going to do about your last request, Mr. Wiseguy. If you want me to give a raise to Colonel White then I'll expect something from you in return sir."

Now, it was General Campanelli who rolled his eyes as he moaned at his Commanding Officer, "I can just imagine what your idea of tit for tat is, sir."

General Weidenbacher smiled, one of those smiles that warned the recipient he was in a world of shit at this point, and the well respected General had the only shovel left in the world.

"Okay smartass, I was trying to find an easier way of springing this load of shit on ya stinking ass for ya General Campanelli, and you just gave me the opening I was searching for, mister. Late yesterday, I was contacted by the President of the United States, and he suggested I take on a young Lithuanian fighter pilot, who their government wanted to give us on a loan basis, in order to train the pilot if you like, General Campanelli Sir. At first, I didn't like the stinking idea in the least, but by the time the President finished speaking with me, I understood his reasoning for the request and I come to respect and believe it was a good idea after all on his part, General."

"Oh, I really believe the President ordered you to take this damn foreign pilot on, right General Weidenbacher?" General Campanelli retorted at his Commander.

General Weidenbacher smiled as he smirked "Exactly General Campanelli, and can you guess who I'm going to stick this pain in the ass foreign pilot with, mister?"

"I can only imagine who's gonna get stuck with this damn foreign pilot, General Weidenbacher Sir." Campanelli grumbled as he lowered his eyes.

"You got that right mister, and I'm going to assign this young pilot to your ass, mister. As far as I know, the transferee is an already experienced fighter pilot, and is reported to be a damn good one at that might I add, sir. General Campanelli, I want him to be by your side, no correct that last remark, sir. He'll be assigned to your personal staff for the duration of this possible military operation sir," General Weidenbacher replied to Campanelli with a smile.

General Luther Claiborne attending this meeting stood and then he requested to speak. General Weidenbacher looked at him and gave him a nod.

Claiborne spoke up as soon as he was recognized by the General, his white teeth shinned in the soft light of the meeting room, "General Weidenbacher Sir, I'd like to clear up one thing you don't seem to understand quite yet about this pilot, sir. This pilot scheduled to be on loan to us from Lithuania, is a female pilot, sir. Her name's Major Aleksandra Klivekaita, sir. She's been in the stinking Lithuanian airforce for almost five years now, sir."

"Jesus H. Christ General Claiborne, I didn't even know the fucking Lithuanians had a stinking active airforce in their damn country, sir."

"Yes they do General Campanelli Sir, and from what I saw and heard about it, their airforce seems to be a damn good outfit at that, sir. The reason the President agreed to the training of this female pilot, is because we're trying to make a special deal with the damn Lithuanian government for us to be allowed to build an airforce and military base in their damn country, sir. So I suggest whoever gets this friggin pilot for training, better treat her with kid gloves, or he'll have to deal with me, and then the President. And I assure you sir, I'll leave very little for the President to pick over by the time I'm done with anyone who insults this damn female pilot, sir," Claiborne specifically glared at Campanelli.

General Campanelli nodded at the General as he realized what he was stuck with.

Weidenbacher laughed at Claiborne's warning, and then went on with his words for his new Commander. "Well General Campanelli, if you want this black, sorry ass sonofabitch raised up to Brigadier General then guess what, sir?" the General gave Campanelli the biggest shit eating grin, and then added. "You're going to get stuck with this foreign bitch as well mister, and you better treat her like fucking royalty if you know what's good for you, mister." Then he turned to Colonel White and grumbled at him, "I guess you're up to Brigadier General when I can sell the idea to the President, sir. I don't know if this is a blessing or not for you, mister." The General gave White a half assed salute as he turned back to General Campanelli and asked.

"Do you have any more questions for me, sir? I want to play nine if I can get out of here mister,." General

Weidenbacher suddenly moaned as he stretched his back a little.

"I do have one other question for you sir. What about our Allies sir? Are they going to back us in this operation, General Weidenbacher Sir? I could sure use the French nuclear powered Aircraft Carrier, or the one Italian Carrier if the shit hits the fan in this operation, sir."

"General Campanelli Sir, I know for certain you can count on the French and Italian government's complete backing, if it came down to any military action taking place in the Asian region, sir. But I'm not too certain about the United Kingdom though this time around General," Weidenbacher offered to his new Commander as he gave him a reassuring smile this time.

General Campanelli stared at Weidenbacher with questioning eyes.

"Close your damn mouth before a stinking fly lands in it on you sir. The reason I said that, is because the damn Chinese government made an offer to the English they can't possibly refuse, sir. The Chinese government offered the English a twenty year lease on Hong Kong, and England has jumped all over the damn idea, sir. And to make the deal even more enticing to the English, the Chinese offered the United Kingdom a chance to buy Hong Kong outright from them sir. That General Campanelli, is quite a fucking offer, sir. For the first time in their history, the Chinese government might allow a foreign government to own a piece of China.

"That's quite a deal General Campanelli especially being England, and the rest of the countries who deal with Hong Kong have over ninety Trillion, that's right General, with a T, Trillion invested in Hong Kong already, sir. The other reason is, it's a great deal for England as all the transactions carried out in Hong Kong, are relatively tax free, saving the investors millions of dollars in taxes. No one has offered to place a true cash value on all Hong Kong's holdings at this time sir. You have to figure in the coin collections, art work, diamonds and what's sunk in Hong Kong to beat out the tax man. Yeah, I think you can scratch the United Kingdom out of our corner this time around, if we're forced to go up against China, sir."

"Shit General Weidenbacher Sir, this has to be the first fucking time in the history of the United States that England won't be standing at our side during any possible war, sir. What about Canada, General? Will they go along with us, or would they go with England if the shit hits the fan on us, sir?" General Campanelli asked his Commanding Officer.

"General Campanelli, Canada's still in our court sir. She's putting her Merchant Marine Navy on full alert, and is also pulling many of her ships out from under the canvass. Canada's with us no matter what sir," Weidenbacher reported to his new Field Commander.

"That's good to know General Weidenbacher," Campanelli replied as he let out his breath.

"Look, it's getting kind of late and I have other plans in mind for the rest of my day, General Campanelli Sir. So if you have no further questions for my ass, I'd dearly like to get the hell out of here and go and enjoy myself some, General. I'll have my beeper with me at all times, sir. But if you choose to interrupt my game sir, you better have a damn good reason to do so, or you'll not have to worry about any damn trouble in Asia, because I'll strangle you personally myself, sir. Here's my beeper number, use it only in a matter of life and death, mister. Any further questions you may have are to be directed at General Claiborne here, sir. He'll man the box while I'm out having myself some fun for a damn change, sir. Now, I have a question for you General

Campanelli. Are you going to treat this damn female pilot with the utmost respect, or are we going to come to blows over this appointment, mister?"

General Edward Campanelli did not answer right off, he just kind of stared dumbly back at the powerful General. He did not know how to respond to that question, without first meeting this female pilot. Then finding out how well trained she might be, before he could possibly draw any conclusions one way or the other over her stay with him.

"I thought so, I didn't think you had a fucking answer to that one, sir. I'll withdraw it so I don't force you to lie mister," General Weidenbacher smirked at his military officer.

The room was filled with laughter, it broke the tension his staff was working under, as the Command Staff watched as the General prepared to leave the room..

"All kidding aside General Campanelli Sir. My staff and I, wish you the very best of luck in this upcoming operation, sir. We're depending on you to protect our children, and use their lives sparingly and wisely, sir. Save as many of my troops as you possibly can on this one mister," General Weidenbacher stood, and then he saluted General Campanelli then he turned and saluted the rest of his staff as he mumbled. "Stick a damn fork in my ass cause I am fucking done, people. Corporal, get my clubs and follow me."

The rest of the Command Staff stood as the General quickly left the room, and then they started speaking to one another, going over some of what was discussed by General Weidenbacher. The officers were pleased to be out from under the eye of their Commanding Officer as they breathed a deep sigh of relief together.

General Campanelli placed one leg on the top of his desk, and the he crossed it over with his other leg, and he moaned out loud, "Shit." As he locked his fingers together behind his head, and then stared up at the ceiling while taking a few moments to himself. He was starting to mull over all the information he was just offered by General Weidenbacher at the meeting.

"Would you like a fresh cup of coffee there, General Campanelli Sir?" one of the aides asked him. "You never got a chance to drink your last coffee while you were speaking with General Weidenbacher, General Campanelli Sir."

"I'd kill for one, thank you," Campanelli replied as he nodded to the aide.

John came over and he sat down on the edge of the desk and spoke to General Campanelli. "Thanks for the increase in rate there, sir. I could sure use the extra money in the old paycheck, Eddy. The kids are getting old, and my oldest has been busting my horns lately for a damn car already, sir. Besides, he'll be heading off to college in two years, so the extra money will certainly come in very handy, Eddy."

General Campanelli laughed without even looking at him as John kept speaking while the General was relaxing for the moment, "What say we put an quick end to this fucking day my friend? We've been working at the top end for the last three days now, Eddy. I'm certain your brain could use a little break about now sir," John offered as he looked at the General.

Campanelli let out his breath in an exhausted sigh, and then replied to his new General and his
Second in Command, "What would I do without you standing by my damn side as always, John? You take better care of me than my wife does, my old friend. I think you're right at that time off though John." The General carefully slid his feet off of the desk and then announced at the same time, "Everyone listen up. We're going to take a stinking lesson from General Weidenbacher, and we're going to go

and have ourselves some stinking fun for a change around here, dammit. Get the hell out of here people, and I don't want to see any sign of you people again until tomorrow morning at ten o'clock sharp. No earlier if you know what's good for ya, got it people? Take some time for yourselves, please."

The exhausted and overworked members of his Command Staff got up to their feet, all agreeing with the idea of some time off, without anything to do but enjoy their families.

General Campanelli watched his new Command Staff literally drag their asses out of the office, and he kicked himself for not realizing his personnel were spent out before this time. The General turned his attention back to his Second in Command and bitched at him, "And what the hell are you waiting for buster, a special invitation, sir? Go home and have some fun with Beth and your kinds, will ya please mister?"

"You got it Eddy, but what about you, man? What the hell are you gonna do with the rest of the day off, sir? Eddy, why don't you come home with me, and have a real meal to enjoy will you please? My wife and kids would love to have you hanging around the house for a little while you know. You look like shit my friend."

CHAPTER 8
JANUARY 16th, 1997;
THE OFFICE OF GENERAL CAMPANELLI AND HIS STAFF IN THE PENTAGON, WASHINGTON DC, TEN HUNDRED HOURS

General Edward Campanelli was the first one to show up at the office for the day. He came up as Colonel Mary Locker parked her car in the North parking lot at the Pentagon. John and Mary came in together by car this time. General Palmieri and the aides were already present, they were at the office since eight o'clock, their regular starting time for the day. The Commanding General nodded at everyone as they entered, each carried a cup of coffee. The General was already seated and he was reading the Washington Post.

At twenty after ten, he folded the paper and put it down on his desk. Saving the best part of the paper for later on, the sports section. He looked around his office at the staff. He noticed John with his head down and said, "Hey guys, before we get down to some brass tacks around here, what say we go and get something to eat." To his surprise, no one wanted to go, and then his aide was picked to get coffee and cakes for them.

General Campanelli had no choice but to start work, even though he was dreading it. The concerned General took the first reports, it was from Naval Operations. Most ships he requested, were being fitted out with food stores, ammunition and man power, and would be ready to set sail by the end of the week. The next report stated the Marine troops were good to go, four Expeditionary Forces finished, or were still presently engaged in training maneuvers of one sort or the other, and Command delayed all soldier's leaves when they issued the Level Three Alert.

These reports made him feel about ready for any operation coming his way. Admiral Owens checked in, and the two clicked together. Owens knew what Campanelli was going to need, and he was offering the troops and ships he requested. Colonel Salsiccia also checked in via the phone, and he promised General Campanelli he would be in Washington later that night, and would report early tomorrow morning on the seventeenth for duty.

The General looked at the phone, one red button was blinking and he picked it up and grumbled into the receiver with a snap in his voice, "General Campanelli."

"General Campanelli, this good General, this Major Aleksandra Klivekaita, mista sir. I report duty for you sir. I come Washington today later on in day. You see soon I come here, no?"

"Yeah I'll see you when you get here Major. When will you arrive, sir, excuse me, Ma'am?"

"I there be twelve o'clock you noon time they say me sir. I fly you aircraft, a YF-27 fighter there, sir. I trained fly plane good for six of you month now, and I feel I ready make you..."

"Look Major, do me a favor, and just get here will ya. I don't like talking on the damn phone. I'll have my private car waiting for you when you arrive, and my driver will bring you here. Until then, stay off the damn phone. Good bye Major," he growled at the Lithuanian pilot.

"Do I do something not you like already General? If so, you tell and I do no more again sir."

"No, you didn't do anything wrong yet that is, Major. You just get your damn ass in here as quickly as you possibly can get here, that's all Major. Good-bye!" General Campanelli hung up not waiting for a response from the foreign female Major.

"Jesus, that's all I fricking needed around here. A fucking foreign pilot who can't talk damn English. Damn, why the hell did I ever agree to get stuck with this foreign bitch anyhow?"

Colonel Locker piped up, "Who told you to be so damn good looking, sir?"

General Campanelli did not appreciate the smart remark and snapped out at his staff, "does anyone have anything new for me to go over with them, dammit?"

No one offered anything up, so he busied himself with the reports and maps on the area that might be involved in a possible war. The coast of China did not offer much in the way of landing a sizable attack force, so he decided to use the west coast of South Korea as a possible military base, if he needed one in that area. The General turned his attention to the small Island of Taiwan. He had a rather detailed map three feet square of it, and carefully searched the coastline with a magnifying glass, looking for any possible landing areas for his forces, in case he had to invade Taiwan in the future.

The General called out over his shoulder at no one in particular, "who the hell do I see if I need a few up to date pictures of a certain location?"

General Palmieri responded, "what kind of pictures do you need sir? Do you want a flyover by the SR-91, or do you want a flyover by one of the satellites, General Campanelli?"

"I want the best pictures possible I can get of the area in question, as fast as I can get them."

"Then I suggest you request a flyover by an SR-91, General Campanelli. You can get the job done by getting General Claiborne in here, and give him your request of the flyover, sir."

General Campanelli turned to one of the aides and asked the young soldier, "Do you know if General Claiborne's in the building yet, mister?"

"Yes sir, he practically lives here lately sir," the aide replied with a grin to the General.

"Good, get him in here right away will ya?" Campanelli ordered as he went back to a report.

"Yes sir." Minutes later, General Claiborne strolled into the office. A smile was plastered across his face as usual as he bitched at the Commander of the upcoming operation. "Shitttt, this here office is no bigger than a damn clothes closet, sir. I suggest you do some bitching bout getting yourself a real office to work from, or the brass will never get you out of this coffin."

The General smiled at the big man as he moaned at him, "General Claiborne..."

"Whoa white boy, let's get something straight right off the fricking bat here and now, sir. Let's cut that shit out right now sonny. If you wanna talk to me right then you betta start calling me Nails, or Clay. Never mind that General bullshit, Edward."

"Yes sir," Campanelli replied as he grinned at the large black General.

"That sir shit hasta go as well mister, if you wanna get along with me correctly, mister."

"Sorry sir... Err... I mean Clay," he said as he shook his head.

"That's a might better there sonny. Now, what the hell do you have on your mind, Ed?"

"Clay, I asked you here because I'd like to schedule a flyover of the coast of Taiwan along with the west coast of South Korea as well, sir. If your pilot has any film left, I'd also like some new pictures of China too, some of their damn military and Naval bases stationed at Tungshan, Canton, and the ship building bases constructed at Shanghai. I'd also like to see what god damn Chinese warships are docked at these three ports, and what ships are presently on patrol, sir."

"Gees Ed, you sure don't mind asking for things do ya. Yeah, I guess I can have a flight up by tomorrow morning at the earliest, and you'll have all your pictures by night. It's the best I can do for you at this time, General. Of course you understand that I'll have to clear the flight with the President, but I see no problem with that request as it stands Ed," Claiborne offered as he relaxed, enjoying getting back in the saddle of being in command of active troops again.

"Good Clay, but I'd also like to know if I could call for a flight anytime I might have need of one, and who I'd have to go to, in order to get the damn over flight when I need them, sir."

Claiborne suddenly glared at Campanelli as he snapped in a sharp tone, "you'll come to me anytime you need a fucking flyover anywhere in the damn world, sir. If I catch you going to anyone else, I'll cut your stinking balls off, sir. You read me loud and clear, General?"

"Yes sir, I read you loud and clear Clay, and I'd never dreamed about going to anyone else but you for this needed information sir." General Campanelli could see the other General was giving him a real warning here just by the way he was staring at him.

"Good. You know, now I have you here, I'd like to ask you a question if you don't mind, Ed?" the wise General asked of his commander.

"Sure thing, anything you want, sir. Ask away Clay. I want my Command Staff to know what the hell's going on at all times," Campanelli replied as he waited for the question.

"How the hell did you ever come up with the stinking nickname of Popeye anyhow, sir?"

General Campanelli laughed as he began to explain how he came across the tag name, "that's a story all in itself, General. You see when my son was born, I was at the hospital, and he was given to me to hold by a nurse. As I was holding him I was looking at my wife to make sure she was okay, and the baby accidently poked me square in the eye. The nurse saw what happened and took the baby from me, and I closed my eye to stop it from tearing up on me. A smartass Second Lieutenant came in at this time, and he made the remark. 'Sir, with your eye closed like that you look like Popeye the Sailor', sir. My wife liked the damn tag name, and another soldier there mention the tag to another, and before I knew it, the damn thing stuck to my ass, sir. So I guess I can say it's my wife's fault for the lousy nickname, General."

General Claiborne bellowed with laughter at the explanation as he shook his head and replied, "General Campanelli Sir, I'll speak to the President now, and get the okay to order up the over flight with a SR-91." He turned and left the office still laughing.

After Claiborne got clearance for the overflight, he got in touch with the airbase stationed in Northern California just outside of Carmel. The base was so secretive it did not have a true name, just the code number of X-227 attached to it. He spoke to the spook (CIA Agent) in charge, and he ordered the flight through a scramble hookup system.

In less than ten minutes time, the super secret SR-91 spy aircraft was charged up inside the specially designed and built and camouflaged hard shelter, as all the base sensors searched the sky, and space, for any possible signs of any unauthorized aircraft or Russian satellite passing overhead of the base. Once this was accomplished, a wave of smaller fighter aircraft suddenly made a number of passes directly over the hard shelter area, trying to hiding the SR-91 aircraft in their tight formation. This was done to help confuse anyone on the ground, who might be keeping a close eye on the base from seeing the plane.

The large SR-91 aircraft was started up with half her fuel stored in her fuel tanks. The ship had what was called breathing fuel bladders, and while it was on the ground, the bladders leaked fuel constantly. Once the sleek aircraft was airborne, it came under tremendous pressures, that would crush the fuel tanks if it did not have this breathing fuel bladder system. The SR-91 was a specially designed reconnaissance aircraft that carried a pilot and a reconnaissance systems officer. The length of the ship was eighty seven feet long, with a height of eighteen feet, and it had a wing span of seventy feet.

Unlike its predecessor, the shape of the SR-91 aircraft was radically altered, to make the ship look more like a flying saucer than an aircraft while in flight. The nose was shortened by four feet from the original hundred seven feet of the SR-71, and the wings were much wider, and actually hooked to the nose and tail sections, thus giving the aircraft a more cylindrical shape. The wings encompassed and covered the engines, making the wings and engines as one.

The redesigned vectoring nozzle ports added much more stability to the sleek aircraft, and the fly by fiber optic computer controlled flight, kept the bird from tumbling end over end, or going out of control on the pilot. It made the pilot feel like he was just coming along for the ride, and to land and takeoff with the plane. With these new innovations, it gave the aircraft greater flying capabilities and increased speed. This version could take pictures of targets while flying at over Mach Four, using the high speed, high resolution camera recently developed by Kodak, with a lens drop down of five inches, that enabled the camera to take a picture of a five inch item from one hundred thousand feet, and read the print on the item.

The specialized aircraft's most important development was in the field of photographing, while flying at speeds of Mach Four taking pictures of the area in question, making it possible for the aircraft to out fly, and or out maneuver most foreign countries missiles. This was the major different from the older and outdated SR-71 aircraft, that was forced to drop down to speeds of six hundred and ninety five MPH, in order to take clear pictures in the past. The SR-91 aircraft was spotted numerous times over the past few years while still under development by hordes of people, who always ended up calling the local police complaining they just saw a flying saucer in the skies above them.

As the SR-91 pulled out of the shelter, six F-16 Falcons blanketed it and paced the aircraft down the runway. As the black ship pulled in the air, the F-16s shadowed it, blocking it from a clear view of ground crew and possible spies. As the plane began its almost straight up arch, and increased its speed, the F-16s went to afterburners in an attempt to try and keep up with the aircraft for as long as possible. In less than three minutes into its flight, the SR-91 rapidly pulled away from the trailing F-16s. The spy plane was swiftly out of sight, she was scheduled for mid air refueling over Guam, and then she was ordered to climb to the ceiling of one hundred thousand feet at Mach Five. The aircraft would have to refuel twice more, before her operation was completed. The reason for choosing this special aircraft rather than a satellite, was its ability to stay in the area for longer periods of time and take more pictures of the area in question.

GENERAL CAMPANELLI'S OFFICE IN THE PENTAGON, WASHINGTON D.C.

General Edward 'Popeye' Campanelli and the other officers with him, were working on checking out the readiness of their troops and other military equipment needed for this pending operation. The General was considering breaking for lunch when a security guard suddenly knocked on his door. After being invited in, the Army security guard informed him the female Lithuanian pilot was in the building, and he had her placed in one of the visitor's quarters, so she could freshen up some from her flight.

General Campanelli asked where the visitor's quarters were located in the building.

"C'mon General Campanelli Sir, it's easier for me to show you where it is, rather than to try and explain it to you where it's located in the building, sir. You might as well get to exploring the building some anyhow sir, being you're going to be hanging around here so much, sir."

The General gave out a laugh as he followed the guard down the long hallway.

Minutes later, the concerned General found himself standing in front of a closed door as the security guard warned him, "General Campanelli Sir, she's in there sir. I have to get back to my post before the Lieutenant comes looking for me, and I end up pulling extra duty because I was not at my post as ordered, sir. I'm afraid you're on your own from here on out, sir. Good luck with her, I have to warn you though sir, she's a real hellcat to deal with General Campanelli."

The Commanding General banged on the oak door and from inside he heard a female voice call out to him. "You come in please, door no be lock to you, sir."

He entered and stared at the naked back of the tall female pilot. His heart skipped a beat, and for the briefest second he thought she was Mendoza. She was the spitting image of her from the back. Her skin was blemish free, and had that olive complexion similar to the Latin Americans. Her hair was dark, almost black, and was as curly as Mendoza's. Even her stance reminded him of Mendoza. General Campanelli breathed fast as the memories, both good and bad of Mendoza, flooded back into his mind while he continued to stare at the back of the female.

He looked her over with his mouth hanging open, her legs were long and slender, and her rearend was smooth and shaped as Mendoza's was. He remembered what he thought the first time he laid eyes on Mendoza's rearend, he said only God could have crafted an ass that perfect. Her waist was narrow, leading to a what he felt was a larger chest than Mendoza's. He had to shake his head to clear the lingering image of his former lover out of his mind.

"Yes, what you want from me this minute, mista? I no need anything right now, I have all thing I need for moment. Did you tell Command Officer I make my ass to his Pentagon like I ordered, and I ask you do?" she said over her shoulder before she turned around to see who just came in her room. When she did turn, she stood staring at General Campanelli, and both officers stood with their mouths hanging open as they continued to stare at each other.

The General's because he was stunned by her beauty, and the Lithuanian's because she did not know who this officer was that was staring at her. Her mouth snapped closed suddenly and she glared at him as she asked, "who you are, and what you want here, mista?"

General Campanelli noticed she made no attempt to cover her nakedness as she placed her hands on her hips and then she continued to stare at him. His stomach turned because of her stance, it was the same exact stance Mendoza always assumed whenever she was upset, or had a point to get across to someone. He stiffened up and then replied to the beautiful young female foreign pilot, "I'm General Campanelli. Edward, Ma'am. I'm your Commanding Officer, and I came here when I was informed you were in the building, Ma'am. To make certain you were comfortable, and the security guards were treating you with respect, Ma'am."

The Lithuanian, Aleksandra Klivekaita snapped to attention and saluted, adding to her beauty.

His eyes opened wide as she stood at attention, her stomach sucked in, and her chest pushed out, she looked like a goddess. Her breasts, though large, looked twice the size and her waist got even smaller because of her stance. Her brown hair encircled her face perfectly, and made it glow. The General was taken by her beauty.

Aleksandra saw the General staring at her body, and she automatically pulled her stomach in even more. She smiled to herself, knowing she already had him right where she wanted him. She remembered her training at the hands of the Russian Communists when they occupied her nation. How she was trained to use her body as a weapon against any breast infatuated American male she wanted to extract vital information from, for her old Communist government. She continued her salute and stand at full attention until ordered otherwise.

The surprised General could not understand why she continued to stand there until he realized she was saluting her superior officer. He returned her salute reluctantly. Immediately, her hand returned to her side, but she still did not make any attempt whatsoever to try and cover herself up, or turn away from his stare as she remarked to him.

"General Campanelli Sir, I have question ask you if no mind, sir. I sure you have question ask me also too, General. You please excuse me because I no speak very good English too much. I no know why my government lend me you for. But I assure you I serve you like I serve my own government, sir. Without hesitate and I obey any and all order placed before me sir. You will find me a very loyal Officer who will do as ordered, and I never complain about order aimed at me. I use to deal with male pilot all time, they think so good betta pilot then we women, sir."

The General could not believe she stood there naked while acting like she was fully clothed. Try as he might, he just could not think of ordering her to get dressed. He tried twice, but the words would not come out his mouth correctly.

Again, she smiled for making her Commander so uncomfortable. The Americans were so easy she thought as she could tell what effect she was having on the man from the bulge in his pants.

"General Campanelli Sir, I have bottle good Stolichnya Russian Vodka I bring with me from native country, sir. I save it for right reason open it for. Would you like join me in drink to our governments, sir?" Aleksandra spent many days learning how to pronounce the General's name correctly, ever since she was first informed she was going to be sent to the United States for further training with their aircraft, and who was going to be her Commanding Officer.

The General could do nothing but dumbly nod yes. He watched her every move as she found her bottle in a flight bag. She moved like a cat, sleek and smooth with no wasted energy, he was certain every movement from her was well calculated. She poured two glasses and picked her glass up in a toast and aimed it at Campanelli. He stared at her as he took a slug of the burning liquid and almost died from it. He did not realize he was taking a shot of booze, he gagged and then coughed as he plopped down in a seat. She dashed into the small kitchen area and retrieved him a glass of water. He quickly washed down the harsh tasting liquid.

Aleksandra laughed as she stared at the big man struggling to get the coughing stopped.

He stared at her bouncing breasts inches before him, and then growled at the foreign female pilot, "what's so god damn funny with your ass, Major?"

"I hear what great drinker America soldier are, now I see me self," She continued to laugh.

The General wiped the side of his mouth, and the tears from his burning eyes as he joined her in laughter.

Aleksandra turned and went back to her mirror, and then she continued what she was doing before the General came into the room. But this time she moved until she could see Campanelli's face in the mirror. She knew well what she was doing, and she was determined to continue until he either raped her, or ordered her to get dressed. It was an old KGB move to gain complete control over one's adversary from the out set.

General Campanelli stared at the perfect, naked young body of the woman staring back at him from the mirror, as he finally found his words and mumbled dumbly, "Err... excuse me Major, but how long have you been a pilot, Ma'am?"

She stopped combing her hair and thought for a second, and then she replied to her new Commanding Officer. "Ten year I fly good aircraft for my government. I start when nineteen I was, for Russia Airforce. I fly every type aircraft Russia has, even Bear Jammer bomber, sir. I love fly all time. If had way, how you say. I would err... yes, live in sky sir."

"How do you find the American flyers, Major? Do they stack up well with their Russian counterpart pilots, Ma'am? I heard a lot of scuttlebutt about how good the damn Russian Pilots profess to be, and I don't believe their load of tripe for a fucking second, Major."

She did not understand what the word 'tripe' mean nor did she really care as she replied, "You flyer good. They fly ring around foolish Russia pilot, I think because you flyer think of you aircraft as their personal friend, err... lover I believe is correct word I look for now, sir. But Lithuanian flyer is another matter, I force offer to my Command Officer. You America flyer no do so good against Lithuanian pilot I afraid, sir. One thing I lot trouble with in you airforce sir."

"Oh, what was that Major?" he interrupted her words as he thought over the typical communist responses.

"You pilot have complicated name each other with, sir. We, in Russia Airforce have number, like one, three and so on, General Sir. You pilot have foolish name like 'Road Runner' and 'Sight Seer', sir. I have much trouble remember you flyer name all time when I spoke to America pilot over radio when train with them, sir. They give me a, how you say, err... yes please, nicker name I believe you say it here in United States, sir."

"Really? And what was the call name they tagged you with when my pilots were training with you, Major?" General Campanelli asked the pilot with a smirk.

She laughed again and the General tilted his head to the side as he stared at her image in the mirror again, "you flyer, as you say, tagged me with nicker name of Twin Peaks, General Sir."

General Campanelli, still smiling but he did not get the inference and he gave her a funny look at her in the mirror.

She noticed the look and turned to face him again, as she allowed her arms to fall down to her sides. Then she raised them, and with her hands she pointed at her breasts using her index fingers and repeated, "Twin Peaks, sir." She announced proudly while moving her chest slightly, drawing the General's attention right to her ample breasts. Then she smiled until she was certain her got the reference she was making to the American Officer.

The General immediately roared with laughter as she stood there pointing at her breasts and he announced between breaths, "I got it and may I add it's a very fitting name as well they blessed you with, Major." He continued to admire her breasts with the up pointing nipples. Perfect, he thought to himself as he continued to stare at her body. And again, he compared her shape to Mendoza. One thing he liked better about her than Mendoza though, Aleksandra had little pubic hair, and no hair under her arms or on her legs. Unlike Captain Mendoza who had a healthy growth of hair below, and under her arms. Not that he found this unpleasant, but with the lesser hair he could see more of her body, and he like looking in that area.

The sound of her voice snapped him back to reality as he heard her saying.

"I sorry, I know how you America feel about human body. You military upset when you see one you soldier walk around with no clothes on. In Lithuanian Airforce, men bunk with woman and share same shower all time. We have no, what you say, let me see, err... hang in about body. We Lithuanian proud of country and body. We think nothing about walk in front of man or woman like this," again she pointed at her body.

"When I come here first, I get you men in much big trouble with their Command, because I walk in their shower alone. I thought I walk in top secret room by way they act against me, sir. You MP take me drip wet to bring back room. I order get dressed quickly and see you Captain. You MP very free with hands though I mind tell you, General."

"I could see that one coming, Major. You were on a Carrier then I take it, Ma'am? What ship were you stationed on during your training detachment, Major?"

"They called it Teddy Roosevelt thing I believe I remember correct. It big ship, I marvel over size of ship. Big I ever see in fool life, General Campanelli Sir."

"Jesus Christ, you did this to Admiral Owens, Major?" General Campanelli said with a grin.

"Yes, that Officer I brought before I remember right, and he angry at me much I worry about. You Admiral was Captain then, and Owens, I hear about Jesus Christ, but I no know he was Jesus Christ, General Campanelli Sir. I believe Jesus Christ was saint, sir."

The General laughed and he mumbled at the female pilot, "No, I didn't mean he was Jesus Christ, Major. I meant I know Admiral Owens very well, that's all, Ma'am. Damn, I could see his face now, as he lost it because of what you did on board his ship, Major. Not that what you did was wrong by any means, Major. It's just our governments not as liberated as yours evidently is, Ma'am. Hell, we just started allowing women pilots in 1995. I'm sorry to say, but some of our female pilots can fly rings around the best of our male pilots, Major." General Campanelli announced proudly, he was all for equal rights for any women, and he was damn glad his government was finally opening their eyes to the fact women warriors were here to stay.

"General Campanelli, I forget myself my manner I afraid, sir. Should I get dressed, or it okay me be in front Command Officer without clothes on any. I hate clothes, but I get dressed if you like, sir. It I get insult when I no take shower with men. I have fun with one of you women pilot in shower once, sir. She show me many thing I never knew before in life, and I thought I know everything about make love to anyone, man or woman, sir. I tingle when remember she show me what and how do it, sir. I almost forgot about men. No, I lie, I never forgot men sir."

"Thank God for that much Major," General Campanelli muttered before catching himself and then he added to his words. "But I better warn you not to talk about your experience with the female pilot in the shower though, Ma'am. If you talk about that sort of shit and someone hears you, there'll be some narrow minded assholes snooping around trying to find out who she was. We're getting better, but we still ain't there quite yet, Ma'am."

"I take you like Lithuanian female pilot, General Sir?" the female pilot asked.

"I like them very much I guess Major," he had to take a quick breath to get a hold of himself, before he got his himself in any trouble, and then he added to his words. "Err... Major, I hate to say this, in fact, I don't really believe I'm about to say it to you, Major. But I do think it's in your best interest for you to get some clothes on please, Ma'am."

She gave him a slight pout, but she did not move to get dressed right away either.

"It's not for me Major. By no means, but I was thinking it wouldn't be too cool for you to be standing there without any clothes on. If someone came in the room and saw us, that's all."

Major Klivekaita smiled as she replied to her Commanding Officer, "I suppose you right in you response to me, General Campanelli Sir. I get dressed before I get you trouble, sir."

The General made a move to leave the room while she got dressed, but he was stopped dead in his tracks as she complained at him. "Where go you now General Campanelli Sir? I like speak you further please, sir. Unless you no like my body see like this, sir?"

He smirked at her as he sat down again and then remarked, "I'd have to be plum out of my damn mind not to like your body, Major." He sat comfortably and watched her as she slowly got dressed, he enjoyed the little private show she put on obviously just for him. She slipped into non regulation nylons, and a garter belt, no bra. Then, the coarse dark green uniform of the Lithuanian Airforce and cap. She was ready.

All the time she dressed, she made certain she bent down just right, and also lingered in one position when she noticed the General shifting his weight slightly, because he could no longer sit comfortably the way he was, and she made sure her breasts were the last thing she covered before him. She had been taught well by her Russian trainers about how the American males felt about a woman's breasts. She thought to herself if she was still working for the KGB, she would have this American General eating right out of her hand and working for her by now. Americans are so easy and she would know all the well guarded secrets locked away in his foolish mind. They make it so easy for us women to own the fools.

General Campanelli stood as she walked towards him and he asked her, "You have a place to stay Major, while you're stationed here in Washington that is, Ma'am?"

"No, I hope you government take better good care of that for me please, sir. I have no idea what do sir, or how buy room here to live with American General Sir," she replied sheepishly.

"Don't worry about it Major. I'll take you over to meet my Command Staff first, and then I'll take you over to the Hilton and get you a room to stay. The Hilton's a half a block from the Pentagon, so you won't get lost unless you try to, Major. To tell you the truth, I was kind of thinking about getting a room there myself, Major. I can't go on sharing a damn apartment with Colonel Locker for the rest of my stay, while I'm stationed here in Washington, Ma'am."

"You talk about Colonel Mary Locker, General Campanelli Sir?" the female pilot asked him.

"Yes, and why do you ask me that question Major? Do you know her Major?" General Campanelli asked the foreign pilot with some concern lacing his tone.

"No personal, but I hear of her and her reputation though. Are you sure you able walk, sir?"

"Yes, I can walk just fine, thank you very much Major," General Campanelli laughed as he wiped at the side of his face with the back of his hand.

Aleksandra stared at him like a farmer would size up a side of beef, even making some noises while she continued to size him up, and then she remarked, "I might reconsider way feel about America military soldier now, sir. Here you General Campanelli, living with less Officer and no marry yet. I all sudden feel maybe hope for America military way of fool think all time, sir."

The General laughed at her last remark as he added, "did you ever live with anyone Major? Here, we're getting to live with a person rather than marry her much too often I believe."

"Yes, twice time in life General Campanelli Sir." She offered matter of factly to her new Commander. She was trying to use his name as much as she possibly could, so she would remember it and pronounce it properly, whenever she spoke to her Commanding Officer.

"Were, or are you married Major?" he asked her as they left the room, and walked towards his office. Her look was more than enough to tell him she was never married. He stopped in front of the men's room and announced he had to go.

She mumbled at him as he disappeared behind the door, "more separation of feelings I see, sir. In Lithuania there no such foolishness as man room, woman room separate. You have to go, you just go, sir. It is that simple in the nation I come from, General Campanelli Sir."

The confused but pleased General went in the bathroom while shaking his head. He mumbled to himself this is all he needed, a foreigner telling him of how wonderful it is in her country, and yet she's learning from my country. He stopped in front of the urinal and took a quick leak, while noticing a hand written note printed on the wall. "In your hands you hold the future. Don't beat it to death." He laughed again as he read the warning and then he finished up. He came back out in the hallway only to find Aleksandra still complaining at him.

"You America waste much good food to also much, sir. You throw away like nothing matter to you people who enjoy too much food to eat. In my country, people would live well on food you throw away and waste in you country, General Campanelli Sir."

The General had enough of her griping about him and his country, while she was constantly bragging to him about her country, and he spun on his heels and actually barked at the stunned young and beautiful foreign female pilot, "will you shut the fuck up for a damn minute please, Ma'am. I'm trying to think and you're bugging the living shit outta my damn ass with all your constant babbling, Major." He glared at her, his face just inches from hers.

A grin slowly spread across her face as she purred back at the angry General once she got control of her emotions and she smirked, "you know, I get turn on by you anger, General Campanelli Sir." Aleksandra then ran the tip of her tongue slowly over her snow white teeth.

Campanelli growled again at her again, "Jesus H. Christ Major, you're quickly getting to be a real god damn royal pain in the can, bitch." He started into his office, followed closely by Aleksandra. He stormed in not taking the time to introduce the Lithuanian pilot to the rest of his Command Staff. He plopped down in his chair, and then he growled at John, "See if I have this one assigned to my staff, or if I just have to be nice to her damn ass, General White."

All eyes in the office went over to the pretty looking female Lithuanian pilot. She stood with her hands resting on her hips while glaring angrily at the General.

He asked her, "yes, do you have anything else to say to me now, Major?"

"I no say what want say because you Command Officer, and I get in trouble if say what want say, General Campanelli Sir," she hissed angrily at him in no uncertain terms.

"RHIP, Rank Have Its Privilege Major," he smirked back at her.

John cut off this slight confrontation taking place between the two by offering, "General Campanelli Sir, here's your latest memo, it reads the female Lithuanian pilot's appointed to your personal Command Staff, sir. She's to serve as interpreter, and is supposed to be fluent in three Russian Dialects, Lithuanian of course, as well as Chinese and some Taiwanese also, sir. She comes highly recommended by the President, and he wants her trained in our ways, sir."

With her hands still resting on her hips, she smiled back at her Commanding Officer, before she added to her snappy words at him, "so much you rank means now to you, sir." She was letting him know he was stuck with her, and there was nothing he could do about it, because she had the American President obviously on her side.

General Campanelli shook his head in disgust, and then he snarled at John, "Since I'm obviously stuck with her ass, put her in with General Palmieri until I can get her a fucking desk, maybe in the outer office if at all possible. This is great, just fucking great, dammit."

"Are you still help find apartment at you Hilton house like said you do for me, General Campanelli Sir?" Aleksandra asked her Commanding Officer with concern in her voice.

"Yeah, yeah right, okay. When I'm done here, I'll take you over to the damn hotel and get you a fucking apartment there, Major."

The rest of the day's work was completed with the minimum of conversation being carried out between the members of the Command Staff. It was General Campanelli who put an end to the day's work as he announced, "well, that's it for today, people. Everyone go home, be back here Monday morning around nine. Good night people." The General stood and then made his way out the office in a rush, with the Lithuanian pilot following closely behind him. He spun around, only to come face to face with her, and she was smiling at him.

"Oh shit, I forgot all about you Ma'am. C'mon, I'll get you your damn apartment Major."

Colonel Mary Locker who stopped in the doorway, stared at the two officers as they walked away. She was angry the General chose not to come home with her for the weekend. General Palmieri, who pulled the weekend duty came up behind, and he tapped her on the shoulder and offered her, "come on Locker, I'll buy you a drink."

Locker turned to him and smiled, "I think I could use one about now, General."

General Palmieri knew how she felt, because he saw she was starting to fall in love with General Campanelli, and he was happy to see the other officers getting along so well until now. He looped his arm over Mary's shoulder, and actually felt her melt against his chest. He found himself questioning his marriage and wondering how it would be to make love to Locker. After their drinks, he walked Locker back to her car, he stayed with her in the dimly lit underground parking lot until she drove off.

General Campanelli allowed the female Lithuanian pilot to hitch a ride with him over to the Hilton in his staff car. Neither officer spoke as the car pulled in front of the Hilton Hotel under the protective awning. It was freezing out, but not snowing yet. He was out of the car first, but the Major got out before he could open her door for her. He shook his head then headed in the building, and she followed him in the hotel without saying a word.

The desk clerk acknowledged the two enter and General Campanelli announced he wanted to rent two rooms in the hotel. The clerk smiled as he spun the wide registry book around and offered, "you can sign in while I get your key cards ready for you, please."

General Campanelli signed in then he signed for the Major as well. She whispered how to spell her name Klevekaita correctly to her new Commander.

The clerk spun the registry around and then he remarked to the two officers, "General Campanelli, you have room 515 and Major, err..."

"Klivekaita,"   the Lithuanian pilot repeated for the concerned looking clerk.

"Err... yes Ma'am. Your room's 517. The elevators are over there please," he pointed towards the other end of the desk and then added. "Do you need a hand with your luggage, sir?"

"No, we can handle them ourselves thanks," Campanelli grumbled as he picked up his bag.

"Very well then sir, breakfast is served from seven until ten o'clock in the morning, sir. It's a buffet and a menu affair, sir.

The dining room's open from five a.m. till ten at night sir, and we have room service until midnight, sir. I hope you'll have a very nice stay with us, sir."

"Yeah sure pal, C'mon Major and I'll get you up to your room. I'll get you all settled in first in your room, before I head for my own room, Ma'am."

CHAPTER 9

Major Aleksandra Klevekaita followed the still angry acting General to her suite. The first thing she did was to look in the bathroom and then she announced excitedly, "A bath, I take bath. You America know to live sure." She giggled as she threw her bag on the bed.

"Major Ma'am," General Campanelli said as he went to complain at her for a moment.

"Aleksandra," the female pilot snapped back at him while cutting him off in mid sentence.

"Yeah sure, Aleksandra. I'm going to my room to freshen up some, and then I'm going downstairs to get something to eat, I'm starving. I'll see you tomorrow morning Major, good night Ma'am," when he was certain she was settled in, he left for his room. It took him fifteen minutes to take a dump and wash up, and then he headed downstairs to eat. The dinning room was empty as he followed the waiter over to a table.

The waiter disappeared and in a few seconds he returned with his glass of cold Pepsi. The General looked around to see if there was someone around he recognized seated in the eating area, but he saw no one. He took a sip of soda, it was plenty cold. He sat waiting for ten minutes before he noticed the Major walk in the room, almost choking on a mouthful of soda as he set eyes on her. She was dressed in civilian clothes, and she was ravishing. She wore a stunningly long dress, black, open to her navel. It was held closed by a thin strand of cloth that ran from the center of one breast to the other. The dress was slit up one side to her hip. She had her hair partially up in a bun with the rest of it hanging down the side of her face, with her blue eye shadow and the red lipstick, she looked like a model.

The stunned General held his breath as she entered the area. At first he thought she was going to sit alone, and was upset until she looked at him, and then she sashayed her way over to his table while wiggling her rearend to beat the band. He could not tell what moved more on her body, her breasts or hips, but he did not care as he enjoyed the show she was offering to everyone sitting in the dining room. It seemed like it took an hour for her to finally reach his table.

"Do mind I join you to eat, American General Sir?" the female pilot asked the General kindly.

Campanelli sat there with his mouth hanging open and did not reply, he could not.

"Sir?" Aleksandra repeated, trying to get his attention away from her body.

He had to shake his head yes. He acted like he was afraid to say anything, for fear of biting his tongue off. When she sat down, it seemed like the entire dining area breathed a sigh of relief. She looked at the General and said sexily, "Sir, you swallow now please before hurt youself sir."

The enchanted General smiled as he offered her, "gees, you look great tonight, Aleksandra. You have to be the best looking Major I ever saw."

Aleksandra nodded her approval of his summary. Their talk was interrupted by the waiter.

He asked the foreign Major if she had eaten yet.

"No, I hope you invite me eat you, err... with you, American General Sir."

"Sure, I'd be pleased if you share a meal with me tonight," he turned to the waiter and asked him. "Can you keep my food warm and bring her a menu."

"Yes sir, I'll bring you a menu in a second Ma'am," the waiter shot off and quickly returned. She read it while he stood hovering over her shoulder, obviously looking down the front of her dress. She looked up at the waiter and then smiled as she announced, "I like Chicken Alfredo and glass you good wine please, thank you very much sir."

The waiter nodded and replied, "very good Ma'am, would you like a salad with that Ma'am?"

Aleksandra flicked her hand in the air at the salad, as she spoke again to the General, "I take by you expression you like dress I chose wear for you special occasion, American General Sir?"

"Very much so Major," he grinned like a school child looking at his first love.

"My name Aleksandra, please sir," she reminded the gawking General once again.

"Fine, if you call me Ed or Popeye," he offered warmly to the stunning young pilot.

"Popeye?" she questioned as she cocked her head to the side and stared at him.

"Nickname, please Ma'am, don't ask me how I got tagged with the damn name Major," the General requested with a smirk.

Aleksandra smiled pleasantly as she carefully spread her napkin out across her lap.

"Do you like the States Major?" he asked her as he watched what she was doing.

"Very good much so, sir. You have no shortage food in country I see. You have marvelous store and supermarket to get food from, General. Grand Union and Publix store I think you store call. Lithuania has no store like that. You traffic scare life out of me, and so do crowd all time be around. You people friend and do anything to me. It good country General Sir."

"If you don't mind my asking, how long have you been working for your government, Major?"

"I be train by Russia government before Russia collapsed on self. I miss Russia, Edward."

"What did you do for the Russian government Major?" he asked forcibly this time.

"Aleksandra please call Popeye. I train for err... what you say, spy work for them, Edward."

"Really, like how Aleksandra?" he questioned, trying to find out more information now.

"I train how get information from men such you, Popeye. I like you nicker name too sir."

General Campanelli completely ignored her last remark as he grew serious, and just about growled back at her this time. "How?"

"How? I taught on how I use body control you foolish men all time. America. How get them to tell me everything Russia government want know from them, General. As you can see for youself General, I have good equipment get job done good and proper for my control sir," again, Aleksandra pointed towards her breasts as she smiled at him.

"You mean you did fucking spy work against my government! And now my government's allowing your sorry fucking ass in here. What the hell's going on around here, Major?"

"I tell what go on General Campanelli Sir," Aleksandra hissed as she got angry and allowed it to show in her tone of voice. "It true I work against you government at one time in life, sir. But that when my government part Soviet Union and no like United State, sir. I gather information from you government, but once Russia government died, I then extract information which you government need to use against Russia. So you government make deal with mine, and I turn information to America over. It you government used me for year, and instead of let go home, they train as pilot in you YF-27 and YF-23 fighter aircraft. Someone must felt I use to you government work if war broke out between America and Baltic nation. I happy much with arrangement made between our governments, General Campanelli Sir." The Major saw the anger etched in his eyes and hissed again, "I suggest you have problem with agreement, you take up with you President. If he no have problem me, you should no angry be me."

He realized he was glaring at her, but it was not a glare of hatred or anger any longer, it was rather one of concentration. Her warning snapped him out of his harsh stare, "I'm sorry Major, err... Aleksandra. I have no problem with you helping my government, Ma'am."

Their conversation was cut short again by the waiter as he returned to their table and began to serve them their dinners and offered pleasantly "Sir, I had the chef prepare another dinner for you to enjoy sir," he said as he laid out the platters of food for them.

"Major, err... Aleksandra, have you been trained in other weapons besides aircraft, Ma'am?"

"Yes, I be marksman with Russia made T-33 Automatic pistol, and Russia AKSU machine gun, and also too Degtyaren 12.5 Millimeter machine gun. I can handle good America M-18 and M-16 rifle, and use Marine K-bar knife which like much good too. I go through Rangers train twice time too. You men got upset when you see naked woman there too I afraid report to you, General Campanelli Sir," Aleksandra laughed more to herself this time.

"Especially one so lovely as you I can believe Aleksandra," the General added politely.

They finished their meal and suddenly, General Campanelli felt a little awkward as he said. "Shall we go?" he noticed the slight frown that crossed her face and he added. "Would you like another drink before we call it a night, Ma'am?"

"Yes, glass wine be nice very much please Popeye," she replied kindly.

He ordered her another glass of wine and himself a Pepsi. When they came, the Major ran her index finger slowly and sexily around the rim of the glass as she stared at the

General before offering to him with a smile, "I wish you be honest total me with all time, General Sir."

"Whatdaya mean by that load of stinking crap, Major? I never lied to you over any reason while we were talking together!" General Campanelli growled, immediately getting angry again at the foreign female Major.

"I wish you tell true to me all time, like you want make mad and passionate love with me all night, General Campanelli Sir. I see it in you eye tonight," the stunningly good looking young female Lithuanian pilot said with a serious expression on her face, as she continued to stare the General dead in the eyes as she waited for his reply to her remark.

He gave out a nervous laugh, and then he began to sweat a little as he replied while trying to control himself and keep his composure, and make like he did not want to make love to her, "oh yeah, and what makes you believe I'd like to make love to you Aleksandra?"

"Ha, you no fool me around in the little mista. I see way eye follow me all over when I walk. You try look front dress down all time too I see, mista. You look at rearend all time when I walk and you drool at what you see. I see this General out corner of eye, mista."

"I guess you got me dead to right and I can't fool ya any, can I Aleksandra? Well, suppose I did want to make mad passionate love to you, young lady? How would I go about getting you in bed, Major?" the General asked her with a smile on his lips.

"Best way start is call Aleksandra or Alex all time. And other way you be very success, be honest and say me, 'Aleksandra, I want to bed you', American General Sir. It easy that much sir."

The General was beginning to really sweat now as he stared at this stunning beauty. He looked deep into her eyes, and then mumbled, "Aleksandra, I'd like to go to bed with you."

"I must say General Campanelli Sir, that no sound convince very too much me, way you say to me like that sir," she smiled back at him again.

There was beads of sweat forming on his forehead now, as his hormones went into overdrive on him, as he continued to stare at the beautiful female Major, and then he repeated to her more convincingly this time, "I really want to take you to bed and make love with you all night long, Alex." He added as he smiled at her again and then held his breath until she replied.

"I believe Edward you now. You get bottle good wine, no cheap, and we go room. I show you how Russia train me, and how I successful in what I did and do sir," Aleksandra stood, and the General followed her like a little puppy, he got a bottle of Chablis and they headed for her room.

He was sticky from sweating, and announced he was going to take a quick shower. She told him to go ahead, and she would pour the wine for them. Campanelli quickly showered and then looked at the only pair of civilian clothes he had in Washington. They were looking a little shabby. He had one uniform in his room, and he knew his orderly was bringing the rest of his clothing and extra uniforms to him tomorrow, now he knew he took a room at the Hilton. He also knew he had to go shopping soon, or he'd be walking around naked.

The shower was hot and he jumped in, and as he washed his hair he suddenly felt someone lightly touch him on his back, it was Aleksandra as she slid into the shower with him. After she washed his back, they made love in the wet mist. He dried her off and then himself, and then he carried her to the bed, and took his time with her. He did everything that pleased Mendoza, and it had the same effect on her. When he finished, she pulled him on the bed and she returned the pleasure by taking him in her mouth. She made him come this way, and he was exhausted by the time they were done with their lovemaking. He crawled up to the pillows and rested his head on them. She laid besides him and took a mouthful of wine.

They laid there staring up at the ceiling and then he said, "I really hate fucking war, it's such a waste of fucking life. I wish some asshole would wake up one day and put a stop to all wars. You know something Major, I once had an Officer who suggested this very same thing to me, and I actually laughed at her. But now, I know where she was coming from. I'm tired of fighting and killing. I'm tired of the whole fucking mess. I tell you, once this possible mess is over with, I think I'm getting out of the damn service all together and then lead a normal life for once."

Aleksandra took his hand in hers and smiled as she replied to him, "you stay night long with me here. I make forget you worry all, and you female Officer you talk much about tonight, sir. I make you feel real good again General." She rolled on top of him and started to play with him. He responded. They made love again and then they turned in for the night.

JANUARY 17th, 1997. SATURDAY, 0635 HOURS

General Edward Campanelli was the first one to wake, he swung his legs over the side of the bed and then looked at the clock then he rubbed the sleep out of his eyes as he stretched and groaned like a bear in heat at the same time. All the noise and movement he made woke Aleksandra, who rolled over and sat up as she leaned against his back.

"What you do up so early my new lover?" the beautiful female pilot asked the General.

"I couldn't sleep, I'm going to order us some room service. What would you like to eat?"

Aleksandra smiled, sleep still clouding over her beautiful blue eyes. She looked like she had something on her mind, forcing General Campanelli to asked the foreign fighter pilot, "is there anything wrong with you Aleksandra? You look a little upset."

"Nothing," she suddenly yawned and said and then stretched herself.

The General could see the concern in her face as she straightened her hair, "I must look mess."

"You look fine to me. Sexy in fact. Now tell me what's bothering you today Aleksandra."

"How well you read me already, wise American General Campanelli Sir. You would been worthy adversary in battle of wits and lovemaking in old days, sir. I think about Colonel Locker, I worry I cut on in her territory, General. I no want angry me for steal her man away from her. I hear story she could rip balls off charging bull without get gored, sir."

General Campanelli let out a laugh as he replied, "don't worry about Locker, she knew where we stood before we started playing around together, Major. She was just a fling, Alex," he smiled in order to take the sting out of his words.

"Am I what you say, fling you to Popeye?" Aleksandra asked with concern in her voice.

"Unless you can make a little more out of this than there is. Aleksandra look, I'm getting a divorce. It's been one hell of a bad marriage for the both of us. I had a girlfriend who I was going to marry before she was killed in a fucking helicopter crash, Alex. It almost killed me when she died on me. I want to coast for a little while, before I get involved in another affair, which might lead to something more than just animal lust, I'm afraid young lady."

Aleksandra laughed at his last remark as she crawled out of bed, and then she sashayed her way to the bathroom, sexily rolling her shoulders and hips as she muttered at the military officer, "my dear Command, I take interest you greatly already I worry me. I intend make lot more of this than as you said animal lust, General. I pick you marry, I marry you soon, mista." She disappeared into the bathroom, seconds later the shower water was running.

The General laughter to himself as he took the menu off the table and called downstairs and ordered breakfast for the both of them and the newspaper. He sat down on the bed and listened to the water running, feeling his luck was again starting to run true for him.

There was a light knock on his door, and a man dressed in a waiter's uniform wheeled a breakfast cart over to the table, and he placed the dishes and drinks on it. He handed the local newspaper to the grinning General as he finished setting the table.

Aleksandra came out of the bathroom dressed in the smallest negligee. The top just barely covering her ample breasts, but the outfit was completely see through. The bottom just covering her private parts, she had on black nylons that needed no support. They accented her long, perfect legs exquisitely. Her bathrobe was also transparent, and she did not bother to close it, and the effect was perfect on both men. The General and waiter both stared at her with their mouths open. She smiled as she said, "you better breathe before hurt youselves, fools."

General Campanelli's mouth snapped shut with a loud click of his teeth, as he dropped his newspaper on the floor and then he continued to stare at her exquisite body.

The waiter could not do enough for them. He poured the coffee and then buttered their toast for them. Then poured the juice, and just kind of started to hung around the table, never once taking his eyes off Aleksandra's superb body for a second.

Aleksandra had enough of the waiter and his rather bothersome attention, and she looked at the General, and then she nodded towards the young man. The General picked up the silent message and suddenly placed his arm on the kid's shoulder, and said to the man, "C'mon son, I can handle it from here on out thank you very much. You better get going before they miss you downstairs, and you get yourself canned mister."

"But sir, I'll wait for the dishes, that way I won't have to come back later on sir."

"No you won't buddy, I'll place the damn things outside the door when we're finished eating my friend," the General actually had to lead the kid to the door.

"Sir, I'd be glad to wait for the dishes until you're done eating if you don't mind sir."

"I bet you will, look kid don't worry about the damn dishes. You seen enough for today son."

The kid let himself be lead out of the room. He noticed his frown as he closed the door, and he smiled as he looked at Aleksandra and smirked at her, "One of these days you're really gonna hurt someone if you keep dressing like that, young lady."

"What you point be America General you? I no hurt no one with way I dress, I just make them want make love with me that all," she purred as she smiled at the General.

They ate breakfast and spoke pleasantly and then they made love again. General Edward Campanelli took a quick shower then decided to get in some shopping for extra civilian clothes he knew he needed. To his surprise, Aleksandra asked to come along with him on his shopping trip. He picked up two civilian suits with her approval. Also a jogging suit and two pairs of lounging pants, a few sports shirts, and even a pair of sneakers. Then Aleksandra took Edward over to Victoria Secrets. The name shot a shooting pain right in the General's memory. This was where Captain Renee Mendoza got most of her sexy outfits from she always wore for him. He stopped outside the store, and she actually had to pull him into the store with her, as she complained at him, "what wrong with you, store no bite you any Popeye."

Campanelli stood up against a wall just inside the store as Aleksandra looked at some bras, panties, and pick out a number of see through robes and chemises. It was not that bad for him to endure because the store was loaded with a gaggle of fine looking young women with great shapes and killer smiles. She showed him a pair of silk lounging pajamas open in the front and asked him, "what you think of these little babies, big boy?"

"I dunno, I have to see them on you before I can decide properly about them, Aleksandra."

"That no problem there, big American General Edward Sir. I try them on special for you to enjoy them sir," Aleksandra quickly disappeared and she returned seconds later, she came out of a dressing room with the items on. She was stunning, and the General gave her a nod and smiled at her and she announced proudly, "I take them."

He nodded like one of those dogs in car rear window nodding their heads.

She brought the outfit, along with a few bras and panties, and then they both left and had lunch at Sparo's. It was here General Campanelli noticed his driver standing just outside the pizza place. He quickly excused himself and headed for the driver, who saluted him.

"Stick that shit up your ass. What's the damn problem Sergeant?"

"Sir, I just got a call from General Claiborne, sir. He ordered me to find you, and inform you the pictures from the overflight are in his office, General Campanelli Sir."

"Shit, this means I'm going to get stuck working today, dammit. Okay Sergeant, get back in touch with the General, and inform him I'm on my way over to the office, will you please. I should be at my office within twenty minutes or so I guess. I gotta dump off the damn pain in the ass Major at the hotel first, before we head for the office, Sarge."

"Very good sir, I'll tell him for you, General Campanelli Sir." The driver quickly disappeared in the crowd of the shopping center mall. He turned and saw the Major paid for lunch and was coming out of the restaurant and she asked, "what happen sir?"

"I have to get over to the office, the latest information I requested just came in, Ma'am. I'll get you back to your apartment and then head for my office, Major."

"No sir you not. I should be with you. In case you need translate something from me, General Campanelli Sir. I know why I given to you government, and this my work I must do for you, sir."

"You might be right at that Aleksandra. The pictures of the coastline of China, North Korea and Taiwan arrived, Major. I ordered them taken to see if there were any reactions to the threat from the other day. I want to see if the North Korean's are placing some of their damn troops on ready alert yet, Ma'am."

"You see sir, I help already you out Edward, sir. I see picture of North Korea during my time with Russia service many times past, and study them good for my Commander and control, sir. I pick out all irregularities for you nice and easy if they changed, sir."

"I guess you might be of some service to me after all, Alex. Okay, let's get going then. The General's waiting for us to get back to him at the office, Ma'am."

It took them twenty minutes to get over to his office at the Pentagon, between the heavy traffic and snow removal operations, they got hung up more than once in the heavy traffic. Campanelli entered his office, and no sooner did he sit down, than Claiborne come storming in announcing.

"General Campanelli Sir, I went over the pictures with a fine toothed comb sir, and I picked up a number of troop movements occurring inside both China and North Korea at this time, General. Strange though, I also detected some troop movements also being carried out in South Korea as well, and the South Korean government didn't bother to notify us about this troop shuffling around crap in their nation, sir. I picked up the South Korean 3rd Army's 8th Corps of two complete Infantry Divisions, along with their 5th and 7th Corps consisting of four Infantry Divisions and their support equipment in the form of tanks and armored vehicles, and one of the Infantry Brigade moving up towards the damn DMZ area, sir. A major violation of their present peace accord with the North, sir." General Claiborne reported as he quickly spread out the pictures he received on his desk, that bore out what he was reporting to him.

General Campanelli picked up the South Korean troops packed tight in trucks and heading directly for the DMZ, and North Korea in three separate columns.

"Shit, I don't like the looks of this shit one damn bit, General. It's opening the damn door to the North attacking the South, and we'll be helpless to react against it. Our troops stationed in South Korea are under strict orders not to attack unless they're hit first. If the South attacks the North, we'll have to withdraw our troops and allow the North and South Korea go at it, sir."

"Exactly Ed," General Claiborne replied as he stared at the pictures on the desk.

"Whatdaya have on the damn Chinese, and how are they reacting to the sudden Korean troop movement in both Koreas, sir? I'm quite certain the Chinese must be up in arms about the fucking movements of these troops," Campanelli remarked to Claiborne with concern.

"It's like they said, we picked up some movement from the Chinese troops she informed us she planned to employ in their opening attack on North Korea. The Chinese have a number of troops on board trains heading north as well. North Korea's responding by moving their Eastern Strike Forces up to the Forty Second Parallel. The Koreans are moving the entire 14th Combined Arms Corps, along with the 3rd and 5th Mechanized Corps, that consists of one Motorized Infantry Division, four Tank and eight Mechanized Brigades, with five Infantry, and three type B Reserve Infantry Divisions, five Mountain Brigades, and four Artillery and Armor Brigades supporting their movements, sir. The Korean government has put out a nationwide alert calling for all able bodied men and women to report to the assigned Officers and Commanders.   A Red Alert countrywide had gone into effect as well, sir. The instant the North Koreans realized China was moving many of her troops towards the North Korean border on them, sir.

"General Campanelli Sir, the North Koreans have also alerted their Western Armies to defend a possible sneak attack from the South Koreans. Their Central Forces have been placed on full nationwide alert, and they could go in either direction, towards the North to defend against an attack from China, or towards the South to help defend their nation from South Korea, a good strategy is being employed by the North Koreans at this time, sir. Their general reserve troops are mustering as ordered. I feel North Korea will be well prepared for China's attack, sir.

"General Campanelli Sir, I took it upon myself to order the SR-91 to do a pass over India sir. I picked up a number of reports stating India's placing a good number of her military forces on alert, and they're moving towards Nepal for some fucking reason. We hope India has no plans to attack China at this point, while China is focusing all her efforts on North Korea, sir. That'd surely put a damn fly in the fucking ointment on us, General Campanelli Sir."

"Are there any Naval movements coming from China yet, sir?" Campanelli asked his General.

General Claiborne moved more of the pictures around on the desk. Then he pointed some out to General Campanelli and remarked, "Yes General Campanelli Sir, seven Chinese Kiangnan Class Frigates, along with three Shanghai Class small fast moving gunboats, and six of the larger Kiangung Class Destroyers shipped out of Port today, sir. They're making way towards the North Korean coast as we speak, sir. One thing causing my damn balls to itch a might though is, the Chinese moved thirty submarines. Both of their nuclear submarines are heading out to sea. Too many submarines for just this operation, I don't like this situation in the least, sir."

"Me neither," General Campanelli replied as he studied the pictures. The female Major piped up and offered her new Commanding Officer. "I no see nuclear powered Luta Class destroyers. They usual birthed right here, General

Campanelli Sir," she pointed to the shipyard stationed at Kiangiun in Shanghai on the pictures they were looking at.

Both officers looked to where she pointed, and noticed the empty births on the pictures. Campanelli growled at the woman fighter pilot, "whatdaya mean nuclear powered destroyers? I didn't know China had any damn nuclear powered Destroyers in their Navy."

"Yes, they took the Russia design for a Cruiser and change and make Destroyer out of them, which be large as Cruiser. They have keel laid for two other ship, sir. Don't you America military keep watch on China and what she do in her own country, friend."

"I can assure you of one thing here Major, the damn Chinese are no one's friends, young lady," General Claiborne growled back at the young female pilot.

General Campanelli looked at the General and then bitched at him, "General Claiborne Sir, I'd like some updated reports on these damn ships she just brought up to our attention A-SAP, sir. What type of armament they have, and what the hell their true intentions might be in this drama slowly unfolding before us, sir. I don't trust the damn Chinese one bit in this mess, sir."

"Right away, I'll have the SR drone look for these missing ships, and once she finds them. I'll have the damn thing keep an eye on them, so we know where the ships are at all times, sir."

"Very good Clay." Campanelli turned to the Lithuanian and told her, "I guess it's good you came along with me after all. Do you have any other surprises you're keeping from us, Major?"

"You aware Russia sold Chinese twenty five S-22N missile with nuclear capabilities, General Campanelli Sir? Along with twenty seven Sukhoi SU-24 all weather attack and reconnaissance aircraft, with plan for Sukhoi SU-29 attack bomber also too. So the Chinese can develop their own breed of the special aircraft, sir?" she offered with a smile to the General.

Campanelli looked at the foreign Major for a moment then he snapped one word at her, "No!"

"Then I think you pay attention much closer intelligence game for youself, if you want be a great Command of this operation, General Edward Sir. It seem you and intelligence group not keep each other properly inform of find, American General Campanelli Sir."

He glared at her and then he casted a harsh look at General Claiborne and grumbled at him this time, "Clay, I trust you'll find out what the fuck's going on here, sir?"

"You bet'cha I will General," he responded to his Commanding Officer's last orders.

"Clay, is Admiral Thomas Standlund inside the damn building by any chance, sir?"

"By all means he is General Campanelli. He and I went over these very pictures before you reported here, sir. He then stormed off saying something about he was going to move a number of his ships around, and not wait to be ordered to do it by you or anyone else, sir. Just push down the blue button on your phone and the intercom will immediately page him for you, sir."

He did as instructed and asked the operator to page the Chief of Naval Operations.

Minutes later, the General, followed by a security guard carrying coffee, came in his office. General Palmieri was keeping a low profile for the moment. Campanelli looked at Admiral Standlund and then asked him, "Admiral, what the hell's going on around here, sir? What are you doing with your ships? I have to know about all your ship movements even before they're taken, sir. This way I can work the rest of my support units around your ship's positions, sir."

"General Campanelli Sir, when I first picked up the Chinese moving so many of their damn submarines around, I became highly concerned over this matter, sir. They have no need for any of their submarines on their proposed land attack aimed at North Korea, General. I took it on my own and ordered the Coral Sea over to the Mediterranean to relieve the Aircraft Carrier Washington on her present search and rescue operations in Israel, sir. I also ordered the older Aircraft Carrier Constellation over to the Persian Gulf, to relieve the Carrier Kennedy from her duty in that region, sir. I also ordered the Carriers Enterprise and Eisenhower to up anchor, and forget about the rescue operations they were carrying out in Egypt and Libya for the time being, sir. I'll also have the Forrestal and Saratoga pulled out of their sleep, and I ordered them to replace these two Carriers assisting in the rescue operations on those two nations, sir.

"General Campanelli Sir, I want all my nuclear powered, and even the newer nuclear Carriers at my command at all times during this present situation, sir. In case anything happens to go rotten in Asia on us, General. As I just stated sir, I don't like the damn Chinese moving around so many of their fucking submarines when they're not going to be needed for what they offered to do, and I don't intend to get caught flat footed by this move of theirs either, sir. Just for the hell of it General, I also ordered the Carrier Washington to make way for Japan at flank speed. I'll clear it with the President, and I'm having this ship pay a sort of courtesy call on the damn Japanese, sir. To show the world we're still friends so to say, sir. I'll also move some of the Destroyers and Frigates out to Guam for a stinking visit, sir. I want to get as many of our ships as possible in this damn Asian region just in case I need their support in a hurry, sir."

"What about that Three, Three, Seven, the Operation Vinegar Joe Platform thing, sir? How the hell are we coming along with that, and how long before that damn thing is fully operational for my needs, sir?" General Campanelli asked Admiral Standlund with concern lacing his tone.

"General Campanelli Sir, I should know a helluva lot more about that damn situation before the deadline's up on the North Korea situation, sir. But I think the damn Platform should be fully operational before we have need of her, sir. I have enough manpower to apply the decks to the tanker ships before they ship out for their ordered position, sir. It's good we stored those damn planks a few years ago, I'd hate to have the damn things made over again, General. The time it would've cost us to have these damn planks duplicated would have been a real plain nuts, let alone the exorbitant increase in cost. Sometimes, things work out for the good, sir."

"Admiral Standlund Sir, I don't have much to do with this shit. I'm afraid this is your problem now, sir. All you have to remember, is if I need any of your damn ships, they better be there when I have need of them, sir." General Campanelli glared at Admiral Standlund.

"Quite right sir. My ships will be where you need them, when you need them General."

"Good, today was supposed to be a day off for everyone concerned with this latest operation, sir. Why don't you Generals call it a day and meet me here on Monday morning. General Palmieri will man the desk, I'm beat up from the feet up and besides, if all hell breaks out there'll be no more fucking days off for the lot of us for a long time to come, people. So go home and enjoy the rest of the damn weekend off sirs, it might be our last one I'm afraid."

Admiral Standlund saluted the General and then he quickly left the office. He did not like the slight reprimand he just received from General Campanelli, and he mumbled to himself all the way as he walked down the long hallway, "My fucking ships will be there mister smart ass fucking Commander. I have got a mind to sail one of my damn ships right up your skinny punk ass for you, shithead. How dare you dump on my fucking ass like you did before the other members of our damn Command Staff, dammit."

General Claiborne smiled at Campanelli as he warned him in no uncertain terms, "you don't really wanna go and rub Woody the wrong fucking way around here, Eddy. He's a damn good Officer to have on your side when the shit comes down sir, and he and his equipment will be on Post when needed, sir. Anyway, what have you been doing with your day off, Eddy?"

Campanelli looked at the Lithuanian pilot then back to Claiborne and replied, "shopping."

A wide grin slowly spread across his face, his teeth were almost blinding white as he grumbled back at his Commanding Officer with a smirk glued to his lips. "Sona fucking bitch, don't tell me you're slipping the old bologna pony to that foreign female Major already, General Campanelli. Shit, you fucking white boys didn't even give her a stinking chance to fucking breathe, before you jumped her damn bones on her, man."

General Claiborne then looked to the female major smiling at him and said to her, "look honey, don't let these little white boys here make you believe they're God's gift to women, young lady. Hell, there are few white boys who can make a woman feel like she should feel."

The smile stayed on his lips as the General continued with his words, "any time you want a real ride, you just come around and look me up young lady. Yes, you come and take a little ride on my bologna pony for yourself. Once you take a ride on my black beauty here, I assure you young lady you'll never think of one of these little white boys ever again, Major."

The female Lithuanian Major smiled back at the huge black man as she offered, "General, secretary already warn me about you black beauty, sir. Any time you want lose inch off that thing of you, you come sniff me up, sir. I known wear down a pony or two one at time, sir." She walked over to the big man, and then she gave him a kiss on his forehead.

"Yeah, she's a pretty good one at that, General Campanelli Sir," he mumbled more to himself and then he added to his words. "I think I'm going to head home and make Betty work for the rest of the afternoon, General. All of a sudden, I'm feeling a little horny myself, sir." He rubbed himself between his legs as he stood to leave the office.

"See ya on Monday morning Clay," General Campanelli called out after him.

"Maybe, if you're lucky enough I guess I'll be here, General," Claiborne snapped sharply as he shot Campanelli a quick grin, and then he gave him a quick wink of the eye.

The office emptied of everyone except for Campanelli, the foreign female Major and General Palmieri, and his thoughts suddenly turned serious as he wondered if he would be able to laugh after the two week time limit given to North Korea ended. He found himself wondering if he would be locked in another shooting war, and having to order even more young American kids to their deaths. Because some so called adults could not work out their differences in a peaceful manner, as he finally grumbled loud enough for her to hear him. "What a world we live in."

"You say something me to Edward?" Aleksandra asked her Commanding Officer kindly.

"No, I was just thinking out loud, that's all Aleksandra," Campanelli mumbled to her.

"How come you General Claiborne no use you nicker name Popeye when speak with you all time, sir?" she asked as she stared at the rather large American officer for a moment.

"Because he's a damn good friend, that's why Ma'am. Almost as close a friend to me as General White is Aleksandra," he said as he allowed his mind to wander a bit, thinking of all the actions he and General John White were in lately.

"You break law of you country, because you be friend with two black men like you are with white men too, is that no right General Popeye Sir? Other no like you if you like black men all time I told sir," she suddenly said as she gazed in his eyes again.

"That fricking bullshit of fucking prejudice is a thing of the damn past, young lady. It ran it ugly course a long time ago, Aleksandra. It's now unfucking cool for anyone to dislike someone just because of the color of his damn skin, or the God they believe in, or who they might be slipping the stinking meat to." General Campanelli snapped at her before calming down a bit himself, he was actually upset by her last words.

"Slip meat to?" The Lithuanian pilot asked the Commander with some concern in her voice.

"Come here little lady, and I'll show you what that means Aleksandra," he was beginning to like using the Lithuanian pilot's first name, it had a nice sound to it.

"Uh-oh, I'm getting the hell outta here and give you two birds the privacy it looks like you're gonna need," General Palmieri offered as he picked up his cover and then added. "I'm heading for the mess to get something to eat, sir. I'll return when I see you two leave the building."

They waited until the other General was out of the office, and then they made love right on his desk, and when they were finished, she looked at him with dreamy eyes and said, "Huh, I think I like much when you slip you meat me some, Popeye General."

She checked his eyes for a response for her calling him by his nickname, and when none came, she decided she was going to call him Popeye any time they were alone. She liked the nickname, and the young and good looking American General as well.

General Campanelli's heart was being torn apart in his chest by the way this beautiful and young Lithuanian pilot said his nickname of Popeye. She said it with just the right hint of her accent, and it reminded him so much of the way Captain Renee Mendoza always pronounced his nickname whenever she used it. Deep in the back of his mind, he had not fully gotten over losing Captain Mendoza in the helicopter crash in the Sudan that claimed her life. Just before the biological weapons release by Libya against Egypt, and the nuclear response from the United States that immediately cleansed the biological weapons from the face of the earth. He even doubted if he would ever be truly over her loss to him for the rest of his life.

The General suddenly pulled Aleksandra close to him and put her in a breath robbing hug as he whispered Captain Mendoza's name to himself. But it was said loud enough for her to hear her name mentioned, and for the first time since she met the American General, she felt sad for him. She rested her head against his powerful chest, while they lay on top of the large desk.

The added weight of Aleksandra lying on top of him, made him sore from lying on the hard surface of the desk, and he had to ask her to move. Once she was off his body, he swung his legs off the desk and then he sat down on top of it. She did the same thing, and they both sat side by side while looking down at their feet dangling just inches above the floor and smiling. General Campanelli broke the moments of silence by reached out and he gently cupped her breast with his hand, and smiled at her pleasantly.

She purred like a lazy cat having her head lightly scratched, as she smiled at the fine looking young American military officer. It was a very tender moment being shared by the both of them for a few seconds. With the severe threat of war hanging heavy over their heads, they were moving their relationship along a much quicker pace than either of them would have normally done. The threat of another war gave the them both a new passion for living, and they were making the best of it. It seemed like the two of them could not get enough of being with the other already, and they were quickly falling in love.

CHAPTER 10
MONDAY, JANUARY 26th, 1997. 0700 HOURS

Monday arrived too quickly and it found General Edward Campanelli and Major Aleksander Klevekaita in the office by seven o'clock, already reading over what reports came in over the short weekend. Nothing of much importance occurred, so he filed the reports with the others. One by one, the rest of his Command Staff started to report for duty, with General John White arriving shortly after the General and Major arrived for the start of their workday.

"Shit, I knew you'd be here already, dammit. What the hell did you two asses do, sleep here over the damn weekend for Pete's sake? I brought you two fools a cup of Java to enjoy." John gripped, and then he looked at the female Major and added to her, "I didn't think you'd be here though young lady, or I would've surely brought you a cup of Java also. I can run down and get you a cup of coffee if you'd like, Ma'am."

"No, I enough coffee drank already for today General White Sir," she said as she held up her hands in protest to his offer.

John went back to his desk and thumbed through some papers he had stacked up on it.

Colonel Locker was the next person to show up for duty. When she came in the office she immediately shot a nasty glare at the female Major, who put her head down and tried to look busy. Locker then sat down on the edge of General Campanelli's desk and snapped at him.

"Well pig, did you enjoy yourself with that new little slut of yours over the weekend, mister?" she hissed just loud enough for the foreign female Major to hear her angry words.

He glared angrily at Locker as he growled savagely at her at the same time, "I thought you were much bigger than that, Colonel. Besides, I don't have to account to you on how I spent my fucking weekend, Colonel. If you have a problem with the way I conduct my personal life, I could always have you replaced so you don't have to watch it, Locker."

It was Mary's turn to put her head down and she replied softly, "I don't have any problems with your personal life, General Campanelli. What do you want me to do today, sir?"

"That's better Colonel. Over the weekend, I read a few reports on increased Chinese ship movement. Find out where those fucking ships went, especially the damn submarines for me."

"Will do General," Locker replied as she went to her desk, feeling ashamed by her words.

General Campanelli glanced over his shoulder and gave Aleksandra a quick and reassuring smile before he ordered her to check on what the Russians were doing, and how they were reacting to the heavy troop movement from the Chinese military."

She went to her assigned desk and looked over some of the latest pictures taken by the SR-91 aircraft on the Russian, Chinese border, and easily noticed the heavy troop movements by each. Russia was taking steps to strengthen all her border patrols. Aleksandra picked up a train letting off a large number of troops in a few picture, and she also picked up a number of Russian main battle tanks moving towards the border towns near by. Nothing was taking place the Russians did not warn they would do at the United Nations meeting against any Chinese troop movements. She placed the stack of photos in the folder, and then she made a number of calls to previous colleagues, to see if they might have heard any threats or troop movements Russia might be involved in. Nothing panned out, and without any new information to offer. she stayed out of the main office to allow things cool off a bit between Campanelli and Locker.

Aleksandra took some solace in the fact she warned the General about how Colonel Locker might react to their fooling around. She knew there was going to be some trouble, because she could tell Locker was staking a claim on his affections, before she came into the picture.

The General could feel the tension in the office, but he ignored it. It had been many years since he had two beautiful women locking horns over him, and he was suddenly feeling like an Arabian Prince making up a new harem. He smiled over the attention he was receiving as he went back to his reports. He was amazed Admiral Standlund had the Carriers Eisenhower and Washington up anchor, and already steaming for the Asian region in less than a day's time. He was also pleased he had such good officers to work with, officers who did what they said they would do and did not have to be checked on to make certain their jobs were being done properly.

General John White came over to Campanelli's desk with a look of concern on his face. Campanelli did not like the look and he knew right off he was not going to like the report John had for him as he offered to his friend. "This is going to make you hitch up your fucking pants a little Eddy. It states here three Chinese Destroyers are currently docking in South Korea, Inchon in fact at this time, sir. The report further explains a number of Chinese military troops are also deploying to the same area. What the hell are those bastards up to in South Korea now, Eddy?"

"I dunno, but I'm sure as hell going to find out what the hell they're trying to pull off here. I hope the stinking Chinese hadn't been able to talk the South Koreans into joining them on their attack against North Korea. That'd be a real helluva mess for us if that took place, sir."

As the officers talked, Colonel Locker came over with a report and then she announce, "You better read this report General Campanelli Sir, I believe something's up, sir."

"Shit, I hate this damn crap," Campanelli growled as he finished reading the report.

"What's up Eddy?" John asked the suddenly frowning military officer.

"The North Korean Ambassador, Kim Sun-neh has notified the United Nations Secretary General he was demanding a second emergency meeting to take place immediately. He's demanding the United Nations to admonish the Chinese government for landing troops and military equipment in South Korea, sir. The North Korean government states this action is a direct aggression move aimed towards North Korea, and she's threatening to react against it, sir. The North Korean's placed their complete nation on full military alert, sir. John, I'm going to have to agree with them this time, sir. This is a direct threat to North Korea, and we have to stop it before things quickly get out of hand on us, sir. Colonel Locker, get me a direct line to err… Ambassador Walters I think it is, the American Ambassador to the United Nations. I want to speak with over this new friggin situation, and see what he thinks about it, Colonel."

"It is Ambassador Walters, General Campanelli. I'll get him on the horn for you, sir."

"I want him to explain to me what the fuck's going on with China, dammit. Maybe we gave them permission to land these damn troops and equipment in South Korea. I dunno, but I'm not going to overreact until I find out what the hell's up for certain," Campanelli grumbled hotly.

"General Campanelli, I have Ambassador Walters on line three waiting to speak with you at this moment sir," Colonel Locker announced to her Commanding Officer.

"Ambassador Walters, this is General Campanelli sir, what the hell are the damn Chinese trying to pull off here, sir? Landing military troops and equipment in South Korea, Sir?"

"How are you General Campanelli?" Walters replied to his angry outburst on the phone.

General Campanelli was thoroughly embarrassed by his angry words and he apologized immediately to the

Ambassador, "Sorry Ambassador Walters, how are you today, sir?"

"Fine, thank you for the consideration, General Campanelli Sir. I have no idea what the Chinese government is trying as you have put it sir, to pull off here sir. I asked Ambassador Chow to come to my office today, and I'm expecting him presently sir. When I find out what his countries up to, I'll inform the President, and when I brief him, I'll also include and inform you of the situation at the same time, sir. Is this satisfactory to you, General Campanelli Sir?"

"Yes, that's satisfactory for my like's sir, and I thank you for the consideration, sir. Then I'll be expecting to hear from you a little later on this afternoon, Ambassador Walters Sir," the General remarked in not so friendly terms to the American politician.

"Till this afternoon then General Campanelli Sir. I have to cut this conversation rather short I'm afraid sir. I have a lot to do to prepare for my meeting with Ambassador Chow today, sir."

"Understood, and I'll be waiting for your call back, good luck with the Chinese Ambassador, Ambassador Walters," General Campanelli offered as he hung up with the politician.

Both men laughed and then General Campanelli looked at his watch. It was already after ten in the morning, and they had not stopped for a morning break yet. He yelled out to the rest of his staff, "Coffee people, get it now or lose it for the rest of the damn day today!"

No one said much as they quickly filtered out of the office and headed for the concession area.

General Campanelli stayed behind to enjoy a few moments of privacy as he placed his feet on his desk, and then he leaned back and laced his fingers together behind his head as he closed his eyes. His thoughts went to the weekend and the fun he had with Aleksandra. He was exhausted, but it was a good exhaustion. He leaned further in his chair with a smile on his face.

Mary came back in the office carrying two cups of coffees and cakes, she saw the smile on his face and realized she lost him to a much younger and prettier woman. She beat back her frown and offered to her Commanding Officer kindly, "General Campanelli Sir, I noticed you didn't take a break for yourself, so I brought you in some coffee and cake, sir."

He eyes opened as he replied, "I don't care what anyone says about you Locker. In my book, you're okay Colonel."

Locker moaned as she watched Campanelli lean forward and take the coffee and cake from her, and then she asked her Commanding Officer with some concern lacing her tone of voice "what do you think is going on with the Chinese, and what they might be up to with the South Koreans suddenly, sir? Is this the start of World War Three, sir?"

He drew a breath and then he replied to the Colonel, "I dunno for sure Locker." For the rest of the day, the concerned General could not concentrate on anything else as he waited for Ambassador Walters to call back. He thought it strange he had not heard from General Weidenbacher, or even the President over this growing situation, but shrugged over the thought.

At three fifteen in the afternoon the phone finally rang, causing the now exhausted General to almost jump out of his chair over the shrill scream. He immediately grabbed the receiver and then barked into it, "General Campanelli here."

"Good afternoon General Campanelli Sir, Ambassador Walters, Sir. I just wanted to inform you I just finished speaking with Ambassador Chow and the President. First off sir, we're going to give North Korea an emergency meeting of the United Nations Security Council as requested, but well after the time limit already set on the North Korean's has passed, sir. We discussed it quite at length and we, by we I mean the President and myself, feel this is a good way to kind of try and force the North Korean's to come to the United Nations after all of the talking is done with, sir. We might even be able to reopen some kind of dialog with the North Koreans at this next scheduled meeting, sir. The Chinese Ambassador Chow has informed me his government sent a number of their troops to South Korea at South Korea's request. He also informed me his government received an emergency request for his military troop's presence in South Korea, because North Korea was massing many of their own troops along the border of North and South Korea along their DMZ, (Demilitarized Zone) sir."

The concerned Commander interrupted the Ambassador and offered, "Ambassador Walters, we picked this troop movements up a few days ago by means I can't divulge at this time, sir."

"Yes, I know this, the President already informed me our government was well aware of the sudden North Korean troop buildup across the borders between the two Koreas, sir. The President also informed me he ordered up a flight by the SR aircraft, General Campanelli Sir," the Ambassador gave the General this information to let him know he was in the loop.

The General grew angry at the obvious attempt to show him up by the elderly Ambassador, and he did not like it one bit as he snapped back at the old gentleman hotly. "Please go on Ambassador Walters Sir, my times very precious as I certain you're well wear of, sir."

"As is mine also I assure you General Campanelli Sir!" Ambassador Walters snapped back and then he took a quick breath before he went on with his words to the powerful military officer on the phone. "A copy of the South Korean's request for these Chinese troops to visit their country was faxed over to me, and I looked it over carefully I assure you, sir. It's true, the South Korean government did request the Chinese help, and they successfully tied our hands behind our backs because of this moment, sir. I placed a personal call out to the South Korean Ambassador, and he was kind enough to inform me his government felt extremely threatened by North Korea's sudden and heavy troop movement so close to their borders, sir.

"Due to the process involved to air her fears in the United Nations meeting, Sir. The South Korean government took it upon itself to beg help from China, General Campanelli. His logic was pretty good if you were to ask me sir. But allowing Chinese troops to mass on the two borders of North Korea, will surely lead to war no matter what we do to try and avoid it, General Campanelli Sir. I formally requested the Chinese leadership remove her troops from South Korea, but I don't think they'll listen to my request. So I suggested United Nations forces be sent over to South Korea, to assume responsibility for the security being withheld between the two Korea's. I feel this request was a waste of time as well General Campanelli Sir. I believe I'd have better luck getting the shit back in the horse, than to get the Chinese out of Korea, sir."

The General chuckled at the Ambassador's remark as he agreed with his summation.

After a quick breath, Ambassador Walters went on explaining what was discussed between the President, Ambassador Chow and himself. "I further contacted the Korean authorities, and I informed the North Korean Ambassador this problem is due solely to their steadfast refusal to stop playing around with atomic weapons, General Campanelli Sir. I also informed him all he had to do was allow the United Nation's inspectors in his country, and allow them to destroy any nuclear weapons they already produced. The Delegate actually hung up on me, General Campanelli. I informed the President I felt he should prepare for an all out war in this region of the world, mainly due to these latest moves of the Chinese troops in South Korea, sir."

"I thought China wasn't to move against North Korea until the two week time limit was up."

"Yes that's true General Campanelli, there are ten days left to the order, but things have changed now I offer you sir. China was given the okay to begin its attack on March 4th sir. We, I mean France, England and the Alliance States, have came to the same conclusion the only road open left opened to us now was of war, and who better in this region than China to get the job done, as they pointed out so well to us, sir. We allowed China to build up her military forces before the agreed to deadline, so she'll be well prepared and had her troops set in place when she starts her opening attacks against North Korea, General Campanelli Sir."

"Then how the hell can we be so damn upset at what China's done in South Korea, Ambassador Walters? You said it yourself, we gave the damn Chinese government the okay to attack North Korea early, sir. We even expect China to attack North Korea, sir."

"General Campanelli Sir, this venture into South Korea by the Chinese troops wasn't fully agreed to by anyone of the Council Members, sir. It was something China and South Korea agreed to between themselves I believe, sir. I hate to think how the Alliance States is going to react to this sudden turn of events in the area, General Campanelli Sir. Balls, I wish we could've worked some of this shit out in the Council meeting a few weeks back, sir. I see many of our children dying on the bloody battlefields again, and I'm powerless to stop it dammit."

"Me too sir, but it's me who has to order their deaths on the damn battlefield, Mr. Ambassador Sir," General Campanelli griped into the phone angrily.

The Ambassador took a breath at the interruption and then remarked, "General Campanelli, I have to go, sir. I have to speak with Ambassador Nicholas Antich of the Alliance States, and let him know what's happening in China, and the two Korea's also, sir. Wish me luck sir."

"Yes, by all means Ambassador Walters, good luck sir," General Campanelli hung up with the politician and then he looked at John as he bitched, "I don't see how the hell we're getting angry with China. We gave them permission to attack North Korea. Now, the Ambassador's concerned how the Alliance States are going to react to China's moves. This is some shit."

The General's staff spent the next ten days shifting American troops, aircraft and warships and other equipment all around the globe, and aiming their assets at the Asian region of the world.

JANUARY 29th, 1997 THURSDAY, 0700 HOURS
GENERAL EDWARD CAMPANELLI'S STAFF ROOM

General Edward Campanelli went to his office early because he had not slept well the night before, mainly because he was so concerned about the United Nations Meeting scheduled to convene at nine o'clock that morning. Aleksandra watched him as he read over the many reports that came in during the night. Nothing was new, upsetting or urgent, many military assets he would depend on to defend any action taken against the United States or any of her allies were already set in place. Many retired officers and manpower were taken back in the services.

He figured by March 4th of 1997, all American forces would be up to the manpower it had been during the Desert Storm vacation. He was satisfied with his troops and other military assets he had available for his operation. He was looking forward to moving his office out to the tanker ship, Blue Whale. It was a super tanker converted to be the center ship of the massive Vinegar Joe Platform system. He was scheduled to be transported out to the ship within the next two days or less, depending on what took place at today's Security Meeting.

General Campanelli's secretaries along with the beautiful and young female Lithuanian pilot, was also scheduled to ship out along with him, and a CV-22 Osprey was already sitting on a runway stationed at Joint Langley Airforce Base, set aside for his personal needs. The Blue Whale ship was already ten miles passed the Island of Guam, while still steaming for her ordered position twenty three miles off the east coast of the Island of Taiwan. All twenty four massive tanker ships making up the huge platform, were scheduled to rendezvous at this exact position by no later than Oh, Six Hundred Hours on March 4th.

The General stared at the clock as it slowly ticked the minutes away. No one was doing much of anything in the way of further work any longer in the office. At ten minutes to nine, he sent one of his secretaries out to get some coffee and either cakes or sandwiches for the entire staff.

Colonel Locker noticed General Campanelli looked kind of upset, and she offered him a newspaper and a large envelope at the same time.

"What's this shit Colonel?" he asked the female Colonel.

"Some information I thought you might find of interest, sir. Read it at your leisure General."

John plopped down in the extra chair and asked the General, "What's up now buddy?"

"Aw, I can't believe this fucking shit for a damn minute I tell ya John. They're picking this poor Senator apart, just because he once stated he was all for the fucking death penalty way back when he was a young pup, man."

John grunted back, "Yeah, remember what they did to that poor black girl, the one picked by the old President. The one who was going to head up the Justice Department I think. Now there's a good play on words, the Justice Department. She didn't receive any fucking justice at all if you were to ask me, sir. The lousy bastards treated her like she was a fucking criminal, just because she wrote some papers in the past about discrimination, or some other bullshit like that, Eddy. I don't remember all the fucking details, it was so long ago sir. I hate this shit, all we do is fight for the rights and freedom of this country. Yet, if you chose to exercise your damn right of freedom of speech, some time later in the damn future, what you said will come back and bite you on your fucking ass for ya, sir. It's all bullshit and bad manners if you ask me man," John thumped the desk with his fist as he allowed himself to get upset by his memory.

General Campanelli looked at the angry man and smiled, trying to calm him down.

"What the fuck are you smiling about, you jackrabbit you?" White snapped at his friend.

"Nothing much John I'm afraid," he retorted with a wide grin to his new General.

"You're a fucking radical, just in case you didn't know it man," John laughed, causing Campanelli to chuckle with him. John stood and stretched his arms and went back to his desk.

General Campanelli leaned forward and then he scratched his head as he opened the envelope Locker handed him moments ago. It contained a book from Saints Peter and Paul RC Church at 211 Ripley Place in Elizabeth, New Jersey. Under the address it read in large print, 'The History of a Lithuanian American Community in Elizabeth, New Jersey'.

He turned the first page, and it was covered by names he could neither read, nor pronounce properly. He gathered up the papers and put them back in the large envelope, he then paged Aleksandra. He looked for Colonel Locker to thank her for the papers, but she was not there.

Aleksandra came over to him with a smile on her lips.

He did not respond to her smile, instead, he growled at her, "here, I thought you might be interested in these papers, Aleksandra. Colonel Locker gave them to me for the both of us."

Aleksandra took the envelope and turned to Locker's empty desk as she started to open it.

"Jesus, don't open it here will ya, take it to your desk so you can read them in private please."

She turned, she was angry at the way he snapped at her, and she vowed to herself he was not going to get what he wanted tonight. She hurried back to her desk and dumped the contents of the envelope on it. Not knowing what she might find from Locker, she was half fearing a bomb. She smiled as she saw the riding Knight printed on the great Shield. She took the pamphlet from Sts. Peter and Paul, and read it happily. As she did, she realized she had not been to

Church since she entered the United States two years ago. She looked at the address then reached for a map and found out how far Jersey was from Washington. It was not that far and she decided to ask Campanelli if he would not mind it if they went to this Church this coming Sunday. She smiled as the thought of going to a Lithuanian Church in a foreign land, but the smile quickly left her as she heard a small commotion coming from the inner office.

Campanelli was acting like a bull in a China shop, knocking over anything that would move. He was steaming over a new report he received. At Oh, Six Thirty Three Hours this morning, the Chinese Destroyer Luta engaged the North Korean Hainan, a small armed patrol craft. The report did not state which ship fired first on the other, but follow up reports blamed each other. But these were not the reports that sent him in a wild rage. It was the report that came in from the United States Guided Missile Frigate that reported the Reuben James was forced to fire on, and then sank the North Korean ex-Soviet Whiskey Class patrol submarine.

It was an old and outdated diesel vessel the Reuben James sank. The report stated the North Korean submarine fired three torpedoes at the James, before it was destroyed by the Frigate's ASROC anti-submarine torpedo system. The Frigates Oliver Hazard Perry, and John L. Hall, along with the Guided Missile Cruiser Valley Forge, instantly moved in, but the Reuben James was the only ship that fired and killed the North Korean submarine.

The extremely upset Commander was screaming angry as he stormed around his office. "What the fuck's wrong with those damn North Korean assholes for the love of the good Christ Child? Don't they understand we're the only damn hope they have left for fuck sake?" As he screamed, a runner came in his office and announced the President wanted him on the Video Telecommunication system in the Command Center immediately.

General Campanelli hustled his way over to the meeting room in the Pentagon, and noticed the President was already speaking to General Weidenbacher. Both men stopped speaking when he entered the Command Center. The concerned General immediately saluted the President, it was not returned as the President moaned at him, "by now General Campanelli Sir, I'm quite certain you're aware that one of our Naval vessels sunk a North Korean submarine, sir."

He nodded in the affirmative to the concerned looking President's last question.

"I have Ambassador Walters sending for the North Korean Ambassador at this moment. He's sending a written protest to the United Nations, complaining one of North Korea's submarines tried to attack and sink a United States warship sailing in international waters, sir. I ordered him to jump all over the bastards. I gave the order for all American warships in this region, to fire on any ship showing possible hostile aggressive action against them, whether they be from North Korea, China or even South Korea at this point, General Campanelli Sir. All they have to do is light up one of our warships with their damn attack radar systems, and they'll get a missile shoved right up their asses for their trouble, dammit. I'll not tolerate any aggression aimed at this country for one moment, General Campanelli Sir. If the Asians aren't careful, I might even start my own offensive against them, and make China stay where she is, sir. I don't trust China..."

He interrupted the President warning by responding to the Commander in Chief, "Mr. President Sir, I'm quite certain you're aware China just sunk one of the North Korean's small surface patrol boats earlier in the day as well, sir."

"No, I was unaware of that sinking General Campanelli Sir, dammit. Here, let me see that damn report General Weidenbacher Sir," the President snapped at the General.

General Weidenbacher watched as the President thumbed through some papers handed him by one of his aides and announce, "ahhh yes, here we go. Yes General Weidenbacher, I have that report here sir, I guess I better read my reports a lot sooner and more carefully, sir. It's a good thing I had this report, or someone was going to find it awful hard to take a crap tonight with my foot up his ass, sir." The President let out a quick laugh and then President Cole turned to Campanelli and bitched at him, "okay General Campanelli, I'm through with you for the time being, you can get back to your office, sir. I'll have Woody get back to you when we finally figure out what warships we're going to get in that region to better protect our interests, sir."

He saluted the obviously upset Commander in Chief and then left for his office. He was fuming over what was taking place in the Asian region, only to be handed another report stating some North Korean Units did a quick and hard hitting probe of the Chinese defense lines on the border between the two countries.

"I believe the fighting's still going on there sir," General White offered to the General.

"Who the fuck sent this damn report to us John?" Campanelli demanded to know.

"The Chinese. We did a quick flyover of the area of concern with the SR-91, and the pictures confirm the fighting's still going on in this region, General Campanelli Sir," John replied.

"Any word from the damn North Korean's about this shit, John?"

"No sir, but we're still trying to get in contact with some of their damn officials, General Campanelli Sir," John was suddenly interrupted, and he was handed another slip of paper by one of his aides, and then he reported to his Commander. "Huh, speak of the fucking devils, Eddy. The first reports in from the North Korean's, sir. It's as I figured all along sir, they're reporting the Chinese Army entered North Korea, and the North Korean troops are forcing the Chinese invaders out of their country, sir. I hate to say this, but the damn pictures by the SR flight, bears out the fact some Chinese troops did indeed enter North Korea, General Campanelli. Well, at least that's where most of the fighting's presently taking place at the moment, sir."

Their conversation was again interrupted, this time a runner who handed a report to General Campanelli this time. He opened it and announced the Alliance States are protesting the fighting taking place so close to her border. "The Russian's, err... pardon me, the Alliance States have gone to combat alert footing throughout the entire area of concern. They're flooding the damn border area with their elite border troops. Shit, this is all we needed sir. Those fucking Russian know what the Chinese are doing, and they agreed to all this shit at the last meeting, dammit."

John cut in and then he offered to his Commanding Officer, "Eddy, this is a damn game of political chess, sir. Russia's in no fucking shape to try and attack anyone, least of all China, sir. This letter's all bullshit and bad manners, and other governments know this as fact, sir."

"Fact or not, the damn Russians could make a helluva mess of it, if they chose to muddy up the damn area with their stinking troops. You put so many armed troops from three different nations in one area, and there's sure to be shooting. I want you to cut a message to the Russian military leader, and see what his intentions are, John. Tell him we'll back him as long as his troops are defending their borders and nothing more, sir. We'll not help them if they attack China or North Korea though. You know how to word the damn thing for me, sir. Get it done John."

"You got it," General White was off in a flash as he rushed out of the office.

General Campanelli looked at the staring eyes of the rest of his Command Staff as they waited for further orders, and he grumbled at them, "Well what the hell are you people looking at me for crap sake? Don't tell me you're surprised at the current events taking place in Asia? You knew this shit was going to happen sooner or later, dammit. Well, it's happening sooner than later, that's all people. I'm warning you people, you better plan on being here all night."

"I have ships and troops being moved around, and I want to know who they are, and where the hell they're going at all times. Locker, find Admiral Standlund, and find out where his damn ships are stationed for me. Incidentally, we sank a North Korean submarine, and China sunk a small North Korean patrol boat, and there's fighting on the Chinese, North Korean border."

He suddenly snapped his fingers as if an afterthought. He instantly scanned his staff until he found his intended target, and then he ordered him, "General Palmieri Sir, see if you can find out if anything's happening on the damn Korean borders, strange we haven't heard anything from them as yet over this mess taking place, sir. Maybe China's planning to start her fucking attack on them sooner than we anticipated, and they have permission to go in action, sir."

Palmieri sat down and placed a call. He was on the phone when John came back in the office.

The Commanding General turned to him and waited for his report to come in.

"I just spoke with a Russian General Oktyabrsky moments ago, sir. He's some ass in charge of Russian Ground Forces Central, sir. He has assured me his troop movement's strictly for show for the Chinese' sake, General Campanelli Sir. He further informed me his government was well aware of the plans made between China, and the rest of the countries in this present situation, and Russia was going to stand by this agreement in principle, sir."

"How the hell do you feel about this damn bird you just spoke with, John? Do you think he was telling us the fucking truth about their stand on this damn thing, sir?"

"Sure, what other fricking course do they have opened to themselves, General Campanelli? They can't possibly attack China for Christ sake. China would walk all over them sir, and who would the United States back if it came down to that shit taking place, sir?"

"I have no idea any longer, John. If we're smart enough, and the shooting breaks out between the two, we should step back and allow the fucking chips to fall where they may. Then we can go in and pick up the damn pieces and reshape the two countries, so they can fit better into the damn future scheme of things, sir." General Campanelli offered with a snap in his voice.

"Yeah, wouldn't that be nice for a damn change, sir. But you know how we are, we'll do something to get involved in the fighting one way or the other, General Campanelli Sir."

The rest of the day was spent with the staff staring at phones. No one ate, and it was nearing Nineteen Hundred

Hours when a report came in the office. It went right to Campanelli, it read.

'Chinese troops are retreating over the border with North Korea. Fighting end. Second train from Central China stopped, many troops departing. Huge convoy of flatbed trucks carrying tanks reached the border. Chinese troops being heavily reinforced. Report based on latest pictures and intelligence gathered by two points, the SR-91 aircraft, and baby drones.

End of report.

General Edward Campanelli let out his breath and then moaned for the benefit of the rest of his Command Staff, "it fucking looks like the worst of the shits over with for the time being, but you can rest assure there is going to be plenty of nations screaming for an emergency Security Council meeting to take place once the stinking dust settles down some."

John interrupted his Commander and remarked, "no sooner said than done sir. North Korea and India just petitioned the Council for a special meeting to be convene A-SAP, sir. North Korea's demanding the latest sanctions be lifted against their nation, and set in place against China for her recent invasion of their country, General Campanelli Sir."

General Campanelli laughed as he remarked to John's last report, "yeah, they have a real fucking case on their stinking hands for themselves with that request, John."

Reports kept flooding into the office for the rest of the day. Some concerning the ongoing skirmishes occurring between China and North Korea, but none of the reports were causing much alarm or concern, although China was successful in sinking two more small North Korean patrol boats. North Korea's demand for an emergency meeting with the Security Council was still being weighed, but General Campanelli knew it was purposely being delayed by the Council Members until after China finally invaded North Korea according to plan.

General Campanelli noticed for the past few days that Aleksandra was acting rather nervous, and he put it off to her worry over the actions taking place in the Asian region. But on Friday she stopped in front of his desk, and then she began to shift her weight from one foot to the other in front of him until he had enough and finally growled at her, "Well what the fuck's wrong with you now for cripe sake? If you have to go to the damn bathroom, just go will ya please?"

She gave him a quick smile, and something warned him he was in for a hell of a request.

He put down his pencil and turned to her and then he grumbled, "okay honey, I have been married long enough to know the fucking look you're dumping on my damn ass right now. You have the stinking floor, sister. Whaddaya want from my ass and make it quick will ya?"

She shifted her feet again as she pulled the pamphlet out from behind her back. The one with Saints Peter and Paul printed on the cover. Again, she tried her best smile on him.

"Will you take that dumb smile off your puss and tell me what the fuck this damn thing is about dammit," the Commanding General growled as he took the small pamphlet from her outstretched hand, and then he quickly thumbed through the few pages.

"General Campanelli Sir, I hope consider you take me Church this Sunday morning, please sir? I no be at Church since arrive first in United State two year ago, sir."

"Sure, which Church do you wanna go to, Major?" he asked as he threw the small pamphlet down on his desk, and then he looked her dead in the eyes.

"I hope you be kind take me to Saints Peter and Paul so I attend Mass in Church of my nationality, please General Campanelli Sir" she actually cringed as she said the words to the angry looking General, w2aiting for the shit to hit the fan, and it did.

He jumped up to his feet as he reached for the pamphlet again, and then he picked it up and began waving it in her face and he snapped angrily at her, "you gotta be shitting me Alex! Do you know how fricking far away New Jersey is from here for Pete's sake? You're out of your stinking mind on this one here girl. I'm not driving that far just so you can go to Church for love of God. Jesus H. Christ girl, can't you settle for a Church somewhere here in fucking Washington. Where the hell's Colonel Locker hiding at anyhow, dammit? I'm going to stick this damn booklet right up her ass for her giving it to you in the first place. She started this damn shit by giving it to me in the first place!" he growled as he threw the book on his desk.

Her blood boiled as she straightened her back while taking her own threatening stance, and then she shot back at her Commanding Officer, "that exactly why I want go Church, for love of God. Besides, my name Aleksandra, no Alex, mista. Just friend call Alex me, and you no take Church, go hell you. I find own way Church if have thumb hitch ride there, mista. And do no you yell at me no more either. I no you bimbo mista. You do no own me, and you want make love to something, find youself ripe tomato and make love to that, because it be hot day hell before you make love me again mista!" She stood with her fists clenched and her nostrils flaring, just daring him to say something else to her so she could knock his block off.

He had no other choice and he smiled as he plopped down in his seat and shook his head slowly as he pinched the bridge of his nose. He knew he was dead in the water because she reminded him so much of Mendoza, and now, seeing her temper in action she looked more like Mendoza than ever before. He knew he was going to fall in love with this woman standing before him and glaring so angrily at him and he liked the thought. She awakened his long dead feelings as he replied to the angry young female Major, "it's a cold day in hell, honey. And a fucking overripe tomato, Christ. I think I'm going to have to try that one someday."

She looked at the General as if he had just lost his mind, and then she demanded from him hotly, "what you say me, mista big shot leader you?"

"When you were yelling at me, Major. It's a cold day in hell, not a hot day in hell, and the other mistake you made is either hitch a ride, or thumb a ride. You better learn the damn phrases right, if you're going to curse me out with them you know young lady," he tried to laugh, but it did not soften her angry stance against him in the least.

"I no give you shit how you say phrase when angry, mista big shot American Officer you. I want go Church, and I go with or with no you I tell you, mista. You want love me then you take me Church, or I no love you longer none, General Popeye Sir!" she growled as she continued to glare at him, now with her hands resting on her hips.

He laughed again as he offered to Aleksander in a much calmer tone of voice this time around, "okay, you win this one I guess Alex. I'll take you to Church, but only if nothing else is going on around here. And if something happens that we have to attend to, we're coming right back here, and I don't want to hear any shit about it one way or the other from you, honey. That's the fucking deal, take it or leave it young lady," he stared at her while waiting for an answer.

CHAPTER 11

A smile spread across her face, "you take me Lithuanian Church in you New Jersey place?"

"Yeah, I'll take you there, okay Alex? Now will you get off my damn back please."

She leaned over his desk and hugged his head to her chest as she warned him, "you wait tonight mista, I make happy you very much for make me happy so. I promise you my word on this, mista." She kissed him on the side of the face and almost skipped out of the office.

He shook his head slowly as he wondered what he might have gotten himself into with this foreign and very good looking female pilot. He looked around his office, and was met by many smiling faces looking at him. Colonel Mary Locker remarked at the General in a pleasant tone, "well sir, I wonder if this is what General Weidenbacher meant when he ordered you to treat this foreign female pilot well, General Campanelli Sir."

John called out from his desk, "I wonder if I offered him my body, if I could work a day off for myself." He was greeted by a twisted up wad of paper striking him on the back of his head.

Everyone in the office laughed, causing General Campanelli to get angry and gripe at them, "I guess you birds don't have anything else to do around here but bust my damn horns like this, so I'll start looking for some extra work for you people to accomplish for your paycheck."

Everyone made moves like they were suddenly busy, and he laughed at the group as he retorted at the group, "yeah you fucks, try and fool my ass now I see will you people. But I know what you people are doing here, you pack of fucking jaybirds."

John, while looking down called out, this time in a disgusted voice, "why don't you read your damn newspaper on the side of the desk and leave us working people alone for a stinking change, you old fart you." Another knotted up wad of paper came whizzing by his ear.

Friday went by without much happening in the Asian region. There were numerous reports filled with threats coming from both North Korea or China, but they were passed over with little if any real concern. Everyone knew where the true outcome of this rhetoric was leading, a shooting war between the two countries, and China would have the blessings of many other nations of the world to invade North Korea. There was one report where India requested a special meeting between the three nations involved, but the request was passed over by the nations of the United Nations.

The only way a special meeting would be convened, would be if North Korea backed out of the nuclear arms development she was involved in, and allowed full inspections from Sweden, France and the United States, to make certain they truly ceased creating any new nuclear weapons, and were dismantling the ones she had already built.

For some reason, General Campanelli was dying for a cold beer, but instead of giving in to his want, he reached in his pocket and took out a roll of life saver candies and popped a wild cherry in his mouth, and then he grumbled as he sucked on it.

Aleksandra was making a real pest of herself, and she asked him at least ten times during the day if he was really going to take her to Church on this coming Sunday, which finally caused him to warn her angrily, "if you ask me one more fucking time if I'm taking you to that Church. I'll make you run alongside the damn car all the way there, now beat it will ya please."

She laughed as she walked away from the general's desk and then went about her business.

He did not know why, but he was in a good mood today. He felt real good about himself, his Command Staff looked happy enough, and they were working well together. No bad news had come in as yet, and there was a smell of coffee coming down the hall. He looked at his watch and saw it was nearing lunch time, and he announced to his staff, "people, people, people you can either eat here, or go home for the weekend. We've been working for thirty hours straight, and we deserve the damn weekend off. General Palmieri Sir, you'll pull the duty for tomorrow, and John will take it for Sunday.

"The rest of you people will check in every three hours, to make certain you're not needed to report back here for any reason. Sunday, I'll not be available for the entire day, except for any emergency that might crop up, and it better be a fucking emergency, people. If I have to drag my ass all the way back here from Jersey just to hold your fucking hands, you're gonna pay dearly for it I warn you pack of crybabies. Got it?"

No one answered to General Campanelli's last warning.

He stood and then he announced to his staff as he wiggled some pain out of his back, "I suggest you people who want to get the hell outta here, do so before I change my stinking mind and make all of you work the damn weekend shift together, dammit." Those were the words his staff needed to hear as they quickly sprang up to their feet, locked files away, jotted down some phone numbers, and then they made a mad dash for the door.

He laughed as he mumbled to himself, "whoever said the dead don't rise, never laid eyes on this bunch of damn crazies I got working for my ass around here, dammit."

Aleksandra came in his office and he looked at her and offered, "C'mon honey, I'll buy ya lunch." They walked to the cafeteria and Campanelli scanned the faces in the lunchroom and he and Aleksandra walked over to Weidenbacher's table when he noticed the General in the room.

The General motioned with his head for the two to take a seat with him. He smiled at the young and pretty Lithuanian pilot, and then he asked the female Major, "how are you today, Ma'am? Is my Officer here treating you well enough, Major?"

She smiled as she announced. "He take me Church Sunday, good deal General Sir."

The General turned his head and looked at Campanelli with a wrinkled forehead, and then he asked him, "aren't you afraid of the roof of the Church caving in on ya, Ed? You going to Church is like me going to the damn Opera, sir." He looked seriously at his General and noticed the light emitting from him to the female pilot and this caused him to moan at them. "Oh brother, please don't tell me you two birds are getting romantic with each other. Eddy, you're taking my orders a little too seriously I see, sir. I know I told you to treat her good, but I didn't tell you to bed her, pal." He gave one of his body shaking laughs, causing his other officers to join him.

"General Weidenbacher Sir, your last orders are the easiest orders I have ever been issued by a Commanding Officer, sir." General Campanelli said between laughs.

"Sheesh General, you're some shit. I'm glad I have no daughters, or I would've had to have you fixed." He raised his hand over his head and the man servant ran over to the table.

"Yes sir, what can I get for you sir," the young Corporal asked pleasantly.

"Not me son. But you better get these two something to eat, besides themselves Corporal. They need to build up their strength some. Do you have any oysters on the menu for today?"

"Sir?" the Corporal asked, not getting the joke the General was trying to make on him.

"Just kidding ya son. But you take their order, I'm picking up the tab for everything today."

General Weidenbacher started speaking when the Corporal was out of ear shot range, "most of the Vinegar Joe system has passed Guam, and your Command Ship has dropped anchor twenty seven miles off the coast of Taiwan. The rest of the ships to make up her deck should be set in position by no later than this Friday, a week from today General Campanelli. I want your ass out on that damn ship by then General, and your Command Staff with you as well, sir. I'll have video telecommunications available by that time, sir. You don't know what a pain in the ass the President's becoming lately, sir. This way, he can bug the shit out of your ass instead of mine for a change, General Campanelli. Woody has the Aircraft Carriers Washington and Eisenhower on station between Taiwan, and the coast of the Korean Peninsula. Their assets are doing a flyover South Korea. We located the submarines from North Korea, and a number of Chinese ones also, sir. You go active Friday, so get your damn Command Staff used to the order, sir."

General Campanelli's burgers came and he dove into them. General Weidenbacher watched both officers, and realized he made the right choice picking Campanelli to Command his forces in the Asian region. He made a mental note to add a comment to General White's 201 file for offering up Campanelli for this Command. He could not believe he was so sound asleep at the switch over missing inviting this office for an interview. He should have picked Campanelli first off, just from his Command abilities he displayed in the Middle East War. He shook his head sadly, knowing he was one of the officers who voted to put Campanelli out to pasture, just waiting for him to get his thirty years in, or die, whichever came first. A sad ending for any good military officer who allowed his feelings for a woman ruin his career. He was not the first soldier who fell into this trap, and he surely would not be the last either.

General Weidenbacher was kind of upset General Campanelli chose to get involved with the female Major romantically, and he found himself searching his mind for a way to try and interrupt this budding romance. He even toyed with the idea of having her transferred out to someone else for her continuing training, he wanted his officers clear headed, and not thinking about some woman. His thoughts were broken by General Campanelli when he asked.

"General Weidenbacher Sir, do you really think China will stop their attack once she destroys the nuclear weapons along with North Korea, sir?"

General Weidenbacher gave a queer look to his concerned looking General, and then he asked him seriously, "and what the hell makes you believe China will destroy North Korea, sir?"

"General Weidenbacher Sir, you have to read between the fucking lines on this one I'm afraid, sir. North Korea's no longer an asset to China, and she might even be a liability to them at this point, sir. A threat if you will General Weidenbacher Sir. If I were in Command of the invading Chinese troops picked to attack North Korea, and I had a blessing from the important nations who had the power to stop China, if she went too far during this invasion of North Korea, sir. I'd sure as hell take full advantage of the present situation, and I'd push it for all it was worth for my country, sir. Especially when I could eliminate one of the only remaining serious threats to my country, sir. Yes sir, I'd surely destroy all the North Korean forces who I'd be forced to classify as hostile in the guise of eliminating the nuclear threat from North Korea, sir."

General Weidenbacher stopped eating as he rubbed his chin. His eyes betrayed the concern his General just brought to light. He took a deep breath and then remarked, "Edward, you're the biggest pain in the fucking ass I ever met, sir." His back straightened up as his face showed the anger building within, and then he added to his words, "I'm going to give my damn Intelligence Officers a hop in their damn asses for not running this scenario by me before you brought it up to my fucking attention, sir. They should've spotted this crap long before one of my Officer's came across it, and he brought it up to me. You know, there's a place for you in the Intelligence game once you decide you had enough playing soldier, and waddling around in the damn mud with you're the rest of your troops. I'd be glad to put you on my staff, General. I assure you Ed, there's going to be a number of openings once I get my hands on these people later today, sir."

General Campanelli shook his head no and replied with a snap in his tone of voice this time, "General Weidenbacher Sir, I'm afraid I have my hands full with the damn ground pounders I have operating under me as it is, sir. I don't think I want to get involved with any of the Intel shits. They're a real strange bunch of people, sir."

"I hear you there Ed, I guess I might have been pushing you a little too hard at that," the powerful General said as he sat back, and then he stuck another french fry in his mouth and added to his upsetting words. "Yeah, there's going to be some mashing of fucking teeth around here when I get back to my damn office I assure you, sir."

He was amazed at how well the General calmed down so much, and he was acting as if nothing else was bothering him lately, when he knew he was burning up inside.

"How long are you planning to be gone on Sunday in case I need your ass back here, General Campanelli Sir?" General Weidenbacher suddenly asked with some concern in his tone.

"I was planning to leave on Saturday night if that's okay with you, General Weidenbacher Sir. Then I was going to spend most of Sunday at the Church, and then head back for Washington by nightfall, and get back here before morning to man my office, sir."

"What, where the hell's this Church at anyhow for the love of Pete, General Campanelli Sir? You're going to need the full weekend to attend this Church, sir?"

"New Jersey sir," he replied as he smiled back at the General.

"You got to be kidding me soldier. Aren't the Churches we have here in Washington good enough for you to worship in, mister?" the powerful General growled as he wiped his mouth and hands with a napkin, and then he threw it down on his plate.

Aleksandra spoke up this time as she replied to General Weidenbacher's last bitch at General Campanelli, "General Weidenbacher Sir, no be angry General Campanelli with please, sir. It fault of mine only, he go to this Jersey new country with me, sir. It only Lithuanian Church I ever find in you country long time for now since look for Church for me go, sir. I want go Church, General Weidenbacher Sir." She purred her words at the well respected General as she flashed one of her soul melting smiles at the staring Military Commander.

General Weidenbacher could not help it and he melted, as did countless men before him had whenever they got locked in her radiance. He turned back to General Campanelli and warned him, "may Heaven protect you from that killing smile of hers, General. Yeah, it's okay for you to go to this Jersey country I guess, sir. I'm glad you brought this up to my attention though at this time. General Campanelli, I'll put myself on call for Sunday and also Saturday night, sir. I'll cover for you, enjoy yourself please, you deserve it sir. And you, you say a few prayers for me will you please, Ma'am? Ed, how are you planning on getting up there, sir?"

"I guess I was going to rent a car and drive out to the Church myself, General Weidenbacher Sir," he offered as he stared at General Weidenbacher.

"What? What the fuck's wrong with your head anyway mister? That's bullshit and bad manners if you were to ask me, mister. You take the damn staff car, and the driver I assigned to you, sir. Let him earn his damn pay for once in his wasted life, General."

"General Weidenbacher Sir, it'll cost a small fortune to allow the government pay for this trip to New Jersey sir," General Campanelli warned his Commanding Officer.

"Look here sir, you're busting your fucking ass for your government with this mess in the Asian region, sir. So sit back and allow the government to show you how much it appreciates the work you're doing for her, will ya please General Campanelli. You use the fucking staff car for as long as you're in fucking Washington, for any reason whatsoever mister."

Campanelli nodded as he started on his french fries, which Aleksandra was helping herself to.

"Now, what's going on today mister?" General Weidenbacher demanded hotly from him.

"General Weidenbacher Sir, my Staff has been at it since yesterday morning straight time, sir, I kept them here overnight, just in case something went wrong on us in this mess, sir. I just gave them the rest of the weekend off. I'm standing duty for the rest of the day, sir."

"Bullshit! You go home, I'll have General Claiborne takeover your office for you, General. That old goat has nothing else to do, and he's been driving me fucking crazy lately, mister. Why don't you make it a whole weekend, and take off for Jersey Saturday morning, and do some shopping over there while you're at it, sir. Sort of help out the economy a little, Ed."

The General finished off his coffee and then he stood and stretched his arms and complained at his General, "I have to get going and straighten out some asses around here, General Campanelli Sir." He then turned to Aleksandra and added with a smile for the young woman, "and you have yourself a good time, but you keep your guard up with this one, I don't trust him in the least."

General Weidenbacher left the room, half way down the hall, he spotted General Claiborne and called out to him, "General Claiborne, would you take over General Campanelli's office for the rest of the day, sir. I'm sending him off on a special little mission over the weekend, sir. Have you heard the latest about that fucking crazy ass dickhead, General?"

"What's he gotten himself into now?" General Claiborne asked his Commanding Officer.

"Major Klivekaita." General Weidenbacher replied with a mischievous sneer on his face.

"You got to be shitting me sir. That there white boy's playing hiding the stinking tube with that Major already, gees General Sir." General Claiborne replied, even though he was already aware General Campanelli was tapping the young female foreign Major. He acted surprised, so he did not rain on the General's high as he played along with his Commanding Officer.

"No sir, I swear it to you Clay. The little crafty fuck's slipping the old meat stick to the stinking pretty Major already, sir. He didn't even allow her to get comfortable with him being her Commanding Officer, before he jumped her stinking bones and started taping her pretty little ass, sir. Damn it to hell and back again, I sure hope to hell General Campanelli didn't use his fucking rank to force the damn Major into spreading her legs for him, sir? I'd pin his stinking ears to the damn floor if I found out he used his rank to get her in bed, dammit."

"I'll be damned, I swear to God that dick of his is gonna to be the death of him yet, General Weidenbacher Sir. But I know the General for a long time now sir, and I know he'd never stoop so low as to use his rank to force any woman to make love to him, sir."

Back in the lunchroom, General Campanelli smirked at the pretty foreign female Major as he offered her with a smile on his lips, "General Weidenbacher's some fucking shit, Aleksandra. Well, it looks like we just got the rest of the stinking day off for ourselves, honey. What do you want to do with the extra time young lady?"

"I want thank you much for offer take me Church, General Campanelli Sir. I fall in love you too much so soon I worry too much for, sir." Aleksandra replied.

They left for her apartment, and another day of making love to each other.

JANUARY 31st, 1997;
ALEKSANDRA'S SUITE AT THE HILTON

Major Aleksandra Klevekaita was the first to rise, and was combing her hair when General Edward Campanelli came in the bathroom to take a leak. She was naked, and she looked so good he came up behind her and gently grabbed her breasts from behind. She purred at his touch.

"It'll take me fifteen minutes to get ready baby." He too was naked, and he started the water for his shower as he called out over his shoulder, "You wanna mess around some baby?"

"Not if want ready in fifteen minute, I do no want mess round right now please, Popeye. I want to get dressed we can so leave for you country of New Jersey, sir."

He took a quick shower, and then he dressed in his civvies and finished his breakfast with her, and then he announced in a matter-of-fact tone of voice to the female Major, "I'll call the Sergeant, and have him bring the car around for us Alex."

Minutes later, they were on their way to New Jersey. It was freezing and there were plenty of pockets of snow and ice still covering the road surface here and there. So the going was rather slow for them. Almost five hours later, and one pit stop, the military staff car entered Elizabeth, New Jersey. After they checked in at the Howard Johnson's Motel, they were back outside as Aleksandra was actually dragging the freezing General down the road.

"Can't we take the fucking car, or a damn cab or something for Pete's sake? I'm freezing my stinking balls off, and I don't like it one stinking bit dammit Major," General Campanelli complained as he allowed her to drag him around like she was doing.

"Nosense you big baby, you can no see store from stupid car, Popeye. Look, look, food store from my old country, let go in please." The store was like an old time New York deli, but it had many Lithuanian dishes which could be eaten right there in the establishment.

She ordered a dish of Kielbasa, and General Campanelli tried to order a plain hamburger. But she would have none of it. She told him he was going to eat some of her Kielbasa and like it. Reluctantly, he gave in again. The sausage was good, a little spicy though. She was in seventh Heaven and all smiles and giggles as she spoke to the proprietor in her native tongue.

General Campanelli could not understand a single word of their gibberish that was being said, so he ignored the two as they spoke together like they knew each other for years.

Next, she dragged him all over the city, finishing with a soda at Akalonis' drug store. The General kept glancing at his watch. It was a little past six p.m., and he complained at the female Major, "Jesus Louise, will you look at the fucking time already."

"I want pass Church so we know where is tomorrow. Then we eat, please Sir."

"What can I say," he waved a cab, and in less than ten minutes they pulled in front of an ancient Church with two large pillars in front. The building was built in 1895, and the pillars were added in the late twenties, the tops of the towers were removed in the late fifties, when fears of the construction were brought out, the cab driver informed them. He looked at the building, the ancient masonry building seemed like it was still in great shape. The front of the Church had a large stained glass window, with a number of smaller ones off to the sides of the large one. The Church had three sets of double doors with the largest in the center.

The doors looked hand carved and were well taken care of over the years.

She stood in front of the Church with her mouth hanging open and her eyes sparkling. For a second, she thought she was transported back to her native land somehow. Her face had a smile that conveyed her longing to be back home. General Campanelli pulled her close to him and she wiggled under his arm for warmth and cried, "oh, it not beautiful Church, sir."

"Yes it is," The rather impressed military officer muttered as he continued to stare at the well aged old building, paying silent homage to the old time builders, who really put their body and soul into the construction of the beautiful Church.

She shivered, and he pulled her closer to his body and said, "C'mon Alex, we better get going before you freeze to death standing here like this, young lady." He led her back to the waiting cab. Once inside, he asked the driver where there was a good place to eat. Aleksandra quickly added kindly, "a Lithuanian place I want eat to, sir."

The driver headed to a restaurant called Zalapukas. Their menu was written in Lithuanian, and no one spoke any English at the place, but the words did not sound like Lithuanian, some of them had a different accent to them. The Commanding General looked at Aleksandra and she replied, "Polish, understand Lithuanian, understand Polish."

He shrugged as he mumbled at her, "I thought you people didn't really like the Pols very much, young lady?"

"You right, long time ago we no like them very much at all, Edward. Now, like you, we no prejudice against no one any longer, life too short to not like everyone meet, General Sir." She smiled as she asked if he wanted her to order for him.

"Please, that's the only way I'm going to get something to eat, I can't read a word of this shit."

She ordered as she ignored the snap in his voice, and the waiter instantly disappeared and she informed him, "I order you stuff cabbage with potato pudding and some beer. He said he see find Pepsi you for drink. I think he take out some one lunch box if has to. I hope you like my pick for food you, sir. I no see any burger on menu, or order you for it General."

He did not respond, he was bored to death and wanted to go to a room and rest.

She broke his concentration by asking him with a little worry in her voice, "I like go nine o'clock Mass tomorrow morning you no mind that is, please sir?"

"Yeah sure why the hell not little lady, whatever makes you happy I guess Alex," he mumbled uninterestedly to her.

The Lithuanian female got angry and she snapped back at him as she glared, "why act like you no good time in least for with me please?"

"I'm having a good time. What makes you think I'm not?" he grumbled back at her.

"You sit with puss reach floor top. Smile little please, thank you very much Popeye."

"Yeah, okay right Alex," he flashed one of his quick fake smiles, and then added to his bitch. "I wish I had a fucking newspaper to read while we're waiting for our damn food to arrive, baby. I wanna keep a close eye on what the crap's happening in Asia, Alex."

"Why we no talk instead you read all time paper for, General Campanelli Sir. Talk me instead of read stupid newspaper all time, tell who Mendoza is John tell me about?" she asked her Commanding Officer while staring right at his face now.

He glared at her before growling because she asked about Mendoza, "John has a big fucking mouth, and he better be a little more careful with the damn thing, or I'm going to kick his fucking teeth down his stinking throat for him, dammit."

"Why you sudden upset so at you long time friend for, mista? I asked who you Mendoza was, that all, General Campanelli Sir. If no want tell, no tell me who was, it up to you, big boy. Who do you think go win the pennant game, the Rams?" she asked, trying to change the subject and get him in a much better mood, or he was going to ruin their lunch on them.

He laughed as he shook his head and then replied to Aleksandra's last remark, "hey honey, the Rams are a stinking football team, not a damn baseball team young lady. How the hell do you know anything about the damn Rams anyhow, little sister?"

"I hear men talk all time, about men who go to how you say, tear team asshole new apart. So get nosy about and ask question, and you men explain me, and I figured rest myself out, sir. Do I make wrong mistake and make fool out of me, sir?"

The amused General laughed again as he mumbled at her, "one day I'll take you to a football game, so you can see what it's all about for yourself, young lady. Hey look Alex, I'm really sorry I snapped at you before. It's just Mendoza's still a rather sore subject for me to talk about, and John had no business telling you anything about her, dammit."

"John no mean anything bad. I asked know about you, and force him tell me about her."

"What the hell did he tell you about her anyway Alex? He knows damn well not to bring her up to anyone's attention dammit," he growled as his mind remembered Mendoza's beautiful smile, the lovely smell of her body, her laugh, and even her voice. He shook his head in order to get her image out of his mind. His throat tightened as he remembered her.

"You no long tell anything more. I see in you face you love her very much, and something wrong happen her terrible. I sorry open stupid mouth, and ask question of past love Popeye."

"It's okay Alex, later, I'll tell you all you want to know about her, honey. Right now baby, I want to keep her private and all to myself, young lady."

Their conversation was interrupted by the waiter. The General stared at his food like it was going to jump up and pull him into it. It looked like hell, and it smelt even worst to him.

She smiled as she told the General, "No be big baby, you try food some for youself, you like it much very more, General. It no bite you, it good for you, eat like this, see sir."

He looked at her, he was surprised she just referred to him as sir.

"Do like this me and you enjoy food you eat? It good like mom make," she said as she took a fork full of her meal, and then she shoved it in her mouth and smacked her lips and purred. "Hmmm... like Mama make home cook." She announced proudly with a mouthful of cabbage.

The General stabbed at his meal with his fork. What did not fall off he stuffed in his mouth, and then moaned, "Jesus man, this shit's great Alex." He stared at the food, he was amazed anything that smelt so bad, and looked even worse, could taste so good as he asked the female Major, "What the hell's this shit called anyway Alex?"

"This shit you call is stuff cabbage, a native dish my country. Is it good, no Popeye?"

"Yeah, it's great yes baby," he whispered as he stuffed more of it in his mouth.

"You wait taste pudding next my friend if you want something good taste. You really enjoy that I assure you, General Sir," she warned her new lover and friend.

He grabbed a fork full of the potato pudding and shoved it in his mouth, and then mumbled with a mouth full himself, "Godddd, this is really good stuff Alex."

After they finished eating, they grabbed another cab, and went back to the Howard Johnson's Motel. As they entered the waiting room, the Sergeant jumped to his feet and reported quickly to his Commanding Officer. "General Campanelli Sir, I didn't know where the hell you two went. So I stayed here and waited for you to return, sir. I'm sorry I didn't keep my eyes open sir, and be ready for you when you wanted to go out for a sightseeing trip, General Campanelli Sir."

He held up his hand in order to stop the excited Sergeant from babbling on as he offered the young man, "it's not your fucking fault or mine Sergeant. It's hers, she's the one who dragged me out in this damn cold looking at the damn town."

Both men turned to Aleksandra and she immediately announced with a smile, "I go upstairs and crawl under warm blanket. Free join me, old grouch General Sir."

He looked from her to the Sergeant and then announced with a grin, "well so much for complaining, that's an offer no one in his right mind could refuse. I'm going up with her."

"I don't blame you in the least General Campanelli Sir. What time are you planning to go to Church tomorrow morning, so I know when to be ready sir?"

"We're going to nine o'clock Mass, Sarge. Be ready by that time please."

"Very good General Campanelli Sir. I'll be waiting outside by Oh, Eight Fifteen Hours, sir."

"You do that. Err... excuse me, but I have to get going, if you know what I mean Sarge."

The Sergeant watched his middle aged Commander quickly disappeared up the one flight of steps to his room, and he smiled after him. Then he settled down in the bar to enjoy a few quick drinks, and then he planned to turn in for the rest of the night.

Upstairs, the female Major and the American General went at it. They made love on the bed, rolling onto the floor then back on the bed. At one point, he held her full weight in his arms, and she had her back up against the wall as they continued making love, until the guests next door pounded on the wall. They dropped back to the floor then on the bed again. When they were done, she wanted more, and tried to jump start him by giving him a blowjob. She continued until he was rock hard again, and they started over again. Once they were thoroughly exhausted, they settled down on the bed and pulled the covers over them and went to sleep. While they slept, the wind picked up and he enjoyed listening to the howling. He loved the sound of the wind, it made him feel cold even when warm and he snuggled close to Aleksandra.

At exactly Oh, Six Thirty Hours sharp, they were awakened by the call from the front desk. Aleksandra sat up and then leaned against his back and groaned and stretched her back and arms. She then grabbed his dick and began to play with it. It did not respond and she looked at him with a frown on her face.

"Oh God, you broke the damn thing. It doesn't work any more. Oh God no!"

For a second, she thought there was something really wrong with him, until she saw him laughing. She growled as she took a pillow and then started to beat him over the head and back with it, and she yelled at him at the same time, "I hate you, crazy American Officer sir." She beat him again with the pillow as she laughed wildly. She kept beating him until he reached around and he looped his arm around her waist, and he pulled her across his legs and gave her a good, resounding slap on her naked rump.

She cried in fake pain as she rubbed the area he swatted and complained at him, "I think you broken it, General." She laughed and then she rolled off him to the floor. She was laughing as hard as he was. He watched her laugh, her breasts jumping along with her laughter. She saw him staring at her and she stopped and watched him in return. Finally, their eyes met and she looked in his and he said, "You're a very beautiful woman."

Aleksandra blushed as she got off the floor and then she hugged him as she purred sexily in his ear. "Talk like that I fall love you with but good you know, mista."

He swallowed, and then he thought for a moment before he said anything else to the beautiful young woman. He continued looking at her as he smiled and then added with a grin, "I think you betta get ready for Church, Alex. It's already getting late honey."

They went downstairs and she quickly spotted the Sergeant sitting in a chair in the lobby, and she gave him the directions to the Church. When they entered, the priest stopped speaking until they were in a pew, everyone turned and looked at them.

He glared harshly at the many staring faces looking back at them, Aleksandra put her head down, she also directed the General as to when to stand, when to kneel, and when to sit. He felt like a puppet on a string as she constantly tugged on his arm, this time to stand.

Some of the people were still turning and giving the two strangers a look. The Church service took over an hour. She received communion, and then she returned to her seat happy as a lark. She saw a paper sitting on the seat near where she was seated. General Campanelli had no idea what the priest, or anyone else was saying throughout the entire Mass, because it was said in Lithuanian.

She unfolded the paper she found, and read the Church was having a special brunch at the Great Lithuanian Liberty Hall on 269-73 Second Street, Elizabeth, New Jersey. She wanted to go, to be with some of her own people for a change. She put her mouth to the General's ear and whispered softly she wanted to attend the brunch right after the Mass.

He angrily growled back in a low and grumpy whisper, "What? You gotta be shitting me for crap sake, Major. I'm not going to any damn brunch and be bored to death for the rest of the friggin day, and you ain't going to make me either Alex."

"People who curse in Church lose voice for good before old man you know foolish mista," she warned the General as she stared him in the eyes.

"That's tough shit, because I'm already an old man, and I still have my stinking voice, so there young lady. That threat didn't work on me either little sister. You have to try some other ploy on my stinking ass to make me go to this damn brunch honey," he retorted angrily.

"You take brunch, or you drive Washington by youself mista," she squeezed his arm.

"Ahhh... that's it, now you're resorting to physical pain I see, huh Alex? You're stooping real low there girl, and am I to believe you're threatening me with going AWOL on me,

Major? I'll have your pretty little ass put behind bars if you try that move against me, young lady."

"You do what you want me, but one way other. I go brunch, with or without you mista!"

He was really pissed off now, but knew he was going to give in again, he could tell just by the way she was looking at him. He looked in her eyes and griped at her "okay, you win this time, but you owe me big time on this one you know, Alex."

"Anything want, ask me and you get in return for you take me to brunch today Popeye," she replied as she placed a huge smile on her lips.

When the Mass was over, everyone stood together and began to walk out of the old Church building. General Campanelli and Aleksandra remained in their seats as everyone quickly filed passed them, and some people shot more glances at the two young strangers to their Church. She squeezed the General's hand as she whispered to him, "let wait until all people out of Church first please, General." She handed the paper to the General, who in turn handed it to the Sergeant, and then he barked at his driver, "find this place for me will you please Sarge."

"You got it sir," he said as he held the door open for the two officers.

It took them two minutes to get over to the Lithuanian Liberty Hall, the directions printed on the back of the card were easy to follow, and the Marine Sergeant did not get lost on the way.

Her face was glowing brightly with wild anticipation and happiness as she pulled and tugged Campanelli through the doors, and into the crowd filling the large room. When they entered the room, most conversations stopped, and everyone stopped what they were doing and stared at the two strangers who invaded their Church, and now their hall. The General and Major were beginning to feel like invaders as they looked at everyone staring at them.

General Campanelli and Aleksandra stood while everyone stared at them. Then an elderly gentleman finally came over to them. He was dressed in the cloth of the Church and asked the man with concern lacing his voice, "may I help you son? Are you lost, do you need help here sir?" He spoke broken English.

Aleksandra answered the priest in Lithuanian. "Father, I am a stranger in this country. I'm Major in Lithuanian Airforce and I have been loaned to the United States by our country, as a sign of their good will, that has grow better between the United States and Lithuania lately, Father. I've been here for two years now, without going to Church until today, Father. Can you please forgive me Father for my sin of missing Church for so many days in a row? I promise you and God I'll try to come to Church more often now I know where Church is, Father. I never knew there was a Lithuanian Church in the United States until this weekend, Father."

The priest smiled pleasantly as he put his hands out and she knelt and kissed his right hand. Immediately, all conversations started over again with the other people standing in the Hall' because their priest just accepted the two strangers. Large rows of tables were quickly setup, and then covered over with all sorts of homemade foods and drinks.

People came over to Aleksandra and talked to her in their native tongue. The General felt a little left out until the priest took his hand and announced, "people, this man doesn't understand our language, so I'd like everyone to speak to him in English please. I don't want to leave him out of our conversations. We owe him much gratitude for bringing our sister home to us."

General Campanelli was instantly deluged with handshakes and conversation, as the old women brought trays of food, and they made him take a sample of their cooking. Most the food was fantastic, while others made him want to spit it out, but he swallowed it as fast as he could to be polite. By the end of an hour, he felt like he was at one of his families usual get togethers, where everyone was happy, well fed and a little tipsy. He was never pounded on the back so much as he was today, and when the Lithuanian's found out they both were military officers in the service, they could not do enough for the strangers.

He had to sit down and stop eating, because he was stuffed to his ears, and he feared exploding if he took another bite of food. It was quite a scene to have so many overly excited strangers making him feel so at home and so respected. They constantly smiled at him, talked or shoved more food in his face. A few times he lost Aleksandra in the madding crowd of people, and he got a little concerned until he picked her up moving around in the crowd, and all the fun she was having speaking in her native language with the others. It was a great day for them both, and he was overly pleased she talked him into coming to the Hall. It was a day that would stay in his mind for the rest of his life.

By later on in the afternoon, the two thoroughly exhausted officers were ready to leave the very pleasing gathering. The grinning General shook hands with as many people as he could, and then the priest's hand, and Aleksandra kissed his hand again as she knelt before him, and the priest blessed them both and said to Aleksandra, "go with God and be safe with the knowledge that God loves you, my little one." Were the last words the proud priest spoke to them as they went out to the car and left, heading back to Washington.

When the pleased General was comfortable in the backseat of the car, he said to the equally exhausted Sergeant, "Sarge, you're free to stop anywhere along the way back to Washington you want, and get yourself something to eat and drink, mister."

"Err... there's no need for that I assure you, General Campanelli Sir," he replied while grinning at his Commanding Officer, as he hoisted up a large bag of food given to him by some of the women from the meeting as he bragged, "General Campanelli Sir, between this large bag of goodies the women prepared for me, and all the food the horde of women kept bringing out for me to eat, sir. I'm afraid I'm actually stuffed to the gills already sir. Hell sir, I don't think I could possibly eat another thing for at least three days, General Campanelli Sir. Some of this stuff is fantastic, they were some sort of people in there, sir."

"You can say that again mister. I don't ever remember being made so much at home by anyone other people than my own mother and family, Sarge. I had one helluva day and enjoyed every second of it as well, Sarge." General Campanelli replied as he looked in the lovely eyes of Aleksandra, and then he smiled at her as he hugged her close body to him, and she automatically snuggled under his shoulder for warmth and protection.

This remark made Aleksandra beam with pride for her good people. She remembered when her Commanding Officer first told her she was going over to the United States for some special training with their American flyers and their aircraft. She was really upset at first, and actually dreading the order also, because of the many terrible stories she heard in the past about the mean streets, and all the nasty people of the United States.

But now she was here and she witnessed their reaction first hand to her presence, it seemed like everyone she met lately, seemed extremely kind and very helpful and pleasant to her and to meet her. She looked at General Campanelli, he had a smile of contentment on his lips that showed her he was truly at peace with nature and his God at this time. She took his hand in hers and then she whispered to him.

"I hope you have much fun like I do today at lunch with my people living in your country, Popeye? I had such wonderful time with my people who share you country, General. It make me feel so much like being back home again, these people reminded me so much of my family and dear friend I left behind in my country, so I could come here for this special training with your great America pilots, General Campanelli Sir," she also informed the still grinning General in his sleep with concern in her tone as she continued to stare at him, and then she smiled at the same time as she listened to the rhythm of his gentle breathing while he laid by her side and then he replied to her question because he was faking sleeping.

"You can bet your sweet little ass I had a great time today in there honey, thanks a lot for sharing some of your people and your traditions with me today, Alex. It was very interesting and it was a good day for me to enjoy with you, and I truly enjoyed myself with them, honey. In fact it was one of my greatest days I had myself in a long time, young lady. And it relieved a lot of stinking pressure from off my damn shoulders at the same time as well, baby. I almost forgot how it was to relax and have a good time with other people, for Christ sake. Not with the crap going down on me lately. Thank you again Alex, it was a real great day for me to enjoy honey."

General Campanelli smiled and then he closed his eyes again as he wiggled deeper into the rear car seat, and within a few seconds later he was snoring away, even though the car was bounding him all over the back seat, and it was freezing inside the car.

She watched the General get comfortable as possible in the rear seat, and then she leaned back herself, and she crossed her arms over her chest and closed her eyes. Moments later, she too was fast asleep inside the car. They both sleep for the rest of the trip back to Washington, as the Sergeant drove them.

The Marine driver did not put the radio on, because he wanted the two officers to sleep for their entire ride back to Washington. He was proud to be the General's private driver, and he also enjoyed being around the both military officers.

CHAPTER 12
FEBRUARY 1st, 1997
SUNDAY NIGHT 2035 HOURS WASHINGTON D.C.

The General's staff car pulled up in front of the Hilton Hotel. But General Campanelli had fallen back to sleep though, so the Sergeant was forced to wake him by calling out softly to him, "Sir, General Campanelli Sir, I hate to have to wake you up like this at this time sir, but we're home. Sir, you have to wake up now so I can park the car, sir." The

Sergeant said in a low voice, as he tried not to startle his commanding officer in the back seat.

His eyes fluttered open and he replied to the worried Sergeant, "who, what was that soldier."

"General Campanelli Sir, we're back at the Hilton here in Washington, sir. It's time you wake up and get out so I can park the car sir," the Sergeant quickly informed him.

"What the fuck time is it anyhow Sarge?" he groaned while trying to see his own watch.

"It's Twenty, Thirty Five Hours sir," the driver replied as he leaned back out of the car.

General Campanelli did some quick calculations in his head, and then mumbled at his driver, "shit, eight thirty five in the fucking morning already, Sarge?" He went to move, and he got a stabbing pain in his lower back for his trouble.

"Jesus H. Christ," he cried out and moved back to the way he was sleeping in the car. His back had not been right ever since the helicopter crash, but he was damned if he was going to tell the medics about the pain he was suffering from. He knew some of the top hats were still looking for any reason whatsoever to put him out of the service, and he was not going to give them one to work with either. He wiggled around for a few seconds in the seat until the pinch in his back went away, and then he moved up in the seat.

All of the moving he was doing finally woke Aleksandra and she complained angrily at him, "dommit, it like sleep top horse drawn cart. You stop move some much huh please will you. You have go bathroom, get up and go then and let me sleep long please."

He growled back at her, "What the hell are you babbling about now Alex, dammit?"

Her eyes opened, and it took her a second or two to realize they were still asleep in the back of the car. She stretched her arms and sat up and admitted, "I forget sleep in dom car."

"You guys want to get out while I get your bags and bring them to your rooms for you, sirs."

"She's getting out here, I wanna get over to the Pentagon and see if anything happened there while we were visiting fucking Jersey Sarge," the General ordered his driver.

"Sure thing General Campanelli Sir, I'll get the Major's bags for her sir," he made a move to get out of the car.

"Hold you position right there where you be seat, Sergeant. I no go nowhere but with General to Pentagon build please," she ordered as she suddenly glared angrily at General Campanelli because she was upset she felt he was trying to get rid of her.

He turned to her, a little surprised by the strength and command in her voice, and he asked her with some concern in his tone, "what did you just say?"

"I told Sergeant hold position where he seat, General Campanelli Sir. I go with you to Pentagon home sir," she growled hotly at him this time.

"I know that Alex, dammit you're one real royal pain in the ass lately! Why the hell did you tell him that for Pete's sake?" he asked the young beauty.

"You think you start work without me at you side be sir? I warn you, you a quite mistake sir."

"Don't tell me you want to come down to the office with me, Alex? Just go and get some rest will you please. Tomorrow's another day, honey."

"That right General Campanelli Sir, I come with you and work by you side as ordered to by you General Weidenbacher, General Campanelli Sir." Aleksandra made certain she refrained from using the General's nickname in front of the Sergeant, or anyone else in the service for that matter. She was reserving the name for them when they were alone together.

"Look at you, you're dog ass fucking tired girl, and you look like a fucking mess to boot, Alex. I think you should stay here and catch up on some of your damn sleep, young lady. There's no sense in the both of us losing the rest of the night's sleep is there?"

"I no care what say you to me sir. If you report work, so I then do too, General Campanelli."

"Like I said, you're getting to be a real pain in the ass lately Major Klevekaita," he let out his breath and then rubbed his stubble covered chin and snapped at the young Sergeant this time. "You heard her Sarge, you better get us over to the Pentagon, son. I know better than to try and argue with any female Officer. Or female for that matter." He muttered under his breath.

As the staff car parked in his North section of the Pentagon parking slot, General Campanelli snapped at his Marine driver, "you wanna come in with us Sarge? I don't think we'll be that long. From the looks of this place, it doesn't look like anything of any real interest happened I should know about over yesterday, Sarge." He quickly scanned the massive parking lot, and noticed only a few cars were still parked in the huge lot, which he figured belonged to the security guards still working inside the building.

The exhausted trio went in the foyer and the sleepy Army guard instantly jumped to his feet as he asked them for their ID's. General Campanelli glared at the guard, to inform him he did not like the fact he was almost asleep while on duty.

The guard quickly scanned the cards then handed them back to the officers still dressed in their civilian clothes. He watched as the three of them went through the metal detector, and then quickly disappeared down the corridor as he grumbled at their backs, "fucking brass babies, I wish they'd all stay the hell home, and leave me the fuck alone for a little while."

General Campanelli opened the door to his office, just as the roaming security guard came rushing down the hall and immediately challenged him, "can I help you sir?" The concerned security guard snapped as his hand automatically went to his side arm.

He turned to the guard and then glared at him.

"Sorry General Campanelli Sir, I didn't recognize you dressed in your civvies sir," the embarrassed guard announced the moment he recognized the General and others with him.

"Never mind that shit Corporal. I'm damn glad you challenged my ass, mister. Don't ever apologize to me for doing your fucking job properly, mister. What's your name soldier?" the powerful General asked the security guard as he waited for his reply.

"Corporal Cruz, James A., sir," the Corporal offered proudly to the General.

"Well Mr. Cruz, James A. Do you feel like getting out of this stinking building for a while?"

"Excuse me General Campanelli Sir?" he asked the speaking officer.

"I'm leaving for active duty later this week, and I need a few good men surrounding me at all times, son. I like how you perform your duty. I'm asking you if you want to follow me to my next Port of Call. Get some sun on your damn ass for a change, mister. What do you say?"

"Sir, I'd like that very much General Campanelli Sir," he responded happily.

"Fine, I'll have your 201 sheet pulled and offered up for your movement over to my new Command Staff position, mister. I'm going to take you along with me Sergeant."

"I'm afraid you made a mistake General Campanelli Sir. I'm Corporal, not a Sergeant, sir."

"You're the one who made the fucking mistake here mister, not me. One thing you betta learn from the start when dealing with my ass, soldier. Whenever a Commander calls you Sergeant, you're a fucking Sergeant. Report to me at Fifteen, Thirty, Hours tomorrow afternoon, and I'll let you know where we're heading, mister. I'll call the duty desk, and inform them you're picked up to Sergeant, effective tomorrow son," General Campanelli grumbled as he started in his office, but he caught the movement from the Corporal. He stood at attention, saluting him.

He shook his head slowly as he came to attention, and then he saluted the new Sergeant back. It was the only way he felt he was going to get him to move off some. Because if he did not return the salute even though he was still dressed in his civilian clothes, he was worried the young kid would have stood there all night long, until he finally came out and saluted him to release him from his salute. The officers watched as the kid quickly disappeared, it looked like he was walking on cloud nine as he left the General's side.

"You very good mood be so tired General Campanelli Sir," Aleksandra remarked.

"Ahh... it's just good to see someone doing his fucking job properly for a stinking change, that's all, baby." They entered his office, the General went to his desk and checked the folder marked problems. There were two reports in the basket, one stated China sunk another small North Korean patrol boat in the open sea. The report stated the Chinese ship ordered the smaller ship to veer off, but when the patrol boat continued to close in, the Chinese ship opened fire on it with its five inch gun, and blew the smaller boat out of the water. The report remarked the Chinese ship found one North Korean survivor, and he was brought to a Chinese port to a hospital. "Lucky bastard," he muttered then added. "At least he's out of the fight."

The second report read, 'USS Wasp, LHD-1 was set in position off the coast of Taiwan. See attached report'. He turned to another page and read the report further, 'The Wasp had one thousand, eight hundred, seventy three combat ready Marine troops stationed on board her, along with thirty Sea Knight CH-46 helicopters, eight Harrier jump jets, and six Super Cobra's, four Sea Hawk SH 60-B helicopters equipped with the Lamps 111 system for anti submarine warfare. The Wasp had an OE 82 satellite uplink along with surface search SPS 67 and sixty air search SPS 52 and 49 radar's with a target acquisition ARS 23 radar.

'The ship's top speed was marked at twenty three knots. She was placed in the Washington Carrier Strike Group. The active Marines on board the ship were all part of the 4th Marine Expeditionary Brigade out of Camp Lejeune, with a complement of twenty thousand troop's part of the 4th Expeditionary Force (MEF). The main body of the MEF was currently stationed at the Rhein Main Air Force Base outside of Frankfurt, Germany. The Marines were air lifted to Frankfurt over the past nine days. It was the first MEF to be put in place at full combat ready condition'. A side note informed the General the Wasp was dragging a TARP, a towed array ranging sonar to help aid in the ship's defense against a possibly submarine attack.

General Campanelli relaxed a bit, knowing he had a strong military strike force of sixty two thousand Marine troops already set in place. They were being backed by a battery of military equipment ranging from two hundred ninety six M-60 machine guns, one hundred towed, and thirty self propelled Howitzers, an unspecified number of Hawk ground to air defense missiles, and a whole array of aircraft and attack helicopters. He replaced the reports in the file, he was that beat. He looked over at Aleksandra sitting at John's desk. She had her head down and was sound asleep. He plopped down in his chair and then rubbed his eyes. Before he knew it, he was also sound asleep. The Sergeant left the two officers sleeping in the office.

The two officers ended up sleeping in the office for the rest of the night, and General Campanelli only woke when one of the security guards came in the office to see why the lights were left on. "It's okay," he whispered in his defense and then added. "I'm working late."

"You didn't clear it with the front desk first you understand, General Campanelli Sir. I have to report this disregard to orders sir. Regs you know sir."

"Yeah, I know, do what you have to do and I'll clear everything up in the damn morning. We're going to sleep in the office for the rest of the night. Inform your Desk Sergeant of this for me please, mister. And order the desk Sergeant we're not to be further disturbed."

"Will do, sorry I woke you sir. I'll keep everyone quiet, sir. Is there anything I can get for you, sir?" the security guard asked, upset he woke the powerful General.

"No, I'm fine, just quiet please," General Campanelli grumbled as he closed his eyes again.

MONDAY, FEBRUARY 2ⁿᵈ, 1997.
THE PENTAGON, WASHINGTON D.C.

General John White was the first one to report in for duty, the Desk Sergeant immediately informed the Brigadier General his Commanding Officer, Lieutenant General Campanelli and the female Major was asleep in the office.

General White growled to himself, 'what the fuck's wrong with that damn asshole anyway? He's going to work himself to fucking death on me, dammit'. He stormed off to the office, but by the time he reached for the handle of the door to the office, he calmed down some. He turned and left for the mess to give them a little more time to sleep.

General Palmieri was the second one to appear in the mess hall, and he went right over to John and complained at him, "Well what the hell do you think about our fearless leader, General White? He's pushing too damn hard if he's down to sleeping at the fucking office now, General White Sir. You want to say something to him, or do you want me to bitch at him, sir?"

"I agree with you. What the fuck are we going to do about it though, sir?" John replied to General Palmieri, knowing neither one of them were really going to get on the General's back about sleeping at the office.

"I'm not going to complain to him, instead I'm going to General Weidenbacher, and see if I can get him to order the damn General to calm down and back off some. I don't want this latest damn assignment to become the death of the bastard."

Colonel Locker came in the cafeteria next, smiling as she came over to the other two officers.

"I see you read the quiet sign left on the door of the office," John groused at her.

"Me, and everyone else who just showed up for work today saw it, John. I saw General Weidenbacher, and he's fit to be tied over it, sir. He's really pissed off Edward slept in the office last night, sir. I think he's going to do something about it as well, sir."

General Campanelli heard the light knock on the door and he jumped up. Then he paid the price for sleeping in the chair all night. His back gave him a shock as he tried to stand, he doubled over and then leaned on the desk with both hands for a moment.

"I brought you and the Major some coffee," General White offered as he placed the cup down.

He looked at his watch as he rubbed his face with his hands, and then he mumbled at his Second in Command, "gees, I must look like shit."

John did not reply, he just smiled at his Commanding Officer for a moment.

"Thanks a heep there my friend. I really needed that," he mumbled as he took a gulp of coffee.

Aleksandra was sitting up trying to fix her hair the best that she could with just her hands.

John handed her a cup of coffee and remarked kindly to her, "you look a hell of a lot better than my old friend over there does, young lady."

She smiled at him as she thanked John for the complement, and the coffee.

He sat back in his chair that screamed in protest as he asked his Second in Command, "anything going down in fucking funny land over the weekend, John?"

John knew what he meant and replied to his Commanding Officer, "naw, we didn't hear a peep from the President all weekend, sir. A few reports came in, and I placed them in your file, nothing immediate though, sir. But other than that, it was quiet as a Church."

"If you think a Church is quiet, you shoulda been with us yesterday General," he moaned as he told John he was going to drain a vein. The Major looked at John with questioning eyes.

"He's going to take a leak," General White informed the foreign female pilot.

"Oh. I see, thank you General White Sir," she replied as she blushed a little.

Campanelli headed for the bathroom, passed the sign warning everyone not to play with themselves, and he went right to the sink. He splashed some cold water on his face and then sucked in his breath as he looked at himself in the mirror and bitched, "ohhhh brother."

He washed up as best he could and then dressed and went back to his office feeling a little bit better about himself. He looked at John as he entered the office.

"It didn't help you very much I'm afraid sir," General White smirked as he grinned at him.

"Fuck you and the horse you rode in on, John. You don't have anything fucking better to do with your damn time around here but look at me and bust my stinking horns like this, buster?"

Both military officers laughed as General Campanelli took his seat, and then he let out his breath in a rush and a deep sigh at the same time.

"I better warn you Eddy, General Weidenbacher knows you slept in the office last night and he was griping about it earlier, sir. He's going to come after you later today I'm afraid, my friend. I felt I should warn you about it before you were blindsided by him," John offered.

"General Weidenbacher would complain about a fucking blowjob if you ask me, John. If he's not bitching then he's not happy, my friend." General Campanelli complained, and then he looked around the office and asked his General, "where the hell's the Major at?"

"She went to clean up some, she left the office after you did Eddy," he smiled back at him.

"What now?" Campanelli asked his grinning friend as he stared back at him for a moment.

"Shit, I guess you're going to hafta make me ask you, Campey. How's she in bed old man? Do foreigners do it any better than our women do, Eddy?" John asked Campanelli seriously.

"Christ sake John, what a helluva of a fucking question to ask me old buddy."

"Yeah, and I noticed you didn't answer the fucking question either my old friend."

General Campanelli suddenly wheeled his chair a little closer to John's desk, and then he leaned forward and whispered low to his friend, "John, I'll tell ya this man, she fucks like a damn bunny, buddy. Two, three, maybe even four times a fucking day sometimes, man."

John was starting to get into it with his Commander and was saying yeah to everything Campanelli whispered to him, as he got excited himself.

"Yeah, I'm telling ya true man, and head, she gives the best head I ever had. Like a fucking Hoover deluxe, with two speeds mind you John," he offered with a grin of his own to his friend.

John's head was just inches away from General Campanelli's forehead now as he was eating every word he uttered to him up. Suddenly, John leaned back and looked in his eyes, and then he bitched at him, "Hey man, are you fucking around with me here buddy?"

"No way in hell, I'm telling you true man. She even gave me a blowjob in the fucking car, all the while we were heading up to Jersey, buddy. When she's dressed in fucking civvies, she never wears any stinking underwear, I can slip in there any time I wanna man."

"Shitttt," John said as he was really getting excited now. He stood and then tried to straighten out the front of his pants, but with little success. He was getting so turned on by Campanelli's words as he went back to listening to what he was telling him.

The General noticed the bulge in his pants and laughed as he added to the obviously excited officer, now that he had him right where he wanted him, "why you lousy sonofabitch you, look at your black ass man, you're really getting off on this fucking shit, man."

"Fuck you Eddy. Tell me more about her and how she is in fucking bed, man. She's real hot looking man," John snapped back at his long time friend.

"One more thing I gotta tell ya about her John. Come here, no, no, get a little closer, closer to me than that man. I don't want anyone else but you to hear this last part, man."

John leaned in real close, and when Campanelli suddenly cut a long loud fart, forcing John to jump back in his chair and bitched, "I fucking knew it, you're bullshitting me all along, you sonofabitch you. Aaahhh gees, you really had me going there for a while you little prick you."

Their conversation was cut short as the other members of the Command Staff started to file into the office, all glanced at their Commander as if they knew something he did not. General Campanelli notice John was using every excuse under the sun to go out of his way to speak with the stunningly beautiful female Major in the outer office, and he laughed to himself. The day was long and boring and every once in a while, he would glance at the local newspaper he found in the bathroom a little earlier, and he brought it with him back to his office.

Lunch came, and everyone except John and Aleksandra went out for something to eat. John was talking to Campanelli when Aleksandra sat down across from them and from then on. John kept trying to look up the Major's uniform skirt. It did not take long for her to realize what he was up to, and finally she spread her legs so he could see all of what he was looking for.

John almost swallowed his tongue when he found out the General was not lying to him, when he told him she did not wear any underwear. General Campanelli saw his chance and he whispered at General White, "you see dopey, I fucking told you so, stupid."

John wiped his lip with a finger and smirked back at the General, "yeah man, but I didn't believe you, you little fucker you. You're always bullshitting on me lately, old buddy of mine."

Aleksandra snapped at the two laughing Generals, "you tell him, I hope two child see enough want see of me? Or want me strip nude for you two stupid fool?"

"A little strip show would be very nice right about now Major," John replied with a smile.

She moved over to John and smacked him behind his head as she announced she was going to get something to eat. But before she could leave, General Weidenbacher stepped in the office and blocked her way as he bitched and Campanelli in an angry voice, "what's all this crap I heard about you sleeping in the god damn office last night, General? You might as well know I just gave the security guards strict orders to pick your sleeping ass up, and deposit it outside in the fucking snow if you ever try that bullshit again, mister. You got it General Campanelli Sir, you listening to me mister?" he did not wait for Campanelli's reply as he added to his angry words, "your damn command ship, the Blue Whale's set in position off the west coast of Taiwan, General Campanelli. The rest of the ships attached to this operation will be there ahead of schedule. You prepared to ship out on Friday morning, mister? What am I asking, you and the rest of your staff will be ready to ship out on Friday morning, General Campanelli Sir."

"Yes sir, my staff and I will be ready to ship out by that time, General Weidenbacher Sir."

"Good General Campanelli, I'll have your damn aircraft put on the ready alert for Friday morning then at exactly Oh, Seven Hundred Hours, mister. I want your ass and the rest of your crew out of my fucking building by no later than Oh, Eight Hundred Hours General, that's when I want to be rid of you. Correct that last statement, I'll have your office and Command Staff transferred out to the damn ship on Thursday morning, so they can have your CIC (Command Information Center) set up by the time you arrive on the Blue Whale. How are you today Major?" General Weidenbacher asked as he turned and gave the Major a quick wink of the eye.

"Very well sir, thank ask me General Weidenbacher Sir," she purred back at him.

"Hmmm... you're lucky I'm an old man young lady. Or you'd really have something to worry about Major," he smiled at her as he spun around and left the doorway he was blocking.

"I go get something eat now General Campanelli Sir," she suddenly announced as she smiled back at the General, feeling a little uncomfortable over the way the conversation was going between the two powerful Generals over her.

"You better be damn careful of that dirty old man lurking about out in the hallway, Alex. He's old but he's still dangerous young lady," General Campanelli called out after her.

"Is he any different than two you any General Sir," she shot right back at him as she had to sidestep in order to get by the smiling General Weidenbacher who was still just about standing in the doorway of Campanelli's staff command room while speaking to another officer.

Both men laughed at the remark as General Campanelli added to his Second in Command, "I guess she's got a pretty good point there John."

John came back with, "no way in hell, I'm a helluva lot dirtier than he is, young lady."

A security guard entered the office with a report in his hand and he announced smartly "General Campanelli Sir, this just came in and I believe it's important sir."

He took the paper and then dismissed the guard with a mere flick of his hand. It was no big deal, the report informed the Command that Admiral Owens took Command of the two Aircraft Carriers, the Washington and Eisenhower. The report further stated the Carrier Roosevelt, with Admiral Owens aboard, stationed itself on the east coast of Taiwan, and he ordered the Carrier Washington to the west coast of Taiwan and the Eisenhower to the south end of the small Island. All three Carrier Strike Force Groups were stationed twelve miles off the coast of the Island.

The Commander let out his breath as he looked at John, and then he offered with a touch of concern in his voice, "I'm damn glad that old sea dog's on the Ocean. Commander

Owens took Command of the situation, and he stationed the Carriers where they'd be the most use to our upcoming operation," he glanced over the rest of the reports then complained at his Second in Command, "John, I don't know how many support ships there are connected with each Carrier Battle Group. I'd think that information should be added to these reports when they're sent, sir."

"Christ Ed, you can't know everything about this massive operation you know, man. Leave some of the shit for the others to take Command of will ya please, sir."

"I think it's necessary to have this fucking list at my disposal at all times John. So I know exactly which ships I can call on if needed, and where they are when I call for them, John."

"Very good sir, if you feel you really want them then you'll have them, Eddy."

General Campanelli looked at the report one last time. Then he screwed it up into a tight roll, and he tossed it at the overflowing waste can, only to have it miss completely and it ended up resting on the floor along with three other misses of his.

"Dammit, it looks like I'm going to have to get someone to empty my damn waste can for me pretty soon mister," he complained at John.

"Don't look at me buddy. I gots me a damn raise, and I no longer hasta dump waste cans. I's only hasta polish yuren shoes Masure," John said as he bowed towards his Commander.

"Get the hell outta here will ya before I hop you in the damn ass, you nut you," he yelled as he threw a pencil at the big man.

"Yes Masure, yes Masure. Please no gets the whips out Masure. I do your bidding Masure. Please don't beat me no mo Masure," John said and left the room to get something to eat.

The rest of the day went by uneventfully, and General Campanelli was never so pleased to see a day finally come to an end, as he was with this one. He took Aleksandra out to eat, and when she went to her room, he stayed behind and canceled his room. He then went upstairs and moved his stuff over to her suite. He never discussed this move with the Major though, and he was surprised by her angry reaction he received when he walked into her room.

"What this you do here, Mista Big Shot Commander you?" she snapped angrily at him as he carried his bag into her room.

"I thought it'd be a good idea for me to move my stuff in your room. There's no sense paying for two rooms when we're only using one, is there Alex?" he offered with confusion.

She put her hands on her hips, just the way Mendoza always did whenever she was upset over something, and his heart instantly skipped a beat when he saw her stance. But the fire in her eyes did not allow him to linger on the memory long.

"No you think should discuss over move you with me first, before move you shit my room like this, mista?" she nearly roared at the stunned looking General.

"C'mon will ya please. What's the big fucking deal anyhow Alex?" he moaned at her.

"I tell you what big deal is about all, mista. Suppose I no want you live in room with me like you want do, mista? You hell of nerve have assume I just allow you move with me in just like that, buster. A hell nerve I tell you think you have to just do this, mista."

"Yeah, and you're starting to get on that fucking nerve too, young lady. What the hell's the problem anyway, Alex? You don't want me here, just say the word and I'll go back to my damn suite, sister. Neither one of us are going to need these damn rooms after Friday anyhow, Alex. Forgive me because I was guilty of trying to save my government a little damn money. Why the hell don't you back off and let things go as they are?" he snapped hotly at her.

"Why arrogant thing you are, mista. I no want live you with me now Mista General buster. You live in back alley I care for you sleep there like old alley cat. You America all like I see. You America think own you world mista," she spat her words at him.

The concerned General suddenly allowed a slight smile to cross his lips, as he put on a sheepish look at the same time, and then he tried to purr like she always did whenever he was mad at her, or whenever she wanted him to do something for her.

She ignored his attempt to be funny, and she growled angrily at him a second time,. "out of room until learn how treat woman well proper, mista."

"Awww come on will ya please, dammit. It's cold out there, I might freeze to death you know, Major. Hell, it's even snowing out there Alex," he pleaded with her this time.

"I no care you do freeze death, you big jerk you. Out my room immediate or I get angry! No worry snow outside, you stay in old room fool," she growled at him as she stared at him.

The grinning General knew he had her now she was responding to his conversation, as he went on with his words, "who the hell is gonna keep you warm tonight while you're sleeping, young lady? Remember how cold it was last night don't you, Alex?"

"no hand me that line of bull poop, mista. Last night sleep in car then you office in. You take me great date out, big time spender you. Sleep in car then office, pew."

"True, true, but were you cold last night honey?" he added in his own defense this time.

"Yes cold, and you nothing do help me be warm, mista. I get warn furry slipper and keep me warm you could better Big Time Spend you," she added as he hardened her glare at him.

He smiled again as he retorted while still smiling at her, "maybe so, but your damn slippers could never make love to you like I can, baby."

"Do no flatter youself so much Big Time Spend you. I cucumber do good you, and never let me down when I need most, and I no have sleep in wet spot after you finish make love me."

He fringed shock and warned her at the same time, "if I ever catch you using a fucking cucumber, I'll stick it up your ass sideways, baby."

"You think so smart you all time, General big shoot. You no scare me in little bit mista," she said as she took a pillow off the couch and threw it at him.

He knew he really had her and jumped her and pulled her to the floor, and then he pulled her blouse over her head and took off her bra and threw it on the couch. He pulled at his shirt as she undid her skirt, and stood up naked with her hands on her hips. He had his pants off then watched as she went in the bathroom and he followed her. They made love in the shower again.

When he was finished with his shower, he wrapped a towel around himself, and then he sat down on the couch as he put on the TV, and watched MTV. He listened to the Aerosmith song playing, it was great, and the next two songs stunk, so he switched over to the adult channels. He smiled as he watched two women as they were taking care of one lucky ass guy sitting on a couch, and he got a hard on again.

She noticed the women on the screen, "you like two women on you once time mista?"

He opened the towel and offered her with a wide grin on his lips, "well whatdaya think lover. I'm as hard as Chinese algebra."

She saw he was stiff and said, "you crazy America, I love it so much."

They made love on the couch, and he ended up on the floor trying to decide if he wanted to sleep there. The next thing she knew, he was snoring away while on the floor.

"Oh no you do not this time I tell you good, mista. I sleep in real bed tonight this time with you mista. No like last night in stupid car or in our office fool!" she tugged and pulled on his arm and he groaned back at her, "what's the matter, you have enough of the fucking bed."

"Get up you old fool you. You no sleep in bed, you sleep on dom floor, you big dummy you," she complained as she continued to tug on the sleepy General's arm again.

The exhausted military officer woke just enough to get up and make his way to the bed, with her help though. Once in bed, she went out and saw the door was not closed, and she became embarrassed. She wondered if any of the neighbors watched them making love on the floor. Still naked, she snuck over to the door and closed it, and then she picked up his clothes and laid them on the couch neatly. She hummed as she straightened his clothes and warned herself.

'Girl, you're starting to fall for this crazy American officer. You better think good at what you intend to do about it'.

She got up and went in the bedroom, pushed him to one side of the bed and then she slid under the covers. She continued to examine her thoughts and admitted to herself she was never as happy as she was when she was with this good looking American Commander. She smiled at the thoughts of falling in love with him and living the rest of her life in the United States, the land of plenty. She thought of a number of different ways to make him love her even more. She gazed at him sleeping next to her and she warned him in a whisper. "You have no chance mista, you'll be mine for the rest of your life."

She failed to notice the slight smile that crossed his lips as he faked sleep, while he was waiting for her to come back to bed with him. She wiggled under his arm, and then she looped her leg over his and fell fast asleep in mere moments. She felt so secure sleeping with this American Officer, at least here she did not have to worry about the secret police come bursting in her room, and taking her off to jail for no reason other than to use her body as their play toy. The training was not all that bad, but the police took full advantage of the young trainees, and sexually assaulted them any time they desired or wanted sex. The police made the women do horrible things to them, and even to other women in the prison.

All the time, the police would tell them they might have to seduce a female as well as a male when they were out working on an assignment for their government, and they better know how to do it properly if they wanted to successfully follow their orders. She remembered the police yelling terrible orders on what they should do to another woman. It was horrible to remember, she never liked to make love to a woman, especially to have a man standing over her shoulder, and ordering her what and how to do something, made the act all the more repulsive to her. Yes, she was pleased to be out of the Communist influence, she closed her eyes as a tear suddenly escaped her eye, and then she fell asleep.

CHAPTER 13
TUESDAY, FEBRUARY 3rd, 1997

General Edward Campanelli's office at the Pentagon was a beehive of activity on this day, with the General supervising the packing of his files in their secured lock boxes, for shipment out to the Blue Whale tanker ship. His scrambling and decipher machine was secured and stowed away, and ready to go under strict security to the ship. His code book was locked securely beneath the decipher machine. John had his papers securely locked and ready to go. General Weidenbacher arranged for Campanelli to use the decipher and scrambling machine in General Claiborne's office, if he needed one until he shipped out to his new post on the ship. It was a pain, but he got used to it easy enough, because his office was a mess now the security guards were coming in and out carrying his file cabinets, maps, machines and the likes.

With all this commotion happening, General Campanelli decided to sit down in the Command Center of the Pentagon for a little piece of mind and quite. As he sat daydreaming, one of the televideo communication screens suddenly flashed in a color test pattern with the words.

"PLEASE STAND BY FOR SPECIAL COMMUNICATION FROM THE WHITE HOUSE."

General Edward Campanelli immediately straightened up, behind him the two oak doors flew open, and Generals Weidenbacher and Claiborne stormed in the room, and they quickly took their seats. Weidenbacher saw Ed and moaned at him, "Jesus Christ, how the hell did you get here so damn fast, mister? I just sent a runner out for your ass, General. Come on over here and sit by me. This Flash concerns you the most I believe, General Campanelli."

He moved closer to the General as he sat down he asked, "what's up sir."

"Dunno for certain at the moment sir, I just got the fucking Flash message myself mister," General Weidenbacher griped and then he looked at the screen.

The doors opened again and Manning strolled down the walkway this time like he owned it.

"Shit, what the fuck's that sack of crap doing in here for crap sake sir?" General Campanelli moaned to General Weidenbacher as he glared at the civilian advisor.

General Weidenbacher grabbed his arm and squeezed it as he warned him in no uncertain terms, "you better calm the fuck down some if you know what's good for you, General Campanelli Sir. The Man read him the riot act, and he's been almost human since the President really got on his damn ass, sir. He's even been helping me for the past two days, Ed."

Campanelli glared angrily at Manning, he smiled back as he gave a slight nod to the Generals.

"I really hate that scumbag with a god damn passion General," he growled at Weidenbacher.

"You better back off on him some like I just warned you, or you're going to be knocking heads with the President over that lousy little prick mister," he again warned Campanelli.

General Campanelli slowly sat down in his chair and then he allowed himself to relax some.

The center screen test pattern disappeared, and it was instantly replaced by the President's concerned looking face. His hands clasped together and he seemed somewhat upset, and he began speaking right off, "Gentlemen, I sent for you because actions have taken place that I feel you must be made aware of. As we speak, there's a major skirmish raging between the Chinese and Russian border guards. I was informed it started half an hour ago. It seems a small patrol of Chinese troops somehow locked horns with a North Korean patrol. From the reports I received, the Korean's took off for the Russian border once they found themselves cut off by the Chinese troops. The Korean soldiers dug in near the Russian border and, as usual, a Russian got hit by a stray round. They, the Russian's then opened fire on the Chinese troops attacking the trapped North Korean soldiers. It's a helluva mess, but one we were half expecting."

President Cole took a quick breath and then began anew, "General Weidenbacher, I sent for you because I ordered

General Palmieri to get the 75th Rangers in the air. I spoke to the Russian Ambassador Nicholas Antich, and I offered him this detachment of Rangers to help support his border guards. He agreed with my offer, and I want the Rangers in the area to help keep an eye on what's happening, and maybe cut off something that could get out of hand on us, if our troops were not present at the Russian border sir. I gave the Rangers permission to fire on Chinese, or Korean troops under the ROE Rules of Engagement if they come under attack from either group. That's why General Palmieri's not sitting in on this briefing, he's attending to business."

"What is it you want us to do Mr. President Sir?" General Weidenbacher asked the man.

"I want you to push up our entire operation to its earliest possible move out time, General Weidenbacher Sir. I want everything set in place PDQ sir," President Cole looked at General Campanelli, and then he snapped at him. "You sir, I want you set in place yesterday, mister. How the hell close are you from shipping out for the Platform, General Campanelli Sir?"

"Mr. President Sir, I should be good to go as scheduled on Friday morning at the latest sir," he reported to his Commander in Chief

The President sat back in his chair, and then he remarked at his officer, "I'm afraid that's not good enough for my wants, General Campanelli Sir. I want your operation in full gear by that date sir. I repeat sir, how soon can you ship out to that damn Platform thing, mister?"

He immediately caught the President's demand and thought for a second, and then he replied to the Commander in Chief sharply, "Mr. President Sir, I'm good to go at this moment if you please, sir." He looked at his watch and then added to his words, "I mean I could be on my way by

Eighteen Hundred Hours today if need be, Mr. President Sir."

The President clasped his hands together, and then allowed his elbows to rest on the arms of his chair as he remarked to his young military officer with a snap in his voice, "okay General Campanelli Sir, this is exactly what I want you to do from this point on, sir. Tomorrow morning will be soon enough for you to get going, sir. You'll use any people you need to get your office and command structure out to the Blue Whale tanker ship, sir. You can have all your people work right through the damn night if need be, General Campanelli Sir. I want you on that damn ship by tomorrow morning at the very latest, you got it sir?"

"Yes sir, I'll be on my way by no later than Oh, Seven Thirty Hours, Mr. President Sir."

"Talk English to me will you please General, give me time in English, not in military terms, sir. It's been years since I last used hours General Campanelli," the President snorted at him.

He straightened up and responded properly to his Commander in Chief, "yes Sir Mr. President Sir, sorry sir. I could be on my way by seven thirty tomorrow..."

The President held up his hand to silence the General as he cut him off in mid-sentence, "I have orders I want you to carry out first, General Campanelli. I'm having a B-1B Rockwell bomber ordered out to Langley Air Force Base today sir, and I'll have your papers and equipment placed on board her. This way, I can get you to Guam much faster, General. The B-1B's the fastest ship that'll hold your entire command party at one time, sir. You'll never get your Osprey packed and out to Guam, so I'll have that aircraft leave immediately, so it can ferry you out to the Blue Whale once you're on the Island of Guam, sir. General Campanelli, I know this is an inconvenience, but I don't give a shit. I need you and your people set in place yesterday, sir."

General Weidenbacher made a move to show the President he had something else to say, and he turned his attention to the military officer and asked, "General Weidenbacher Sir?"

He stood and replied right off, "with all due respect Mr. President Sir, I'm rather concerned about the Army Rangers being attached to the damn Russian border guards, sir. What's their duty and who'll command these troops in Russia, sir?"

"I already informed you during this conversation General Weidenbacher. The Rangers are going to attack any hostiles who threaten them, or the Russian soldiers they are detached to sir. I don't want the damn Russians to engage any hostile troops themselves. I feel if they do, things will rapidly get out of hand fast on us, sir. At least I'll control the Rangers, and if I tell them to stop their attack, they'll do as ordered immediately, sir. I have no such control over the Russian guards, General Weidenbacher Sir. In this way, it allows me some form of control at what's happening at the Russian, Chinese border sir," the President glared at the General for making him go over something he thought he already explained.

The President turned back to General Campanelli and added, "you, you're the Supreme Commander of all combat troops and their support units in this Asian region, sir. If I like the way you're operating General, I'll give you that last star, sir. The future of Asia, and perhaps the world will rest in your hands General Campanelli. Don't fuck it up on us sir."

He smiled back at the seated President on the large screen.

"Okay, now that much has been settled, I suggest you get out of here sir, and get to your office and see what's happening there, General Campanelli. Get your civilian affairs in order, because you'll not be returning to the States until North Korea's sterilized, and we find out what other intentions China might have in mind, sir. We may have to fight them too before this mess runs its course, sir. I hate like hell the United Kingdom's currently sleeping with the damn Chinese on this one General Campanelli, but ever since the Chinese told One Downey Street they were thinking of allowing the English to actually purchase the Colony of Hong Kong out right from them. Nothing China has done since has upset England in any way, shape or form on us, sir."

Campanelli immediately left the room, pleased to be getting away from the angry President.

General Weidenbacher responded to his Commander in Chief words over the United Kingdom and their actions so far in the Asian affair, "Mr. President Sir, I don't think the United Kingdom would ever go against anything we decided to do in the region, sir. No matter what the Chinese might offer her in the short term, sir. The United Kingdom has been too good an Ally through to many years, for them to go and leave our side now sir."

"Maybe so General Weidenbacher, but I wish to hell and back I had your confidence about this damn situation though, sir. I don't feel that confident about the United Kingdom and China being so damn chummy together sir," the concerned President put his head down and then he let out his breath in a sort of sigh.

General Campanelli stepped back to his office, only to see the place a complete mess. All the security guards were rapidly packing up his papers into special lock boxes, and then loading them on heavy four wheeled metal platforms.

He was amazed his office had accumulated so much paperwork in so short a time period. A guard accidently backed into him as he tugged on an overloaded platform truck, growling before he knew who he was yelling at.

"Will you get out of the way, dammit. Can't you see me moving this damn shit the hell outta the office?" the angry security guard snapped, and then he looked over his shoulder. He immediately let go of the hand truck and snapped to attention and immediately apologized.

"Sorry General Campanelli Sir, I didn't realize who was blocking my way, sir. I have orders to get this equipment shipped out to Langley from the President ten minutes ago, sir."

"Yeah I know your orders so see to them, mister. You look like you just shit yourself, didn't ya buster?" he then smiled at the soldier, as he instantly stepped out of his way. When he was aside, the security guard grabbed hold of the overloaded hand truck, and then he tugged hard on it to get it moving forward again.

He knew the soldier would have picked up the hand truck and carry it off on his back, just so he could get out from under his angry glare. He laughed as he entered the office to make certain everything he needed was going to be moved out of the office.

General John White was standing right in the center of the room of sheer mayhem, and he was dishing out orders to anyone working in the room by him, "hey you that goes along with this bunch of fucking papers and crap over here buddy. Here, put this crap on that damn hand truck over there will ya, soldier. I need another damn lock box moved over here for this other shit I have stacked on that counter, someone. That's important papers and I have to be protected from any possible prying eyes, dammit."

General Campanelli acknowledged his presence to John, who immediately worked his way over to him and complained, "man Eddy, what the fuck happened? Are we at war or what buddy? Who the hell are all these stinking shitheads in here for crap sake sir? One minute I was working at my desk, the next minute a flood of guards and CIA Spooks charged into the room and were pushing me outta the damn way, and packing up my papers and security machines, and moving the damn things out on me, sir. Are we still the Command Staff, or did something go wrong, and we got dumped outta the operation, sir?" John asked in an excited voice.

"Christ sake John, will you calm down a little please. We're still the man for this action, some shit happened and we're moved up a little, that's all John. We're leaving for the Island of Guam by Oh, Eight Hundred Hours tomorrow morning, sir. Look my friend, you better bug the fuck outta here and get home. Play a little patty cake with your lady, and let her know you're gone as of tomorrow morning, buddy. I don't want Beth to find out at the last moment, sir."

"Don't go worrying about her, she's used to this kinda shit, sir. Here today, gone tomorrow Ed. I wanna know what the hell happened to stir up so much action this time?" John replied.

"China just attacked North Korea, and the North Koreans were smart enough to scramble their asses towards the Russian border, once they found themselves cut off by the attacking Chinese forces, sir. The Chinese troops kept dogging the North Korean asses, and they ended up firing on some of the Russian guards. The Russians responded with artillery and rockets and small arms fire, it got a little hairy for a few hours, but the last reports I read stated the fighting stopped, and the Russians took the North Korean soldiers prisoners. The President's sending a detachment of Rangers over to Russia as support troops, and a sorta buffer force. He made some good sense to me when he said he could order the Rangers to stop fighting, but he was powerless to order the Russian troops to stop fighting if more stupidity breaks out in the region, sir."

"Sounds like pretty good sense to me General. But we're still sending United States Rangers to Russia, sir. Is that a wise idea Eddy?" he asked as he shook his head slowly.

"Sure is, we're getting more of our first strike forces set in this damn region without any serious fighting taking place. Think of it John, to have more of your forces set in place if and when needed, is the best possible situation you could ever ask for when fighting on some other land, sir." General Campanelli waited for the information to sink in.

"Yeah, I see what you're driving at sir. But I'm still rather uncomfortable about having some of our Army Ranger's linking up with the damn Russian border guards sir," he remarked as he absorbed the new information from his Commanding Officer.

The two military officers were forced to move out of the way by a security guard, as he entered the room with an empty hand truck. One guard came over to the two officers and suggested they both go and get some coffee and get out of the way.

Campanelli looked to John and then shrugged. As they were leaving the office, they heard someone running up behind them. They turned and saw Aleksandra rushing at them and she called out, "where you two bird go now, and how come no you ask me along with you please? I no long have place to work from. I feel like thrown out in cold by you security guards."

John was all for her coming along with them, he wanted her around him so he could sneak a peak up her dress again, as he offered to the beautiful female fighter pilot, "we're going for some coffee, you can come along if you want, in fact, I want you to come along Major."

"Just as long as you keep your dress hitched up and your legs spread," Campanelli added.

She turned to General Campanelli and asked him, "what you say to me sir?"

"Nothing, I was just clowning around with you a little that's all, you coming along Alex?"

She shook her head and then she fell in line with the two American Officers and friends.

The coffee room was nearly empty, and the General took a corner table for them to use.

No one spoke, both John and Aleksandra could tell Campanelli was more than a little antsy. They both watched him chow down his burger, and then suck down his Pepsi in a rush. John took the lead and said to his Commanding officer, "say Eddy, I think I'm going to take you up on that last order to go home a little early, and making nice nice to my wife, sir. You know, one of the boys have been giving Beth some grief about school lately, and I was going to take the time to get his sails set right to the wind again for his little ass. I guess I better have that talk with him before I ship out later on tonight sir." John offered as he stood up from the table.

General Campanelli stopped drinking long enough to share some wisdom with his old friend, "ahhh... yes, teenagers, God's punishment against us adults for enjoying sex man."

All three military officers laughed at his remark as John went to leave, and he said, "I hafta remember that one and share it with my wife, Eddy." He then walked over to the soldier behind the counter and paid for the coffees and then left for the day.

Major Aleksandra Klevekaita remarked to General Campanelli as they watched John leave the lunchroom in a rush, "You amaze sir. All time I grow up in Lithuania, I told by Russia control white man and black man in America no get along good never all the time. I attend training class told us be patient, wait long enough, see great America land crumble under weight of civil war between black and white man. I see they teach wrong all time me. I find amaze so many soldier get along no matter who deal with, Black man, White man or even woman. I see there never be civil war in America again over race like told many time over year. I like what see about United State so long. I no think I want ever go home until my country come up America standards. We worst than you country ever is, we hate same race people just because they come different town, or come out mountain instead live in city all time, sir.

"We have no problem of race our country, because we have little black people live there in Lithuania. We just hate other Lithuanian, and is worst any kind racial hatred different races, General Campanelli," she shook her head sadly as she took a quick breath in, and then she continued. "Oh, I no know what mean any far. I want live life America if can, sir."

He had to swallow, she used the same phase Mendoza used whenever she became stumped in a conversation, even though she left out the 'don't' in the phase as he replied to her words, "Look Major, are you telling me you want to defect to the United States?"

She smiled as she replied to his last question of her, "I happy defect if had someone nice live with, General

Campanelli. Someone like you live with and be happy with, sir."

He tried to act like he did not understand what she just said to him as he remarked, "are you trying to make a pass at me or what, Major?"

"I no know what mean make pass you mean? I no walk any no where here, General Sir. What you mean I make pass by you for, sir?"

Ed laughed, "I mean, are you trying to pick me up. Are you asking me to live with you?"

She smiled again as she announced in a much happier tone of voice this time after she realized what he was talking about, "for suppose smart America Officer you thick big head you know, sir. I know what mean try pick up now, mista. I want stay in United State here, I want loved by good man. I want live free, do what think, what say what want do all time, sir. I tired military life, want live like other woman of world do all time. Get pregnant, raise family, and make home and stop have someone look over back all time, and order me what do all time, sir." She looked like she was suddenly on the verge of tears as she stared at her Commanding Officer.

"You know something young lady, I just might be able to help you out with this little problem of yours. It's funny girl, but I was thinking very much the same thing you know. That I was getting kinda tired of living the military way and life. I don't know if I'm really ready to live with a foreigner though, and I'm still legally married you know Major."

She purred as she said, "I make forget you all marry, big American soldier you."

Ed rubbed his eye as he moaned, "I just bet you could at that young lady. I think we can work something out here to the satisfaction to the both of us. You wanna stay in the

United States, and I can fix that by giving you my last name, Alex. That'll automatically make you an American citizen you know. I have a home in Carmel, New York and another one in Florida. I can give the house in New York to my wife, and take the home in Florida. You'll have a house, and just think of all the damn fun we could have trying to make some children. Yeah, I think we can work something out we can both live with. After all, you're kinda easy on the eyes Alex."

She cocked her head to the side as she asked him, "easy on eyes? What that mean by easy on you eyes? You use word I no understand all time, Mr. big shoot you."

"Yeah, you're real good looking there Alex. We can make this thing work out for the both of us easy enuf I guess. But it's gonna be your job to convince me on just how much you really want to be an American, while we're stationed in Asia baby."

"Why have do all the work time all mista? I always have prove how much love you, big head mista you," she protested at the grinning General.

"It's only fair, look at what I'm bringing to this here relationship, young lady. I have a home, the name you need to become a United States citizen, and I know the language as well baby," he looked at her until he could no longer hold a straight face and suddenly laughed at her.

She cried at him, "oh, you pull wool over shoulders me on I see, this joke, no?"

"It's a joke yes, and I'd love to have you move in with me, but we have to put everything on the back burner for the time being, until this damn operation's over with honey. Another thing I should tell you about before you find out about it yourself baby. My government pays rather handsomely for any defectors who want to live in the United

States. You'll be well paid, and well taken care of, even if you don't wanna have anything to do with an old man like me."

"You no old man, you good look man for America I see. You easy on eye too, I think take you please," she replied as she looked deeply in his eyes.

"Gees, thanks a helluva lot there young lady. I think I just got hit with the bad end of the stick. You have any other slugs you wanna take at my ass before we get the hell outta here, baby?" General Campanelli moaned as he tried to look like he was just insulted.

A security guard showed up at the door and he informed the powerful military officer. "General Campanelli Sir, I hate like hell to bother you like this sir, but we need you back at the office sir. You have to unlock your file cabinet from the floor chain for us, so we can load it up for immediate transit out to the airfield, General Campanelli Sir."

"Shit, I forgot about the damn thing," he got up, followed by Aleksandra and they both headed for the office. He was amazed his room was almost completely emptied already. Everything was gone except for two file cabinets and the desks stacked one on top of the other in the center of the room. Even the phones had been removed from the room. General Campanelli walked over to the chain and unlocked it, and then he went to John's cabinet and unlocked his.

Four security guards quickly moved in, and they loaded the two heavy file cabinets onto one of the hand trucks. An armed CIA Agent stayed with the two guards at all times, and he followed them as they headed down the long hallway now.

Aleksandra remarked. "You America people careful very much I see all time, sir."

"Hafta be baby, you never know who might be working against you, Major. C'mon, I think we should get back to our room and pack up our stuff. I'll have the Sergeant come by with a truck so he can get our stuff out to the airport for us, Alex. I want to call my wife and let her know I'm shipping out again, honey. She deserves that much from me baby."

The two left the Pentagon, with General Campanelli driving the car for himself. His usual driver was going to get a pickup van, and meet them back at the hotel. It was late, he looked at his watch, it was ten minutes to three already. They rapidly packed up their belongings in two separate sea bags, and then they marked them personal belongings, and placed them aside. They would be stored until they returned to the United States from the Asian region.

Next, they packed up their uniforms and military items in two other sea bags, and did not mark them except with their names and ranks. Their bathroom articles were packed up together in another bag. They were done with their packing in no time, so the two officers had a little extra time to burn off before the Sergeant showed to pick up their belongings. So General Campanelli made a real pest of himself by sticking his hand down the front of Aleksandra's blouse, or hitching her shirt up and over her hips. She howled in laughter and delight in reply to the attention he was showering her with. Finally, he got her blouse off, and she started to run around the apartment topless. They did not notice the two other soldiers come in the room, they were so involved in making so much noise and having some fun at the same time.

She was actually standing on top of the bed doing a sort of can can dance with her dress hiked way up, and exposing herself to General Campanelli, when she happened to notice the Marine driver, and another soldier staring at her. She let her dress down, but made no attempt to cover her breasts by placing her hands on her hips, and then she stared at the two stunned looking soldiers standing in the center of the room now.

The General saw her looking at something, and he turned his attention in that direction and immediately offered to his driver and the other soldier with him, "ahhh... Sergeant, you made damn good time with getting your ass back here my friend. We were just having a little fun waiting for you to get back, Sergeant."

"Yes Sir General Campanelli Sir, I can see that for myself sir, and I found this other soldier walking around looking for you also, sir. He states you ordered him to report to you here today, sir. His name's Jim Cruz, sir. He's a security guard over at the Pentagon sir," the grinning Marine Sergeant replied to his Commanding Officer with some concern in his tone.

"Yeah, I remember him alright. Sergeant Cruz, how the hell you doing today son, and are you all pack up with your crap and ready to ship out with the rest of us? Because in case you're interested my friend, you're shipping out tomorrow morning along with us at Oh, Seven Hundred Hours at Langley mister," he warned the new Sergeant.

"Yes sir. I'm packed and am aware of my orders of being shipped out tomorrow morning, sir." The Sergeant snapped as he instantly turned and quickly left the room.

"Sergeant, you're coming with me too, buster. Do you have any problem with that last order, mister?" he actually snapped at the other Sergeant who was with him ever since he was first placed in Command of this operation.

"Sir?" the surprised looking Sergeant mumbled at the General.

"Yeah, I want you to be my personal aide while I'm in Command of this damn operation, mister. You'll be lifted up to Sergeant Major if you come along with my ass, mister."

"Yes sir," the suddenly happy Sergeant replied with a wide grin.

"Good Sergeant, I want you to store the seabags with tags with property until we return to the States. The other two bags are to go out to the airbase with the little bag sitting over there on the couch, Sergeant. Then I want you to go home and pack up your crap, and get ready to ship out with us tomorrow morning, Sergeant. You married mister? Please tell me you're not fucking married, Sergeant?" General Campanelli asked the Sergeant.

"No Sir General Campanelli, never was sir. I kinda like my freedom the way it is sir," he replied with a snap in his tone to his Commanding Officer.

"Good. It's better if you aren't married to be shipping out for this crap detail in the Asian region, mister. One never knows what might happen when one is ordered out on a military operation Sergeant," he remarked as Aleksandra climbed down from the bed, and then she moved the two bags around for the other soldier to take care of for them. She never once tried to cover herself up, and both men enjoyed the lovely view she was offering them as they worked on removing the officer's items from the hotel room. She shared a beer with the Sergeant, and they sat at the table after the other soldier left the apartment with the bags.

The two men were staring at her breasts, and she loved having them off stride and stumbling over all of their words and actions, just because she exposed her breasts to the two fools. She also enjoyed the attention the three men were giving her because she was showing them a little skin. Finally, she announced she was going to take a quick shower.

Neither man made a move as she quickly disappeared in the bathroom. Then, she was standing in the doorway completely naked and she grumbled at the General, "am I have wash own back now round here all time sudden, mista?"

"I'll do that for you honey," General Campanelli offered as he instantly jumped to his feet, and then he headed for the bathroom in a rush.

"If you don't do it General Campanelli then I'd be most pleased to volunteer for the duty sir," the Sergeant joked while watching the grinning General nearly run for the bathroom, and the stunningly beautiful woman in a rush who again disappeared in the bathroom. In seconds, he heard the water running in the shower and the two officers laughing and her screaming over what he was doing to her as they obviously showered together and he smiled.

He almost broke his neck running to the bathroom. The Sergeant smiled again as he gathered up the other bags for the officers going with them on the plane, and then he brought them out to the truck, and then drove off to his apartment. He was going to top off the load with his stuff, and then bring everything over to Langley.

The General would keep the staff car overnight, and then he would use it to drive out to the airbase in the morning when it was time for them to leave for the airbase and their next duty station. He left the number where he could be reached at the main desk of the Pentagon, just in case any new reports came in that needed his immediate attention, about anything erupting between China, North Korea and even Russia now.

No new reports came in, so he was able to get a full night's sleep for a change. Aleksandra was not going to allow the General to go to sleep until she had all she wanted from him first. After they made love, she was able to fall off to sleep.

Even though he was able to sleep without anyone interrupting his sleep because of something happening in the Asian region. The excitement of shipping out the next day, robbed the exhausted General of his sleep. He ended up spending most of the night staring at the ceiling, and listening to the rhythm of Aleksandra's breathing.

General Edward Campanelli showed up a little early at the Joint Edwards Airbase with Aleksandra in tow, she was neatly dressed in her Class A full dress Lithuanian uniform, and he in his Class A Army uniform. His chest was covered with twenty different campaign ribbons, announcing to the world of the many medals he had been awarded over his number of years of service. He looked good whenever he was dressed in his class A dress uniform, and this uniform made him look even better. But uniform or not, he was ill prepared for all the mayhem that immediately greeted him at the massive military airbase.

A horde of soldiers, civilians and excited CIA Agents alike were running in all directions, as security was kept high because of the B-1B bomber resting on the tarmac of the airfield. News leaked out the bomber landed, and reporters were all over the place, trying to take photos of the elite craft. More than once, General Campanelli was bumped by an excited reporter or camera crew, and he was getting pissed off over the situation, and when a second cameraman bumped into him, he gave the guy a hard shove away from him and he went sprawling to the ground in a heap. A reporter rushed over and helped the cameraman back up to his feet, and then he glanced over his shoulder and growled at the military officer who just shoved his cameraman. "What the hell's wrong with you buddy? Didn't you see my man trying to get by you, asshole?"

General Campanelli was not used to being talked to in this manner by anyone, and he responded angrily at the man doing all the complaining at him, "you fucking guys shouldn't be allowed on the damn airbase in the first place, Spudhead."

The reporter snapped back just as angrily as he glared at the man dressed in a military uniform, "and who the hell do you think you are buster? The fucking President or someone mister?"

He was still angry as hell as he warned the reporter who suddenly assumed a threatening pose against him, "go ahead motherfucker make your stinking move on my ass, so I can have your hospitalization kick in for ya ass, buster."

The reporter saw this officer was not backing down, and he did not want to get in a fight and lose his military pass. Besides, some security guards were heading for them to see what the hubbub was all about. The reporter stepped back and warned the angry looking General, "you make a move on me, and I'm going to hawk you up a new ribbon for your uniform, mister."

He ignored his crude remark, because he knew when the reporter took a step back, nothing more was going to come of the slight altercation. The cameraman was on his feet and pulling the reporter's arm, to get him out of trouble with the angry officer. He knew he would lose his press ID if his reporter got in any trouble with the military officer.

The General glared harshly at the two of them until they were completely out of his vision. Aleksandra grabbed his arm and leaned against him and remarked in a concerned voice, "what nasty man he be, sir. Are all America new reporter nasty he was sir? I no believe how rude that man just was to you, General Campanelli. He has no respect for good Military Officer, sir."

"Not really, most of the damn reporters are pretty good at what they do. It's just some of the younger ones are constantly trying to make a name for themselves, who are the nasty ones. You take a reporter like Jensen there's a professional, I'd stop what I was doing to speak with him."

More commotion stopped their conversation, as they watched a staff car pull onto the tarmac, and two Generals, and one Admiral quickly stepped out of the vehicle. The reporters instantly moved in on the new group of military officers, and they immediately shoved their microphones in their faces, in an attempt to get any possible information from them.

He laughed as he watched General Claiborne hunch up his shoulders and nastily slapped a microphone out of his face, and then he gave the reporter a harsh shove backwards with his hands. General Weidenbacher held his hands over his head and roared in a commanding voice at everyone gathering around him, "I don't know what the hell all you damn people are doing around here dammit, but nothing happening here I assure you people. It's just one of my Officer's going on a little training mission, that's all. It's no big deal people."

From out of the crowd of reporters, someone called out to the General, "sir, if there's no big deal then how come you have a modified B-1B bomber resting on the tarmac, sir? The last time anyone saw one of these babies up close and personal, it was during the war in the Middle East. Is the United States preparing for another such war, General?"

General Weidenbacher glared angrily at the reporter as he snarled at him, "don't be a god damn asshole, buster. Who the hell would we be going to war with for the love of God."

"General, we see a nest of other Officers gathering around on the base, sir. Are these Officers the ones going on this supposed new training mission, sir?"

Before the General had a chance to answer, another reporter cried out, "look, one's a Russian." All the reporters left Weidenbacher, and they ran towards Campanelli and Aleksandra.

The way the reporters charged towards her, Campanelli thought they were going to gang up on him for the way he treated one of the reporters earlier. He raised his hands and clenched them in fists, as he prepared for the onslaught. As the reporters circled the two, Aleksandra became scared and she actually tried to hide behind his back. Questions were shouted out loud and furiously at the female officer, and neither one of them could make out what was being yelled at them so quickly by so many excited reporters. Everything sounded like one huge roar.

The large group of news reporters completely ignored the American General as they rudely stuffed their microphones right in the Major's face, with one reporter after the other shouting out questions at the scared looking female officer. The General pushed a microphone out of her face and bent the shaft of another one, when the reporter accidently hit Aleksandra in the shoulder with it. Nothing dissuaded the horde of reporters.

One question the Major heard shouted at her made her respond angrily against the question. She was asked if she was a Russian Officer and she growled angrily at this reporter. "I no god dom Russia soldier, mista. I good Lithuanian pilot loan to you great government for special training with some of you fighter aircraft, mista."

More of the questions were shot back at her with a new intensity by the horde of excited reporters. "Why would we be training a Lithuanian pilot in the use of our military aircraft for? Is Lithuania going to become an Ally of the United States?"

General Campanelli answered this question with a snarl, "the last I knew, Lithuania is already an Ally of the United

States, as well as Russia is. Why the hell don't you people back off some and give us some room to move and think for crap sake, so we can get our job done!"

Another reporter called out in an excited voice, ignoring the General request. "Yes, and we want to know what that job is, General? Who are you anyway sir? Are you a General? I don't recognize you, and I know all the Generals stationed here in Washington, sir."

"My name's General Edward Campanelli people, and that's all you're gonna get from me."

"Hey, I know you, General Campanelli. Aren't you the guy that was in Command of the Middle East mess a couple of years back, sir? I'm certain that was you, General." Another news reporter called out over the voices of the masses talking at the same time.

"It's General Campanelli Sir to you buster. Yes, I was in Command of that operation mister."

"Then what the devil is an Army General doing with that Airforce B-1 bomber, sir?" the same news reporter called out this time.

CHAPTER 14

"If you must know what's happening in my life bud, I was happily retiring when the General," Campanelli pointed towards General Weidenbacher standing along with General Claiborne and Admiral Standlund. "asked me to reconsider my decision of retiring, he told me there was a place opening in training the next breed of troops in trench warfare. He's sending me to Germany in that there thing." This time he pointed at the bomber and added, "to check on the readiness of the troops stationed overseas, and to see what they may need in the way of any military equipment and manpower. I don't have to tell you of the threat coming from North Korea at this time, and we have to be prepared for any contingency."

"Are you saying you're going to Germany to increase the status of the troops stationed there sir? And if so, does this mean we may take a more active role in this budding Asia mess going down between North Korea and China, sir?" a female reporter called out this time.

Campanelli laughed at the remark because the woman was closer to the truth than she realized as he replied to her question, "you have an overactive imagination there for yourself, young lady. As I just stated, I'm going to Germany to review the troops there, and to make certain they don't need any extra military equipment, in case a war does happen to break out in Asia, or anywhere else in the world for that matter, Ma'am. Which we don't see happening in the very near future either may I add, young lady." He was starting to sweat a little, because he was not prepared to give a news briefing, and he was trying to mark his words very carefully as he spoke.

"General Campanelli Sir, you didn't answer the question of why our government's training the Lithuanian pilot for, sir. Doesn't the United States have enough of their own pilots to train, instead of taking the time to train some foreign pilots in the use of our aircraft sir?" the reporter who started the questioning called out this time to the General.

The General glared at the reporter and snapped at the abrasive female reporter, "you're getting to be a real pain in the damn ass whether you know it or not, young lady."

"You're sounding like her editor now, General," a rival reporter smirked at him.

She cut in and snapped, "very funny sir, but you still didn't answer my question, General."

General Weidenbacher had enough of the reporters and he suddenly pushed his way through the group and stood next to Campanelli and announced in an angry tone of voice, "the General didn't answer the question because he didn't know the answer to that question." He then turned to Campanelli and ordered him in no uncertain terms, "General Campanelli Sir, I'll take it from here, sir. It was the President and myself who discussed it and thought it a good idea to respond favorably to the request from the Lithuanian government to train some of their fighter pilots in our tactics and aircraft, Ma'am. Ever since the demise of the old Soviet Union, Lithuania, and a number of other countries from the Baltic region lost their airforce capabilities. The Lithuanian's contacted our government and informed us they'd be willing to buy some of our fighter aircraft, if we're willing to train their fighter pilots in the use of these certain aircraft, Ma'am.

"Now, I don't have to explain how bad a shape our economy's in, and a potential sale of this size would definitely help put more of our out of work Americans to work. This deal would also serve to strengthen our ties with the smaller countries that once made up the old Soviet Union. If you need any more questions answered in this area then I suggest you speak directly to the President. He knows a lot more about this deal than anyone else does, Ma'am."

General Weidenbacher turned back to Campanelli and warned him and saluted him at the same time, "you better get going then General Campanelli Sir. I don't want to keep the aircraft on the ground for any longer than is absolutely necessary at this point, sir."

The General's salute was returned by Campanelli, and he and the Major walked to the aircraft.

A horde of news reporters started to follow the officers towards the aircraft, but they were stopped by a number of armed MPs who informed them they were not allowed any closer to the specialized aircraft than they were currently standing. The reporters rushed back to where General Weidenbacher was still answering some of the reporter's questions.

"Sir, can we get some pictures of the inside the aircraft please?" a reporter asked the General.

"C'mon, you stinking shitbirds know better than to ask me that stupid a question. No one's going to get a picture of the cockpit of that aircraft buddy!" he said with a smile.

"Sir, can you please tell us where in Lithuania this female pilot comes from, and how long she's going to be on loan to the United States, General?" a second reporter called out to him.

He looked at his new inquisitor and then responded once he was able to pick the person out of the large crowd of other reporters, "I know she comes from the capital of Lithuania, Vilnius it is, and she is known to have flown the Russian SU-29, along with the Mig 31s. I think she even flew the Bear, the Soviets version of our B-52 bombers. She's a damn good pilot with plenty of flight time already, mister."

"If she has so much flight time in an aircraft already then why the hell are we wasting our time and money training her in flying, General Weidenbacher?"

"Christ Almighty you people are thick as a plank, that's Russian training I was speaking about, buster. We want to train her on the American fighter aircraft, Mac. If we're planning to sell her country our fighter aircraft then she has to know how to fly the damn things damn," he snapped as he turned his back on the reporter who just asked the dumb question.

General Edward Campanelli walked over to General Claiborne and the two officers watched General Weidenbacher interacting with the horde of news reporters.

"How was it over there sir?" the large black General asked the new General.

"Rough, I didn't expect to see any damn news reporters hanging around the airfield like this, sir. How the hell did they ever get permission to walk out on the damn tarmac, sir?"

"Arr... the pain in the ass reporters started to turn up right after the damn bomber touched down on the tarmac, sir. One day someone's gonna find out what type of stinking radar these motherfuckers, use to know what the hell we're doing. Even before we know it ourselves, for Pete's sake sir." General Claiborne complained to the other General.

Luther laid his hand heavily down on Campanelli's shoulder, and he could easily feel the weight of his arm, and wondered how strong this old man truly was, as Clay offered him with some worry lacing his voice. "General Campanelli Sir, I'm really sorry these damn jaybirds jumped on you like they did, sir. I had no way of warning you in advance they were staked out here, sir. Besides, the way the damn reporters had been hanging around every since this big bird landed. There was no way in hell of sneaking you two officers on board the damn aircraft on your way out to your Asian vacation, without the reporters picking you two up and then jumping on your backs like they did, Eddy."

Aleksandra stared at the massive aircraft with her mouth hanging opened, and her eyes glistering with awe. Nails picked up her amazement and laughed as he said to the foreign female pilot, "she sure is a big bird, isn't she Major? I bet you can't wait until you get inside that big bird and give her the good once over real close up like, Major."

"Yes sir. You bet boots I can no wait to see her controls, General Claiborne Sir. I dream of fly an aircraft of this size and capabilities sir," she replied as he moved in a little closer to her and she added to him. "I certainly like try fly her some if possible, sir."

"Let me see what I can do about that request for you, Major." General Claiborne said as he walked over to the pilots standing next to the crash truck charging the batteries of the aircraft. He engaged them in a conversation, he then returned to General Campanelli and Aleksandra and informed her, "you're in luck Major Klevekaita Ma'am, the pilot said he'd allow you to tickle the controls a bit when we're over the Pacific. You see, no sooner said than done, young lady."

He then turned to Campanelli. "You sir!" he growled as he stuck out a callused paw and shook hands with him and then added. "You look after yourself out there sir, and I'm still looking forward to that party you promised you were going to throw for me, mister. I want to mess up your carpet like you did mine, mister. Do you know the grief you caused me, getting sick on my wife's carpet like that, sir?" he slapped General Campanelli heavily on the back, almost knocking him forward a step as he continued. "All kidding aside mister, you watch your ass out there sir. This one could turn into one helluva damn mess on ya before you know it."

"Will do sir," The pleased General Campanelli replied as he smiled back at the rather large black General.

"C'mon, I'll take you aboard her so you can see what she really looks like inside." Claiborne put his arm out to show the two officers where they were to go aboard the specialized aircraft. He stood aside while Campanelli climbed up the narrow ladder into the bomb bay area of the huge aircraft. The General gave the Major a hand, he stood under the ladder until she was on top, and then he started up.

The Major knew what he was up to, and she called down to him, "do no look my skirt up sir."

The General's eyes were the picture of innocence as he offered the grinning female fighter pilot, "I assure you young lady I'd never stoop so low as to look up a Major's dress for a moment, Major Klevekaita. Especially when she's standing over me, so I don't have to stoop."

She laughed as she called down at him, "dirty old man are you not General Sir?"

"Yes Ma'am, and proud of it, and I'm going to be a dirty old man until the day I die, Ma'am."

General Campanelli lead the way down the walkway of the aircraft, and then to the door leading to the flight deck. He moved until he was standing alongside the pilot and co pilot's seats. He marveled at the comfort of the odd shaped chairs, they were almost like resting in a reclining position. Between the seats, there was a mass of dials, switches and gauges. Above their heads was the same thing, the windows were tinted, and they had a series of screens, that the pilots were to close when a nuclear device was detonated. It guarded them from the flash, that could lead to blindness if one looked directly at the detonation. The amazing aircraft had the smell of new, the navigator sat to the back of the co-pilot, and his wall was covered with small screens, along with many more dials and switches. The cockpit was smaller than it looked.

"Some fucking plane, huh Ed?" General Claiborne said proudly as he looked at the craft.

"Yes sir," she answered for the General as she enjoyed looking at the cockpit.

"I'll show you where your equipment and luggage is stored on board the aircraft, people."

General Campanelli followed Luther to the rear of the aircraft, passed the forward bomb bay section to the second bombay area. His computers and deciphering machines were strapped in securely for the long flight, and Claiborne informed him, "the flyboys had to remove the rotor Cruise Missile system, so you people would have this room for your equipment, Eddy. They setup a number of seats here and here for your comfort, it was the best they could do, after all, this aircraft wasn't setup to carry any fucking passengers, General."

General Claiborne pointed towards his right, and then to the left side of the bomb bay area and announced further, "these here seats were installed for you and your staff's needs, sir. It was a helluva thing, to transform this great war machine into a fricking flying bus, but that's what the President ordered, and that's what the Man got, sir. He wanted to get you and the rest of your staff out to Guam as quickly as humanly possible, sir."

There was a slight commotion up front of the aircraft, and all three military officers looked up and noticed the pilot, co-pilot and navigator enter the ship and head in the flight deck.

"I guess that's my cue, I have to drag my ass the hell out of here before I find myself flying to Guam with you, General." General Claiborne offered his hand again, and as they shook he added, "you be damn careful out there General Campanelli, and give them hell for me sir."

Not waiting for an answer, he turned to Aleksandra and shook her hand and offered her at the same time, "young lady, you gave me a helluva raise, and I thank you for that pleasure, Ma'am. I'm looking forward to seeing you again, Major. I know I'll be making many trips out to that Platform thing in the future. Is there anything you'd like me to bring out with me, Ma'am?"

"Vodka," Major Aleksandra replied with a large smile on her lips to the black General.

"Yes Vodka, of course, Russian I trust?" Luther replied as he smiled back at her.

"Is any other kind drink good sir?" she added as she watched him leave the plane.

"I like you Major, you'll go far in this life, I'll see you soon. Good bye," he left the ship.

General Campanelli and the Major took the chairs set alone, and as they sat down. She looked at Campanelli and asked him with some concern in her voice, "you tell me what General mean when said me gave him raise? I no pay him anything with money, Edward."

He laughed as he asked her if she really wanted to know what he meant by the remark.

"Yes?" she replied as she stared back at the General and her lover.

"Okay, but remember you asked for this Alex. He meant you must have given him a hard on when he followed you up the ladder to the aircraft. He was looking up your dress, Alex."

"I know this, and why stood over him when come up ladder. I want give him raise as say."

"Well you succeeded beyond your wildest dreams Alex," he laughed back at her.

"I happy my government sent here America. If no, I no never meet you, and be with you."

Their conversation was interrupted by General White, who just entered the aircraft and he grumbled at the two officers, "can you believe all those fucking news reporters out there for crap sake. They don't give a shit what they ask or say to you, dammit. I almost slugged a fucker out there because he was really starting to get on my dick nerve, man. The lousy bastards got an ear full when they tried to jump on Colonel Locker's backside I can tell ya, sir. Shit, I thought she was going to eat a few of them asses alive, and then spit them out later. I think the damn MPs saved a few of them damn reporters when they separated them from Locker. I never saw the Colonel so fucking angry before, sir. She even threatened some of the reporters with a firing squad, until General Weidenbacher ordered us aboard the damn aircraft, sir."

The three officers turned as Colonel Locker next came climbing up the ladder while yelling angrily at someone who was below her they did not see, "and don't you go and stand there while trying to look up my damn skirt on me, you old fart you. I know what the hell you're doing down there by offering to help me up the damn ladder, mister. You're not fooling me in the least, you black devil you."

All three officers called out at the same time, "General Claiborne."

Colonel Mary Locker came over to General Campanelli and bitched at him, "can you believe that old fool out there, standing down there like he was giving me a hand, the damn fool he is. When all he wanted to do was look up my damn skirt. I should've farted in the face of the damn fool. Did you have as much trouble as we did coming on board the aircraft, Sirs?"

"Yeah, the damn reporters jumped all over us too, the pains in the asses they are, dammit." General Campanelli growled back at her.

"I wonder where the devil General Palmieri is at, sir. He was standing right behind me as I came up the damn ladder to the aircraft, Campey." Colonel Locker said as she looked over her shoulder to see if the General was following her on board the aircraft.

"Dunno, I wish this damn aircraft had windows in it, so I could see what the hell's going on there, dammit." Campanelli griped as he stared at the female Colonel for a moment.

Just as he said that, General Palmieri's head came in view, and he was up in a flash and complaining all the way, "it's really crazy out there, people. I think they should ban all damn news reporters from any military bases, dammit. This way the dumb asses wouldn't be getting in our way, and I wouldn't have had to dump that one popinjay on his fool ass."

"You hit one of the stinking reporters General Palmieri Sir?" Locker laughed at him.

"Damn right I did, the dopey ass hit me right in the fricking mouth with a damn pocket recorder he shoved at my puss. I though the ass busted my damn tooth on me, and I let him have it. It felt real good, here look, my damn lip's bleeding." The still angry General pulled his lip out to shoe the Colonel he was really injured.

All four officers leaned forward and Locker cried, "I think I do see a small trace of blood there. Yes, yes it's a trace of blood alright. The poor thing you are, General Palmieri. Wait a minute, it wiped off. I think it was some jam what did you have for breakfast, General."

"I didn't think I'd get much sympathy from you stinking guys dammit!" he ran his tongue over his lip and then added. "It's blood, not jam Locker."

General Campanelli laughed as he remarked this time, "you know where to find sympathy in the dictionary sir, right between shit and syphilis."

Next up the ladder was Sergeant James Cruz. He was carrying a green camouflage bag, and he dumped it on the deck like a sack of potatoes. He looked at Palmieri and laughed as he remarked, "gees General Palmieri Sir, you sure hit that bugger in the chops, they brought up an ambulance for the guy to get him off the tarmac, sir. He's crying like an old whore in heat sir."

"Good for the dumb bastard," Palmieri snapped as he grinned at the young Sergeant.

Sergeant Cruz turned to the General and put his hands out from his side and said, "well sir, what do you think of it? I make a good looking Sergeant, don't I, General Campanelli Sir?"

"You were cut from the old Sergeant's tree out back son," he laughed at the kid.

"I thank you sir for the raise in rate General," he added as he headed for a seat.

"No need to thank me Sergeant. I appreciate it when a soldier does his job well, mister."

The Sergeant dragged his bag passed the officers, and took one of the two farthest chairs.

Sergeant Willis was the last up the ladder of the aircraft, he was Campanelli's driver and he was dragging his heavy duffle bag behind him, as he went to the back of the aircraft. He strapped his bag to the back of the seat, and then he settled in for the flight.

Locker, Palmieri and General White took their seats and readied themselves for the takeoff.

An airman came up the ladder and pulled it up and called out, "all clear in the bombay sir."

A second later, General Campanelli heard the loud whine of the hydraulics, as the bomb bay door closed, and the chamber they were in, instantly became dark. When the hydraulics stopped, the chamber was next bathed with the makeshift lighting system strung up by the aircrew in the compartment, that was usually used to carry the bomb payload for the aircraft.

The Airman looked at his captive audience and then he announced, "good day sirs, I'm Airman First Class, Peter R. Carpenter, and I'll relay all orders from the pilots to you. Sirs, I have to inform you to strap yourselves in, and there's no smoking on the entire flight. As you must have realized by now, this aircraft's not prepared to carry passengers. I had the base cooks prepare some sandwiches for you for the flight, and I have plenty of coffee and sodas. Sorry, but we're not allowed to have any alcohol on board the aircraft, sirs. We have a makeshift bathroom set up behind that screen behind you, it's a portable john from a boat sirs."

The Airman pointed towards a canvass curtain hanging to the floor behind the Sergeants and then continued with the orders, "I apologize because I wasn't informed there would be any females on board the aircraft. I'm afraid you'll have to make the best of our poor facilities as they are, sirs. I have air pills if anyone gets sick, and there's some books in the corner for your pleasure. Parachutes are stored over there if the need arises." The Airman pointed towards the chutes hanging on a wall of the aircraft, and then he finished up with his orders, "any questions sirs? Now is the time to ask them of me. We'll be taking off shortly sirs then I'd be severely hampered to further assist in any wants and needs you might have, sirs."

He quickly scanned the group officers while ignoring the two Sergeants, and none of them made any motion. The Airman then turned on his heels and headed in the cockpit.

Campanelli's hands clutched the handles of the seat for dear life, as he held his breath in preparation for the takeoff.

He considered asking the Airman to help him into one of the chutes, but he changed his mind when no one else asked for any help. He was damned if he was going to be the only one on board asking for a chute, not with this group of jokers on board.

Aleksandra felt him tense up, and she turned and looked at him. She sensed he must have been scared of flying, and tightened her grip on his hand and he turned to her and smiled.

"There no thing ashamed or afraid of, plenty people no like fly," she told him.

"Leave me the fuck alone will ya for Christ sake. I'm just fucking fine Alex," the upset General hissed back at her, embarrassed she picked up his fear so easily.

"You pick fine place want alone be, mista. What suggest you I do make you alone on aircraft sir? Use chute and get out you sight General Campanelli Sir?"

He looked at her and she instantly flashed him one of her soul melting smiles.

"Thanks, I needed that. I hate flying, and all I ever do is get stuck flying all over the place."

"Would like something drink or eat, no sir?" she asked the General with some concern.

"Yeah, that might help out some I guess, Major. Something to drink please Alex."

"Airman Carpenter, can see moment you please," she called out to the Airman.

He poked his head out of the cockpit into the makeshift compartment and then he offered, "can I help someone please?"

"Yes, like some drink, you better have Pepsi in bag mista, or you go have bad flight on hand." She remarked and warned at the same time as she looked at the Airman.

He did not reply as he looked through his bag of sodas until he found a Pepsi.

"Here you go sir," he said with a smile as he handed the heavy glass to the Major.

"No, no me, for General Campanelli Sir," she informed the airman.

He offered the soda to General Campanelli then.

Now the General had a real problem on his hands, because he had to let go of the handles of his chair to take the soda. Yet he was still scared to death to let go even though the engines of the aircraft were idling so low he could almost not tell they were running. He finally let go with his right hand and grabbed the glass. The airman smiled, letting him know he realized he was afraid of flying. He made a mental note to show this General some extra special attention during the flight, to make it a little easier on General Campanelli and himself.

He took a good slug of the ice cold soda. The Airman looked at the Major and then he asked her, "Major, I have four more cans of soda, Pepsis. Will that be enough for the General for the entire flight to Guam, Ma'am?"

"That do just fine I believe Airman. Do have you have any bottled water on you aircraft to drink, sir? I little thirsty myself, sir." She said.

"Yes Ma'am, I have one full bottle of water Ma'am. Would you like some water, Major?"

"Yes please thank you Airman," she replied as she smiled at the young man. She took the glass and then thanked the Airman again.

"That's not necessary Major. I'm here to help you out Ma'am."

General Campanelli watched the Airman as he quickly disappeared back inside the cockpit, and then he growled at

Aleksandra, "crap, I wish to hell and back again that damn bugger would stay the hell out here with us, so he can tell me what the fuck's going on up there, dammit. I hate not seeing where the crap we're going inside this damn thing, Alex. "

Without warning, the aircraft vibrated as more power was added to the once idling engines.

"What the fuck's that damn shit about for crap sake, dammit?" he snapped angrily as he almost dropped the soda, and then he tried to grab the handle of the chair while still trying to hold on to his glass of soda at the same time.

"Give me you glass please before you spill it all over aircraft. They only start power to engine so we take off, that all happen General Campanelli."

The aircraft bucked as the pilot moved onto the runway. It was a bumpy movement and the worried General immediately tensed up. The Major leaned against him and offered, "General Campanelli Sir, no problem. You want me get motion pill for you, sir?"

"Christ sake Almighty, what the hell do you think I am, a fucking baby Major? I don't want a damn pill to hack this damn plane ride out to the fucking Island. I can hack it easy enuf Major!" he fired right back at the concerned female pilot.

"Oh stop it you big baby, if pill help you relax on aircraft, why no you take one and be more comfort for flight out to island, General Campanelli Sir?"

"I'm not going to take one of the damn things so back the fuck offa me before I throw up all over your damn lap, Major!" he warned her as he turned green.

She stared at him for several long moments while smiling.

"I'm only kidding Alex," he smiled at her, and she immediately returned his smile.

The aircraft slowly taxied down the runway, and then it shot up in the air like a dart. Although Campanelli could not actually see what was happening, it was easy for him to figure it out. His grip was so tight on the handles of his seat that she thought he was going to tear them free of the chair. It took the aircraft ten minutes to level off, and the General finally relaxed.

There was some small talk going on between them, and even John left his seat to get in on the conversation. The continuous roar of the engines was deafening, and it made most conversation almost impossible to follow in the Bombay section of the aircraft. The General wanted another soda and the Major got up and got it for him this time.

The Airman saw her move and he instantly came out asking if he could help her.

"Yes, General Campanelli want soda again. I want do you favor big me. You dissolve air sick pill in soda before give him please for me. He has calm down before he get sick on aircraft."

The Airman looked at the Major and then gave her a quick wink of the eye and offered, "sure thing Ma'am, I was planning to do the same thing myself, Major. I saw he was having a hard time with flying in the aircraft, Ma'am. These ground pounders like the earth, Major."

"Yes, I know what you mean, I like glass water also if you no mind much please?"

"No problem there Ma'am." The Airman smiled back at her pleasantly.

The foreign Major took the glasses and then went back to her seat.

"I wonder where we are." General Campanelli asked as his mouth became moist again.

"Airman inform me we over you country Oklahoma, Chichashaw he tell me name of place be. He say me we no go to refuel until over Pasadena, in you California country area, sir. He explained me why we wait we over Pasadena place before take on needed fuel, General Campanelli Sir. We take enough fuel on there to make all way out Guam country, with no have refuel again in flight. Pretty good okay, no General Campanelli Sir?"

"Damn, you're just a stinking wealth of fucking information there lady aren't you. I don't like refueling in flight. Shit, I really hate like hell flying, dammit."

"There no problem flight refuel. It do hundred time day and you no know it happen, sir."

"I don't give a shit about the hundreds of time. I care about this one fucking time, sister."

"You impossible be fly with General Campanelli Sir," she complained as she sat back and then stared off into nothingness. While she sat, she did not notice General Campanelli yawning, it was just moments before she heard him snoring.

John snuck up behind her chair and whispered, "how the hell did you get him to Z out?"

She winked at the concerned looking General, and then she smiled at him.

The flight was smooth, as the large aircraft shot though the air at Mach One point Two Five. Aleksandra just got comfortable when she felt the aircraft suddenly start slowing down some. The Airman immediately stuck his head in the Bombay compartment and announced their tanker aircraft, a KC-135 was cruising a hundred yards off their right wing tip of the aircraft and reported, "he'll accompany us until we finally reach Pasadena where we'll top off for the trip over the Pacific. Major, would you like to see the tanker aircraft up close, Ma'am?"

"Yes, much very please thank you," she replied and was out of her seat in a flash.

"Would you mind following me then please Ma'am," the co-pilot said to her.

She went in the cockpit and looked to the right and easily picked up the massive tanker aircraft now actually pacing the bomber. She looked around the cockpit and realized it was tighter than she first thought. With her and the Airman in the flight deck, no one could move around much. The massive aircraft was pressurized so no one had to wear an oxygen mask, but the pilot and co-pilot were on oxygen anyway. The Airman noticed what she was looking at, and he told her it was SOP for the pilot and co-pilot to both be on oxygen while the aircraft was in flight. He smiled as he told her if anything happened to their oxygen supply, everyone on board was expendable except for the pilot and co-pilot of the aircraft.

She nodded, but she had already deduced as much herself as she replied to the Airman, "that way it should be, the pilot and co-pilot must stay alive to land aircraft safely, sir.

The pilot suddenly bent his head back and he growled something to the Airman, and he immediately ushered the Major back to her seat in the Bombay section of the aircraft.

The aircraft slowly increased power for what seemed like twenty minutes to the Major, and then the plane slowed down again. She could actually feel the aircraft making some movement, and knew it was lining up with the tanker aircraft for the fuel transfer. There was a sudden high pitch whine from hydraulics, and General Campanelli's eyes instantly flew open, and he growled, "what the fuck's happening? I heard something, we landing this damn thing yet, dammit?" He cried as he grabbed the handles of his chair again.

"No land, we just take some fuel on, that all we do at this time, General Campanelli Sir." The grinning Major reported to the sleepy looking Commander.

"Great, I had to wake up for this crap," he moaned as he held on the handles for dear life.

There was a slight buck from the aircraft when the umbilical cord hookup was completed, and everyone on board could hear the rush of JP-8 Kerosene based fuel being pumped in the wing tanks of the aircraft. They then heard the pilot speaking with the Boom Commander, but they could not make out what was being said. A second whine started that warned the pilot his tanks were almost full already. The high pitch whine grew louder until there was a sound like someone slammed a door. A loud buzzer screamed as the co-pilot announced, "all fueled up sir."

"Good, disconnect the lead and close the penis plug then sir," the pilot snapped, and then they removed their oxygen masks, and everyone was able to hear what the pilot was saying again.

General Campanelli leaned over to Aleksandra and asked, "what's the penis plug thing?"

"No know nothing about aircraft and refuel I see sir. Penis plug extension come out when aircraft accept fuel from tanker aircraft. It like gas cap of you car, General?"

"I see Alex." Just then, the hydraulics started again, and the General looked at the Major.

"Close penis plug door that all to hear, American General you," she smiled at the upset looking military officer.

General Campanelli shook his head in complete understanding this time.

When the refueling tanker aircraft was out of the way, everyone on board the slick bomber could feel the massive aircraft's power immediately increase, as the pilot went for air flight now. It was exhilarating to feel the awesome power of the huge aircraft, as it skimmed through the air like a huge kite. The pilot climbed the aircraft, and then leveled off as he opened the engines full bore now. The Airman came in the pressurized compartment and informed everyone they were now flying at the top of the line Mach One point Two Five, and were already over the Pacific Ocean. Then he disappeared back inside the cockpit.

The General leaned his head back, and closed his eyes and fell off to sleep again.

The Airman came out and whispered to Aleksandra, "Major, are you up Ma'am?"

She opened her eyes, and focused them on the soldier's face.

"Major, I didn't want to bother you Ma'am, but the co-pilot has to take a dump, and the pilot wanted to know if you wanted to work over the controls for a little while he's gone, Major?"

She nearly jumped out of her chair, and then she headed right to the flight deck without replying to the Airman.

The co-pilot stood, and she snaked passed him and plopped down in his seat. She was amazed the seat felt like it actually wrapped itself around her body completely. She strapped the face mask and helmet on and heard the pilot's voice, "hello Major, I'm Captain Thomas E. Abelson, glad to meet you and have you on board my aircraft, Ma'am."

"Yes, I Major Aleksandra Klivekaita from Lithuanian Royal Knight Air Guard, sir. I too am pleased be on board you fine aircraft and enjoy the flight with you, Captain Sir."

"Major, would you like to take over the controls for a little while, Ma'am?"

"Much, please thank you sir," she could not hide her grin that was on her lips now.

"Okay, but first I have to warn you of something you might not be aware of, Ma'am. Did you ever fly an aircraft that's controlled by wire, Major?"

"No sir." The female pilot offered while she cocked her head to the side and stared at him.

"Okay, you're in for a little surprise then Ma'am. The aircraft responds to the controls much quicker than most fighter aircraft so be careful. Another thing I must warn you about Major, she likes to fly away from you, so you have to keep a close eye on her at all times, Major. Don't allow her drift off on you any, I'm going to give you Command of the aircraft now so be aware, Major. Are you ready to accept the control of the aircraft, Major Ma'am?"

She was so excited that she shook her head yes rapidly in response as she locked her hands on the wheel, and then glanced at the pilot. She saw him release and place his hands on his lap, but she did not feel anything happen to her control.

The pilot picked up her puzzlement and he offered her with concern in his voice, "she's real light on the arms, Ma'am. That's the fly by wire controls, Ma'am."

"She feel real good in hand, light, like small plane, fighter aircraft, and no bomber, sir. Very light on arm also I feel as you say, sir."

"Major, you can take her up to Angels Forty Two Thousand Feet if you like, Ma'am. That's our allotted flying altitude for this entire flight out to the Island of Guam, Ma'am."

She did not respond as she gently pulled back on the stick a little. She was astonished at how quickly the massive aircraft responded to the slight change in the controls. The Major banked the aircraft slightly to the left, with just the slightest of movement of the wheel. The aircraft responded immediately to her slight pressure and she said excitedly to the pilot, "she respond just like small fighter aircraft to controls of the aircraft, sir."

"You're absolutely correct Ma'am.   The aircraft was developed for low level attack operations. She flies better at a lower altitude Ma'am, and the aircraft can accelerate fast, turns and climbs out of a low level Mach point Nine flight so quickly, that it'd leave even the best of most fighter aircraft in the dust, Ma'am. The cockpit's shaped like a fighter aircraft as well, this gives us all around vision of the aircraft so we can react to an attack or a bombing run much easier, Major." The pilot could tell she was leveling off the plane now.

"I no believe we climb up eight thousand feet quick and smooth so, sir. I like feel able see much from flight deck, it very important for pilot able see so much of aircraft outside cockpit, sir. She so beautiful and easy to fly, Captain."

"Yes she is, and she can get our ass out of trouble in many different ways, Ma'am. She has chaff canisters, with free fall black chaff. She also has a missile system that fires from the backend of the aircraft, so tail attacking fighters or interceptors will be in for quite a surprise if they try to attack her from her Six or rear, Ma'am. She also has tail radar with air to ground, and air to air missiles support. She also has a special bounce imagery, so on tracking radar's, she appears to be in a different location than she really is flying at, Ma'am. Ground launched missiles would be chasing illusions if they try and go after her, Major. We also have two

Sidewinder missiles for self defense, with electronic and counter electronic measures to better confuse any attacking missiles and aircraft. Yes, she protects her crew very well at that Major."

"I see for self. What type bomb and missile she carry on board aircraft, Captain Sir?"

The Captain looked at her for a moment and then he responded with caution lacing his tone of voice, "I'm sorry Major, but most of that stuff's still classified Ma'am."

"I sorry step my limits over. It no happen again I assure you Captain Sir, I no get over how handle she so good, sir. Like fly pippercub aircraft."

"This baby's a little harder to fly than one of those little paper planes, Ma'am."

The excited female Major stared out of the windshield as she moved the stick slightly to her right and then to her left. She then pulled back on the stick, and the aircraft instantly climbed again. She leveled off quickly then punched it forward. The aircraft started a slight dive and she cried out in an excited voice to the pilot of the aircraft. "I no believe well handle for huge plane like she is, sir. America put aircraft together."

The Captain smiled at her words. He thought to himself, 'yeah, and I bet you buggers would love to get your stinking hands on one of these here babies. I don't understand why the damn head honchos want to allow one of you fuckers on board my damn aircraft. You're sucking up a lot of top secret stuff here, bitch'. Suddenly, he found himself angry she was in his cockpit, he growled to himself, 'fuck what those damn assholes say, I'm getting this piece of shit the hell out of my flight deck before she memorizes the damn instruments'. He shot a hot glance over his shoulder. With a quick head movement, he motioned for his co-pilot to get her out of the cockpit and back to her seat after he returned from his bathroom visit.

The co-pilot nodded and then he tapped the excited female Major on the shoulder as he offered her. "Major Ma'am, I have to get you back to your seat now, sorry Major."

The female Major pouted as she reluctantly unstrapped her helmet and seat straps. Then she stood as she offered to the co-pilot, "I like have fly little more time please. Maybe I fly her later in flight again if am allowed to enjoy, sir?"

The co-pilot smiled, "you're going to have to ask the Captain for that permission, Ma'am."

She turned to the pilot. "Captain, what say? Will get another turn control? Please."

He made like he did not hear her, so she repeated the request, this time louder.

He looked at her when the co-pilot was strapped back in his seat and ready to assist him if needed, and his hands were lightly resting on the controls, "afraid not young lady. This is a special flight, and I think I might have overstepped my bounds by allowing you take over the damn controls as it is, Ma'am. I think you better go back to your seat and strap yourself in for the rest of the flight out to the Island of Guam, Major."

She easily detected the anger etched in his voice, so she shrugged then she turned and headed back to her seat. When she was out of earshot, the co-pilot snapped at his Commander, "what the hell was that shit all about, sir? She seems like a pretty good Joe to me, sir. Why the cold shoulder with the female pilot, Captain?"

"She's a fucking Russian owned bitch, and any damn Russian I ever came across was a fucking spy who wanted to kill then cook and eat my fucking ass, sir."

"She's a Lithuanian pilot, not a stinking Russian, sir. I think you're dead wrong on this one sir. If the brain thrust says she's okay then you should go a helluva lot easier on her, sir." He grumbled at the commander of the aircraft.

"Russian, Lithuanian, they're all the same, just different fucking beds they're sleeping in, sir. I don't give a rat's ass what you might think is right or wrong here, mister. When you get Command of your own aircraft, then your opinion will mean something, you got it mister?"

The co-pilot glared angrily at his Captain, but he did not respond to his last angry words though. He knew better than to get involved in an argument with his Commander, but he still could not understand why the pilot was being so hard on the female Major.

The pilot snapped again just as angrily at the other pilot, "I didn't fucking hear you co-pilot. You got that right mister?"

"Loud and clear, I got it loud and clear Captain," he fired back at the pilot.

General Campanelli was groggy but he noticed the Major's sad eyes, and he asked her what was wrong with her this time as he sat forward in his chair still strapped into it.

"I no know, I think I upset you Captain little bit some, but no understand what did I wrong at him in the least, sir. I so enjoy fly aircraft little too short time though sir," she cried as she took her seat and smiled at her Commanding Officer.

"Ahhh... don't take it to heart pretty lady. I was a little surprised he allowed you anywhere near the stinking flight deck of this aircraft anyhow, Alex. This aircraft is still a top secret aircraft. These pilots are a real fucked up bunch of buggers to try and understand, Major."

"Perhaps right you after all General Campanelli. I wish just to know what I do so wrong that pilot so upset with me for reason I no know why sir," she replied as she leaned back and then strapped herself in her chair, and then she added to his Commander. "I say you awful calm on flight all sudden. Are you get used to fly maybe, sir?"

"No way in hell sister, I still hate fucking flying, dammit. I just can't keep my damn eyes open for some stinking reason, that's all Alex. I almost feel like I'm fucking drugged up on something I'm so damn tired. I guess the past few week's work has finally taken their damn toll on my ass. Once I sit back, all I want to do is fucking sleep for a while, Alex."

She smiled as she closed her eyes and allowed herself to remember the thrill of flying the large plane even for those few minutes she had the controls in her hands. In her mind she was already comparing this aircraft with the Russian built Bear aircraft.

The two slept for the rest of the flight, and they did not wake up until the airman called out that everyone better have their seat belts set. They were heading on their final approach at Guam.

CHAPTER 15

General Edward Campanelli suddenly sat up in his chair and shook his head in an attempt to try and clear the cobwebs clouding over his mind, and then he checked his seatbelt as did Aleksandra. The huge aircraft slowly banked hard to the left, and the General tightened his death grip on the handles of the chair again. The aircraft then leveled off and it started its slow descent. The Airman called out the height of the aircraft as it came in for the landing. "Twenty Three Thousand, Nineteen Thousand, Fourteen Thousand, Eight Thousand."

General Campanelli leaned over to Aleksandra and complained to her, "I wish to hell and back that stinking popinjay would shut his damn mouth for a little while, dammit. I don't wanna know about anything until we're back on the damn ground, and I can get out of this death trap."

"Will you please General Campanelli Sir, you act like big baby all time lately when we fly in aircraft, sir. You safe in this aircraft as you safe in mother's arm I assure you, General Campanelli Sir." She complained at the General and she gave him the look.

"Look honey, I have the rank to act any way I want," he griped as he crossed his hands over his chest and pouted. He glanced at her and they both laughed because of the way he was sitting.

"We're at Five Hundred Feet and received the final to land, sir. We'll be on the ground in less than a minute." The Airman pulled down a small seat behind the navigator and strapped himself in as he crossed his hands, and then leaned into the uncomfortable looking chair.

The pilot barked out loudly, "speed's down to Three Hundred knots, flaps at full, fuel mixture full rich, wheels are locked down and set in place, sir. We look good for landing, Tower."

The navigator called out, "sir, we have a mild cross wind coming at you at five miles per hour sir, and it's gusting up to nine from the northeast, not enough for you to worry about though sir."

"Yeah," was the only remark the pilot replied as he paid close attention to his landing.

The next words the General heard called out from the cockpit were, "touchdown, brakes, full reverse thrusters, release the chute and extend the air breaks. Speed decreasing, we have control of the aircraft, taxiing down to One, One, Three, sir."

General Campanelli knew it was coming, but he still jumped as the wheels touched down, and he did not breath regularly again until the aircraft came to a complete stop. When the bombay doors opened on the side of him, a rush of cool fresh air flooding into the compartment, instantly revived them. He unstrapped his harness before the Airman lowered the ladder in the Bombay area, and he stood over the Airman's shoulder as he locked the ladder in place.

"Would you like to go down the ladder first, General Campanelli Sir?" he asked as he gave way to the excited acting General.

"Fucking A I want down first sonny, get out of my way mister!" Campanelli actually sped down the ladder, and then he moved out from under the massive aircraft and quickly went some fifty feet away from it, before he turned and waited for the others to join him.

John came down the ladder next, and he was laughing all the way to where he was having a little trouble catching his breath as he cried out to his Commander, "Jesus Christ Eddy, that's the fastest I ever saw you move your lilly white ass since we first saw that broad walking down the street with no top on, while we were stationed in Italy man. For an old man, you still have quite a little spring in your damn step when you want one, sir."

"Fuck you buster," he growled at his laughing friend, but could not help joining him. There was something about John when he laughed, anyone nearby would automatically laughed along with him. Probably because he put so much into it.

John hung around the aircraft making himself look busy until Aleksandra and General Palmieri came out. The two were laughing but made sure they did not aim it at Campanelli. Everyone knew he had a good sense of humor, but no one wanted to push their luck and make him come out of his tree against them. They all knew of his temper in the past as well that was kept on a hair trigger one time or another, and no one wanted it aimed at them again.

The General shook his head and gave them their laugh as he scanned the small Island. To his right, there were a number of bulldozers busy leveling some small buildings and filling in a number of slight depressions. The dozers were cutting down small hills and it looked like a group of SeaBee's were setting some explosive charges on the base of a low mountain. The more he looked around, the more workers he spotted. He wondered what it was all about.

John and Aleksandra walked over to him as he surveyed the area. The General spotted two officers bent over a blueprint table and he decided to see if he could find out what was up. The two caught up to Campanelli as he reached the other soldiers. The officers snapped to attention and saluted Campanelli, who returned their salute as he asked them, "what the hell's going on here Captain? Why all the work sir?" he coughed from the dust.

"Sir, I'm sorry to say but I'm not at liberty to inform you of our orders, sir. If you want to find out what's going on with the Island, I suggest you go to H.Q. and speak to Colonel Paulette Tomlinson, sir. She can answer all your questions much better than I can, sir." The two other officers remained standing at attention until the General walked off in the direction he pointed.

General Campanelli came across a small wooden hut and banged on the door. A female voice from within boomed out, "come in and make it quick."

The General walked in the hut like he owned the place while John and the female Major remained standing outside the small building. John mumbled at Aleksandra as he smiled at her. "I guess he has to be a pain in the ass wherever he goes, young lady."

As Campanelli entered the building, the female Colonel noticed he was a General, and she stood and gave him a weak salute, she was not intimidated by his presence as she barked at him, "yes, and what can I do for you General Sir? I'm rather busy as you can plainly see sir."

"I won't take up too much of your damn time on you, Colonel. I just landed on your shithole of a fucking Island of yours Ma'am, and I saw all this work going on around here, and I was wondering what the hell was up here, Ma'am."

"Who the hell are you, and what the hell business is it of yours what's going on with my military base, General Sir?" the female Colonel grumbled at the nosy officer.

The instantly upset General spat out with all the venom he could muster in his voice, "allow me to introduce myself to you, Colonel. I'm General Edward Campanelli, Supreme Commander of all Allied Forces in the Asian region, that's who I am sister, and if you want to keep those damn chickens you have pinned on your collar. I suggest you tell me what the fuck's going on around here, and I warn you to use a little caution in your damn tone when addressing my ass, Colonel!" he glared angrily at the Colonel while waiting her response.

She immediately straightened up a bit as she apologized for her transgression aimed at her obvious Commander, "please allow me to introduce myself to you, General Campanelli Sir. I'm Colonel Paulette Tomlinson, Sir. I've been pushing my people both day and night, trying to accomplish what the government wants finished before your operation goes into effect around here, sir. I wasn't prepared for a visit from the Commander of this operation for quite a while from now sir. Would you like a cup of coffee sir?"

"No!" the General snapped with anger in his voice, he was still upset with the female Colonel who he did not like very much already.

"Very well General Campanelli Sir, I can tell you what you want to know, sir. My job is to level the entire Island of Guam to convert the entire Island into one huge airbase for this upcoming operation, sir. This is a contingency plan, we're going to displace the inhabitants of the Island and then level everything. Mountains, houses, trees, the works, sir. I have orders to make the Island a huge parking lot to accept the B-52 Hs and B-1 B bombers, that might have to be used in possible attacks against China or North Korea, sir. This is in response to losing our military bases once stationed in both Japan and the Philippines, and now in South Korea, sir."

"We lost the South Korean military bases? I wasn't aware about that damn situation, Colonel. When the hell did this move take place against us, Colonel?" Campanelli asked, stunned the military bases in South Korea was being pulled from him now.

"Yes Sir General Campanelli Sir, as of early this morning, we were requested by the South Korean Military Command to close down all our military bases stationed in South Korea, sir. This is their response to our demand they stand down from a war footing aimed at the North, sir. Guam's our closest military base to the theater as of point now, sir. Except for all the scuttlebutt I keep hearing about some kind of a Floating Island thing we're supposed to be setting up off the coast of the Island of Taiwan someplace, sir. Perhaps you can answer a few questions for me this time around, General Campanelli Sir?"

"Sure, why the hell not, shoot Colonel. What's on your mind, Colonel?" General Campanelli barked at her, interested in this new information now.

"Is it true the crap I keep hearing about this supposed super Floating Island Air and Military Base thing, I heard so much about lately, sir?"

"I knew that question was coming at me Ma'am. You seem to have a pretty good intelligence network working for you out here on this damn Island of yours, Colonel Tomlinson. Yes, it's true, that's what my assignment is, to setup this damn floating base thing, Ma'am."

"Jesus, Mary and Joseph, I bet that must have cost the government a pretty penny, sir."

"More than you'll ever know I believe, Colonel Tomlinson." General Campanelli smirked back at the female officer.

"Is it feasible sir?" the Colonel asked the General, trying to draw any information from him.

"I have no idea because I didn't see the damn thing first hand yet. But if I was to respond to your question, I'd have to offer Colonel. Yes, it's very feasible, Colonel Tomlinson. From all I read about the damn thing, and what I seen about the damn thing so far. I think it's one hell of an idea, and someone with some mighty big balls has put it all together for us, Colonel."

"Whose baby was it General Campanelli Sir?" the female Colonel asked him this time.

"President Bush, he was the only man with the guts to put something like this together."

"You're right sir. He was our best President in quite a while sir, he put pride back in our military forces sir. A good man there sir."

"Yeah, right, anyway Colonel Tomlinson, when do you plan to complete your operation, Colonel Ma'am? I should know of this if I'm forced to rely on this airbase any, Ma'am."

"Right now, all we're doing is leveling out the least populated areas of the Island, General. Just in case it's not necessary to clear the whole damn Island off, sir. We have the power to force all civilians off the Island at a moment's notice though, sir. But as I said, all I have permission for at this time sir, is to merely level the least populated areas, and any areas I might determine vital for our immediate use, sir. That means the highest mountains and hill areas sir. So far, the civilians have been cooperating pretty well with us for the most part. Most of the displaced people have moved in with their relatives on the other side of the Island. I know I'm going to have some trouble when I have to get them off the Island, but that's my problem to deal with sir."

"You got that right Colonel," he grunted at her this time.

"Sir, how long do you intend to stay on my little Island, General?" the Colonel inquired.

"Can't wait to get rid of my ass already I see, huh Colonel Tomlinson? I kinda have that effect on most people I happen across I assure you, Colonel."

The female Colonel smiled pleasantly at the General for the moment.

"I thought so Ma'am. Look Colonel, I'm kinda sorry I came on to you so heavy before, I have been cooped up inside a damn aircraft, and I hate like hell flying for some time now, Ma'am. I was just stretching my legs I'm afraid, Colonel."

"And your mouth sir," she retorted as she informed the General she was still angry at him.

"Touché' Colonel. I'm afraid you got me there Ma'am," he smiled at her this time.

Both officers laughed as she poured him some coffee, and then she offered General Campanelli a shot of Brandy to go along with his coffee, but he immediately waved it off. The coffee was good as the General offered to the Colonel for her information.

"I don't know how long I'm going to be on the god damn Island, Colonel Tomlinson Ma'am. I guess I have to wait for my CV-22 to arrive to take me out to my damn ship, Ma'am."

"What's the name of your ship sir?" she asked, still looking for some information.

"Most of the operation is still TS,(Top Secret) at this time but since you know about as much as I do about it, I don't think it'd hurt if you knew the name. After all, I have a foreigner who has her nose stuck in the middle of this mess. I can't see keeping secrets from my own people. The name's the Blue Whale. Colonel Tomlinson, once the operation's completed, I'll send my plane back to the Island and pick you up, and you can spend the day on the Joe, and you and I can go exploring the damn thing together, and find out what this Floating Island's all about Colonel."

"I'd like that General, how long do you think it'll take to get the operation in effect, sir?"

"You got me there Colonel," he said as he rubbed his chin, and then continued with his words. "I was told the entire damn thing would be put together by March 4th. Then I was told it'd be completed by the time I shipped out to the damn thing, and now I'm told only seven ships will be linked together on it Ma'am, when I touch down on the Platform. I don't think anyone has any idea what's really going on, and no one will until the damn thing's completed, Ma'am."

"Sounds typical to me, General Campanelli Sir. Would you like something to go along with your coffee General Campanelli Sir? We have a well stocked mess here sir."

"I could sure do with something to eat, I'm starving. By the way Colonel Tomlinson, I have two other Officers standing outside, and another one who I'm sure is roaming around the Island with two of my enlisted men. They could stand a meal as well Colonel."

"Then I suggest we go and get them and hit the mess hall together, General Campanelli Sir," she stood and General Campanelli followed her out the building as he offered.

"Colonel Tomlinson Ma'am, may I introduce you to Brigadier General John White, and Major Aleksandra err... Klivekaita I think you pronounce it properly Ma'am" he looked at the female Major and she nodded yes to her Commanding Officer.

"Very good General Campanelli Sir. You say last name almost as good as my people of Lithuania say it," the Major replied as she smiled at his attempt to pronounce her name.

"She's on loan to us from Lithuania for some special flight training and other crap, Ma'am." General Campanelli continued to explain to the Colonel.

Tomlinson shook hands with them, as Campanelli scanned the open end of the Island for any sign of General Palmieri and Colonel Locker. He spotted them watching the SeaBees setting up some of their explosive charges. He called out and they turned and then walked over to them.

"Colonel Tomlinson, this is General Palmieri, and Colonel Mary Locker, they're from the Joint Chiefs of Staff assigned to my Command, so watch your mouth with them please."

Colonel Tomlinson laughed as she shook hands with them and she invited them to the mess. When they entered they saw the Sergeants found the mess and Campanelli remarked, "shit, I shoulda known the street fighters would find the food first. I think we should follow them."

"One thing I learned a long time ago General Campanelli Sir. The foot soldiers take good care of themselves at all times, sir." Colonel Tomlinson replied, making the officers chuckled as they took their seats after joining the two Sergeants.

Once seated, John asked his Commanding Officer if there was any word about their CV-22.

General Campanelli looked at Colonel Tomlinson and then remarked, "I think the Colonel's in a much better position to answer that one for you, sir."

All eyes went to her and she offered, "I have no word on a CV-22, but I'll call the Tower and find out if they have any information on the aircraft for you, sir." She got up and quickly disappeared behind the counter and then she returned.

"Your CV-22 Osprey has refueled from a tanker aircraft over the Pacific, and it should be landing within the next two hours, General Campanelli. Their ETA's Seventeen Fifty Hours, they're scheduled to spend the night on the Island, so it looks like I'll have to make arrangements for your outfit to bed down on the Island overnight, General Campanelli Sir."

"If it won't be too much trouble for you to do that for us, Colonel Tomlinson Ma'am."

"No trouble at all General Campanelli Sir, it's not every day we get members of the Command Staff spending the night with us, General. I'll order the Officers Club to stay open late for this occasion, sir. If you'll excuse me sir, I have some accommodations to arrange, General."

John absentmindedly said, "I bet she broke some backs in bed in her day, Eddy."

Both Locker and Aleksandra complained at the same time at the General, "John, don't you have anything else on your mind but sex and who's getting it?"

"Is there anything else to think about ladies?" he retorted with a wide grin.

Locker snapped at the General "you're impossible you know that mister."

"And you love it, this old Alabama black snake has never been as busy as it has been lately."

Both women laughed as Locker added, "you wish it was, you mean General White Sir."

The General loved it when his officers bantered back and forth like this. It showed him they not only respected each other, but they cared much about one another. Besides, he liked it when they went after one another, because it meant they were leaving him alone for a change.

As the officers and NOCs ate, a soldier came in and announced the quarters were placed at their disposal, and the base security was off loading the B-1's special cargo. Their equipment was placed in the brig for safe protection. Two armed guards were to be stationed at the gate of the brig at all times, while the General and part of his Command Staff were visiting the Island.

General Campanelli was pleased with this security arrangement. As they spoke, the B-1 bomber took off. From where they sat, they could see the plane takeoff and the soldier asked the officers. "Would the Officers like to see their quarters now, sir?"

"Not now, I think we'll walk around the base to see the sights first, son." Campanelli replied.

"Very well then General Campanelli Sir, I'm to inform you I'm to act as your personal guide while you're visiting the Island, sir. Anything you want to know about the Island, please feel free to ask, and I'll try my best to answer it for you, sir. Colonel Tomlinson wished me to inform you that she'll join the Generals for supper, sirs."

Campanelli ignored the Corporal as he, and the other officers talked amongst themselves. The corporal took a seat behind them and waited. He hated having so many officers hanging around with nothing to do for themselves. He had to watch his Ps and Qs, not to mention his mouth. He stared at the officers as they laughed and talked to one another, he was already bored to death.

Suddenly, the small group of officers got up and they started out the mess, with the Corporal following close behind them in silence. General Campanelli was interested in the construction and he went to the workers and watched them.

From out of nowhere, the General heard someone calling out his name to him in an excited voice, "Colonel, you fucking remember me sir?"

General Campanelli looked around until he spotted a large SeaBee waving wildly at him. He could not tell who he was from this distance, so he slowly drifted over to him. When the General got close to the soldier, he instantly realized who it was. The SeaBee Chief who stole him an air-conditioner when he was stationed at Base Easy Money in Ethiopia. The old Chief was walking towards him now in a rush while grinning from ear to ear.

General Campanelli put out his hand and remarked, "Jesus Christ Almighty, you still driving fucking nails for the Navy, you old bastard you. I thought by now, the Navy would've put you out to pasture, mister. Whatdaya do, whatdaya know, whatdaya say Chief? It's a real pleasure to see you again, Chief. How the hell's life been treating ya lately sir?"

"Holy shit, look at you will ya now sir. A fucking three star General. What the hell ever happened, sir? The Army had some extra stars hanging around doing nuthin, so they gave them to you just to get rid of the damn things, General Campanelli Sir?"

The two men laughed as they shook hands and patted each other on the backs as Campanelli offered, "say Chief, I'm gonna look and see if I need any of you pains in the ass Bee's on my staff, sir. And if I do, I'm gonna draft your damn ass as one of them like I did in the past, mister. I could sure use you standing behind me and making certain I didn't screw up again, Chief."

Chief, Robert W. Kirby became serious as he grumbled at the General in a concerned tone of voice, "sir, I couldn't think of any other Officer in the service I'd rather serve under than you, sir. We sure tied one on a few times over there didn't we sir?"

"I have news for you Chief. I stopped drinking sir." General Campanelli told him.

The surprised Naval Chief stared back at the General for a long moment, and then he offered with his eyes displaying the concern he had. "You don't say, bad liver sir?"

"Nothing like that thank God, Chief. I felt I was getting my ass in too much trouble, and that's why I gave the crap up, that's all sir."

"Looks like I'll have to do all the drinking for both of us then from now on, sir. Where's your damn shadow of a pain in the ass Captain, General? He still hanging around, or did the Army finally come to their senses and dump his black ass out of the damn service, sir?"

"You mean John, he's hanging around here someplace, he's a General too now Chief."

"Jesus H. Christ, I can't believe that crap for a second, sir. It looks like I'm wasting my time in the stinking Navy I see, sir. Shit, if you two birds made General then they woulda surely made me a fucking President or something, with the way I hafta keep getting the two of you SOB's outta trouble all the time, General. What a pleasure seeing you again sir."

"No doubt Chief," General Campanelli accepted the insubordination from the overly excited Chief because he was that good a friend and worker. He did not like to be saluted, and would rather be treated like a soldier than a General as he added, "say Chief, if you come with me you won't have to deal with any stinking civilians this time around, sir."

"Jesus H. Christ sir. What the hell did I do, just die and go to Heaven or something suddenly, sir. Those damn civilians were really one royal pain in the ass back there in Africa, General Campanelli Sir. They were like shit stuck on the bottom of your damn shoe General, you couldn't get rid of the assholes no matter how hard you shook your foot, sir."

"You got that right Chief. Look Chief, this operation's going to be strictly military this time around, and we're going to be stationed at sea to boot, sir. So if anyone bugs ya butt out there, you can just chuck his stinking ass overboard, and that'll be that sir."

"Jesus, that's the best deal I have ever been offered while in the service, sir. I'd give a damn month's pay to ship out with you again, General Campanelli Sir. Hey, what ever happened to that hot little Latino number you were slipping the old log to on Easy Money, sir?"

General Campanelli swallowed hard and then said sadly, "she didn't make it Chief. She got killed in a helicopter crash right at the end of that fucking war, sir."

"Sorry to hear that, you and her got along real well. Yes sir, war's hell, that's why I never married, General. Besides, no woman with half a brain would give me the time of day, sir."

"You never married I take it Chief? Gees I can't believe that shit for a minute, not with the way you were constantly playing with all those children back in Ethiopia, sir. Someone who likes kids as much as you do, has to be married and have a gaggle of kid to play with along the way, Chief. I never thought you not being married for a minute, sir." General Campanelli replied, trying to get the subject off Mendoza and her death.

The Chief laughed as he remarked. "General Campanelli Sir, I said I didn't marry, but didn't say I didn't make any children in my many years of debauchery and sinful living, sir. I have a number of kids running around the country, correct that sir, the world."

"I bet you do Chief Kirby Sir." General Campanelli replied pleasantly with a wide grin.

"Sir, I'd really like to spend the rest of the day jaw jacking with you like this sir, but I have a helluva lot of work to accomplish before I can call it a fucking day, sir. You staying on the Island for a while, or are you gonna disappear on me again, General Campanelli Sir?"

"I'm going to be on the Island for a coupla hours, and then I'm off for my new station, Kirby."

"That's a real shame, I wish your stay was a little longer on the Island, sir. Yes Sir General Campanelli Sir. It's been a real pleasure bumping into your ass again, sir. Look General, I'll try and have my people set up to work by themselves, so I can sneak away before you ship out. Then I'll look you up and we can talk more about this other shit, sir." Chief Kirby offered him.

"You got it sir, I'll let you know if and when I can use you by then, sir. I have the power to draft any soldier I feel would be a useful cog in my future operation, and you sir, are a major cog in anything I might be involved in, Chief."

"Thank you for a vote of confidence General, you were always a sharp knife to deal with, sir. I have to get back, I'll see you later if possible, General Campanelli Sir." The Chief slapped him on the back as he left. The General could easily feel the strength in the old man's body as he thought to himself. 'Yes, a good man to have on your side in a fight'. He hung around until the SeaBees set off their charge, and a hilltop disappeared in a cloud of dust. Then, the three dozers moved in and leveled the ground until it was smooth enough for a fighter to land on.

General Campanelli walked around the Island for about an hour, he found the site of birds trying to land or take off rather comically. They were far from agile as they crashed into the ground, or ran as they tried to get airborne. A local told the General they were called Gooney Birds, but they were really Albatross. He could not get enough of watching them, especially when they tried to land. He thought the birds would fare a lot better off if they just tucked themselves in a tight ball, and allowed themselves to roll along the ground instead of crashing the way did. He tore himself away from the spectacle and walked the coastline. He came across a group of fish near the shore and one shark fin, and then he spotted some women swimming, and warned them of the shark. Four women no older than twenty came out of the water without a stitch on to avoid the shark. He enjoyed the sight before he moved on until he came across John, Locker and Aleksandra coming at him from the other way.

He happily joined the other three officers, and in no time flat he was holding hands with Aleksandra. John was the first one to see the strange looking aircraft as it came out of the clouds from the east and announced, "will you look at that damn thing coming at us sir."

As the CV-22 Osprey came in for a landing, Aleksandra stared at it in stunned disbelief. This was the first time she ever saw one of the Tilt Rotor aircraft in flight.

General Campanelli was being tugged on his arm by an excited Aleksandra, she tried to force him towards the weird looking landing aircraft as she cried at him, "I want see that plane. I never see anything like it in life before, it wonderful sight to see, sir."

The General was nearly dragged across the tarmac as they headed directly towards the aircraft when it came to a stop. She ran up to the side then walked around the ship, running her hand lightly on the metal skin, touching it with her fingers, and smelling it's odor. General Campanelli felt if she could, she would make love to the aircraft.

The tail loading ramp slowly lowered, and the Major stepped back and bent down to look inside. Her face told the pilot she was in awe of the aircraft. The pilot never saw her uniform before and for a second, he felt slightly threatened by her presence, until he spotted the American General standing directly behind her. The pilot immediately saluted the General and relaxed.

Campanelli walked up to him and said, "sir, would you do me a tremendous favor here?"

"Sure thing General Campanelli Sir, just name it and if I can, I'll get it done for you sir." The pilot knew who he was supposed to pick up and was aware this officer was the General.

"You mind giving the Major here the grand tour of your aircraft, sir? Otherwise, she'll never leave me alone for a damn second, sir. It's okay Captain, because she's scheduled to be station on my ship and she'll be traveling out to her on your aircraft anyway, sir."

"In that case General Campanelli Sir, yes sure thing, sir. Major would you follow me please Ma'am?" The officers circled the ship, as the Captain talked to them. He gave Aleksandra the complete low down on the specialized aircraft.

She did not look at him as she listened to everything he told her about the aircraft and stood thunderstruck, never aware an aircraft like this ever existed. She had her hand resting on the plane, maybe to make her believe the aircraft truly existed.

"Would you like to go inside the aircraft and really check her out from there, Major Ma'am? It's quite the aircraft, and seeing it from outside is not doing her justice, Major."

"Could we please sir?" she replied with a wide smile plastered on her lips to him.

"Sure thing Major, follow me please Ma'am," he offered pleasantly to her.

They walked up the wide tail ramp, the co-pilot was already on board and called out. "Jesus Capt, we haven't been on the ground for ten minutes yet, and you already found yourself a good looking piece of ass to play around with, sir."

"Put it back in your damn pocket, she's a fucking Major you asshole you." General Campanelli warned him in an angry voice as he followed the Major into the aircraft.

The Lieutenant snapped to attention and saluted the strange looking uniformed Major.

She was flattered by the salute and she returned it proudly to the American pilot. The Captain let her get in front of him and snapped at the Lieutenant, "you don't have to salute her inside the damn aircraft, asshole." The Lieutenant snuck out, brass always made him feel uncomfortable no matter what country they came from.

"Here you go Major Ma'am. There's a special system designed into the V-22 Osprey aircraft. If we come under enemy attack, and one engine becomes disabled, this here baby has a unique system that transfers power from the good engine, over to the damaged one, and both engines will continue to turn at full power until we land safely, as long as we land quickly that is. This system isn't made to keep the aircraft flying for long under those conditions, Ma'am. The aircraft just about does anything to protect her pilot and crew, and the newer models are coming through equipped with a titanium shell surrounding the cockpit and engine compartment. The engines comes with an exhaust suppresser to protect the ship from possible heat seeking missile attack. We can do a vertical liftoff, and convert to a turboprop aircraft while in flight, and we can land and takeoff quicker than any helicopter can. Do you have any questions Ma'am?"

"I hundred question I dare to ask Captain Sir, but I no know where start, please. In life, never see aircraft like this one, never sir."

"There's no aircraft quite like this here bird anywhere else on the entire earth, Ma'am. The only other aircraft that comes anywhere near the capabilities of this craft, is the A-8 Harrier Jump aircraft, Ma'am." The proud Captain offered to the staring female Major.

She scanned the many dials, control sticks and gauges and then she asked the polite pilot in an excited voice, "what this stick used for sir? I never see a stick like this in any other aircraft. What does to control in the aircraft, Captain?"

"This one's moved up when you want to free the wings to close her up for tight storage on a base, or if she's being stored on board a ship where space is in short supply, Ma'am. So the aircraft's can be placed one against the other, and this stick here is moved whenever you want to go from turboprop flight to helicopter mode, or hovering Major Ma'am."

"Aircraft hover like helicopter I believe, sir?" the stunned foreign female officer cried.

"Yes Ma'am, this ship can do everything a helicopter can do, and a helluva lot more as well, Ma'am. It can fly twice the speed of most helicopters, Ma'am." The pilot said with a smile.

CHAPTER 16

All the while the pilot was giving the Major a grand tour of the aircraft, Campanelli remained standing outside the craft speaking to the other officers with him. It was getting late, and he wanted to get this dinner date with the female Colonel over with so he could catch some sleep. He felt this dinner party was going to be a very boring affair. He was right, the dinner was boring. The Colonel did nothing but pump him for information on the Vinegar Joe Platform. He waltzed around most of her questions, and the others he could not dodge, he simply replied by the stock answer that he was not at liberty to talk about her questions. After dinner, they went to the quarters while Colonel Locker and Major Aleksandra went to the room they shared together.

Locker took a quick shower and she returned dressed in a silk bathrobe. Aleksandra noticed she was angry so she took her shower, and there was little talk between them. She opened a bottle of whiskey and sipped from a glass. She offered Aleksandra a glass, and Colonel Locker told her about her past, and all the trouble she was having hooking up with a man who could please her. She also informed Aleksandra most men were afraid of any women in power, and being a Colonel sure put a severe kink on her love life.

As they spoke Aleksandra's towel slipped, and she did nothing to cover herself. She noticed Locker staring at her, she could not keep her eyes off her breasts and the Major thought as she continued to stare at Colonel Locker. 'I thought so, you substituted women for men I see, I could own you if I wanted to waste time on you, bitch'.

The two female military officers continued to drink and talk together, until Aleksandra finally announced she was done in, and was going to sleep. She stood and removed the towel, and felt Locker hold her breath. She smiled as she thought, you fool Americans are so easy, but she was stunned when Locker asked if she wanted any company between the sheets. She smiled as she replied to the female officer. "Not this time, maybe next time Colonel."

Locker purred, "that's a shame, I could teach you a few things about love making, Major."

Aleksandra smirked back at her, "I doubt, you no be first woman slccp with in life, Colonel."

Now it was Locker's turn to be stunned. She gulped down the remaining liquor, and then she slipped between her covers and mumbled to Alex, "see you in the morning Major."

A slight snore was her only replied from the already sleeping foreign female Major.

At exactly Oh, Six Hundred Hours, General Edward Campanelli alone with the rest of his Command Staff stood gathered together on the tarmac of the airfield. The CV-22's massive motors were already spooling. Chief Kirby was standing with Colonel Tomlinson's small group, and they saluted the officers as they got on board the waiting Osprey. Then Kirby broke ranks and quickly ran up the ramp to be with General Campanelli's group as ordered. The General was much more comfortable in this aircraft mainly because this one hand windows he could look out of this time and much better seats for the group.

Aleksandra was excited at flying in the weird looking aircraft. She looked over every inch of the interior aircraft again as she was trained to be by her Communist Commanders. The flight out to the Blue Whale cargo ship was quick and smooth. It took five nearly hours until the pilot announced over the aircraft intercom. "If you people look off to your right, you'll see our landing zone, sirs. It's one helluva sight to see sitting on the water, people."

Everyone was surprised by the sight. What they saw appeared to be one huge, flat massive sea of gleaming steel, floating easily on the Ocean surface. They could easily see three of the massive commandeered super oil cargo ships that made up the unusual metal Island.

The pilot announced proudly, "we just made contact with the ship, and Command has informed us seven of the twenty four ships are already bolted together, and they're decked out for landing aircraft and command structure. The rest of the ships are scattered all around the area while waiting to be called in for hookup to the floating Island, sirs."

As the officers watched all the action taking place below them, another massive converted fuel tanker ship came in close to the Island. General Campanelli ordered the pilot to stay in flight as they watched the ship prepare for hookup to the ever growing Island. They observed hydraulics raise the long extra sections of decking hanging over both sides of the large tanker, as drag lines were setup and three huge winches were ready to drag the massive tanker into position. Once the added decking was set in place and connected to the decking covering the entire deck of the tanker, the drag lines were launched from the Island to the eighth ship.

General Campanelli noticed the decking from the Island side looked twice as long and a hell of a lot wider than the decking from the ship being slowly pulled in place with the heavy drag lines. The entire operation was something to witness, and it was being completed in no time and it did not leave much to the imagination on how the entire project was going to look once finished. The amazed Commanding Officer could easily tell it was going to be one massive flight deck once all the huge ships were set in place.

Chief Kirby moved nearer to the window and then he looked over the shoulder of General Campanelli and said after he let out with a low whistle, "looks to me like they added some extra section of decking between each of the damn ship, sir. Damn, this is some system they're working on below us, General. If it works out the way it looks like it will, it means the United States could have an operational airbase close to any possible military conflict throughout the rest of the world, sir. It's a great idea, someone sure did their fricking homework on this one, sir."

It took half an hour for the flight deck workers to drag the huge once super oil tanker ship into position. Then, a horde of deck workers attacked this ship to the deck and worked like hell bolting the ship securely and placing the expansion joints in place, and then connecting hundreds of wires and pipes to the newly set in position tanker, to make all the ships act as one.

The pilot interrupted the observation and called out, "General Campanelli Sir, we're going to have to set down pretty soon sir, or we're going to become the Vinegar Joe's first emergency situation to deal with, sir. I'm afraid we're quickly running low on fuel, sir."

The General yelled back without taking his eyes off of what was taking place below him on the expanding flight deck of the Vinegar Joe Platform, "well, then set the damn thing down will ya please. I don't swim too good you know mister."

The vertical lift aircraft circled the massive Platform once more and then began to slow its speed down until they received final clearance for landing. For a moment it felt like the aircraft was going to fall right out of the sky as the engines started to angle up into hover mode. They vibrated and shook a bit until the landing aircraft was set in full hover mode, and then she started its slow descent to the flight deck.

"I no believe ship, it fantastic see sir. I never believe something like this possible, General Campanelli Sir!" she squeezed the General's arm, but he did not respond. She looked at him and saw he was glued to his chair as he held onto the handles of his seat as the plane stared to land.

The aircraft lightly touched down as smoothly as if they just hit a slight bump in the road, while riding in a luxury car. A loud hydraulic sound started as the rear tail ramp slowly lowered, flooding the interior of the aircraft with daylight and a rush of fresh air. The noise served to scare the General, and most of the others who were not prepared for the ramp lowering in the aircraft. He actually jumped up and ran out of the plane, only to be met by a group of other officers and enlisted men standing at attention, waiting to greet their new Commanding Officer.

A Captain suddenly stepped up and immediately saluted the General, and then explained what his duties were. "General Campanelli Sir, it's great to have you on board the Vinegar Joe Platform, sir. Allow me to introduce myself sir. I'm Captain Carl Hoffman, and I've been placed in Command of this operation until your arrival on the Platform, sir. I have your private quarters prepared for you sir, and your CIC, Combat Information Center's ready below deck also, sir. Workers are standing by to off load your equipment, and bring it over to the CIC and hookup your computers and other machines for you. You have Televideo and Telecommunications, with Teleconference capabilities along with data up, and down links, with all communications, and reconnaissance and spy satellites from your CIC Chamber, General Campanelli Sir.

"Oh yes one more thing I have to inform you about General Campanelli Sir, before I happen to forget to tell you about this other stuff, sir. Chief of Naval Operations, Admiral Thomas Standlund sent a special memo over, to inform you he was able to pull some strings, and he's releasing the Aircraft Carriers Stennis, and the United States along with the Kelso. Our latest super Aircraft Carrier to your Command, sir. He's also pulling back the Carriers the Kennedy, America and Constellation, to replace the other Carriers presently on station in the Middle East region of the world, General Campanelli Sir."

The Captain read from a paper as he continued with his reports for the Commander, "the Admiral said he's going to re-commission the older Carriers Midway, Coral Sea, Forrestal, Saratoga, and the Ranger in order to make room for these ships, and to also stay well within the guidelines set down by the past Administration, sir. I can't believe all our Nuclear Powered Aircraft Carriers are under your Command, sir. It's amazing the Admiral pulled up these last ships, especially since the Kelso hadn't had her shakedown cruise as yet, sir."

General Campanelli smiled and he offered the Captain, "there's nothing better to forge a ship's metal, than to have her damn shakedown cruise be a trial by fire and blood, sir. It'll strengthen her keel. Perhaps you could have some of your men show my Command Staff where everything is, and show me around this damn thing. This is sure some helluva ship, Captain."

"Sure thing sir. Sir, what would you like to see first on the Platform, General Campanelli Sir?"

"I want to see the workers hooking up that ship we witnessed being docked up with the Platform when we were about to land on this damn thing, Captain."

"Okay General Campanelli Sir, if you'll follow me please sir," Captain Hoffman offered.

The overly interested General followed the proud Captain as he walked over to a mass of flight deck workers. The crew immediately stopped what they were doing in order to salute the two officers, but General Campanelli did not want them to stop their work. He always felt a salute marked him out as a person in Command, and a sure target for any possible enemy sniper to pop a cap off at him. As he walked through the mess of workers, more of them stopped what they were doing and they saluted him, he was getting really pissed off over this situation. He spotted a First Class Petty Officer with a bullhorn tucked under his arm, and made his way over to him. The Petty Officer saw the General coming at him and immediately yelled out, "Attention on Deck." All the workers came to a stop again and they snapped to attention.

General Campanelli walked up to the man and snarled at him, "give me that fucking bullhorn, mister." He tried to talk in it, but it did not work, so he glared angrily at the Petty Officer and he hissed at him at the same time. "Don't make me ask you how this fucking thing works, mister!"

He jumped as he offered to the General in an excited voice, "yes Sir General Sir. Here you go sir, let me show you how to work it correctly, General Sir." He pushed the switch to on and then he announced to the angry and glaring officer. "There you go General, it's ready to use, General Sir. All you have to do is pull the trigger and then speak into the back of it and you're good to go, General Sir."

General Campanelli grunted at the officer as he put the horn to his mouth and he barked into it, "listen up people, everyone stop whatever the hell you're doing for a minute and pay attention to me, dammit. That's better, in case you're unaware of this fact, I'm General Edward Campanelli, and I'm the Supreme Commander of this here little operation. If you people want to get off on the right foot with my ass. Then I suggest you stop saluting me, or any other officer on this damn thing until further notice. I want you people to work, not waste your damn time with saluting any damn brass walking around this here thing until it's fully operational.

"I have to get this damn Platform thing completed, and ready to accept aircraft A-SAP, and until that time, you people are going to hate my damn guts, and my Officers as well. Once this damn Platform's completed, I'll make it up to you people by giving you a party that you'll never forget, and plenty of leave time also to enjoy to go along with that damn party. The phone lines to home will be opened for you people, and any other suggestions you people might think up can be written down, and then placed inside my damn mail box. I promise you all that I'll read each and every suggestion I receive from you guys, even the ones telling me to kiss your stinking asses, people."

Laughter from the men and women workers as they remained staring at the new officer.

"I can't impress on you people how important this damn Platform is to this entire operation, and the sooner it's completed the better for the United States and her Allies. Now get back to work people, all I want to see assholes and elbows from you people," he lowered the bullhorn and scanned the horde of workers and then turned back to the Petty Officer. "You too mister. Find something to do." He growled at the young man as he actually threw the bullhorn back to him and he added to his angry words, "get working on something around here mister."

"Yes sir," the Seaman replied as he walked over to the men and watched them.

The General looked to the Captain and smiled, "I must say sir, you do have a way with words."

"You're not the first one to ever tell me that shit sir," he replied with a grunt.

The officers moved between the workers, no one saluted but the workers remained civil.

General Campanelli looked at a number of the heavy bolts joining the tanker ship to the main section of the Platform, they were nearly two full inches thick and made of chrome alloy steel, to avoid possible rusting and snapping. It had threads on both sides of the bolt, with a narrow section of the bolt with no threads. The Captain explained this was to tighten the bolt and still have some movement between the deck planks because the bolt could only be tightened so tight. The General's attention was drawn over to a jagged section of metal planking, and it fitted neatly into another section of planking shaped the same way. It looked like the mouth of a giant alligator with its teeth fitting together correctly. The Captain explained it was called a Tiger's Tooth expansion joint, and the teeth were there to enable the planks to spread out, and yet not allow the wheels of the fighter aircraft to slip into any of the opening.

"Amazing." Was the only word General Campanelli muttered, as they moved onto the last ship's section of flight decking. There was still a lot of movement here because the ship was not completely and properly secured with the rest of the Platform yet. He heard engines running below deck, and he asked the Captain what they were for.

"General Campanelli Sir, they're the generators and the one desalination plant we have is already up and on line, General. What we branded as the shitter ship hasn't been installed yet, that's her over there sir, she's the next ship scheduled to be set in place, sir. Right now most of the men are shitting in cans, and we're just dumping it overboard, sir."

"I don't think I like the sounds of that last remark Captain," General Campanelli growled angrily at the man as he glared and then waited for his response.

"Neither do I sir, but for right now. We don't have much of a choice in the matter, sir." Captain Hoffman replied to his Commanding Officer with a little concern in his tone this time.

"When do you plan to have the entire Platform complex completed by, sir?"

"I figure at least another week to a week and a half to have all the tanker ships connected up completely, and then another two months at the least until all the catwalks, and the other connections are complete, and then we're at one hundred percent fully operational, General Campanelli Sir." Captain Hoffman reported proudly to his Commander.

"Shit, that's a helluva long time from now before this damn thing is finally going to be fully operational for us Captain," General Campanelli mussed as he shook his head.

"General Campanelli Sir, once you see this Platform complete, you'll realize exactly what size this operation truly is, sir. We'll have a Floating Island over twenty times the size of our largest Aircraft Carrier, and we'll also have more fighting aircraft stored on board this ship, than most countries have in their entire ground arsenal, General Campanelli Sir."

The General totally ignored the Captain's explanation as he growled back at the other officer. "I want that stinking shit tanker ship brought up immediately, and if you have to, I want temporary ramps sent out to her so she can take care of these damn workers, mister. That ship's doing us no damn good sitting off our damn beam like that, mister. It's demoralizing my people by making them shit in god damn buckets, and I'll not stand for that for another damn second, sir. If these men and women have to shit, I'll not have them shitting in fucking cans, mister. Now order that damn shit ship moved closer to this damn thing at once, sir."

"It's not that easy to accomplish I'm afraid General Campanelli Sir, we'll have to hookup another desalination plant, because the workers are going to want to shower once they see the shower stalls inside the latrine ship, sir. And we're going to have to have power out to the ship in order to run the waste treatment plant on board the shit tanker ship as well, General Campanelli Sir. Besides General, the ships have to be connected to the Platform in a certain order to make this Platform work out properly as per the instructions, sir."

"What the fuck are these people doing for a damn bath around here, mister?" he suddenly roared at the once Commander of the Platform.

"General Campanelli Sir, they're taking a swim in the Ocean, and washing in the salt water until we have the shitter ship set properly in place, General Campanelli Sir."

General Campanelli openly glared at the Captain as he snapped at him angrily, "you got to be fucking shitting me with that damn order on your part, mister. I have my people bathing in the fucking sea. It must be freezing in the water dammit, what the hell kind of operation are you running around here anyhow, Captain Hoffman? I have a good mind to bring your ass up on fucking charges, which I'll do if any of my people get sick while bathing in the damn cold Ocean water, mister. Or because of the unfit sanitation situation you have established around here as well for crap sake Captain!" the fuming General actually yelled as he started to pace back and forth in front of the stunned Captain.

Captain Hoffman immediately snapped to attention and then he replied to the extremely angry acting Commanding Officer, "yes Sir General Campanelli Sir, I'll get right on the shit tanker setup immediately, General Sir." Captain Hoffman actually ran from the General's side, and he started to bark out a flood of new orders to a radio operator. Seconds later, the General saw the so called shit tanker ship start up her engines, and then slowly begin to edge her way closer to the Platform. Other officers quickly moved in and they pulled a number of the workers from their already assigned jobs, to have them help out with the shit tanker linkup.

General Campanelli stood by while they moved the shit tanker ship in place. It took nearly an hour for the ship to be pulled and dragged up alongside the Platform. The excited Captain used his head while trying to get back on the good side of the Commander, and he had the ship pulled in the position where it would have in the scheduled Platform lineup. The heavy drag lines were fired out to the waiting ship as the side planks were raised, and then locked and secured in the proper position. The extension planks were set in place in this area, so the ship was able to be pulled in place quickly. When the ship was set, a horde of workers bolted it in place.

The angry General muttered to himself while still fuming at the Captain, 'that's much better you fucking asshole you, making my people uncomfortable like this'. He turned and walked away, while leaving the Captain at work as he explored the rest of the ship.

The General watched as the workers quickly unbolted the super structure of the last tanker to be hooked up to the Platform, and then they immediately covered over the opening with more of the six inch thick specially designed manganese deck planking. General Campanelli walked over to the edge of the rapidly expanding flight deck, and then he looked down at the sea that was over sixty feet below him and he moaned aloud, "whoa boy, I won't do that fucking move again you can bet the bank on it."

John came on deck and found General Campanelli and reported to him, "Say Eddy, you should see all the stinking equipment that's stowed below deck of this damn thing, man."

General Campanelli was still steaming over the Captain and the way he was treating the workers and he bitched at John, "I can't believe this dumb shit of a fucking Officer, making his people shit in god damn buckets and swim in the cold Ocean to get clean."

"What's all this shit about Eddy?" John asked him with some concern in his voice.

"Arrr, this fucking Captain who was in Command of this operation until we showed up, was having his people swim in the damn Ocean and shit in cans, and then dumping it overboard, instead of having the shit tanker ship set in place first on the damn Platform, John. If I were running this fucking operation, I would've built the Platform around the damn shit tanker first. That way I coulda made certain our people we being treated properly, dammit. I can't get over that fricking Captain forcing his people to shit in damn buckets for Pete's sake," the General moaned at his lifelong friend this time as he shook his head in disgust.

"Campey, in case you don't realize it yet sir, you're in Command of this entire god damn operation, sir. So do what you gotta do to the Captain to set his ass straight on course again, Eddy." John immediately informed Campanelli as he flashed him one of his best smiles.

General Campanelli glared back angrily at John, and then snapped at him, "Fuck you wiseass. You always have to point out the stinking obvious to my ass all the damn time, don't you John? What's your problem around here anyway, mister?"

"I think you better get laid Eddy, it might put you in a betta mood, my friend. As I was saying sir, the CIC Chamber they have setup on board this damn thing. It's complete with all the hookups, so we can actually speak in real time to the Air Force, Navy, Army, and Marines in the field of battle, at the same damn time sir. We're even patched through into each of their satellites and computers at the same time as well, Eddy. It makes our headquarters back at Base Sentry in the Sudan, look rather primitive compared to this one, General Campanelli Sir. We even have air conditioning below deck, and we also have separate rooms equipped with computers, so we can remain in constant contact with the CIC at all times, sir."

General Campanelli calmed down a little and then he asked John if he was getting a little familiar with the decks below the flight deck.

"A little bit, but I warn you Eddy you can easily get lost down there sir, as Colonel Locker has already found out, sir. It took our escorts over fifteen minutes to finally locate her, once she went off exploring on her own and she was madder than a wet hen when they finally found her, sir." John again smiled at his friend of many years.

"I could bet on that John," General Campanelli laughed as he looked all around the deck.

"You want to come below deck and see what we have stored down deck, Eddy?" General White asked him as he tried to get Edward to come below deck with him.

"Nah, I'd rather stay top side for now. How long until we're operational in the CIC, John?"

"I figure not for another hour or so, the lighting bellow deck is pretty good. We have a ton of supplies and tapes, so we can record all incoming and out going communications. There's a threat board, that covers most of China and lower Russia, North and South Korea, and Japan and Taiwan sir," General White reported to his Commanding Officer this time around.

"Why the fuck do we have Japan covered for, John? How the hell did she get involved in this damn situation now and why are we thinking of protecting Japan, after what she did in the African war?" General Campanelli asked his Second in Command with concern.

"From what I've been hearing lately Eddy, there's some concern China might push through South Korea, all the way down until she becomes a serious threat to Japan. China would love to get her hands on Japan for what she done to that nation during World War Two, sir. China has a very long memory, and there's a lot of anger still held by them against Japan, Eddy."

"You really think China's still carrying a stinking grudge against Japan for their actions of almost fifty two years ago, John? I seriously doubt that very much John, but if the brain thrust thinks China might attack Japan if she got half the chance to. Then why the hell don't they put a damn stop to their stinking attack against North Korea then? After all, the United Nations just gave China permission if you will, to sanction an attack against North Korea. I really don't believe they gave enough thought to this clearance to attack North Korea by China, myself John. There's too many loose ends left dangling around if you ask me, sir."

"Dunno for sure at this time, all I know is there's more rumors floating around here than I can shake a fricking stick at, Eddy," he complained, he then looked over Eddy's shoulder. Out of the mist covering the sea came a massive ship, it was an Aircraft Carrier, she turned a bit and John saw the numbers CVN-69 and he announced proudly, "that's the Eisenhower now Eddy."

"What the hell's she doing so stinking close to the damn Platform thing, John?"

"Looks like she's changing position. Evidently, the ships waiting to be linked up to the Platform, knew she's going to move stations. Look at how the tanker ships hanging around, are sudden no longer in sight, Eddy. Besides my friend, from what I was lead to believe, the Carriers can dock with this Platform for added supplies, as well as any Destroyers and Frigates. It has a special dock below deck where submarines can even dock up to us, and off load and or take on provisions, sir. This damn thing has taken everything possible into consideration. There's even a number of portable catwalks which mount in the sides of the ships, enabling us to go from one ship to the other from below deck. Every tanker has an elevator stationed in them, to send aircraft, armament or provisions from below decks to top side, sir."

"Look John, what the hell are you trying to do around here my friend? Are you trying to sell me the damn thing or what, dammit? You sound like a frustrated real estate agent trying to sell me a stinking home I have no interest in buying, man. I read most of what you're telling me already, and the rest of it I'd like to find out for myself, mister. After all, I like surprises just as much as the next person does, John."

"Jesus Campey, what the hell's up your ass man?" John bitched as he looked at his friend.

"I guess I'm still a little pissed off about this damn Captain Hoffman making his fricking people shit in buckets and swim in the damn Ocean to clean themselves. Christ, what the hell does he think this shit is, the stone fricking ages or something, sir? I'm surprised his people didn't rip him apart over that dumb ass order of his, dammit to hell and back again."

"Why don't we stand behind the ass, and drive him a little crazy while he dishes out orders."

The Commander smiled, it was a devilish smile that spelt serious trouble for the unsuspecting Captain as he replied, "you know something, I like the way you're thinking lately

John, that's a good idea sir. I want the fucker to know he made a mistake, and an asshole out of himself. Once this Platform's fully operational, I intend to ship his ass back stateside. With that in his 201 file, the reader will know he screwed up, and his Commander was kind enough not to write down his fuck up. He'll remain a stinking Captain for the rest of his time in the service with that report stuck in his report jacket. He deserves it, I can't believe he allow his people work under those conditions." Campanelli stopped speaking for a few moments, and then he added.

"John do me a favor, I want you to go around and find out if there's any beer stored on this damn tub. If you find some, I want you to commandeer it and get it chilled off, and then have it sent up to the flight deck. When the workers are finished hooking up these last two ships today, I'm going to call for a rest period, and allow them to tie one on if they chose.

"I might as well start off on the right foot with them. Hmmmm... see if they have any burgers while you're at it, if not, order the cooks to make some up. We'll cut up a few of those metal fifty five gallon drums stacked over there, and make them into sorta barbecue pits, and cook the shit for the work crews. Hell, we might as well turn this thing into a damn party for them for Pete's sake. Sort of go all the way and give the crews the rest of the stinking day off. Let the bastards enjoy themselves some, and then we can work them to death the day after."

John smiled as he replied to his Commanding Officer, "I got ya man, and I happen agree with you on this one Eddy. It pays off when you give the crews a stinking day off every once in a while, sir." General White took off like a shot to carry out his new orders. John liked to make waves whenever he could much like Campanelli, and he knew he was going to give the supply Sergeant below deck and the cooks some real fits with these new orders.

General Campanelli watched with much concern in his expression as the massive Aircraft Carrier slowly went off into the thick mist again. Some of the sailors from the Carrier were standing on the huge flight deck, and they were waving to his workers and also watched all the going ons on the huge and ever growing Platform deck. The worried General looked off to the east and began to grow more concerned, he wasn't a weather man, but he sure could feel the bad weather coming in quickly on him.

Even the rapidly massing clouds looked like they were angry at the earth, as they quickly bunched up high in the sky overhead his new toy. He next made his way over to Captain Hoffman, and he watched the officer as he barked out more orders nastily at his people as he tried to drive them harder than he ever did before General Campanelli arrived on the Platform.

The workers were a good mix of young Sailors, SeaBees, Army and Airforce personnel. The General smirked as the upset Captain continued to scream harshly at his people as he ran from one work crew to the other, all the while continuing to yell at the toiling workers.

The General mumbled to himself, 'yeah, go ahead you asshole you, and make your people hate you even more now than they ever did before, mister. That way it'll make it that much easier for me to walk in, and give them the rest of stinking day off, and make them respect me for the order like they should've been respecting you all along while you were constructing this damn thing, mister. This just goes to show me you're really a piss poor damn leader of any military troops, or workers' you have Command over mister',   he shook his head in disgust as he watched the Captain work on his people.

A sudden and loud roar overhead made everyone stop what they were doing and look up. Two sleek F-22 Raptor stealth fighters launched from the Aircraft Carrier Eisenhower, flew directly over the entire flight deck of the Platform. The crews cheered as the fighter aircraft dipped wings to the men and women working below. An angry Captain Hoffman brought the quick break to an end by screaming at his workers to get back to work, or their asses would be placed on report. The crews grumbled angrily at the Captain, but they when back to what they were doing.

General John White ran up behind General Edward Campanelli while out of breath, and he reported to his Commander in an excited tone of voice. "Hey Eddy, I found a full skid of beer stowed away in the damn cooler, that works out to two beers for everyone working on the deck with a few left over for good measure, sir. The cooks have three hundred pounds of chopped meat, and they didn't mind in the least the extra work of cooking the stuff outside on the flight deck, sir. One cook even offered he knew how to make a barbecue outta the drums, he followed me up to the deck. He's working on the first drum right now sir," John pointed at a man busy cutting a metal fifty five gallon drum in half the long way with the help of one of the SeaBee's who was obviously a welder.

"That's great, I'm watching this stinking Captain bury himself deeper and deeper with his damn people, sir. He's making my job of taking over Command a whole lot easier, John."

News spread like wildfire throughout the horde of workers that the Platform cooks were up to something special on the other side of the flight deck. One by one, the workers sneaked little peaks at the new activity, every time someone stopped to take a look at what was going on. It brought another flood of curses from the fuming Captain, who was trying desperately to save his ass by working his crews to death now. General Campanelli kept a close eye on what Captain Hoffman was doing, adding to his frustration with his men that made him yell all the more at his crews. One worker saw the welder attach legs to the bottom of the halved fifty five gallon drum and he yelled out, "holy shit, they're making a barbecue pit over there, people!"

All the workers stopped what they were doing this time as they watched the cooks going at it. Some of the workers cheered, and this made the Captain go more nuts on them. He threatened them with court marshals and much worse. But the workers were too excited now, and they did not pay much attention to the Captain's ranting and raving.

Although the General did not feel good about destroying a man in front of his troops, but he felt this foolish officer deserved it. He did not feel too bad knowing he was going to stop this Captain from making any further rate in the service once he filed his report, but this was how the Armed Forces remained strong. He suddenly feared the crews might even revolt against the angry Captain and he stepped in. He raised his hands and waited until everyone stopped working and looked at him then he announced. "I think you people have done enough work for today. I'm having a cookout and tomorrow is a day off for everyone on the deck crews."

The exhausted workers yelled out in excitement over the offer of a day off tomorrow.

General Campanelli growled at the workers, "shut up and let me finish addressing you people will you please, dammit. There's more to this than just what I told you people."

Some of the Chiefs and other deck officers yelled at the crews to quiet down and listen to the General. When this was accomplished, he continued with his explanation. "I watched you people work, and I think you're a helluva crew. To show you people my appreciation, I'm having the cooks make up a ton of burgers, there'll be beer coming up from below deck for you guys, but I don't want anyone to get nuts on me, or I'll throw your ass in the damn can. I want all you men and women to get these two ships locked in position, and then the party begins."

"Get the hell outta our way and watch us go to work on the damn things then General Campanelli Sir," someone called out from the crowd. The crews went back to work with a new vigor, men yelling, some actually singing and cursing at the same time.

The General watched the workers go at it. The angry Captain came over and then he snapped at General Campanelli. "You really stuck it to me just then you know General Campanelli Sir, thanks a helluva lot for the knife in the back, sir."

General Campanelli got right to the point with the angry Captain, "don't debate with me mister, you'll lose every time, sir. You're the ass who fucked up royally by making these people work under these animalistic conditions you created, and I'll never forgive or forget you for that mess up, Captain. I'll have your transfer papers drawn up by tomorrow afternoon at the latest, and I want your ass off this damn Platform thing by no later than Saturday evening, sir."

The Captain was stunned by what he was hearing from his Commanding Officer and he cried, "sir, you're putting a nail in my damn career on me, sir. If you transfer me like this, I'm dead in the water sir. Step on me yes, but don't destroy my career General Campanelli Sir."

"You should've thought about your damn career when you first forced your people to shit in fricking cans, mister. I had a crew in the deep jungle in Ethiopia, and they had bathrooms setup before the fighting started. You have to keep your people comfortable if you want to work them to death like you're doing here, Captain. I saw your stinking act, and I didn't like it one bit sir, you tried to drive them by treating them like damn animals. So get the hell outta my face before I have you chucked overboard so you can bathe. I said get out of my face mister!"

The Captain instantly backed off, and he went back to the workers, and watched them perform their duties as ordered. All the while, he was cursing the angry General under his breath. A Lieutenant stepped up and he took over the workers. He snapped out a bunch of new orders to the Sergeants, who in turn drove the crews the correct way.

General Campanelli mumbled more to himself than anyone standing near him. "Ahhh, give me a hand full of stinking Sergeants, and I could conquer the stinking world with them."

A cook came over to General Campanelli and offered, "General Sir," he said not knowing his name and he came to attention and saluted him.

"Can the salute, whaddaya want from me Corporal? C'mon man, I'm rather busy as you can plainly see for yourself, mister." He snarled back at the man.

"General Sir, I wanted to inform you the coals are hot and ready for cooking sir, when do you want me to start the burgers going for the crews, General Sir?"

Campanelli looked at the amount of work the crews had left ahead of them, he then stated, "don't start cooking the damn things for another hour mister. What about the beer?"

"General, we won't bring up the beer until the crews are finished working, sir. I hope I did the right thing for you with that order, sir?" The grinning Corporal offered as he looked at what the General was looking at, and understood why he wanted the delay cooking the burgers.

The Commanding General suddenly laughed as he replied to the young man staring him in the eyes, "you did fine Corporal, and my name is Edward Campanelli, inform the others you speak with. I'll introduce myself to the crews when they stop to eat. Tell you what mister, when you see the workers stop working then you can order the beers to be brought up to the flight deck."

"General Campanelli Sir, I can't do that sir. There's a Sergeant below deck, and he'll get really pissed off if I tried and order him around any, sir."

Campanelli let out his breath and then he nodded after hearing the Corporal's concern, and offered the kid, "Look kid I'm telling you to order the beer brought up to the flight deck level when you think it's the right time to do so, and don't worry about the damn Sergeant. Let him get pissed off Corporal, it's better to be pissed off than pissed on, mister."

"Boy sir, you can say that again. I have to remember that one, General Campanelli Sir."

"Do that, now get back to work will you mister." He ordered as he turned and then went back to watching the workers again. He noticed the still angry Captain placed plenty of distance between himself and the General. He shook his head and grumbled at no one in particular. "Just as I thought, no god damn balls an obvious book brass bastard."

He watched as one after another, the workers finished up their work assignment, and then they started to drift over to the barbecue area if they could not assist any workers still going at it. Some workers stayed behind to help the others.

Soon, all hookups and bolting were completed. He decided this was good enough, the wire and pipe connections could be completed after tomorrow. He looked to the east and swore he could see rain coming in. He smiled, sure tomorrow was going to be a wash out, and this way the workers would feel he gave them the day off, and not the rain. He yelled out, "that's enough today guys, let's go and eat people."

The soldiers ran their tools over to the gang boxes, and then ran over to the cooks.

As General Campanelli strolled towards the cookout area, a short young soldier dressed in an undershirt and khaki pants two sizes too big for him, walked up alongside the General and said to him. "Say General Sir, not for nothing but do these babies look like they belong to any of you ugly guys, sir?" she grabbed her breasts with both hands while shaking them slightly.

He gave a grunt, "you got me there soldier, I apologize for my words. I promise in the future, I'll be more careful with the way I address my people, young lady. Point well taken soldier."

The young female shot him a quick smile that would have melted ice. Then she quickened her pace leaving him behind, knowing she made her point with the new Commander of the Platform. She did not want to linger around in case she might have rubbed the Commander the wrong way.

General Campanelli thought about Mendoza, he always felt she was too sensitive when it came to her being a woman in the service, but now he saw it was not only her. All the women wanted the respect do them. He made a mental note to add women to his speech whenever he addressed his forces, it was a good point to remember. His attention was drawn to the cooking area, a lift truck was delivering a skid of Budweiser beer to the deck. The men and women cheered as it came nearer. It stopped in front of an ugly Sergeant whose white undershirt was covered with grime, and he needed a shave as well. He yelled angrily at the gathered soldiers.

"Okay ladies, beer's here. Form a line from this point on," he pointed in front of him, and the lift truck and then he added. "If you birds want any beer, right now, two to a customer. Any leftovers will be dealt out on a first come, and first serve basis. Let's get her going people, I'm hungry." He threw his cigarette butt on the deck, and then ground it into the metal.

General Campanelli came over and got himself a burger and just as he took a bite, John walked up to him and offered his Commander. "Say Eddy, we're up on line and a few new reports have come in that I feel deserves your immediate attention, sir."

"Shit!" he groaned and then he ordered his Second in Command. "Hey John, why don't you grab yourself a few burgers, they're pretty damn good man."

"We have some burgers stowed below deck already sir. Someone up here was kind enough to send down a number of the damn things to us, before they started feeding the work crews, sir." John burped and then he pounded his chest with his fist while trying to catch his breath, and then he grumbled. "These damn things always give me gas, sir."

The Commanding General laughed as he followed him to the CIC chamber. Moments later, he read a report marked urgent, that stated the English Jump Jet Carriers R05 Invincible, and R09 the Ark Royal, had taken up position off the coast of North Korea, and the two British ships were now being escorted by a few Chinese gun boats, and some of their Destroyers. The report further stated the North Korean government was up in arms at the knowledge the English Carriers were sailing along their coast with a number of Chinese Navy ships as their escorts.

He growled in response to this new information, "what the fuck are the English up to, damn? These flaming assholes are actually sailing with the damn Chinese ships. Locker, get me the damn Commander of the Invincible on the double quick, Colonel."

A second report he read stated a wing of CV-22 Osprey's would be landing on the Vinegar Joe Platform, dropping off new supplies and a horde of special engineers and their support crews. He put this report aside and told John it was no big deal.

Colonel Mary Locker cut in and offered. "General Campanelli Sir, I have the Commander of the Invincible on the horn, and he's waiting to speak with you General Sir."

"Good!" he growled as he reached for the phone and snapped it on and then replied into the receiver. "This is General Edward Campanelli, Supreme Commander of the Allied Forces in this region. Who the hell am I speaking with sir?"

The voice on the other end of the line snarled back at him just as hotly, "and this is Vice Admiral Robert Middleton, KCB sir, and I don't like to be spoken to in that tone of voice, sir."

"And I don't like finding out from my Command that your damn ships are sailing with the fricking Chinese ships, Vice Admiral Middleton, Sir!"

"General Campanelli Sir, a little more care in your words and remarks if you please sir, this is not a secured communication hookup sir," the English Admiral warned him.

"Then switch over to a secured line sir," he looked at the setting. "Turn to CC1CR."

A series of annoying screeches and clicking came over the mike as the setting changed. John remarked to his Commanding Officer. "Campey, if you hang up, you won't hear all the damn screeches, sir. The phone will ring when the Admiral's back on the line for you, sir."

"Oh," he said and he followed John's instruction as he hung up on the Admiral.

Seconds later, the phone rang and he barked in it, "yes Admiral Middleton, yes, yes, I know, but you have to realize I don't like your ships sailing with the damn Chinese, and nothing you say can make me feel any better about it, sir. What the hell's England up to for crap sake? Are you going against the United States if things go from bad to worse in this region, sir? Yes, yes, I don't give a rat's ass about Hong Kong at this time sir. I only care about my soldiers, and my country. I'd hate like hell to have to pit my forces against those of the United Kingdom, considering how England has always backed the United States in the past, and we your country, sir.

"Yes, I'll contact your Command, in fact, I'll report this to my President, and have him contact your Prime Minister to see if they can straighten this mess out between them. Incidentally, we're having a cookout on the flight deck, and you and your Officers are more than welcome to join us if you like. I'd like to meet with you personally, so I know the man I'll be dealing with over this situation, sir. Oh, I'm sorry you can't make it, yeah, that'd be great. I'll be looking forward to meeting you tomorrow then, sir. I can send my CV-22 to pick you up. Oh, that'd be fine, a helicopter can land on the flight deck easily, sir. Good, until tomorrow

Admiral, good-bye sir." he hung up and snapped at John who was standing right by his side.

"Crap, for the first time in my stinking life, I find myself not trusting the English as far as I can throw them for crap sake. This one gonna be bullshit and bad manners, these damn rice dimpled bastards are pitting friend against friend this time around, sir."

A SPECIAL MEETING BETWEEN THE CHAIRMAN OF THE CHINESE COMMUNIST PARTY AND THE MEMBERS OF THE NATIONAL PEOPLE'S COURT

Chinese Chairman Mao Cheng-yu was addressing Minister Chou Shu in an angry tone of voice, "I don't care the dom American Carriers are now in our waters, sir. They'll all suffer the same fate as did the Independence in the war in the Middle East. If they choose to send their aircraft and foolish pilots against our shores and pilots. These American tit suckers are in for a rude awaking if they choose to dare attack China. We're well prepared to fight the American fools with every drop of our blood, and every man, woman and child in our country."

Minister Chou Shu-teh remarked in a concern voice as he bowed slightly to the powerful Chinese leader, "Chairman Cheng-yu, can we really afford to go to war with the powerful United States and their military might, sir? True we have plans to war with the United Kingdom, when we're certain they have returned their great wealth to the worthless banks of Hong Kong and the land of China. I agree with this part of the plan completely, sir. May I remind you we're still looking for the lowly criminals who put us in this position in the first place, sir."

The Vice Chairman, Chao Tso Jen interrupted the conversation as he asked Minister Shu-teh if he came up with the exact total on the amount of money the six missing bankers successfully stolen from the People's Bank of China.

"Yes, I'm sorry to inform the Vice Chairman and Chairman the amount of money the lowly god cursed banker dogs stolen from our banks is well over thirty six billion in American dollars in true worth, sir." The extremely concerned and upset sounding Minister stopped speaking, and put his head down in a totally submissive stance.

"I shall have their skin freed from their foul bones, once we find the mongrels who stole so much money from the people of China. Damn banker's anyhow." The Chairman snarled.

The Chinese Vice Chairman continued with his questioning of Chu. "Minister Chu, this is exactly why we have to wait until the United Kingdom brings all their foul funds back to Hong Kong. They removed this money when they thought they were going to be thrown out of Hong Kong when the People's Republic of China was scheduled to take over Command of Hong Kong. Once we're certain all the monies are returned then we shall invade Hong Kong in force with our military and drive the worthless fools into the sea, and confiscate their ill gotten money.

"We estimate there'll be well over at least six trillion and eighty three billion dollars worth of cash, precious metals, diamonds and bonds in Hong Kong once it is returned to the banks by the English. If we don't get all this cash, we'll be bankrupt far worse than Russia is today in a few short years. We'll be destroyed as a nation, and a world power and neither I, nor the Chairman will stand for this for one moment. We're quite prepared to do whatever is needed to get our hands on that United Kingdom worth sir," the Vice Chairman warned him nastily.

"Vice Chairman Chao Tso Jen Sir, I feel that I must warn you, sir. If we continue to sail down this path of war, China will be shunned by the rest of the world at large. Every country of the world deals with Hong Kong one way or the other, and in essence we'll be taking Command of their great worth as well when we drive the English from Hong Kong, sir."

"You're wrong Minister Shu-teh Sir. We shall have all their god dom money. But you seem to forget one thing, any nation will want to deal with a country that has money, even if it's theirs, you fool you." The Vice Chairman growled at the always cautious Minister.

"Maybe so Mr. Vice Chairman Sir, but I still don't like the idea of having to go up against the military power of the United States. They are truly a force to be both feared, and respected, sir."

"Again you seem to have forgotten these most important points here Minister. The United States no longer has a conceivable military base operating on any land in the Asian region, or the surrounding area at this time, sir. No matter how powerful a nation is, it cannot possibly win a war without military land bases in which to operation their Commands and weapons of war from, sir." The Vice Chairman hissed through clenched teeth at the concerned Minister. He hated the always cautious and refined Minister always going against anything he wanted to do.

"This is something I wish to discuss over with the Chairman. Over the past few days, many of America's large fuel tanker ships for some reason have been showing up on the east side of Taiwan, along with other warships from the United States. The fuel tankers were reported to be nothing like any other tankers which have ever sail the seas before. We have no idea why these ships are here, and what they might be up to so near the hated island of Taiwan, sir."

The Vice Chairman cut him off as he actually barked at the timid Minister, "then I suggest you find out what the devil these Americans are up to, if you're so worried about their presence off the coast of Taiwan, sir. No matter what the foolish Americans try to do, they shall never establish another operating military base in this region in time to block our actions. Thus, insuring our success, and once we're in complete Command of Hong Kong, Taiwan and Japan. No nation on the face of this earth will be strong enough to make us leave the conquered lands. China will be in complete charge and Command of most of the world's finances, sir.

"We have a plan on how we'll soon deal with the cursed United States that shall make them eat our rice and enjoy it. I'll explain my plans further to you Minister. Once China takes over Japan, we'll offer to forgive the great debt the United States owes to Japan, sir. In essence, we'll be offering the United States over two hundred and fifty billion dollars, for them to turn their backs on Japan, and what we're doing in the Asia region, Minister Shu-Teh. I think the god cursed Americans will trip all over themselves because of this kind offer we shall give the great fools. We would, besides, with the hard feelings currently existing between the Americans and Japanese, no American would want to lose his of her life for them. It's a foolproof plan we'll offer them, sir. Here, we'll be offering the hated United States the chance to be one of the most financially strongest countries in the entire world, alongside China that is.

"Together, our two nations could control the entire world if the god dom United States looks the other way, while we attack these few worthless countries here in Asia. The world knows in their hearts that Taiwan truly belongs to China. If it was not for that filth eating rebel, Chiang Kai-shek, who snuck onto the Island to avoid his just punishment at our hands. That Island would still be under our control, and everything made on that Island would be ours, as it should be. I cannot wait until we finally settle up with those Taiwanese fools, and the criminal bankers also. I'd be willing to bet the foul bankers are hiding somewhere in Taiwan at this very moment, and that's why we cannot find the motherless bastards anywhere inside China soil, sir."

The old Chinese Chairman had to laugh as he warned his Vice Chairman and Ministers in no uncertain terms, in an attempt to calm down a little, before he herniated a vital organ on himself. Other members attending the meeting also laughed at this remark.

The Minister of the People's Congress was not to be stifled so easily though, as he continued to voice his many fears and deep concerns over the Americans and their military might, "Mr. Chairman Mao Cheng-yu Sir, I don't feel so confident the hated Americans will be so willing to deal with us, if we take Japan during our intended war with Taiwan and North Korea, sir. The United States have invested far too much money and time into that foul country, for them to just walk away from Japan just like that I believe, sir."

"Nonsense!" the elderly Chairman laughed, and then he continued with his angry words at the concerned Minister. "We shall offer the foolish Americans anything of Japan they might want from that worthless nation, once we have successfully destroyed that country completely. Their factories, information systems, anything the Americans want to remove, they will be free to do so, sir. We may even allow them the right to operate factories inside Japan. We shall offer the Americans far too much, for them to possibly refuse our offers to them. They're a people of much greed and lust, and they'll come around, just as the other countries of the world will, and soon they'll be bending over backwards to deal with China again I assure you, sir."

The Minister let out his breath in a rush as he cautiously offered to the Chinese Leader, "Mr. Chairman Mao Cheng-yu, you offered the United States presence in this region is far too weak for them to mount much of a defense against our military moves. I beg to differ with you sir. What about the American Aircraft Carriers? They could be deployed off our coast in a mere week's time. They have eleven active Carriers in operation, and each ship carry up to ninety attack aircraft. That's almost a thousand aircraft, which could be sitting off our coast within a week's time, sir. Not to mention the other air wings they have stationed in England, Italy, Spain, Germany and Sweden, that we know of, sir. The Heavens knows what else the United States have stationed elsewhere that we're not fully aware of as yet, Mr. Chairman.

"I worry seriously we're moving much too fast, and we're planning to grab too much to control. We can only stretch our military forces just so far before they're too weak to maintain proper control of the lands we'll soon conquer. I'd desire to hold back some. Perhaps take Hong Kong then maybe Taiwan, and be happy with that much, sir. I feel we should leave Japan alone for the time being, Mr. Chairman. If not forever, at least for the time being. I pray we have not underestimated the American's will to defend the Islands of Japan, sir. If they become crossed with us as we propose to do, sir. They'll rise up against us like a wounded dragon, and their unconquerable rage will be uncontrollable, this history already teaches us, sir."

"You're truly a dreamer and romantic Minister Chou Shu-teh. You offer we should leave Japan alone, and if we do, allow the Americans build up their military strength in Japan again to defend against our forces, once we decided to turn them loose against Japan. You offer us wait until the United States is powerful enough in the region again to make us not want to attack Japan at any time, now and in the future sir. From there, the hated Americans will deploy their cursed military forces until they drive us out of Taiwan, and maybe even Hong Kong in the future, sir. No, I want the Americans kept far from China's shores and our interests. Minister Shu-teh, if you're getting cold between your foul legs. I could always have you replaced, so you can spend the rest of your foolish life living in a Monastery, contemplate your foul errors in the wisdom you offered me, if you'd like sir?"

The concerned Minister looked to each of the other Minister attending this meeting for their support, but as he looked at each face, each Minister quickly looked away from him, or they cast their eyes down to the floor and refuse to look at him again. He understood, by standing alone, he just placed himself in a precarious position by resisting the powerful Chairman. Reading he was defeated, he looked to the Vice Chairman. The Minister read the unspoken warning, and bowed as he took his chair again after announcing he no longer had reservations against the pending attacks China would soon be engaged in with the other nations just mentioned.

Chairman Mao Cheng-yu rose swiftly to his feet and said calmly. "I knew it was only a matter of time, before my Minister saw his error in foolish judgment. I thank you for taking the time, and reuniting our war council, sir. I look forward to give the order for our patrol boats to sink the English Carriers the Invincible, and the Ark Royal in our opening salvos of our war against the United Kingdom. At that very moment, our ground forces will begin the overwhelming invasion of Hong Kong, and then our troops will take over all the banks in one swift move.

"Blocking all foreigners from removing anything of worth from China's shores. Our soldiers will also remove the jewelry from the foreign whore's we'll be expelling from our country. It shall be their price to pay, for China giving them a boat on which to get back to their loathsome and foul country." The Chairman's smile returned, he then laughed. He laughed and laughed, until his entire Council looked at one another, worried about the Chairman's sanity.

One by one, the shaken Chinese Ministers quickly filtered out of the room. Each of them heading for his respective post, to prepare for the war China would soon find herself locked in. No Chinese politician gave a second thought to the war their troops would soon be engaging in North Korea. They knew of the weapons the North Koreans possessed, and her troops also knew how North Korea would react, when they came under attack by their troops. The Chinese leadership knew everything they had to know about the North Korean military and their tactics. They had not only sold them most of their armament and military equipment, but they also taught them how to fight, and how to react to being attacked. The Chinese military was preparing to use this knowledge quickly to destroy North Korea in one swift and hard hitting military operation. She would not stop her attack until North Korea no longer existed on the face of the earth.

The Vice Chairman waited in the room until the powerful old Chairman stopped laughing. The old man looked around, and then he stated, "the weak dog eaters are gone from my presence. My Ministers are weak, untrustworthy and too cautious. I'm pleased the worthless fools are gone, when the fighting is over with, I'll have all of them shot for their weakness. I'll replace them all with men I shall hand pick, men I can trust like yourself. I'll rule China with an iron hand. I'll put a stop to this democracy movement burning the heart and soul out of my country. Mr. Tso-jen, you'll be the new Chairman of North Korea, and you can do what you will with the foul country of dog eaters, once we have taken over complete command of that entire worthless Korean Peninsula. Take it as my gift to you, for your loyalty for me."

The proud Chinese Vice Chairman bowed politely towards the old Chairman, and then he offered him with a slight smile on his lips, "may I obey all your orders with equal enthusiasm and pleasure as these orders offer me, Mr. Chairman. I shall await further word when I can have the Ministers replaced at your favor, sir. I'll allow the internal Army of the People's Republic lose upon the foul heads of any and all troublemakers who might wage problems against me and your Command, sir. I assure you Chairman Cheng-yu, we'll have the China, Mao Zedong had only dared to dream about come true, Mr. Chairman Sir."

CHAPTER 17
ON BOARD THE VINEGAR JOE PLATFORM

The cookout was going very well, until the first raindrops began to fall. Some of the soldiers made passes at the women, and the women were delighted over the surprised attention they were suddenly receiving from their counterparts. General Edward Campanelli looked at the weather report and smiled as he read there was rain forecast for that night, and it was supposed to continue for at least the next twelve hours. Some of the workers were exhausted and they slowly began to filter below decks to bring the party out from the rain and picking up wind, the noise from the rec room was loud, and General Campanelli looked to John.

"They're coming down from above sir, it must be raining already General Campanelli Sir."

"What's the story about the damn shit tanker ship being fully operational, John?" General Campanelli asked his Second in Command in a serious tone of voice.

"From what I have been told, the Captain pulled some of the usual fuckups from the cookout, and made them get to work on the tanker's final hookups, sir. He's pushing the shit out of the poor bastards though," John reported to his Commanding Officer as he stared him in the eyes.

"It's about time he did something right to earn his damn pay this time, dammit. I'm going to go see what he's up to, and make certain he's not taking his stinking anger out on his people, sir. He's the type of prick to try and blame anyone else but himself for his short comings and failures, John." Edward snorted as he returned his smile.

"Yeah, I picked that up for myself, Campey ." John added as he nodded his head at him.

"If he is, he's going to find himself buried dick deep in horseshit and flies I tell you sir. I'll not stand for it for one damn second, John." General Campanelli started out and when Aleksandra asked him if he wanted company. He looked at her and then replied, "sure, you can come along if you want, I could sure use the company in case I get my ass lost on this damn thing."

She immediately fell in behind him. It was raining heavily now and the General almost turned back, but he thought better of it and he went out to the last ship being connected to the Platform. It was a good jog for both officers to get up to the super structure of the tanker. When they were in the cabin, they both could hear powerful engines running. General Campanelli listened for a moment until he finally heard someone yell at the top of his lungs and he followed the noise, walking down six flights until the two officers finally came across a number of men working on the countless under the flight decking hookups to the so called shitter tanker ship, and the upset and angry Commander growled, "where the hell's the damn Captain at sir?"

"General Sir, he's below deck working on the waste plant water hookups, sir. Some parts were broken on the trip out, and he's waiting for a metal worker to get down there, to see if he can prefab any of the broken parts so he can complete the connections, General."

"How the hell do I get to him from here mister? I don't know my way around this damn thing yet, mister" General Campanelli demanded hotly from the young Seaman.

"I'll be pleased to guide you down to where Captain Hoffman is working if you'd like, sir." The Seaman stepped forward to lead the way for the two officers. General Campanelli was amazed, he saw waste treatment plant constructed on many land military bases, but never anything on this scale. Everything looked like it was overkill for the massive Platform. The circular brushes and chemical batching plant that treated the wastewater before it was released into the wells, looked like they were ready to go at the drop of a hat.

The angry Captain picked up the General coming towards him, and he did not salute him but he did stop working in order to speak with him.

General Campanelli snapped at the grim covered and exhausted looking Captain, "what's the fucking problem here?" He omitted the sir on purpose this time.

"Sir, the sprocket to run the heavy rotor brush systems was obviously somehow cracked during transit out to the Platform, General Campanelli Sir. I sent for one of our metal workers, to see if the sprocket can somehow be duplicated, or at least welded back together for a quick fix repair, until we can get a replacement sent out from stateside to us, sir."

General Campanelli looked at the damaged sprocket connected to the six inch wide stainless steel shaft of the brush assembly, and then he grumbled. "Shit!"

A worker also covered in grime came down the ladder and he called out for the Captain.

"Over here mister. It's about time you got down here!" Captain Hoffman called out.

"What do you have for me sir?" the worker offered while ignoring his attitude against him.

"Over here Chief, this sprocket's cracked, and I can't run the brush unit without it in place."

"Hmmm... I see what you mean Captain Hoffman Sir. Whatdaya want me to do about it sir?"

"Are you shitting me mister, I want you to fix the damn thing for me, Chief. That's what I want you to do about it mister," he snapped at the elderly Chief who was busy carefully studying the broken gear while rubbing his chin at the same time.

General Campanelli laughed as the Chief jumped over the force in the Captain's voice, and he replied to the angry officer, "okay, okay sir, but I can't fix this one, sir. It's a cast item and it can't be welded properly, sir. I could probably make up a jury rig until a replacement comes from stateside. I could have it ready sometime later tonight I guess, will that do sir?"

"That'll do fine Chief. Do me a favor and install your makeup when you finished it, sir."

"I had every intention of putting the thing back together for you once I make up a replacement, Captain. Do you think I'd allow one of your heavy handed butchers working on this damn thing touch something I made up by hand, sir? Not on your life sir," the Chief grunted.

"I know better than that Chief." The Captain said with a half a smile.

The General pointed out, "looks like you seem to have everything under control down here for the time being Captain Hoffman. I'm going to take this Seaman, and let him give me a grand tour of the interior of this ship. I wanna see what I'm dealing with in here, sir."

No sooner did he say this than a powerful engine suddenly started and slightly startled the military officer, "what the fuck's that damn noise now for cripe sake?" General Campanelli spat out as he looked in the direction of the engine running.

"General Campanelli Sir that must be the desalination plant that purifies the salt water for the bathrooms and showers for the crews, sir. I have a number of workers working on the boilers that'll heat the water for the showers for the crews, sir. Most of the water will be recycled over there inside that system, General Campanelli Sir." The Captain pointed towards a number of large sealed tanks sitting off to their right and then added, "the water gets purified and filtered in those tanks, and then it's reheated and pumped back into the pipes for reuse in the showers again, sir. This way the desalination and purification systems won't be overworked any, sir."

General Campanelli was not that impressed by the system as he turned to the Seaman, and he snapped at him this time, "you ready to get going again mister?"

"Yes sir," the Seaman replied as he turned and headed out of the area with the General.

"Let's get going then mister," General Campanelli mumbled as he followed the Seaman out of this tanker ship, and they headed for their next destination on the Platform now.

"What do you want to see first, General Campanelli?" the Seaman asked as he lead the way.

"The shitters, what else Seaman. That's what started all the damn problems between myself and your Captain in the first place mister," he fired back at the waiting Seaman with a snap.

Minutes later, he was looking at row after row of toilets in the men's section of the latrine ship, he counted four rows of fifty five toilets, and there were three more rooms to this ship area. Two other areas were set aside for the women stationed on board the Platform.

"Where the hell's the damn shower area mister?" he said in a demanding tone to him.

"Follow me please, General Campanelli Sir." The Seaman replied in a calm tone back.

"Where the devil's the men's showers stationed at inside this here tub, Seaman? I especially want to see them during this little tour of ours mister," General Campanelli growled as he followed the Seaman over to the shower area of the Platform.

"Sir, the men's showers are on the other side of the ship for the obvious reasons, General Sir."

"That's good, I didn't like having the damn showers too near each other, that'd surely lead to some trouble between the two sexes I'd imagine, mister."

"Yes Sir I agree with you there General Campanelli Sir." The Seaman smiled at the concerned General as he started to lead him to the other section of the ship he requested to visit.

The shower stalls were extremely clean, the floors tiled and walls were made of metal. Even though, General Campanelli was pleased his wardroom came equipped with a private bathroom and shower stall for his private use as he asked, "where does that room lead to here, mister?"

"That leads over to the Officer's section of showers and their private toilet area, General Campanelli Sir." He reported to his Commanding Officer sharply.

"Let's go, I wanna see brass land as well this time around Seaman," he ordered.

The officer's territory was much better prepared, the shower areas were tile all the to the ceiling, and the shitters had wall dividers between each toilet, and the sinks had mirrors before them. There was no communal urinal in the center of the large room as was in the enlisted soldier's area. Water was already dripping from a few of the faucets in officer's country.

"The Captain musta gotten the desalination plant up and on line already I see General," the Seaman offered. Neither man noticed the lights were on line, meaning the generators were also up and on line and running. Suddenly, there was a low rumbling sound from deep within the bowels of the shit tanker ship as it had come to be known.

"Sir, that noise has to be coming from the boilers stocking up, obviously we're making hot water for everyone now, General Campanelli Sir."

"It's about time we did mister!" General Campanelli grumbled at the Seaman.

The rumbling soon became no more than a low growl as the boilers finally quieted down, and then they ran correctly.

The smell of diesel fuel spread throughout the bowels of the ship.

"General Campanelli Sir, there's three more decks to this one ship sir, and they're identical to this one, sir. Would you care to see each of the decks, sir? I can take you to every area of the entire platform if you want to visit each section of the system, because I was one of the first ones to be stationed on board the Platform when they started assembling it, sir."

"Nah, I believe I saw enough of this damn ship already, I want to get back to my Command and see what might be brewing there, mister. But I do have a question for you. Is one desalination plant going to be enough to run an operation this size? I mean just the shitter ship?"

"General Campanelli Sir, we have three other desalination plants up and on line at this time, and two more are waiting to be fully operational, sir. We figure at the peak of operations, we might be using somewhere in the vicinity of maybe a million gallons of water per day, every day of operations, General Campanelli Sir. Each plant is more than capable of producing over five hundred thousand gallons of drinkable water a day, every day of operation, sir. We should be able to produce a surplus of somewhere around five hundred thousand gallons of drinkable water a day from the shitter ship alone, sir. Then you have to also add what the other two plants will produce once they're up and on line and running, General Campanelli Sir."

"Hmmm... that's good to know Seaman. How many of the damn desalination plants will be spread throughout the rest of the Platform for us, when she's complete son?" Campanelli asked the man calmly this time, as he held him in his gaze for the moment.

"Sir, I recall the number being placed at twenty I believe was, General Campanelli Sir. With another five being held in reserve sir, in case of a breakdown, or by a lucky hit by the enemy during an attack on the Platform, sir. Mosta the plants are stationed well below deck, but four portable units are scheduled to be setup on topside as well, General Campanelli Sir."

"I saw and heard enough for my liking. Get me back over to the CIC Chamber, mister."

"Follow me General Campanelli Sir, I'll have you back to the CIC Chamber in a jiffy, sir."

The two headed upstairs and onto the massive flight deck, and the General did not realize Aleksandra was missing until he noticed it still raining. He looked over his shoulder back at the stairwell and then he asked in a form of a bark "Where the hell's the damn Major at Seaman? I thought she was right behind us, dammit. I didn't notice her break off from us as we checked out that damn ship below, mister."

"Dunno for certain sir, she left us when the boilers came back on line, General Campanelli Sir. Does the General want me to go back and look for her, sir? I can find her easy enuf I believe, sir. Even though the Platform is massive, there's only a few places to really get lost in, sir."

"Nah, if she gets lost, it'll teach her to leave without informing me she was going off on her own for a while, dammit. You should've told me she separated from us though, Seaman."

"Yes sir, sorry for not keeping a closer eye on her for you, General Campanelli Sir."

General Edward Campanelli headed directly for the walkway leading up to the CIC Chamber of the Platform. It was raining steadier now, and he had to actually jog the remaining few feet. He shook his head to get the water out of his hair, sending a chill down his back in the process. It was cold on the massive flight deck with a strong wind blowing across it.

Both General John White and Colonel Mary Locker were playing with the IBM computer. When the General walked into the CIC, he noticed an IBM monitor and a fold down lap top IBM computer on his desk. He was pleased the government changed most of their computers over to the IBM models. He liked how easy and fast the machines worked. Coming from Upstate New York, where just about all the smaller counties owed their very existence to the huge company, he was grateful the government changed over to the IBM computers. Most track and search radar on many of the warships were also controlled by IBM computers lately.

Colonel Locker looked at the General and immediately offered to her Commanding Officer "nothing new to report to you at this time, sir. Where's your shadow at sir?"

Campanelli ignored her rude remark, so Locker quickly changed the subject, "General, we're hooked up to all communications and intelligence data linkups, and we're also trying to get..."

"Can you get me in contact with General Weidenbacher for me, I want a secured line hookup, Colonel Locker? I have a few things I want to speak over with the General."

"Sure can General Campanelli Sir. Within ten minutes, if he's at his desk where he should be back in the States at this time, General Campanelli Sir."

"Get it done for me then Colonel. I need to speak with him as soon as possible, Locker."

"Yes Sir General," her fingers danced across the keys like she was playing a piano. Instantly, one of the screens showed a test pattern coming up on it. Its brilliancy lighting up the entire CIC Chamber instantly. This was quickly replaced by a harsh white blank screen for a few seconds until General William Weidenbacher's face appeared, sharp and clear on the screen.

"General Campanelli Sir, I'm damn pleased you placed a call to me, sir. I was just about to get in touch with you myself, sir. How the hell do you like the Vinegar Joe thing so far, General? How do you like what you're seeing out there, General Campanelli?"

"The Platform is amazing General, I can't believe what I'm seeing of it so far, General Weidenbacher. I'm doing real fine sir, but shouldn't we be using a secure hookup, sir? I asked for a secured line when I ordered to communicate with you, General Weidenbacher Sir."

"Your people didn't inform you General Campanelli? Any communication coming to the Pentagon, or to the White House from your Platform system, is always held on a secured line, sir. What's the reason for this requested communication, sir?"

"General Weidenbacher, I want Captain Carl Hoffman transferred from the Platform A-SAP sir," this subject was causing the General anger and he wanted to handle it as fast as possible.

"Why do you want to do that for sir? I found the man to be a pretty good Officer, Edward."

General Campanelli remained quiet, and General Weidenbacher broke the silence by adding to his question, "Edward, you're destroying the man's career if you go through with your request, and refuse to make a written report along with your reason for the requested transfer out, sir. I hope you're not reacting a little too hastily here, General Campanelli Sir."

"I'm not General Weidenbacher Sir!" was all that he would remark to the General.

"Very well then, he's now a Captain for the rest of his life, General. I guess I could find him a job some place in Alaska if I look hard enough that is, sir. Anything else you have for me sir?"

"Yes Sir General Weidenbacher Sir." General Campanelli said as he stiffened up some.

"Can the sir shit, if you don't want to be saluted, I don't want to be called sir, when we speak, mister. You can call me Rockjaw or Bill, and I'll call you Edward. Is that clear sir?" General Weidenbacher said with some anger lacing his tone. He was rather upset his General was choosing to destroy the Captain's future in the service.

"Clear as a bell sir. I guess news travels pretty fast around here sir, even from across the damn Ocean I see, sir. I didn't expect you to know about the saluting bullshit so quickly, Bill." General Campanelli offered to his Commanding Officer as he flashed him a quick smile.

"You forget, I read your damn 201 file, and there a number of references to you not liking to be saluted when on active duty in Injun country, sir. I know the reason why, you still blame yourself for that Captain's death when you saluted him in the Nam, sir. I guess we all have our damn crosses to bear, Edward. Continue your report please, General."

"Very well Bill, I called for a holiday for tomorrow sir, and it worked out very well for me, because it's supposed to rain for the entire day anyhow, General Weidenbacher Sir. The reason I placed this call to you, was because I didn't like the report about the two British Carriers sailing with the damn Chinese warships, especially so close to the coast of North Korea, sir. I requested the Vice Admiral of the Invincible, Admiral Middleton to get his ass over here on board the Joe, so I can find out what the hell they're up to out here for crap sake, sir."

General Weidenbacher interrupted again, "I already read the report, and I assure you I don't like the Brits sleeping with the damn Chinese either, General Campanelli. I know the President's going to have lunch with the British Prime Minister next week. I spoke to him on this issue, and he informed me he was going to set the Prime Minister straight on this concern. I think he's going to threaten him with cutting off any Intel and military support with the United Kingdom, if they continue down the path they're presently sailing on, sir. The Boss told me he's going to tell him he wouldn't keep England informed of our moves until we can ascertain if England's still on our side or not, sir. The President was plenty pissed off about this shit I can tell you, Edward."

General Campanelli breathed out a deep sigh of relief, knowing it was no longer up to him to sort this mess out.

"Is this the real reason you wanted to speak to me today, Edward?" the General asked him.

"Yes Sir General Weidenbacher Sir, I wanted to see how you wanted me to handle the Vice Admiral when we meet tomorrow morning, sir. I knew I had to react, and I'm sure the United Kingdom was waiting for our response as well to happen, sir."

General Weidenbacher smiled as he added to his conversation with General Campanelli, "you can bet the damn barn on it they're waiting for us to react to what you just brought up to my attention, sir. I don't know why the devil the damn Brits didn't inform us of their intents first, before they carried them out with the Chinese, dammit. Strange, very strange if you were to ask me, sir. Anyway, when will you be accepting any aircraft to deck down on the

Platform, Edward? I have a new toy I want to send out to you for your approval, sir. It finished its Baptism, and I want you to try it out in a combat situation if any happens out your way, sir.

"I also have some more supplies I want shipped out to you as well, and there's another little gem that has been released to the Airforce you're unaware of, General Campanelli. So you see, while you're out there getting yourself a damn sun tan and a sea breeze at the government's expense. I've been busting my ass here getting these new weapons released to the forces, in case you might need them if the shit hits the fan on us, sir. See how good I take care of you mister. And this was the reason I was going to get in contact with you, but you got to me first General."

"I believe I can probably start accepting the first fighter aircraft for landing on our deck by February 6th. I think all I need is one more ship hooked up to the center line of the Platform, and the runway will be complete, sir. But right now I can easily take any CV-22s, sir."

"Shit, that's right dammit. I forgot all about them damn things already Edward." The well respected and powerful General growled at himself, and then he went on with his words, "Look Edward, I'll have one takeoff tomorrow morning to you, sir. I want you to see this new toy as soon as possible, sir. It's some shit sir, you're going to love it I warn ya, sir. The supplies I want you to have will be on the Platform along with this other item I'm speaking of. okay Eddy, there are some things I have to get to at this time, sir. I'll be back to you right after this little toy decks down on the Platform sir," he signed off without further word.

"I wonder what this little toy is the General has for us, and wants us to try out for him."

John laughed as he remarked, "I guess you can bet the bank on it, it's gonna be a real humdinger if the General's involved with the damn thing, sir."

Just then, Aleksandra came strolling into the CIC Chamber looking rather upset.

"Where the hell did you get off to Major?" General Campanelli said abrasively at her.

She shrugged as she remarked to Campanelli, "I go explore expedition, I check on armament tanker ship please. Every weapon aircraft possible carry store below deck sir. There one steel door with armed security guard stationed right front and sign on door state, 'Authorized Personnel Only. All Others Will Be Shot'. Wonder what behind it door, General?"

Now it was John's turn to smile so he offered with a smirk to the female Major "I can tell you if you really want to know what it is all about Major."

"I do," she said dryly to the large black General as she stared back at him.

John looked to General Campanelli and then he said at the same time, "it's up to you sir. It's classified top secret, but if she wanted to know, all she has to do is punch it up on the computer she controls, sir. Top secret information's accessed through all our terminals, sir."

"That's a dumb question then John, if she has access to the TS files, and she's questioning a top secret door mark. Then I think you have to answer her. Besides, I'm interested myself, sir."

General John White let out his breath in a rush, and then he began to explain for his officer's information. "Aleksandra, behind the first door there are three other armed Marines stationed, with the power to not only kill anyone who tries to gain entry into that area without the proper permission by Command to do so, young lady. But the Marine guards can also flood the entire armory section laying behind the last door, to keep any intruders out of it, and compromising our stores of weapons and special equipment stored inside this secured area, Ma'am."

"Why do that for?" she whispered as she cocked her head to the side, not understanding.

"Because behind that secured door there are a number of nuclear devices that can be delivered by either the F-15 E two seater warplane, or by any of the F-111 light bomber aircraft, Ma'am." General White paused for anymore questions from the foreign female officer. But no one said a word back to him, the CIC Chamber was mired in dead silence, as if no one was even daring to breathe again. The mere mention of nuclear weapons being stored on board the Platform made everyone silent and reflecting.

General Campanelli was the first one to speak ominously after being informed about the nuclear weapons resting inside the bowels of the Platform. "Fucking nuclear weapons, didn't we learn anything from the damn war in the Middle East for the love of God? I thought after that one, every civilized country in the damn world would bury any nuclear equipment they had control over, sir. I can't believe them damn things are on board this Platform right under my stinking feet, dammit." He raved about the terrible effects the weapons had on civilians. John had to place his hand on his shoulder to try and calm the General down some.

"Eddy, no one has more of a right to hate nuclear weapons than you have, sir. But you have to remember something, sir. Two of our potential enemies in this region of the world, also have nuclear weapons on hand, and you can rest assure they have them sitting in aircraft and on top of missiles as we speak, sir. Aimed at us right this minute, and probably at the

United States as well, sir. As long as we have the damn weapons stored on board the Platform, and the enemy knows this, they'll think twice before trying to attack this Island, sir."

The General pushed John's hand off his shoulder and bitched at him, "there's still no reason on this earth that'd make me accept those filthy things. I saw what they can do first hand. And from what I was lead to believe, China has no idea this damn Island even exists, sir."

John got hot as he snapped back at his friend, "What the hell do you want us to do with the damn things then, Eddy? Ship them back to the States and tell them thanks, but no thanks, sir?   You know where that'll get ya in a fast hurry, General Campanelli Sir. The funny farm sir."

General Campanelli glared harshly at his lifelong friend for a long moment. The only man on this earth that he would ever allow to speak to him in this fashion. He then took in a deep breath, and moaned at him in an exhausted and angry tone at the same time. "I see what you mean, what the fuck can I do about the damn things now, John? They're on board this damn thing and I guess that's that then, dammit. I just hope against hope I'd never see another one of those fucking things for as long as I live, John."

Aleksandra rested her hand lightly on the General's powerful shoulder, and he immediately covered her hand with his as he mumbled up at her in a labored tone of voice. "I guess you really don't know what the fuck I'm talking about here, young lady. I had the terrible privilege of being the second Commander in the history of mankind to order a nuclear detonation on the face of the earth, Major. But I'm the only Commander who allowed forty seven nuclear explosions to be launched, and the death of over fifteen million people while I was at it young lady, civilians most of them were at that." General Campanelli suddenly leaned forward, and then he rested his head in his hands and applied pressure on both of his temples.

She did not remove her hand from his shoulder, as she offered in a kind tone to him as she genially squeezed his shoulder, "It no you fault at all, General Campanelli Sir. I know terrible war and devastating effect war cause to all people involved in war, especially civilians, sir. You forgot Alliance States too involve in that war also, and Lithuania sent number of doctor help wounded out there too, sir. I no blame you for what happened in that ugly war, and no I think you blame youself either, sir. Was war, and nuclear weapon launch in order to kill bacterial weapon other side let loose on earth and her civilian, sir. It necessary do this so many more civilian no die in that terrible war, sir." She suddenly moved her hand from his shoulder, and she rested it on his neck. The movement caused him to shudder a bit.

"I heard all of this stinking bullshit said to me before young lady, but it still doesn't make it any god damn easier for me to sleep at night I tell you, Major. And now I have the same fucking weapons that caused all that damn destruction and death in the first place, resting right here under my damn feet, and knowing this bugs the living shit out of my stinking ass, dammit. I can actually feel the death emanating from the damn things as I think of them things being stored on board this damn Platform, dammit. Crap, how the hell did I ever allow myself to get snookered like this for crap sake." General Campanelli grumbled angrily at himself as he slowly shook his head no and breathed out again in a deep sigh.

"You come on now General Campanelli Sir, I believe you let imagination get best you of right now, sir. The weapons harmless kitten sit below deck of this Platform thing, sir. Come on General Campanelli and I buy cup coffee you and hope you relax a little, sir. I know what is good for you to make you forget all you trouble over stored nuclear weapon, sir."

General Campanelli smiled at her as he replied, "I could sure use a cup of coffee right about now, but I don't feel like going out for one though, Major."

"Come on, I make worth you problem well if you come with me, sir. You need take break from all you worry about everything you have rest on you trouble mind I see, General. I worry this operation is taking too much from you and you need little time relax and enjoy few minute of pleasure, help you forget all you trouble all time worry about, sir." She actually bumped him slightly with her rearend, and then she smiled at him.

"Since you put it that way, let's get going Alex," he stood and they both quickly left the chamber together, but they did not head for the mess. Instead, they went to her wardroom, and she loved the trouble out of his mind.

As they left the CIC Chamber, General White turned to Colonel Locker and remarked with a wide grin on his face to her, "well Locker, it looks like you're gonna be thrown out of your room for a little while there, Colonel." John waited for Colonel Locker to catch up with him, as he waited for her to follow him over to the mess hall for a quick cup of coffee.

CHAPTER 18
FRIDAY, FEBRUARY 6th, 1997.
ON BOARD THE VINEGAR JOE PLATFORM

General Edward Campanelli was up early on this morning, because he had a hard time falling sleeping because he was anticipating the arrival of the CV-22 aircraft all night long, and he was still wondered what General Weidenbacher was sending out to him. He left Aleksandra sleeping and headed for the mess on the same deck he was on. Every once in a while, he would get a quick whiff of old fuel oil, and it forced him to remember the ships the Platform was constructed on, were all converted oil super tankers. He rubbed his nose to get the stink out of it.

John was already eating as the General entered the mess, so he headed right for the man. When he sat down, a Seaman immediately came over to him and asked.

"Can I get you something to eat General Sir?"

"Coffee would be great son," General Campanelli snapped as he stared speaking with John. "Whatdaya think this new weapon's all about the General's sending out to us, John?"

"I haven't the foggiest idea what it could possibly be, but if the General's shipping it out to us on a special flight just so we can gawk at the damn thing, you can bet this thing must a real humdinger then, Ed." John snorted as he gnawed at a biscuit.

General Campanelli's coffee came, and he took a quick gulp, almost melting his face off as he complained back at John, "Jesus h. Christ John, this shit's hot as the gates of hell, man. Any idea when this damn aircraft's due to touch down, John?"

John looked up from his breakfast and replied with a mouth full of food, and point his fork at his friend. "No, but I'll check with the Tower to see if they were notified when I'm done, sir."

"I'd appreciate that John, I'm going to get myself some chow, I'll be right back sir."

The Tower was exactly that, the deck workers turned the super structure of the first tanker ship of the massive Platform, into a sixty foot high Control Tower. This was what Captain Hoffman wasted so much of his time on. It was well equipped, as most Control Towers usually was, and at sixty foot above the massive flight deck of the Platform, it gave the controllers an excellent view of the surrounding air and the Platform deck at the same time.

General Campanelli returned with a tray of food and John immediately griped at him, "couldn't you get any more damn eggs piled on the thing for yourself, sir?"

"C'mon man, you're getting worse than my ex-wife for fuck sake. Always nagging my stinking ass all the damn time, just eat your food and shut up will ya man."

Once they were finished eating, John left Campanelli standing in the hall, and headed for the Tower to see if they had an ETA on the CV-22 flight. The General went to the CIC to see if anything happened overnight. He noticed his basket was empty, and breathed a sigh of relief. He was dreading what he thought he might find sitting in his basket, the report informing him he was involved in another shooting war. As he sat there, John came in and he reported, "hey Eddy, the CV-22's due in at Thirteen Hundred Hours sir. Anything happening out here Ed?"

"Quiet as a Church on Saturday night John," he reported back to his friend with a smirk.

A MEETING BETWEEN\ THE CHAIRMAN OF THE PEOPLE'S REPUBLIC OF CHINA AND THE CENTRAL MILITARY COMMISSION

The powerful and feared Chinese Chairman Mao Cheng-yu sat quietly in his office when the Central Military Commission President, Yang So came strolling in his office.

"Ahhh... sit please," when the President was seated, the Chairman, the most powerful man in all China, began speaking. "I guess you're wondering why I have sent for you, sir."

"Yes Mr. Chairman, I was wondering that sir. Has anything happened on the war front?"

The Chairman laughed, and then he stated, "nothing as dramatic as that I assure you, Yang So. I called you here to see if you, excuse me. I mean your military forces, are well prepared to commence their opening attack on the foolish North Koreans, sir."

The younger President hesitated until the old man glared at him, and then he responded, "my forces are set in place, and ready to go to battle at a moment's notice, Chairman Cheng-yu. My soldiers are backed by armor and aircraft. We're taking a page from the American's strategy, and we have saturate the entire area with bomber aircraft and missile for the opening attacks. We shall drive the worthless North Korean defenders underground, and then we'll simply roll over the top of the worthless fools. We made maps of all their inferior defenses, and we'll take out their tracking and attack radar's first. Then we shall attack their missile installations and all their airbases. All defenses of North Korea will be destroyed in three week's time. Of course, there'll be many small pockets of useless defenders to be dealt with, but deal with them we shall, sir."

"Good, we shall then be able to turn our full attention towards the foolish English then. I have intelligence that assures me most of the foul money was moved back in the banks on Hong Kong, sir. I gave orders to the soldiers to secretly takeover the duties in all banks throughout Hong Kong. When we're ready to strike, the soldiers will merely lock the doors of all banks, and then the foolish English will not be able to get at their foul money, our money I mean out of those cursed banks." The Chinese Chairman laughed and then continued with his words.

"I want to move up our attack against North Korea, we shall begin our opening efforts on March 4th, but I want to go along with the attack by no later than February 20th. That is a Friday, I want to go on Friday because their worthless soldiers will be looking forward to a weekend off, and will not be at their sharpest. Can you be ready at this time? Don't tell me you are ready if you'll not be ready to attack at this time, sir. If this attack fails, I'll hold you personally responsible, President So." He glared at the President of the military commission.

He swallowed hard as he wiped his hand over his bald head, and then he offered calmly, "Mr. Chairman Cheng-yu, my military forces will be well prepared to launch their opening attack against North Korea on this day, sir. Of this I promise you, sir."

"Very well then, remember it's your neck in the noose if your troops fail my demands, sir." The Chairman warned as he dismissed him, and went back to reading over his latest reports.

01035 HOURS: ON BOARD VINEGAR JOE

Aleksandra strolled into the CIC Chamber looking rather refreshed and relaxed. General Campanelli did not pay much attention to her as she entered the area, but John looked up and smiled at her as he offered, "Well Major, good afternoon Ma'am."

She looked at her watch and replied, "It no afternoon yet, General White Sir."

John laughed as he said, "It was a bit of sarcasm, sorry for the barb Major Ma'am."

"Oh," she laughed, not having any idea what she was laughing about.

Colonel Locker was at her computer moving troops around the Asian region, so her forces assets are a finger's touch away from any possible outbreak of hostilities. She moved a Battalion of Marines from the 5th Marine Division over to Germany, and having their gear stored on board the Amphibious Cargo Ships, Charleston, LKA-113 and the El Paso LKA-117, and then she ordered the ships to station off the coast of Japan to standby. This put, the Marine tanks and artillery pieces less than a days sailing to any needed area in the Asian region. Colonel Locker smiled to herself, knowing if China had something planned aside from their attack on North Korea, the United States would have enough troops and weapons in the region, to put a quick stop to any further aggression from China, or any other country in the region for that matter. By March 4th of 1997, the United States would have all her troops and their military equipment and assets in the region needed to fight a six month, all out war.

General Campanelli suddenly called out to Colonel Locker, "Hey Colonel, what the hell are you doing over there, dammit? All I see is you making entries in your damn computer terminal at lighten speed, and no reports ever coming back to me from you, Ma'am."

Colonel Locker snapped at her Commanding Officer. "Jesus Christ General Campanelli Sir, I'll give you a report when one comes out on the damn printer sir, calm down will you please." She took the paper out and she handed it to him and then grumbled at her Commanding Officer. "If you would've waited a few seconds longer, I would've had the damn thing for you without you getting on my ass and getting me upset, because you were riding my ass sir."

"Yeah, yeah, yeah," General Campanelli muttered more to himself as he read over the rather lengthy report from the Colonel, and then he offered her. "Hey Locker, I approve of all your moves here." He placed the report in the file.

Time passed slowly for the Command Staff, and no one admitted it but everyone was waiting for this aircraft from the States to land, so they could see what the General sent out to them. Noon passed with no one from the staff going to lunch. After Twelve, Thirty Hours, some of the staff members slowly drifted out of the CIC and up to the massive flight deck of the Platform. The deck workers had two more tanker ships moving, one already locked in place while the other was being pulled to position by the heavy drag lines and powerful winches.

General Campanelli looked around the CIC Chamber and discovered he and John were the only ones still left below deck. John smiled at the General and asked his Commander. "Whatdaya say, do you wanna go topside or wait here until the incoming aircraft lands, sir?"

"Ahhh shit, I might as well go topside myself, I could sure use a little sun on my face, along with some fresh air to breathe. I hate being stuck down here without a fucking window to look out of. Grab the damn radio, this way we can stay in contact with the damn Tower, and we'll know when the damn aircraft's gonna land." The Commander grumbled as he stood up.

"Good idea," John replied as he took a handheld portable radio and snapped it on his belt.

The two officers hustled up the six flights of steps to the deck, the General was instantly hit by a brisk wind coming from the south, southeast. As the cool breeze hit him, he cursed himself for not taking his heavy overcoat with him. He scanned the deck and saw men pulling another ship in place, and he drifted over to the workers. Most of his Command Staff was watching the workers struggling with the huge tanker ship. They were having a little trouble with this ship, because the water was rough. The waves were making the ship pitch to where it was dangerous to try and linkup the deck plating from the Platform to the shifting tanker's deck planking.

General Campanelli did not notice until now, but there were two large Ocean going tugs on the side of the tanker ship, and they were helping the winches by pushing the tanker towards the Platform. He smiled as he realized these men would not be able to horse this massive ship to the Platform by themselves, no matter how many men they had guiding on the drag lines.

The three tugs were having major problems controlling the tanker and at one point, the General thought the ship was going to get away from everyone and possibly crash into the Platform, because the sea was so rough. The tanker ship actually rode up on one of the tugs and broke some rail, but the Captain quickly swung his tugboat around and came against the tanker nose first. The tug kicked up foam as the huge engines worked on pushing the much larger ship. It came up against the Platform with a loud thud, and the three tugs and drag lines held the tanker in place. Then a horde of workers attacked, placing the bolts that would hold the ship to the Platform. Workers placed the temporary pins in so other workers could bolt the lose planks together once the holes were properly aligned. The General's attention went to Chief Kirby, he was screaming out orders at the workers over the roar from the straining tugs and huge winches.

Kirby noticed the General watching him and made his way over to him and complained bitterly, "Shit sir, this is fucking nuts, man. I'm ordering a stop to trying to set any more damn ships in place until this damn sea calms down a little for us, sir. I ain't gonna lose any of my damn people because you had to have a damn ship set in place today, General Campanelli Sir. We'll hook up the two we have moving and see how the weather is before I try another one, sir. I have to take in consideration the safety of my workers at all times, sir."

General Campanelli leaned his head over until his mouth was an inch away from the Chief's ear and he screamed. "That's why I got you here, mister. To get the work done, and not have anyone hurt in the process, mister. One thing you have to keep in mind at all time around here Chief, I need this fucking Platform done yesterday, sir. I have fricking ships being bounced all around out there, because they're not hooked up to this damn thing yet, mister."

"Yeah sir, that's something I've been meaning to ask you about, General. How the hell did a stinking ground pounder ever get placed in Command of a barge like this one, sir? What the fuck gives around here anyway, General Campanelli Sir? Shouldn't some damn Fleet Fag be in Command of a Naval operation, if that's what this damn thing is, General Campanelli." The wise Chief growled as he struggled to communicate with the Commander of the operation.

"Shit, it was just my dumb luck to be picked to run this damn operation, Kirby. Besides Chief, this operation doesn't belong to any one branch of the stinking service, sir. We're gonna have Marines, Army, Airforce and Navy personnel stationed on board this damn thing once it's been completed, and we're gonna run the entire operation from this ship solely, or whatever you want to call this fucking thing, Chief." General Campanelli yelled back at him.

"Ahhh, it beats the shit outta my ass why any stinking ground pounder's in charge of something like this, General Campanelli Sir." The old Chief grumbled at his Commander.

"Would you like someone else in Command of this stinking mess, Chief?"

A smile quickly spread across the tobacco stained teeth of the older sailor as he replied, "not on your life sir. As far as I'm concerned, they picked the right crud to run this damn thing sir."

"Good, why don't you get your ass back to work then, before I have you pitched overboard."

"Yeah I'll do just that sir, but I'm not gonna hookup another damn ship until this stinking sea calms down a little, and neither you nor God can make me change my fucking mind about it sir. Even if the thumbscrews and whips come out, sir." The Chief glared at the General, enforcing the order he was not going to try to hookup another ship today.

General Campanelli saw the look and he knew right off it would be a waste of time to try and talk him into moving another ship in place as he replied to the man, "Say Chief, I dunno why the hell I ever allowed myself to be talked into taking you along with me on this damn mess, sir. You're a bigger pain in the ass than my ex-wife was, you old fucker you."

"Don't hand me any of that shit sir. You let yourself be talked into taking me along, because you wanted the best man for the job, and you know I'm the best there is sir. So don't try any of that flattery shit on my old ass, sir. Too many of you brass asses tried that shit in the past, it didn't work then, and it ain't gonna work now I assure you, General Campanelli. Now get the hell out of my sight before I have you slamming bolts along with the rest of my workers, sir."

Campanelli looked into his eyes and snapped at him, "you fricking Bee's are all alike." Then he let the Chief get back to his work. He picked up John waving his arms and he jogged towards him and then asked the excited officer, "whatdaya have for me sir?"

"Eddy, the CV-22 is holding in a landing pattern, sir. There, you can see it off to the right, out there. About three hundred feet up. She's coming in for a landing right now sir," John pointed out to sea and drew Campanelli's attention to the aircraft coming at them.

He picked up the ugly looking aircraft as she lined up with the two freshly painted white lines on the flight deck. Aleksandra was standing by his side and he jumped when he saw her and grumbled at her at the same time, "where the hell have you been all the fricking day?"

"I in CIC Chamber before, I come see plane land and want see what it had inside her, sir."

"I didn't see you below deck when I was down there Alex," the General complained at her.

"I be there same time you be there. I see you, but you no see me," Aleksandra snapped back.

He expected the CV-22 to land like most of the aircraft do on the flight deck of the Platform. Because of the long runway the Platform offered any landing aircraft. He was a little surprised when the aircraft leveled off fifty feet above the deck, and then slowed down and transition her massive engines up to where the aircraft went into a hovering mode over the lightly pitching flight deck. Slowly, the aircraft descended, adding to the wind sweeping over the flight deck.

Major Aleksandra cried out excitedly, "is it not beautiful thing to see, General Campanelli?"

He turned to her and replied with a smile, "yes, it's a beautiful thing to see Alex?"

"The way aircraft land, mean I sir," she added, making sure he knew what she meant.

General Campanelli did not respond, instead he watched as the props stopped spinning then the tail ramp slowly lowered, and three soldiers walked down carrying boxes. A Marine Major, looked around until he picked up the General standing with the other officers.

He walked up to General Campanelli, and placed the two plastic cases down right at his feet and sharply saluted and announced, "good day General Campanelli Sir, General Weidenbacher sends his regards, sir." The Major barked orders to the Marines standing behind, who in turn unpacked the boxes and setup a series of targets a good distance from where they were working.

"What the hell is it now, Major pain in the ass?" Campanelli asked the female pilot harshly.

The Major spoke over the conversation going on between the Commander and the female pilot as he offered, "sir, it's a new weapon system, unlike any you have ever seen before in your life I assure you, General Campanelli Sir." The Major picked up an odd looking helmet, and offered it to the General for his inspection as he added to his explanation.

"General Campanelli Sir, this here little baby is the HR-334 system. HR stands for Hyper Reality, sir. With this helmet, the weapon shows you what you're aiming at, it has the same aiming device as does the Apache helicopter, sir. You simply look through this aimer with one eye, and you'll see everything the barrel of the weapon sees, General. With the other eye you look out this visor here, sir. If you turn up the intensity here, most of the leaves of the trees sort of disappears from your view, and you can spot the enemy a helluva lot easier, sir. The helmet hooks to the sight, and you can aim it without having to put the sight up to your eye, sir. The weapon actually becomes the catalyst for the shooter, instead of the shooter becoming the catalyst for the weapon system, sir. The helmet increases the vision of the shooter, so he no longer has to carry binoculars with him or her, sir.

Here sir, let me show you, you put the helmet on and I'll hook it up to the weapon for you, General Campanelli Sir."

When the Major hooked up the sight, it was the weirdest thing he saw. He moved the weapon in all directions and every time he moved it, he saw a tiny screen in the helmet visor. The sight automatically focused on the target. He placed the circle on ten different spots, and felt the bullet would go where he aimed without using his eye to aim. His head was sweating in the helmet.

The Major removed the helmet, and then he asked the General for his opinion of the weapon.

"It's something, if it works like you say it does, Major," he said skeptically.

"General Campanelli Sir, the targets are set up, would you like to take a few shots with the weapon and try your luck with it, sir? There are three targets out there, here you go sir." The Major said as he handed him the helmet again.

"I can't hit a backside of a barn with a street car Major." General Campanelli smirked smartly.

"Try it, sir. You might be surprised at how easy this system works, General Campanelli."

He put the helmet back on, and the Major placed the weapon in his hands and then warned him. "Use the weapon to aim the scope, not the scope to aim the weapon, sir."

He moved the weapon around until he picked up the target set up well away from anyone on the flight deck. The scope automatically focused in on the target until he could actually read the writing on it. Made in Canada on the base of the duck. The weapon rested on his hip and he pulled the trigger. The target instantly disappeared, and he smiled as he moved the rifle until he found the second target, a pig. With the weapon resting on his hip he pulled the trigger. The second target disappeared. He handed the system back to the Major, he then took off the helmet and scratched his matted hair vigorously as he growled in delight to have the heavy helmet off his head, "damn I can't believe this thing Major. Normally, I can't hit anything, and yet I hit two out of two targets, sir. How far away were they from us?" he beamed.

"General Campanelli Sir, the targets were placed over one thousand fifty yards away from us, and they were only six and a half inches tall, sir."

He looked at the Major and grumbled with surprise, "you're shitting me Major."

"Afraid not sir, this weapon system can hit a target that small from over two thousand yards away. You see sir, most problems with firing happen because the shooter can't hold the weapon steady, and aim at the same time. We made it so the shooter doesn't have to aim, he just fires from the hip, than try and hold the weapon high and shoot. The HR-334 uses caseless bullets sir."

"Caseless bullets Major?" he asked with some wonderment in his tone.

"Yes Sir General Campanelli Sir, the brass is no longer needed, this makes the bullets much lighter, and the foot soldier can carry more ammunition on his or her person, sir. There's no waste from the shell other than a mere cap, and the shells are much more accurate, because they're not gripped by the brass as they used to be, sir."

"How the hell are they fired at the target, Major?" the rather surprised General grumbled at the military officer, not believing the Major's last words in the least now.

"Here sir, the side of the shell's made of paper, the leads inside it as you can see, just the tip of it here, sir. The powder's off to the sides of the lead, and when the primer's struck, all the action happens along the side of the bullet, and is funneled to the back, which sends the projectile flying faster, and less violently than the brass shells did, sir. I don't quite know all the physics involved in the process, sir. All I know is it works, and the shells are lighter than they used to be, sir. All the bugs aren't quite worked out of the system as yet sir, and for now, just the snipers will get the HR system for their use, sir. A spotter's no longer needed by a sniper team, but one will always go along with the sniper, we want a team spirit at all times sir."

The General looked at the new weapon lying in the box and asked, "Major, if this weapon can make me hit these two targets so far away from us. Then it can make any soldier a damn shooter, sir. I can't even see a thousand yards yet alone hit a target that far away from me, Major."

John stepped forward and asked if he could try the weapon out this time.

"Sure thing sir, here, put on the helmet, and I'll adjust it properly for your head General."

John moved a little, but before he had his head inside the slightly heavy helmet, General Campanelli grumbled at him, "hold on there for a minute will you please, John. Do you mind if Aleksandra tries the weapon out first, sir?"

"No problem Ed." John replied as he removed the helmet and handed it to the female pilot.

She stepped forward and put the helmet on, and the Major adjusted it, "look into the lens and move your hands until you see the target in the screen between the cross hairs, Ma'am."

"I see it, thank you for all you assistance, Major Sir." Aleksandra said back to the Major.

"Good, now you see the target, pull the trigger and see how you do then, Ma'am," the concerned Marine Major told the female Major.

The target disappeared, she moved the weapon around until she discovered the next target, and pulled the trigger and hit the second one and then she cried out in an excited voice, "marvelous, no believe see target clear and hit easy, sir. Can use weapon night?"

"By all means Ma'am, just push the button on top of the sight, and you'll be transitioned to the night vision capability mode, Ma'am."

She pressed the button, and everything immediately took on a bright reddish orange glow about it. It was a good thing it was heavily overcast out, or she could have blinded herself momentarily. She moved the weapon around until she finally came on the massive engines of the CV-22, that clearly showed up bright in the soft infrared glow of the sight. She sent a number of soldiers working on the flight deck scurrying around for their lives, when she moved the loaded weapon around the flight deck so recklessly.

The Major immediately grabbed the barrel of the weapon and forced it towards the ground and growled at the woman fighter pilot at the same time, "what the fuck's wrong with you damn noggin, Major!" He pulled the weapon from her hands and then added angrily at her. "The damn thing's loaded, you could have killed someone with that dumb ass fucking move, dammit."

She removed the helmet and looked at the angry Major, and then she replied to him, "I terrible sorry, forget had loaded weapon in hand, sir."

The Major took the helmet and placed it back in the box and then he snarled at her again, "you're fucking done Major, say General, do you still want to try the weapon out, sir?"

John stepped forward, and the Major placed the helmet on his head and adjusted it for him.

Aleksandra looked around until she noticed Campanelli grinning at her as he offered in an attempt to calm her down some, "take it easy, Alex. We all fuck up every now and then."

The General noticed how the weapon sounded when fired. It was more like a spit than a round being fired, and if you were not listening for it, you might even have miss the sound all together as he asked the Marine Officer, "say Major, is the weapon equipped with a silencer, sir? I believe it has to be because I can barely hear the weapon being fired off, sir."

"No sir, and that's the beauty of this new weapon system sir, because that's the way it sounds whenever the weapon is being fired, General Campanelli Sir. It's because of the caseless bullets, it actually takes away the violent explosion that always took place in the old style weapons and ammunition, General. Isn't this weapon something, sir?"

"Yeah, we're damn good at making weapons that will end someone's life alright, sir. But we still can't do anything about fricking war before it leads to more stinking death, sir."

"General Campanelli Sir, this weapon gives a big boost to the SSKP ratio and we..."

"What the hell's the SSKP ratio, Major?" the General snapped while growing impatient with the demonstration and the boring Major explaining the new weapon system to them.

"Sir, the SSKP means the Single Shot Kill Probability, General Campanelli. It means there will be a lot less bullets flying around, possibly hitting civilian's toes. One shot one kill is every Army's dream, General Sir. It brings down the collateral damage scenario way low, sir."

General Campanelli stayed with the demonstration until John had the helmet on, and fired the first almost silent round off, and then he turned and headed back for the CIC station. He did not even get off the flight deck when Sergeant Willis ran up to him and warned excitedly, "General Campanelli Sir, General Weidenbacher's on the screen and wants you STAT, sir."

He increased his pace a little as he followed the concern Sergeant below deck. He entered the CIC chamber in a rush, and noticed General Weidenbacher's face being displayed on the side screen, meaning the President of the United States was going to speak as well during this communication, and he would be on the center screen shortly. A test pattern suddenly appeared on the center screen as General Campanelli got comfortable inside the CIC station.

General William Weidenbacher started the instant he saw General Campanelli's face on his screen, "Ed, there's been some new developments in China. I have…"

President Cole's face appeared on the screen and he overrode the General words as he started speaking the instant he was able to communicate with his Commander on board the Vinegar Joe Platform. "General Campanelli, it's good to see you again sir. I'm sorry to inform you, but I believe I have some rather disturbing information I feel you must be informed about immediately sir. We just picked up a number of communications, and it looks like the Chinese are moving in for the kill against North Korea, well before the time specified in the United Nation's mandate, sir. This in itself is no big deal sir, but we also noticed via satellite observations, and a number of manned and unmanned recon flights showing an extraordinarily high amount of people are being moved in, and around the Hong Kong area at the same time, sir.

"Now we don't know exactly what this latest movement's all about yet, and who most of these people might be, General Campanelli. But some of the military and civilian advisers are seeing ghosts hiding behind every tree now, sir." President Cole glanced over to General Weidenbacher for a moment, and then he continued with his words of concern. "These advisors are warning me most of this sudden movement's more than likely military in nature, sir. General Weidenbacher feels the Chinese are trying to sneak troops into this area. Which I hope is true, because I feel these troops are being sent there to better protect the British investments in the Colony of Hong Kong, sir. In case the North Koreans try something stupid like attacking the Province. General Weidenbacher believes these troops are a serious threat, and he feels they might have something to do with the Navy Shipyards stationed in Talien, General Campanelli Sir.

"Now I don't know exactly what these troops might be up to at this time sir, I don't even know if these are troops, or if they're just a vast number of displaced citizens being moved from the public's eye, sir. That's why I have the General here, and it's why I chose to speak directly to you before the General got to you first, General Campanelli Sir. I didn't want him pressing any panic buttons with you at this time, sir. But I want you to go to a Ready Alert Two, General Campanelli Sir. Get that Platform completed, and get ready to accept and launch aircraft as soon as possible, sir. I'm ordering the Platform to move off the coast of Taiwan. I want a hundred miles between that damn Platform thing, and the Taiwan coast, and then we'll take the same procedures for our Carrier Strike Forces, one hundred mile kill zone, General Campanelli Sir.

"I believe General Weidenbacher will explain further of this rapidly developing situation for your better understanding, General Campanelli Sir. I'll also keep you well informed of any new developments picked up from my side of this damn mess, when they become available to me, sir. Thank you and good luck, and may God be with you and our fighting men and women in this here new mess, sir." The screen instantly went dead, and the General turned to General Weidenbacher to see if he had anything else to add to this one sided conversation.

General Weidenbacher slowly rubbed his chin for a brief moment, and then he offered with much concern lacing his tone of voice "I wish to hell and back that the American public would choose a military man to run this country once in a damn while, dammit. This guy can't see a bad guy lurking about until he sneaks up and kicks him right square in the damn nuts, sir. General Campanelli Sir, I don't like any of this military movement we picked up by the Chinese troops and despite what the President might believe, this is definitely Chinese troop movements we're picking up sir. I was so concerned I got in contact with the English, and it looks like they don't give a shit what we have to say any longer about this damn situation either, sir.

"They're putting in with the Chinese, and I fear if it came down to it, and we go up against the Chinese in any way, shape or form. We'll also be fighting the damn English on this one, sir. We're taking this newly discovered threat extremely seriously and tracking all English warships and submarines in the Asian region at all times now, sir. This ones going to suck the big one on us, Edward. How soon are you going to be ready to accept and launch aircraft from that damn thing of yours, General Campanelli Sir?"

"General Weidenbacher Sir, we can accept aircraft as we speak now sir. The workers just secured the tanker controlling the arresting cable systems for the flight deck, and we have a runway nearly twice the length of any normal Aircraft Carrier in the force, sir."

"Hot shit, that's outstanding to hear General Campanelli. I'll inform all parties involved in this damn thing, you'll get aircraft starting tomorrow morning, sir. General, I feel the Chinese are going to commence their attack on North Korea by no later than the middle of February, I got the feeling, sir. We don't care when they actually attack though sir, but we're a little concerned the Chinese haven't informed us of a possible change in their attack plans for North Korea yet sir. By the way Ed, have you looked into the tanker ships marked R-7 and R-13 yet mister?"

"No sir, I haven't have had the time to do much of anything just yet sir, as well as exploring the rest of the Platform, sir. Why do you ask General Weidenbacher Sir?"

"We have some new military equipment stored in those two tanker ships, sir. A special aircraft and tank, I suggest you see them immediately, sir. What the hell did you think about the damn HR-334 weapon system, General Campanelli Sir?"

"That ones something General Weidenbacher Sir. I hit the target twice, and if the damn thing can make me hit a target twice without missing it, sir. You have a winner on your hands, sir."

"I thought you'd like it General. Go and check out those damn tanker ships I just mentioned, if you liked what you saw about the damn rifle system, you'll love what you're about to see stored in there, sir. I'll be back to you when any new information becomes available to my attention, sir. Hell

General Campanelli, I might even come out to that damn Platform for a little visit some time next week, sir."

"Looking forward to your visit General Weidenbacher Sir. It'll be a pleasure to see you again, sir." General Campanelli was trying to sound very pleasant to his commanding officer.

"Yeah, I bet you are mister," the General growled at General Campanelli as he signed off.

Colonel Locker and General Palmieri both asked if they could accompany the General to the two tanker ships mentioned by the General. Campanelli agreed and sent the Sarge out to get General White and Major Klivekaita, so they could check out the tanker ships with the rest of them. He did not realize he had to go top side to get to the two tankers. John and the female Major met them topside, and they fell in line as they all went over to tanker R-7. The super structure was already removed, and the only way they knew they were on the tanker R-7, was because someone painted the number right on the massive flight deck over the tanker walkway.

The group went down a scuttle and entered a huge opening, on each side of the ship there was a tier of compartments, seven high and thirty across, each compartment contained a fighter or small bomber aircraft stored in them. The center of the tanker was cleared, and a large elevator moved the full length of the ship, and also up and down. So it could take an aircraft from any compartment, and move it up to the flight deck through either openings in the massive flight deck that could be sealed over to make the Platform completely decked out. The process was much like one that delivered the aircraft up to the flight deck of any modern day Aircraft Carrier.

An Airman noticed the brass enter his domain and he ran over to them and snapped to attention and offered as he saluted the group, "can I help the General Sir?"

"Yeah, I was told there was a new type fricking aircraft being here that I should take a gander at down here someplace, mister."

"Yes Sir General Sir. Please Follow me sirs," the Airman led them over to the elevator and he ordered the operator. "Take me to up Two, Oh, Five, Level Three."

The elevator lifted and move to the left at the same time. It stopped after going three tiers up. The General was able to tell the elevator could easily take an aircraft from either side of the ship at the same time as the Airman offered, "right this way sirs."

The officers followed the Airman to a requested hanger. Sitting by itself with men working on it, was an aircraft unlike any General Campanelli had ever saw before in his life. It looked like a triangle, with markings on either side stating F-22Y Raptor. It was fantastic, nearly forty five feet long, with a wing area of five hundred and forty eight square feet. The wings swung for better performance while in flight. In all essence, it looked like a baby SR-71 aircraft.

The motors of the aircraft could not be seen, because they were constructed up against the body of the aircraft. There were twin stabilizers, and an edge that went completely around the front of the sleek looking aircraft. The cockpit sat one and was rather long, with two bands of metal crossing over it. The pilot sat high, giving him a clear view of his surroundings and aircraft. The body of the aircraft looked like it was ten feet wide. The General felt the skin and to his surprise, it was kind of soft to the touch, it almost felt alive to him as he offered to the young Airman. "By the way mister, my name is General Edward Campanelli. You might want to pass it on because I didn't have the time to introduce myself to all the crews before, son."

The Airman piped up as he nodded to the powerful military officer, "pleased to meet you General Campanelli Sir, the reason why the surface of the aircraft feels that way sir, is because the skin's made up of a composite metal of magnesium and steel, with a heavy coating of RAM material. (Radar Absorbing Material) Any sharp points of the aircraft are layered over with the composite to help absorb, or deflect any radar detection possibilities aimed at the aircraft, sir. The engines are set up towards the front of the aircraft, and the exhaust is funneled through specialized heat absorbing and reduction ports, in order to help hide its infrared signature from most radar detection capabilities, sir. This here little baby will show up on enemy radar as a blimp the size of a football, or maybe even a little smaller sir.

"In most cases, the aircraft's signature will most likely be taken for a possible bird in flight by most radar operators, and not a true aircraft detection, sir. Her top end's over Mach Two point Six, sir. But this speed hurts her Stealth abilities though, sir. She has forward and back air breaks, with two breaks on either side of the fuselage of the aircraft. Which are used to help in high speed turns with her diving and climbing abilities, sir. She'll also easily out maneuver any enemy aircraft, and leave them in the dust at the same time, and she comes equipped with the specially designed MSCM (Mini Smart Cruise Missile).

"This new missile system's about the same size and weight of the old and outdated Phoenix missile system sir, and it comes equipped with an effective range of up to and over fifty miles, but the missile is also designed to circle the target area for up to twenty minutes, while searching for any pre-assigned targets, sir. The missile is also equipped with a small on board computer system, that can be programmed to attack say a single tank, or a special armored vehicle, or even a communication center that has shutdown features, because of a possible air attack being employed against the enemy installation, sir. The missile also has the capability of hanging around the area in question until the operator either communicates or on picking up the radio emission, the missile will immediately attack, killing the Command Post and all working inside it, sir. This weapon's as close as we can possible come to the proverbial bullet with your name printed on it, General Campanelli Sir.

CHAPTER 18

"Nothing will be safe from her attack, General Campanelli Sir. The on board computer can determine if one tank's already disabled, and the missile will not commit to attack any already disabled target. Hell sir, this weapon's so good, we can take out one tank from a column of tanks. Any command tank or armored vehicles dead with these babies. The F-22's equipped with the standard, but newer version of the AMRAAM, long range Sidewinder and Sparrow missiles as well, sir. She has three in wing hard points, and four belly hard points, along with a thirty mike mike rotor cannon sir, and a tail stinger of two rear mounted sidewinder missiles for her rear protection and defense. The aircraft has it all sir." The Airman announced with a grin.

General Campanelli absorbed the information, he heard some stories about this specialized aircraft before. But this was the first time he ever saw one in person as he asked the Airman, "how many of these damn things do we have on board this thing, son?"

"We have every one made, forty five in all. I heard there were twenty five about ready sir."

"Damn," The Commander muttered and then he looked at the rest of his Command Staff accompanying him on the tour and asked them. "Do any of you guys have any questions?"

No one responded either way.

"Okay, let's see what other little fucking surprises this damn tanker R-13 has in store for us, people," the officers got back on the massive elevator, and the Airman yelled out a number of orders in the speaker. "Hey Ray, take us down to the main deck please."

Instantly, the massive elevator went back to the base of the tanker. Once the officers got off it, they immediately headed for the stairwell then over to tanker R-13.

General Edward Campanelli was now armed with a map showing him where all the ships were attached to the Platform, he took it from the Airman. It took five minutes to get over to the second tanker R-13, this one, like the other ship was near the exact center of the Platform. When the officers got to the bottom deck, they walked into the main room and they saw a center tier with tanks stacked on both sides of the massive ship, five high, fifty long on either side. There were a thousand tanks in one section of the Platform. A filthy Marine Sergeant slowly rambled over to the group of officers and he growled at them as he cautiously eyed the Airman who immediately took off like he was not allowed in this section of the Platform.

"Okay, what the hell's this crap all about, this ain't no fricking playground down here, sirs. If you don't have any business down here then I suggest you people go back topside before you get your purdy new uniforms all dirty, sirs." The Sergeant chomped down on the stub of an unlit cigar that looked like it was days old. He was about to send a gurb of spit to the deck, when he noticed the officers he dumped on were Generals. He swallowed the tobacco juice and shuddered as he instantly snapped to attention and offered, "Sorry Sirs, we ain't used to Officers coming down to purgatory, Sirs. We work down here, and we have no time for visitors in uniforms, sirs."

General Campanelli laughed and watched the Sergeant turn green from the juice, and then he barked at the Sergeant, "get rid of that juice before you get sick on the crap, mister."

"Thank you General," he said as he sent a gurb of spit to the deck, and then he placed the stub in his pocket and looked at the group of officers.

"You're gonna hafta take the damn time to entertain some visitors this time, Sergeant. I've been ordered from the Chief of Staff Chairman to examine a new tank stored down here, mister."

"General Sir, we have no new tanks stowed down here sir, but I think I know what the General wanted me to show you, sir. It's something we just added to many of our tanks that'll defeat most infrared and laser aiming and missile attack systems, sir."

Colonel Locker piped up this time as she remarked, "I gotta see this shit, if anything saves my troops during any enemy engagement, makes me happy as hell Sergeant."

"Yes Ma'am, would you follow me, and be careful where you're stepping down here. There's things down here that could hurt you real bad if you ain't careful, and I'm not going to get stuck carrying your ass up to the damn flight deck for medical care if you get hurt down here."

"That's be quite enough of that bullshit from you, Sergeant. I gave you a little leeway because we invaded your fricking space here mister, but now keep it civil or else Sergeant!" General Campanelli growled angrily, as he shot a hot glared at the Sergeant, and then he added to his angry words, "we're not any babies here, mister. If we're stupid enough to get hurt down here then we'll get our own asses up to the flight deck for attention. Now, lead the damn way mister."

The angry Sergeant let out with a grunt of disgust as he headed to one of the two massive elevators in this section of the huge super tanker. He was trying his best to get rid of the brass following him. He lead them through the dirtiest and most dangerous areas below deck. He went by the first elevator over to the second one. It contained an oil spill that had not had been cleaned up yet, and then he bitched at the officers, "here we go sirs, get on board and I'll take you up to a tank with the special equipment installed on her, sirs."

General Palmieri was the first one to get on the massive elevator, and he almost took a spill when he stepped in a small puddle of oil he did not notice on the deck. If he did not grab hold of the hand rail, he would have ended up landing flat on his back.

General Campanelli suddenly grabbed the Sergeant by the arm and looked into his weather beaten face and growled savagely at him, "I warn you mister, if one of my people gets hurt because you're screwing around with us, I'll skin your fat ass alive real personal like, and then I'll feed the rest of your stinking body to the friggin fish. Take care of my people or you'll be cleaning the bilge of this tanker with a fricking tooth brush. Do you read me mister?"

"Loud and clear General, maybe we should take the other elevator up to the damn tank you wanna take a look at, sir. I'll have the workers clean up this mess before someone falls and gets hurt General," he turned to General Palmieri and asked him. "Are you all right sir?"

"Fine, just get me over to this damn tank so I can then get the hell outta here, Sergeant. And in one damn piece might I add if you don't mind, mister."

They rode the huge heavy duty elevator in silence, each officer looking at the tanks sitting in the separate bays. This tanker ship held two thousand tanks between both massive holds. The group of officers passed by the old Abrams tanks, and went over to the newer Abrams M-65 tanks. The elevator stopped in front of one of the M-65s.

"We're here, all out, and watch your step please sirs." It was tight to move around the tank stored in the bay. The Sergeant moved between the officers to the side and then announced, "gentlemen and ladies as you know, when a laser's aimed at a tank, ninety five percent of the time the laser's aimed right here." He lightly padded the side of the steel monster and then went on with his explanation. "This is because it offers the largest area of target to the incoming missile, and the tank cannot get out of the way of the missile in time to save herself, sirs. Someone has come up with a nifty and rather easy solution to the threat, sirs. Let me show you how it works, sirs." He went to the rear of the tank and took out a heavy wire lead with a box hooked to the end of it. It had a number of buttons and toggle switches on it.

"Inside the machine there's a small sensor that screams when the tank's zeroed in by a laser tracking device, sir. Imagine you're the driver of the tank and the alarm goes off. Now you know the tanks under missile threat, and what do you do? Up until a few years ago your tank died with you still in it, sir. Now, all you hafta do is hit this here little button. I have to do this manually in this instant, but if the tank was under attack, this would happen automatically from inside the machine, sirs." He hit a button and a edge of the tank over the fender that ran the full length of the machine dropped down, and a piece of metal snapped out, and it dropped down to the side of the tank in one motion. It's finish was as highly polished as a mirror.

"Here you see the panel. Say a laser hit the turret sirs." He hit another button, and the mirror moved up in order to deflect the laser from the turret area of the tank. This item cost fifteen hundred dollars to manufacture, and so far it has stopped ninety five percent of laser aimed missiles from hitting its intended target, sirs. And not to worry about the mirror giving away the tank's position. Because if you have to use this here little device then your position's already compromised, and if your tank has to die, sirs. You might as well make them work for it, sirs." Again he lightly padded the tank and then added, "this hear little baby ends the threat from most laser guided missiles such as the Hellfire missile. Simple sirs. If you were to combine this simple trick along with the sprinkler system, you couldn't hit this here baby with laser or infrared aimed missile system. Pretty good isn't it sirs?"

Aleksandra stepped forward and asked the Sergeant, "what you mean sprinkle system sir?"

"I'm not a sir, Ma'am. I still work for a living around here," he grumbled as he looked to the General, to make sure he was able to tell this officer about the sprinkler system.

Campanelli gave him a slight nod and the Sergeant replied with a nod of his own. He then let out his breath in a rush and explained the sprinkler system to the concerned female officer, "Ma'am, this system will be activated when the tank comes under attack by an infrared aiming missile attack system. Along both sides of the machine, and on the front and the back of the tank, are a number of small ports that pump a fine spray of cool water over the entire tank's shell. The water comes from a special tank stored inside the rear of the vehicle, and the water cools off the outer shell of the tank, thus reducing the infrared signature to the missile's seeker warhead, and the missile becomes confused after losing the signal. The cooler the tank becomes, the more invisible it becomes to the tracking missile system. The tank then fires off a flare from the tubes constructed underneath the machine, and the missile goes after the flare, while leaving the tank alive." He smiled at the young and good looking female officer.

"Huh Sergeant what happen if out water for this new system, I do no think this system good as other one with mirror thing, Sergeant." She asked and complained as she studied the massive war machine she was standing next to.

"Sorry Ma'am, I can explain this part of the system a little better for your understanding, Major. If you'd look here for a moment, Ma'am." He pointed to the ports under the ones that sprayed the water out over the machine. There were small troughs that made the water running down the tank collector, and head for this other hole in the tank.

"You see Ma'am, the water's collected and then recycled back to the holding tank, to be continuously sprayed or just stored back in the holding tank until its needed once again for the tank's defense. It's a completely enclosed system, and there's a cooling coil inside the holding drum, that keeps the water cool or even cold. Depending on how heavy the attack is against the war machine, Ma'am. Another simple solution to a once complicated problem, Major."

"I see, and I impressed very by what you work out protect tank from enemy attack, Sergeant." The foreign female Major commented as she smiled at the filthy Sergeant.

Edward was growing grumpy and tired and he growled at everyone with him, "I saw enough of this shit and at the end of your shift, I wanna see you in my office, Sergeant. I have a bone to pick over with you mister." He was still angry as hell the Sergeant brought them to the oil covered elevator, he knew the Sergeant did not want to waste his time with them, and almost got one of his officers hurt because he did not want to be bugged by them.

"Yes sir, I'll be there General Sir," he said in a low voice, knowing that his ass was in a sling.

"My name is General Edward Campanelli and remember it Sergeant. Get us down, I want to get back to my office." The officers got on the elevator, and the machine went down. Once on the deck, Campanelli lead the way out, but not before he gave one last harsh glare at the Marine Sergeant, to enforce his warning he wanted to see him later on today. No one spoke as they climbed the stairway, but once on the deck outside, everyone talked at the same time.

"What the hell did you think about the mirror system, Eddy?" John asked his old friend.

"How about the sprinkler system?" the Major asked her Commanding Officer excitedly.

He had enough and he bitched at the two excited officers, "for Christ sake, you two birds sound like a coupla children fighting over a new stinking toy, dammit."

"Whew, what the fuck's up your ass today, Eddy?" John griped back at him.

"Arrr... I don't like where this damn operation's heading. It seems like we're preparing for an all out war, and no one knows if one's coming at us or not. I thought this operation the Chinese were going to pull off, was to avert a possible major war from taking place. But yet, all I see are preparations for a heavy conflict in the fricking region. I thought I'd never have to send another young kid to his death. It's bugging the shit outta my ass, that's all." He increased his pace, leaving the other officers in his wake. As he walked, he looked around the deck and picked up over three hundred workers still putting the finishing touches to the last two tanker ships to be hooked to the Platform decking. He looked out to sea and noticed another ship making its way towards the Platform. He looked around until he spotted the old Naval Seabee Chief covered with grime, with his once white cap cocked over to one side of his head.

He knew the Chief had decided to hookup another tanker ship to the Platform and smiled to himself over the fact, knowing he made a good pick pulling the growly old Chief from Guam, and bringing him out to the Platform. He continued his scan of the ever enlarging flight deck, and noticed the CV-22 and the three Marines still wrapping their weapon system up.

Aleksandra caught up with Edward and asked him, "is thing bother you, sir? It no me?"

He stopped walking and then turned to face her and said in a calm voice along with a sharp smile, "You young lady is the only ray of damn sunshine I have around here you know, Alex. You could never do anything that'd get me pissed off at you, baby."

She smiled and they walked off together with her still complaining at him, "I get little hungry, I think time to eat something, Edward." She announced absentmindedly.

"Jesus, you're right you know Alex. I forgot all about eating again, no wonder I'm so damn jumpy and angry. C'mon Alex, I'll buy you lunch young lady," he laughed at her.

"I afraid it more supper now than lunch if you look at watch and see time it is, General Campanelli Sir. It took much time to visit two tanker ship and see weapon systems General Weidenbacher wanted us see, sir," Major Aleksandra Klevekaita purred back at her lover.

"Whaddaya mean by that crap, it's still plenty early yet, Alex." The General griped and then he looked at his watch and whistled and grumbled at the same time, "where the hell did the damn day go anyway, it's after five already, dammit."

"I told you, let go get food and then go bed," Aleksandra wiggled her hips at him sexily.

"No, you know what I'd like to do tonight, honey? I'd really like to take a little stroll around the Platform as it starts to get dark out, Alex. It looks like it's gonna be a real nice night out, and I bet we can see all the damn stars in the night from here. Whatdaya say Alex?"

"I like much that Edward, it good idea sir," she smiled at her new love.

They went below deck and ate quickly, Edward made up for missing lunch by the amount of food he ate at this meal. Then they practically ran up the stairwell leading to the massive flight deck. There were a number of workers just finishing up their last minute assignments. General

Campanelli saw a young Seaman walking with a sea woman and he smiled, wondering if the two were going to make love like he was planning to do with Aleksandra on the flight deck. The sun was just about down, and both military officers could feel the sudden chill kicking up in the air. She shivered and the General pulled her close to him.

They could hear the waves lapping at the ships below the Platform deck, there was something soothing about the sound and motion of the Platform. In the distance, they saw a soft lighting from the moored tankers waiting their turn to be bolted up to Vinegar Joe. He heard a low cry and looked for the two sailors, fearing one of them might have fallen and got hurt.

She squeezed his hand lightly, and when he looked at her she said, "I think sound might come from whale or dolphin, Edward. I no know for sure which one though, sir."

They both looked at the revolving light on the Control Tower, and then he pointed out the lights from the Aircraft Carrier Eisenhower, he knew immediately it was a Carrier because he could actually see an aircraft landing on her flight deck from this distance. There was a shower of sparks from the tail as the aircraft landed on the Carrier. He thought it was having some trouble landing until she explained the sparks came from the steel tail hook of the aircraft being dragged along the flight deck to grab the arresting cable.

The sky was getting dark, but the lights from the massive Platform were bright enough to light their way. A light marked each of the stairwells leading below deck and they were casting an eerie, colorful hue across the massive Platform flight deck.

The two military officers came to a place that looked secluded enough near a heat vent, and General Campanelli put his hands under her blouse. She pushed him away, but he persisted and the next thing she knew, they were going at it behind the stack of fifty five gallon drums. It was nice to make love under a sky covered with stars. When they finished, they leaned up against the stack of drums and stared at the sky. He smelt smoke and looked around, he saw a soft glow and someone move. It was the two sailors he noticed moments ago. They also made love under the stars, and they were now enjoying a cigarette together.

"Is no love beautiful thing?" Aleksandra asked Edward as she looked towards the two lovers.

Campanelli did not answer and she mumbled, "I wish had America made cigarette smoke."

"I didn't know you smoked Alex," He asked her, a little stunned by her last comment.

"I no usual do, but after make love like this, and sky beautiful so, feel like have cigarette, sir."

General Campanelli looked for the sailor he saw walking with the female sailor before, he was still there and he called out to him, "hey sailor by the life raft. Do you have a spare butt on ya?"

He popped his head up like he was just caught doing something wrong, as he searched for who was calling him. General Campanelli saw the sailor looking at him and he called out again to him, "I need a stinking smoke, can you spare one buddy?"

"Yeah, yeah sure Mac," the sailor got up and started over to the two people by the drums. He almost shit himself when he saw it was the General he was speaking to, and he quickly offered why he was on deck. "General Sir, me and my friend were having a little stroll around the deck, it was too close below deck and the smell from the oil was..."

"Cool it friend, I hope you were as lucky as I was tonight, mister. If so, I hope you were doing it safely young man." He groused with a smile, bringing a sharp jab to his ribs from Aleksandra, and a laugh from the two men.

"Yes Sir General, I made certain I used a dick balloon sir. We don't want a family until we get back to the States, sir." The grinning sailor offered to his Commander.

"I'm damn glad you're using your head wisely around here, young man." General Campanelli ordered a number of condom machines installed in all bathrooms and gathering places like the rec room, and reading rooms on board the Platform.

"Is she good?" he asked the young man with a grin on his lips this time.

Aleksandra hissed, "What question terribly ask him." And gave him another jab in his ribs.

"Yes sir, she's real good General Sir. She can suck start a Harley sir, if you know what I mean sir." The two men laughed while Aleksandra glared at both of them, and then the General asked the sailor, "you guys wanna join us for a few moments, son?"

"Are you sure General Sir?" The sailor asked, stunned the officer wanted him with them.

"Yeah sure why the hell not, come on over and we can talk some more if you'd like, mister. By the way, I'm General Edward Campanelli, and I'm the Commander of the entire operation."

The Seaman was really impressed and he called out to his girlfriend, and she immediately popped up while quickly fixing her blouse, and the sailor asked. "General Campanelli Sir, you don't mind we were, err... playing around a little on the flight deck, General Sir?"

"Not unless you mind we were doing the same damn thing over here, sailor." Campanelli laughed as he got another jab in the ribs from Alex as she glared back at him again.

The kid looked at the General like he was shocked the officer made love to a woman, and the General joked at him. "Yeah son, General's make love to women the same way you do buddy."

The Seaman's mouth snapped shut as he realized he was staring at the two officers with his mouth hanging open. A cool breeze suddenly washed across the flight deck, and everyone shivered this time as the sailor offered his Commander. "General Campanelli Sir, I'm Seaman Second Class, Peter Kelsey, and this is Sea Woman First Class, Terry Allen, sir."

"Glad to meet ya both," he introduced the Major to the two young sailors, and then asked them where they came from. The sailor explained his girlfriend came from New York and he came from New Jersey and they met and fell in love while on active duty in California.

He was pleased the two kids got along so well, and they talked until way into the night and only when it got too cold to remain outside, did they finally go below. The kids separated and finally went on their way. Edward and Aleksandra headed for her room, but Colonel Locker was in and she was already sound asleep. So he pulled lightly on the Major's blouse and whispered to her at the same time, "C'mon, you're spending the damn night with me tonight, Alex."

She tried to protest but he added while overriding her protest. "That wasn't a request Major, it was a direct order, young lady. So let's get going will ya please, Alex."

She wanted to stay in her apartment for the night, because she feared Edward and herself might get in some trouble, if she stayed every night in his private wardroom. Again, they made love before turning in for the night. Tomorrow being

Saturday, he planned to sleep in late for once, and he wanted a little company while he did.

Seven a.m. John lightly tapped on his door.

"Go away unless you want to lose your stinking life for bothering my stinking ass this early this damn morning, fucker." General Campanelli growled out from his bed.

"Whew, still in a bad mood this morning I see sir," John called out from in the hall.

Edward jumped out of bed when he heard John's voice. Thinking something was wrong and he needed to be informed about it. He dashed over and opened the door naked.

"Damn, from the looks of you two, I sure hope I wasn't interrupting something going on around here, Herr General Sir." John smirked at his friend.

"Get your damn ass in here before I catch a fucking draft, will ya please."

John walked around him as he smirked at his long time friend. "Only if you put on pants, mister. I don't want anyone getting the wrong idea about us, sir." John stopped dead in his tracks when he noticed Aleksandra in his rack with a cigarette. She was topless.

General White announced when he laid eyes on her, "may the god of bad habits bless you young woman. I knew you had perfect breasts lady."

She smiled at him as the General growled at his lifelong friend. "C'mon man, get to the damn point that brought you here so fricking early on my damn day off, buster. I know you didn't come all the way down here just to discuss the Major's stinking tits, mister."

"I always want to discuss a woman's tits sir," John retorted with a grin at his friend.

"Yeah, yeah. What the fuck do you want down here, you pain in my ass you. I wanted to sleep in today if you don't mind asshole," General Campanelli griped in a hot tone of voice.

"Oh yeah, some of the Officers are talking about getting up a little game of baseball later on this morning Eddy, and I was wondering if you might be interested in playing some, sir? I remember you play a mean short stop position many years ago, General. I think it'd be a good thing for everyone wanting to play the damn game, sir." John offered with a grin again.

"You mean to tell me you woke my ass up for that bullshit, buster. I ought to put my stinking foot up your ass for ya for waking my ass this morning, dammit." He snarled at John, but Aleksandra was all smiles as she added to the conversation now.

"I love see play this ball base thing, Ed." She got out of bed, making John almost come in his pants as she walked right by him naked as the day she was born.

"I ain't gonna do anything until I get something to eat for crap sake around here. Will you get back in bed before you set this stinking guy off on me, honey? I know what he's like when he gets a hardon, and take it from me he's no fun to be anywhere around him, young lady. No ones safe until he buries that black snake of his in someone, be it man, woman or even beast." The General complained at his best friend of many years now.

The two officers laughed as Aleksandra wrapped a towel around her hips, and put her legs up on the tiny wall desk and said, "I like something eat self, but no want go for it and get."

"That's easy enough," he smirked at his new girlfriend, and then called over to the mess. He told the Mess Sergeant he was feeling a little under the weather, and asked him if he could possibly make something up for him to eat, and have it sent up to his room.

The Sergeant immediately exploded as he growled into the phone, "what the hell do you think I'm running down here for Christ sake, General Campanelli Sir? God damn room service or something, sir? I ain't got nobody down here I can send to get you some food, sir"

He laughed and replied to the angry sounding Mess Sergeant, "it's no big deal Sergeant. I was just feeling a little under the weather, I'll come down to the mess to eat I guess."

"Whoa, hold on there a second General Campanelli Sir. I think I can make you up a little tray of food to satisfy you sir, and I'll have one of the usual fuckups run it over to your wardroom for you, sir. What would you like to chow down on this morning, sir? I have everything under the sun on the menu for today, sir." The now not so angry Mess Sergeant asked his Commanding Officer, now he trying to make some points with his Commander.

"Some scrambled eggs," he looked at the Major and she mouthed flapjacks and he added. "Some flapjacks and sausage would be fine." He then looked at John and he mouthed, eggs, bacon and some orange juice. Edward glared at him as he said in the phone. "Some more eggs, along with some bacon and more sausage and orange juice."

"What the fuck kinda crap are you trying to spoon feed me down here, General? You can feed half the damn crew with the amount of stuff you want sent up to your private quarters, General Campanelli Sir." The Sergeant griped and then he added in a much calmer tone of voice this time, "look sir, why the hell don't you do me a little favor, and tell me how many people you're entertaining in your quarters this morning, and I'll make up a cart and get it over to you sir."

He laughed again as he announced, "three people are in my living quarters Sarge, and we're gonna be working in my wardroom and I was..."

"Yeah, yeah sure, I guess you just wanted to be pampered a little today, am I right General Campanelli Sir?" The Mess Sergeant grumbled at his Commanding Officer.

"What can I say to you man. I guess you got me dead to rights on this one Sarge." He laughed for the third time into the phone.

"Yeah, I thought so General Campanelli Sir. Look General, the next time you decide to sleep in, would you be so kind as to let me know the night before, and that way I'll have some stinking food sitting outside your damn door as you first wake up, sir." The Sergeant offered to his Commanding Officer as he nodded to a Seaman to come over to him.

"You'd do that for me Sergeant? That'd be real cool of you if you can do that for me, Sergeant." He asked him in a serious tone this time.

"Yeah sure why the hell not sir, and I'll have it served to you by Sally suckum silly from Philly too, sir. Good-bye General Campanelli Sir, your food will be up to you shortly, sir."

The General hung up while laughing over the Mess Sergeant's last remark as he announced to the two other officers with him, "like I said, you give me a hand full of fucking Sergeants, and I'll get any job done with half the stinking trouble, and half the fucking time too."

John and Edward engaged in some small talk, all the while John kept glancing over at Aleksandra who was busy filing her fingernails, she was still topless and sitting on the edge of the bed. A knock on the door, and a scruffy looking Seaman appeared who just lost a stripe, the strings still hanging from the empty space on his arm. He pushed the food cart in the tight room, and his eyes shot open when he got a good look at Aleksandra sitting on the General's bed. The guy instantly lost over ten pounds from his waistline, as he sucked in his gut for all he was worth. He offered to set out the dishes, but the General stopped him, and then he wanted to pour the coffee for the officers in the room. Edward had to actually order him out of the room.

The gawking Seaman slowly backed out of the General's wardroom, all the while he keeping his gut pulled in tight, and his eyes glued to Aleksandra's exquisite breasts. Once he was gone, Edward remarked, "one of these fricking days you're going to kill someone with those damn cannons of yours, young lady. You gotta keep those puppies covered once in a while, honey."

"It be done more than once already mista," she retorted absentmindedly to him.

Both military officers looked at one another as they grasped the meaning of her last remark. General Campanelli now found himself wondered how many men lost their lives to this once enemy agent, who used her body like a soldier used his weapon in a war. Edward shook his head as he thought, 'well, I guess it's too late to worry about that shit now and besides, if the United States had no problems about what she done in the past then I sure do not'.

"C'mon, are you going to eat something before it gets cold on ya young lady?" He asked her with a little concern as he waited for her to eat something.

She pulled her chair over to the small cart and sat down, Edward and John sat on the edge of the bed, and they dug into the mound of food. The Sergeant set up a real good meal, with everything from flapjacks to toast resting on the food cart.

After he finished eating, Edward sat back on the bed and let out with a loud belch.

She turned to him and said, "my God, hope you no hurt youself with that one, Eddy."

"Ha, ha," he smirked as he stuck his tongue out at her.

John sat back and grumbled at his lifelong friend, "man Eddy, I have to admit it buddy, you sure do know how to live while stuck on active duty, old buddy. I bet you're the only sonofabitch I know who can have his breakfast served to him in his stinking wardroom, and have a beautiful woman naked to share it with also, man."

"Eat your heart out, always remember one thing around here mister, rank does has it privilege, John." General Campanelli smirked back at his friend this time.

They both laughed as the General pushed the small food cart out in the hall. Seconds later, they heard it being wheeled away.

Aleksandra stood and she stretched her arms over her head, and then let out with a loud groan. This instantly got the men's attention, and they stared at her until she said she was going to go and take a quick shower for herself by her own living quarters. She removed the towel and threw it at John as she quickly slipped into her dress and blouse, and then carried the rest of her clothes in her arms. She went back to her room for a change of clothes, and then she headed for the officer's head and showers setup for Edward's private staff members. The General's room was the only one on the entire Platform that had its own private shower and head in it.

As she entered the shower area, she heard the water already running, and then she noticed Colonel Locker washing herself. She shrugged and then she stripped down and entered the shower and turned the other shower head on.

Colonel Locker stared at her as she snuck by, and she asked her in a sarcastic tone of voice. "Well, did you enjoy yourself last night with the General, honey?"

She did not respond, she lathered herself then said, "yes, thank you much Colonel."

"I see why he likes you so much Major. You have a gorgeous body." Colonel Locker said as she rubbed one of Aleksandra's breasts with her hand. To her surprise, Aleksandra did not pull away from her and she bitched, "you would make love to anyone, wouldn't you?"

"If make love you, you never try man ever again I warn you, Locker. I ruin you for men after share lovemaking together I assure you, Colonel." She declared angrily at her.

"Hmmm... I'd like to take you up on that little threat of yours, Major." Locker purred as she reached out with the other hand and fondled both her breasts now. Aleksandra allowed Locker to play with her for the moment. She also allowed her to really get into it, just long enough before she suddenly shoved her away from her body and then she snapped angrily at her.

"No when you want make love me, I tell when you do that me again, Colonel Locker. If you want ever do that again with me, you treat me better much than you do now, Colonel. Now, you stand and come over to me. That it, you do right, stand and put hand down at side." She moved her face right next to the Colonel's as she put a finger in her mouth, and then she moved it around. Then she removed it and put her hand down betic `between` Locker's legs. She pushed her finger in Locker and warned her hotly. "You treat better me now, right Colonel Locker?"

Locker was instantly reacting to her finger movement as she replied in short puffs of breath, "yes, I'll treat you much better Aleksandra, don't stop please."

"I stop and no do ever again to you until feel you be nice to me, Colonel. If you want do again and more to you, you earn it from me, Locker." She said in a sarcastic tone to her.

"Please don't stop Major." Colonel Locker begged the stunning and much younger woman.

Aleksandra smiled to herself as she thought and stared deeply into Locker's eyes for the long moment. 'Control, you America fool so easy to control and conquer all the time'. She suddenly shoved Locker away from her a second time, and this time she ended up falling on her rearend on the tile floor of the shower, as Aleksandra said again to her, "you earn right I do this you again and good better too, Colonel Locker. I have lot able to teach you how be with woman when you want to play with one, Colonel Locker." She hissed angrily as she now turned her back on the slightly older woman, and then she lathered herself up again.

When she finished with her shower, she left the older woman still sitting on the floor of the showers, without saying another word to her as she left the area with a towel wrapped around her exquisite body. For just a brief instant, Locker suddenly felt extremely threatened by this foreign young and beautiful female pilot. She wondered if she was still working for the Russians, and they were controlling her actions, while finding out America's latest military secrets and military equipment. At first she was going to discuss this possibility with General Campanelli, but she quickly thought better about that idea, and then she made up her mind to speak to General White first, and let the General direct her as what to do next about her sudden fear of this extremely dangerous and beautiful woman.

Then she calmed down a little and rethought the situation over in her mind. She realized if she did question Aleksandra's loyalty to the General. Then she would have to admit to making a lesbian advance towards the foreign Major in the shower area today, and Aleksandra could easily dispute her claims by merely saying she refused her advances in the shower, and that was why she was trying to hurt her with the American government because of Aleksandra's not wanting to engage in a sexual affair with the other woman.

Colonel Locker shook her head slowly, knowing she was stuck right in the middle of a no win situation, and she decided not to pursue the issue any further, unless she detected some evidence to successfully accuse Aleksandra of espionage against her country. She got up and quickly dried herself off, and then she dressed, still wondering how it would have been to make love with the female Major. She headed back for her room.

Aleksandra went back to General Campanelli's private wardroom, it was the largest one on entire deck, probably on the entire Platform. She decided to move in with him after all, and she was going to share the large room with him. She was also going to leave most of her clothes and other personal items in the room she shared with Colonel Locker though. But she would spend most of her time in General Campanelli's private room with him.

It was late by the time she headed back for General Campanelli's wardroom. That was because she stopped by the mess and ate supper, and then she checked on the CIC and found nothing new came in, so she smiled and then headed for Campanelli's room.

General Campanelli already ate while she was doing her act, and he laid down on the oversize bed in the room, and he was sound asleep by the time Aleksandra came back in his room to be with him for the rest of the night.

She actually had to shove him over with her arms to get enough room for her to lie down on the bed comfortably, and then she wiggled into his bed with him. She was looking forward to the baseball game that was going to pit the officers, against the enlisted men of the Floating Island. She loved it whenever men played like little children in front of her.

CHAPTER 20
SUNDAY FEBRUARY 8th, 1997 O910 HOURS
ON BOARD THE VINEGAR JOE PLATFORM

The enlisted men were ready to play ball, other crew members had just pulled two tanker ships in place. The officers were to one side talking over their strategy against the enlisted men's team. The game started, first up was General Campanelli and he quickly struck out. The game did not get any better for the officers, and by the time the five innings were over, the enlisted men had a thirteen to two win. The General took to even threatening the enlisted men, letting them know he would be extremely unhappy if he was on the losing side of the ballgame. He said it in a pretty joking way, but the next time the General came up to bat, he got a hit that easily turned into a home run, because no enlisted man would dare pick up the ball and try to get out the slow rumbling military officer, who looked like he was going to die before he reached homeplate.

The losers had to give the winners a cheer that sounded more like a death chant to everyone involved in the game. The game did what the General hoped it would do, cause everyone playing to laugh, and banter back and forth with each other. He walked over to Aleksandra, Colonel Locker, and the young and pretty sea woman they were with last night. Her boyfriend was the one pitching for the other side. The women laughed at the General, and he joined them with their laughter. The pitcher came over and apologized to the General for striking him out three times in a row during the game. He simply waved him off while telling him he had more fun today than he had in the past few years.

General Palmieri was left behind to man the CIC Chamber just in case something went down with the Chinese and North Korea. When the other officers filtered in, General Palmieri informed them a number of new reports were coming in hot and heavy. General Campanelli went to his desk and pulled the pile of reports from his basket, he read reports stating a few skirmishes between Chinese and North Korean troops occurring more and more frequently. Fourteen in all, each worse than the last and growing in intensity, along with the troops involved.

One report stated a number of Chinese tanks engaged a unit of North Korean troops and a heavy tank exchange broke out. The report further stated twenty three North Korean tanks and armored vehicles were destroyed in the brief but extremely deadly exchange, to three Chinese tanks killed in the skirmish. The General went to another report, he did not like this one any better. This report stated a number of South Korean tanks attacked North Korean troops having exercises near the border. The South Korean Units penetrated the North by three miles.

General Campanelli turned to General Palmieri and growled at the other officer, "order all United States troops the fuck out of South Korea immediately, sir. If these damn cocksuckers want to start a war then none of my people will be in harm's way, sir."

"Sir, I think we need..." Palmieri went to offer, but was cut off by his Commanding Officer.

"No if ands or buts about it General, I want the troops the hell out of South Korea. I don't wanna be drawn into another shooting war because the South Koreans can't control themselves. Order it, have the troops transferred over to Japan and Germany. I'll have the junk haulers (cargo ships) brought up to take their equipment off the Korean Peninsula. Most of the troops will head for Japan, you got it General? I'll clear the order with the Japanese and General Weidenbacher."

General Campanelli thumbed through a second report as he ordered General Palmieri, he glanced down and held his breath. He stood as he read from the paper and growled at no one in particular working inside the chamber. "What the fuck's this crap all about, dammit? What the hell are the damn English up to anyhow for crap sake? John, look at this damn report, will ya."

"I don't have to sir. I read the damn thing already. I was the one who placed it on your desk."

Colonel Mary Locker asked the upset acting General with concern what the report said.

General Campanelli glared at her as he barked in an extremely angry tone of voice, "I'll tell ya what the damn thing says. The damn English Jump Jet Carrier Ark Royal, just launched aircraft, and they're flying attack shorties over North Korea along with the Chinese aircraft, dammit." As he read on, another report came in over the printer. Everyone became quiet, until the machine finished printing. General Palmieri let out with a low whistle as he read the new report.

"What the hell is it? Give me the damn paper will you, General." Edward hissed at him.

General Palmieri handed the latest report to Edward and his face turned red. He sat down and leaned back in his chair and let out his breath in an angry hiss as he steamed. "The North Koreans just declared war on England for invading her country, and I don't blame them a bit. John, when is Vice Admiral whatever the hell his name is, supposed to get here sir? I gotta go over this last report with him and try and find out what the English are doing in this mess."

"Admiral Middleton Sir, he changed his visit until later on this afternoon at Thirteen Hundred Hours, General Campanelli Sir." General White reported to his Commanding Officer.

"I'm looking forward to meeting with this bugger, and see what the hell the United Kingdom's up to, sir. I'm gonna clean up and shave for his visit, inform me if any new reports comes in, and I don't mean reports about a stinking small tank skirmish, important reports like this last one, people." General Campanelli angrily threw the paper about England attacking North Korea on the floor then he stormed out of the chamber. He took a quick shower then shaved and got into his class A dress uniform. Then he went to the VIP room and waited for the English Vice Admiral to arrive. The United Kingdom Admiral was early and ushered to the air-conditioned lounge. Edward offered his hand, they shook then seated themselves across from each other.

"Coffee Admiral Middleton Sir?" The General offered the United Kingdom Officer politely as he stared at him for a moment.

"Tea please," Admiral Middleton replied in a pleasant and calm tone back to the General.

"Yes of course tea, forgive me please, I forgot how you English were about your tea, Vice Admiral Middleton Sir." A Seaman in dress whites took off instantly almost running. He returned and sat the tray on the table between the two officers, and then he quickly left again.

Edward watched the English Vice Admiral fix his tea, and then sit back while holding the cup over his lap. He waited until the English Officer was comfortable, and then he snapped in a sharp tone at him. "Admiral Middleton Sir, is England going to back China in this damn operation, and if so, how far is that support going, sir? Is England willing to turn her back on the United States, and the rest of the free world, just for a chunk of Chinese real estate sir?"

Admiral Middleton laughed as he replied, "General Campanelli, my country will never turn her back on the United States, sir. We've been Allies far too long for that to ever happen, sir. I wish you Americans would realize just how important Hong Kong is to England's future, perhaps then you'd understand our position in this strange situation, sir. Nearly a third of all economic transactions that takes place in Hong Kong's for England interests, sir. Hong Kong has the twelfth largest economy in the entire world, sir. If we ever lose Hong Kong, over forty five billion dollars of monetary trade would be instantly lost to the United Kingdom, sir.

"I've been told catastrophe of this size would increase our inflation rate to over sixty five percent, and the value of the pound sterling would be at an all time low, and it'd take four pound sterling to make just one United States dollar, sir. This disaster would completely destroy the United Kingdom as an economic powerhouse while putting over five million people out of work, and possibly cause a civil war in my nation at the same time, sir. This is why we're trying to protect our investment in Hong Kong, General Campanelli Sir. China has shown us the reports that prove North Korea was preparing to attack Hong Kong, this is why the Ark Royal and the Invincible are taking up position with the Chinese ships at this time and we are working with Chine, for the time being, sir." Vice Admiral Middleton said smugly to the American Officer.

"I see why you're here, but what happens if China decides to attack South Korea, and maybe even Japan after she has destroyed North Korea as a working nation, sir? How will the United Kingdom react to a scenario like that takes place, Admiral Middleton Sir?"

Admiral Middleton's eyes opened wide, and Edward saw the fear etched in them. The English Admiral placed his cup on the table and remained sitting as he mumbled barely over a whisper. "My God, you have information about China going after Japan, sir? I could not image a situation like that taking place, General. Arrr... if something like this ever occurred, you can rest assure England would do everything in her power to prevent such an attack against Japan, sir."

"It's been suggested to me that's what might be in the back of their mind, Admiral."

The confused English Admiral could not help himself and he stared at the General, and then cried. "Gawddamned bloody hell, I'm certain if China dares to attacks Japan.

England would live up to her agreement with Japan, and intervene on her behalf, General Campanelli Sir."

"What about Hong Kong and all England's money you people are so damn concerned with that you people have hidden away in Hong Kong, sir?" The General asked the Englishman.

Admiral Middleton instantly got nervous as he replied cautiously to the General. "Bloody hell General Campanelli, I don't know what England would do about that one sir. I know there's possibly a couple of trillion dollars of worth of England's inside Hong Kong, and my government could ill afford to lose it, sir. I'm quite certain my government would send in troops to get our money out of there, if we had to go up against China and her troops, General Campanelli."

"Would England go to war against China if she moved out against Hong Kong, Admiral Middleton Sir?" General Campanelli nearly roared his last question at the English Officer.

"Yes, I'm positive of that much happening General Campanelli Sir. We would have no other choice in the matter if that scenario ever took place, sir " The English Admiral replied.

"Well sir, what are you going to report back to your government about this conversation, sir?"

"Hell, I'm going to suggest we remove our money from Hong Kong, like we was doing before China gave us a new lease on Hong Kong, sir. I don't know what my government would do now, maybe even put off draining the banks for fear of showing the Chinese we don't trust them any longer, but that's why we have politicians, sir. Gawddamned Bilkers anyhow sir." Admiral Middleton said in sheer desperation over what General Campanelli was informing him of.

"You have some things to talk over with the rest of your people, Admiral Middleton Sir. I'll be here if you need my help, sir. Your military forces will be free to use this installation if needed Admiral. I hope for your sake it doesn't happen though, sir. Would you care to take a quick tour our little Island project, sir? I'd be pleased to give you the grand tour of the place, free of charge at that, sir." General Campanelli offered as he tried to lighten up the moment now.

The English Admiral gave out with a sort of nervous laugh as he declined the kind offer by replying. "I believe I better get back to my ship, and send a message out to my people, informing them of what you just informed me of, General Campanelli Sir. Bloody hell, there's going to be a terrible reaction, maybe they'll put some of our troops in Hong Kong, sir."

"Putting troops in a foreign land without invitation? I seriously doubt that ever taking place Admiral Middleton." Campanelli exclaimed and then added, "it'd be sheer suicide, and I'm certain China would have England before the Security Council before the spit hits the floor, and England would be proven wrong if she placed any military troops in China without a state of war existing, sir. It'd be classified as an invasion of China and we would have to go against you sir."

Admiral Middleton glared at Campanelli, he did not like being told the United States would go against England at a Council Meeting for any reason. He milled over what the General said and he replied with a snap in his tone of voice. "General Campanelli Sir, you're right about your last assumption, sir. I'm quite certain my government would never take to invading China under any circumstances, sir." Admiral Middleton stood and offered Edward his hand.

General Campanelli shook it then offered, "I was kind of hoping you'd at least stay for some supper, Admiral Middleton Sir. I ordered something prepared specially for your visit, sir."

"I thank you much sir, but I'm afraid not at this time, General Campanelli Sir. I think it's more important that I get back to my ship and speak to my Command, and see what they might want to do over the information you just shared with me, General Campanelli Sir."

"Very good then sir, I understand this Admiral Middleton Sir and good luck sir." General Campanelli replied as he stood and began walking the Admiral out of the meeting room.

"Next time I'll take the time to see your entire Platform operation sir, I'll be back on board soon I promise, General Campanelli Sir. These damn bilkers will see to that, sir."

"I'll walk you topside then Admiral." Campanelli offered as he lead the way for the man.

The Seaman waited outside, and then asked when he noticed the two officers come out of the lounge area. "The General and Admiral are leaving already, sirs? I took the liberty to prepare a table for you to dine at in the mess hall, sirs."

General Campanelli smiled at the man and responded, "not this time Seaman. Thanks."

The Seaman instantly saluted the two officers as they slowly made their way up to the main flight deck area of the massive Platform. Once there, General Campanelli picked up the Westland Sea King helicopter resting on the flight deck, and the English pilot immediately started his engines spooling, the instant he noticed his Admiral coming towards the aircraft.

Admiral Middleton turned back to General Campanelli and said with concern lacing his tone. "Sir, I thank you for this important information, and sorry if my government gave you a sort of start, General Campanelli Sir. I'll be back in contact with you once my people direct me as to our next course of action over this situation, sir. I hate politicians, and it seems I'm being forced to act like one myself lately, I'm a much better soldier than politician, General. I thank you once again sir." He saluted the General, turned and crouched while holding his cap as he ran towards the spooling helicopter. The engines went to full power the instant the Admiral was on board.

The American Commander watched the chopper until it was completely out of sight while enjoying the brisk fresh air. It was getting colder with each passing day on the Platform, and he shivered and then he headed back for the warmth of the CIC Chamber.

"Get me General Weidenbacher on the damn horn immediately mister!" the General ordered Sergeant Willis the moment he entered the CIC center.

Seconds later General Weidenbacher was on the screen and General Campanelli offered. "Good day General Weidenbacher Sir. I just informed the Admiral from the Invincible we have information that offered China might attack Japan after they destroyed North Korea, he almost shit his pants, sir. I further informed him this information was unsubstantiated for the moment, but confidence is high an attack could take place, General Weidenbacher."

"I'm a little eager to know, what was his response to this information, General Campanelli Sir? We have to try and keep England on our side as this mess is starting to shape up, sir."

"He offered he's getting in contact with his people, and inform them of what I informed him of, General. He felt his people would live up to their bargain, and protect Japan if she happens to come under attack by Chinese forces, sir. But he didn't know what his people were going to do about the massive amounts of funds they have in Hong Kong. The Admiral stated he was going to suggest his government start to filter out the money quickly in drips and drabs I guess, General Weidenbacher Sir. He wasn't quite certain on this part of our conversation, sir."

"That'd be like fashioning paper airplanes out of lead, it's not going to fly well, General Campanelli. They might as well be spitting in the damn wind on this one. They won't move any of the damn funds the hell out of Hong Kong until it's too late for them to do so." General Weidenbacher growled and then added, "I'll be back to you when the President informs me how it went with his meeting with the Minister." With this, the General killed the communication.

He found himself staring at a blank screen for a long moment, thinking of what his next move was going to be, he then turned to John and asked with concern lacing his voice, "how many of the damn tanker ships do we have locked together on the damn Platform so far, sir?"

John looked through a stack of papers and then responded, "we have five of the six tankers with fighter aircraft stored on them hooked up, along with three armament, four fuelers, three troop tankers, three food, and one shit tanker ship, General. Nineteen out of twenty four ships are already set in place at this time, sir. We'll have the remaining few tanker ships together by Wednesday, barring any bad weather conditions or any other crap hitting us, sir."

"Good, I like that, I like that a lot, John. Does this estimate include the wire and pipe hookups to these remaining tankers as well, sir?"

"I think you better allow ten to fifteen extra days for secondary hookups to be completed, sir."

"Arrr... that's too damn bad, we look in pretty good shape other than that though sir." The General clasped his hands behind his head as allowed himself a slight breather. He wanted a cigarette so bad he could taste it. He looked at Aleksandra and then glared, he was blaming her for his weakness and want to smoke again. She started smoking yesterday, and had a cigarette dangling from her mouth as she typed.

He laughed as he complained under his breath if she made him start smoking again, he was going to boot her in that lovely little ass of hers. It was good to have someone around to shift the blame for his weakness on.

The next few days dragged by at a snails pace, the work was hard, and never ending for the General and the rest of his overworked Command Staff. They sifted through mountains of papers, sorting out important reports from the less important ones. Conversations between the General and his Command were strained, as the situation in North Korea grew more intense day by day. The more General Campanelli did, the more there was to do. He was having less time to spend with Aleksandra, and she was getting more edgy with each passing day on him.

SATURDAY, FEBURARY 14th, 1997

General Edward Campanelli was up early and already inspecting the Platform from one end to the other. The super structures were removed from all the tankers already hooked up and making the massive flight deck of the Platform. The painters were working at putting down the direction lines for the vehicles driving and aircraft landing on the deck. All the desalination plants were up and on line already, even though one of them had to be replaced when its motor suddenly exploded. He was pleased even though he lost two men caught between some of the planking when the last tanker ship was pulled into place, and two others lost some fingers the same way. All in all, four casualties were not that bad for a massive project of this size.

The overworked General lost some of the equipment overboard, the largest was a fork lift truck, knocked over the side by a crane. He was having frogmen from stateside flown in and the divers were offered, and the General knew how he was going to put them to use. They were moored in the water over one hundred and fifty feet deep, and the divers were going over the side in order to hookup lines to all the lost equipment, so he could retrieve it and then get it back in proper working order, or scrapped all together.

General Campanelli still had to move the Platform to only one hundred miles off the coast of Taiwan as ordered, he was going to move it earlier, but his engineers suggested it would be much wiser and easier to move the entire Platform, once all the super tankers were bolted together to the Platform. That was the reason he had decided to move the Platform on Monday after General Weidenbacher's scheduled visit to the Platform.

The CIC Chamber was quiet for the first time in a long time, and General John White and Colonel Mary Locker were the only two people still manning the room.

"Where the hell is everyone else at, for crap sake, mister?" The General asked as he looked around the chamber after he entered the large room.

"I gave the rest of the staff the morning off sir, nothing was happening out there, and I thought it was rather foolish to have the entire Command Staff sitting in here wasting their damn time on nothing, when it's so damn quiet in North Korea at the moment, General." John replied.

"I guess you're right at that John, it's better to have people well rested, if and when something breaks loose on us. Good call on your part sir." Campanelli remarked, but his mind was already elsewhere, all this quiet in China and North Korea did not go unnoticed by him. He saw this a few times in his life, it was the calm before the storm. He saw other warning signs as well, he was having some trouble sleeping, and noticed many of his Sergeants were slightly edgy, and snapping at their men. This was a sure sign the shit was going to hit the fan. Anytime General Campanelli wanted to know what was happening in the world, all he had to do was look for his Sergeants, these soldiers always seemed to know what was coming even before Command did.

"say John, I'd sure like you to call in for a quick flyover of both North Korea and China by the SR-91Bird for later today, I have an itch I can't scratch, sir. Hell, you might as well have the aircraft continue on and do a run over South Korea at the same time as well, sir."

"Uh-oh, I don't think I like the sound of that last request, sir. Every time you get a stinking itch in your jockies, all hell usually breaks out, my friend. I'll see what I can do for you sir."

"Do better than that General White Sir, I want the damn flight over China as soon as possible, sir. I want to see if the damn Chinese are moving anymore of their stinking troops around, where they shouldn't be moved to, John. I don't trust them as far as I can throw them, sir."

"You and a lot of other people involved in this damn thing sir," John added with a smirk.

General Campanelli looked at Colonel Locker for a moment, she looked like she was really worn out and he griped at her, "what the hell's up with you Mary? Where the hell did your spirit go on you, woman? You look like you were shot at and missed, and shit at and hit. I want you at your fricking best, Colonel. I don't want your ass moping around here all damn day, young lady. You have to make certain all the damn personnel are in full dress uniforms. This goes for the personnel not working, the workers are to be in clean uniforms. I don't want anyone looking like a sack of shit today, and that goes for all the Officers too. All brass will be polished so I can see my stinking puss in it, and all metals and ribbons will be on. Got it Locker?"

Colonel Locker remained seated at her computer as she replied over her shoulder without looking at her Commanding Officer. "Sir, this is the tenth time you're busting my damn horns about this same damn shit, sir. I told you ten times already I'll see to the dress uniforms, they'll be fine General. You'll be proud of them, now get off my ass will ya please, sir."

For a second, Edward got really steamed at the way she just spoke to him but then he wrote it off as to being that time of the month.

"I'm going to lay down for a while," he mumbled as he dragged himself to his room, it was empty, and he dropped down in his bunk like a sack of potatoes. His little while turned out to be over eight hours, he woke with a start at Zero, One Twenty Two Hours looking for Aleksandra. He was horny, she must have noticed he was tired, and she went to her own room for the night.

General Campanelli wanted to take a shower in the enlisted men's quarters, because he wanted to see how it was there. He went to the shit tanker through the below catwalks that linked the ships together, so no one had to go top side to get to any one tanker of the system. It was cold and every time he came to a exposed catwalk area, he shivered. He made a mental note to order the catwalks enclosed and heated. He made it to the showers, stripped and then started the water, it never got as hot as he felt it should have been, and he made another mental note.

Campanelli headed back to his wardroom but he was not tired, so he went on the main deck to see what was going on there. It was a clear night, and he looked for constellations he knew. He smiled as he saw a shooting star then noticed some aircraft flying in tight formation. Their tail beacons blinking to ward off any possible mid-air collision. He watched until they were out of sight, he then scanned the huge flight deck and picked out seven flash light beacons from the fire watch teams. He shivered and decided to go back downstairs, he heard the TV room was working, there was a fifty seven inch RCA TV, VCR, and loads of tapes. He made for the room, a satellite dish made sure his ship got all the stations and sporting events from back in the States.

General Campanelli plopped down heavily in a chair like he was just shot, and then he put the TV on. He did not realize how loud it was up until the OOD (Officer Of The Day) rushed in the room and he lowered it on him, and then the officer complained at the General at the same time. "Gees General Campanelli Sir, I have people sleeping down here, dammit sir."

He merely smirked at the excited officer and then checked out the channels, stopping at MTV just in time to hear a song sung by AERO-SMITH. Then he flipped through the channels again and announced excitedly. "Holy shit, we have the stinking Playboy Channel, hot damn man." He said as the screen filled with one massive looking breast and he added, "now that's what I call a fricking picture, son." He mumbled to the OOD who laughed with him.

The camera backed off, and they were suddenly looking at a naked woman with a great shape, no fat, no marks, just perfect and he remarked. "They have to touch these pictures up before they air the damn things, no woman could possibly have a shape like that, General Campanelli Sir. At least where I look for them they don't, sir."

"How could they possibly touch them up dummy? I was at an old Playboy club a number of years ago, and those women were as good looking there, as this one is on the damn boob tube, sir." Just as he said that, the camera did another close up of the woman's breast and then he added, "right choice of words at the moment sir, boob tube sir."

Both men laughed, and they watched the Playboy channel for over an hour. Both were ready for a woman, the OOD said reluctantly to his Commander, "General Campanelli Sir, I guess I have to get going now sir. I have a watch to walk, and I dogged it long enough, sir."

The General paid little attention to the OOD as he continued to stare at two women playing with each other. He spent the rest of the night watching this channel until it finally went off the air at five a.m. He stood and then stretched as he growled out loud.

One of the fire watch personnel was walking down the hall, and he rushed into the room and cried out at the same time, "gees sir, are you all right General?"

"Yeah, why?" The General looked at the young man with questioning eyes for a moment.

"Jesus sir, for a minute I thought there was a bear in heat in here. The way you growled sir."

He waved his hand at the fire watch soldier as he mumbled something about taking himself a dump. He headed for his room, and after dressing he looked in the mirror. He still looked good when he was in a full dress uniform. The touch of gray gave him a distinguished air about him. His shape was good despite the slight roll. He put on his cap and over jacket with his ribbons, and then headed for the CIC Chamber. He looked around the almost empty room, John had the graveyard shift. The General nodded, he then spotted the newspaper in the can. He made a rush on it, he looked at the date. It was two weeks old, it must have been brought over to the Platform by the Marines who showed off their new weapon system a few days back.

Edward read the paper and then looked at his watch, it was seven thirty. The General and his guests were not due on the Platform until eleven thirty. He was bored and tired, the constant motion of the ship bothered him, and the constant slight odor of fuel oil bugged the hell out of him. No matter how many clean up crews he put on the job, on some days the odor was almost overpowering. He hated there was no sunlight in the CIC, the only sun he saw lately was when he went topside. He longed to feel the earth under his feet again. He missed the smell the dirt as all good foot soldiers enjoy as he griped at himself. "What the hell am I doing on this damn thing anyhow for crap sake? I'm a damn ground pounder, not a saltwater taffy, dammit."

Aleksandra strolling into the CIC Chamber and asked her lover, "what you just said sir?"

He spun around and looked at her and then he replied with a snap in his voice. "Nothing, I was just talking to myself, that's all Major."

"That no all do with youself lately big boy. When last time we make love each other last. It been day and I no use wait for what want all time. I warn you I find cucumber, what wrong with you? You get tired on me so ready? Do you no love me any longer, General?"

"I've been pretty fricking busy lately you know," h complained in a hoarse whisper.

John heard the two bitching at each other and he instantly made himself look busy.

General Campanelli rubbed his eyes, trying to massage away the beginnings of a headache, that always happened to him whenever he got in an argument with the opposite sex. It happened all the time with Captain Renee Mendoza and was now happening with her as well. This was all he needed, a headache with the powerful Chairman of the Joint Chiefs of Staff coming out to the Platform for a visit. "Jesus, cut me some slack will ya?" he bitched at Aleksandra.

"See ever try I speak conversation you any again mista." Aleksandra snapped back at him.

"A conversation I don't mind in the least baby, but don't go and accuse me of something stupid, will ya huh? Just because you want to make love with me, and I've been too damn busy to service you, sister." The General growled angrily at the foreign Major.

John hunched his shoulders as he mumbled, "oh bother, the shits gonna fly now."

"Service me! Service me! What hell you think am, cow need bull service stud? Do no flatter youself so much good, mista. I get serviced by any man, or woman for fact matter on fuck ship any time want one. I thought we fall love each other, no service you, mista!" she said as she started to cry, something that she had not done since joining the KGB.

John knew when he was in the way, and he snuck out of the CIC center as quietly as he could.

"Jesus H. Christ lady." General Campanelli muttered as he went over to her. He then pulled her close to him. But she resisted this offer, but not for long though as the General said to her. "Alex, I love you baby and I'm sorry. It's just with this damn major inspection scheduled for today, and the other horseshit that's going on in China and North Korea. I've been pulled in all fucking directions at the same time lately, honey. Sometimes I wish there were three of me, so I could be in all three places at one time people want or need me there, dammit."

"Would like cup coffee hot? I glad get one for you?" Aleksandra asked as she wiped her eyes.

"I'd love one Alex," he offered as he flashed one of his best smiles at her.

She took off while Edward went to his desk, he checked his basket and then his lock box. No new reports were in and he complained at no one inside the CIC. "Where the hell's the damn Sergeant at, one of the birds was ordered to be stationed inside the CIC at all times, in case something came in when none of us were in the damn room." He looked for John now.

The Sergeant came in with John, and both of them seemed like they did not have a care.

"Where the hell were you two birds at for crap sake, dammit!" General Campanelli growled one of his favorite phases, glad to have someone to finally yell at again.

"General Campanelli Sir I had to get in my uniform sir. I asked General White if it was alright and he gave me permission to leave, sir." The excited Sergeant offered his Commanding Officer.

General Campanelli let his breath out in a rush as he turned and then looked to John who nodded as he remarked the instant the upset looking General looked at him, "Say Eddy, I was hiding on your ass sir, because you and the Major were…"

Aleksandra came in with two coffees and the conversations ended as the trio sat down and talked, until it was time for them to get up on the main deck of the Platform. The rest of his command was already on deck milling about and waiting for the General's aircraft to land.

General Campanelli smiled, pleased his crew had gone so far as to make sure they looked real good for this inspection, and if they looked good, he would come out smelling like a rose over it.

The Captain in charge of the Control Tower announced proudly that they just picked up the General's aircraft approaching the Platform from the east on their radar.

General Campanelli took the megaphone from the Sergeant and he growled into the machine, "okay people listen up, I want you to form sharp lines as you rehearsed before, look sharp and know your damn assigned positions at all times. Where's the damn band at, dammit?"

Some men moved and Edward saw what he called the band, all six of them. They took up the position, the lines looked like a group of people waiting for tickets to a rock show or something as he mumbled to himself, "God damn I hope they look a helluva lot better than this when the stinking General gets here for shit sake."

The Control Tower Officer called out the distance of the aircraft heading for the Platform. When the Controller finally announced General Weidenbacher's aircraft was less than ten miles out. General Campanelli instantly got on the megaphone and barked in it again, "the damn time is now, sharpen up those fucking lines people. Look good out there people."

The band tuned up, and the Tower gave the small leer jet permission to land of the Platform. As the aircraft came to a stop on the massive flight deck, the band broke out in the Texas State National Anthem, as the Texas Representative accompanying the General out to the Platform, came down the ladder. He turned towards the band and smiled at them. General Weidenbacher followed, and they walked over to General Edward Campanelli saluting them.

"Mr. Gonzales Sir, may I introduce you to General Edward Campanelli Sir. He's the Supreme Commander of all American assets currently stationed in and surrounding the Asian region, sir."

"I'm pleased to meet you at long last, General Campanelli Sir. I heard quite a bit about you General. Mostly good, some err... no so good I'm afraid, sir." He said as he put his hand out.

General Campanelli shook his hand and then he replied to the Representative. "Congressman Gonzales Sir, I've been looking forward to meeting you for a long time now, sir."

"Oh yes, and why is that may I ask, General." Gonzales replied to the military officer.

Edward looked to the General who looked off in the air, as if to tell him his foot just got stuck in it, and it was up to him to get it out. General Campanelli shrugged and then he went on with his words, "Congressman Gonzales Sir, ever since I saw you on TV, you were straight forward and holding no punches back, sir. I came to respect you for that position you always assumed, sir. I watched you as you went up against everyone trying to get their damn point across sir, and you always weathered the storm they aimed at you, sir. Afterwards, when no one was on your side you still stood strong against the lot of them, sir. That took some real balls sir."

General Campanelli noticed the other General put his hand up to his eyes and he wince. So he stopped talking to see what Congressman Gonzales's reaction to his last words would be.

Mr. Gonzales let out with a soul shaking laugh as he remarked, "my boy, I never heard it put quite so eloquently, it's very refreshing speaking with you General Campanelli Sir. You should consider politics once you leave the service of our country, sir."

"Not on your life sir, a politician's damned if he does, and damned if he don't. I like it here in the service, where you can do your job, sir. And no stinking second guessers sneak behind your back and burns you down to the ground, at least I know where my enemies are coming from sir."

"Refreshing and true sir." Gonzales added and stepped back and gave the floor to the General.

General Weidenbacher put out his hand, and the General's shook it. Then he leaned forward and whispered at Campanelli, "remind me to have a little heart to heart with you on the proper way to speak with a damn Representative of our fucking country, mister."

The band hit a sour note and the General winced and then complained at the Commander of the Platform. "And a word about this damn band of yours also, General Campanelli Sir."

Both officers heard Gonzales remark. "Interesting." While looking at the band.

General Campanelli shrugged as he offered politely to his Commanding Officer and the others with him, "would you gentlemen like to take a little tour of this installation?"

"We didn't come all this way out here just to see you, General Campanelli Sir. Though I must admit it was a real pleasure to meet you because I have heard so much about you lately, General Campanelli Sir." Mr. Gonzales retorted with a grin.

Before they started, Edward introduced Gonzales to the rest of his staff. When he introduced him to the Lithuanian Major, Congressman Gonzales shot a quick look at General Weidenbacher.

"Congressman Gonzales Sir, she's on special loan to our government for selected training with the YF-23 aircraft, sir. We're selling certain aircraft to the nation of Lithuania, and to close the deal we offered to train one of their pilots with the aircraft, sir."

"Why is this ship, err... it is a ship isn't it, named the Vinegar Joe, sir? If you don't mind my asking you that question, General Weidenbacher Sir?"

"Congressman Gonzales Sir, yes it's being classified as a ship because we didn't know what else to brand the system, sir. The name Vinegar Joe was given to this operation to honor General Joseph Stillwell, sir. After the Pearl Harbor attack he was named Commander in Chief of the United States Forces stationed in China, India and the Burma Theater of War during the start of World War Two, and he acted as President Roosevelt's personal Liaison Officer with General Chiang Kai-shek, sir. He was relieved of Command in late 1944 because of irreconcilable differences growing between him and Chiang Kai-shek, sir. General Kai-shek ordered an attack General Stillwell was set against, but Kai-shek wouldn't listen to him, and he ended up losing a hundred men and worse. General Kai-shek gave away his position and the freedom fighters were driven deep into the hills of China, and had to start a guerrilla campaign against the occupying Japanese forces, until they were reinforced and were able to go on the attack again, sir."

"Ahhh... I see you know your history very well General Weidenbacher." Gonzales laughed and then offered, "I seem to remember hearing about this Officer when I was a young pup, he was a hell of an Officer, sir. I'm pleased our government's honoring him this way, sir."

"Much like yourself I'd like to offer sir." Edward added politely to the Representative.

This remark made Gonzales smile and say, "I thank you for your vote of confidence, sir."

General Campanelli showed the two men the ships below the main flight deck, all twenty four massive ships were now set in place. Congressman Gonzales talked to most of the workers they came across below deck. Everywhere they looked, it was clean and rather fresh smelling, except for the occasional whiff of old stale fuel oil. The tour went off very well though, and there were few gripes from General Weidenbacher and Congressman Gonzales, and General Campanelli told them he would have those minor situations taken care of immediately. He smiled and then he announced the tuna lunch the cooks were preparing in Mr. Gonzales' honor was done.

They headed for the cookout pit. "General Weidenbacher Sir, I had a few Marines catch these fish just yesterday sir," General Campanelli offered as he lead the way for the others.

The meal was a great success, and a full Gonzales and Weidenbacher followed Campanelli over to the CIC. The last part of the ship to be visited by the group. General Weidenbacher was pleased to see how well his General set himself up in the Command Center. Generals White, Palmieri, Colonel Locker and Major Klivekaita were stationed at their positions. Sergeants Willis and Cruz were in their corner at the ready to serve the other staffers.

Congressman Gonzales immediately noticed Sergeant Cruz standing with the other Sergeant, and he walked over to the young man with a smile. Campanelli and Weidenbacher watched as he spoke at length with the Spanish Sergeant. General Weidenbacher suddenly leaned a little closer to his General and whispered to him, "I guess he's pleased to see one of his own in a position of authority, a good call on your part with getting him on your personal staff, sir. I'll make a special note of this in your jacket when I get back to Washington, General Campanelli Sir."

Edward leaned his face away from the General and gave him a disgusted look. Then he whispered back at his Commander, "I didn't pick the little fucker up because of the color of his god damn skin, sir. I picked the little sonofabitch up because he had his eyes open when they shoulda been opened, sir. Do you have a problem with that sir?"

"Jesus Christ and miracles General Campanelli, would you calm down a little until I can unload this old fart from my damn hands, sir."

Congressman Gonzales came back to the two Generals and placed his hand on Campanelli's back and announced, "General, I must compliment you on the way you treat your people. That young kid over there thinks an awful lot about you sir, and that's the best any Commander can expect from his troops, sir. You look me up next time you're in Texas, and I'll show you how to really put on a barbecue, Texas style son. With beef this time, good, thick beef steaks, and racks of baby back ribs. Some corn on the cob, look at me, I'm getting hungry all over, sir."

"Congressman Gonzales Sir, what do you say? It's time we leave, and get out of this fine young Officer's hair, sir.

General Campanelli, I must say I truly enjoyed the little tour of this installation, sir. I think the combined forces have spent the taxpayer's money wisely, and I'll enter that on my report to Congress next week, sir. I'll include a remark about the selection of the Officer picked for Command. All in all sir, I feel this is going to be a very useful weapon to be included in the United States arsenal, sir. Good work Generals."

Congressman Gonzales took the time to shake hands with General Campanelli and the rest of his main Command Staff people, before he started for topside. General Weidenbacher followed, and General Campanelli took up the rear, and once topside, Congressman Gonzales shook hands with every soldier he passed in the true form of a good working politician. General William Weidenbacher did the same thing as well.

General Campanelli followed the men to the waiting leer jet, and as General Weidenbacher stepped on the ladder he turned to his General and offered him, "Edward, you did real good here, and I have a little present for you and the rest of your staff inside the damn aircraft, sir."

General Weidenbacher ducked inside the aircraft and a few seconds later, he was back. He handed General Campanelli three flat boxes, they were cold to the touch as he offered, "here you go sir, twenty one Filet Mignon steaks in each box, they were corn fed, none of that hormone shit for my Officers I tell you, sir. They'll melt in your mouth if cooked just right sir. They come from Texas, compliments of Mr. Gonzales and his State, enjoy them General, you earned them sir. Quite frankly General Campanelli Sir, I didn't know what the hell I'd find out here, after speaking to Captain Hoffman, who is one of your favorite people might I add, sir.

"I'm pleased I didn't put too much stock in what he had to say about you and this damn Platform, sir. When I get through with him, he'll beg to be sent to Alaska, dumping on my damn Officer like he was, the asshole. Ahhh hell with him I have to go, we have a meeting scheduled in Honolulu tomorrow, and I'm looking forward to catching up on some sun with those scantily clothed young babes. I'm damn pleased the Mrs. stayed behind, if you know what I mean, sir."

"You're a dirty old man sir." Campanelli laughed at the much older General.

"And I plan to stay a dirty old man until the day I die, God's speed General. May you return home safe and sound General." Weidenbacher straightened up and then he saluted his General.

The troops standing directly behind their Commander instantly snapped to full attention and saluted the powerful General. Campanelli did not know what to do because his hands were full of steaks, and he could not salute the General, so he finally just nodded to his Commander.

Weidenbacher saw his dilemma and smirked at Campanelli, "You owe me one mister." With this said, he stepped inside and the boarding ladder picked up and closed, and the aircraft taxied to the runway. The pilot stopped at one point and increased power to his aircraft. Campanelli picked up the pilot speaking to the Tower and then it shot down the runway into the sky. The takeoff was perfect, and the pilot dipped the wings as a final salute to the soldiers below.

CHAPTER 21

The General was being flanked by four of his Sergeants, he looked at them and then ordered them, "here, give the troops a well done for me." Then he ordered the workers below to stop their work by bellowing out at them. "Every soldier on this fricking Island has the rest of the day off. Sergeant Curtis, see if you can talk the cooks into preparing something steaks outside for tonight, music is okay on the flight deck area for the rest of the day. Whatever the men and women want to do, they can do it Sarge. I'm sorry it's so damn cool out today, or they'd be allowed to go swimming if they so chose to do so, mister."

"I'm sure there'll be some assholes going swimming, sir." One of the Sergeants offered.

"I'm sure of that myself Sarge, make damn certain if any fool take a dip, he or she has some sort of bathing suit on. Workday starts at exactly Oh, Six Thirty Hours tomorrow morning gentlemen. First order of the day's to prepare this damn Platform to sail to the new position sixty five miles off the coast of the Island of Taiwan, people." The General warned them.

"Why is that sir? I thought we were suppose to take a position of one hundred miles off the coast of Taiwan, sir?" one of the Sergeants called out from the from the rear of the group.

"We were until those orders were changed, now it sixty five miles off the damn Island. This is so we can setup a Carrier defense zone around this damn installation closer to the Island, mister."

"What's that General Campanelli Sir?" another Sergeant asked the Commanding Officer.

"I didn't think a ground pounding Sergeant would know what I was referring to. It's a zone of defense that every Carrier employs, we're being classified as a Carrier, a very big Carrier at that. The zone consists of three, the first and furthest out is usually the one hundred mile zone from the center of the CIC of the ship. This zone will be defended by aircraft only, this zone's one hundred to eighty miles out. The second zone extends out ten to eighty miles, this zone's defended by aircraft and missile systems. All Carrier support ships will participate in this protection zone Sarge, all supporting Destroyers and Frigates are ordered to run interference for the Carrier, I mean us. The last zone extends to ten miles out from the center of the CIC, this is our last line of defense guarded by aircraft, all missile systems and the CIWS, or Close in Weapons Support system, along with the shorter range surface to air missiles, and also the sea skimmer defense weapons, all designed to protect this damn thing from attack.

"Needless to say people, if the enemy cracks this zone of defense then we're dead in the water. There are a number of special chaff launchers that will flood the area with aluminum foil, as a last resort defensive attempt, to try and confuse any incoming enemy missiles and aircraft, this is a standard protective ring usually installed around any Aircraft Carrier, and it's installed around this Platform as well. I'll give you people the rest of the day to prepare to get this damn Platform on the move. Do your homework people, I want everything to go off smoothly without a hitch. Thank you gentlemen for your time and patience in this matter."

There were many moans and groans from the four Sergeants listening to their Commander, and General Campanelli snapped at them, "Yeah, I know I just gave everyone the day off. But you guys make more money than the damn crews do, so it looks like you have to earn it, people." The General turned away from the group and headed for the stairwell, a Corporal ran up to him, and offered to take the steaks from him. General Campanelli handed the boxes to him and said, "Officers mess right away, and guard that shit with your life, mister."

As the General reached the down stairwell he spotted an officer hanging around and he called out to him. "Hey Lieutenant, can I see you for a second sir?"

"Sure thing General Campanelli, what can do for you sir?" the officer replied to him.

"I want a meeting ordered with all Officers and Junior Officers at." He looked at his watch and then added, "We can do this better, all Officers will take mess together for supper tonight, sir. I'll also hold the meeting while we eat, this way I won't cut into anyone's day off time, and we can kill two birds with one stone while we're at it, sir. Mess will commence at Eighteen Hundred Hours sharp, sir." General Campanelli picked up the disgust in the Lieutenant's eyes as he told him of the meeting and he snapped. "Do you have a problem with this order mister?"

"General Campanelli Sir, you have to understand, I just informed the other Officers that they had the rest of the day off, sir. Now I have to inform them they have to show up at a special meeting to be held at Eighteen Hundred Hours in the mess hall, sir."

"Stop your whining, you wanted to be an Officer, and with that comes certain responsibilities, mister. If you want, I can have you replaced like Captain Hoffman, and that goes for any other Officer I can't rely on twenty four, seven. And you can tell them this, any Officer who wants out, all they have to do is request it, and I'll process their request on the first working day after receiving it. I have no time or patience for any Officer who thinks he or she can give me a hard time. Shove off, any Officer who fails to show up for the meeting, won't have to ask for a transfer. I'll have his ass shipped out before he realizes what happened to his ass." The General saluted the Lieutenant as a final warning for him and the rest of the officers to show up.

"The only excuse I'll accept for missing this damn meeting's duty call or death, because any Officer missing the meeting will wish he or she was dead I tell ya, sir." General Campanelli turned on his heels and walked away from the Lieutenant without any further words to him.

The Lieutenant waited until the General went down ladder, and then flipped the bird at him as he quickly jogged off. He decided to go to communications and have the officer announce the meeting over the intercom to save himself from having to address each officer personally.

General Campanelli was in the CIC when he heard the orders to officers and he mumbled, "it's about time he used his head for more than a damn hat rack around here, the asshole."

John heard him gripe and asked if he had any trouble with the young officer.

"The usual crap when you ask any young buck Officer to do some extra work around here, dammit." General Campanelli laughed and John drew in his breath and then asked his Commanding Officer "I guess it's up to me then to ask what this meeting's all about, sir?"

"Nothing, you know we have to move the Platform and install the defense zone around it, sir."

"I knew that General Campanelli Sir." General Palmieri replied matter of factly to him.

Colonel Locker looked at General Palmieri and remarked with a smirk, "well look at you will ya, all of the sudden you're a wealth of information aren't you, Mr. Palmieri Sir."

"Enough crap, I wanted to discuss the defense zone with the Officers at the meeting, so they all know exactly what I want from them, dammit. It's necessary, it shouldn't take long, I combined the meeting with mess," he looked at all the faces and then bitched at them. "Yes, you birds have to attend the damn meeting also, I don't want any Officer not knowing what they're doing tomorrow, until we get this damn thing set back to position again." General Campanelli saw the looks and he got angry until he remembered the steaks. "Look guys, I'll make it up to you birds, I'll have the cooks prepare a special meal for all Officers tonight at the meeting."

"More damn fish sir?" Colonel Locker complained at her Commanding Officer this time.

General Campanelli grunted with a smirk on his face, "No more friggin fish. What do you people say to a nice thick Filet Mignon for each of you damn shitbirds. Cooked specially to your liking, if you guys get off my damn ass, that's what you'll get for attending my meeting tonight."

"Where the hell would you get your greedy little hands on some steaks you're talking about, mister?" John asked as if he did not believe his commander's offer of the steaks.

"They were a special present from General Weidenbacher and Mr. Gonzales, wiseguy."

"And how long were you going to keep this crap from us, mister?" Colonel Locker griped with a smile at her Commander.

"Hell, for one of those steaks I'd attend a staff meeting every day," General Palmieri offered.

"Then it's all settled people, no more stinking gripes from any of you people, especially at the damn meeting, guys?" General Campanelli asked the group of officers.

The special meeting at the mess came and went without a hitch. Most of the attending officers became quite mellow once they saw the steaks being prepared for them. It went well with much bantering going back and forth from the group of officers. Some jokes passed across the tables, and the officers quickly understood what their responsibilities were, pertaining to the moving of the massive Platform to their new ordered position. After the meeting concluded, Edward, John and Aleksandra went up on deck for a quick breath of fresh air.

A Sergeant was going over a few things with Chief Kirby. When the two men spotted the General and they stopped speaking and waited for the group of officers to join the noncoms.

"What's up Chief Kirby Sir? I hope there's no problems with moving this damn thing out to the new ordered position, Chief?" General Campanelli asked with concern lacing his tone, he did not recognize the Sergeant who was speaking with the Chief.

"No problem there sir, we were just discussing the release points of the securing lines to the Platform, in order to get this old big bucket moving, sir. We're gonna hafta disconnect some of the stabilizing computers, the ones controlling the ballast intakes and exhaust systems, sir."

"I don't know what the hell you're talking about, but I'll take your word for it, Chief."

Colonel Locker cut in and offered to her Commander. "General Campanelli, the computers control the amount of water drawn in, or expelled from the ballast tanks while we're sitting stationary in the water, sir. This ballast keeps us stable and the flight deck safe for the landing and takeoff aircraft, sir. I don't know if you noticed it or not General, but we're very stable on the surface of the water sir. I saw more movement from a Carrier then we have with the Platform, sir. All movement from the water has been kept down to an absolute minimum by the ballast.

"We could hardly have a fighter aircraft land on flight deck when one ship's heaving high, while the next one's heaving low, sir. This action would cause the fighter to leave the deck, and then crash as it came back to the deck on a low swell, sir. The computers flood parts of the tanker, while draining others instantly, sir. This gives the deck absolute minimum of movement sir. From all I read about this

Platform sir, this problem was the biggest one the engineers faced and corrected. The computers removed this problem pretty well for us, sir."

"That was what we were just discussing General Campanelli Sir. The way I figure it sir, we'll have the computers make one final adjustment before we take most of them off line, sir. We'll then order the computers to empty all ballast and then close them off, so no more water can get in. We have to back off a number of flight deck bolts, if we move this barge without backing off them. We're going to end up snapping the lines, and creating some big problems for ourselves later on, when we setup in our new position, sir." The old Chief offered cautiously.

"You know, I seem to remember reading something about this ballast thing when I was first handed the reports of this damn thing. Chief Kirby, you do whatever you gotta do for us to move this damn thing safely, sir. This is exactly why I drafted your ass for mister. Earn your damn money for once in your old life, mister." General Campanelli laughed at the elderly Naval Chief.

"I always earn my fricking money General Campanelli Sir," the Chief fired back at him.

"Don't tell me you started up one of your little poker games again, Chief. Remember what I told you the last time about you and your damn poker games, mister?" he warned him.

"No, no, I'm not playing poker any longer sir. I swear to you General Campanelli Sir."

"What the hell did ya do then, find another way to relieve the men of their money, mister? Look Chief, I think the President should have you in his damn cabinet. If anyone could pull the United States out of this depression we're stuck in, you surely could mister. All you have to do is get in one of your damn card games with the stinking Prime Minister of Japan, and all our national debt would be eliminated in less than a week's time, mister."

"General Campanelli Sir, you're kinda flattering me sir. It'd take me at least two full weeks for me to win that much money from the damn Japanese Leader, sir."

"I bet. Chief, is it going to be a big problem to move this here old tub or what?"

The Chief chomped down on the end of his cigar, and then he grumbled at his Commanding Officer. "Hmmm... I see no real problem with moving this damn thing, as long as we're careful about it and we go real slow, sir. Is there any time limit on getting to our set position, sir?"

"None that I know of, all Command told me was where to go, not how long to get there, sir."

"That's good, because I'd like to keep the speed under, or at just five knots for the trip sir."

"You got it Chief, in fact mister. I'll leave you in complete control of the mess. You pick the speed, stop us when you want us stopped, just handle it Chief. I'll put the ship in your hands, sir. You work with the damn engineers, and keep them on their stinking toes, mister."

"You did pick the best time to move this thing along at that, General Campanelli Sir. From all the water maps and weather charts I read through, it looks like the weather will work out well for us with this ordered move, sir. The undertow will be going in the same direction we'll be heading in, and that'll take much of the pressure off the damn ship, General Campanelli."

"I leave it entirely in your hands, Chief." Edward said as he turned with his entourage, and they went over to the center of the ship. As he entered the CIC, he noticed John was taking to General Weidenbacher on the special hookup from his aircraft, he was leaving from his second meeting. When he noticed General Campanelli enter the CIC, General Weidenbacher said. "One thing I forgot to tell you Edward, I'm having Admiral Owens transferred out to the VJ Platform. I think he'd be more valuable operating from there than from the Carrier Roosevelt, sir."

"I agree with that order General Weidenbacher Sir, although I never worked with the man side by side, I think it'd work out just fine for all concerned, sir. I'll have some private quarters especially set aside for him today, when will he be shipped out to me, sir?"

"I'll have his ass shipped out on the VJP by mid-day tomorrow, Edward. When I informed him I was transferring him out to you, sir. You'd think I just stuck him with a damn pin right in his ass, he bitched so much at me, sir. I told him he'd have until tomorrow morning to get all his affairs in order, and then transfer his authority to his next in Command on the Carrier, sir. A Lieutenant Commander Philip J. Stoner, he's not bad and he knows the ship and men under him very well, sir. He'll do fine, all he has to do is follow Admiral Owens orders to the damn letter if he wants success, sir." General William Weidenbacher grunted at him with a smirk on his lips.

"I don't know where I'm going to put him here in the CIC though, General Weidenbacher."

"I don't care if you have to put him on top of your damn desk, Edward. He has to be stationed inside that damn CIC and comfortable to boot, mister. Move out your damn Sergeants, they have no business being stationed inside the chamber in the first place, General. The Sergeants can set up a waiting room just outside the CIC if needed, sir." General Weidenbacher snapped at him.

"That sounds like a wise move to me, sir. General Weidenbacher, we'll be on our way tomorrow to set coordinates of Six, Six, Three by Three, One Two. My Chief figures it'll take us two and a half days to get out to this new position, he wants to move us real slow, sir. He checked the weather charts and feels there'll be no weather to hinder our move out, sir."

"If it's going to take that long to get to position then your damn Chief must be planning to row the damn thing out to this new position, mister." General Weidenbacher bitched and then added. "I have to go, this call's costing the taxpayers a mint. I'll be back to you when I return to Pearl, keep me informed of any new events, General." Weidenbacher broke off the communication.

General Campanelli leaned back in his chair until he hit the side of the ship with the back of the chair, the coolness of the steel hide felt good against his back as he mumbled, "I wish this damn shit was over with already, dammit." He looked at his watch, it was late and he did not feel like anything to eat. He felt all he was doing since he came on board the VJP, was eating and working. "I'm going to go and lay down for a little while, I'm beat out people."

"Are no you get something eat before turn in for sleep you. You have eat to keep up you strength you know, General Sir." Aleksandra nagged him from her chair.

"No, I'm gonna turn in for the stinking day, tomorrow looks like it'll be one helluva damn day for all of us concerned with this damn move. I suggest all you people grab some shut eye as well. Tomorrow we're going on split shift schedules. General Palmieri Sir, you and Colonel Locker will pull the graveyard shift, while General White, Major Klivekaita and myself will take on the days. We'll work twelve hour shifts a day until I get some extra help ship out to us.

" Admiral Owens will work the day time shift. General Palmieri, you can have Sergeant Willis for your runner, and I'll keep Sergeant Cruz with me. Colonel Salsiccia should be out here in a day or two, and you can have him for ballast. I'll draft a few extra people, so we can go on an eight hour shift within the next few days, people. This is the best I can do for now. I don't think there'll be any trouble tonight, so I suggest the Sergeants man the CIC chamber for us. One sleeps while the other takes command of the console, we start the spilt shifts as of tomorrow morning, people." General Campanelli said and he turned and started out of the chamber.

Aleksandra caught up with him and she whispered, "No want any company when you sleep?"

Edward laid a hand on her shoulder as he looked in her eyes, "I always want your company."

She beamed as she replied, "Why no lay down, I go mess and get you something eat."

"I don't feel like eating anything tonight, honey." He offered in an exhausted voice to her.

"Nosense, you eat must do, I no want you get sick on us mista," she replied at him.

He gave a grunt and then mumbled at her, "Suit yourself." He slowly made his way to his little world split up in two small rooms. He pulled off his shirt and went to the sink and threw some cool water on his face. Looking at his reflection in the mirror he moaned at himself. "Man, I could get the damn lead in a stinking horror show looking like this, wow."

He rubbed his hand over his face, his eyes burned from strain, his back ached from sitting and standing all day. "Yuk." he grumbled as he kicked off his shoes, and then he plopped down heavily on his bunk with all the grace of a sack of potatoes being thrown from the rear of a fast moving delivery truck. In no time, he was snoring away and did not wait for Aleksandra to return to his room with the food she offered to get for them to share together.

She came in the room and found the General sprawled out across the bunk. She frowned as she stared at him, and then she put the tray of food down on the bureau. She ate what was hot and left the fruit, bread and soda for him for later. The Major was going to move him to one side and sleep with him, but quickly thought better of it. Seeing him sprawled out like he was, she decided he needed his sleep, and he might as well have the whole bunk to himself tonight. She shrugged and then she gave him a kiss on the forehead and left for her own assigned room.

Colonel Mary Locker was there, she showered and was wrapped up in a towel, and she smirked at Aleksandra as she remarked to the foreign pilot. "Couldn't wake him up I see, huh?"

"He out for entire night cold," she took off her clothes and when she was naked, she slipped into a robe and then announced. "I shall take shower for self." She took a steaming hot shower, feeling a little blue about not sleeping with Campanelli for the night. She did not make love to her General for the past two days now, and she was getting a little horny herself. Aleksandra thought about waking him so they could make love together, but she quickly talked herself out of that thought. She came out of the shower and quickly dried herself off, and then she slipped into her short robe and headed back to her room she was sharing with Colonel Locker.

Locker let out her breath when she saw Aleksandra, "I was worried you weren't going to sleep here tonight, Major. I was hoping we could explore each others bodies." She tried a smile on her.

"I no mood for woman tonight." Aleksandra hissed as she laid down and fast fell asleep.

General Campanelli was awakened to the sound of rhythmic rumbling from seventeen of the twenty four massive tanker ships that made up the massive Platform structure. The ship was already underway, he looked at his watch and cursed the old Chief. It was Zero, Five, Fifteen Hours and he already had the Platform moving. 'That old sonofabitch shoulda informed me he was ready to get underway, dammit', he growled to himself as he put on his overhead light. He rubbed the sleep from his eyes as he swung his legs over the side of his metal bed. He subconsciously looked around his room for Aleksandra, half expecting her to be in the room.

He could feel the deck vibrating under his feet, he wished he had a porthole he could look out to see what was going on outside. He ran his hands through his hair and got a whiff of his underarms. "Phew," he mumbled as he got up and started the water in the shower, he dressed in fatigues and headed for the massive flight deck. It was cold as he scanned the deck for the Chief, he spotted him and a few others looking over the side of the deck and jogged over to them.

"Jesus Christ Almighty Chief, what the hell did you do for Pete's sake, sir? Work all stinking night long to get this damn thing moving so quickly today, sir?"

The three men laughed at his remark. The upset General then glared at each of the other two men, but he did not recognize either of them.

"Just about sir. I don't think you know these men with me General Campanelli, this is Captain Williams from engineering and Lieutenant Gallagher, also from engineering sir, and the last man behind the Officer's is Seaman Third Class Lawrence, he's a navigator. General, I decided to work all night to get this thing underway early today, sir. We turned about Zero, Three, Twenty this morning and once that was done, I didn't see why we shouldn't get going at that time, sir."

General Campanelli kind of only half paid attention to the old Chief's words as he drank his morning coffee to help warm his insides. He looked to the right of the Platform, and noticed two other ships were sailing very near the VJP and he bitched at the Chief, "whose god damn ships are those out there, mister? Dammit, they look too fricking close to us, no Chief?"

"General Campanelli Sir, the larger ship is the Virginia, sir. She's a Guided Missile Cruiser, and the other one is the Waddel, a Guided Missile Destroyer, sir. The both ships are assigned to our support group and our security as we move the Platform to the ordered position, General."

"Aren't they sailing too damn close to the friggin Platform, Chief?" he repeated angrily at him a second time as he stared at the massive ship steaming so close to his Platform.

"Normally they are sir. But they're running an attack operation exercise, and are playing out a missile attack on this here old Platform, sir. They're also running interference for us at the same time, sir. It's standard operations for our support ships to run an exercise like this, and with us being in motion, it adds to the training maneuver and experience for the crews, sir."

Campanelli did not look at the officer, he just stared at the ships and added, "maybe so mister. But I still don't like having them so damn close to us while we're in motion, mister."

"General Campanelli Sir, I can easily order the two ships to back off some on us, if you'd like and feel more comfortable sir."   Captain Williams offered as he got into the conversation now.

"No, no, let them have their little fun and games for the fricking time being I guess, Captain." He bitched as he turned back to the Chief Kirby and grumbled at him this time, "Chief, I'm counting on you to keep us out of harm's way during this damn move, mister."

"I'll do my best at it sir." They were now looking overboard, it was mystifying to stare at the sea as the bows of the lead ships sliced through the water, even at this slow a speed. From out of nowhere, a small pod of dolphins suddenly appeared off the lead bow of the Platform, and the pod seemed to be actually guiding the ship forward.

"Look at that will ya for crap sake." General Campanelli exclaimed and then asked the Naval Chief. "What the hell are those stupid fish doing down there, mister?"

"General Campanelli Sir, no one seems to know for sure why the dolphins do this, sir. Most of the scientists think the dolphins are merely playing. I never saw one of them get struck by a ship though through all the times the mammals do their act with any ships, sir. But they always seem to be out there, sir. They'll stay with us for miles sir." The smiling Chief offered.

Now, they were all watching the dolphins swimming out in front of the ship. Suddenly, the ships to their right moved out, and they joined with another two warship, and they started a distinctive search pattern, like they were suddenly looking for something. General White ran over to General Campanelli out of breath and offered in an excited tone of voice.

"General Campanelli Sir, sonar just picked up a submarine some twenty thousand yards off our port bow, sir. It's signature identifies it as an older Russian boomer. Our ships are moving out to intercept, and politely drive the bastard off us sir. We informed the Russian and Chinese government of our action. We explained it off as mere ship exercises, and their submarine was interfering with the exercise, sir. Right now, I hope this is a damn Russian submarine, not a fucking Chinese one, sir. We'll find out once our ships make contact with the damn thing, sir."

Now, the group of officers intensely watched as the four American warships crisscrossed back and forth, the Destroyer Waddel slowed down her speed, and she started to pace itself. The Chief pointed out the Destroyer must have taken up position right over the suspected submarine. Everyone on deck could feel, and actually hear the sonar pounding away from the Destroyer hitting the submarine. Campanelli saw the Destroyer move a little further from the Platform at this time, and he felt the suspected submarine must be moving off from their present position.

General Palmieri showed up next and he reported to his Commanding Officer. "General Campanelli, reports from the Waddel states the submarine's moving off at full speed now. It also reports the submarine didn't make it to periscope depth, and our signature shows up as twenty four separate tanker ships heading in the same direction and at the same exact speed, sir."

"Good deal for us I take it General Palmieri Sir," he remarked as he continued to stare at the American Destroyer as she moved even further off from the Platform's portside and then he added. "Well, there goes one of our stinking problems, people."

The group of military officers remained standing on the flight deck and watched the waves as the massive Platform made its way slowly towards her new assigned position for over an hour. None of them realized just how cold they were until they decided to move, and then the shivering started for them. General Campanelli was the only man dressed in his heavy watch.

PEKING CHINA. A MEETING BETWEEN THE CHAIRMAN AND THE MINISTER OF NAVAL AFFAIRS, GENERAL LIU CHUNG

"Chairman Mao Cheng-yu, one of our submarines has just been driven off by a United States Destroyer. The submarine was assigned to find out what the hated Americans were up to on the other side of the Island of Taiwan. There are quite a few American warships presently gathering out there, and we're trying to steal any information from Russian or American satellites on their motives. But we have not been able to make direct contact with any of them as of yet, sir. But we shall fine the key to gain this access needed to access the satellites soon. I must report we no longer have access to any satellites, not since the Russian dogs have cut our feed against us, sir.

"We have nothing but stone walling by the godless Tongzhi, sir. I checked with the Xichang Satellite Launching Center, and the Fengyun X134 has not launched yet as ordered. I'm tired of this fool promising us he's going to launch his spy satellite any day, sir. Well, now is the time we have need of the satellite, not later. I suggest you remove Tongzhi from his present post for insubordination, immediately sir. I need the extra eyes in the sky if I'm ever going to wage a successful war against the worthless British, and possibly the foolish Americans, Mr. Chairman."

The old Chairman smiled at his rather upset and concerned Minister, out of all his Ministers, he trusted Liu Chung the most. He always had China, and the Chairman's best interest in his heart and mind, as he replied to his upset Minister, "Minister Chung, I know of your feelings against the fool Tongzhi over his failure to launch the requested satellites. But I must say this in his behalf, sir. It is not entirely his fault, he has not been given the satellites for launching. There has been a failure throughout the entire system. We have to resign ourselves that we'll not have these satellites to work with when we need them the foul things the most. We shall have to sacrifice some of our submarines and warplanes, to find out what the hated Americans are up to in the Philippine Sea. What has the submarine that made contact with the American Destroyer, been able to pick up for us, before the submarine was driven off by the hated American ships?"

"I'm afraid there's not very much to report at this time, Mr. Chairman Sir. The Captain of the submarine reported at least twenty American warships were heading away from Taiwan. The submarine reported contact of two Carrier Strike Forces, and a number of other American surface warships operating in the same vicinity. We have no idea why these American ships are there, and why so many of them would be sailing so close to one another, risking a collision sir."

"I've been notified the United States was going to hold a number of Naval war games and exercises in and around the Philippine Sea, sir. If these ships are heading away from Taiwan then their foolish war games must have been completed, and the threat of so many of these dom American warships being in the area, is over with now." The Chairman replied strongly at him.

"Mr. Chairman Sir, I read the notification of the American war games as was reported. But I feel there is too much a coincidence the foolish Americans have chose this very time to play their little war games. I don't like one convoy of ships sailing so close together, all turning at the same exact time and sailing at the identical speed, and in the same direction. I want to send out another submarine, I know their course plotted, and I'll have the submarine wait on the Ocean floor to count the god dom American warships as they sail over our submarine, sir."

"Minister Chung, this is a very wise idea if you're so worried about these hated American warships. I don't share your same fears though. I feel if the American warships are heading away from the Island of Taiwan and our country then why all the fear?" The Chairman asked.

"I too am relieved the foul American warships are heading away from our country. However, the warships are still too close to our shores, especially since we're going to attack North Korea in a few short days, sir. I have an ominous feeling about all these god cursed American ships of war sailing so near our vicinity, sir. Mr. Chairman, may I have permission to send a number of aircraft to fly over this rabble collection of American warships, and let them take a number of pictures of them, so we can determine what is truly going on with them, sir?"

"Yes, I'll give you permission to send these flights out if you so choose to do so, sir. But first, I'd like you to try some of our Ocean going Junks. Send out a number of them, let them drift into this ring of defense the foolish Americans have set up around these warships that concern you so much. Perhaps the worthless Americans will pay little attention to these harmless looking ships, and we can get all the pictures you want of what they might be up to, Minister. If they fail, you'll have my permission to use ten flights of two aircraft each, and three submarines to get your needed pictures of their actions, sir. Do you agree with these terms?" The Chairman asked.

"Yes, I happen to agree with these terms you have just offered to me, sir. I'll have some of the Junks operating by the Philippines to sail out so they can to easily intercept some of these hated American warships. I thank you for your time and patience in this matter, Chairman Mao Cheng-yu Sir," the worried Minister of Naval Affairs bowed his head politely as he stood, and then he prepared to leave the meeting with the chosen leader of all of China.

"And I thank you for your vigilance to my many concerns aimed against the hated American's actions, Minister." The Chairman added as he watched the Minister leave his office.

THE PHILIPPINE SEA

A fleet of fifteen large Ocean going Chinese Junks immediately set sail from their previous positions, armed with orders to intercept the fleet of American warships. It was calculated it would take the faster moving larger Junks over an hour to get near enough to where this American fleet was sailing. The Chinese submarine that had been driven off by the American Destroyer, circled around and then got in front of the oncoming American convoy.

The submarine pushed at full steam until it was just ten miles out in front of the furthest oncoming American ship, and then the Chinese submarine silently sank below the waves to come to rest on the Ocean's floor, six hundred and fifty feet below the waves. There, the Captain resigned himself to wait for the American convoy to past by his present position, and count the number of United States ships passing over her position, paying close attention to the pack of ships sailing so close together right in the middle of the large American convoy.

The group of Ocean going Junks pushed themselves to get to their new assigned position, once they were certain the Junks were sitting right in the path of the on coming American ships of war, the Junks then began to disperse and make like they were busy fishing in the surrounding waters. The Junks were flying the flag of the Philippines, and they even set out some of their fishing nets, in an attempt to try and carry off their little deception further against the American warships and the United States Command.

CHAPTER 22
ON BOARD THE MASSIVE VINEGAR JOE PLATFORM

General Edward Campanelli was forced below deck because he was freezing his back side off standing topside, he just entered the CIC when a class three Flashed came through. It was the lowest Flash traffic message. He pulled the paper free of the machine, it was from the Frigate Francis Hammond, riding the point guard for the convoy, the message reported;

:::FROM FRIGATE FRANCIS HAMMOND:::

'Am presently tracking twelve small surface contacts, apparently said contacts are taking up positions stationed directly in front of our convoy, Command. Am moving out along with the Frigate Stephen W. Groves, and United States Guided Missile Frigate Samuel B. Roberts, with the intent of intercepting said vessels, and then intend to drive off said contacts at time of engagement, unless instructed to do otherwise by Command.

:::END OF REPORT:::

The General read the message over for a second time, and then he turned to Sergeant Cruz and grumbled at the young man in an extremely angry tone of voice this time, "Get me the Commander of the Hammond on the damn horn STAT, Sergeant."

A few seconds passed and then the Sergeant replied to his Commander. "General Campanelli Sir, Captain Charles Farrell's on line two for you, sir. I patched it through the secure line sir."

"Err..., this is General Campanelli, Captain Farrell Sir." He had already forgotten the Captain's first name as he asked the officer, "what the hell's the present situation out there, sir?"

"General Campanelli Sir, I'm presently tracking up to fifteen separate, small surface Tangos (Targets) at this time, sir. I take these Tangos to be Ocean sailing Chinese Junks, sir. I'm ordering them off our beams at once, or risk possible military consequences against them, sir."

"What are you gonna do if the damn things don't move off our fricking beam, Captain?" General Campanelli asked the officer with much concern in his voice.

"Dunno for certain sir, I was kind of hoping to get word from you as to my options, General Campanelli Sir. I guess I'll do anything I hafta do to get these damn thing far away from our slow moving Platform, sir. You understand the Chinese are trying to find out what we're up to on this side of the Island of Twain at all cost to them, General Campanelli Sir."

"Shit, I wish Admiral Owens was here already. Captain, warn them off verbally first, if this fails, you're to fire a few warning shots over their bows, if this fails, hold tight. I'll order up a quick flight of F-18 Hornets, and let them deal with the damn Junks if your attempts to move them off, failed. Good luck Captain and remember, I want to keep the security of this Platform a secret for as long as possible, sir. Even to the point of our having to sink these damn pieces of junk, no pund intended, sir." General Campanelli offered as he broke the connection with the Captain and turned he to Locker and ordered, "get me the Commander of the Washington."

Seconds later. "Yeah Ned, Campanelli here sir, I need a flight of Hornets up A-SAP, sir. I have fifteen small surface contacts taking up position directly in front of my Platform. Three of our Frigates are closing in on the contacts as we speak, they'll try and move them off us, sir. If the Frigates are unsuccessful, I give the Hornets permission to splash the Junks on my call, sir. The safety of the damn Platform's of the utmost importance to this operation, and I take full responsibility for the actions of your aircraft, sir. Get those damn birds in the air for me, sir."

Without further word, Commander Ned Watson turned to his Boatswain's mate, and then the Captain ordered him, "Scramble Ready Caps One, Two Three and Four immediately, mister. We have unfriendlies in front of us that have to be dealt with immediately, sir."

"Yes sir," The Boatswain immediately keyed the ships intercom and bellowed into it. "All hands, man your battle stations, General Quarters, General Quarters. This s not a drill!" he then repeated the orders a second time before he continued with his orders.

Instantly, the massive flight deck of the Aircraft Carrier Washington was a beehive of activity, as Ready Air Cap One, Two, Three and Four were quickly lined up, and then fired off the flight deck of the ship two at a time. The four fighter aircraft then quickly marshaled off the fantail of the Washington, and there waited for Ready Air Cap Two to launch and their further orders. Their call name for this mission was Rainbow Flight One through Six. The Pry-Fry Commander Murray informed the Air Wing Commander of his mission, and then he ordered the six pilots where they were needed. Then the aircraft instantly shot off to the east on full afterburn power in to intercept the small fleet of Chinese Junks with orders to sink them if needed.

A Starfisher aircraft was still working over the area where the Chinese submarine had parked below the surface of the water. The Starfisher was a LRAACA (Long Range Air Anti Submarine Warfare Capability Aircraft) that replaced the old and outdated P-3C Orion Submarine Killer aircraft. The Starfisher laid down a wide sonar buoy net to try and relocate the hiding Chinese submarine, if it was still in the vicinity. Ten buoys were in the water, and buoy three and four instantly displayed a positive contact report. The Starfisher then circled these buoys and dropped two more buoys, but much closer together this time. The four buoy markers was positively identifying the contact as a submarine, and they had it zeroed in for a possible attack against it.

The Chinese submarine Commander heard the low level pinging coming from the buoys now stationed on both sides of his submarine, and decided to get out of the area before his submarine came under attack by the American forces in the area searching for his boat. The Chinese submarine came to the surface so the Starfisher could see him, and the aircraft followed him off.

Once the Minister of Naval Affairs, Liu Chung heard about the American aircraft locating his submerged submarine. He immediately ordered his Junks out of the area, before the American warships attacked and sank the specially equipped group of small sea going crafts.

The American Frigate Hammond instantly picked up the sudden change in direction of the much smaller Chinese surface fishing boats, and they kept sailing directly towards the Chinese Junks as they began to pull back away from the approaching American convoy and massive Platform. The Captain of the Hammond immediately notified General Campanelli of the change in direction of the Junks. The General breathed a deep sigh of relief as he ordered the Hammond to continue dogging the small Chinese crafts, until they were well away from the area.

The Carrier Washington recalled the flight of Hornets when the General informed the Captain of the Carrier the present danger to the Platform had been eliminated by the picket ships.

Campanelli looked at his watch and then bitched, "Hey Sarge, can you get some food sent over to us, I don't want anyone leaving the CIC unit until this mess is completely over with."

"Working on it General Campanelli." Sergeant Cruz was in contact with the Mess Sergeant, and informed him from now on, if the brass stationed inside the CIC Chamber did not make it down to the mess by Thirteen Hundred Hours. He was to have something sent up to the CIC center for the officers to eat without having to be asked to do so.

The Mess Sergeant agreed to have meals sent up every day if needed to the CIC.

"Your meals are on the way over, General Campanelli Sir." Sergeant Cruz announced proudly to the Commander, once he was informed the meals were on their way up to the CIC.

The tension filling the CIC chamber moments before was lessening quickly, even some jokes were being offered up by the people manning the CIC Chamber as his staff relaxed a bit.

In a Sikorsky CH-53-E Super Stallion helicopter, a very grumpy and extremely upset Admiral John 'Bear' Owens was being ferried out to the Aircraft Carrier Eisenhower from the Carrier Roosevelt, while on his way out to the massive Platform he heard so much about already. The cramped Admiral was snapping at everyone he laid eyes on. He did not like being transferred out to a Platform made to look like a ship or massive Aircraft Carrier. He also did not enjoy taking apart his current CIC center either, transferring his entire Intel system out to this Platform thing with him. He did not like this young pilot accompanying him as well. He glared at him, and the pilot automatically put his head down to get out of the Admiral's harsh glare.

The fighter pilot was Charles B. Wright, Lieutenant Commander, his stay in the service was not the best for him. First he had to live down the Wright last name, and being a fighter pilot he heard all the jokes made about his last name. The officers seemed to expect more from him because of his name, even though he was in no way related to the famous fathers of flyers.

Lieutenant Wright had to also live down his nickname as well, given to him by accident by the then Commander Admiral John Owens. It seem every time Owens wanted something done by Wright, he would start the sentence off with. "Jesus Christ, will you get your ass over here?" Or, "Jesus Christ, don't you understand anything I tell you young man?" So even though his name was Charles B. Wright, he was nicknamed J.C. Wright. It stuck, and now, anytime Commander Owens wanted him he would bellow out, "J.C., get your ass over here."

Admiral Owens stared at the young man, and then complained at him in an angry voice. "Jesus Christ, of all the damn flyers under my Command and I had to pick from. I had to get stuck with in my life, some damn young wiseass had to stick me with you again, J.C."

"Luck of the draw I guess sir." J. C. bewailed with a half assed smile, because he really liked the elderly and always grumpy but extremely wise Naval Commander.

The Admiral put a smirk on his lips as he looked back at the young kid. He did not really mind having him as his personal pilot. He was good and much like himself, the rest of the guys picked on him endlessly. But if any flyer needed a great Wingman, they always picked J.C., a good testament to a great, young combat flyer.

The helicopter lumbered to a landing on the slightly heaving deck of the Eisenhower. The Admiral was the first one to get out of the spooling chopper. A Lieutenant met him, snapped to attention as he offered, "Admiral Owens Sir, the Commander's off the ship, there's a problem with the support ship Bennington, sir. Their tow array sonar's out, and we depend too much on her communication systems to ignore this problem, sir. The Commander's due back on board his ship within the next two hours at the latest if they can work out the kinks, Admiral Owens…"

Admiral Owens held up his hand and offered, "say no more about it son, I know what he's going through, dammit. It's a crying shame I'm going to miss him dammit, I was looking forward to sharing a cup of coffee with the man before I had to report to my new Command."

"Admiral Owens Sir, I guess you haven't heard, today's his last day on duty call, sir. The Commander's to be replaced by a new Admiral appointed by the Naval Chief of Staff, sir." The Lieutenant quickly informed his Commanding Officer in a rather calm tone of voice.

"Oh, I hadn't heard of that order, whose the new guy? I knew the Commander was looking forward to retiring, I just wish he could of held off though until this present situation was over with, Lieutenant." Admiral Owens bitched at him over this bit of information he was just told of.

"We all do sir. We don't like breaking in a new skipper right in the middle of a possible shooting war, sir. The new Admiral's named, Admiral Sarah McKinnon, sir. No one knows very much about her and her abilities of Command as yet, sir."

The Admiral smiled and then grumbled, "I have son, I know she's a damn good Commander. I crossed swords with her in a war game once, and she almost got the best of my damn ass as I remember correctly, Lieutenant. Between you and me sir, she did, but I'll never admit it though. Your ship has nothing to worry about if she's at the helm. I'm damn pleased you gave me this information, when she's settled in, I'll send for her and have dinner with her on the Platform."

"Commander Owens Sir, what's she really like, if you don't mind my asking Admiral Sir?"

"Lieutenant, do your damn job and you'll work out just fine with her, a word of warning though mister. She takes no shit, no horse play, and especially, no prejudice from anyone. Be damn careful about any woman in high places jokes, she has a sense of humor, and once she gets to know everyone on board, and sees how you people kid around with each other. She'll relax and you'll all get along just fine with her. Just remember at all times Lieutenant, respect, she's a real stickler about respect, sir." Admiral Owens looked to the helicopter, the flight deck crew was topping off the fuel and checking on a noise picked up on the way over.

One of the workers rushed over to the Admiral and quickly informed him, "Admiral Owens Sir, we found the slight problem with the helo sir. It was just a slightly loose small inspection plate, sir. It's dogged down and it won't give you any further trouble on the flight, sir."

"Good Chief, how soon can I get back in the damn air, sir?" Admiral Owens shivered and then added, "what the hell gives, the last weather report said it was going to be a good day today. Where the hell did all this damn wind come from, sir? I don't like the looks of the sea today either, Chief. If I didn't know any better, I'd swear we're in for a hard blow, sir."

"Admiral Owens Sir, they just revised the forecast from Taiwan. We're now expecting heavy showers and winds later on today, sir. I don't think it'll affect your flight any, or the Platform, sir. You'll be going away from the weather all the way sir," the Chief reported to the Admiral.

"Thank God for that much I guess Chief, from what I read about this damn Platform thing, sir. It won't hold up very well to much bad weather, unless it's already set in position and moored to the sea floor, before the onset of any bad weather, mister. Hell, I already hate the damn thing, from the all damn scuttlebutt I've been receiving lately about it, it's reported if this damn thing works out well, it just might replace our entire damn fleet of Aircraft Carries, sir. What a helluva thing to fear, all our damn Aircraft Carriers a thing of the past, sir. These damn pencil pushers just can't leave well enough alone around here, dammit." Admiral Owens grumbled as he stared back at the Chief who just informed him of the change in weather.

Their conversation was interrupted when a second member from the flight deck came over to the Admiral to inform him his helicopter was ready to lift off now. Admiral Owens climbed in board the vibrating machine and immediately looked for his pilot and called out. "Jesus Christ, where the hell is J.C. at, dammit. C'mon J.C., we're about to lift off, mister. If you're not on board this damn thing in two seconds then you can swim out to our new station, mister."

The door guard snapped to attention and then he replied to the angry Naval Commander. "Admiral Owens Sir, your pilot informed me he had to go to the head, Sir."

"Jesus Christ, couldn't he hold it until we're out on that damn Platform thing for fuck sake? Of all the damn times to have to take a damn leak, mister."

"I guess not Admiral Owens Sir. J.C. said he was floating and had to go, sir." The door guard replied while trying to will J.C. to get back to the craft quicker.

"Get out there and find him and drag his ass back here on the double quick, mister. I want to get under way ten minutes ago for this damn thing I just got stuck with, sir."

"Yes Sir Admiral Owens Sir." The guard jumped off the helicopter and he went looking for the young Lieutenant who was already on his way back to the spooling helicopter.

The door guard warned him the angry Admiral was bitching bad about him going off to the john.

The Lieutenant laughed as he replied, "damn sir, the Admiral would growl at me if I stayed where I was for Christ sake. Don't worry any bout him any sir, he's not happy unless he's growling and bitching at someone, I'm afraid it's in his nature man."

The Lieutenant climbed on board the spooling helicopter to the Admiral bitching angrily at him. "Jesus Christ J.C., why didn't you tie a fucking rubber band around the damn thing, rather than tie me up like this, mister? Get your ass in here so we can get going, dammit."

When the door guard was back on board the helicopter, he said something in the headset, and then the helicopter instantly lifted off and headed east. The trip was spent in silence, with Admiral Owens keeping his head glued to the window. He was dying to see what this Platform looked like. He was looking forward to being teamed up with General Campanelli again. He spotted the Carrier Washington, and off to her south he saw what looked like a small Island floating in the water. As the helicopter neared, the massive Island increased in size dramatically, until he saw the whole Platform. An Island was exactly what it was, it was enormous. He saw many different types of aircraft resting on the enormous flight deck. As his helicopter slowed, the Admiral ordered the pilot to make a quick flyover, so he could view the entire Platform.

"I'll have to get permission from the Tower before I can do a quick flyover the damn thing, Admiral Owens Sir." The pilot offered to the Admiral.

"Jesus Christ, just get it then will ya please. I want to see what this whole damn thing truly looks like here, mister." Admiral Owens snapped back at the pilot.

It took over a minute to get from one side of the Platform to the other. The pilot then hovered for a few seconds over one of the internal elevators currently bringing a fighter aircraft up from the bowels of the tanker ship to the flight deck crew waiting for it to arrive.

The Admiral counted twenty elevators, missing a few of them in the massive flight deck. The helicopter hovered by the Command Tower before touching down where General Campanelli and General White stood waiting to greet him. When Admiral Owens spotted the General he walked over and put his hand out as he offered, "Jesus Christ, how the hell are you sir? It's great to see you again sir. There's only one thing I wish I could change when we meet, sir."

"You don't say Admiral Owens Sir, and what might that be sir?" General Campanelli asked.

"I wish we could stop meeting only when a damn war's about to break out on us, General Campanelli Sir. I'm damn pleased to see you finally got the rate increase you so richly deserved because of that little fracas we both shared in the Middle East and Egypt, sir." Admiral Owens glanced at John and added to him. "Jesus Christ, will you look at this sonambitch, the Army must be getting real desperate if it has to make a black bastard like this one here, a baby General, sir." The Admiral slapped him on the back and remarked, "Jesus Christ, it's good to see friends sticking together like this, John. Are you going to keep him out of any trouble this time, sir?"

"Admiral Owens Sir, he's the one who always gets my ass in the stinking shit, sir. Then the wiseass pulls rank on us, and then he gets his ass out of the grass, and leaves me to burn it down, sir." John complained at the Admiral about General Campanelli's antics.

"Jesus Christ, I see it's still the same crap between you two birds." Admiral Owens laughed.

"Hungry sir? You must have been in the air for quite a while now, Admiral Owens Sir. We have a great mess on board the Platform, sir." General Campanelli asked the Admiral.

"Starving," the Admiral replied as he looked around the massive deck of the Platform.

"Good, I have a few Filet Mignon's cooking up for ya, Admiral," he announced proudly.

"Where on the good earth did you ever get your damn hands on them blessed things from, mister? Shit, you people really knows how the hell to take care of yourselves on this damn thing I see, sir." Admiral Owens grumbled as he smiled at the General.

"Gifts from General Weidenbacher on his visit out to the Platform sir," the General replied.

Lieutenant Wright got off the helicopter carrying Admiral Owens' seabags and he walked over to the three officers and asked the Admiral, "where should I put these for you, sir?"

The General looked around until he spotted a Seaman watching what was going on with the officers, and he called out to him. "Seaman, take these bags over to the VIP room below deck will ya. And who is this fine looking young Officer who is obviously with you, Admiral Owens Sir?" General Campanelli asked as the Naval Lieutenant joined the other officers.

"Him, he's J.C. Wright sir, my personal pilot for quite a while now, General Campanelli Sir." Admiral Owens snapped while looking at the young polit.

"What's the J.C. stand for Lieutenant?" Campanelli asked as he put out his hand to the flyer.

"General Campanelli Sir, my name's really Lieutenant Charles B. Wright, sir." The pilot answered as he gave a quick glance at Admiral Owens standing right next to him now.

"Then where the hell did the J.C. come from son?" he asked with a smirk on his lips.

The Lieutenant made a quick motion with his head towards the grinning Admiral.

"I gave him the damn tag name and he deserves it General Campanelli. It stands for Jesus Christ. Without knowing it, every time I spoke to the young Lieutenant, I always added Jesus Christ. He was a real fuckup when he was younger, sir. Anyway, the other flyers tagged him J.C. He's a good man who turned into an outstanding pilot though, sir." Admiral Owens offered.

The General looked to the good looking pilot and then offered him. "Pleased to meet ya, Lieutenant J.C. Wright, I too have a nickname, sir. It was given to me by my Lieutenant, the name's 'Popeye', and you can call me that anytime you choose to, son. It's good to see someone else stuck with a damn tag name, hey Bear," the General said to the still grinning Admiral.

"Bear?" The Lieutenant laughed as he turned and looked at the Admiral.

"Yeah! Bear! And if I ever hear you using it mister. I'm going to have your gonads ripped from your damn body, and then I'll have the damn things ran up the miserable flagpole for all to salute, mister." The Admiral warned his young flyer in no uncertain terms.

"Yes sir! Admiral Bear Sir!" J.C. smirked at the grinning Admiral this time.

"Let's go and get ourselves something to eat sirs," General Campanelli said with a grin.

A table was setup in the mess in honor of the Admiral's arrival on board the Platform. General Palmieri and Colonel Locker were already seated at their table, and Major Aleksandra was getting herself something to drink, she automatically sat down next to the General.

Admiral Owens stared at her for a few moments, and then he offered in a concerned voice. "Say, don't I know you, yeah, I remember you now. You're the nut who tried to take a fucking shower with my damn male Officers, and you almost caused a riot on board my ship, young lady. General Campanelli." The Admiral offered as he turned to look at the General, and then he added, "Yes Sir General Campanelli, my SPs had to actually pull her naked ass from the damn showers. Young lady, you still have the men on board my Carrier talking and drooling all over that little stunt of yours. I hope you never try that one again on another Commander, Major."

Aleksandra smiled pleasantly at the Admiral who returned her smile.

General Campanelli laughed as he introduced the Admiral to his other Command Officers. Admiral Owens watched as Colonel Locker got up and walked over to the food counter, and then he leaned over to General Campanelli and whispered to him. "Who is the female Colonel, sir?"

"Colonel Mary Locker sir. She's unattached Admiral." General Campanelli whispered back.

"Man, she's got some damn trunk you can smuggle things out in, General Campanelli Sir."

Both men laughed, Aleksandra heard the conversation and she gave Campanelli a quick kick under the table, for laughing with the wise cracking American Admiral to his right.

"Say Eddy, did you get a showing of the new HR-334 rifle system sir?" the Admiral asked.

"Yes, I sure did Admiral Owens Sir. It's some system, made me hit the damn targets, sir."

"Yeah, it's some shit, huh General Campanelli?" Admiral Owens asked the General.

"Yes sir. It sure is Admiral Owens," he replied for a second time to the Navy Officer.

The meal was pleasant and filled with a ton of small talk. Aleksandra loved listening to the men talk and brag about their past experiences together in the service. The more she thought about it, the more grateful she felt for no longer living under the heavy Communist thumb and pressures. She made up her mind to discuss with Edward what was needed to request political asylum in his country. Deciding to live in the United States, and share that life with this American General nick named Popeye. She looked at him and Edward caught it and returned her gaze and smiled, a smile that heated up her soul. All of a sudden she had an overwhelming desire to make love to him. It was because of his smile.

The Admiral had to cough to get General Campanelli's attention back on their conversation as he said, "whatdaya think this shit was about today, sir? You think this damn submarine's Russian or Chinese? It's hard to tell anymore, because the old Russia has sold so many of her outdated submarines to the Chinese and other countries who want to give us some fits, General."

"Dunno, but I have a gut feeling this one was Chinese. If I were them and planning to attack North Korea within the next few weeks, I sure as hell would want to know what any country had floating around the soon to be fighting theater sir," the General offered with a smirk.

Colonel Locker came back to the table and took her seat and began sipping her coffee.

"Hmmm... I see what you mean General Campanelli Sir, but I don't happen to agree with you it was a Chinese submarine though, sir. I think it was more a damn Russian one, but her mission was the same though sir. To find out what the hell was floating around them in the Ocean, and how much of a threat it posed against her shores and military activities, sir."

The talking stopped as the group of officers ate, once finished, General Campanelli offered the grand tour of the Platform to the Admiral. All the while, the Vinegar Joe Platform kept creeping slowly along towards its new mooring position off the Island of Taiwan.

Slowly, the Platform walked its way to position, the CIC was constantly received one report after the other, and the threat board was dotted with many probes from the small Chinese Junks, to a possible new submarine contact. No targets got close enough to make out what the Vinegar Joe Platform was all about though. The General had doubts about the first submarine being Russian. The Russians had satellites, and if they were interested in finding out what the Platform was about. They just had to make a few passes over it with their satellites, and they would know all they wanted to know about the Vinegar Joe. General Campanelli decided to put his thoughts down in a report, and then send it off to General Weidenbacher.

WEDNESDAY, FEBRUARY 18TH

The Vinegar Joe Platform finally ceased all forward movement, it was Oh, Ten, Twenty Three Hours when the engines of the Platform were finally shutdown. The General immediately noticed the silence and he looked up from his desk and then listened for a moment.

Admiral Owens announced as soon as he heard the motors shutdown, "we must have just reached the new position, the engines have stopped sir."

"Let's see what's going on topside people," the General announced as he got up.

Chief Kirby was already at work barking out a flood of new orders and curses at the officers and enlisted men alike. He spat on the deck as he growled at anyone he saw not working, or was caught up in his sight as he tried to push his people to completely secure the Platform.

General Campanelli walked over to the old Chief and then he commented to the man with a snap in his voice, "Chief Kirby, I was just thinking..."

"Not fucking now sir, I have enuf god damn work to do, General Campanelli. If you wanna help, grab a damn tag line and tug on the damn thing. If not, get the hell outta my way sir."

The suddenly fuming Admiral Owens tried to push General Campanelli out of the way in an effort to get at this insolent Chief as he roared at the old man. "How dare you speak to the Commander of this operation like that, Chief? I'll have your leather hide tacked up on the damn yardarm, so the General can take some pock shots at the damn thing at his leisure, mister. I'm going to put your old ass on report and have you drummed out of the service, and then..."

The General intercepted the enraged Admiral and offered in an effort to calm him down some. "Admiral Owens Sir, I expect to be told off good an proper whenever I'm in the damn way by my people, sir." He rested his hand against his chest to stop him from going at the Chief.

The Admiral stared at General Campanelli for a minute, and then he bitched at him this time, "Dammit sir, this man's like you were. Arrr... I'll respect your Command, but I'll not allow this old fool to speak to me like this I tell you that much, General Campanelli Sir."

The General ran his hand across his chin to stifle a smile as he remarked, "I betta keep you and the Chief well apart for now I see, Admiral Owens Sir. I gave him the run of the work crews and the entire flight deck until we're fully secured and operational again, and I can't have you interrupting his work for a moment, Admiral Owens Sir. Let's step back so you can see him in action, sir. Then you'll understand why I gave him this amount of leeway, sir."

The two officers backed off and then watched the Chief and workers going at it securing the Platform. The angry Chief ordered the divers over the side, and the submergence vehicle DSV-3 Turtle, slowly came out from under the massive Platform to rendezvous with the waiting divers. Slowly, the small submarine disappeared below the surface of the water, with the divers hanging on to the sides of it. The water where the Platform was presently positioned, was nearly two hundred feet deep, and the divers and submarine were on their way to locate possible positions for mooring lines to be set in the Ocean floor. In the event of bad weather, these lines could be tightened or released, so the Platform could weather any storm thrown at it.

Electrical leads were dropped in the water as small electrical charges were sent through the Ocean surrounding the Platform. This light trickle charge was a very effective shark repellent system, it interfered with the shark's electric field like they were being attacked with itching powder it was believe by the developers, and made the sharks stay far away from the area.

General Campanelli noticed the bubbles breaching the surface as the submarine and divers worked under the sea. In less than half an hour, the dive team installed three of the very heavy mooring hookups into the hard rock below the water. With each cable mooring completed, he felt the stability returning again to the massive floating Platform.

Admiral Owens grunted at his Commanding Officer. "General Campanelli, I don't get this crap for an instant, if this damn thing's supposed to be a sort of Aircraft Carrier. Then how the hell are you launching fighter aircraft from the flight deck, sir? How do you get the nose of this damn thing into the wind to add to the lift of the small fighter aircraft as they takeoff, sir?"

General Campanelli looked to John, and he allowed him answer the Admiral's last question. "Admiral Owens Sir, we don't have to move the ship to get the lift from the wind, sir. All we do is change the direction the aircraft are taking off or landing. We do have nine catapult systems setup on the east side of the VJP, just in case we have to get more aircraft in the air then by merely launching them into the wind. Our runways took away the need for catapults in many instances, sir. We don't have to have the aircraft fire their afterburners to get off the deck either, sir. The deck is long enough for normal takeoffs and landings of the aircraft involved, sir."

"Arrr... all I know is I don't like this damn shit one god damn bit I can tell ya, dammit mister. I liked it when you had to make Command decisions, and get the ship heading in the wind, and shit like that sir." Admiral Owens griped at General White.

General Campanelli laughed as he groused at the rather upset acting Naval Officer. "C'mon Admiral, let's get back to the CIC Chamber and see what's doing there, sir."

More reports already came in on some minor skirmishes raging between the Chinese and North Korean military forces. The fighting was surely becoming more intense of late, and much more frequent than in days past, and General Campanelli could feel the hair in the air, and the blood on the ground, as he complained to anyone within earshot of him, "shit, dammit, I think there's going to be fighting before the fricking week's end, dammit."

"Really General Campanelli Sir? I thought the damn North Koreans had until March 4th to comply with all the United Nations mandates, sir? I was informed on the 3rd of March, the Council President, Bartlett was going to get in contact with the North Korean Representative, Kim something or other, and request his presence at the United Nations meeting, before allowing the Chinese to open any hostilities with the North Koreans, sir. Sort of giving him one last chance to come around, and stop screwing round with their damn nuclear toys and other crap like that, General Campanelli Sir." Admiral Owens complained at the General.

"I heard that also, Admiral Owens," the General replied and then added. "But I don't think the Chinese will wait that long, sir. Too much is happening for this thing to hold together before war finally breaks out in the damn region, sir. You can smell it on the stinking wind, sir."

"I know what you mean, I got the same damn feeling myself, General Campanelli Sir." Admiral Owens added in a disgusted tone of voice.

Colonel Locker looked at the two officers as if they were losing their minds. The Admiral picked up the look and smiled back at her. He had been keeping a close eye on the good looking Colonel Locker as he mumbled at her, "I see you think we're all nuts here, Colonel Locker?"

Locker nodded her head yes in agreement without thinking about it first.

"Have you ever been in a war zone before all hell breaks loose on the damn battlefield, Colonel Ma'am?" Admiral Owens asked her with concern in his tone.

"I was in Panama, if that's what you mean, Admiral. That's the closest I ever got to an actual war zone and all out fighting, sir." She offered to the powerful and well respected Naval Officer as she continued to stare him dead in the eyes.

"Bah, that was only a stinking military exercise over there, Colonel Locker. I meant a real fucking war, where hundreds and even thousands of lives are at stake, Ma'am?"

"No sir, I haven't been involved in any such action like that Admiral Owens Sir."

"That's why you're looking at us as if our heads are coming loose on us, Ma'am. It never fails, just before a war, certain things take place on the soon to be battlefield, Colonel. I don't mean the obvious things like these here minor probes being carried out by both sides. I mean the many things that you can't see, you can't really put your finger on it, just kind of sense or feel the changes. The tension, the quiet that spreads across the battlefield before the battle and deaths begins. We call it the praying time. Hell, even the damn animals and bugs feel it. They get well out of the area before the shooting starts. That's why a battlefield's so quiet before the killing starts. Did you ever wonder why there are so few animals killed during any shooting? That's because they're out of harm's way. My dear Colonel, you'd have to have been in a real war to know what we're sensing here, Ma'am." Admiral Owens smiled at her as he let out his breath.

"I hope I never get the chance to understand what you're talking about here, Admiral Owens Sir." Colonel Locker said softly, suddenly afraid of the horrors a war might bring with it.

"Me too Colonel Ma'am. But as things are starting to shape up before us at this time, I believe you're about to see the true effects war brings with it, first hand at that might I add Colonel." Admiral Owens said in a low voice as he agreed with her last words.

Colonel Locker suddenly put her head down, sorry she ever made the Admiral explain about these so called feelings he and the other officers was suffering through.

The rest of the day went by mostly uneventfully. The deck workers successfully secured the Platform to the Ocean floor, and other workers brought up a number of F/A 18 Hornet fighter aircraft from below deck, and prepared them for immediate armed flight. The aircraft were designated as Ready Cap Workload One through Six. They were assigned to the Platform protection and security systems. Aircraft from the Carriers Washington and Stennis maintained the hundred mile Barrier Cap patrol security area for the Platform for the time being.

"Do we have any aircraft up as an operating Ready Air Cap cover over the damn Platform yet, sir?" Edward asked General White with a snap in his voice.

"Yes sir, we had them launched the instant we stopped moving and secured the Platform, sir. We have other aircraft overhead at all times during our entire move operation. The protection aircraft were launched from the Carriers trailing us to our new position, sir."

The Sergeant piped up as he offered this time to the Commander, "General Campanelli Sir, we have a ship requesting permission to moor up with us, sir."

"Who the hell is it? And what the hell is the reason for this requested linkup to the Platform, mister?" he snapped as he turned to face the Sergeant speaking to him.

"Sorry General Campanelli, the ship requesting to moor up with us is the Transport Oiler Ship The Falcon Leader, sir. She's been ordered to top off our fuel tanks from our supplies, she informed us the provisions ship Elizabeth Lykes will pull in to replace some of our used stores. Sir, Marine troops are scheduled to board as well, sir. We're ordered to expect two full Divisions of just short of two thousand Marines in the next coupla of weeks, General Campanelli Sir. Also sir, two C-17 junk haulers (transport cargo aircraft) will try their luck at a deck landing on board the Vinegar Joe Platform, sir. This operation's scheduled to take place early Friday morning, sir.   They err... sorry sir.   General Weidenbacher wants to see if we can land a cargo aircraft safely on our flight deck, sir. If this is possible, this would surely ease the stocking of the Platform, and enable us to use the Marine troops on board us as a quick strike force, instead of having to wait for ship transportation to get the troops to any hot spots that might develop, General."

General Campanelli grunted at the Sergeant in an angry tone, "I think the General's losing it on us if he's planning to deck down a cargo aircraft on our deck. He's gotta be kidding me, if he intends to land one of those damn aircraft on this ship. It'll go right off of the fricking side."

"Not exactly sir, we have enough runway for it to land and takeoff rather safely, General Campanelli Sir." Sergeant Cruz offered confidently to his Commanding Officer.

General Campanelli glared at him for interrupting his conversation with the other Sergeant.

The technicians had the computers back up and on line now, and the ballast intake and exhausts were working perfectly again. The Platform sat soft and level in the sea beginning to show some anger in it. The waves were at a six foot crest, and the winds were picking up rapidly from the northwest at fifteen miles an hour, with gusts clocking in at over thirty five mph.

CHAPTER 23
FRIDAY, FEBRUARY 19th, 1997:
ON BOARD THE VJ PLATFORM

General Edward Campanelli was up early, mainly because he did not sleep very well, he was really worried about trying to the land one of the huge cargo aircraft on his flight deck. He showered quickly, ate and then checked the CIC for any new reports, and then he went topside. Aleksandra was already on the deck along with Admiral Owens dressed in khakis. He made his way over to the two officers and scanned the deck and noticed John and Locker standing with General Palmieri, who was talking with Chief Kirby and some of the other deck workers.

They had to have a RAC, or Ready Air Cap set to launch at a moment's notice at all times while the Platform was at station of call. So the sleek aircraft were moved out to the catapult section of the massive Platform flight deck. Any aircraft not classified as part of the Ready Air Cap was brought below decks, along with all unnecessary military equipment and supplies. The deck was cleared off of anything that might get in the way and interfere with the large incoming C-17 transport aircraft's landing.

Admiral Owens looked at General Campanelli as he walked up to them, and he mumbled at the Commanding General, "we're all set for this crazy ass stunt of General Weidenbacher's, sir."

"Yeah, I wonder what Easter Egg this hair brain idea was hatched under? I'm gonna find the damn puke who dreamed this damn thing up, and shit on him for causing me all this extra work and worry, dammit." General Campanelli growled, causing the Admiral to laugh as he added.

"I think we'd get a better look at this mess from the Control Tower."

The small group of military officers headed over to the Tower, and stood alongside the Air Traffic Controller, Captain Francis Myers. He snapped to attention when he noticed the other officers come into the Tower center. Neither of them returned his salute, they were too busy looking out the plate glass windows surrounding the Tower on all sides.

"Where the devil will the damn transport aircraft come in from, sir? I don't see a damn thing yet, mister." Admiral Owens asked the Air Traffic Controller.

"Low sir, she's scheduled to come in from the south southeast at us sir," the Captain said as he pointed in the general direction of the incoming aircraft.

"Would you Officers care for a cup of coffee sir? It's hot sirs." Captain Myers asked as he nodded towards a pot sitting on a table in one corner of the control tower observation deck area.

General Campanelli took a cup and then had a swig of the terrible smelling and over perked brew, and shuddered as he scowled at the cold coffee, and then he plopped his cup down on the little side table, not to be touched again by him.

The Air Traffic Controller Captain smiled as he saw the look from the General, because he knew the coffee was cold and bitter and not very drinkable any longer.

Time passed slowly, and it was the Air Traffic Controller who suddenly announced in a booming tone, "I got him sir, there he is sir. He's coming in low from the south southeast as scheduled, sir." The excited Captain pointed to a small blinking light on the radar screen.

The Admiral looked at the General and then asked him, "I meant to ask you how the hell you ever hooked up with Chief Kirby again, General Campanelli Sir. The last I heard of the always troublesome old and angry Chief, the Navy was planning to put him out to pasture, sir."

"I shanghaied his salted old ass when I spotted him working in Guam, Admiral Owens Sir."

"I wonder what he did wrong to end up on Guam, General." Admiral Owens snorted.

"I got him on my eyeball now, Captain." Said an Airman as he looked through a pair of binoculars while pointing out the window towards the southeast.

The General stared in that direction until he finally spotted the tiny speck in the air.

"The huge C-17 Globemaster transport aircraft has a two fighter aircraft escort for security purposes, sir." The same Airman cried out this time to his Commander.

In a matter of minutes, the huge aircraft was slowly circling over the massive Platform flight deck, and the pilot was already communicating with the Tower Air Traffic Controller.

"Daydream, am requesting permission to land on the Platform, sir. Over." the pilot requested.

"Daydream, this is Homeplate. You're cleared to land, you're instructed to approach us from the northeast. Use runway One Fiver for landing, the winds are out of the south at twenty knots, with strong gusts up to thirty five knots, sir. I have a good cross wind whipping up at over thirty knots, sir. Do you have an umbrella brake capability on board your aircraft, sir? Over."

"Yes sir, and I see no problem with this landing attempt at this time, sir. I've been practicing for this landing for over a month now, Air traffic Controller, sir. Over."

The umbrella break was slang for the parachute braking system for the large aircraft.

"Daydream, you're clear to land, start your final approach now. I have an LSO (Flight deck Landing Signal Officer) with the paddles at the ready. Watch the ball sir. Good luck sir. Over."

"Roger that last, I copy all as offered and received, Air Traffic Controller Sir. I have the ball in sight at this time, Homeplate. Out."

"You're instructed to take all orders from the LSO now. Out Daydream, good luck sir. Over."

"Daydream to Tower. I roger that last and will comply with all as instructed, sir. Over."

The LSO or Landing Signal Officer took Command of the C-17 transport landing, neither General Campanelli nor Admiral Owens heard the communications going on between the LSO and the aircraft pilot. The General watched as the incoming aircraft lined up with the flight path, and slowly lowered in the sky. It looked like a giant cloud descending. The General watched the wheels lightly touchdown on the flight deck, and the pilot immediately threw his engines in reverse. Then the pilot put the aircraft to full power, the engines screamed as the plane slowed on the deck. The powerful vibrations actually rattled the windows of the Tower so violently that the General instinctively moved away from the glass for fear of them shattering.

The large aircraft continued to slow down as the powerful engines continued to roar, and the pilot popped out his chute brake. Then the aircraft finally came to a complete rest with another five hundred feet of flight deck to go, before it reached the edge of the massive Platform flight deck. The General let out his breath in a rush as he whispered. "Whew, that wasn't so bad."

"Shall we see what our new friends brought us this time around people?" Campanelli offered.

The tail ramp of the large aircraft lowered, and a flood of Marines dressed in Kevlar helmets, chest and leg guards marched down and took up security position by the aircraft. A Captain came down the ramp next. General Campanelli watched as Colonel Locker shook hands with this officer, he looked a little familiar to Edward and he carefully studied his face. Suddenly, he recognized Colonel John Salsiccia, and the General put a grin on his face as he started for him right off. He was pleased to have the well liked Colonel back in his command again.

The Marine guard instantly straightened as the General walked over to them. When he spotted the General, he yelled out in a commanding tone. "Atten huh." Colonel Joseph Salsiccia instantly snapped to attention and saluted the General coming directly at him now.

"Stow all that crap, fella. How the hell are you Captain, sir? Long time no see sir. Good to have you on board again with my sagging ass, sir." The General was so used to calling the Colonel a Captain, he did not notice he was a full bird Colonel now.

"It's Colonel now, remember General Campanelli Sir." Colonel Salsiccia replied with a grin.

General Campanelli stepped back and said, "so it is. How the hell are you, Colonel Salsiccia?"

"Fine sir, looks like every time I see you lately, we're preparing for another damn war, sir. I have two full Divisions of Marine troops scheduled to come on board this Platform thing within the next few days, General, Campanelli Sir. Where will I place them sir?"

"You can have them settle down in tankers R-16 and R-17 for your troop's comfort, and I ordered another shit tanker ship to link up with the Platform, and you and your men can use that one for their showers and shits. How do you like my new toy here, Colonel Salsiccia Sir?"

Colonel Salsiccia looked around and then he remarked, "you got one helluva damn plaything here sir. What the hell is it anyway, sir? Every time I heard anything said about this damn thing, it was always replied to as a Platform, but I see it's a helluva lot more than just a Platform, sir."

"It's called a Floating Island, and that's exactly what it is sir, a two layer Island at that, sir. Everything we could possibly need to wage an all out enemy engagement, is stored below her decks, sir. The only thing missing is the capability to grow its own food. Other than that, we're rather self sufficient out here, sir. We can even wage an all out war for at least twenty full weeks from here, beginning this very moment, before we need any resupply sir." General Campanelli sort of bragged as he was starting to think of the Platform as his personal battle Platform.

"Twenty weeks of all out engagement, sir? Damn, we didn't have that capability when we were stationed in the Sudan on dry ground, sir. All we could do there was run a war for six weeks before we ran out of supplies and equipment, sir. This place must be something, sir."

"Get your gear stowed, and I'll give you the grand tour, you're gonna shit when you see all we have available for our needs, sir." Edward boasted then he turned and left the Colonel and his troops and headed to the CIC. He did not like leaving the center for so long, the rest of his command staff caught up with him without being ordered as he entered the CIC Chamber.

"Some fucking landing that was, Colonel. Glad to have you aboard sir." John said to him.

"Yeah, I'm damn glad I wasn't on the thing when it landed." General Campanelli griped.

The day was spent monitoring the computers and communications from the Asian countries.

THE CHINESE, NORTH KOREAN BORDER

At exactly Oh, Six Hundred Hours sharp three full military Divisions of Chinese troops rapidly invaded North Korea from their south. Over one hundred bombers, and a thousand fighter aircraft joined in on the attack. Chinese Naval Cruisers and Frigate stationed off the coast of North Korea, launched hundreds of missiles at the country. A second Army of five full Divisions of troops and equipment and support vehicles, attacked North Korea from another position on the Chinese, North Korean border. Heavy probes from the Chinese troops stationed in South Korea, attacked the north from the south. The invading Chinese troops moved out so quickly, they were unable to take many prisoners, crushing the North Korean defenders underfoot.

Hundreds of Chinese tanks, armored vehicles and rocket launchers attacked from three different points from mainland China. The first coming from the forces stationed at Antang, the second wave came from China, and the third one from Linchiang. The tanks caught hundreds of North Korean defenders trapped in their foxholes. This lightening quick movement led the main charge, followed by the foot soldiers that rooted out all the surviving North Korean soldiers, and slaughtered them in their rush to attack Pyongyang, the capital city of North Korea.

As clouds of Chinese aircraft, tanks and troops launched their opening attack from China, North Korea fell under attack from a second force. The Chinese warships stationed in the Korea Bay, Kyoggi Bay in the west, and Tongjoson Bay in the east, opened fire on key North Korean military positions and equipment, and also fired on the civilians in villages and cities under attack by the Chinese Naval warships. Within the first few hours of the main and all out attack, many North Korean border cities and towns fell to the rampaging Chinese troops.

Chasong was the first North Korean city to feel defeat, seven thousand North Korean troops and civilians, fell to the swords wheeled by the Chinese attackers. Thousands of North Korean troops and civilians took to the road in a mass exodus towards the south, making it almost impossible for the North to reinforce its beguiled troops tied down in

Chasong, Musao, Manpo, Wiwon and Sinuiju. These cities were completely cut off from any possible reinforcements from North Korea, and these troops and civilians were slaughtered to the last by the Chinese soldiers.

The North Korean port cities of Chingju, Sinanju, Sunchon and Hamjong ni, Nampo, Changyon and Ongjin, came under heavy missile and shelling attack from Chinese surface ships and submarines stationed on the west coast of North Korea. The east coast of North Korea had not escaped the onslaught by the Chinese forces either. The North Korean port cities of Najin, Chongjin, Kyongsong, Yongan, Kimclaek, Tanchon and Sinpo felt the awesome sting from the deadly Chinese sword. The major port city and harbor of Hungnam, was completely destroyed, catching much of the North Korean Navy while still moored at port for the weekend.

In the first three hours of fighting, the Chinese forces estimated over twenty nine thousand North Korean forces were destroyed, with another forty five to fifty thousand civilians killed by the attacking Chinese troops and armor. The Chinese airforce pounded every airbase spread throughout all of North Korea. A number, estimated to be set at nearly seventy percent of the North Korean airforce, was caught on the ground and quickly destroyed. In the forth hour of fighting, the North Korean forces stiffened, and the Chinese invader's advance slowly ground down to a mere crawl in their ongoing march towards the capital city of Pyongyang.

0650 HOURS: ON BOARD
THE VINEGAR JOE PLATFORM

All sorts of bells and sirens suddenly sounded inside the CIC center, as Flash messages flooded into the chamber by the handful. The groggy General was still half asleep while sipping his coffee in the mess. Sergeant Willis ran in calling out his name excitedly.

"General Campanelli, General Campanelli Sir, where are you sir?"

The General picked up his head and looked at the screaming young man, and stood and called out, "over here Sergeant, what the hell are you screaming about, dammit? Calm down will ya."

The Sergeant ran over to him and snapped to attention and saluted him as he reported in an excited tone to his Commanding Officer. "General Campanelli Sir, the damn Chinese troops are attacking North Korea in force, sir. First reports coming in state the Chinese troops are out right slaughtering the North Korean soldiers while they're still trapped in the foxholes, sir. Other reports state the North Korean civilians are suffering the same fate, outright slaughter sir."

The General glared at the man as he suddenly growled angrily at him. "Shut the fuck up will ya, dammit! Let's get the hell outta here before you start a damn panic in here asshole." General Campanelli actually pushed the Sergeant on the shoulder as he steamed at him. "What the fuck's wrong with you, pisshead. Giving me a damn report this important like a shrieking bitch. You're a soldier, and you're to act like one, or I'll have your ass shipped the hell outta here."

Campanelli doubled timed it over to the CIC Chamber, and almost crashed into General White heading in the same direction as General White moaned at his Commanding Officer.

"Well I guess the shit just hit the damn fan as we feared it would all along, sir."

"I know, I heard the Sergeant, sir. Are the Admiral and General Palmieri in there yet mister?"

"No sir. I have no idea where they might be at the present time, Eddy." John replied.

He stopped the Sergeant by placing his hand against the kid's chest. "Stop!" he growled.

The kid actually came to a sliding stop and he immediately stared at his Commanding Officer while waiting to see what the Commander wanted of him.

General Campanelli glared harshly at the Sergeant again, and then he snarled at him, "I want you to go and find the Admiral and tell him to get over to the CIC A-SAP, mister. Give him this message, 'There's a fire on the water', and that's it mister. Then you're to find General Palmieri and give him the same damn message. Then, I want you to locate Major Klivekaita, she's somewhere below deck, and you're to tell her I want her back here at the CIC on the double quick, don't tell these Officers what has just taken place in North Korea yet. Zip your lip mister. Then go over to the mess and have the Mess Sergeant send up a breakfast for each Officer responding to the Command Center. You know who and how many will man the damn center, and also order a gallon of coffee to be sent up to the Chamber. Get going and keep your damn mouth shut, and only speak to the Officers I ordered to the CIC, Sergeant."

The Sergeant left in a rush and found the Admiral and General Palmieri standing together, and they were watching some of the flight crew working on one of the aircraft resting on the flight deck topside and he reported. "Sir, there's a fire in the water," was all he said to the two officers before they ran over to the stairwell, the Admiral chucking his cigar overboard.

Sergeant Willis then looked for the female Major. He asked a female Sea person he spotted if she would go in the showers, and tell Aleksandra she was wanted back in the CIC Chamber immediately. But she could not take the time, she was already on special duty herself, and she could not leave for post to carry out the Sergeant's request.

Sergeant Willis was trapped in a dilemma as he walked back and forth in front of the female officer's showers area. He was scared, but he also knew he had to get in there and order the foreign female Major to the CIC. He suddenly drew in a huge lung of air and then he ran in the showers while calling out, "Major Klivekaita, where are you Ma'am? Major."

"Over here. Who want me now, I take shower please." A sexy voice called back to the excited and embarrassed Sergeant as she continued washing herself.

The Sergeant stopped dead in his tracks when he realized she was still showering. He turned his back as he talked to the female fighter pilot over his shoulder.

"Sergeant, I no hear word say to me, you turn and tell me what want here so I finish shower."

A second officer showering, laughed as she said, "Well will you look at this, a shy Sergeant. Now I seen everything, girls." The other women laughed from out of the steam.

Sergeant Willis turned and informed the female Major she was wanted back in the CIC Chamber A-SAP, his eyes wandering over to the other women also showering with the Major. They were all standing with their hands resting on their hips while listening to his report. A dream come true for the Sergeant as he quickly checked out the other women's shapes.

The foreign female Major waited not so patiently until the Sergeant quickly finished his report for her, and then as she casually walked passed him, she reached out and grabbed his crotch and then purred at the same time at him. "Big and dangerous Sergeant, you bit shy I see, mista. Refreshing, very refreshing Sergeant. I never think for second any Sergeant in United State military ever be shy like you, mista. Remind me to invited you to the woman shower again real soon Sergeant. So you see more a lot of us women soldiers here. By way fool Sergeant, you can swallow now before you hurt self, fool you. I go get dressed and see you back in CIC Chamber once dressed proper, Sergeant. Please inform General Campanelli I'll be at CIC soon as dressed proper for duty at CIC. You may leave now mista, unless you want watch me dress, Sergeant. I promise you enjoy what I show you as I get dressed in front you, mista."

The Major laughed over her shoulder as she slowly walked naked away from the still gawking and rather confused Sergeant, leaving him watching her as she left him. Some of the other female officers started giving the Sergeant cat calls, while others asked him to wash their backs for them as they continued to shower with him in the area.

Sergeant Willis shook his head in an attempt to try and get his wits back operating for him again, as he mumbled under his breath at himself, "What the hell am I waiting for, dammit. I better get my ass the hell outta here and back in gear while I still have some clothes left on my stinking ass." He rushed to report back to the General at the CIC.

PEKING, CHINA: CHAIRMAN MAO CHENG-YU AND VICE-CHAIRMAN CHAO TSO-JEN IN THE ALTER CHAMBER ENGAGED IN A PRIVATE MEETING

Mao Cheng-yu sat back while smoking a cigar and listening carefully as his excited Vice Chairman laid out his further plans of war. "Mr. Chairman, we're going to use a staged attack on the keel of the old junk Aircraft Carrier Varyag we so foolishly brought from the worthless Russians, as an excuse to jump to an earlier attack date against North Korea, sir."

"I don't remember this deal with our foolish Russian friends. Was I involved with this great blunder of an obvious mistake?" The slightly confused Chairman asked his Vice Chairman.

"Not in the least Mr. Chairman. The Navy handled all the foolish negotiations with the hated Russian Navy for the useless transaction we so foolishly brought from the lowly dogs, sir."

The Chairman suddenly glared angrily at his Vice Chairman as he snapped in a surprisingly strong voice at him, "Explain this so called foolish deal with the hated Russians to me a little clear then you speak of. I don't like finding things out after they had taken place on me, sir."

"Chairman Cheng-yu Sir, early last year, the Russians got in contact with our Naval Minister sir, and informed him Russia was willing to sell us the bottom section of a nuclear powered Aircraft Carrier called Varyag they and the Ukrainians had been constructing for two years. The reactor was set in place, and some of the decking was also installed on the foul ship. The Naval Minister fell all over himself with trying to get the twenty million dollars the hated Russians demanded for the useless hull of the ship. I was the one who gave the final blessings of this office to close the deal, sir. At the time it looked like an excellent deal for us to do, sir."

"What happened to this so called excellent deal we carried out with the Russian dogs then, Mr. Chao?" The still rather angry Chinese Chairman whispered as he exhaled the cigar smoke.

"Once we took Command of the worthless hull, we quickly discovered the useless ship would take five billion dollars to correct the countless mistakes and flaws the foolish Russian workers committed, to complete the work needed to finish the Carrier and make it sea worthy, sir. By the time we would've finished this foul project, it would've been so outdated it would have been a terrible embarrassment to us to put this worthless ship out to sea, sir. We done little to the hull since it was first brought to the shipyard at Shanghai. We even considered cutting up the rusting hull for scrap, sir. There was a little interest from the French to buy the worthless keel, but when they saw the condition of the worthless thing, they immediately backed out of their offer."

"It seems like the Russian's have pulled the wool over our eyes again I see, you old fool you. Once this foolish problem with North Korea and Hong Kong is over, heads will roll for this blunder I assure you, sir." The Chinese Chairman snarled savagely at his Vice Chairman.

"Yes, they truly did take advantage of us on this worthless deal, Mr. Chairman Sir. But now we could use this great blunder to our favor, and we employ it against the North Koreans, sir." The Vice Chairman said with more of a leer than a smile on his lips.

"Continue with this nightmare you're offering to me, sir." Chairman Cheng-yu snapped as he took another drag from his cigar, and then he openly glared at his Vice Chairman, displaying his displeasure over what he was hearing about this Russian ship they brought from the Russians.

"Mr. Chairman, we're planting charges in and around the rusting hull of a wreak as we speak. I intend to destroy the hull and then blame it on the North Korean fools. We have three North Korean prisoners held in custody for months, and our doctors worked on them endlessly. The three fools were fishermen who strayed in our waters, and were arrested in possession of a camera when we searched their Junk. These foolish fishermen are in such a state, the fools will admit to anything asked of them. Once they admit to the sabotage, we'll publicly execute the three so no one else can ask them any further questions. No country will blame us for attacking North Korea, once they see they have destroyed a ship we were working on, sir. It'll constitute an act of war at the time when most nerves are stretched to the limit." The Vice Chairman sat and then waited for a response from his Commander. He stared back at the well aged Chinese Chairman for some time before he showed any sign of a reaction to his offer and words.

The elderly Chairman held his cigar locked between his fingers and stared up at the ceiling for a few long moments while collecting his thoughts. Slowly, a smile crossed his lips, and it quickly turned into a laugh as he suddenly roared at his worried Vice Chairman. "You have come up with a plan worthy of my approval, Vice Chairman Chao. You have done very well for yourself, carry out your plan, and we'll then attack North Korea in force, sir." He laughed again and added, "when will you put this plan of yours into full action, sir?"

"Mr. Chairman Sir, I plan to detonate the charges at three a.m. on the twentieth day of this month. Then I'll order our troops and aircraft massed on the Chinese, North Korean borders to attack North Korea. I'll inform all Army Group Commanders of the North Korean attack on our soil. This should be more than enough to cause the Commanders to be ruthless to China's enemies no matter who they are." The Vice Chairman sat back and smiled, pleased with his plan.

The Chairman pulled his bulk forward on the handles of his seat. The Vice Chairman made a move to stand but the old man motioned for him to remain. He walked to a table and picked up one of his favorite cigars, and handed it to the Vice Chairman. "Care to join me in a smoke?"

He saw the chest of his favorite politician swell with pride as he put the cigar in his mouth. The Chairman shocked the Vice Chairman as he struck his solid gold cigarette lighter and lit the cigar and offered his Second in Command. "I like your plan Vice Chairman Chao, I see my faith in you was not unfounded sir. Are your troops ready to begin their attack on North Korea?"

"They're chomping at the bit to begin their opening attack on North Korea now, sir." The Vice Chairman bragged proudly as he removed the cigar and blew the smoke towards the ceiling.

The Chairman returned to his seat and plopped down in it like the old man he was.

ON BOARD THE VINEGAR JOE PLATFORM

Major Aleksandra Klevekaita dressed quickly and then she rushed to the CIC Chamber, she was shocked to see so much activity taking place inside the center as she entered.

General Campanelli was busy screaming at everyone working in the chamber, and the Admiral was bellowing in the radio as he squeezed it to death in his hands. General White was also yelling at someone over the phone. "What go on?" She cried.

General Campanelli looked at her and then bitched, "the damn Chinese just attacked North Korea in force." He turned to a small screen as he yelled at the operator. The box, direct hookup with the White House, buzzed, and activity inside the CIC center came to an instant stop. The fuming General roared. "Okay people, all none essential personnel get out of here." General Campanelli waited until the only people left in the room were members of his command staff.

The screen suddenly turned into a test pattern then it quickly cleared to the Military Command Center in the Pentagon. General Weidenbacher sat with General Claiborne off to his right, and Marine Colonel Marianne Matteoni, the Senior Military Officer sat to his left. General William Weidenbacher started to speak the moment he saw Campanelli's face come on the large screen.

"Ahhh... General Campanelli how the hell are you doing today, sir? I'm quite certain you're well aware of what's going on by now in both China and North Korea, sir?"

General Edward Campanelli nodded slightly then he stared at the General while waiting for him to begin his latest briefing on the present situation taking place in North Korea.

"We know why this action has taken place before the scheduled United Nations meeting, sir. We, I mean the President has been in constant contact with the Chairman of China, and he explained the reasons for the early attack leveled against North Korea, sir. If he's not lying then China has a damn good reason to attack North Korea before scheduled, sir. I don't believe the explanation from the Chinese at all though, General Campanelli. I don't see the logic to the supposed attack from North Korea against China on her own soil at that, General Campanelli.

"The President's scheduled to address the public at ten a.m. sharp. He's also calling for an emergency broadcast to inform the people what's happening in North Korea, and he'll demand a cessation of all hostilities, and both parties come to the United Nations, sir. It's quite entailed and you'll have to wait until the press conference to find out what's up, General Campanelli Sir. The Chinese notified us they were going to test a nuclear device, and we're monitoring Lop Nor Nuclear testing site for it, sir. The President's pissed off at their timing for this test. I got in touch with you, so I can order you to Alert Level Two status. Secure your installation. I think..."

The General's communication was suddenly interrupted, the President was preparing to address the public. The picture switched to the podium in the press room off the Oval Office. Then it was quickly replaced by the words, 'Please Stand By'. Campanelli took this time to grab a soda.

President Albert Cole took his place at the podium, and began to address the public in general. "Good morning ladies and gentlemen, I'm pleased you were able to attend this news briefing. I called all you here today, to inform you of the events currently unfolding in Asia. Earlier today, three Armies from the Socialist Republic of China, have invaded North Korea and..."

The room immediately erupted into many conversations, the President had to raise his hands for silence, and then he began anew, "the reason given for this attack was at three o'clock this morning, Chinese time, North Korean Sailors blew up a ship under construction in China." President Cole purposely omitted what type of ship it was as he went on. "The ship was destroyed in the attack at the shipyards in Shanghai. This was classified as a wanton act of war committed by North Korea against China. The fighting started at exactly six o'clock China time. We deplore this attack on Chinese soil, but the United States is asking both sides to lay down their arms, and come to the United Nations to try and work things out in a peaceful manner.

The United States realizes tensions were high in this region due to the fact North Korea chose to continue her experiments in developing and the miniaturizing of nuclear weapons.

"At the United Nations meeting we'll air all sides of this matter, and hopefully come to a peaceful solution. I'm prepared to go to China myself, and or North Korea if need be if this will stop the fighting. I have also ordered our American Forces stationed in Asia and Europe to an Alert Two Status, which will remain in effect until both sides stop fighting. That is all I have at this moment for you, I ordered Mr. Walters, our United Nations Ambassador to request an emergency meeting of the Security Council. So we can discuss all options in an attempt to stop this war, before the shooting gets out of hand and other nations come involved. I want to thank you for coming today." The President moved from the podium but was inundated with questions.

"Mr. President, Mr. President Sir." The calls from the gathered news reporters cried out.

President Cole smiled as he held up his hands again, and quiet quickly returned to the briefing room as he announced in a much calmer tone of voice this time. "I'm sorry ladies and gentlemen, I wasn't planning to answer any questions from you reporters at this time please."

Again the calls started, "Mr. President, Mr. President." As the hands shot up in the air.

The President let out his breath and his shoulders sagged a bit as he gave in to the pressing news reporters. "Okay gentlemen and ladies, I'll answer a few of yours questions. But I warn you I have prior commitments I must attend to." Before he started, he turned to his Press Secretary and moved his hand behind the podium, and opened his hand quickly and closed it, and opened it again as he brought his hand up to his face and wiped his eye with one finger. It was a silent message sent to his press secretary to cut off the questions after ten minutes. The press secretary nodded in compliance to the President's last orders.

President Cole turned back to the gathered news reporters and looked at the many concerned faces. He was forced to squint his eyes because of the harsh glare coming from the lights, and he could also feel the first pangs of an oncoming pounding headache hitting him.

"Mr. President Sir." A reporter from channel seven started and then went on with his question. "What's the position of the United States in this sudden war in the Asian region, sir? Are we going to takes sides with China, seeing she's attacking the only serious threat to the world with nuclear weapons, sir? Isn't China doing the world a favor here by attacking North Korea, with the intention of destroying all of North Korea's nuclear ambitions, sir?"

The President glared harshly at the male reporter, sorry he chose to speak to him as he replied, "I'm rather surprised by your question young man. In a war no country does another a favor by attacking another nation with armed troops, sir. War is not to be looked on in terms of a favor, young man. As for taking any sides in this military action taking place between China and North Korea. As always, the United States takes the side of peace, sir. We'll do everything in our power to try and get both sides of this damn conflict back to the peace table."

President Cole picked up an old friend's face in the group of reporters, and he smiled pleasantly at him as he gave him the slight head nod, and then he offered to the well liked news reporter. "Mr. Jensen Sir, as always, a real pleasure to see you again sir."

Jim Jensen stood and then he bowed slightly for his kind introduction as he started speaking, "With all due respect Mr. President Sir. Where will Japan sit in this extremely dangerous situation taking place in Asia, sir? Are we going to continue with the sanctions that are enforced against Japan for her part in the Middle East war, sir?"

President Cole smiled as he thought to himself 'that's a real good question sir, I should have known he would hit some of the nails right on the head' as he replied. "Err... yes Jim. If we feel Japan's threatened by any armed conflict taking place within this region of the world. Yes, we'll live up to our past agreements with Japan, and protect her shores from any possible invading forces, no matter who or where they may come from, sir. As for the sanctions imposed against Japan for her part in the Middle East and Northern Africa war. I'm going to ask Congress to remove them, and bring Japan back into the fold of friendly nation status again with the United States. I've been giving Japan much thought lately, and I was about to suggest that Congress lift those sanctions anyway, and this sudden war has only served to hasten my decision."

The President scanned the other gathered reporters, he settled on a pretty female reporter he did not recognized. She stood and announced she worked for the Washington Post, that made the President wince as he listened to her first question. "Mr. President Sir, we've been working on a story that uncovered certain evidence that the United States was well aware China was preparing to attack North Korea, sir. The evidence we uncovered makes us believe the United States and the United Kingdom were giving China the nod to go on with this attack against North Korea, Mr. President. Is there any truth in these statements I just made, sir?"

President Cole gave out with a nervous laugh as he replied "Err... Miss... err?"

"Wilson, Mr. President Sir," the female reporter replied as she waited for his answer.

"Yes Miss Wilson, the United States has been monitoring movements of the Chinese forces, and we were aware she was massing her troops on the border with North Korea for some time now. Just as every other nation has known of these facts, Ma'am. We were hoping this was just a threat against North Korea, and both sides would come back to the peace table, before any shooting had taken place. Obviously, we were wrong with this assumption, young lady. As for any underhanded actions, we were in complete control of what was going on at all times, Ma'am. We didn't sanction any such attack from one nation against another nation, for any reason whatsoever. In fact young lady, I take exception to the remark from your newspaper, Ma'am." The President turned abruptly away from her and glared at his press secretary.

The press secretary walked over to the podium and whispered something in the President's ear.

The President again raised his hands and then he announced with a snap in his voice, "I'm terribly sorry ladies and gentlemen, but I have an emergency and I have to place an end to this briefing. I thank you all for coming here today on such short notice." The President turned away from the podium and walked between his guards and the press secretary.

General Edward Campanelli was rather surprised the President did not mention anything about the Chinese testing a nuclear device. His screen suddenly went dead right before his eyes.

When the President was in the hallway of the White House, he growled angrily at his press secretary, "who the hell was that damn bitch, and where the devil did her damn paper get hold of that information, mister? I don't know where the hell the damn Washington Post gets their god damn information from. But I promise you one thing right here and now mister, one day I'm going to find this damn leak, and I'm going to block it with the informers head for Pete's sake."

They made their way to the Oval Office where the President plopped down heavily in his chair very angrily, as the Secretary of Defense, Jerry Levenhagen, and the National Security Director, Norman Griffin took their seats surrounding the President's massive antique desk.

"Well gentlemen, what the hell do you think of this damn situation so far? Do you think North Korea really attacked China the way they reported this attack to the world? And if so, for what reason would North Korea take it upon themselves to attack China? What did they intend to get out of it besides a full-fledged war on their hands. If North Korea didn't attack first and this ploy was on China's side. Then what the hell are the Chinese up to? They knew we were going to back their attack on North Korea two weeks from now. Why on earth the early start, and why didn't the Chinese inform us if they intended to start their invasion early, dammit. Something's rotten in Denmark here, and I want to know what the hell it is before this damn thing gets out of hand on us." The President then sat back and allowed his brain thrust have the floor.

"Mr. President Sir," The Security Director stated as he spoke first and then continued with his words. "I don't think the North Korean's attacked China in the least, sir. I don't believe this for a god damn minute, sir. It doesn't make any sense to a sane man, China could do an easy walk over, over North Korea and wipe her from the face of the earth in under three week's time, if China goes all out militarily against North Korea, sir. No sir, I think the damn Chinese had staged this supposed incident to start this war off early for some reason, Mr. President Sir."

"What the hell would they go and do that for, dammit?" The President demanded hotly, "I don't understand this for the love of God, they knew they had our approval for their attack."

"I don't know why the hell they did what they did, sir. Maybe they knew something we don't, Mr. President Sir. Maybe the North Korean's were moving some of their nukes around and the Chinese discovered this action and reacted, sir. I just don't know why China jumped off so early against North Korea, sir. It had to be something that spooked them into action early, sir."

"Then I suggest you find out what the devil it was that spooked the Chinese into early military action against North Korea, mister." The President growled at the Security Director.

"Excuse me for a moment please sir, but I happen to disagree with the Director on this one, Mr. President Sir." The Defense Secretary suddenly piped up as he now got involved in the conversation, "I think the North Koreans are so damn cock sure of themselves, that they're willing to cross swords even with us, sir. They did it once already in the past, Mr. President Sir."

"Yes, and that was with the fucking help of China though if my memory serves me correctly, Mr. Secretary." The Security Director snapped back sarcastically.

The Defense Secretary glared back at the Director for his nasty interruption of his words.

The President noticed the terribly look going on between the two Directors and he quickly intervened, "Gentlemen look, I don't need any damn fighting between you two now. I need answers, and we're going to stay here until I get some answers from the two of you. Coffee?"

ON BOARD THE VINEGAR JOE PLATFORM

The floating Platform was extremely active, with fighter aircraft landing and taking off almost constantly now. The Carrier Washington docked with the Platform and took on stores and weapons. Many support ships of the Washington Strike Force, and the Platform closed in and watched the military activity. General Campanelli and Admiral Owens were stationed inside the CIC Chamber while viewing the countless reports of the fighting as they came flooding in. The Secretary of Defense ordered the orbit of two spy satellites to be altered, so they would fly directly over the trouble spot. Reports came pouring into the CIC center almost two at a time.

China was in complete control of the northwest section of North Korea in so short a time of heavy fighting. The North Korean cities of Sinuiju, Uiju, Sakchu, Changsong and Chosan, along with the port cities of Sonchon, Chongju, and the Naval port of Sinanju, were already in the hands of the invading Chinese troops. What the reports failed to state however, was the Chinese soldiers were slaughtering any military forces from North Korea they came across. Mass graves were hastily dug, and the captured North Korean soldiers were being shot, and then dumped into the long pits in much the same way the Nazis murdered and buried the Jews.

Chinese aircraft attacked hordes of civilians as they fled the fighting and walked out in the open on the roads heading towards the south, in an effort to try and slow down any North Korean reinforcements from getting to their besieged fellow soldiers. One report stated at least two missiles from a Chinese submarine struck the capital of North Korea, Pyongyang.

General Campanelli turned to General White and General Palmieri, and then he asked them with concern in his voice, "well whatdaya think about this shit, gentlemen?"

"I think if the damn Chinese soldiers continue at this pace, within two weeks they'll have destroyed the whole of the North Korea nation, sir. Then we're going to have to sit back and see where the devil the damn Chinese forces are going to head off from there, sir."

General Campanelli stared back at John, "whatdaya mean by that bag of shit, mister?"

"Eddy, I'm convinced this present military action is just the first step of many the Chinese Command have up their damn sleeves, sir. I think the Chinese are using this military action as a sort of stepping stone to another attack they plan someplace else in the damn region, sir."

The General let out his breath in a rush and bitched at his military officer, "Jesus John, why the fuck didn't you say something before this, man. I felt the Chinese was up to something also. Explain your last statement further. Admiral Owens, Colonel Locker, Major Klivekaita, I want you guys to pay close attention to John's remarks, I want your input too here. Go ahead John."

"General Campanelli Sir, I think these rice dimpled bastards are up to something, and I've been doing a lot of thinking about it of late, sir. Remember the report we read a while back about some Chinese bankers stealing nearly twenty nine billion dollars from the banks of China? I done an investigation into this report, and I found out the bankers took off with over forty billion, and it could even reach fifty billion when all is said and done, sir. Judging by how bad the economy of China has gotten since they haven't been able to sell any military hardware to the Arab nations, I think China's in serious trouble financially, sir. They might even be on verge of a civil war, sir. The Chinese offered to attack North Korea over the nuclear situation to cover up their real reason as to what they might be up to in the Asian region, General. I think they intend to go after Japan and takeover that country, and then loot their god damn banks, sir. Either Japan or Hong Kong's their true target in this stinking mess, General Campanelli Sir."

Admiral Owens let out with a low whistle as he asked General White in a stunned tone of voice, "Jesus Christ John, if that's true then how the fuck is China going to get at Japan for the love of God, with South Korea still standing in their way, sir? Uh-oh, I think I might have just answered my own damn question there, sir."

"Exactly Admiral Owens Sir, I believe China will continue her march right through North Korea, and then right through South Korea as well, until they have complete Command of the entire Korean Peninsula, sir. Then they'll merely attack Japan from South Korean soil. That simple man," he offered the Naval Commander as he stared back at the man.

"For Christ sake, why the crap did you choose to keep this bullshit under your damn hat for so long?" General Campanelli snapped at his lifelong friend, and then continued with his angry words, "I had a bad feeling all along about the damn Chinese and what they might have been up to in this region, but not like this, sir. I felt they wanted to take over all of North Korea, and eventually South Korea.

But I never gave thought they'd ever threaten Japan or Hong Kong with invasion, sir. Shit, could you imagine what'd happen if the Chinese took over Hong Kong, sir? I shudder to think of it, sir. I warned that pompous ass Admiral Middleton about this as an after thought, to get the English to stop sleeping with the damn Chinese. Looks like I have to get Middleton back out here again, and run this new shit past his ass. Locker, tapes running?"

"Yes sir," Colonel Locker offered back to her Commanding Officer.

"Good, I want a copy of this damn conversation sent out to General Weidenbacher at once."

"Consider it done already sir," Colonel Locker replied smartly to her Commander.

General Palmieri butted into the conversation and he offered flatly, "General Campanelli Sir, I think you might be interested in this latest report we just received in, sir."

"Shit, these English, the Invincible and Ark Royal launched aircraft to attack Korea. They're flying shorties, hitting radar and airport installations throughout the lower half of North Korea."

"Another report just in sir," General Palmieri said as he handed another paper to Campanelli.

The extremely upset General quickly read the report, and then he announced angrily, "This tears it all to hell, England has just declared war on North Korea, for their sinking of an English warship. It's going to be hell for North Korea now. Word has it three of England's heavy Cruisers are underway for Korea, and who knows how many submarines and ground troops."

CHAPTER 24
IN THE KOREAN BAY

The English warship Invincible, and twelve of her support ships, took up position in the Korean Bay. An old Russian made Chinese submarine successfully worked her way into the defensive net of protection surrounding the English warships, and picked out her intended target. The light forces English ship Dumbarton Castle lagged behind the Invincible seven miles, sailing in a zone that was reported to be free of any possible enemy submarines. The Russian built Chinese submarine moved in until she was well within firing range of the English ship. The submarine got position on the British ship, and fired two torpedoes and then went in a deep dive.

Two Chinese Frigates were tracking a North Korean Russian built submarine, and when the Dumbarton Castle exploded, one of the Chinese Frigates announced she was now tracking the North Korean submarine that had just attacked the English warship. Two English Frigates, the Marlborough and Sheffield, backed by the British Destroyer Cardiff, joined the Chinese Frigates in the search and destroy mission on the suspected North Korean submarine.

When the English Destroyer started to pound away at the classified enemy submarine with her sonar, attempting to drive the submarine to the surface. The North Korean submarine replied and fired two torpedoes at the English Destroyer, in an attempt to escape the now enemy Destroyer tracking her. The Destroyer easily escaped the North Korean attack, and then went all out after the supposed enemy submarine. In its first pass on the submarine, the Destroyer launched two submarine seeking missiles and upon hitting the water, the missiles instantly turned into seeker torpedoes, and they both began pinging away at the North Korean submarine with their own built in active sonar systems as they began hunting the fleeing submarine.

Almost immediately, the two torpedoes locked onto the North Korean submarine trying to escape the area by going into a deep dive, as she popped off a number of noise makers to try and confuse the searching torpedoes, but all of this maneuvering was in vain. The English torpedoes were not to be denied, they immediately zeroed in on their target, and overtook and destroy the enemy submarine. Reports from both Chinese and English sources stated emphatically the attack on the Dumbarton Castle was perpetrated by the hunting North Korean attack submarine.

The United Kingdom had no idea the Chinese submarine that actually attacked the English warship, was now trailing one of the two Chinese Frigates, and the Chinese Frigate was running interference for the submarine. Both submarines were identical in nature, and both were built by the Russians and were both sold to their once allies.

THE VINEGAR JOE CIC CHAMBER

Colonel Locker informed General Campanelli all incoming reports were blaming the North Koreans, for the attack on the English warship. Even American Intel placed the blame squarely on the North Korean shoulders. "General Campanelli Sir, this makes about as much stinking sense to me as trying to buy the damn Brooklyn Bridge, sir. What the hell reason would the North Koreans have for attacking the Chinese then the English, sir? It doesn't make any damn sense to me, sir." Colonel Mary Locker mumbled to her Commanding Officer.

"I know and understand that Colonel Locker. Admiral Owens, what are your forces doing, sir? Are you or your forces responding to what's taking place here for fuck sake, sir?"

"General Campanelli Sir, I have the Aircraft Carrier Washington docked with this vessel at this time. The Carrier Eisenhower's steaming for the southern end of Taiwan, while the Carriers Stennis and the United States have turned, and they're currently heading back for the northern end of Taiwan, sir. I'll have two complete Strike Forces set in place off the coast of South Korea by late this afternoon, General Campanelli Sir. I also have the Carriers

Lincoln and Carl Vinson heading here at flank speed. These Carrier Strike Forces will then take up position between us and Taiwan. We'll have enough strike forces set in place to protect Taiwan and this installation, while offering South Korea and Japan security of our forces in case something goes wrong.

"I also have the Carriers Kelso and my old ship the Roosevelt moving around the Islands of Japan, and they have orders to take up their new position between the Korea's and Japan, sir. The Kelso will also position herself off the coast of South Korea. I want these forces set in place to keep the fighting confined to where it's currently taking place, in Korea and China, sir."

"So do I Admiral Owens Sir. Do we have any assault ships moving out as yet, sir? I want to know where any of our ground forces are going to be stationed at this time, sir."

"I think you should really direct that question more to Colonel Locker, sir. She controls them."

General Edward Campanelli instantly turned to Colonel Locker and asked her in a sharp tone of voice, "well what the hell are you doing with your damn forces, Ma'am?"

"General Campanelli Sir, I have the Wasp moving up to her new position along with the Carrier Roosevelt, she has two thousand Marines stationed on board her craft, sir. I also have the Nassau moving to a new position along with the Carrier Kelso. The Essex and Kearsage are also moving up to rendezvous with the Carrier's Vinson and Lincoln. Sir, the Eisenhower will have the Pelelieu with her battle group, while the Stennis and the United States Carriers will have the Amphibious warfare ships, the Belleau Woods, and the Iwo Jima as support ships, sir. So that leaves the Saipan sailing with the Carrier Washington Strike Group, sir. These ships are normally stationed along with these Carrier Battle

Groups, but we have reinforced them, just in case of any military action as is taken place currently in the region in question, sir.

"I want at least two thousand Marines supporting each of the damn Carrier Battle Groups from now on, sir. Just in case we have to go to a full out attack mode against either North Korea or China, or both of these nations, sir." Colonel Locker replied to her Commander and then she took a quick breath and added, "General Campanelli Sir, I trust that you're aware there are two thousand Marines on station on each of the Aircraft Carriers we have sailing in this possible Theater of War as per General Weidenbacher's orders, General Campanelli Sir."

General Campanelli smiled at her and then offered, "I thank you for reminding me about the Marines stationed on the Carriers, and I happen to agree with you on all these preparations, Colonel Ma'am. I think we should stand pat for the time being, and take a wait and see position, to see what takes place next in this damn drama. I want a memo sent out to all ships under my Command, if they come under attack from any forces, known or unknown. They're to engage and open fire first, and ask questions later, and that includes any English ships of war. We have a sea full of bad guys out there, and we won't know who they are until the smoke clears. Submarine contacts are to be treated as enemy, unless the sub identifies itself immediately. All American submarines are free to roam the sea at random, and the same go for them.

"If they come across any possible contacts, these contacts are to be regarded as hostile in nature, if the damn contact doesn't immediately back off, and it's to be fired on. No one waits until they're fired on under my watch, we're on a Second Stage Alert here people. So let's act like we're ready for a fucking war. Any aircraft coming across another aircraft in flight is to react as if they're under attack, and act accordingly. I don't wanna lose one aircraft, one ship, or one trooper without that aircraft, ship, or trooper taking out the opposing attacking forces, people. I'm warning everyone in this damn CIC. No one here is going to run off to any god damn newspapers and offer them something that'll save their asses if things goes wrong here.

"We're all in this damn mess together, so if there's any discontent over any of my orders or this operation. I want it aired here and now or forever bite the bullet and die with your mouths shut. We all have to hang together throughout this mess or we'll all surely hang one at a time later. You people read me loud and clear on this here?" Campanelli warned as he watched his command staff relate the orders to their subordinates, and then he leaned back in his chair, feeling he and his forces were as ready as they could be to engage in war with either warring side.

Every military officer and Sergeant working with the General's Command Staff inside the CIC Chamber readily agreed with his last orders.

BEIJING CHINA, OFFICE OF THE CHAIRMAN

The Chinese Minister of Defense was giving his latest report to Chairman Cheng-yu, on the attack presently raging inside the always troublesome nation of North Korea. He warned the elderly Chairman of the sudden and massive movement of many of the American Aircraft Carriers basically surrounding the Island of Taiwan. Along with the information his radio operators were picking up, issuing stern orders for all American Naval and ground forces to fire upon any ship or aircraft taking a threatening posture aimed against any American warships stationed in the Asian region.

The elderly Chairman ran a hand slowly through what used to be his hair as he closed his eyes, while going deep in thought for a long few moments. He found himself wondering if he might have possibly underestimated the response of the United States military forces stationed in the Asian region, if he was to go through with his plans to run the hated Englishmen out of Hong Kong. So he could order the complete confiscation of all the money and worth the United Kingdom stored in the Colony of Hong Kong by his attacking ground forces. He could not help but wonder if the Americans would go to war for the sake of the United Kingdom, and if so, how would the United States Command justify it with the American people. If they attacked his country over England and what China was doing to the English from Hong Kong.

The extremely exhausted elderly Chinese Chairman looked at the Minister of Defense while he continued to try and think, and then he snapped at him angrily, "fool, you will continue to prepare our military forces to drive the foolish English out of Hong Kong as planned. I have decided to continue on with our original plans, no matter how the hated American military forces might respond against our military actions taken against the worthless English. After all, the loathsome American Military Command have no major land military bases to wage war with us from in the entire Asian region."

"Yes Sir Mr. Chairman Cheng-yu. I shall issue your last orders as you have stated them to me, sir. I cannot wait until we can finally run the cursed English out of Hong Kong, and then we can once again be in complete control of that always troublemaking little Colony of ours, sir. And then we can really start to control the rioting youth of Hong Kong we have so long ignored. It's time the foolish youth of the Colony of Hong Kong realize that it is China that is the nation who is truly in Command of Hong Kong, not them or the hated English, Mr. Chairman." The proud Chinese Minister replied as he stood, and then he bowed properly to the well aged Chinese Chairman, and then quickly left the office to carry out his latest orders.

THE VINEGAR JOE PLATFORM

General Edward Campanelli's eyes burned him like the devil, because it was after four and he had been at it since six o'clock in the morning, none stop. He sat back and pinched the bridge of his nose and grumbled at his Command Staff members, "okay people, I want everyone to review all of today's reports, and make damn certain we didn't miss anything important, dammit. Then I want a written account of your assumption of what the Chinese plan might be, and your best guess as to where they might be going once they have successfully knock off North Korea for crap sake." Edward looked for Colonel Salsiccia, he spotted him sucking down some coffee.

"Colonel Salsiccia, I want you to prepare an offensive with a two case scenario, sir. Make up a plan for defending Japan from the Chinese military forces currently beating the snot outta North Korea and then between you and me. I want you to run a workup using the assumption the Chinese forces went after Hong Kong and then the damn Island of Taiwan in that order, sir. Something's still bugging the living shit outta my ass about this Chinese attack being ran against North Korea, and I can't put my stinking finger on what's bugging me about this shit, dammit. I want all options covered here. Use Locker, she knows where the ground troops are deployed in Europe and Asia, sir. I'm going to order Camp Zama in Japan, reopened and reinforced whether the Japanese government likes it or not. I need some ground bases operating if this mess gets further outta hand on us. Hell, I think I'll even order the Roosevelt to pay a visit to this base."

The General looked at his watch and then continued with is orders, "tomorrow will be soon enough for this report to be offered up to me, sir. But first I'll have the damn Wasp transfer her Marines over to the Roosevelt, this will put some four thousand Marines on her deck, sir. These Marines will disembark Camp Zama to reinforce that military base against attack, once she's fully operational again. I'll have the junk haulers ferry in as many Marines as I can get there."

"That sounds like a pretty good plan to adopt to me, General Campanelli Sir. I'll get started on my workups right away for you sir, and inform you on what forces and military equipment we'll need to effectively defend both Japan and Taiwan from a possible Chinese attack, sir."

"Get it done for me A-SAP Colonel Salsiccia, you're going to be in Command of any engagement that we get involved in if you're interested, sir. All ground forces, both Army and Marines. Yeah, yeah I know, I can see by the puss on your face, you're expecting some trouble with the Army, if they have to fight side by side with the Marines. Colonel, I don't want any of that bullshit inter service superiority crap taking place here if the shit hits the fan, sir. The Army has to rely on the Marines, and the Marines are going to have to rely on the Army like it or not, sir. We're all American soldiers here, and we'll help each other, or you'll find yourself buried dick deep in horseshit and standing tall before the man, sir. Now get a move on it toot sweet Colonel, I know I told you your report doesn't have to be submitted to me until tomorrow afternoon sir. But I suggest you get a move on it about now, sir."

"You got it General Campanelli Sir, but for some reason I get the feeling I kind of heard this little pep talk of yours not so long ago if I remember right, sir." Colonel Salsiccia laughed as he moved off to carry out his latest orders.

"You better get outta here before you hear a lot more than that crap coming at ya ass, mister." General Campanelli offered with a laugh and a smile of his own.

"General Campanelli Sir, I just received a report stating a number of Chinese and English warships are really pounding the living shit outta the North Korean city and Naval yard stationed at Nampo, sir. The report is very weak sir, I'm quite certain it's a lot worse than the report states it is out there, sir." General Palmieri reported to his Commanding Officer in an excited voice.

"Shit!" General Campanelli growled over this new information, and then he asked, "Do we have any fricking word as to how we're to treat the English warships, if any of our warships happen across their path from General Weidenbacher, sir?"

"General Campanelli Sir, we operating under direct orders to attack any English warships, if they come a little too close to one of our own ships, sir."

"I know that already dammit!" the General snapped at General Palmieri and then he added. "Did anyone get in contact with Central Command, to see if we have any side orders to that damn order? I'm quite sure our government doesn't want us to sink any British warships."

"I'll get through to Central and see what they want us to do if the Brits come a little too close to any of our warships, sir." General Palmieri offered and he immediately placed a message out to the Pentagon, and he spoke directly to General Claiborne.

The Joint Chief General confirmed the order any American warship coming in contact with a British warship, is to order the ship off, and if the ship refuses to move off. Then the British ship's to be regarded as an enemy and dealt with accordingly.

"General Campanelli Sir, I spoke with General Claiborne a few moments ago at Central Command at the Pentagon, sir. He has informed me General Weidenbacher has been in conference with the President since the first shot was fired off between China and North Korea, sir. The word is we're to react against any British ship of war accordingly, sir. I asked the General to clarify what was meant by accordingly sir, and he replied strongly. 'If the damn British warship doesn't veer off as ordered, she's to be sunk, period sir.'" General Palmieri reported to his Commanding Officer as he offered him the report so he could read it for himself.

General Campanelli was stunned by the word "Sunk" and he mumbled low as he sat down heavily, "What the hell type of fucking war are we getting ourselves involved with here, dammit? Shooting at our long time Allies like this. I hate this shit for crap sake."

Photos and video recordings came into the chamber from the Keyhole spy satellite K113. General Campanelli saw the Chinese and North Korean troop movements on the ground, as if he was watching TV. He watched the last two hours of Chinese and North Korean troops fighting all out. He even blinked when a tank exploded violently, obviously hit by an anti-tank missile. He noticed the crumbling North Korean forces along the border with China and North Korea, and was shocked at how far the Chinese troops had penetrated North Korea in so short a time. He carefully studied the tape, and noticed the Chinese troops were not taking any prisoners. Instead, they were just steam rolling right over the entrenched enemy defenders, and a second wave of Chinese soldiers rooted out any remaining enemy troops missed, and engaged them.

"Look at this damn shit will ya for crap sake, those damn Chinese soldiers just killed over thirty North Korean soldiers standing before them with their hands up, sir. They plain outright murdered them all and we got it all on fucking tape, sir. We'll own their stinking asses when we file charges of murder against China." General Campanelli muttered to General White.

"If you're upset by that then you're surely not going to like these stills we just got in, Eddy." General White replied as he handed General Campanelli a new stack of prints.

General Campanelli quickly skimmed through the stack of photos, the first few clearly showed the Chinese troops digging a wide deep trench for what was believed to be some kind of military fortifications and he announced, "it looks like they're preparing to stay there for a stinking while, sir. Where the hell's this shit taking place in North Korea, General White Sir?"

"Between the North Korean cities of Sakchu and Taeyu-dong, sir. But I don't think those damn trenches are military fortifications in the least Eddy," General White remarked.

"Oh? Then what the hell do you think they are for, John?" Edward said as he flipped to the next picture in the stack and he closely examine them with a magnifying glass. He picked up a bulldozer making the trench a lot longer by not wider. The next picture clearly showed the earth digging machine out of the trench, and a number of Chinese military trucks pulling up along it. The next picture showed a good number of bodies lying in the bottom of the open trench.

"They are bodies I take it John?" Campanelli asked his Second in Command with concern.

"Yes sir they sure are Eddy, and I truly believe they're civilian bodies from the North Korean city of Taeyu-dong, sir." General White reported.

"What the hell makes you say that John? That's a damn serious charge you're making here, General White Sir. To kill a number of unarmed soldiers is bad enough for any soldier to commit, but when they start slaughtering civilians in mass numbers. Then they're taking this shit to the next level and asses will fry over it." Campanelli warned him.

"If you look at the next picture in the stack Eddy then you can judge for yourself what I meant by that last remark to you, sir." John replied sadly to his friend as he looked over his shoulder at the next picture that the stunned General was going to look at.

This picture clearly showed a number of Chinese soldiers shooting what looked like a long line of North Korean civilians. The victims were not dressed in any type of military uniforms. The fallen people were picked up, and then thrown into the rear of the waiting trucks. It looked like most of the civilians being shot when herded over to this killing area. The stunned General saw the road was heavy with trucks going and coming into this area of the slaughter.

"You better look at the next picture before you make any further judgments over what you're seeing in them damn pictures, sir." John said in a flat voice and did not look the General.

General Campanelli saw the long trough was now being back filled by the bulldozer, with hundreds of bodies still exposed in the open end of the pit. He stopped looking at the pictures because he was suddenly having some trouble breathing, because he saw horrors like this before. First, from films of World War Two when the Nazis killed the Jews by the thousands, and the second time was when the rescue workers moved in the Middle East and upper Africa, after the nuclear and biological war there. He looked at John with disbelief etched deeply in his eyes as he complained, "this can't be true John, this just can't be happening at this time in our civilization for the love of God. It just can't be happening again, damn this all to hell and back again."

"General Campanelli Sir, it sure is happening again, and we have to do something about it, and we have to do it in a fast hurry for Christ sake. What the fuck do you suggest I do with these damn pictures we have here in our possession, sir?" General White asked him.

"I'll tell you what I want done with the damn photos. I want you to make copies of them for us to hold then send the originals to General Weidenbacher, he'll know what the fuck to do with them. I think this information has to make its way to the United Nations." Campanelli growled.

All the while the two Generals spoke, the tape of the Chinese invasion forces continued. The angry General turned his attention back to the large screen. The Chinese troops were already in Sinhung, and had the whole of upper North Korea cut off from any possible support troops. A contingent of Chinese mop up forces were working their way to the northern end of North Korea. He noticed the Chinese and English ships of war were firing at North Korea and aircraft as they flew over North Korea. The screen was dotted with numerous hot flashes from the explosions taking place throughout the entire area under observation by the satellite taking the pictures.

"Man, the damn Chinese troops are really taking it to the god damn Koreans during this attack against them, sir. Everything, man, woman and beast are all under their weapons."

"General Campanelli Sir, we have another spy satellite just coming over the horizon, sir. It's scheduled to fly directly over the eastern edge of North Korea, General. There are some reports stating a number of Chinese warships are working over the eastern section of North Korea, sir. The Chinese are using more forces than they originally informed the United Nations about, sir. I think they're going to try and wipe North Korea right off the face of the damn globe, sir."

General Campanelli glared at the excited Sergeant and then barked angrily at him, "I don't remember asking you for your opinion here, mister. You run the damn machine and let me make the damn assumptions around here." The General hissed and immediately felt bad for snapping so angrily at the young NCO. He knew the Chinese used more troops and equipment than were permitted by the Security Council meeting two months ago. He was searching his mind in an effort to try and figure out what the Chinese wanted from this operation. All of a sudden, he felt like he just had the wool pulled over his eyes, and he did not like the feeling at all.

The General let out with an exhausted sigh, fatigue robbing all his strength from him as he closed his eyes to get his wits about him again. Aleksandra saw his exhaustion, and was heading for him when General Palmieri got to him first, and he took the seat right besides General Campanelli. He sat down and waited for the General to open his eyes again.

Aleksandra was angry General Palmieri cut her off, she was going to try to get Edward out of the CIC for a little while, and make him eat something and get some sleep. He suddenly opened his eyes and instantly noticed a smiling General Palmieri and griped at him, "oh God, what a fucking sight to see, sir. Do I look as bad as you do, General Palmieri Sir?"

"You look a helluva lot worse sir," General Palmieri tried a smile on the exhausted General.

"Great, I really needed to know that shit my old friend. What's your problem anyway General Palmieri Sir?" General Campanelli moaned in an exhausted sounding voice.

"General Campanelli Sir, I just worked out what the Chinese might be up to with these damn attacks sir," he stopped speaking and took a quick breath and then continued. "General, the Chinese are cutting central North Korea off from the rest of the country, sir. Look at what she done so far in this opening attack, sir. China attacked from three separate points of penetration in the North, and their forces successfully dissected the northeastern section of North Korea in just nineteen hours. To say they caught the North Korean troops flatfooted is a gross understatement here, General Campanelli Sir. Now the Chinese military split their forces. There's two separate Chinese Armies currently heading down the west coast of North Korea, taking over seven port cities. The Chinese are being aided by Chinese and English Navies and aircraft, and clearing the way for the ground troop's rapid advance through North Korea. The Chinese are forcing the North Korean troops to head for the center of the country. We have a force of Chinese and South Korean troops attacking the North Korean defenders from South Korea now, sir."

"I didn't hear anything about this Army coming in from South Korea. When did this happen?"

"This took place while you were looking at the damn tapes sir." General Palmieri answered.

"Shit, continue with your assumption, General Palmieri Sir. I like what you set forth so far here sir, so I believe you're truly on to something here, General Sir."

"General Campanelli Sir, the Chinese troops are attacking North Korea from three separate points. From the north with three Armies from the west with two Armies backed by Naval guns and aircraft, and also from the south with a joint Army of Chinese and South Korean soldiers. We have some reports stating the Chinese and English warships are hitting the east coast of North Korea with a constant heavy barrage of mixed shells and missiles. All this action's effectively forcing the North Korean troops stationed on the coast to the center of North Korea, like I said before sir. I think the Chinese troops are doing this on purpose, General Campanelli.

"Once the North Korean troops are gathered in one central location, I think the Chinese troops are intending to shell them into oblivion, sir. I believe this has been planned from the very beginning, and I don't think the Chinese Command give a shit about any civilians trapped in their sights either. I think as John does, the Chinese troops are planning to eliminate the North Korean troops, and they're not stopping until they're all the way to Japan and laughing at us, sir."

"You bet they need Japan, think of what China could do to the world's economy, if they took Command of Japan, sir. It'd ruin the world. I like what you put together so far, but I want it all down on paper, and I'll get it off to General Weidenbacher to see what he thinks about the scenario, sir. Until then, we have to sit tight and see what happens next in this drama, sir."

The Sergeant came over and reported, "General Campanelli, sorry for interrupting sir. But the birds over Korea, and the pictures are coming in, they're being sent over to your safe box, sir."

General Campanelli headed for his lock box and he removed the pictures and looked at them, and then he asked the Sergeant, "what the hell are we looking at here Sergeant?"

"General Campanelli Sir, the Chinese troops are attacking the east coast of North Korea in force sir, and these shots should clearly let us know what forces the Chinese and English are employing in their main attack against North Korea, General Campanelli Sir."

Other pictures displayed North Korea was clearly under heavy attack by combined Chinese and British warships stationed off their coast. The General did not recognize the Chinese ships, but he immediately recognized two English ones easily. The third English Carrier Illustrious, and the largest of their Destroyers, the Bristol. One of the photos showed the bow of a ship just coming into the frame, and it looked like the bow of the English Destroyer Glamorgan. The Sergeant whispered communications picked up the code name for the Destroyer Fife as well.

"I'd imagine these few ships have all their support ships in tow with them, and they are also aiding the Chinese forces in their opening attack against North Korea, Sergeant?"

"Affirmative General Campanelli Sir. We've been able to pick up much of the radio chatter coming in from the British warships known to be support ships for their main battle wagons, sir. Looks like the Brits are committing more of their ships here, than they did during the entire time of Desert Storm, and the Middle East, African War, General Campanelli Sir."

"Yes, and I'm going to put a fucking quick stop to it too I tell you Sergeant. Get me that damn English Vice pompous ass Admiral on the damn horn, Sergeant. I want to talk to him right this minute, mister." General Campanelli snarled at his NCO again.

The Sergeant quickly moved off and he repeated the General's orders to the radio operator. Moments later he reported to his Commander. "General Campanelli Sir, Vice Admiral Middleton stated he's too busy, and is unable to come out to the Platform for a quick visit, sir. But he'd be pleased to visit our ship at his first opportunity, he states sir. He used the scramble to inform us the Platform was still secret from the Chinese, General Campanelli Sir."

"Sonuvabitch, did you tell this damn marmaluke it was extremely important I see his lousy ass A-SAP, mister?" The General added in an angry voice at the Sergeant.

"Yes sir, and he replied again that he was too busy at the present time to visit with you, sir."

General Campanelli plopped down in his chair, he was fit to be tied but too tired to react. It was after ten p.m., and his eyes were getting heavy from the strain of reading so many reports. Before he knew it, he was sound asleep with his head resting on his folded arms at his workstation. Everyone still inside the CIC center was trying to be as quiet as possible.

THE SECOND DAY OF THE WAR, FEBRUARY 21st: SATURDAY

The invading Chinese forces worked down the west coast of North Korea all the way to the port city of Hamjongni. The city was under siege with Chinese ground forces attacking it from the north, while heavy Naval guns and missiles walked through the city, and surrounding areas with deadly accuracy. The grid shelling was taking out certain sections of the North Korean city at random, and the combined Chinese and British aircraft worked over the other areas the Naval weapons could not reach. The first reports coming to the CIC stated the North Korean city of Hamjongni was going to fall within the next three hours. No one, civilians or soldiers alike would be able to live through the horrendous shelling and air attacks for very long.

General Campanelli awoke at six o'clock, and he was stiff as a board from sleeping in his chair all night. He stretched his arms and back, and instantly paid the price as a sharp pain ran up his spine and into his both shoulders. He was quickly informed about the fate of the North Korean city of Hamjongni, from General Palmieri, and he asked him sharply. "Whatdaya think? Do you think we should try to help the stinking North Korean city out any, sir?"

"Sure I do, the Chinese are slaughtering North Korean civilians. But how can we possibly help them, General Campanelli Sir? We'll be going up against two of our Allies if we tried to assist any North Korean city or her troops, sir. We have no orders from the Pentagon to allow us to lend any assistance to the North Korean soldiers or civilians, so we have to sit tight and wait for something to happen, or we get a change in orders, General Campanelli Sir." General Palmieri reported quickly to his Commanding Officer as he merely shrugged his shoulder at him.

"Yeah, I guess you're right General Palmieri Sir." General Campanelli's stomach suddenly growled and he offered, "pardon me sir, I guess I'm gonna go and grab me something to eat, and then I'm going take a quick shower. Hold the fort down until I return, General Palmieri Sir."

"Sure thing sir, take your time getting back here, General." Palmieri offered back to him.

General Campanelli ate, showered, and then returned to his stateroom to find Aleksandra sitting on his bed naked and she purred at him, "I know you come here." She said with a bright smile. They made love quickly, and then General Campanelli rushed back to the CIC. As he walked in, General White got his attention and General Campanelli asked him. "Whatdaya got?"

"Sir, the North Korean's are screaming bloody hell for an emergency meeting of the Security Council to be convened immediately, General Campanelli Sir. They requested help from the Russians, and even from Cuba as well, sir. Asking the two countries for any possible troops and or military equipment, sir. They even been begging anyone and everyone they can for any help, sir. They're even asking for help from us at this time, General Campanelli Sir."

"Do you blame them General White Sir?" Campanelli hissed as he went over to his desk.

"No, not in the least sir. China has turned it up a notch as well while you were away from your desk, sir. They just announced any aircraft flying over North Korea would be a target, even commercial ones, sir. Every country has suspended all civilian air traffic over the entire Korean Peninsula, sir. It cut off any possible exodus from the country, leaving North Korea's leaders stranded in the middle of a war zone. When the fighting's over, the Chinese will get their hands on the leaders of North Korea and then execute them all simply because they can, sir. This has assured us North Korea will fight to the very last man or woman and child, and it also opens the door for the Chinese to eliminate them as a whole. A good ploy on their part, sir."

"What the hell are we trying to do about this fucking mess, sir? We can't possibly just be sitting on our fucking thumbs, sir" General Campanelli snapped angrily at him.

"General Campanelli Sir, President Cole asked for all fighting on the entire Korean Peninsula to stop immediately, and for both sides to come to the United Nations today, sir. Other than that, we're just kind of sitting with our fucking thumbs shoved up our damn asses, sir."

"Jesus Christ Almighty General Palmieri, we'll never learn will we, sir? I want some damn action on this tub. Let's conduct some air operations, I want everyone on board doing something. Let's get the damn pilots to do some air time, so they know how to land and takeoff from this damn thing. Do we still have those damn Marines stationed on board, General?"

"Yes sir, they're stationed below deck at this time, General." John reported to his angry friend.

"Good, then get their damn asses topside, and let them exercise or do something for their damn pay, let them start acting out a fucking war game or something, sir. Let's get some damn sand maps made up, and workout some attacks scenarios on China, in case we need them mister. I want to see assholes and elbows moving around here in a damn hurry it up, dammit."

"You got it sir." John quickly left the CIC Chamber, and he immediately jumped on the lesser officers, and within minutes from receiving his orders to do so. Fighter aircraft from below deck, were being lifted up to the main flight deck, and then the aircraft were prepared for immediate launch. The Marines were brought up on deck, and a drill instructor was putting them through their paces. After two hours, General Campanelli went topside to see what was going on. The deck was freezing, and it was being swept by a strong twenty five mile an hour wind, and the temperature was dropping below sixty already. Edward's attention was drawn to a fighter aircraft as its engines were brought up to full military power as it prepared to be launched from the flight deck of the Platform. It was a YF-27 Advanced Tactical Fighters, he watched as it fired off into the dim, overcast sky and quickly disappeared in the heavy cloud bank.

Another fighter aircraft just taking off caught his attention, something about the pilot struck a nerve with the interested General. Maybe it was the way the pilot looked at him before he took off. He took note of the aircraft's number before it disappeared into the clouds, and he headed for the Control Tower. He entered the smoke filled area and then he asked one of the Air Traffic Controllers. "Say buddy, who is in Command of Flight Seventeen, sir?"

He instantly stiffened up when he saw the Commander of the complex and then he replied. "Sorry General Campanelli Sir, but you have to ask the TAC for that kinda information sir. He controls all flight operations from the Platform, sir."

"Where the hell is he at son?" General Campanelli asked in not so pleasant a tone this time.

The kid pointed towards an officer intensely looking out the window with field glasses.

The TAC noticed the General looking at him and he stiffened and then he gave him a quick nod as he asked his commanding officer. "Can I be of any help for you sir?"

"Are you the Tactical Air Commander for the day sir?" the General growled at the officer.

"Yes sir, what can I do for you General?" the TAC replied as he stared at the general's stars.

"Who the hell is the pilot of Flight Seventeen, Commander Sir?" Edward continued his angry words as he waited not so patiently for the TAC's to reply to his question.

The TAC Officer put down his radio and then he quickly checked his clipboard and then he offered to the interested Commander. "Hmm, here we go sir. The pilots name's Major Aleksandra Klivekaita, sir. She's on loan to us from Russia, General Campanelli Sir."

"Jesus H. Christ, what the hell's she doing up there dammit? By the way Commander, she's a Lithuanian pilot not a damn Russian one, sir. Can you raise her for me on the damn box, sir? I need to speak to that little pain in the ass pilot STAT, sir."

"Sure thing General Campanelli Sir, standby a moment sir. Twin Towers, this is Homeplate. How do you read me? Out. Sir, we're transmitting on the UHF Ultra High Frequency of 300 MHz to 3 GHz in order to avoid any possible interception of our radio communications by any unfriendly forces, sir. Not even the Russians can go that high up, they're not equipped sir."

"Good, I want to keep this damn installation a secret from the friggin Chinese for as long as possible Commander," General Campanelli grumbled at the TAC Officer.

The TAC's radio came to life. "Twin Tower, Homeplate. Read you five, five. What up sir?"

"Err... Twin Towers, Homeplate. I have someone who wants words with you, Major. Out."

"Twin Towers to Homeplate. Put someone on radio for me please sir. Out."

The TAC Officer offered the General his radio mike and then he informed the Commander, "General Campanelli Sir, just press down the button here and you have communications, sir."

The General's glare was more than enough to warn the officer this was not the first time he used a radio in his life. The TAC Officer took a step back to give the General some privacy.

"Twin Towers this is your Commanding Officer, Ma'am. What the hell are you doing up there dammit!   And I don't like your damn call name either, Major. I already told you this..."

"Twin Tower to Homeplate. I clock in some fly time for myself, sir. I no be in air over three month now, so I follow you last order to do something with self or else, sir. You one who make order pilot in air for some serious stick time, General Campanelli Sir."

"Don't give me any of that stinking shit, Major. I want you back in the CIC chamber in case you're needed. You should have discussed this with me before you went off and took a flight..."

"Twin Tower to Homeplate. No regulation response and no respond no military response me. Out." Aleksandra broke off the communication with her Commanding Officer.

"You get the hell back down here double quick, Major Klevekaita! And don't give me anymore fricking lip shit about it either, Major. Get your ass back to base immediately..."

Again the Major snapped at her Commander over the radio, "Twin Tower to Homeplate. Was last call direct me, if yes, call name Twin Tower, and I no respond unless call name used by you, sir. For all I know, you be could Chinese pilot draw me in trap and then kill me. OUT!"

General Campanelli drew in his breath, he was really pissed off now as he held the radio mike locked in his hand as he tried to choke it. All of a sudden, he felt like he had done this before with another female pilot, who always drove him just as crazy. He thought of Captain Renee Mendoza and then talked to her memory. "Christ Maz, do you know how much this pain in the ass kid is just like you? Did you arrange this so I wouldn't miss you so much, dammit?"

The TAC Officer leaned a little closer to the angry sounding General and he whispered to him, "Did you just say something to me, General Campanelli Sir? I didn't catch it sir."

"No, I was just cursing this damn flying pain in the ass female pilot, that's all Commander."

"Join the club sir." The TAC laughed, causing the General to smile in response.

General Campanelli pressed the button again and he hissed in the mike, "this is Homeplate to Twin Towers. When do you intend to finally land Major, so I know when I'll have you back inside the damn CIC Chamber? Over."

"Twin Tower to Homeplate. I schedule forty five minute flight time, and then engage simulated dogfight with Flight Three fighter aircraft. I deck down one hour thirty five minute from now after in flight refueling, sir. Over." she reported to her Commander.

"Homeplate to Twin Towers. When you deck down, you report to the CIC. Got that! OUT!"

"Twin Tower to Homeplate. I report CIC Chamber on double quick when deck down. Out."

General Campanelli then handed the mike back to the TAC and headed out of the Control Tower. He could hear him already speaking with his pilots again as he grumbled over his luck. "Pain in the ass damn women pilots. I wonder if all of them are like the two I hooked up with."

A MEETING BETWEEN THE MINISTER OF DEFENSE AND THE CHINESE CHAIRMAN IN BEIJING CHINA

"Chairman Mao Cheng-yu, I requested this meeting to take place, because of a series of most conflicting reports I just picked up from the Sea going Junks I ordered to the Philippine Sea. All the Junk's reports point to another American Aircraft Carrier stationed in this region, sir."

The old man slowly leaned forward in his chair and put his cigar in the ashtray, and then he asked in a weak and exhausted voice, "what are you trying to telling me Mr. Minister?"

The Minister straightened up and then he replied to the very powerful Chinese leader, "Mr. Chairman, either the Americans have a new, and much larger Aircraft Carrier, one we have no knowledge of its existence, sir. Or they're playing a great hoax against us, to try and make us believe they have another Carrier stationed some place behind the cursed Island of Taiwan, sir."

"And why do you feel this way Minister?" The old Chairman asked the Minister angrily.

"I have asked the Minister of Naval Affairs to join us along with his reports from the past twenty four hours of fighting, sir. I need his reports to prove my concerns to you, sir."

There was a knock on the door, and the Minister of Naval Affairs, Liu Chung, walked in the private room. He took a seat off to the right of the Chairman, and laid out the reports on the desk, bowing to the Chairman and Minister before he began to speak, "Chairman Cheng-yu, for the past twenty four hours we have picked up a series of radio communications in a frequency we cannot define clearly, sir. All transmissions were unable to be deciphered, but they seem to be coming from ship to aircraft, or aircraft to ship, which leads me to believe the hated Americans have another Aircraft Carrier stationed somewhere behind the miserable Island of Taiwan."

"What is the great importance of this new discovery Minister? I fail to see the emergency you are hinting at over this possible new American Aircraft Carrier," the Chairman complained angrily as he stared at his Minister before he continued with his words. "We know the foolish Americans have eight of their eleven Aircraft Carrier Groups on station in and around Asia at this time. As I stated, I fail to see the concern here. All the Americans have done is move another one of their worthless Carriers into position behind that mongrel little Island of Taiwan.

"We were well aware the loathsome Americans were going to try to overpower the area with their worthless aircraft and warships. Remember gentlemen, as long as the foolish Americans don't have an active military land base to conduct their military operations from, they'll be extremely limited in the support they can possibly offer to the foolish English, when we finally attack Hong Kong against the fools. The way the Americans have spread themselves out, when we finally attack the Island of Taiwan, the Americans will never get in a successful position in time to stop, or even hinder our moves against Taiwan. I failed to understand what all the hubbub is about over this other Aircraft Carrier you have obviously discovered hiding behind Taiwan. This other Carrier has to be one of their lesser and older and outdated Aircraft Carriers.

"All the American nuclear powered Aircraft Carriers are already positioned, and are accounted for in our invasion plans, once we open our attacks on South Korea, Japan and Hong Kong." The old Chairman sat back in his chair and then folded his arms across his chest, and he stared at his two Ministers. It was a warning sign that did not go unnoticed be either Chinese politicians. The Minister of Defense allowed the Minister of Naval Affairs to carry the ball and continue his report, "Mr. Chairman, the amount of air traffic and radio messages we're receiving..."

"That you cannot understand? As you have just stated to me!" the Chairman growled at him.

"Yes Mr. Chairman, this is true we cannot decipher any of their god dom communications as of yet, sir. But what we have been able to determine all points to this new and undiscovered American Aircraft Carrier is either much larger than any other Aircraft Carrier in the American Fleet, sir. Or this is some sort of a sham the loathsome American Military Command is trying to playing against us, sir. We have no real intelligence on a so called Super Aircraft Carrier in the American arsenal if it truly exists or not, and we see no other reason for the loathsome Americans trying to make us believe they have such a ship available to them.

"We have no idea what the devil the hated Americans might be up to with this god cursed deception, if it is a deception they're trying to pull off against us, sir. However Chairman Cheng-yu, we have sent out a submarine, but the submarine was driven off by a superior force of American surface warships. We also tried to have a submarine get in the path of a good number of these oncoming American warships, but the foul submarine was detected and was also driven off again. So we then employed our Ocean going Junks and we have..."

"Foolish Minister, I was the one who gave permission for that operation to take place, sir. So I'm fully aware about this god dom submarine of ours being driven off by the hated American warships, and I still don't see what the problem is concerning this possible other so believed American Aircraft

Carrier the cursed Americans might have, and it might have been moved somewhere near the miserable Island of lowly mongrels of Taiwan."

The concerned Minister took a quick breath for himself, because he understood full well there was no sense holding back anything now, as he added to his report to the Chinese Leader, "Mr. Chairman, we have a report we obtained from one of our spies operating within the foul United States, sir. He has reported the god dom Americans have developed some kind of a Floating Island type warship, and they're also in the process of deploying this supposed Floating Island in this god dom operation aimed against us, sir."

The Chairman suddenly sat forward in his chair and then he stared hard and long at his Minister for a few moments as he snarled at him, "do you have any other information about this supposed Floating Island ship you have just offer me, Minister?" His face showing some concern. An Island base would severely hamper, maybe even stop the plans he had for China.

"Mr. Chairman, our operative working in the United States has reported this so called Floating Island. If it truly exists mind you, Mr. Chairman. Is reported to have enough weapons and military forces based on the foul thing, to wage a three week war from. Everything the foolish Americans would need to wage a successful war from, is believed to be stored on board this one supposed massive ship stationed somewhere off the coast of Formosa. Aircraft, tanks, troops, fuel, food, water facilities, everything the Americans may need is supposed to be part of this new Aircraft Carrier, sir. But I find this spy's foolish words rather hard to believe for myself, sir. I feel and I truly believe all he has offered to us, is impossible to accomplish, even for the foul Americans. The hated Americans are good, but to build such a ship as this one the great fool has reported to us might be, I believe is completely impossible and out of the question, sir."

Chairman Cheng-yu rose to his feet and then he started to pace around the room as he growled nastily at the Minister, "we have to find out if this report is true, do we not Minister?" He rubbed his chin with his cold hand as he went deep in thought for a moment. Then he sat down and stared at his Ministers and then ordered him. "I want you to order two of our fighter aircraft up, and have them search this entire area in question, until they can either confirm or deny the existence of this believed to be Super Aircraft Carrier, Island thing of the American military, sir. These god dom pilots are to disregard any and all Commands from the Americans to veer off until they have established if the presence of this supposed Super Carrier is true. The pilots shall keep going until they have either seen this supposed great warship, or they get shot down." Chairman Cheng-yu then sat back and watched as the two Ministers quickly left the office.

A specially ordered flight of two Chinese Shenyang F-12 B fighter aircraft, made from the body of the older and outdated Russian Mig-23 Flogger, immediately lifted off from the airbase stationed at Tungshaw, China. The two aircraft were specially equipped with a pair of extra belly fuel tanks, and also lacked much of their usual armament, in order to ensure the two aircraft could make it out to their assigned target area, and then have enough fuel to search the area in question for a reasonable amount of time, before being forced to leave for need of fuel.

A Russian built in flight refueling tanker, was scheduled to refuel the pair of Chinese aircraft during their homeward flight back to their base in China. The Chinese aircraft flew just south of the Island of Taiwan, and they steered well clear of the American Carrier Battle Group lead by the Eisenhower, stationed so near the Island of Taiwan.

Radar units from the Aircraft Carrier Eisenhower and all her support ships instantly picked up the Chinese flight, but the two aircraft stayed well out of the claimed hundred mile threat zone of the Aircraft Carrier. So the four F-18 Ready Air Cap Hornets sent out from the Eisenhower to intercept the two Chinese fighter aircraft, never saw hide or hair of the two planes coming or going from their area of assigned responsibility.

CHAPTER 25
ON BOARD THE VINEGAR JOE PLATFORM

Flight Commander Paul Sanders moved a little closer to the radar screen inside the CIC. The radar officer of the E-2 Hawkeye with the call name of 'Eight Ball', informed the CIC operator of the two unidentified Zappers rapidly approaching the Platform from the southwest.

"Who the fuck are these two birds, and what the hell do they want coming this close to us Eight Ball, dammit?" The CIC radar operator barked at the Hawkeye radar operator.

The overcrowded CIC unit was just a jumble of radar screens, clear plastic plotting and threat boards, computers, radios, sonar scopes and a mess of sailors and soldiers smoking, talking and plotting the two inbound aircraft course, while marking where the American aircraft were in the sky. A Seaman marked the plotting board with a white grease pencil, showing the exact course and distance the two inbounds were at, away from the Vinegar Joe Platform's present position.

"Eight Ball, this is Homeplate. Can you get a stinking visual on the damn pair of possible inbounds yet sir? Over." Flight Commander Sanders roared in the radio after taking Command from his radar operator, and he was now responding to Eight Ball's reports.

"Homeplate, Eight Ball. That's a negative on that request at this time, sir. The twin inbounds are too far out as yet for me to make any kind of positive ID on the inbounds, sir. Over."

There were two large E-2 Hawkeye early warning radar aircraft circling overhead the Platform twenty four hours a day. Eight Ball was orbiting at thirty six thousand feet, while the second Hawkeye aircraft was circling at thirty four thousand feet. The plane's radar was strong enough for the aircraft to detect any approaching aircraft, missiles or surface ships, for a range of up two hundred and fifty square miles out, using the Platform as dead center of their scope.

Flight Commander Sanders checked out his chart, and picked up Admiral Owens was dining with General Campanelli, and Colonel Salsiccia. He did not want to interrupt the General's meal on him over Eight Ball's reports. He was kind of hoping the twin inbound planes would soon veer off, before they entered the first zone of defense of the Platform. He glanced at the threat board again, the two inbounds were currently thirty miles from the first zone of defense. The Flight Commander was searching his mind as to what the aircraft might be up to, and who they belonged to. His thoughts were suddenly shattered by a voice on the radio.

"Homeplate, Eight Ball. I have a positive ID on the twin inbounds, sir. I mark them as two Mig-23C Floggers, or they could even be the Chinese Shenyang F-12 B aircraft, sir. Both Chinese aircraft are almost identical in structure, and are hard to call, sir. In this case I'd bet the barn the inbounds are Shenyangs, sir. They're on a direct intercept course with the Platform, and will pierce the first defensive zone within two minutes, sir. I repeat sir, two minutes. Over."

"Dammit to hell, Eight Ball, Homeplate. Can you tell if the aircraft are armed sir? Over."

"Armed. I see their markings now sir. They're Chinese all right Homeplate. Over."

"Eight Ball, Homeplate. Launching Ready Air One and Two to intercept the inbounds, sir. The Flight Lieutenant in Command of Ready Cap's call name's Baseball One and Two. They're F/A-18C Hornets, I want to leave the Air Cap over the Platform where they are, sir. Over."

"Roger that last, copy same as called Homeplate. Call's Baseball's One and Two, sir. We'll control the Ready Air Cap from here, sir. Out."

The moment the Flight Commander stopped speaking to the Hawkeye Radar surveillance aircraft radar operator, he immediately hit the scramble button, and in mere seconds later. Two sleek F/A 18C Hornets shot off the massive flight deck of the Vinegar Joe, afterburners hot.

Eight Ball instantly picked up the aircraft as they climbed in the sky and the Commander made contact with the pair of Hornets. "Baseball One, Eight Ball. Targets running at

Angels Thirty Seven and are traveling at Mach One point Two. Coming in fast from south, southeast, sir."

"Baseball One to Eight Ball. Copy that last sir, I got'em already, I have them on the scope now, sir. Over." The pilot Lieutenant Roberts, replied as he brought up the HUD (Heads Up Display) and then put his targeting and attack computer on line.

Admiral Owens sixth sense told him something was up and he offered with a bit of concern in his voice, "Err... excuse me a second will you please General Campanelli Sir." As he threw his napkin on the table and then added, "I have to see what the devil's going on in the CIC Chamber, sir. I believe we might have just launched Ready One and Two for some reason, sir."

"By all means do Admiral Owens Sir. Do you want any company Admiral?"

Admiral Owens removed the phone he carried, and rang the CIC center. Sanders answered.

"Good, Commander Sanders, Admiral Owens here sir. Did we just launch the Ready Air Cap from the flight deck, mister? And if so, why?"

"Err... yes Sir Admiral Owens Sir. Ready Cap's on an intercept with two Chinese Shenyang F-12 Bs, and they're armed, sir. The inbounds just entered the rim of Zone One Defense, sir."

"Jesus Christ, go to GQ immediately, launch Ready Flight Three, and notify all support ships for a possible intercept situation here, sir. Where the hell's the Washington at mister?"

"Admiral Owens Sir, the Carrier's presently positioned to the south in the zone, and so is the Eisenhower at this present time, Admiral Owens Sir."

Admiral Owens had to wait before he answered, because the mess area and Platform was being assaulted by the God awful blaring horn, followed by a Boatswains Mate screaming into the intercom system, "General Quarters, General Quarters. All hands man your battle stations. This is not a drill. General Quarters, General Quarters, fire watch to your stations, I repeat."

General Campanelli jumped up and placed his hand on the Admiral's shoulder, and then he asked him in a concerned voice. "What the fuck's up Bear?"

"General Campanelli Sir, we have a pair of inbounds, fucking armed Chinese, and they're entering the first zone of defense for the Platform system, sir."

"Shit!" the General growled angrily as he and the Admiral sprinted off for the CIC Chamber. Admiral Owens was the first one to enter the center and he immediately called out, "Commander Sanders, report present situation on those two damn inbound Chinese aircraft, mister?"

"Admiral Owens Sir, the two inbounds are still coming directly at us at this present time, sir."

General Campanelli noticed Aleksandra sitting in the CIC and he grumbled at her angrily, "I see you finally landed, little miss smartass. Why didn't you do like I told you to do, dammit?"

"Because I order take seat and monitor computer terminal first, General Grouch Sir."

"You always have a fucking excuse huh, Twin Towers." Edward grunted back at her angrily.

She turned her head away from him and went back to her work station again.

"Jesus Christ Almighty, what's the stinking status of the damn defense systems of the friggin Platform?" Admiral Owens spat at Sanders this time.

"Admiral Owens Sir, all RAM missile systems are up and on line and good to go, sir."

The RAM system was the rolling airframe, a box of twelve small intercept missiles that defended the surface ships from any sea skimming anti ship cruise missiles.

"The ten ASROC systems are also up and on line and ready for action, Admiral Owens Sir."

These were the anti sub missile systems stationed on the Platform for added defense.

"All eight CIWS are armed and ready for defensive purposes sir."

The CIWS, or Close In Weapon System also referred to as the Phalanx, fired 76/62 HE-PFF, a fragmentation shell with a proximity fuse which exploded when the shell got close to its target.

"Admiral Owens Sir, all contact and defensive computers are up and on line and are active, sir, and sonar's activated and pinging away also, sir."

"Any fucking word from the damn inbounds? Are they in trouble sir? Are they requesting political asylum? Anything coming in from them rotten bastards, Commander Sanders?"

"Not a damn peep, Admiral. The Chinese pilot's are not responding to any of our radio contacts, we know they're picking us up though, sir. We tried a game, and made false contacts with fighter aircraft s supposed to be off to their right, and the inbounds immediately changed course to give the fakes a wide birth, which proves they hear and understand our hails, sir."

"Okay, we know they're listening to us, warn them again. Let'em know they're entering a secured defensive zone, and they're about to be shot down, sir." Admiral Owens ordered hotly.

Sanders did as ordered. "No response from inbounds. Either they can't, or won't respond, sir."

"Okay, we have some time left to us yet, so there's no sense with pushing any panic buttons at this precise time. Can the Hornets see the damn inbounds yet, Commander Sanders?"

"Yes sir, the Hornets have them in their sight sir," Sanders replied smartly to the Admiral.

"Jesus H. Christ, tell them to back the damn inbounds the fuck off of us then, dammit."

Commander Sanders immediately keyed the mike and bellowed into it. "Baseball One, this is Homeplate, sir. You're instructed to back the Chinese inbounds off us, sir. Out."

"Homeplate, Baseball One. Copy that last, have a good eyeball the two Chinese inbounds at this time, will warn them off in no uncertain terms, sir. Out."

Admiral Owens turned to General Campanelli and complained at him, "Jesus Christ sir, I wish to hell and back again I knew what these assholes were up to out there, sir."

The aircraft branded Baseball One pulled up to the first Shenyang aircraft, and he tried to get the Chinese pilot's attention. The American pilot waved frantically, but the Chinese pilot completely ignored his efforts. The Flight Captain then moved his wings up and down next. Still no response came from the Chinese pilot. Exasperated, he called home. "Baseball One to Homeplate. Either this asshole's blind, or dumb or both sir. He won't even look at my ass, sir."

"Baseball, Homeplate. I want you to do a flyby. Make it close, I want you to get this asshole's attention. Make it close so he understands what you want, sir. Back this sonofabitch off us."

"Will do as ordered, Baseball Out," the Baseball pilot banked his fighter aircraft hard to his left, and smacked his throttles to afterburner in the same motion. He did an offset head on pass directly at the Chinese plane, and then he pulled a mile ahead of the slower flying Shenyang aircraft. Then he came back and shot across the bow of the Shenyang at Mach Two point Five. This dangerous move made the Shenyang aircraft waver, but it did not alter its course.

"Baseball to Homeplate. We just hit our bingo state at this present time, sir. Over."

"Roger that Baseball. I have a KA-6D Aerial tanker on station for you, fuel's no problem sir."

"Baseball to Homeplate. Roget your last. Man, this guy's thick as shit sir. Famished. Over."

General Campanelli turned and asked the young Airman who happened to be standing behind him, what the pilot meant by the word famished.

"Sir, Famished means he needs additional instructions from us, General Campanelli Sir."

"I knew that mister," the General replied as he smiled back at the Airman.

"Stand by Baseball One. Commander Sanders, how far out are the damn inbounds at this point, sir?" Admiral Owens demanded from the radar operator.

"The two inbounds are eighty six miles out, and closing fast on us, Admiral Owens Sir."

"Yeah, okay, fine. This is what I want you to do, Commander Sanders. At seventy five miles out, order Baseball to fire a Sparrow missile across the bow of the lead inbound aircraft. Then Baseball's ordered to veer off, and let them think that one over for a little while. If the inbounds don't back off at the sixty five mile marker. The Hornets are cleared to splash the damn inbounds. There's no further radio communications needed from or to Baseball at this time."

"Yes sir." Sanders replied as he contacted Baseball and he relayed all the Admiral's orders.

Baseball's pilot stationed his aircraft four hundred yards off the right wing of the lead Chinese Shenyang aircraft, and then he counted off the miles. General Campanelli and Admiral Owens both listened to the communications between Homeplate and Baseball flight.

"Crossing." Baseball One pilot informed Baseball Two pilot, meaning he was changing his position on him so they did not get involved in a mid-air crash between the two aircraft.

"Beacon on and warning at this time, Roger that last as received, Baseball Two. Over."

"Baseball One, Homeplate. Where the hell are you at the present time, mister? Over."

"I'm cruising at Angels Three Eight Thousand feet sir, and am dropping down to Angels Three Seven now sir. Over." The lead American aircraft pilot reported to his Command.

"Roger that last as received, keep me advised of your present situation, sir. Out."

At exactly seventy five miles out from the Vinegar Joe Platform, Baseball One fingered the trigger on his control stick, and a sleek white Sparrow missile instantly dropped off the right wing rack, and it went soaring directly across the windshield of the Chinese aircraft at over Mach Four. The thin vapor stream left no doubt in the mind of the Chinese pilot he just received the final warning from the American pilots flying so near his aircraft.

The Chinese pilot looked around the sky now frantically, trying to locate the shooter.

"Baseball One to Homeplate. That got the lousy little bastard's attention but quick, sir. That was a good call because I think the Chink pilot just shit himself, sir. Over."

The Chinese pilot placed a call to his control, and informed the Commander he was just fired on by a stalking American fighter aircraft. He was ordered to ignore the missile and to continue on with his mission. A fatal mistake, the Chinese pilots armed their missiles next.

"Baseball One this is Two. Inbounds have just armed their fucking missiles, sir. They're going active on us, sir! Requesting permission to engage the enemy inbounds, sir. Over."

"Roger that, weapons are free (Fire on any enemy aircraft) Laser tracking working, locked on target, enemy's taking evasive action, sir. Too late sucker, your ass is grass and I'm the fucking lawnmower, so kiss it good-bye, buddy. Distance out, Two."

"Baseball One, this is Baseball Two. At the sixty five mile mark out sir, and the two inbounds are still coming at us but fast, sir. Over." The second pilot informed his Flight Commander.

"Baseball Two, this is One. Roger that last, Fox away, Fox Two, Fox Two. Fox on the way sir. Over." The pilot of Baseball One just fired the kill missile at the inbound Chinese aircraft.

A deadly Sidewinder missile streaked the sky, and it instantly killed the now running lead Chinese aircraft. As the Baseball One aircraft did a quick victory roll while still moving away from the trailing enemy plane, he heard in his head set.

"Baseball One, this is Baseball Two, Fox Two, Fox Two away, sir. Out." The second enemy aircraft immediately disintegrated while still in flight.

"Baseball One to Homeplate. Grand Slam. I repeat sir, Grand Slam, sir. Splash two! I say again, Splash Two sir. Both enemy aircraft have been eliminated at this time, sir. Out."

Commander Sanders keyed the mike and then he offered to the Baseball One pilot. "Good job Baseball One and Two. Exxon's hovering overhead at Angel's Forty Five Thousand. Fuel up, and then get back to base immediately, sirs. Well done. I repeat, well done gentlemen. Out."

Baseball One immediately headed for the fuel tanker aircraft. As he pulled up behind the tanker aircraft, he noticed it had a painting of a charging Bengal Tiger on its tail, thus the name Exxon. The co-pilot of the KA-6D tanker opened the radio communication with the pilot. "The hell with a little pussy in your tank, try a little tail in the air, sir. Fill her up sir?"

Admiral Owens laughed as he ordered the closest Destroyer in the area of the downed planes, to search and pickup any survivors. At least two chutes had been reported by Baseball One.

BEIJING CHINA: THE OFFICE OF THE CHAIRMAN

The Chinese Minister of Defense informed the Chinese Chairman their two aircraft were ordered to continue their flight. Even though the aircraft were just fired on by American pilots sent out to intercept them. "There are four more American fighter aircraft heading for our two planes, sir. We'll lose them to the hated American aircraft. Our two aircraft don't have a chance with six American warplanes prepared to attack them, Mr. Chairman."

The Chairman did some quick thinking, and then he remarked to his Minister, "contact the American Command at once, and inform them this flight is an unauthorized flight, and they are to take any steps necessary to protect their warships. Of course, you'll delay this message until our pilots have seen what these sneaky tit sucking American fools are up to, and they reported back to us about it. The planes and their pilots are expendable for this mission, Minister."

ON BOARD THE VINEGAR JOE PLATFORM

General Edward Campanelli immediately sent a Flash message out to General William Weidenbacher, the Chairman of the Joint Chiefs of Staff. Informing him of what he classified as an attack on his ships by two Chinese armed fighter/r aircraft. The General was immediately cut off in the middle of the complaint by the calm speaking Chairman of the Joint Chiefs.

"Calm down a little there General Campanelli Sir, because we just received a Flash message from the Chinese Command, and they informed us this was an unauthorized flight. I think the two Chinese pilots were trying to defect or something like that, sir."

"That 'something' is the part that worries the shit outta my ass, General Weidenbacher Sir." General Campanelli interrupted and then went on, "I don't think this was an unauthorized flight in the least. The damn Chinese knew sure as hell what these two aircraft were up to, sir."

General Weidenbacher interrupted his extremely upset military officer a second time as he offered. "I agree with you General, I think the Chinese caught wind of our Platform, and they were willing to sacrifice two of their aircraft to see if what they heard is true. I know they weren't planning to attack the Platform, that move had to be the furthest thing from their minds. I'm quite certain this flight was strictly a recon mission, and nothing more than that General Weidenbacher. I hope the damn English didn't let the cat out of the bag about my ship out here sir. I warned their Admiral Middleton not to inform the Chinese about the Platform's existence."

"I don't think so. I spoke with Admiral Middleton, and he has assured me he was zip lipped about this operation, sir. The English want us in their corner, just in case something goes wrong with their new Chinese fucking friends, sir. They don't trust their Chinese friends either I see."

"True, I agree General Campanelli Sir. What the hell are you doing right now, sir?"

"Running some fighter aircraft training missions, and the Marines are working up a good lather exercising on deck. I want assholes and elbows doing something on the Platform, sir."

"Ed, have you been able to identify any Armies the Chinese have fighting in North Korea yet?"

"Yes sir, we located all their active Armies used in their invasion of North Korea, sir. I'll give you a complete run down at this time if you like, General Weidenbacher Sir."

"Go, I should've had this information reported to me already, General Campanelli Sir. I warn you sir, don't allow any damn grass to grow under your feet on this one, or you'll pay hell for it, sir. These damn Chinese buggers can do anything they set their minds on, and we're the only force in the fire region powerful enough to stop them, sir. If we remain on our toes that is, mister. Report sir." General Weidenbacher suddenly snapped rather angrily in the radio, his voice was weighed down heavily with both sarcasm and anger.

General Campanelli took a quick breath, he did not like the General being cross with him as he replied, "General

Weidenbacher Sir, elements of the 11th Group Army supported by one hundred and fifty tanks, one Motorized Division, and one Infantry Division from the 15th Group Army encircled the city of Hamjongni. While elements of the 21st Group Army consisting of on Tank Division backed by two Infantry Divisions, are currently marching towards the Naval port of Nampo. Two Destroyers are pounding the crap outta the city from the sea. Panmunjom, Haeju and Changyon have been taken by the Chinese lead elements, a mix Army of the 13th and 14th Group Army backed by 3rd Army. Also the South Korean VIII Corps sir, with two Infantry Divisions, and VII Infantry Brigade, along with the 1st and 2nd Armies of South Korea, General. Two Mechanized Divisions, and 1st Marine and the 11th Infantry Division.

"These combined military Divisions of Chinese and South Korean Armies are attempting to linkup together with the leading elements of Chinese Armies attacking the North Korean city of Nampo. If they're successful in this effort, they'll completely cut off North Korea from two sides, actually three, General Weidenbacher Sir. From the north along the Chinese, Korean border, along the west coast of North Korea, and from the border of North and South Korea.

"The North Korean's could be starved to death, if they aren't careful, sir. We have reports certain elements of the Chinese Army are working down the east coast, and if this is completed, the strangle hold the Chinese would have on North Korea would be comprehensive, General Weidenbacher. Then, all they have to do is sit back and wait for the North Koreans to slowly starve to death, which wouldn't take very long General. Knowing the Chinese tactics they'll close the damn noose, until they have completed what they set out to do, sir. I feel they want to eliminate North Korea from the face of the earth." General

Campanelli stopped talking and took a sip of water, giving General Weidenbacher the time to respond to his analysis.

General Weidenbacher listened to his General's report intensely, his index finger lightly tapping his desk as he complained, "General Campanelli, you have any reports on the status of the damn North Korean Army, sir? How they're faring under this massive Chinese attack, sir?"

General Campanelli quickly shuffled through a number of papers, and then he reported to his Commanding Officer. "Here they are sir. The North Korean Army's not holding up very well against these combined attacks aimed against them, sir. I have a report stating the North Korean XIV Combined Arms Corps and III and V Mechanized Corps defending the west coast, were completely destroyed. We have no idea if any prisoners were taken. I fear not many sir."

General Weidenbacher let out with a low whistle and then he grumbled at his General, "shit, over one hundred thousand North Korean troops are gone, sir."

"Plus all their damn military equipment as well in this attack, General Weidenbacher Sir." General Campanelli added with some caution in his voice this time.

"Damn, any more bad news you have for me today?" General Weidenbacher asked hotly.

"Yes, afraid so General Weidenbacher, four tanks and five Mechanized Brigades, and the 4th Army Artillery North Korean Brigades sir, were totally wiped out, along with three regular, and two type B North Korean Infantry Reserve Divisions were wiped out by the rapidly advancing Chinese troops, sir. This leaves the North Korean Western Strike Force, with just one Motorized Division, and the remains of two others still left intact, General. No Tank Divisions, but three Mechanized, two Infantry Divisions, and one type B Infantry Division, along with two Brigades of the Special

Purpose Corps are left to the North Korean Command to defend the western and northern coasts, and the damn border with China, a monumental task for them, sir.

"Elements from the North Korean Central and Eastern Forces are being moved around, but these areas have their own problems to deal with, General. I don't think the North Koreans will move many of their remaining Armies from these few positions, leaving their flanks open to a seaborne attack. This would leave the entire country open to being overrun by the combined Chinese and South Korean ground forces almost uncontested, General Weidenbacher Sir."

"I can't believe I'm feeling a bit sorry for the damn North Korean troops on this one, Edward. I always hated the North Koreans because they were so damn hard to communicate with. But I never wanted their entire nation to be wiped off the face of the earth. Damn, we should've never agreed to what China was offering us." Weidenbacher complained, he stared at the image of General Campanelli for a moment then asked, "what are the English doing with the Chinese?"

"General Weidenbacher Sir, they're flying a number of sorties from the west, by aircraft from the Ark Royal, and the Invincible, sir. I requested Admiral Middleton come out to the Platform for a quick question and answer visit, but he declined, stating he was busy sir."

"I can understand that shit easy enough Ed," General Weidenbacher griped back at him.

"The aircraft from the two English Carriers are pounding the radar and communication centers, and electrical plants of North Korea, sir. The English destroyed the two nuclear power plants in Nampo. Reports of radiation escaping from one crippled plant in Pyongyang only partially destroyed by the British attacks. The English aircraft destroyed the nuclear research and uranium processing plant, and pounded the uranium mines at Yongbyon, and the British aircraft are now concentrating their efforts by turning their attentions against the nuclear power plants constructed at the North Korean cities of Taechon and Sinpo. Along with the uranium processing plant stationed at Kusong. Other reports we have been able to pick up, state the uranium processing and mine, are under heavy attack by the English warplanes, sir. It seems the Chinese are allowing the British to work over all the North Korean nuclear facilities and mines for them, sir.

"We just sent a Flash message out to Admiral Middleton, demanding he send his aircraft back and completely destroy the nuclear processing plant they only crippled, sir. The English are also concentrating their efforts on destroying the major bridges and roads in this region of North Korea, in an effort to try and cut off any possible North Korean reinforcements from reaching the trapped Armies of the Western Army Group. Looks like the plans of the Chinese, English, and South Koreans have been well thought out here on this one, sir. They're stealing some pages from our workbook during the Desert Storm war, sir. Conforming to a grid bombing pattern, and they're employing their aircraft to soften up the fortified ground positions of the North Korean troops, before committing their own ground forces to their ground attack on the North, sir."

"Where the hell's the North Korean airforce at dammit? They had over a thousand fighter aircraft they brought from the damn Russians, and they had a pretty fair size airforce beforehand as reported, General Campanelli." General Weidenbacher growled and then added, "what the hell are they holding back for, dammit? What the fuck do they want to do, save their damn aircraft? It's now or never for them. Doesn't their Command realize this shit, sir?"

"General Weidenbacher Sir, most of their aircraft were caught on the ground, a number of the planes headed for South Korea, and their pilots were arrested as they landed, and their aircraft confiscated. The English are making short work of the rest of the North Korean airforce, sir. China's SAM missile batteries have been devastating on the aircraft they can get at. For all intents and purposes sir, the North Korean airforce no longer exists, and the North Korean Navy's about destroyed as well, sir. There are a few ships still afloat, but the Chinese and English ships are dogging the hell outta them, sir. A few of the North Korean ships requested, and received permission to port in Japan. The Korean submarine fleet's the only effective attack force they still have left pretty much intact. The submarines are raising some kind of hell with the Chinese and English ships, sir. They sunk one Chinese Destroyer, and a number of their Frigates, they're successfully dodging the Chinese and British ships assigned to their pursuit sir."

"I'm damn glad we're just spectators on this one for now, General Campanelli Sir."

"Yes, but for how long is that going to be the fact, General Weidenbacher Sir?"

"As long as we can be General Campanelli Sir. The North Koreans are crying for a special meeting of the Security Council, and it looks like they're going to get it some time next week. Once we're talking to their Diplomats, we'll know a helluva more about what's truly going on. Until then, we sit and watch, sir. I'll stay in touch with you, you're doing all you can, General. Keep the fighter aircraft up, and the Marines on their damn toes, sir. I want a written report on the Chinese troop positions, and keep me informed of all events as they happen, General. You have the power to fire at any ship, aircraft or soldier who fires on any American, or

Allied forces, sir."   With this remark said, General Weidenbacher broke off the communication.

General Campanelli suddenly leaned back in his chair, and then he let out his breath in a rush, as he slowly ran his right hand over his forehead.

"You look all done in sir. Why don't you catch up on some shut eye, Ed. We'll takeover for a while, and if something happens. I'll have you sent for on the double quick." John offered.

"You got a good point there my friend, I'm gonna shower and then hit the hay for a little while John." General Campanelli started out of the CIC, but before he left he looked for Aleksandra. She was nowhere to be found. He was to tired to ask about her and headed for the showers. He allowed the hot water to run on his face as he leaned against the steel wall with one hand, and then lowered his head and had the water beat on his neck. It felt good, he let out a groan as his body relaxed. He toweled off and headed for his room naked. No one passed him, and he did not care if someone did. He opened his door only to bump into the table covered with food. Aleksandra sat on his bunk, naked except for a robe which hung loosely over her shoulders.

"I looked for you before I left the CIC Chamber, I was wondering where you went off too."

"Knew come you room back, you no eat much well past three day now, my lover. I no let you sleep before you ate something good to keep up you strength for you, mista." She said as she stood and then placed her hands on her hips and stared at him.

"Eat what?" General Campanelli laughed as he looked at her long, slender and muscular legs.

She purred and offered. "I leave you imagination mista." She widened her stance so he could see all what she wanted him to see. "I think should have some eat might fill you stomach first."

Campanelli sat on the fold down chair and said, "I gotta thank the mess Sergeant for this one."

Again, she placed her hands on her hips as she faked being angry with the General as she offered him with a smirk on her face. "Thank mess Sergeant bullshitty! I go down mess myself, and I had cook prepare especially you for mista to eat proper good okay. I place on cart by hand and push here self with own hand, sir. You thank me Mr. Wiseguy General Sir."

Campanelli stared at her, her breasts looked great pointing up like they did as she stood with her hands resting on her hips. "Pardon me." He said as he took a steak and he put it on his plate.

"You take some vegetable also too mista. You need them make healthy good again General."

"Yes mummy," General Campanelli laughed as he put two pieces of carrots on his plate, and then he popped the top of his Pepsi and took a good swallow of the cold soda.

Aleksandra sat down on the edge of the bed, and she allowed the robe to fall away from her shoulders and come to rest on her arms. She filled her own plate with food.

"You're making it mighty hard for me to eat like this Alex." The General smirked back at her.

"You no comfortable enough. I move cart away you have more room little if like me to do."

"No Alex, I think you might have misunderstood me. I mean, you're making it mighty hard for me to eat like this, honey." He motioned with his chin at her lovely breasts.

She blushed and looked down and then giggled pleasantly. She knew what she was doing, and she was having a good time doing it. After eating the General felt a little better, and he was ready to enjoy her fine treasures. He shoved the cart to the side as his towel fell to the floor.

She howled at the condition Edward's member was in, standing at full attention now as he rapidly moved in on her. He grabbed her around the waist and then pulled her down on the bunk. He cursed as he bumped his knee on the metal rail, and then he jumped her bones. They made love then slept wrapped up tight in each other's arms. She awoke in the middle of the night, and started giving him some head to try and arouse him, because she was a little horny still. They made love for a second time. It was the best night of sleep and sex the General had enjoyed ever since the Chinese had first invaded North Korea.

DAY FOUR OF THE FIGHTING.
FEBRUARY 23rd, 1997: MONDAY

Many other countries joined India in her demands the fighting and slaughter occurring in North Korea be stop immediately. India went so far as to even threaten to join forces with North Korea against China, if the fighting did not cease instantly. Pakistan, Burma, and Thailand along with Mongolia and Tibet, also threatened to join India if she attacked China. Both Mongolia and Tibet would do anything to give China fits, and these two s mall nations felt they owed it to North Korea, and they offer their full support, even if it was only in words.

Russia became extremely concerned about the heavy fighting taking place so close to the border with their nation. There were fifteen different skirmishes taking place between Russian and a number of Chinese border guards. One skirmish was so severe in nature that the American Rangers stationed on the border, had to join in helping the

Russian guards fend off the strong Chinese probe of their defenses. Russia launched an official complaint with the United Nations over the Chinese troops firing at the Russians border defenders.

Russia took steps to heavily reinforce her border, and this move caused the President of the United States to become deeply concerned over the heavy military buildup on the Russian side of the border. President Cole sent a request for a special meeting with the Chinese Chairman to take place at the earliest possible moment. The worried American Leader got a run-around from the Chinese, promising the meeting would take place in the next two weeks, but he pressured the Chinese for a exact date and the Chinese leadership finally gave in. The meeting would be held in two weeks on March 23rd, 1997 a Monday. President Cole was angry at how long he would have to wait, and he informed the Chinese he was not very pleased over the amount of time before their meeting. It had no effect on the outcome, the date remained the same.

FIGHTING IN NORTH KOREA:
THE FOURTH DAY

Elements of the Chinese 21st Group Army, met up with the Chinese 13th and 14th Group Armies, and they immediately tightened their stranglehold on the besieged North Korean city of Nampo. The Chinese and South Korean forces successfully cut off the North Korean soldiers and civilians from the west coast. The North Korean cities of Unggi, Onsong, Chongson, Hoeryong, Musan, Puryong, Hyesan, Chasong, Manpo and Wiwon were completely overran, and the Chinese forces were in total control of this entire region of North Korea. Pictures came flooding in to the CIC unit of the Platform, displaying a number of long, wide, open trenches hastily dug in the earth by bulldozers, and forced labor from the North Korean prisoners.

The Chinese troops continued on with this mass murder unabated in the open, and under the vision of American satellites, recon flights, and countless eye witness. News reporters from FOX, CBS, CNN, and the Washington Post, transmitted film of the fighting taking place in North Korea. One film crew made their way to a slight knoll overlooking the new killing fields, and filmed the Chinese soldiers lining up hundreds of North Korean soldiers and civilians alike, and then machine gunning them to death. The bodies not falling directly in the pit when shot, were unceremoniously kicked into it by the angry Chinese soldiers. The disclosure of this film prompted the Chinese government to place a bounty on any new reporters caught in North Korea. Other than that, the Chinese military and Command completely ignored the world's disgust over the mass killings. The only time any Chinese Commanders acknowledged the mass killing, was with a quick note passed to a reporter from CBS news stationed in China.

China sent a hand written complaint to the United Nations viva the news reporter: The world complains China is slaughtering civilian, and many nations now view the Chinese government under a different microscope than it did the Serbs of what used to be Yugoslavia. The government of China warns the people of the world, until the eyes of the world opens to all killings of the world. Then the eyes of the world should not be looking at only China. This was a war, unlike the so called war in Bosnia being waged mostly against only civilians of that nation.

The reporter gave the hand written note to the United States Ambassador, and he in return sent in on to

Washington. The President did not allow the note be shown to the general public.

When the three large Chinese Armies finally linked up together, the fighting seemed to lessen some throughout the entire of North Korea. The massive Chinese Armies waited for the rest of their troops to reach their assigned positions, before starting their march inland to destroy the complete nation of North Korea. Meanwhile, on the east coast of North Korea, other elements of the Chinese 11th Group Army backed by the 35th Group Army, started down the eastern coast of North Korea, in the final attempt to cut off the entire North Korea country from the outside world. These rapidly advancing Chinese Armies were being assisted by a newly organized Chinese Army Group trying to come up from South Korea side on the east coast. The Chinese 9th Group Army consisting of four full Infantry Divisions, and the 23rd Group Army including one full Tank Division and a heavy Motorized, and two Mechanized Divisions, along with the 1st South Korean Army, attacked in force the port city of Kosong in the North.

What remained of the North Korean Army realized what the Chinese forces were attempting to do against them, and they reacted against it. The North Korean soldiers took to firing Scud missiles with HE (High Explosive) warheads at the invading Chinese Army from the south. The missile attack took a staggering toll on the invading army. Within hours of heavy fighting, nine thousand dead or wounded Chinese and South Korean soldiers lay scattered on the ground.

The North Korean Command ordered their remaining Scud missile systems to be fitted with their few nuclear warheads. These few warheads were of the low yield capable of destroying only five square miles of the earth.

The American satellites instantly detected the activity at the North Korean nuclear research facilities still operational in the nation, and realized the North Koreans might resort to the use of their own nuclear weapons against the Chinese invaders.

Washington sent a Flash message out to the English Command, and warned them of this latest fear. The English Command ordered their Aircraft Carriers further off the coast of North Korea. The United States started its debate on whether or not to inform the Chinese government.

THE SITUATION ROOM OF THE WHITE HOUSE, WASHINGTON D.C.

President Albert Cole sat in his chair in the Oval Office, his hair was a mess as he fumbled around with a small plastic ruler, absentmindedly bending it back and forth in his hands. He was waiting for the Security Director to bust ass over to the meeting. The Secretary of State, Maria Hernandez was already seated and she was speaking pleasantly to the Secretary of Defense, Jerry Levenhagen. Finally, the out of breath Security Director showed up and the President bitched at him in an angry tone of voice, "nice of you to attend this here meeting Mr. Griffin Sir."

"Sorry Mr. President Sir, I was attending a special meeting of the Joint Chiefs when you called for this special meeting, sir. General Weidenbacher's on his way also Mr. President Sir."

"We're not waiting for him, let's start this damn meeting. I called you all here, because I have evidence the North Koreans are preparing to employ their nuclear weapons against the Chinese forces." The President paused to allow this information to sink in. There was dead silence in the room, and the President looked to the Director of the CIA, "Mr. Raincloud Sir, this is your field of expertise I believe. Would you like to explain this information a bit further for us, sir?"

Director John Raincloud was a full blooded Indian, and he slowly rose and straightened out his jacket, and then walked over to the screen. The well respected Director picked up a wood pointer and then he turned to the Sergeant at Arms in the room and ordered. "Turn on the machine son."

The Sergeant instantly turned on the video system as Director Raincloud quickly scanned the many faces of the attendees at the meeting staring back at him. The Deputy Secretary of Defense, Harold C. Clifton, was still speaking privately with Manning.

"Gentlemen, ladies, if I could have your full attention for a moment please. Here we have five mobile missile launchers made in Russia. You can clearly see the North Korean technicians removing the warheads of the missiles. If you keep watching, you'll see a truck appear, ahhh, here it comes now. Watch, when the technicians remove the tarp covering the rear of the truck. Here. You can plainly see this is a nuclear warhead. We have enhanced the picture a might." A second screen came to life, and Raincloud moved over to it and pointed at the enlargement next.

"Here, you can plainly see the radiation insignia painted on the side of the warhead."

The Security Director interrupted the conversation between the President and the CIA Director as he offered, "is that shit the only evidence you have that it's a nuclear warhead the North Korean technicians are going to attach to one of their missiles, Director Raincloud Sir?"

"No, not really Mr. Griffin Sir, we also confirmed this by the warhead's shape as well."

The Secretary of Defense cut in this time and asked, "Mr. Raincloud Sir, why is it you're delivering this report to us? I thought it'd be delivered by the National Security Director, sir."

President Cole spoke up in Director Raincloud's defense, "I'm afraid you have to blame me for that one. Because I had the film go directly over to the CIA, because I wanted them to do the enhancements of this certain section of the damn film. Director Raincloud, please continue sir."

Director Raincloud nodded to the seated President, and then continued on with his report for the other members of the meeting. "Gentlemen, ladies, if you watch closely please, you'll see the North Korean technicians remove the installed warhead of this missile, and then place it on the wooden skid by a truck. There, now the truck containing the nuclear warhead moves in, here." The Director tapped the screen with the pointer stick as he clearly showed everyone at the meeting the truck move up against the launcher, and then he went on with his report.

"This is a rare moment to witness, a nuclear warhead actually being changed out in the open, in the field. Keep watching, here, there are more North Korean technicians starting work on the other missiles. The airforce backed up this video bird for us, so we could keep a close eye on the entire operation as it took place. We launched two other video birds, and the space shuttle Nova's being moved over to the launch pad to join the Discovery as I speak. They'll launch later on tonight, and will stay in space on the longest mission of any shuttles to date. Thirty days, longer if we need them, sir. Their task is to send down real time coverage of any action, or troop movement in North Korea, South Korea, and most of China. Getting back to the picture at hand gentlemen, ladies. Here, you see the North Korean technicians have the first new warhead set in place on this missile. We figure it'll take the North Korean technicians over two hours to install the hot warheads, and add another hour for them to remove the first warhead, sir."

"What the devil are we going to do about this new god damn situation you just brought up to our attention, Director Raincloud Sir. I don't think the world's ready for another such nuclear exchange, no matter how small the yield of the damn explosion might be, sir. A nuclear release is a nuclear release, sir. Not after what took place in the Middle East and Northern African war not even a year ago with nuclear and biological weapons, Mr. President." Ms. Hernandez hissed as she openly glared at the powerful CIA Director, and then waited his reply.

"There'll be no nuclear exchange this time around I assure you Ma'am, dammit. Once was more than enough for me to witness in my lifetime, Ma'am." The obviously upset President growled harshly as he turned his attention back to Director Raincloud.

"What the hell are we going to do about this new batch of information and threat then, Mr. President Sir? We can't possibly allow the North Korean troops to start attacking the Chinese troops with their damn nuclear weapons, sir. The Chinese will immediately reply in turn and the next thing we know, Russia will be pulled into their fricking conflict, and they too will be employing their own damn nuclear weapons against both of these warring Asian nations, Mr. President Sir." National Security Director Griffin called out while remaining seated.

President Cole let out his breath in a rush as he replied to Director Griffin's last question. "This is the reason why I invited you all here today. I wanted your input before I spoke to the Commander of our troops and military equipment stationed off the coast of Taiwan." The President looked at the screen and asked no one in particular. "Why the hell isn't the Supreme Commander General Campanelli sitting in on this damn meeting? He's our first line of defense if anything goes sour on us in the Asian region, dammit. Sergeant, send a Flash message out to the Vinegar Joe thing, and tell them I want General Campanelli on the screen, STAT."

CHAPTER 26
CIC CHAMBER ON THE VINEGAR JOE PLATFORM

The Sergeant monitoring the radio for the CIC Chamber on board the Vinegar Joe Platform, picked up the word Flash light up across his screen, and he immediately called out, "someone better get General Campanelli in here quick, there's Flash traffic coming in for him people."

General Palmieri rang General Campanelli's private quarters, and when he answered, the voice on the other end stated, "flash traffic coming in at the chamber, General Campanelli Sir."

"I'll be right there General Palmieri Sir. Thanks." The General placed his hand on the female Major's fine rump, and then he gave it a slight shove.

"What it now be from you now mista? I no mood to make love you now mista. I still sleepy very and do not want to wake yet, sir. Let me sleep or I bite you on finger for you, mista." She moaned in a very sleepy voice as she shifted her weight on the bed.

"I have a Flash message coming in, and I gotta get down to the CIC center STAT, honey. I didn't want to wake you, but I have to climb over you if you don't move some, Alex."

She rolled out of bed and half stood as she got out of the General's way.

General Campanelli got up and grabbed her breast as he passed her and mumbled. "Nice."

"Hmmm... no try start motor to run now if plan to leave me now right, buster. If start, finish please." She purred as she fell back on the bunk, and then she pulled the sheet completely over her head. A second later she was breathing deep, sound asleep again.

General Edward Campanelli put on his shirt as he watched her sleep, he pulled the sheet off her face, and she snuggled in better. The General smiled because he could not believe this good looking woman would be the least bit interested in him romantically. In seconds he was in the CIC Chamber, and the General went over to the Sergeant and asked him. "What's up mister?"

"The President's coming in any second on screen two, General Campanelli Sir."

The Commanding General looked at the screen and then called out to the other members of the chamber, "okay people, all non-essential personnel you know the drill, outta the damn box." No sooner did he make this announcement than the screen came to life, and the upset President remained silent and watched as the few stragglers quickly filed out of the CIC room, and then he offered. "Good morning General Campanelli it's good to see you. How are you today sir?"

"Good morning Mr. President Sir. I'm fine, thank you for asking sir. How are you sir?"

The President did not answer, he merely got right to the point with the Commanding Officer on the Platform. "General Campanelli Sir, I wanted you to sit in on this briefing, because the results will include you as well sir. Allow me to brief you as to what was already covered at the meeting before we included you in on the meeting, sir. We have strong evidence, correct that, positive evidence the North Korean's are arming their Scud missiles with nuclear warheads, and we're discussing what we intend to do about it, sir. I don't think any nation's willing to have another nuclear exchange take place. Not since the Middle East War, General Campanelli Sir."

The General no longer heard the President's voice, or his words for that matter. His mind was already screaming at him not to go through another nuclear war. He was sweating as he quickly mulled over the ugly ramifications of a nuclear exchange occurring in a region so heavily populated by the North Koreans. He was brought back to reality by the President, as he asked him with much concern in his voice. "General Campanelli Sir, I know it's rather early over there sir, and I'm sorry about it. But if you don't mind General, please pay better attention to this report, sir? This is very important for you to hear and react to, General Campanelli Sir."

"I beg your pardon Mr. President Sir, I but was praying I don't have to use anymore god damn nuclear weapons again in this mess, sir."

"Yes, yes of course you were, General Campanelli Sir. I forgot about you having lived through one such nuclear exchange already a few short years ago, sir. I'm terribly sorry General, but if it happens again, I have to know if you're going to be able to pull the damn trigger if needed, General Campanelli Sir. If can't do your job then I'll have you replaced quickly, sir." President Albert Cole stared at the extremely upset General, while waiting for his answer.

He thought to himself for a long second, and then he replied to the American Leader's remark. "Mr. President Sir, I'll do whatever's expected of me, without hesitation I offer, sir."

The President nodded and then he turned his attention back to Director Raincloud and asked him, "Director Raincloud Sir, do you have anything else to add to your summary, sir?"

"Yes I do sir, one important question has to be asked here, Mr. President Sir. What the hell do we do about the damn Chinese, sir? Do we inform them about the nuclear warheads being prepared inside North Korea, sir? What's going to be their reaction once they're aware nuclear missiles are being aimed at their troops in the field. The Chinese already lost a number of troops to missile attacks we figured took one quarter of North Korea's missile stores in the attack."

Campanelli spoke up, "I was unaware a missile attack on Chinese troops took place sir."

"Yes it certainly did, nearly an hour ago General Campanelli Sir. Your Intel people should be picking up the report by now, sir. If not then I suggest you get on your people, and have them update any and all information coming into your center, sir." The President growled at him.

General Campanelli was sweating as he asked his Commander in Chief, "what type of missile attack was aimed at the damn Chinese troops, Mr. President Sir?"

"Calm down some please General Campanelli Sir, it was a conventional attack reported with high explosive warheads, sir. It did massive damage to two attacking Chinese Armies, and it put the kibosh on any further movements of any more Chinese troops along the coast, sir."

General Campanelli nodded as he breathed a deep sigh of relief and then let it our slowly.

National Security Director Griffin was stewing while the President explained the missile attack to the concerned General. When the President finished, Director Griffin spoke before anyone could cut him off, "Mr. President Sir, I think Director Raincloud brought up a very valid point here, sir. Are we going to inform the Chinese government about the missiles and warheads? And how do you think they'll react to this information, once they're made aware of it sir?"

Secretary of State Maria Hernandez responded to the Director's question, "of course we're going to inform the Chinese about the damn missiles and nuclear warheads, Mr. Griffin. We have to, it's an absolute must, sir. If we don't inform the Chinese Command, they're going to find out sooner or later, and we'll lose our credibility with them, because we didn't inform them of the nuclear threat, especially once the nuclear tipped missiles hit their troops, sir. I have to add this though, I fear the response from the Chinese Military Command over this information."

Director Raincloud spoke up and he offered the worried looking Security Director. "Director Griffin Sir, the missiles we're talking about aren't the long range kind, sir. Besides, the Chinese troops already stationed in North Korea, are the more pressing threat to North Korea..."

"You mean the North Korean Command are going to hit their own damn country with these fucking nukes, sir?" The stunned Security Director asked his counterpart from the CIA.

"Sure they will without any hesitation, if it's the only way they have to try and stop the damn Chinese troops from taking over their entire country on them, sir. As far as I can see, this is the only door left open to the North Korean Command, if they want to salvage some of their country that is, sir. A move of this sort might be enough to stop the Chinese onslaught of their nation. It's very dangerous but it's the only one left open to them. I don't think the Chinese will retaliate with their nukes though. It's too close to their own country and besides, Russia will get into it if China dares to employ nuclear weapons in this mess." Director Raincloud offered the members.

"We're suddenly taking an awful fucking lot for granted around here, Director Raincloud Sir." Secretary of State Maria Hernandez complained, and then she added to her angry words, "all I know is if my enemy has resorted to the use of nuclear weapons against my troops out in the field, sir. Then I'd sure as hell reply in much the same manner, and I'd be damned to hell and back again, if any of my neighbors would stop or even change my damn mind, sir."

"What the hell do you mean by that last remark Ma'am?" the President demanded hotly.

"Mr. President Sir, I'd certainly employ the use of nuclear weapons in a flash, if say Russia was my neighbor, and I didn't see eye to eye with them, sir. I'd be dammed to hell..."

"I don't think for one minute you'd ever have the damn balls to fire off nuclear weapons at any neighbor and possibly killing thousands, and maybe even millions of lives, both military and civilian, Ms. Hernandez." Director Griffin snapped back angrily at her.

"Don't you tell me I haven't got balls, mister. I just happen to wear mine on my chest instead of between my legs, and I guarantee you that mine area helluva lot larger than yours, Mr. Griffin. I assure you sir, if any nation dared threatened my soldiers or nation with nukes, they'd be sucking on my nuclear tipped missiles before they know what's happening to them, sir."

"Enough of this kind of talk. Maria, that kind of thinking will only lead to one outcome in this damn nightmare we're mired in, Ma'am. A nuclear exchange between both Russia and China, Maria." Director Raincloud vented angrily as he stared at the ailing female Secretary of State.

"I don't think China's very afraid of Russia, or her opinion for that matter. Or what she might do or say against China's response to a nuclear exchange in North Korea." Hernandez shot back.

"I agree with my Secretary of State on this one Mr. Director Sir," the President added, still laughing under his breath at what Maria had just aimed at the Security Director Griffin.

"What if our Marines do a surgical strike before the North Korean's can use them damn things sir." Director Griffin commented as he suddenly turned his attention to the American Leader.

"You mean commit an act of war on a foreign land?" Hernandez asked the Director angrily.

"Christ Almighty woman, I'm trying to find a damn solution to this mess we have exploding right in our damn faces here, Ma'am. At least we could avoid a possible all out nuclear exchange in this entire region if we hit these damn Scud missiles ourselves." Director Griffin snapped back at her, and then continued his complaint, "we'll have to base the aircraft in Russia, and we'd have to inform the Russians about our possible attack, Ma'am. I don't believe they'd react kindly to a bombing mission being operated off their land though." Director Griffin added.

"I don't understand, why the devil would the attacking aircraft have to come out of Russia? We have eight Aircraft Carriers and the Vinegar Joe Platform stationed in the Korea region. We could always use one of these ships to launch the damn attack from," The President offered.

"Mr. President Sir, I wouldn't want to launch this possible attack from the Carriers, sir. If we did, Japan would demand they move off her coast, fearing a retaliatory attack from North Korea. Once we launch an attack from our ships, they become fair game from North Korean submarines, even from many of their still active surface ships and aircraft. I wouldn't want to launch an attack from our Carriers unless we're prepared to go all out in the region." The Director warned.

The President let out with a deep sigh that was loud enough so everyone quieted down, and then he went on with his words for the members of the meeting. "Gentleman, and lady, I'm not going to entertain any such attack on North Korea except as a last resort, people. I don't want to commit our military forces and if we're talking about a surgical raid on their nuclear facilities, we should've thought about this damn solution in the first place before this damn war started. Instead of going along with China's offer to destroy the nuclear weapons and installations of North Korea. I think you people should've saw this shit coming at you, and had some plan set in place, to counter this damn problem before it bit us on the ass. Our most pressing question is, do we tell the Chinese North Korea's preparing missiles with nuclear weapons, and aiming them at their troops or not? This has to be answered before we do anything over this arising situation."

Secretary of State Maria Hernandez piped up and remarked in an excited tone of voice at the American Leader, "we absolutely must inform the Chinese Military Command of this nuclear threat from the North Koreans, so they can get their people the hell out of the damn area, sir."

"I agree with all you just stated Ms. Hernandez Ma'am," the Security Director said and then added. "But I don't think the damn Chinese will use this information to move their people out of harm's way. I think they'll use this information to form an attack on the missiles themselves."

"I go along with Mr. Griffin's thoughts here, Mr. President Sir," the Deputy Secretary of Defense added as he turned slightly so he could see the seated President a little better now.

All eyes fell on the face of General Campanelli on the screen, the President smiled at his military officer as he commented at him, "General Campanelli Sir, you've been strangely quiet throughout this entire debate, sir. Do we have your full attention at this meeting, sir? And do you have anything to offer to this conversation that might shed some more light on what we should do with the damn information we're considering at this meeting, sir?"

General Edward Campanelli laughed as he offered to his Commander in Chief. "Mr. President Sir, as the Secretary of State has just offered us, we have to notify the Chinese Command about the nuclear warheads plain and simple, sir. There's no question about it in the least Mr. President Sir. We must share all our information, even the location of the damn North Korean missiles, sir. The Chinese are doing the world a big favor as it is by going after these damn things in the first place, being developed in North Korea against the rest of the world's opinion, sir. After the Chinese troops get the damn missiles, and destroy the nuclear weapons. We can then demand the Chinese forces stop where they are, and then begin to withdraw from North Korea at once, sir.

"I'm angry as hell the damn Chinese forces chose to carry out such a heavy war against North Korea as it is, sir. I felt they should've gone right after the nuclear weapons, and avoided most of this damn ground war, and the terrible slaughter of the North Korean civilians at that, sir. As far as I'm concerned, the damn Chinese troops went well beyond what they were supposed to do in Korea that gained them the ability to invader North Korea in the first place, sir."

"Hmmm... that's a good response from you General Campanelli Sir." The President said and then continued with his words, "but what if the Chinese Command resort to using their own nuclear weapons to destroy the North Korean threat of nuclear weapons aimed at them, sir?"

"With all due respect Mr. President Sir, I seriously doubt this scenario will ever take place, sir. First off sir, China has too many of her damn troops out in the field of North Korea, for her to dare respond with nuclear weapons of her own against the North Korean threat, sir. I think they'll react much the same way we're thinking, the Chinese, along with the help of the Brits, will do a surgical strike on these damn missile sites, and then eliminate the problem for us, sir."

"Does the Chinese military have the capability to do such a precision attack against these damn weapons we're talking about General,?" the President asked his officer with concern.

"They couldn't possibly pull it off by themselves Mr. President. That's why I said for them to attack with the

English support, sir. The British have the technology for such an attack to be successful, and I'll make damn certain my information will be leaked to the English Command first, sir. I'll even allow their damn pilots to have access to our laser guided bombs and aiming equipment, to insure them of getting the job done properly and quickly, and with the least amount of collateral damage to the North Korean forces." The General offered his Commander in Chief.

"The British already have their own laser aiming systems that are sort of compatible with our own aiming systems, Mr. President Sir. It'll be good to offer them limited access to our computer systems, so they can pull up the needed information from our satellites, and they can locate the nuclear tipped missiles in question here, sir. They'll need some real time information though, because if I'm not mistaken, these damn missiles are stationed on mobile missile launchers, and they're ready to fly at a moment's notice, sir." Security Director Griffin added.

"I didn't know that," the President growled angrily. "How the hell are they going to catch up with a mobile missile launcher for the love of God? They'll give the damn British aircraft the same fits the damn Iraqi Scud missile systems gave us during the Desert Storm War, sir."

"Mr. President Sir, our technology has grown much better now than it was back in 1991, sir. We have the video capable satellites, and we can easily track the damn missile launchers as they move to their launching positions, sir. Then we can send this intelligence information over to the United Kingdom aircraft while in flight, so they can make their corrections while in flight in order to intercept the damn mobile missile launchers, sir." The Security Director offered.

"General Campanelli Sir, how the hell do you feel about giving the damn English military direct access to our intelligence gathering satellites and computer systems, sir? Are we going to compromise any of our security and Top Secret information with this offer to them, sir?"

"No Mr. President Sir, I have no problem with giving the English any of this information, and as for giving away any Top Secret material to them, sir. We'll be in complete control of the information that's going to their computers at all time sir, and we can easily cut off any material we don't want them to have access to before they get it, sir. The only thing still bugging me a little is, Mr. President. The damn English are working so damn closely with the Chinese. It's hard to accept the English and Chinese ships of war are sailing side by side in this one, sir."

"I understand how you must feel General Campanelli Sir," Secretary of State Hernandez responded. "I assure you I feel the same way as you do, sir. But war makes rather strange bed fellows of us all, sir. We're involved in saving lives now, and in the future sir. I wish we we're able to make North Korea understand this fact before the shooting started, sir."

"General Weidenbacher Sir, how do you suggest I get this vital information out to the English? I have my own idea how, but I want to make certain you have nothing else in mind, sir." General Campanelli asked the powerful General, having no idea he came late to the meeting.

"I have no plan as yet in mind, so let me hear what you have in mind to offer before I come up with a conclusion to the plan, General Campanelli Sir."

"General Weidenbacher Sir, Mr. President Sir, I can hop a plane from the VJP out to the Invincible, and give Admiral Middleton the information in hand myself, sir. I have the stills of what the North Koreans are doing to their damn missiles, and I can take along the video, and simply run the information we're in possession of for the English Admiral, sir. I'll give him the clearance to pass this information on to the Chinese if needed, General Weidenbacher Sir."

General William Weidenbacher slowly ran a finger over his lips as he thought about General Campanelli's suggested plan then he replied, "I don't think I can come up with a better way to get the shit over to the Chinese myself, sir. I say it's a go, if the President agrees that is, sir."

All eyes went over to the President this time, as General Weidenbacher was standing and waiting for his reply to what they had just come up with. He was late for the meeting, and he had no intentions of walking in front of the man in order to get over to his seat.

"I have no problem with the material passing over to the English in this manner. I can contact the Prime Minister, and have him order Admiral Middleton to report to the Platform. It'd make it easier for you, General Campanelli Sir." President Cole offered with concern in his tone.

"Mr. President Sir, I'd much rather go out to his ship if you don't mind, sir. I want him to forget about the Platform for the time being, sir. Besides Mr. President Sir, I always wanted to see one of the English Jump Jet Aircraft Carriers in person, Mr. President." General Campanelli replied as he stared at the President's face on the large screen inside his CIC Chamber.

"I see what you're up to here sir, and like it mister. You get out to that damn English Jump Jet Carrier, and give him your information, General Campanelli Sir. I'll notify the Chinese we're giving the English some important material for both parties concerned with this present situation, sir. I want to stay on the good side of the damn Chinese for the time being, sir."

The conversation was suddenly interrupted by a Marine who entered the Situation Room with a message for the President, who unfolded the paper and then turned white as he moaned to the other members of the meeting. "The problems already started, the Japanese picked up the North Koreans arming their missiles with nukes by one of their own satellites. They sent us a Flash message about it." The President held up the note and then went on with this new information, "they're informing us they're going to react against any nuclear exchange with one of their own, people. The Japanese are going to Alert One Status, meaning they'll open fire on any ship except ours. They'll be keeping a close eye on the Chinese, and they will react accordingly against any of their military actions, sir." The President sat back and he wiped his upper lip.

General Campanelli was dumbfounded by this new information, he had no idea Japan had any nuclear weapons in their country. He could not fathom why in good conscious, the Japanese would dare ever develop them after seeing firsthand, what they're capable of doing to the civilian population of any nations attacked by the ugly weapons of mass destruction. He wondered if the civilian population of Japan knew there were nuclear weapons stored on their soil.

President Cole noticed the expression on General Campanelli's face, and he responded to it, "I see you're shocked by the news the Japanese have a number of nuclear weapons under their command, General Campanelli Sir. Where do you think that plutonium was going when France sold it to Japan, sir? We're aware the Japanese were developing a number of defensive nuclear weapons, sir. We even helped them in their quest, because we felt the Japanese would need them to defend themselves in the event of an attack from either Russia or China, sir. We gave the Japanese an observation and surveillance satellite also, sir. They launched two of their own birds with our complete compliance, we stand by the Japanese government in all aspects sir."

General Campanelli stared at the American Leader in stunned disbelief, and then he asked him with much concern lacing his tone this time, "Mr. President Sir, I believe and aren't all the damn nuclear weapons supposed to be classified as offensive weapons in nature, sir?"

"In some cases, yes that's absolutely correct General Campanelli Sir," the President replied cautiously to him as he smiled reassuringly at his General.

"If they're being classified as offensive weapons in nature, does the fact that the Japanese have the damn things stored in their arsenal, go against the surrender terms of the World War Two peace accord, Mr. President Sir?" General Campanelli added while keeping the conversation going for the time being with his Commander in Chief.

President Cole smiled and nodded as he replied to the General's most interesting words. "General Campanelli Sir, those terms were signed when nuclear weapons were in their infancy stage, sir. The agreement's well outdated, and has to be altered in order to enable Japan to survive in this new and extremely hostile world we now live in, sir. Japan needs these weapons to better protect herself from attack from her troublesome neighbors. This knowledge states the intended use of these nuclear weapons are for Japan's protection as a nation. Which makes them defensive weapons in nature, they're developed under this intent General Campanelli Sir."

"But the nuclear weapons could also be used offensively against any other nation in the world, including our own, sir."

General Campanelli warned the President in no uncertain terms.

"Don't start and debate with me General, just concern yourself with carrying out my orders to the letter for this latest situation, sir. I don't give a damn if you agree with them or not, mister!" the President suddenly snapped hotly as he glared angrily at General Campanelli.

The General immediately put his head down to avoid the harsh gaze coming from the rather upset looking President of the United States as he replied softly, "yes Sir Mr. President."

"That's better General Campanelli Sir. You handle the English and Chinese, and I'll handle the Japanese and any political questions that might arise, sir. Now you have a job to do. So I suggest you get on with your assignment, General. Lives are depending on your speed sir."

"Right away, I'm on it Mr. President Sir." General Campanelli replied as the President's screen suddenly went dark right before his eyes.

THE CIC CHAMBER ON BOARD
THE VINEGAR JOE PLATFORM

General Edward Campanelli stood, never in his life did he ever want a cigarette more than he wanted one at this very moment. He looked around and noticed a young Seaman with a pack of butts stuffed in his top pocket, and he barked at the man, "give me one of them fucking smokes will ya Seaman."

John, standing alongside Campanelli interrupted, "belay that last order Seaman, continue with what you're doing, son. Ed, I think you better contact Admiral Middleton right away sir."

General Campanelli glared harshly at his Second in Command for a long moment. Then he let out his breath in a sight as he mumbled at his friend, "yeah, perhaps you're right there John. Seaman, open up a channel to the Invincible, a secured one for me mister."

"Yes sir." A few seconds later he reported, "sir, I have their CIC sir, the blinking light sir."

"This is Lieutenant Byerns here sir. Can I help you out any please sir?"

General Campanelli snarled in the phone at the British sounding voice, "this is Lieutenant General Edward Campanelli, and I wish to speak with Vice Admiral Middleton at once, sir. It's most important I speak with your Commanding Officer immediately, mister."

"Right away sir, will you please hold the line while I get him for you, General Campanelli Sir. He's rather busy, but I'm certain he'll spare the time to speak with you, General Campanelli Sir."

"Yeah, I'll hold on, just get him for me will ya Lieutenant." Campanelli snapped again at him.

A moment later, "good day General Campanelli Sir. What can I do for you today, sir? I kind of have my hands full at the moment as you can well imagine, sir."

"Admiral Middleton Sir, I'd like permission to pay you a quick visit at this time sir."

"It'd be a great honor to see you again, General Campanelli Sir. This time please allow me to show you some of our British hospitality, sir. When do you want to come on board sir?"

"Today some time sir. I could be out to your ship within three hours at the latest, sir."

"Yes, err... okay, that'd be fine with me, General Campanelli Sir. Is there a problem sir?"

"Yes, but I won't discuss it over this hookup. The time is seven ten, I'll be there by ten sir."

"Very good, but we're in day five of a conflict, sir. I trust this meeting will be brief, General?"

"Yes, I think the satellite information I have will show you why it's imperative for us to meet."

Admiral Middleton became extremely concerned when General Campanelli mentioned he had satellite information to share with him. His mind raced, he wondered if the film it took would show information about China, or the North Koreans as he offered. "Sir, I'll be expecting you by ten o'clock today then, sir. Until then, thank you for calling General Campanelli Sir."

Admiral Owens piped up when the General broke off the communication with the British Admiral, "you can have J.C., he can fly you out to the Invincible, General Campanelli Sir."

"Very good Admiral Owens Sir, have him on deck, I'm gonna change and then we'll be on our way, Admiral." The General replied and then he left the CIC chamber and headed for his wardroom, where he had the motion sickness pills Mendoza gave him when he was about to fly.

The Admiral's pilot was watching the flight deck crew bring his aircraft up from below deck, it was serviced and armed, and ready for flight with the external power cart already hooked up to his aircraft and running. He walked over to him and Lieutenant Wright saluted his Commander as the General asked him, "do you have your flight path worked out, Lieutenant?"

"You bet I do sir, we'll be ready to go in five minutes, sir." The pilot replied.

"Great." General Campanelli moaned, he did not like going as the WIZZO on this flight though. The radar and weapon systems operator in the YF-27 fighter. He climbed up the ladder, and then he squeezed his body in the rear seat of the sleek fighter aircraft, as the pilot took his place. The canopy closed and the pilot immediately increased power to his engines, and he warned the General, "you better hang on sir. They're disconnecting us from the power cart sir."

"You bet your ass I'll be holding on for dear life mister." He replied hotly as the aircraft slowly moved out to the flight line. The pilot known as J.C. lined the aircraft up properly, and then added more power to the engines until they were screaming. The General could feel the incredible roar from the engines as they went to full power and then into afterburner.

"Grasshopper to Homeplate. Requesting permission for flight takeoff at this time sir. Over."

"Homeplate to Grasshopper. Granted permission for flight takeoff, good luck sir. Over."

"J.C. saluted the colors of the flag, and then he saluted the flight deck crew Chief as he held on to the breaks of the aircraft, locking the screaming aircraft in place and then he announced to his Commanding Officer over the roar of the engines, "here we go now General Campanelli Sir."

"Nice takeoff kid." The General muttered as he opened his eyes and looked out the window, to make certain they were in flight, and immediately he got sick to his stomach. J.C. leveled the nose of the aircraft off to add more speed to the aircraft. He climbed to forty thousand feet and then announced. "General Campanelli Sir, this aircraft flies by light, that's why she handles so smoothly, sir. This one, and the F-22 are the only aircraft in the world that fly in this manner."

"Whatdaya fucking mean by flight by god damn light, mister? Whatdaya have up here? A fucking flash light or something, mister!" he grumbled at the young flyer.

Lieutenant Wright laughed as he replied to his Commander. "Not exactly General Campanelli Sir, this aircraft flies by fiber optics, the optics react to the computer commands much faster than any fly by wire, or fly by muscle aircraft, sir. Everything inside this here little baby's controlled by an FS Forty Five Computer with backups, there's a total of forty five computers on board this here little old aircraft all together, sir. This plane responds to any Command given to her forty percent quicker than any wire controlled aircraft, sir. This is the last step before the 6th generation thought controlled family of aircraft are finally born, General Campanelli Sir."

"Thought controlled aircraft you say, pilot? What the hell is that crap all about, you just think flying your plane and it flies, buster." Campanelli asked the flyer with some concern.

"I know it must sound like pure bullshit to you, General. But I heard they're trying to make a command helmet that'd control the aircraft by pure thought, General Campanelli Sir. All the pilot has to do is think he wants to go to Port, and the aircraft would automatically go left with no other movement from the pilot, sir." The smiling pilot informed his Commanding Officer.

"I believe you, after seeing that demonstration on the damn HR-334 weapon system, which shoots where the aimer is just looking through that tiny TV screen inside the damn helmet, sir. I think I'd believe almost anything just about now, Lieutenant Wright Sir."

The rest of the flight was completed in silence, with an occasional call from the pilot, drawing the General's attention towards a ship below their aircraft. To General Campanelli's left was the west coast of North Korea, he looked hard and swore he could actually see a number of explosions taking place on the coast. Lieutenant Wright's radio was full of chatter.

"Baker's Oven to Grasshopper. Come in please sir. Over." An Air Traffic Controller called.

"Who the hell is Baker's Oven for Christ sake, mister?" General Campanelli growled as he demanded to know over the ICS (Intercom system) at the pilot.

"I believe it's the call name of the British Carrier we're heading for, General Campanelli Sir."

"You betta answer them then mister," he warned the Lieutenant as he tried to see him.

"Grasshopper to Baker's Oven. Come in please sir. Over." The General's pilot offered and then he waited for the controller's reply.

"Baker's Over to Grasshopper. Jolly good to hear from you, sir. We have an aircraft recovery situation presently being carried out on board the ship that should be completed within the next few moments, sir. Please stand by until advised to do otherwise, sir. Over."

Lieutenant Wright put his fighter into a hovering glide path, and waited for Baker's Oven to give him final permission to land on the British Carrier. Wright and Campanelli watched the Invincible retrieved a wing of four Sea Harrier jump jets, and one AEW Sea King helicopter. Once they were decked and out of the way, the call came in. "Baker's Over to Grasshopper. You're cleared to land. Pay attention to our LSO officer. Good luck Grasshopper. Over."

The pilot listened to the control officer, and immediately aligned himself with the flight deck of the British Carrier as instructed. Once he was in the pipe, he was turned over to the British Carrier's LSO. The LSO lined Lieutenant Wright up with the Meatball, the Optic Light Landing System, and his on board computer handled the rest for him.

Lieutenant Wright called back to the worried General, "sir, have you ever done a Carrier landing before, General Campanelli Sir?"

"NO!" was all the General snapped back in the radio as he looked at the back of the pilot.

"Dammit, those friggin birds shoulda told me that crap first, sir. Look sir, there's no time to waste here, General. Pull your harness straps as tight as you can possibly stand them sir, and then allow the straps to pull you back in your seat, General Campanelli Sir."

The concerned General heard the urgency in his pilot's voice, and he immediately pulled on the lead strap as hard as he could pull on it, until he could barely breathe any longer. Once this was completed he gasped and complained at his pilot. "Done, now what mister?"

"Grab hold of the damn crash bar in front of you sir, and hold on with both hands for dear life, General. We're going to be landing at half power, so we'll be coming in at three hundred miles an hour, sir. General Campanelli Sir, there's no way in hell for me to explain the feeling of going from three hundred miles an hour to zero, in less than four hundred feet, sir. General Campanelli Sir, you're going to swear to God someone just pulled your stomach out through your damn nose on you, sir. Tighten your oxygen mask, and then lean your head against the back of your seat headrest, and keep your mouth closed as well, sir. I'll increase your oxygen level so you don't get too sick on me, when we hit the deck of the ship sir. Here we go General."

General Campanelli felt the aircraft rapidly descending while maintaining level flight, the roar of the engines was deafening. He opened his eyes and gave a quick look out the side of the cockpit, he could see the fantail of the ship coming straight at him, and he swore their aircraft was going to crash right into the tail end of the British ship. He felt the landing gear go down on the aircraft, and the pilot say something in the radio. "Hook locked in place, sir."

The sleek American made advance fighter aircraft landed and for just a brief second, General Campanelli's mind registered a rather smooth landing on the British ship. That was until the arresting cable finally tightened. The awesome force of the landing made him feel like his balls were some where up in his mouth, and the harness almost ripped right through his skin, and the pressure actually stole the breath from his lungs. The Commanding General tired to suck in huge gulps of pure oxygen with little if any success to his attempts.

The aircraft suddenly jerked back some twenty feet, making his stomach join his ball in his mouth. General Campanelli's eyes felt like they were going to pop out of his head. His teeth slammed shut, and his neck felt like someone just tried to twist it off his shoulders violently. The plane finally came to a complete stop with another jolt, forcing more air out of his lungs.

The canopy popped opened as Lieutenant Wright called back to the General while grinning at his Commanding Officer. "Are you alright back there General Campanelli Sir?"

"That fucking depends on what you call alright, Lieutenant. I'll have to take an inventory of my damn body parts, before I can answer you truly on that last question, son. What the hell do you call that fucking landing anyhow, Lieutenant?" General Campanelli asked him.

"General Campanelli Sir, in pilot talk, that's what's known as a controlled crash of an aircraft, on deck, sir." Lieutenant Wright laughed as he drew in a huge gulp of air himself.

The stunned General went to move and he got a stabbing pain in his shoulder for his effort, and he complained against at his pilot, "what the hell makes you believe this was a controlled crash we just did, son. Have you seen my stomach lying around here anyplace, sir?"

"We're still alive and in one piece aren't we General Campanelli Sir. That makes it a successful controlled crash on the flight deck, sir." The grinning pilot offered him.

"That remains to be seen," he went to get out, but his harness stopped him from moving.

"It works much easier if you take the damn harness off ya first sir, before you try and get out of the aircraft, General Campanelli Sir." Lieutenant Wright smirked as he grinned back at the angry looking General for a second time after their landing.

The General glared as he quickly undid his harness, and then rubbed his shoulders which felt like they were separated, and he groused at the pilot this time. "I don't know how you madmen go through this shit every fucking day. I'll tell you this much kid, I have a new respect for you crazy ass young pilots after living through that landing, and I use the word landing loosely."

Lieutenant Wright laughed as he offered to his Commander. "C'mon sir, we gotta get out of the aircraft in case of any invisible fire in the internals of the engines, regulations sir." The pilot stood and then turned to the General and added, "need a hand getting out sir?"

"No way sonny, you just watch my dust getting my ass outta this damn coffin of yours, mister." General Campanelli snapped hotly as he was up, and out of his harness and climbing down the ladder with Lieutenant Wright laughing at how fast he moved now. There was no fanfare waiting for the two American Officers, not with a launch and retrieval of aircraft in progress on the Jump Jet Carrier. A flight deck officer met the General as he stepped foot on the flight deck, and he quickly ushered them both through a bulkhead lateral hatch to the Conning Tower where Admiral Middleton was watching the launch operation below. When he spotted General Campanelli, he walked over to him and then he shook his hand. The General introduced Admiral Middleton to Lieutenant Wright, and then he got right down to business.

"Admiral Middleton Sir, I have some extremely important information my government wants me to share with you, sir. Is there a place where we can go that's secure, sir?"

"Yes, if you'll follow me please, we can talk in my private wardroom General Campanelli Sir."

The Commanding American General followed Admiral Middleton, while Lieutenant Wright stood by and he watched the landing of one of the British Jump Jet Aircraft.

Admiral Middleton sat down and then he offered General Campanelli a chair, along with an offer for a drink. "A brandy sir?"

"I guess you wouldn't happen to have a Pepsi on board your ship that I can have, sir?"

Admiral Middleton announced with a slight smirk on his lips, "I was warned in advance about your soda kick from General Weidenbacher, sir. I had a number of cans of Pepsi placed on board my ship just for your enjoyment, General." The Admiral then pressed a button and a Seaman rushed in while carrying a cold soda and a chilled glass, and he sat it down on the table before General Campanelli. He took a gulp, it was cold and made his teeth and throat hurt.

Admiral Middleton had a cup of tea laced with just a slight a taste of brandy. After a few moments of some small talk, Admiral Middleton took the incentive and he asked the General about the obvious intelligence information the American General had for him.

General Campanelli offered Admiral Middleton the tape. The Admiral took the tape and from out of nowhere another officer appeared. Admiral Middleton whispered to General Campanelli. "M-5 Officer sir. The picture will appear when he's ready to run the tape for us, General."

A screen automatically came up from a shelf and the second officer called out, "Ready sir."

Middleton replied, "start the tape and General Campanelli will tell us what it's about."

Admiral Middleton immediately knew what he was looking at the moment he saw the North Korean technicians working on the missile warheads. General Campanelli watched as Admiral Middleton slowly sat forward in his chair and he stared at the screen intensely. His breathing was noticeably labored, and his forehead showed beads of sweat as he grumbled at the General. "Bloody hell, do you know what this means to us, General Campanelli Sir?"

"Why do you think I'm here for Admiral Middleton Sir? My people know what this damn threat means to you and the rest of the world, and what it could possibly lead to, sir. I've been authorized to offer you direct access to one of our birds, and we'll help direct a surgical attack against these missiles and nuclear sites, sir. Once these sites and missiles and warheads are eliminated, my government wants me to demand an immediate cessation of all aggression in North Korea. The elimination of the nuclear threat from North Korea was, and still is the only objective the Chinese were allowed to invade North Korea in the first place, Admiral

Middleton Sir. Once this is accomplished, all fighting has to stop immediately Admiral."

"I assure you General Campanelli Sir, once the nuclear threat's eliminated from North Korea, Britain will stop fighting, sir. We'll pull all our forces back to a safe zone, and allow the politicians to takeover this mess. Do the Chinese know of these nuclear tipped missiles, sir?"

CHAPTER 27

"That's a question the British can help us with, Admiral Middleton Sir. The Chinese don't know of the nuclear tipped missiles presence, sir. But we're sharing this information with you, so you can inform them of their presence, and what we plan to do about them, sir. We'll not give the Chinese any direct access to our birds for security reasons, sir. We'll work with you, and you can work with them, Admiral Middleton Sir. But we want the Chinese Command to be aware this information Is coming from the United States for the obvious reasons, sir. We want some control over this present situation. I've been ordered to inform you we'll grant access to certain bombs and guided missiles if requested by your Command. We're prepared to offer you British all the assistance we can possibly offer short of giving you access to our CIC chamber, sir."

Admiral Middleton smiled pleasantly as he replied to the American General kind offer of military assistance to his forces and responded, "I'll gladly take you up on that kind offer you just made me General, and I know what weapons I'd need to accomplish the attack on these missile systems, General Campanelli Sir.   What about the Chinese Command, sir? Do they know of this fantastic Platform of yours out there yet, sir?"

"No Admiral, not as yet at least, and we'd like it to stay that way for as long as we possibly can, sir. Until we see the outcome of the fighting taking place in North Korea, sir. We also want to keep the installation as our trump card, in case something goes sour in this region, and we have to react militarily on our own sir," the General offered to the British Officer as he sat back in his chair, and allowed himself to relax for the first time since landing on the British Carrier.

Admiral Middleton also sat back in his chair as he replied, "right now the Chinese have no idea you have a Floating Island on which to wage war from, sir. I've been told many times by them that the United States is no threat to them, sir. Because you have no land base in which to operate from sir. I hope they never have to find out they're wrong in that assumption, General."

"So do I Admiral Middleton Sir. I had quite enough of this damn fighting to last me for the rest of my damn life, sir. It's nuts and has to stop, sir." General Campanelli replied as he laid out all the still photos taken by another one of the satellites.

Admiral Middleton leaned forward in his chair again, and the second officer went over the pictures with a strong magnifying glass while saying to himself. "Hmm, yep, yes I see."

Admiral Middleton stacked the pictures up in a neat little pile and then he leaned back and remarked in a calm voice, "can I offer you something to eat, General Campanelli Sir?"

"Not if I have to fly back to the Platform, I don't want to have anything in my stomach, sir."

"You don't like flying I gather, me too, I hate it sir. General Campanelli Sir, on behalf of my government, I thank you for sharing this vital information with us, sir. We'll be in touch with you when I had a chance to speak with my people, and then the Chinese, sir. I'll let you know if we need any of your weapon systems, and what our plan of attack will be, sir. We'll be going after these damn missiles and nuclear warheads, and once they're destroyed General Campanelli, I feel rather confident that all the fighting in this region will come to a rapid conclusion, sir."

The Command General lightly tugged on his ear as he quickly collected his thoughts, and then he offered, "Admiral Middleton Sir, I have to warn you that we're not the only government who knows about these damn North Korean nuclear tipped missiles, sir."

"Oh," Admiral Middleton said as he leaned forward again and stared at the American General.

"The Japanese also detected the presence of these nuclear tipped missiles, and they sent us a coded message they have armed their own nuclear missiles in reply to this latest threat from North Korea, sir. They also warned us they're well prepared to use them on any ship other than Japanese or American that comes to close to their country. The Japanese missiles will have no problem reaching into the heart of China, or Russia for that matter, sir. Admiral Middleton, I suggest all your ships use extreme caution when sailing anywhere near the Japanese coastline."

"Gawddamned bloody hell, I always believed the Japanese had some sort of nuclear weapons in their arsenal, sir. I never thought they'd have an effective delivery system in operation though, General Campanelli Sir. Do the Chinese know of these nuclear weapons presence in Japan, sir?" Admiral Middleton asked with concern in his voice.

"No, I don't believe so, and we'd rather they didn't know of them at this time, sir. Let the Chinese Command worry about one country at a time, sir. I don't need them using the same excuse they used on North Korea, to invade Japan. We have a feeling China might make a run at Japan once she finishes off Korea and has all her troops still on the Korean Peninsula, sir."

"Why on bloody earth would the damn Chinese military ever want to go and attack Japan for, General Campanelli Sir? What the hell would the reason be for such a foolish and rash attack against that nation net them, sir?"

"Think about it for a second Admiral Middleton, control of a strong economy. With Japan in their possession, the Chinese could pick and chosen what countries to ally herself with, while controlling others at the same time, sir. There are many other reasons for this suggestion to work out in China's favor, sir. Let's just say we're going to keep a close eye on all of China's military moves in this region for the time being, and we also plan to act accordingly against any possible threat China levels at any other country in the Asian region, Admiral Middleton Sir."

"If the Chinese move against Japan, I hope your government will give my people enough time to pull back, before you react against them General Campanelli Sir." Admiral Middleton asked.

"By all means sir. I hope you keep your eyes open, so you know when it's time for you to pull back your forces to a much safer position if China forces our hand, and we have to react against their actions, sir?" The concerned American General suddenly stood and said he had to get back to his Command and then offered, "You can keep the tape and pictures, they're copies sir."

"I can share this information with China then I take it, General Campanelli Sir?"

"As I said before Admiral Middleton Sir, yes by all means please do sir. But first I must request you must keep the Platform a secret for the time being, sir."

"Yes, and I thank you again for this most vital information, General Campanelli Sir. I'll walk you topside General. Your aircraft has been refueled and checked out, sir." Admiral Middleton lead the way up to the flight deck. He left the tape and pictures resting on the table, and the M-5 officer immediately scooped them up and then quickly disappeared with the evidence.

The two officers shook hands as General Campanelli headed for the YF-27 parked on the fantail of the ship. The upward sweep of the far end of the flight deck would be enough to throw the aircraft in fight. The Invincible did not have catapults, but she had arresting cables, in case one of the Harrier jump jets had to land without it usual hovering abilities.

The American fighter aircraft easily shot up in the sky as smooth as silk. Lieutenant Wright climbed up to thirty seven thousand feet, and then headed directly back for the massive Platform. Cruising at twelve hundred mile per hour, without the use of afterburners. General Campanelli took one last look at the huge English Jump Jet Carrier through the twin vertical stabilizers of his aircraft, and then he shook his head over the sight he witnessed behind him.

The M-5 Officer joined Admiral Middleton when he returned and he reported. "Admiral Middleton, I just spoke to Command, the Americans have been in touch with our Prime Minister, and he has given us the clearance to work up a surgical attack against these nuclear tipped missiles with China, using the American intelligence offered us from their Command, sir."

"Thank you Colonel, contact the Chinese Command Ship Luta and inform them I want to meet with Admiral Hui Ching at his earliest possible convenience, and let him know that I have vitally important information to share with him which needs his immediate attention, sir." Admiral Middleton then went below, he wanted to change uniforms before he took a helicopter flight out to the Chinese warship Luta, the Destroyer that was the command ship for the entire Chinese Navy. In less than an hour, Admiral Middleton was on his way.

General Edward Campanelli landed on the fully operational and massive Platform with the young pilot, and he immediately swore to himself the only way anyone was ever going to get him back in a fighter aircraft again, was to kill him first. He went directly over to the CIC Chamber, and he instantly ordered all non-essential personnel out of the room, so he could make contact General Weidenbacher. General Campanelli placed a scrambled call out to the General at the Situation Room, after he was informed the General was speaking with the President. He waited until he saw General Weidenbacher's face on the screen, and then he started right in with his report. The President was on the center screen with the two officers.

General Campanelli quickly informed the President and General Weidenbacher of how it went with his meeting with the English Admiral. Once he finished, the questions began.

President Albert Cole wanted to know if the North Korean nuclear tipped missiles were a surprise to the English Military Command, or if they were aware of their presence.

General Campanelli assured him the English did not have any idea the North Koreans were preparing the missiles with nuclear warheads for an attack against them.

The always troublesome civilian advisor to the President, Raymond Manning, wanted to know if the English Command was still to be trusted at this point.

"Yes!" General Campanelli answered in an extremely hostile voice, as he openly glared at his civilian inquisitor that brought an instant and harsh stare from the President. The unspoken warning was more than enough to back the obviously angry military officer down some.

A messenger came in the room and he waited silently for the President to request the memo he was holding in his hands. He read the report and then the President announced Admiral Middleton was on his way out to meet with Admiral Ching, who was in Command of the attack on North Korea. The President looked to General Campanelli and he asked him.

"Well, what do you think they will be talking about sir?"

"Mr. President Sir, I'm certain they'll be discussing the alternatives, and how they're going to attack the missile sites in North Korea, sir. That's what I'd be doing at least, Mr. President Sir."

President Albert Cole snapped angrily at his military officer. "I didn't ask what you might be doing, mister." He was sorry he allowed General Campanelli's flare of anger at Manning to upset him so. His attack on General Campanelli brought a harsh glare from General Weidenbacher as well. The President noticed the concerned look, and he nodded slightly towards the upset General Weidenbacher, who nodded back that his point was well taken by the American Leader.

President Cole turned back to General Campanelli and asked his Supreme Commander of the Asian Theater. "General Campanelli Sir, what's your plan of action from here, sir?"

"With all due respect Mr. President Sir, I intend to get the level of awareness as high as possible, sir. I'm afraid we'll be joining the fighting before too long, Mr. President Sir."

"Oh, and who'll we be fighting sir?" the President grunted as he stood and began to pace.

"Mr. President Sir, I think we'll be fighting the god damn Chinese in this case..."

"For what reason will we be fighting the damn Chinese forces, General Campanelli Sir." The President suddenly bellowed as he held him in his gaze over the television hookup.

Campanelli was sweating because he did not want to get involved in an argument with the President a second time. Not with all going on around him at the moment. "Mr. President Sir, China will not only march through North Korea, but she has enough troops positioned in South Korea already, to takeover that country without much trouble from them sir. I think China's real motive in this game of theirs is to attack Japan, and possibly Taiwan also, Mr. President Sir."

President Cole turned white as he stared at Campanelli on the screen as he asked, "are you mad? Where are you getting these crazy ideas. Do you have proof to what you are offering, sir?"

General Weidenbacher interrupted the two by offering to the American Leader in a calming tone of voice this time. "Mr. President Sir, the General and I have discussed what the Chinese military forces could be up to in this operation at length, sir. He has discussed this with me on a few separate occasions, and I believe he may have locked onto something rather important here, sir. We don't like so many Chinese troops suddenly showing up in South Korea, and Japan's getting rather nervous over this situation as well, sir. Japan has informed us she has armed her own nuclear missiles, and is standing poised to attack any possible threat to her land offered against them by any nation in this region, sir."

"God dammit sir, how the hell come I wasn't informed about this damn conversation of yours before this time, General Weidenbacher Sir. This is a helluva fine time to bring up this concern to my fucking attention for the love of God, sir. We're into this damn thing too deeply to change course now, sir. We're locked into what is happening with China and North Korea, sir." The upset President demanded angry from his top military officer this time around.

"Mr. President Sir, I didn't bring this subject up to you attention until now, because it was still at a discussion stage, sir. I don't think you want to know every conversation I have with any of my damn Officers, sir. You couldn't possibly absorb all this information. I..."

"I warn you sir, don't try and fence around with me mister, because you'll lose every time General Weidenbacher Sir. I don't enjoy it when you try that kind of shit on me, sir. A conversation of this importance should've been brought up to my attention immediately, sir."

"It's like I said in the past, Mr. President Sir. The Army wants to do whatever the hell it wants to do, and answer to no one but themselves while they're doing it, sir. I think we should really investigate the Armed Services, and see if there's any other important information that might have been withheld from you at this point, sir. Like all soldiers, when they fail with the sword, they ask for more swords to fight with, Mr. President Sir." Manning growled angrily.

All eyes stared at him, and General Weidenbacher glared hotly at Manning while the Secretary of State quickly stood and she actually yelled at him this time, "I don't really believe this meeting should be opened to any civilians at this time, Mr. President Sir. Civilian will only get in the way of any military solutions that we will come to an understanding of. We have to be able to speak our minds in the open, without fearing upsetting a civilian, and then have him interrupting our conversations like this. This situation is much too important to have any hysterical civilians attending the meeting, Mr. President Sir. I believe Mr. Mann..."

President Cole cut the obviously upset female Secretary of State off by raising his hand, and then offering to her. "That'll be quite enough of this kind of shit from everyone attending this damn meeting. I don't need anyone throwing any more gasoline on this damn fire on me but me. I need everyone here with a clear head and open minds for this meeting, people." The President turned to Manning, and then he barked at him only, "will you sit down and keep your mouth shut unless you have something constructive to add to the conversation, sir." The President then turned to General Campanelli and added as he got his emotions under his control again.

"I believe you're done here General Campanelli Sir, do as you offered and get your troops ready for all options coming at them, sir. I want you well prepared to respond to any possible attack on Japan or Taiwan for that matter, sir. If you need anything in the way of added troops or supplies.

Let General Weidenbacher know, and I'll make certain you get what you need and request, General Campanelli Sir. Now go back to your people, sir."

Manning started to add something else in his defense, but the President immediately snapped at him, cutting him off in mid statement as he growled at him angrily. "I just said that'll be more than enough out of you for the time being, Mr. Manning. General Weidenbacher Sir, you and the Director in my office immediately please, sir. The rest of you people get something to eat for yourselves. I want all of you in constant contact with the White House from this point on. Until the damn fighting currently taking place in North Korea's over with, people. I should've had my head examined to ever allow myself to be talked into allowing the damn Chinese to attack North Korea in the first place, dammit. I should've known damn well they were up to something no damn good around here. Gentlemen, to my office right now please." The President quickly marched out of the Situation Room and up to the Oval Office, and he was followed closely by the smirking General Weidenbacher and a concerned Director Griffin.

The President charged through the door to his office, and he went right over to his desk and dropped down in his seat, and then let his breath out in a deep sigh at the same time, as he got comfortable and then he waited for the other two to be seated.

CIA Director John Raincloud and the Chairman of the Joint Chiefs of Staff, General William Weidenbacher followed the President into the room and they both remained standing until they were offered seats by the upset looking American Leader. Once he was able to get his breathing under control, and he was much more calmer. That was when the two powerful representatives finally relaxed and they took their seats, and then they waited for the President to address them. The National Security Director Griffin sort of snuck into the room behind the two others and he quickly took a seat.

DAY SIX OF THE FIGHTING IN NORTH KOREA

British Admiral Middleton returned from his meeting with the Chinese Commander Admiral Ching. Ching just got back to his ship from a private meeting with the powerful Chairman of China, Mao Cheng-yu. Admiral Middleton requested and received from General Campanelli, three dozen GUB-10 E/B MK-84 two thousand pound LGB Paveway 11 series laser guided smart bombs, and forty AGM-109 MRASM cruise missiles. All were promised when Admiral Middleton informed General Campanelli his meeting with the Chinese Admiral went off very well, and he was all for a joint mission to destroy these North Korean nuclear tipped missiles.

BEIJING, CHINA
AN EMERGENCY MEETING BETWEEN THE
CHAIRMAN OF CHINA AND ALL HIS MINISTERS

The well aged Chairman, Mao Cheng-yu, sat with his younger Vice Chairman Chao Tso Jen in his private office. He was enjoying a cigar, the only one at the meeting smoking, and the only one allowed to smoke. Chairman Cheng-yu rose, scanning the many faces of his other Ministers at the meeting staring at him, he was looking for his Minister of Nuclear Industry. When he spotted him, he said in a slightly shaky voice. "I believe the floor is yours at this time Mr. Chi-mao. Explain why I have asked all the Ministers to attend this special meeting, sir.”

Minister Chi-mao stood as the Chairman took his seat while bowing slightly at him, and then to the others Ministers at the meeting as he began explaining to the others about the missiles in North Korea, and how they were being turned over to nuclear warhead tipped missiles now.

All the Ministers sat in complete silence as they looked from one to another. The Minister of Civil Affairs, Lao Tsi-tan stood and then he waited until he got the nod from the Chairman to speak, when he did he offered quickly. “Is there a threat to the mainland by these god dom North Korean nuclear missiles you’re speaking about, Minister Chi-moa? Should we move some of our civilians away from certain areas of China, in case we come under attack from them?”

The Chinese Minister of State Security, Hong Kuo Feng bounced up to his feet and cried. “The mainland is not threatened by the substandard missiles from the lowly barbarians to our North. The only thing these foul animals are doing is threatening our fighting soldiers operating in North Korea with them. This opens many doors to us, sir. We would be within our rights to resort to the use of nuclear weapons ourselves, if we so choose to take this path that is, sir.”

The Minister of National Defense rose, and the elderly Chairman allowed him speak over the protest of the angry Minister of State Security. “I fail to understand why the State Minister has offered his opinion of what we can, and cannot do since this threat was brought to our attention. I say what is open, and how we react against it. We can respond with a nuclear attack, but it’d be in China’s best interest to use a conventional response against this sudden and terrible threat, sir. Thanks to the foolish Americans who we can now make use of, and have them work with us along with the worthless British. We know where these North Korean nuclear tipped missiles are being prepared, and where they are also being moved to, sir. The foolish Americans have offered to supervise our attack efforts for us, aided by their satellites and recon aircraft. They gave the worthless English fools some of their special breed of weapons to make this attack successful."

"What type of weapons did the Americans offer to us sir?" the Chairman asked with concern.

The Minister of National Defense checked a list and he replied to the Chairman confidently. "The hated Americans gave the English fools a large number of their laser guided smart bombs, a good weapon. They have also given them a certain number of their advanced cruise missiles that are capable of being carried by some of their fighter aircraft. Each fighter can take four of these smaller missiles. The important fact is, one of these missiles can be fired with a preprogrammed target, and the missiles will fly around the target for twenty five minutes while hunting the set target. It's a perfect weapon to employ against the worthless North Korean targets, it'll not attack a damaged launcher system sir. If the North Koreans make dummy launchers, if the proper radar and electronic signals are not being emitted from it, the missile completely ignores it, sir."

The Chairman interrupted the report as he snapped at his Minister, "how come the worthless Americans gave these weapons to the English only? How come we didn't get any of them?"

"I believe it's because the Americans don't quite trust us very much, Mr. Chairman."

Laughter quickly filled the room. The Chairman had to stand to quiet the room again as he remarked with a touch of anger in his voice, "I wonder why the not so foolish Americans don't trust us very much, sir. I'll prove to them that their fears are well founded in truth, sir."

Mr. Chung continued with his report for the other members of the meeting. "The English are being very guarded with the American weapons. I've made two requests so far to have a number of the cruise missiles released to us, but the hated English responded they did not have enough missiles for their own aircraft, to enable them to be shared by us sir. I know the god cursed British don't want us to have any of these American made weapons for ourselves, sir."

Chairman Cheng-yu slowly almost threateningly rolled his cigar in his fingers as he responded. "I want a few of these god dom missiles, and I don't care how you go about getting us some, sir."

"Mr. Chairman, when I first spoke with the English, they made it known to me in no uncertain terms. Once we successfully destroy the North Korean missiles and nuclear sites stationed at Yongbyon complex, sir. They and the Americans want the war to end immediately sir. What excuse will we have to carry on with the war any further unless we openly attack Taiwan, sir?"

"What the devil do I care what the worthless English, or even the hated Americans want and don't want from us. Who the devil are they to tell China what they are to do, sir? I shall teach the loathsome Americans what to do in Asia shortly myself, sir." The old man caught himself, and he took a quick drag on his cigar, as his eyes studied the paintings hanging on the wall.

Minister Chung looked to the rest of the Ministers attending the meeting, everyone waited for the powerful Chairman to return his attention to the meeting and them.

The Minister of Justice, Qing Tu-wei made a quick motion with his hands for Chung to continue with his concerns to the Council of Ministers, "Mr. Chairman Sir, the Americans are continuing to build up their military presence in the region as we meet here, sir."

"Yes I understand this as fact, and I don't like it one bit either I add for your worthless ears. I intend to order our Ambassador to offer a protest at the next meeting of the United Nations, against the American military buildup in our region, sir. I want it stopped right now."

Minister Chung bit his lip as he replied with caution in his voice. "Mr. Chairman, as you said, as long as the hated Americans have no military land base in which to operate from, how much of a threat can they possible be against our military might? We could wear down the Americans with a war of attrition, and make them use up weapons and supplies until they run out sir."

"I know what I said in the past, I don't like being reminded about it either, and it does nothing to change my feeling of not wanting so many American soldiers in Asia, does it Mr. Chung?"

"No sir, it certainly does not at all sir. I'm sorry for bringing the matter up to your attention again Mr. Chairman." Minister Chung offered as he bowed slightly to the Chinese Leader.

The old man smiled at the contrite Minister as he leaned back in his chair, pleased he had just put this younger upstart in his place in front of the other Ministers at the meeting. Now they understood they better side with him no matter what he chose to do about the English, Taiwan or the hated

Americans. "Continue!" the Chairman suddenly hissed at the concerned Minister.

"Mr. Chairman Sir, our nation's military troops are set in place in, and around Hong Kong. The bank tellers have been replaced mostly by our loyal soldiers, and they have orders to close down all the banks as soon as the word comes from us to do so, sir."

"What do you intend to do with the god cursed foreigners who have flood our land, once we have completely taken over all of our Colony of Hong Kong sir, and how do we go about supporting the takeover of Hong Kong, sir?" the Minister of Civil Affairs asked.

The Minister of National Defense snapped hotly at the Minister, "we have gone over this at length at a number of prior meetings, sir. We're going to drive out all the lowly mongrels from the land of China. We'll have our guards check all passports, and any English, or foreigners will immediately be deported. But first they are to be searched, and all valuables confiscated from the fools. Then the god cursed devils will be placed on board transports, and shipped out to sea where ships from their own country can pick them up. No foreigners not our allies, will be allowed to remove anything of worth from the land of China once we take over Hong Kong, sir."

There was a sudden commotion as a messenger entered the room, and he handed a paper to the old Chinese Leader. Anger instantly flashed across his wrinkled, weather beaten face.

The Vice Chairman easily caught the silent message from the obviously angry Chairman, and he immediately announced the meeting was closed. He ordered the Central Military Commission President, Yang So, to remain with the Ministers of Naval Affairs and Defense.

No one spoke as the other Ministers quickly filed out of the meeting room.   Once they were gone, the wise Chairman told the remaining ministers to move to the forward chairs, so he did not have to raise his voice for them to hear his words. The old man suddenly clapped his hands, and a number of women servants marched in with tea and biscuits, and a damp towel for the Chairman and Ministers to wipe the sweat from their faces.   The women quickly disappeared, and when the tea was finished, the old Chairman stood on shaky legs. He walked the length of the table three times before he took his seat and then looked to each of the chosen men.

"Gentlemen, my most trusted of Ministers, once this foolishness is over with, all but you few will be replaced, and we will rid ourselves of the weak Ministers. I have a dilemma, we started this war to gain the trust of the worthless English, and to coax them to bring back billions of their worth to Hong Kong. The English were removing this cash when they knew we were not going to allow them to remain in control of Hong Kong past the year 2000. We have gone to great lengths to get them to bring this money back to Hong Kong. Our plan has worked out very well for us, but I have just received a report from the Chinese First National Bank, and it states that the flow of cash coming back to Hong Kong has gone down to a mere trickle, and some of the god cursed English investors are again actually removing their money from our banks.

"I have an estimate of the exact amount of money that has been returned to our banks in Hong Kong, it's figured to be well within the range of nine hundred and forty billion in worth. Two years ago the worth was placed at well over one trillion and eighty billion. This report states that within the past week alone, a billion in worth had been withdrawn by these lowly mongrels again. I feel it is because of this war we have entered against the worthless North Koreans."

The old man took a quick breath and then he went on, "we have to act against the British before we had planned to. I want to stop anymore of this great worth from being withdrawn from the banks of Hong Kong. So I'm ordering our bank tellers to delay any further withdrawals, and I don't care if they have to close the banks in order to stop this foolishness. My concern is we have to act very quickly against the god cursed English, and go ahead with our plans to attack Taiwan as well, sir. I leave this up to you as to how we're going handle the problems with the foolish British, and start our next operation to make the world believe we had just cause to confiscate the English monies. I'm open to any and all suggestions here, gentlemen." The Chairman took his cigar from the ashtray and blew out a ring of smoke around his head.

The Military Commission President bowed politely and then offered to the Chinese Leader. "Mr. Chairman Sir, we planned to take Hong Kong in force, once we have finished our war with North Korea, sir. We had no plans on how to accomplish this other than just march in and force the English off our land of Hong Kong with just the clothes on their worthless backs, sir."

"I'm well aware at what we intended, but we can no longer merely march in without just cause, we'll look bad once we keep our military forces in North Korea, and make our push into South Korea, and then mass our forces against the hated Nation of Japan. I want the world to think we're going after Japan rather than Hong Kong, this was to allow the hated British to get their worth back to Hong Kong." The old man gasped for air as he stopped speaking.

"We can do this, we can mass our military forces in lower South Korea, sir. We're on good terms with the great fools now, and we know the South Koreans are not on the best of terms with Japan either. And I seriously doubt their government would stop us, if we told them we're going after Japan, sir. They might even join us on the attack sir." The Defense Minister offered.

"Do you really believe the foolish South Koreans are still that angry at Japan they'd join us, if we attack that worthless nation that is?" Vice Chairman Chao Tso Jen asked.

"Yes, I've been in constant contact with the worthless South Korean government over the past few days, and observing their opinion of the fact our military troops are in part of their god cursed foul country under the guise of protecting South Korea, in case the North Koreans attacked their nation, sir. The great fools have no problem with this situation, sir. I got the feeling the more of our troops are in their foul nation, the better as far as they're concerned, sir." The Chinese Defense Minister offered to the Vice Chairman confidently this time.

"Good, this is exactly what I wanted the foul fools to believe." The Chairman leaned forward and then added, "I shall order a full flotilla of transport ships sailing for the southern end of South Korea by no later than this afternoon. Ha, we'll give worthless Japanese some serious fits when our troops land so close to their foul country. We'll tell the world that these troops are on liberty, but the foolish Japanese will see they are making an active military base, and also taking permanent residence in the South of Korea. I'll further send the 71st Group Army, a Class C Army made up of old, untrained men and women, who don't know how to shoot properly.

"Their presence will accomplish what we had in mind all along, and we'll allow the world to digest this, while we continue to prepare to invade the cursed Island of Taiwan. I want this country of hated Mongrels, I'll slaughter all who followed that lowly dog, Chiang Kai-shek and the rest of his bastard sons who betrayed China in her times of most need of these fools, sir."

"We have not come up with a positive way to begin our opening hostilities against the United Kingdom, Mr. Chairman." The Civil Affairs Minister said. Silence immediately filled the room while everyone thought of a successful attack plan to try and impress the Chairman.

The Naval Affairs Minister offered in an excited tone of voice, "we can always create a situation over the British knocking down one of our warplanes, or we could even have our troops request an air strike in North Korea. Then we can have our criminals brought there and killed, and blame their deaths on the British warplanes, and use this to start a dispute with them."

Chairman Cheng-yu looked at the Minister as he grumbled in an upset voice, "we're going to need an incident much stronger than that one, fools. We need an incident to cause us to take Hong Kong, without problem from the rest of the world sir. I want quick action, and once we're our troops are in place in both Hong Kong and Taiwan, I'll not care one grain of worthless rice what the world has to say, but they have to leave us alone until our forces are set in place, sir."

The Vice Chairman's eyes were ablaze as he offered in an angry voice, "since when did China ever care about what the rest of the world thought, or had to say about our actions in the past. We react when we chose, I say we go into Hong Kong and Taiwan at the same time, and the hell with what the rest of the world has to say about our actions. And I offer we do it now, before the lowly mongrel English have a chance to remove more of their worth from our banks, sir."

The old man raised his hand to silence his Minister, and then he announced, "it does my heart good to see such agreement between you Ministers, but we didn't answer the question on how to justify our attacks on these two locations we have aimed our eyes upon." He turned to his Vice Chairman and moaned at him, "Mr. Chao Tso Jen, I know in the past we have reacted, and never once cared what the rest of the world said or believed about our motives, but here we have to think differently I believe. We're planning to steal enough money to make China the power she should be, and we're not really stealing it. Our bookkeeper's feel England has removed, and made three times this much money, and they never shared a cent of their profit with China or her people. The English owe us this much and more, think of it as past due taxes and interest owed to China by them. I want China to look like she was right, I'll ask the Ambassador from Japan to leave our country once our troops are set in place in the lower section of South Korea."

No one understood where this comment came from, but it got everyone's attention quickly.

"We're going to pick on the Ambassadors from the Philippines and Vietnam. This will cause the American military to split up their forces. If the Philippines cry, the United States will have no choice but to send one of their worthless Aircraft Carriers to that nation to shut them up. Now that the Americans are on peaceful terms with Vietnam, and we're creating a problem with that miserable country of lowly dog eaters, the American pride will dictate they send another Carrier Group to the coast of that worthless country to help protect that nation from us. We'll stretch the forces of the United States so thin the foul fools couldn't possibly defend the Philippines and Vietnam, and also offer a good defense against our plans aimed against the English and Taiwan."

"What about the god cursed Russian animals? They've invested great interests and money in that nation of Vietnam too, Mr. Chairman." The Naval Minister cried out from his chair.

The smile appeared again on the elderly Chairman's face as he smirked at his excited Minister. "Don't make me laugh, Minister. I'll tell you about Russia, this so called Alliance State they now call themselves, no longer have the money to sail one of their worthless warship on the Seas to defend their country of less worth any longer. Their nuclear threat is spread out through the Middle East, sold to the highest bidder time and again, along with their foolish pride as well. All that's left of the once great Russian Empire is the black market, that exists only to sell off their lowly remains. The Great Bear has been defanged, and they're no longer to be feared by us."

The Naval Minister was scared by the Chairman's words as he remarked, "Mr. Chairman, I hope you're not underestimating Russia, and what is left of her god cursed nation and military defenses. She retains enough of her nuclear missiles to destroy all of China in one attack, sir."

The Chinese Leader laughed a second time as he snarled at his Minister this time. "If the foul Russians have these missiles you fear so much, they no longer have the fuel to make them fly, sir. Their population has drained off all the fuel of everything, even their missiles, to use in their rotting automobiles. Russia is the land of thieves and black marketers for sale to the highest bidder. Look at the United States, they've stolen the top Russian scientists, leaving the dregs to sell off the rest of their knowledge to the lowly Arabs. Look at the once great Russian Navy, sir. With no fuel for their warships, it's left rusting in ports, to be picked over and taken apart for sale for nothing. Don't fear cursed Russian fools, sir. Tomorrow, maybe another government will be installed, only to be overthrown by another one next week. Bah, I fear Russia as much as I fear South Korea, and what that nation could offer our fighting forces once we engage the fools."

Vice Chairman Tso Jen looked around and then snapped in an angry voice. "Gentlemen, as of this moment, we haven't heard any positive solutions on how to commence our hostilities with the nation of England!" he glared at the remaining Ministers to enforce his anger at the delays.

All but one of the Ministers lowered their heads in order to avoid his hard glare again. The Vice Chairman's attention went over to the one Minister daring to continue looking back at him. "Minister of Defense, Mr. Chung, you seem to have something on your mind I see, would you care sharing your thoughts with the rest of us?" Tso-Jen said sarcastically to him.

The Minister rose on shaky legs as he offered meekly to the angry looking Second in Command and well feared Chinese Leader. "Mr. Vice Chairman, if we want to start something with the hated English fool than I suggest we sink one of their precious Aircraft Carriers on the fools, sir."

The old man's body jumped out of his chair like a man who had just received an electrical shock to his rump, as he roared at his Minister as the angry Chairman took over the conversation, "are you in full command of your faculties, you great fool? How dare you suggest to me that we dare to sink an English Aircraft Carrier. That would be an all out act of war. I don't want to start a war with the hated English, I just want to create an air of mistrust with them, so we can have our soldiers take Hong Kong, and the English worth, you fool." The Chairman lowered himself back in his chair as he looked for his cigar that had rolled to the floor. He opened another.

"Mr. Chairman, you did not allow me to finish what I have to offer you, sir. I don't propose to attack the United Kingdom Aircraft Carrier outright, sir. We have a good number of our submarines in the area of conflict, sir. We even have two of our submarines trailing the English Aircraft Carriers at all times. I merely suggest we stir up a North Korean submarine, and drive it at one of the English Aircraft Carrier Groups. Then one of our submarines could fire a number of torpedoes at the British Carrier, and then we merely blame it on the North Korean submarine, and the English could not possibly be angry at us for moving against the enemy submarine, sir.

"Yes of course, the foolish English will accuse us of firing the torpedoes, and we'll blame the North Koreans. We'll build up this incident into a full blown situation where we could break off our relations with the English fools, without having to fire a single shot in anger at them, sir. We could use this ploy to drive the English out of China, and use their money while the courts tie up their request for the funds to be released to them for many years to come, until we finally tell the English to die, and we keep the money outright, sir. The world will be so tired of hearing the English crying about this unending case, that no one would raise a finger to help the fools, sir."

The Vice Chairman went to add something, but he was instantly cut off by the Chairman as he added, "I like this idea very much, I believe it'll work. I like the idea of keeping this situation tied up in the worthless courts for a long time to come. I shall allow you put this plan of yours in motion, sir. How are we going to get our submarine to attack the foul English Aircraft Carrier without being detected by the English ships protecting that ship, sir?" the Chairman asked him.

The Defense Minister smiled as he offered to the powerful Chinese Chairman, "that'd be the problem of the Minister of Naval Affairs to work out for us I believe, sir."

The Minister of Naval Affairs immediately responded as he rose to his feet. "I have two of our submarines sitting right on the bottom in the Korean Bay in case they're needed, sir. I know of their exact position, and can have Admiral Ching stationed on the Destroyer Kuta, move the British Invincible over to their location. I can have a second Destroyer move a North Korean submarine it has been tracking for the past three days now, towards the position Admiral Ching will order the Invincible to. We can then attack, and make it look like the North Koreans have sunk their precious warship, but the English would not be sure, sir. They'll try and blame us, because we moved the Invincible to this position, and would have it in the back of their worthless minds we sunk their great warship sir. Either way, it'll serve to create ill feelings towards us."

Chairman Cheng-yu's smile was spotted with missing and rotted teeth. He then turned to his Vice Chairman and ordered him to make certain the Naval Minister had everything he needed to complete this operation, and sink the English Jump Jet Aircraft Carrier. The old man totally ignored the other Ministers attending the meeting, he was relieved they had the plan needed to accomplish what had to be accomplished. He was actually overjoyed he was going to put both the English and Americans in their place. He looked to the portrait of Mao Zedong, and smiled as he gave him a silent salute. His train of thought was broken by the Minister of Naval Affairs.

"Mr. Chairman, I'd like to know how far I can go with this latest operation, sir?"

"What do you mean by that question?" the old Chairman snarled back at his Minister.

"Mr. Chairman, how should I react if the foolish English are able to detect our submarine, and they realize we moved them into a trap, sir?" The concerned Minister of Naval Affairs asked with some concern in his tone, as he stared at the leader of the Chinese government.

The Chairman snapped back at the concerned looking and acting Minister, "I've done everything I can think of to make this happen like it was our fault, but not our fault, sir. If one of your god dom submarines are discovered by the English then you'll continue with the attack. If we're found out, we'll make it an all our war then with the great fools, and be done with it sir."

The remaining Chinese Ministers looked to one another, none of them knew how to react to this last statement uttered by the elderly Chairman. Was China strong enough to stand alone against the awesome combined powers of the United Kingdom and the United States?

CHAPTER 28
ON BOARD THE VINEGAR JOE PLATFORM

General Edward Campanelli immediately looked for Aleksandra, she was not inside the CIC chamber, so he checked out the mess hall for her. He finally resigned to eating alone because he could not find her anywhere he looked for her on the massive Platform. He filled a tray and sat down then spotted Sergeant Cruz sitting with a young female Sergeant at another table. Sergeant Cruz looked in his direction and then General Campanelli immediately motioned him over.

"Yes sir, what can I do for you General Campanelli Sir?" the Sergeant asked his Commander.

"How are you doing Sergeant Cruz? I was looking for the pain in the ass female Major again, have you seen her out and about? Who is the new hen you're sitting with mister?"

"Sergeant Harding, General Campanelli, I'm trying to talk her into taking a quick ride on the old bologna pony, sir. The last I heard, the Major's flying sir, she went up with the other female pilots on a training flight, sir. General, they musta been up for three hours now. That means they musta tanked up while in flight, I guess they're trying to stay sharp, General Campanelli Sir."

The upset General grabbed the chunk of meat and slapped it between two slices of bread, and then he slugged down the rest of his Pepsi and headed topside for the Control Tower. The Flight Controller was speaking to an airborne pilot, and the General was forced to wait until he finished with the pilot before he could ask the controller if the foreign Major was airborne.

"Sure General Campanelli Sir, she and a group of pilots are doing in flight exercises in Red Sector Four, sir. You want to listen in on them as the pilots carry out their exercise, sir?"

"Yeah sure why the hell not sir." He growled, he was pissed off because she went up again without informing him first, he then laughed at himself, "sonofabitch you're still just a damn male chauvinist pig after all these years, old buddy."

"Excuse me sir?" The stunned Airman asked the General with a little concern in his tone.

"Nothing, I was just thinking out loud I'm afraid. Airman, open up a communication with the pilots for me will you please?" he ordered as he shook his head at himself and smiled.

"Hold on a second Airman." The Flight Commander immediately snapped at the young man, and then he went on with is gripe to his commanding officer. "General Campanelli Sir, any requests to speak to a pilot while in flight, has to come through me General Sir."

"Okay if we're going to start splitting hairs around here. Then you open a communication with the Major for me, sir. I need to speak to the Major immediately, Flight Commander Sir."

"Yes sir, right away General Campanelli Sir. I'll get her on the horn for you, sir," he picked up the mike and grumbled into it. "Homeplate to Blue Flight Leader. Report in. Over."

"Homeplate, this is Twin Peak, sir. Report in as order to sir. Over." Aleksandra replied.

"Twin Peaks, Homeplate. I have an important message for you. Please stand by. Over."

The again fuming General took the mike and growled at his female pilot, "Major Klevekaita, General Campanelli here, Ma'am. I need you back at Homeplate at once Major. Over."

"Twin Peak to Homeplate. Sorry sir, can no do as order you me at this time, sir. Over."

"Whatdaya fucking mean by that load of crumbled cookies, Major? I just ordered you to get your ass back here on the damn double quick, and that's exactly what you're gonna do, that's an order, Major." General Campanelli snarled, realizing she did not changed her tag name.

"Twin Peak to Homeplate. Improper radio transmission I receive from you, sir. I no return base now for surely, sir. I engaged in Vector Three exercise, and no able to break off exercise for you at this time, sir. I have three chicks engage against and am fight them off, sir. Over."

"What the hell's a Vector Three exercise dammit? Disengage your Vector Three immediately. I need you back here right now, Major!" he ordered, turning red as he squeezed the plastic mike.

"Twin Peak to Homeplate Flight Commander Sir. Over." She said in her radio.

"Homeplate to Twin Peaks. This is the Commander, go with your traffic Major. Over."

"Twin Peak to Commander. Explain Vector Three to General. Out." The radio went dead.

The Commander smiled as he turned to the extremely angry General, and offered him with a snappy tone of voice. "She's got some fucking balls there, General Campanelli Sir."

"Yeah, steel balls and fucking brass ovaries, Commander!" he interjected.

"General Campanelli Sir, a Vector Three exercise is an operation where we pit two sets of three attacking aircraft against each other in a simulated dog fight situation, sir. Twin Peak's right sir, once this operation commences she can't possibly pull out until she's either killed off, or the exercise is called to a buster signal and ended, General. Blue Flight's all setup, and so is Red Flight sir, this is an expensive exercise, and unless your need for her is an emergency, sir. I'll have to override your request for her to deck down at this present time, sir. Is it possible for you to wait for the Major until the exercise has been completed one way or the other, General Campanelli Sir? It shouldn't take more than ten to fifteen minutes to complete, sir."

General Campanelli suddenly drew in his breath, and then he hissed in an angry tone at the Flight Commander, because he was not used to having any of his ordered overrode like this. "Yeah, I guess so sir." He knew the Commander could easily override him over this demand, and then resigned himself to wait until the mission was over with. He pulled a chair a little closer to him, and sat and watched as the Flight Commander did his act with the pilots.

"I thank you much for your understanding of the present situation, General Campanelli Sir. Homeplate to Twin Peaks. You're now instructed to disregard your last transmission, Major. Continue on with you Vector Three exercise as instructed, Major Ma'am. Out."

"Roger. Blue Flight One to Blue Two and Three. Over." She used her squadron's frequency.

"Blue Flight Two in. Blue Flight Three in. Over." The other two pilots reported in.

"Blue Two, Mastercard. Take mid cap patrol at Angel Five. Blue Fight Three, Manhunter. I want you take high cap patrol at Angel Ten Thousand Feet. I take low cap patrol at Angel Two Thousand Feet. Ladies, keep you eye open, Red Flight attackers come at us from any direction during exercise please. Blue Flight Two, make noise and get their attention. Over."

"Roger that last, will commence my noise making as of now, Major Ma'am. Over."

"Blue One to Two and Three. You have you climb corridor, and have you mosaic, keep eye open. Beacon double, we go use beacon riders and gun for intercept, let boogie out here. Out."

General Campanelli realized all of a sudden how well Aleksandra's English was getting lately.

"Roger that last Blue One Flight Commander. This is Blue Flight Two heading for Angels Five Thousand Feet to begin ordered patrol as instructed. Out."

"Blue Flight One this is Blue Flight Three. Heading for Angels Ten to begin hunting. Out."

"Blue Flights Two and Three. I head for Angel Two for protect of you aircraft. Out."

The three sleek fighter aircraft split their ranks and the three aircraft headed for their assigned positions. The pilots were expecting an opening attack from three F-22 Raptor Stealth fighters. Blue Flight was in the attack zone for five minutes now.

Blue Flight One was the only aircraft in the flight that had her radar search on and working for her, looking for the first sign of the attackers to show up on her scope. Aleksandra kept glancing at her radar scope, hoping to spot the F-22 Raptors before they found her flight and attacked and killed them off. She had her other aircraft set and marked on the screen, and was still picking up her Exxon fuel station circling at Angels Forty Five Thousand Feet. She radioed in.

"I check port and starboard area with radar search, Blue Flight Two you check you six with visual check for possible enemy contact. I show all clear, no contact other friendlies then nothing but clear sky head and behind us. Out."

Twin Peaks suddenly got a quick bounce echo on her radar. Then a second one, and a much stronger bounce this time, with a clear height showing at Angels Seven, and she immediately reported to her other two pilots in her group. "I have bounce echo contact, confused, stand by. Multi contact, target acquisition complete. Duck, trouble coming you way ladies. Out."

Aleksandra had two targets locked up in her attack radar, one at Angel Three even, and the other at Angel Seven Thousand Feet. "Blue Flight One to Blue Flight Two and Three, I have positive bounce at Angel Seven and Three, they come in from south, southeast at, I peg Mach Two. You instruct increase speed Mach Two point Five and intercept course come in from north, northwest. Be advised, I no pick up target three, be aware of possible trap ladies. Out."

RED FLIGHT

"Red Flight Leader One to Red Flight Two. Headhunter, get your black ass up to seven thousand feet on the double quick, sucker. Red Flight Three, Triple Cross, get up to Angels Four and start hunting man. I'll stay at Angels Three. I have a positive radar read at Angel's Five, and they're holding true and even, and a second read at Angel's Two. That's two targets accounted for, Headhunter and Triple Cross, attack target at Angel's Five. I'll work on the radar contact holding steady position at Angel's Two. Move out niggers." All three of the attacking Red Flight aircraft had black pilots at their controls for this exercise engagement.

Twin Peaks picked up the radar echo emitting from her target at level flight at Angel's Three, and figured this aircraft was the Red Flight Leader for this exercise. Just as Red Flight Two and Three went after the Blue Flight Two target patrolling at five thousand feet, a third clear contact suddenly showed up. As this target dropped down from Angel's Ten to Nine. Red Flight One Commander smiled to himself, this was the missing Blue target pilot.

Red Flight One went after this target first, and he had the Blue aircraft patrolling at Angel Two picked up and locked in on, because this one lone aircraft was employing it's attack radar. By this he knew this was Blue Flight Leader, and he decided to save her for his last kill of the day. The Red Flight One Commander pulled back on his control stick, and then he turned his aircraft to show the narrowest possible radar cross section read on Blue Flight One's tracking and aiming radar. He now showed up as a radar target no bigger than the size of a football to the Blue Flight One Commander, who had not noticed the aircraft employing his climb corridor in order to attack the other Blue Flight aircraft in flight. The Red Flight One Commander easily got on top of the Blue Flight Three aircraft, and he was coming at her from out of the sun, a perfect strike position for his opening attack against this supposed enemy aircraft.

"Blue Flight One Leader to Blue Flight Two and Three. Target Angel Seven move to Angel Eight. Keep eye opened. I believe he prepared to attack from you six. Close rank and team up and defend each other against the possible attack. Over."

"Blue Flight Three To Blue Flight Leader. I copy last, and am dropping down to Angel Nine in order to intercept target. Over." The pilot of Blue Flight Three replied to his Commander.

"Blue Flight One to Blue Flight Two and Three. I have fade out of supposed enemy aircraft, I lost contact from radar, switch to Doppler uplink and go active against miss aircraft. Good, there are the bastard is, I reestablished contact on you attacker please. This free lance mission, you each have control of you own aircraft so attack accordingly ladies. Out."

A third radar bounce suddenly appeared on Blue Flight Leader's radar for a brief second before it instantly disappeared again. The contact was located briefly at Angels Four and moving up quick against her. Twin Peaks increased her speed and moved in for the kill.

"Go to gate, maximum power afterburners to intercept contact. You weapons are free to engage. All Blue Flight Fighters, you cleared to arm and fire at attack aircraft. Out."

This exercise was to be a close in attack, using guns and short range Sidewinder Simulated Attack Missiles. The two upper radar bounces closed in fast together, and they made a direct charge at the Blue Flight Two aircraft. The F-22 Raptor came down after Blue Two.

"Blue Flight Two, you target indicate speed contact Mach Two. Increase, they arch over to attack you flight. Get out there Blue Two and protect you six please."

Aleksandra pushed her power to the stops, and went to full attack speed, and then she pulled back on her stick as she climbed her aircraft at full power. The two F-22 Raptors came in on top of the Blue Flight Two aircraft. The Blue Flight One pilot watched her radar, and realized the enemy aircraft had Blue Flight Two dead, there was nothing she could do for her fellow pilot.

"Blue Flight Two. Call is Popeye, Popeye." Aleksandra suddenly yelled like her aircraft was in danger of being killed.

The Commanding General's head instantly popped up from his sort of daydreaming, as he looked to the Flight Controller and then he asked confused. "Why the hell is she calling for me for, dammit? I can't do anything for her from down here for Pete's sake."

The Flight Controller chuckled as he offered to the Commander of the Platform. "No Sir General, she's not calling you sir. She's warning Blue Flight Two to get her ass in the clouds to reduce visibility for the supposed enemy aircraft, and possibly lose her attacker in the fluff, sir."

"Oh." General Campanelli replied with a smile as he tried to fake like he knew it all the time.

Both attacking F-22 Raptors opened fire with their simulated guns, and they instantly killed the Blue Flight Two aircraft, but both attacking aircraft were traveling too fast, and they were obviously overshooting their intended target. A mistake that was going to cost them dearly.

Aleksandra, picking up their mistake and she immediately leveled off her aircraft at four thousand five hundred feet, and then she began hovering and waited for the two attackers to cross before the bow of her waiting aircraft. She targeted them both with her the simulated Sidewinder missiles and open fire, and she received a positive kill read on both rapidly passing planes.

Blue Flight One called in over her radio. "Lock on, beam true. Tally ho, Fox Two way, Splash Two. I repeat, Splash Two. Am go after contact three now." Aleksandra saw the twin vertical stabilizers of Red Flight flash by her as she fired at the two other planes at the same time.

"Where hell is other sonofabitch hide." She mumbled more to herself than into her radio as she checked her radar again, and picked up the two killed F-22s head down for the hard deck to join the two killed Blue Flight Two aircraft mustered at their standoff positions for the exercise. This was in order to clear her radar as if they were truly killed during this exercise.

While she attacked the Red Flight Two and Three aircraft, the Red Flight One Commander looped up from under her, and he easily killed Blue Flight Three. The remaining aircraft contacted each other, and engaged in an aerial waltz of simulated death, as each pilot tried desperately to out maneuver the other pilot, in order to try and gain some valuable position on his enemy pilot. Neither pilot could out do the other's flying abilities, it was a checkmate situation rapidly developing between the two remaining pilots still alive in this exercise.

The Flight Commander kept a close eye on his watch, and at the exact time limit set to end the exercise, he called. "No Joy." Into the radio, then added, "What state?" Meaning how much fuel, oxygen and ordnance each aircraft had left on their air platforms.

Blue Flight One responded first, "Fuel is passed bingo, air down less forty percent, sir. Out."

"Roger that last as received." Then the Flight Commander ordered all aircraft involved in the last exercise to tank up, and then get back to base. All six aircraft took on six thousand pounds of fuel to enable them to get back to the Vinegar Joe Platform safely.

General Campanelli listened in as the radio was suddenly jammed with pilot chatter. The pilots were joking around with each other, as one pilot complained the other pilot attacked her out of synch, and it was not a fair attack against her. She complained she had no time to properly respond to their attack. The pilots of the F-22 Raptors that Aleksandra killed, tried their best to try and convince her she was just lucky to get both of them so easily, but she was not buying any of their shit. She razzed them both right back that she was a lot better pilot than both of them combined. She snapped at one of the male pilots.

"You go home and check between you leg, make sure it still there, big shot fly boy you."

General Campanelli stood and then he stretched his arms and yawned and then grumbled at the Flight Commander. "I'm ordering you to inform the Major I wanna see her when she's down."

The Flight Commander looked at General Campanelli, and then he responded. "That's impossible sir, I have to do a complete debriefing with all pilots before I can dismiss them, sir."

General Edward Campanelli's eyes instantly flashed pitch black as he hissed at the young Airforce Commander in a sharp tone, "look fucker, you had the fricking chutzpah to override my ass once already today and lived through it, don't try it again mister. I'm warning you sir, I'll not stand for it for a second time sir. I said I wanted to see the Major upon landing sir, and that's exactly what you'll order her to do buster, or you might find yourself landing planes up at the damn North Pole for the rest of your stinking life, sir. Is that clear to you on my orders mister?"

The Flight Commander instantly snapped to attention and he saluted the angry Command General sharply as he replied quickly. "Yes Sir General Campanelli Sir. It's as clear as a bell to me sir. I'll order a written report from the pilots involved with this last exercise for later evaluation on this exercise, sir. Will that do for you, General Campanelli Sir?"

"That does just fine Commander." General Edward Campanelli growled angrily, and then he headed out of the Flight Control Tower while saying behind him, "Tell Twin Peaks she's to report directly to the damn CIC Chamber immediately upon decking down, Commander."

"Yes sir. Homeplate to set Blue and Red Flight pilots. I want written reports and evaluations of this latest exercise on my desk by no later than Oh, Eight Hundred Hours tomorrow morning, from all you birds on your assumption of this last exercise, or you'll wish you mothers never met you fathers. Well done Blue Flight Leader, you have two confirmed kills, and two loses to your Flight Wing. Red Flight One Commander, you have one confirmed kill to two aircraft, and a one on one kill as well, sir. You birds have people really pissed off down here I want to tell ya guys. I want to see you people A-SAP, now get back here on the double quick. The F-22 Raptor Wing made some serious mental errors which caused you to lose two of your damn aircraft to this exercise. The taxpayers are going to get mad as hell if you birds lose aircraft two on one to any enemy aircraft you people engage at a cost of over seven hundred million dollars apiece, pilots. I want some god damn good answers from you, Red Flight Commander Sir."

The F-22 Stealth Fighter Aircraft were expected to make short work of the older and much slower and less maneuverability YF-27 ATFs, while suffering no losses to their much superior Air Wing. These pilots were in a world of shit from their Commander this time.

General Edward Campanelli returned to the CIC Chamber in an angry huff, and by the time Aleksandra finally got back to him. He was suddenly too busy to realize she even entered the room on him in the first place, and he was still angry as the devil at her at the same time.

The CIC Chamber was beginning to smell real bad from all the body odor, and the heavy smoking being carried off inside the Command Chamber. It was actually beginning to burn the General's eyes, and he started thinking about banning smoking inside the chamber all together, for the entire duration of the Chinese attack on North Korea. He decided he was also going to order everyone to take daily showers to cut down on the stink in the CIC.

He was so busy with going over the countless reports flooding almost constantly into the CIC Chamber about the continuing fighting occurring in North Korea, he even forgot all about the smoke burning his eyes. Every report he read lately, stated the attacking Chinese troops were really putting it to any North Korean soldiers they came across. The attacking Chinese troops were even doing in all the civilians they came across during their heavy invasion of that country as well as they marched right through the entire of North Korea so swiftly.

DAY SEVEN OF THE FIGHTING IN NORTH KOREA

At exactly Fifteen, Fifteen Hours, the United Kingdom Jump Jett Aircraft Carrier The Invincible, was suddenly struck by six torpedoes. Ships of war from China, along with the support ships from the English Carrier Strike Group, raced to assist the rapidly sinking ship.

American Admiral Owens after picking up the Invincible's SOS distress signal, ordered two of his Destroyers from the Stennis Carrier Strike Group, the Charles F. Adams, and the Claude V. Rickers, off to aid the stricken English warship. The American warships were immediately dispatched to the area to see if the British Carrier was in any danger of truly sinking.

The radio waves were being flooded with requests for assistance, from any and all ships in the area responding to this disaster. Even two North Korean Frigates, that had successfully eluded the Chinese and British Navies, offered their assistance to the stricken British Carrier.

General Edward Campanelli asked Admiral John Owens if he thought the English Carrier was in any danger of sinking from the unprovoked attack leveled against the massive ship.

"Jesus Christ, how the hell would I know if she'll sink or not, sir. We have to wait until the damn recon flight Walter, makes a few passes over the stricken ship to see what kind of shape she's really in, sir. I don't think she'll go down though, at least I hope to Christ it don't, sir."

"You seem rather worried about the damn English ship sinking, Admiral Owens Sir? Why so much concern for her, sir?" General Campanelli asked the Admiral with concern in his voice.

"If you remember right General Campanelli Sir, I lost the Carrier Independence in the last fucking war, but that's got nothing to do with this shit at all, sir. I really don't believe the North Koreans attacked this ship in the first place, sir. What reason would they have to hit her except for expanding the war against their nation, dammit? They know damn well it'd cause the British to go for their damn throats to they hit her ship. The fighting in North Korea's almost over, I don't see the Koreans attacking this ship. It just don't make any stinking sense to me, sir."

"Who the hell do you think attack the English Carrier then, Admiral?" The General asked.

"You want the truth, General Campanelli Sir? I kinda have an opinion on who was really responsible for the attack on the English ship, sir." Admiral Owens asked his commander.

The General nodded slightly as he snapped at the staring Admiral, "of course I want your gut feeling about this fucking mess, Admiral Owens Sir."

"I think this British ship was attacked by the damn Chinese, General Campanelli Sir."

"Why? What the fuck would they get out of it, dammit. Christ I hate this damn shit."

"Jesus Christ, if I knew the answer to that question sir, I'd play the fucking lottery, General Campanelli. It's just the way I feel, and I don't think the damn North Korean submarines could possibly get close enough to attack the English Carrier, without being detected before they could get off even one torpedo at the damn ship, sir. They don't command the technology needed to pull it off, unless the British were sound asleep at the switch, and I seriously doubt that sir."

Their conversation was interrupted by a sudden test pattern on their communication screen. Then the pattern went to water. "The Walter Flight's reporting in General Campanelli Sir."

Both military officers stared at the large screen as the recon aircraft made its first pass over the crippled British Carrier and started her film running.

General Campanelli drew in his breath as he picked up the Carrier, and what he saw left no doubt in his mind. She was going down by the fantail, fast. The water was fifteen feet from her flight deck. He saw a number of aircraft actually sliding off the deck into the water.

"I give her two hours at the most before she slowly sinks under the waves, sir." Admiral Owens said in a low voice and then continued with is words in an extremely sad tone. "I'll order the damn recon aircraft make another pass over the crippled ship, General Campanelli. I think I want to keep her covered until she's gone from sight, sir."

"No can do Admiral Owens Sir. The recon aircraft was just warned off by a British fighter aircraft. They want the entire area clear for the rescue workers, sir." An Airman reported as the screen was covered by the word Flash, and the airman called out.

"Flash message traffic coming in General Campanelli Sir. You'll need your key to retrieve the report sir, it's probably from the White House, sir. They musta heard about the British Carrier getting hit by the torpedoes, sir." The Airman was wrong.

The Flash traffic reported three Chinese troop carriers had just landed in the port city of Masan in southern South Korea. Directly across from the coast of Japan. The report estimated up to six thousand Chinese troops had just landed, and there was a follow up report, stating an airlift was also heading from China, and making way towards Masan.

General Campanelli moaned as he rubbed his eyes with his hands. "What the hell else can go fucking wrong for today, god dammit. What the fuck are these sonsofbitches up to, dammit?"

Admiral Owens quickly read the report, and then he complained to the General. "Jesus Christ General Campanelli, it looks like the damn Chinese are massing more troops inside South Korea, possibly as a prelude to an all out invasion of Japan I make it, sir. This is going to add some stinking fuel to the fire on us, sir. When the damn British come up with the same conclusion as we did, and they start to blame the Chinese for sinking their damn Carrier, dammit General."

The main screen came to life filled with General Weidenbacher's angry looking face, and he was talking even before the screen cleared up. "Ed, we just received a Flash about the Chinese landing troops in South Korea across from Japan. What's the hell going on over there sir?"

"We got the same stinking message ourselves a moment ago, General Weidenbacher Sir. Add this shit to the sinking of the damn British Aircraft Carrier, and I think all hell's going to let go in the Asian region sir, and real soon at that General Weidenbacher Sir."

"What the hell are you talking about mister? What god damn British ship just got sunk?"

"The Invincible was just hit by a number of torpedoes, and she's going down by the tail, sir."

"You're shitting me General. Who got at her dammit?" the General asked Campanelli.

"First reports blame the damn attack on the North Koreans, a submarine attack as it's reported, General Weidenbacher Sir. But we think it was sunk by the Chinese, sir."

"Jesus General Campanelli, don't you think you should've informed me about this shit before I made contact with you, sir? I have to get my ass over to the White House toot sweet, and brief the President on this latest shit. I'm sure as hell he's going to want to speak with the Chinese Chairman, and see if he'll tell him what the hell they're really up to in this mess. Got to go sir."

"Never seen him so damn upset since I have known him sir." Campanelli told the Admiral.

ON BOARD THE NUCLEAR POWERED SUBMARINE FUCHOU ALONG WITH HER SISTER SHIP THE SWATOW

Two Chinese submarines sat on ocean floor for over fifteen days in a row. The Fuchou, picked to fire her torpedoes at the British Carrier, was ordered to move into the Korean Bay just off the coast of the city of Nampo, North Korea. The Fuchou listened to the constant rhythmic sounds coming from the powerful engines of the English Aircraft Carrier Invincible. The submarine engines were rigged for silent running, her nuclear power plant was up to ninety five percent power, and her torpedo tubes were already loaded, and flooded. As soon as she was ordered to attack and sink the Invincible sailing for her new position. The Chinese Captain of the Fuchou, Captain Chong laughed as he told his next in command this was going to be easy as picking up a whore in Shanghai.

Both men laughed as they listened to the sound of the engines of the massive English warship, as the ship rapidly closed in on their current position. When it was determined the Invincible was just two thousand yards off their bow. The Chinese Captain ordered his submarine up to torpedo depth. In five minutes, the submarine raised to sixty feet. The Chinese Captain ordered the periscope up, and then he looked for the British Carrier. He instantly got a firing solution on the slow moving Invincible, and then he ordered the torpedoes fired.

Once the torpedoes were fired, the Captain of the submarine ordered his sub into a deep dive, and then turn to a new heading of Zero, One, Zero. The Chinese submarine immediately headed for one of two Chinese escort ships assigned to guard the British Carrier from any possible attack. The second Chinese submarine headed for the other escort. Both Chinese submarines took up position directly underneath the Chinese ships actually running interference for them.

At a depth of one hundred feet, avoiding all sonar hits from the hunter ships moving in to kill the attacking submarine. The Destroyers from China pushed the North Korean submarine in front of the hunter ships, and when the Invincible violently exploded, announcing her soon to be death to the world. The Chinese Destroyers dropped their depth charges on the trapped North Korean submarine, and then requested assistance from the British warships involved in the search.

The North Korean submarine was being pounded by six warships, and finally killed, exploding under the sea. The Chinese submarines now made their presence known, and their Captains requested permission to join the search for the North Korean attacker. It was an almost fool proof maneuver created by the Chinese ships and submarines, as the confusion of the moment removed all possible blame to be leveled against the Chinese submarines or their command.

ON BOARD THE BRITISH JUMP
AIRCRAFT CARRIER INVINCIBLE

"Sonar to CIC, Admiral Middleton Sir. We have a possible submarine contact just off our portside at two thousand yards out, and she's closing rapidly on our present position, sir. It looks like she's preparing to fire at us sir." The sonar operator warned his Commander.

"Does he have his torpedo tube doors open mister?" The Admiral asked the sonar operator.

"No sir, not at this exact time sir, but I'm picking up sonar location beams right now Admiral Middleton Sir." The suddenly scared and concerned sounding sonar operator reported, as he quickly read the sounds he was hearing coming from under the water and the submarine.

"Go to GQ then. Order the Invincible up to full military power, rudders mid-ship, hard right to starboard. Let's give them our rear if they intend to fire at us. Get those damn Chinese ships moving between us and that damn attacking submarine. I want our ship out of here on the dou..."

"Sonar to CIC, the submarine's ranging us... Oh God, they just fired at us! Torpedoes lose in the water! Two, three, four, still firing Admiral Middleton Sir. Six torps in the water running true sir, they have acquired us sir, we have..." The Seaman's voice was cut off by a sudden explosion, the Invincible shook from the force of the explosion, one blast after the other rattled the massive British warship. It felt like the ship had been lifted up and out of the water, shook, and then thrown many feet to her side. Admiral Middleton screamed. "Get damage control."

"Damage control aye Admiral Middleton Sir." The crew man replied to his call.

"How bad we hit mister?" the Admiral roared at his engineer over the radio set.

"Bad sir, maybe even fatal from the looks of it as far as I can tell at this time, Admiral Middleton Sir. We're taking on heavy water from..."

"What the hell are you saying fatal to me? My Ship has not received a fatal wound, I'm going topside, what's the status on that bloody submarine?"

"The Chinese ships are on top of it Admiral. They're pounding it with depth charges, our ships are moving in to attack the submarine, sir. There's no chance for them to hit us again sir."

Admiral Middleton ran out of the CIC to the ladder leading up to the main deck of his Carrier. His shoulder slammed into the bulkhead, and for the first time he realized just how bad his ship was listing to her starboard side. There was a deep rumble from below deck, and then a powerful explosion. He thought his ship was under attack again, and another explosion quickly followed.

It was at this point he realized his ship was quickly ripping herself apart. He smelt diesel oil, sea water and smoke rising to the deck. He pulled himself up the ladder, and had to lean against the wall in order to walk. He plowed out of the water tight door to the huge flight deck and instantly got sick at what he witnessed. The ship had a list around seven degrees, the flight deck was covered with debris, with burning aircraft spotting the buckled flight deck of his Carrier.

The radar mast from the tower laid across one of his smashed aircraft. He spotted a body then he scanned the deck, and picked up more bodies as the firefighter's pumped water from three hoses below deck through a gaping hole ripped through the flight deck. Creaks and rumbling came from below deck as the fire buckled many of her bulkheads. His ship was crying in death. Admiral Middleton's eyes were wide with fright, he was trying to decide if damage control could save his ship. Then a tremendous explosion suddenly shook the Invincible, and threw Middleton down to the deck. He struggled back to his feet as his ship continued to shake violently under his feet. An excited and grime covered Chief ran up to him and announced in an excited voice. "Sir that was a boiler. Engineering thinks the keel just snapped, we have to abandon ship sir."

Admiral Middleton stared at the Chief for a minute, stunned he was unable to speak.

The Chief repeated his warning to his Commanding Officer. "Admiral Middleton Sir, I think we should abandon ship, she's going down and we're powerless to do anything to stop it. Sir, what do you say sir? Should I place an abandon ship order out, sir? Admiral Middleton Sir, you have to transfer the flag out to one of our support ships, sir." The Chief returned the stunned Admiral's blank stare, and then he rested his hand lightly on the officer's shoulder to try and bring the staggered officer back to reality.

Admiral Middleton suddenly shook his head and then asked, "What was that you said Chief?"

"Admiral Middleton Sir, we have to get off of the ship before she goes down, sir."

"Yes, abandon ship. Make sure every one gets off. Any estimate on how many men we lost?"

"There's three hundred dead, with five hundred still missing, mostly from below deck, sir. We lost seven bloody aircraft from the deck, all aircraft stored below deck are lost. We have eight hundred wounded, most walking, the Destroyer Bristol's steaming to our side, along with two Chinese Destroyers, sir. The men should not be in the water for long, Admiral Sir. I think you should go below and retrieve the log and flag for transport off the ship, sir."

"Yes, see to the abandon ship order then Chief?" Admiral Middleton moaned as he shook his head again to try and clear his thinking as he turned and headed below deck.

"Right away sir," the Chief left the Admiral and went off to carry out his last orders.

Admiral Middleton headed below deck and back to his CIC Chamber, as he walked the hallway, a voice came over the intercom, "Abandon ship, all hands abandon ship immediately."

ON BOARD THE VINEGAR JOE PLATFORM

"Sir, I just picked up a report stating they're abandoning the Invincible, sir. She's going down fast now General Campanelli Sir." The radio man reported to his Commanding Officer.

The General was stunned, he was deeply concerned over the latest information the Chinese were landing their ground troops in South Korea so close to Japan's coastline. He did not know where to turn to next. He was pleased the joint Chinese, English operation to bomb the nuclear tipped missiles throughout North Korea was a complete success, and he was anxiously awaiting first word from China she stopped all her aggression being carried out in North Korea. It had not come in yet, and it had been three hours since the United States confirmed the total destruction of the nuclear warheads and missiles in question in North Korea.

General Campanelli's train of thought was suddenly interrupted by the radioman who reported to him in an extremely excited voice, "whoa boy sir, here's a damn report you better read right off, sir." He tore the sheet free of the machine and then he handed it over to the General.

It stated Admiral Middleton, who was now reported stationed on board the British Destroyer Bristol, was demanding the two Chinese submarines surface, so he could board them and check on their inventory of torpedoes. General Campanelli laughed as he handed the paper over to Admiral Owens and then he replied as he tried not to laugh over the report.

"Uh-oh, it looks like Admiral Middleton smells a rat too I see, General Campanelli Sir."

"Jesus Christ I guess so Admiral Owens Sir, you can bet the damn bank this is going to create some hard feelings between our two once lovebirds, sir. Let's keep our heads down and see what comes of this latest message, sir." General Campanelli offered as he looked at his Admiral.

For days eight and nine of the fighting in North Korea, things were pretty much quiet. The British stationed a Destroyer over each of the Chinese submarines, and everyone waited for a response from them. It never came, instead, the Chinese continued their attack on North Korea, while continuing building up their troop strengths in South Korea. Even though there were mounting cries from many nations who begged, ordered and even demanded all the fighting in the Asian region stop, it fell on deaf ears of the Chinese command and leadership. The Chinese troops continued their outright slaughter in North Korea. As all this was going down in North Korea, no nation spotted the heavy troop buildup slowly taking place in and around Hong Kong.

On day ten of fighting in North Korea, a special meeting of the Security Council was convened. The members of the Council demanded the Chinese Delegate appear at the meeting.

CHAPTER 29
SECURITY COUNCIL MEETING: NEW YORK CITY.
MARCH 1st, 1997 10 A.M.

All the member nations of the Security Council were seated and talking amongst themselves, when the Delegate from the United Kingdom requested permission to speak before the Council. The French Delegate and still acting President of the Council, banged his gavel and immediately called the meeting to order. Silence quickly filled the meeting room as everyone watched the British Delegate as they waited for the Secretary General to acknowledged the

United Kingdom's politician want to speak to the members. The French President stood, as he said.

"Ladies and Gentlemen, I'm pleased everyone was able to attend this meeting convened at the United Kingdom's request. I have a few questions I'd like to ask the Chinese Delegate, before I turn this meeting over to the Ambassador from England, to hear what is on her mind."

The Chinese Delegate bowed slightly to the Council President as he replied with a snap, "I'd be most honored and pleased to answer any of your questions for you, Mr. President."

"Thank you kindly Ambassador Chow, and to start I'd like to know what your next course of action might be in North Korea, sir? As I'm certain you're aware of Ambassador Chow, once the nuclear threat from North Korea was ended, all fighting was requested to end immediately, and all Chinese troops were supposed to leave the soil of North Korea as quickly as possible. So we can start working out a truce in the region between the nations involved in this action, sir."

"I assumed you were aware my government was trying to rid North Korea of all the nuclear weapons, that North Korea was planning to use against our troops just three days ago, may I add sir." The Chinese Delegate replied smugly to the President of the meeting.

"Did not the Chinese and English forces destroy all the nuclear weapons and missiles in question over three days ago, Ambassador Chow Sir?" President Bartlett asked in a polite tone.

"I believe that was accomplished as per the Council's mandate, but there is no way of telling for certain at this time, if we got all the nuclear weapons with those surgical raids, sir."

"Is it safe to say over ninety percent of the weapons were destroyed in those raids then, sir?"

"As I already stated, who can tell for certain, Ambassador Bartlett? Our intelligence informs us maybe that amount was destroyed true, sir. But we're not certain of the exact tally at this time, Ambassador Bartlett Sir." The Chinese Delegate smirked with confidence.

"Is this why your military forces are continuing to fight on in North Korea, Ambassador?"

"Yes, this and the fact that the North Koreans are still fighting our troops as well as we follow the mandates of this Council sir. Are the only reasons for the continued fighting currently and still taking place in North Korea, sir. We requested on numerous occasions, for the North Korean warriors to put down their arms."

"How the devil do you expect the proud North Korean soldiers to put down their arms, when it's your country who has invaded their land and are continuing to attack them, Ambassador Chow? My country would fight to the last man, and woman before we would put down our arms if another country invaded India, sir." The Delegate from India, Ambassador John Dutrow hissed at the Chinese representative from his seat.

Ambassador Chow glared harshly at the once supporting Indian Delegate for a long moment as he scolded him "Ambassador Dutrow Sir, if you remember correctly sir, my government was invited by all the members of this Council, to invade North Korea with the desire to destroy their nuclear weapons and aims, sir. Until we're absolutely certain all these nuclear weapons and missiles have been totally destroyed by my Chinese troops, we'll continue to fight on, sir! If you like the North Korean people so well then why do you not see if you can get them to lay down their arms, and the fighting will stop immediately in their foolish nation, it's that simple sir."

The Indian Delegate jumped up to his feet and roared angrily at the Chinese representative. "Ambassador Chow, your country is no longer looking for any further weapons of the nuclear nature, sir. I suggest to you that your government is trying to destroy all North Korea as a whole, and your country is using this hunt for nuclear weapons as an excuse to get the dirty deed done before the eyes of this Council. I demand all the fighting in North Korea end immediately sir."

Ambassador Bartlett stood and stated. "Gentlemen please, let's not cast any unwarranted aspersions at this meeting. We're here to discuss different ways to try and end the fighting in the Asia region." President Bartlett saw the Delegate from Japan make eye contact with him, and he decided he was going to allow him to speak before the representative of the United Kingdom.

The Indian Delegate growled extremely angrily at the President of the meeting, "I think China should stop all her troops from fighting in the country of North Korea, I offer this. If China stops fighting, I'll ensure the North Korean's will do the same, and if they don't. Then I and my nation will join forces with China. I'll send troops to fight alongside those of China, until any possible threat from North Korea is completely crushed. I say we have to start someplace and this is as good as any?" He looked at Ambassador Chow and waited for his answer.

"That is an interesting offer sir. How would you react if I was to tell you if you guarantee the North Koreans will stop all their fighting, I'll immediately order a cease fire to take effect at twelve o'clock midnight tonight throughout all of Korea, sir." Ambassador Chow offered.

The Chinese Delegate spoke the words every nation was waiting to hear from his lips. Little did the Indian Delegate know by this time. The noose would be drawn so tight, and North Korea would be an all but a non-existent nation in the matter of the world's eyes.

Ambassador Dutrow suddenly bowed slightly to Chinese Ambassador Chow as he offered, "I'll guarantee North Korea will stop fighting by midnight tonight, sir. I thank you for this kind offer, and I have nothing further to offer to the members of this meeting at this time, sir."

The Japanese and English Delegates stood together, each hoping to be recognized first. Bartlett made up his mind who would have the floor next. He looked to the Japanese Delegate, and gave him the slight nod. Ambassador Alexander sat down and waited her turn to speak.

The Japanese Delegate was red in the face with anger as he barked angrily as soon as he was recognized by the Council President, "Ambassador Bartlett Sir, ladies and gentlemen of this meeting, I demand to know what reason the Chinese government has for building up military troops in South Korea? We're taking this action extremely seriously and as a direct threat to the security of Japan, and I'm here to advise every nation at this meeting. Japan will act accordingly to protect her shores from any possible invasion, like the one sweeping through North Korea at this time. My government has ordered me to inform all the members of this esteem Council, if China does not remove this present threat across from Japan shores. It'll leave Japan with no other alternative but to prepare for all out war with the nation of China, sir."

All eyes went from the Japanese Delegate over to Ambassador Chow who stood, a smile across his lips as he offered sarcastically, "My dear Ambassador Lang Sir. I fear your government is overreacting a might to Chinese and South Korean troops having a rest from the terrible fighting taking place in the North, a little fun for the soldiers only guilty of doing what this Council has requested China's troops to do, sir. I cannot believe for one moment that Japan wants to take this little bit of enjoyment from the fighting men and women of my country.

"It's bad enough Japan controls and has a strangle hold on most nations' economies, now she wants to control where Chinese fighting men and women take their pleasures and relaxation. I think Japan owes China an apology. After all, Chinese fighting men and women are dying in the mud of North Korea to secure this region of the world, and free this area from all possible nuclear threats and ambitions. Japan has even offered to help China pay for this war, yet China hasn't received one copper from Japan as of this time. How easy she forgets her commitments once the fighting and dying had started, sir." Ambassador Chow glared at Ambassador Lang.

"Huh, this only goes to show China is acting in a most threatening manner towards the nation of Japan, and all her people. Leaving us with no other choice in the matter but to prepare all of Japan for war. I do this with a very heavy and sad heart, but I must do it for the protection of my nation and her children. I came here with the sincere hope and desire that I, along with the other esteem members of this Council, would be able to talk sense into Ambassador Chow to remove his fighting troops from so near the coast of Japan. I now understand that was a mistake in my assumption, and I'll leave this meeting immediately to inform my government of what has transpired at this meeting, gentlemen and ladies."

Ambassador Bartlett offered in an attempt to try and keep the Japanese representative at the meeting. "Ambassador Lang please sir, if you leave this Council, sir. We'll not be able to get a variable solution solved to these new threats you have just brought up to our attention at this meeting, sir. If you stay, we shall continue to talk and try and work out a mutual understanding that would be most satisfactory for both nations involved. Please sit back down sir."

Ambassador Lang looked from one Delegate to another attending the meeting, and then he placed his briefcase back down on the desk and took his seat again. He then folded his arms across his chest and sat staring angrily at the Chinese Delegate.

"Thank you for remaining Ambassador Lang, that is better. Ambassador Chow, I'd like to ask you a question please?" Bartlett asked as he turned his attention to the Chinese Delegate.

Ambassador Chow nodded towards the acting President of the Security Meeting.

"Thank you much Ambassador. Now Ambassador Chow, is it at all possible for your great fighting soldiers to take their pleasures and relaxation someplace other than directly across from the Island of Japan, sir?" President Bartlett asked with concern in his voice.

"I believe it'd be possible for the Chinese troops to enjoy themselves elsewhere, yes. But why does everything have to be the way Japan wants it to exist in this world, sir? Does Japan now tell China where she should allow her elite troops rest, sir? What next will Japan want and demand for us? To tell China where she may make money, sail her ships, which crops to grow on her own soil, sir? Is this how arrogant the Japanese people are getting about themselves? If China gives in on this request, what is Japan going to want and demand next from China, sir?

"I'm terribly sorry to offer the members of this Council Ambassador Bartlett, but my nation of China is actually helping protect the foul nation of Japan from a possible nuclear attack from North Korea, sir. And this is how Japan wants to thank the good People of China, by telling her fighting men and women where to rest and play and getting away from the death and fighting of this war you people sanctioned. I think Japan wants too much from China and her proud soldiers, but if Japan chooses to prepare for war with me country then so be it, sir. The people of China will respond to any and all threats aimed against the soil of China, and her people. Allow me ask Ambassador Lang who he is preparing to war with, sir."

Ambassador Lang snapped hotly. "We're taking this Chinese troop buildup in South Korea directly across from Japan's shores as a very serious military threat against my country, sir. We are preparing for war against the Chinese troops stationed in South Korea, Ambassador Chow."

"Those are military troops from the People's Republic of China, Ambassador Lang. Then I'm forced to take it that in essence, your country of Japan is declaring war on China as we sit here and speak of peace at this meeting, sir. I believe you should rethink your foolish position here, Ambassador Lang. If you continue with daring to threaten China with as you have put it, all out war. I assure you Ambassador Lang, China will prepare for war with Japan. You're leaving my country with no other option if you continue to threaten China with war at this meeting, sir."

Ambassador Lang did not know what else to say. His government informed him if he demanded the Chinese remove their troops from Masan, they would comply. He had no other instructions, and now the Chinese Delegate called his bluff. He had one trump card left to play, to walk out of the meeting. He knew nothing was going to happen as long as he showed no reaction, this talk of preparing for war went no further than Japan putting her nuclear missiles on alert. But once the North Korean nuclear tipped missiles were destroyed, Japan stood down so as not to threaten any nation in the Asian region. Lang was sweating, he could feel it run down his back, he scanned the worried faces of the other Delegates. He turned and walked out to Bartlett egging him to retake his seat and keep talking. It took control for him walk out on shaking legs.

Ambassador Bartlett turned to Ambassador Chow and asked him. "Ambassador Chow Sir, am I to take it China just declared war on Japan on your word, sir?"

Ambassador Chow gave out a nervous laugh as he replied with a smirk. "Ambassador Bartlett, China has not declared war nor wants war with any nation, sir. You seem to forget it was Japan doing all the threatening of war at this meeting, sir. It was Japan who just declared war on China and then walked away from this meeting so we might have been able to talk Ambassador Land from continuing with his threat of war against China, sir."

"I concede that much to you Ambassador Chow. But I have to know what China plans to do about Ambassador Lang's declaration at this meeting, sir. I have to admit Ambassador Lang had a claim, and I believe it wouldn't be that much of a problem for China to have her military go to even a different location in South Korea to enjoy themselves, and relax from the toils of war, sir. A different location not so directly across the water from Japan's shore, Ambassador Chow Sir, does China have any claims against the nation of Japan or her people, sir?"

Another nervous laugh came from the Chinese Representative, he then replied, "Ambassador Bartlett, China has no intentions of attacking Japan for any reason, unless Japan is foolish enough to dare engage China's troops currently enjoying themselves in peace in South Korea, sir. I fear Japan is a victim of her own imagination here, sir." Ambassador Chow said all he wanted to say on this issue, so he took his seat as an aide moved up to him whispered something in his ear.

Everyone sat in silence, no one wanted to say anything for fear of saying the wrong thing. It was Bartlett who broke the silence, "gentlemen and ladies." He nodded at Mrs. Alexander, and then went on. "I think we should take a break and eat some lunch. This will give me a chance to speak a little further to Ambassador Lang in private, and see if I can get him to come back to the meeting. I put it up for a vote, all in favor of a two hour lunch break in the meeting say 'Aye'."

All but one of the Representatives replied 'Aye' to the latest offer put before them.

Ambassador Bartlett turned to the United Kingdom Ambassador Ms. Alexander, and saw she was staring hard and long at him. He tried a smile and quickly realized it was wasted so he said. "I know you wanted to address this Council Ma'am, but I'm asking for a well deserved break. This will give everyone a chance to cool down so we can regain our wits. Please?"

She slowly nodded in compliance with the Security President's request.

"Thank you Ma'am. It's now twelve fifteen, I suggest we meet back here at two p.m.. Enjoy your lunch please." With the bang of his gavel again, Bartlett stood and left the meeting. Separate conversations erupted as the Delegate's filed out of the room. Time crept by, but by one, forty five the Delegates slowly filtered back, filling the meeting room with conversation until Ambassador Bartlett called the meeting to order again.

"Ladies and gentlemen, I spoke further to Ambassador Lang over the break, and was unable to talk him into coming back to the meeting. However, he did offer he'd attend tomorrow's meeting, once he spoke with his people. I'm quite certain we'll be able to talk this thing through, and stop these preparations for conflict. I thank you all for your patience over this matter." French Ambassador Bartlett made certain he made eye contact with Ambassador Chow, and he gave him a slight nod. He and Ambassador Chow met during the break as well, and he received reassurances from him that his government was not the least bit interested in attacking Japan.

Security Council President Bartlett sat back in his chair and then rubbed his temples because his head was beginning to pound on him. He was dreading the next confrontation he knew was coming at him, because he spoke to Ambassador Alexander yesterday, and hoped she and the Chinese Delegate would get together on their own, and then worked out something between themselves. Obviously, they were not able to come to an understanding, because she looked as nervous as ever. He let his breath out in a rush as he raised his eyes up to the ceiling as if to find an answer there, and then he moaned to the other members of the meeting. "The floor recognizes the United Kingdom Ambassador Alexander, who originally requested this meeting take place.

She stood quickly and nodded to the other Delegates then she turned to the Chinese Delegate and began speaking directly at him, "as everyone here is aware, HMS Invincible was sunk off the coast of North Korea earlier this week by an unknown submarine attack."

"It was a North Korean submarine that attacked your ship!" Chow corrected from his seat.

Ambassador Alexander glared angrily at him for daring to interrupt her as she continued. "Yes, this is what we believe, ships from the Chinese Navy along with a few English ships, have attacked and sunk a North Korean submarine in the area of the attack against our ship, sir."

"Excuse me Ma'am please, but a North Korean submarine was sunk right next to where the Invincible was attacked and sank, Madam Ambassador. Within half a mile of the incident if I'm not mistaken, and shortly after the attack I remind you also." Ambassador Chow grumbled.

Ambassador Alexander hissed, "if the Delegate from China is going to continue to interrupt me every time I say something to the other members of this meeting. We're going to end up being here all day, and nothing is going to be accomplished. I hope Ambassador Chow would allow me to continue uninterrupted then he shall be free to ask me any questions he desires."

Ambassador Chow glared terribly at Ambassador Alexander, and then he retook his seat.

"As I was saying, early yesterday, divers from the Waveney, a British mine sweeper ship. Has successfully located the shell of the North Korean submarine believed to be responsible for the sinking of the Invincible. The divers did an inspection of the forward end of the North Korean submarine, especially the forward torpedo room area. The divers did a count on the number of torpedoes remaining on board the submarine, and they discovered the submarine still had a full complement of torpedoes held in their racks. This discovery was most confusing, because it was believed this North Korean submarine fired the salvo of six torpedoes which sunk the Invincible. We have more divers investigating the shell of the submarine with cameras, so we can document all the evidence we found inside this sunken North Korean submarine."

Ambassador Chow jumped up to his feet and bellowed at the United Kingdom Ambassador. "What evidence are you talking about, woman? What does the English think took place in the Korean Bay? I don't believe I like the direction the English Delegate is heading with her conversation and unspoken aspersions. I..." Ambassador Chow's narration was cut short by President Bartlett who banged his gavel, and ordered Ambassador Chow to wait his turn to speak to the council members. Chow stared at Bartlett before backing down, he was steaming as he tapped his foot impatiently, while waiting for the English Delegate to finish with her complaint.

"Thank you sir." Ambassador Alexander said as she took a quick breath and then added. "As we speak, ships from the English Navy are shadowing two known Chinese submarines stationed in the Korean Bay area. The Destroyer Bristol had been stationed over top of the Chinese submarine Fuchou, and is following her, while the Swaton's being shadowed by the Destroyer Glamorgan. We're requesting the members of this Council direct the Chinese government to allow our inspectors to board these two submarines in question, and count their torpedoes."

Ambassador Chow actually screamed at the United Kingdom Ambassador from his seat this time, "you daughter of a motherless whore." In Chinese slang and then he continued to roar. "What are you saying at this foul meeting? That China was responsible for the sinking of your god cursed precious warship? China does not treat her Allies in this fashion. I demand a...”

Ambassador Bartlett banged his gavel five times loudly on his desk, before getting Delegate Chow's attention and then he sort of snapped at him. “Ambassador Chow please sir. I have to ask you to sit down please sir, and allow Ambassador Alexander to finish what she has to offer us at this meeting, sir. Then you'll have all the time you need to respond to her words, Ambassador. Please Ambassador Chow, take your seat and be quiet, please sir.”

“I'm terribly sorry we have to make such a request of our Ally, but we have to find out what happened to our ship, and who is truly responsible for the lives of our sailors who died in the attack. Even if we find out a Chinese submarine fired and sunk the Invincible, we're not saying it was on purpose, it could have very well been a terrible mistake. That would be left up to the investigators to determine. All I'm saying is, we have to find out who fired on our ship, Ambassador Bartlett. My government is making plans to raise the North Korean submarine, so the Representatives of this Council can examine the remains, and draw their own conclusion as to if this is the North Korean submarine that attacked and sank the Invincible. All England wants is the right to board, and examine the two Chinese submarines in question.

“If all their torpedoes are intact and accounted for. Then they have nothing to worry about, and England will apologize to China. If the investigators are not allowed to inspect these two Chinese submarines, the United Kingdom will have to take matters into her own hands.” Ambassador Alexander sat down and took a sip of water, refusing to look at Ambassador Chow.

The Delegate from Italy stood even before Ambassadors Chow and Bartlett allowed him to speak, and he replied.

"Ambassador Alexander Ma'am, am I to believe England might take it upon herself to board, or even sink either of the two Chinese submarines in question, Ma'am?"

Alexander snapped, "I guess England will have to leave that up to your own imagination, sir."

The Delegate from Spain remarked in an excited voice as he also joined the conversation now. "I don't believe I like the way the Delegate from the United Kingdom is speaking before the members of this meeting. I was under the impression that once all the fighting in North Korea was completed, all fighting in and around the Asian region would likewise be over with as well, members. Why is there still fighting taking place if our mandates are covered."

"We're not the ones who is the cause of more fighting to take place, but the United Kingdom demand the right to know what has happened to our ship. Any nation would demand the same when one of their warships is attacked and sunk, sir." Ambassador Alexander replied.

Ambassador Bartlett looked to the Chinese Delegate, but Ambassador Chow angrily looked away from him. He truly liked the direction this discussion was taking. It was exacted what he wanted to take place at the meeting. All the Delegates were now dumping on the United Kingdom for making threats against China. He was most pleased to allow the other Delegates to fight for him and his country. But his happiness was short lived. His eyes suddenly opened wide when the Delegate from the Alliance States stood, and then he requested the floor.

"The Chair recognizes the Delegate from the Alliance States at this time please."

Ambassador Nicholas Antich spoke without recognizing Ambassador Chow "I remind all at this meeting, I was against allowing the Chinese troops to invade North Korea in the first place. We realized what might happen if the Chinese were allowed to run wild, and our worse fears are coming true. Not only has China completely destroyed all of North Korea, but now their troops are threatening the Islands of Japan, and we'll not stand by and allow this to happen. Japan has invested heavily in the Alliance States, and we will not forget this."

Chow interrupted Antich's speech by remarking angrily from his chair. "The Russian Delegate forgets we're going to stop all hostilities presently taking place in North Korea tonight, sir. This hardly constitutes threatening the peace of the region, does it Ambassador Bartlett?"

Ambassador Antich dismissed this remark with a sharp snap of his head as he continued with his words to the other members of the Council. "The Chinese Delegate wants us to believe China is being magnanimous, by offering to stop the killing and slaughter tonight. What other choice does China have in this instance? North Korea is virtually a dead nation. The North Korean Armies are defeated and about non-existent, and their civilians are being slaughtered in uncountable numbers as we sit here and speak of China's crimes. I demand China removes all her troops from the entire Korea Peninsula immediately. Immediately I say to all the members of this Council. The Chinese forces done what they set out to do, and more I add. I warn China, the Alliance States will send aircraft and cruisers to the coast of Japan. Here, our ships will take position, and attack any Chinese or English ships coming too close to the coast of Japan."

Ambassador Alexander addressed the Russian Delegate rather than the other members of the Council, "Ambassador Antich, why is it Russia is threatening England in his words aimed at China? England is no threat against Russia or any of her interests in this region of the world, and we're no threat especially against Japan. The United Kingdom is stopping all military action being carried out on the Korean Peninsula. My country is ordering a full pull back of the Royal Oak and Illustrious to a standoff position of one hundred miles off the coast of Korea.

"The support ships of our Carrier Groups are ordered to follow, we have flown no flights over North Korea for the past six hours. All British aircraft has been ordered grounded, except for our recon and Air Cap aircraft. We intend to keep our aircraft on the deck until we find out what truly happened to the Invincible. At this moment, we desire no further connection with the Chinese forces in, and on any North Korean soil, until this present situation is settled."

Ambassador Antich bowed to Ambassador Alexander and he offered. "I apologize to my English colleague, I had no intention of making the United Kingdom think we consider them a threat to the Alliance States, or against the Islands of Japan for that matter, Ma'am. We're only concerned about China, and what her next move might be in the Asian region, Madam."

"China has no next move to engage in I assure you, Ambassador Antich." Ambassador Chow called out nastily from his seat, "it's only your own foolish imagination that has you dreaming of next moves and further threats, sir. My Russian friend sees shadows in the dark, and he's preying on the fears of others to make him feel strong again. Russia would be better served tending to her own needs and business, rather than trying to threaten the power and military might of China. I suggest you get your own house in order, before you dare start to criticize others on how we conduct our nation's business, sir." He gave an angry leer to the Russian who leaped to his feet and barked at the Chinese Ambassador.

"How dare you speak to me in this foul a manner, I shall have my military forces ordered to full alert, Ambassador Chow. If China is so foolish as to dare think the Russian bear is no longer capable of defending herself or her interested anywhere in the world. Then I suggest your forces give the Russian military a try Ambassador Chow, and see what that nets you. You shall be shaking hands with your ancestor's if you dare, sir." Ambassador Antich openly glared at the Chinese Delegate, who gave him a mere wave of his hand, dismissing him rudely.

Ambassador Bartlett banged his gavel and warned the members of the meeting. "Gentlemen, ladies, we're trying desperately to avoid any further confrontations here, not to start new ones. Ambassador Antich Sir, I'm quite certain your government would be most displeased with you, if they knew you were here making threats towards Ambassador Chow."

Ambassador Chow smiled as the President admonished the larger Russian politician.

Bartlett picked up the nasty grin and he turned to Ambassador Chow and snapped at him. "Ambassador Chow, you're no better here I warn, sir. I'm as certain your great country of China would be as angry with you over your conduct being displayed here today, sir. If they knew you were speaking with such disrespect towards Ambassador Antich, sir."

The Japanese Delegate stood and spoke before being recognized. "This is good, but it's still not addressing the real problem at hand. My government wants all troops in Masan removed, nothing but their removal will be accepted by Japan." Ambassador Lang demanded hotly again.

Ambassador Bartlett drew in a deep breath and then offered, "Ambassador Lang, I assure you we're trying our best to work out a suitable solution for all parties involved in this current situation, sir. Without making any further demands or threats leveled against China or any other nation of the world. I assure both of you Ambassadors, and also Ambassador Alexander, that all your concerns will be addressed before this meeting concludes here today."

Ambassador Chow snapped angrily at him "Ambassador Bartlett Sir, I feel we, the people of China made a terrible mistake by offering to help the world, by eliminating the nuclear threat from North Korea. It's an appalling shame now most of the fighting in the Korean Peninsula has been completed, and thousands of Chinese troops have died in the fighting. The nations who begged my nation of China to attack, are now attacking us for carrying out the directions of the Council. What is China to think now, when we were dying our attack was sanctioned by all here today. Now it's over, we're the ones being treated as if the criminals, not the North Koreans." The Chinese Ambassador sat down and took his ear phones off, lit up a cigarette and then stared off in the distance, completely ignoring the other members of the Council.

Ambassador Bartlett took this time to respond to Ambassador Chow's last inflammatory remarks. "Ambassador Chow, no member here is blaming your great fighting men and women for the problems we're discussing at this meeting, sir. But you must agree there are some serious questions raised here that must be addressed, for the sake of peace to return in the Asian region, sir. It'd surely be in the best interest for you and your nation to be as open as you possibly can, sir. We're here to help all concerned, even North Korea at this point, sir."

Ambassador Chow completely ignored the concerned Ambassador Bartlett's words, he reached the limit of his patience over this latest Council meeting. He had permission to say whatever was on his mind from the Chairman of his country, and he had his final act well rehearsed, and was just waiting the proper time to deliver it. The Chinese troops were set in place, paused to begin their opening attack against Hong Kong, and then the Island of Taiwan. His trend of thought was suddenly interrupted by Ambassador Bartlett, repeating his name.

"Ambassador Chow, please Ambassador Chow Sir. I'd like your full attention here as we try and work out a peaceful solution to the questions being raised today at this meeting please. Ambassador Chow, this is most important to your country, and the rest of the world, sir."

Delegate Chow looked at Ambassador Bartlett as he said in an almost excited tone of voice. "Ambassador Chow, we're trying to work something out that'd be most satisfactory to all parties concerned here today, sir. I'd really appreciate your undivided attention to this situation, so we can end this debate and then get on with other business concerning this Council, sir."

Ambassador Chow stood and snuffed out his cigarette in disdain, and then he looked at the many faces staring at him while waiting for him to speak. He yawned without covering his mouth, he then commented in a controlled and calm voice, "Ambassador Bartlett Sir, esteemed colleagues of this Council, fellow Delegates. I sat here for many hours while listening to certain members of this Council call China a cheat, a liar, and a sneak. I resent this foul treatment of my people, my country. If this was the United States involved in this foul war, no members of this Council would dare complain about one warship being sunk, or about the harsh actions leveled towards North Korean soldiers, and their rioting civilians engaging my soldiers in combat.

"Allow me to inform you about war. In war, the first death starts the killing, and to bring a war to a speedy end, you have to react, and sometimes, overreact to what is happening on the battlefield. You have to release the savagery of war lose to end a war as quickly as possible. The more savage the war, the shorter it is in duration, and, as always, civilians die during any war.

"This is a most regrettable and painful byproduct of the war, the death of the innocent, sir. But nevertheless it happens in all wars, past, present, and it'll be repeated in the future wars, sorry to offer. China has done everything within her means to protect, to try and keep the civilian death down to an absolute minimum during the fighting taking place in North Korea. Yes, civilians have died in this war, and I'm truly sorry for this happening. But all attending this meeting must remember at all times Chinese troops, China's sons and daughters have also died in this short lived but hard hitting war. I don't hear anyone here remarking about how tragic it was China's children are dying in the mud and blood of North Korea. China's children have carried the complete burden of fighting for world peace in this region of the world.

"All nations represented here today at this meeting must further remember North Korea is the aggressor in this drama, not China. War is an extremely terrible thing for any civilized nation to witness and endure and be forced to engage in, and as in all war, warships, as well as human beings expire because of combat situations that took place during the Fog of War. Such as is in the case of the British warship Invincible. I'm truly sorry for the terrible loss of life to the United Kingdom warriors, but look at the terrible loss of life to the Chinese people, and to the North Korean soldiers I must add as well. Yes, and in war, sometimes one's troops find themselves stationed, and relaxing in or near another country to get away from the killing, and the terrible stresses war brings to a country's soldiers even for the shortest period of time.

"I'm also extremely sorry a number of China's troops have found it most pleasurable for them to rest so close to the Japan Islands. I wish Japan would understand, it's far better to have these Chinese troops so near their country enjoying themselves. Than to have North Korean troops in the same position, and aiming their nuclear tipped missiles and weapons and artillery pieces at the Japan Islands with anger in their hearts and evil intents in mind.

"No, I truly think Japan should reexamine their conscience, and weigh this question much more carefully, before they continue to condemn China, and what her soldiers have accomplished to end the nuclear ambitions of North Korea and their foolish leaders. It's not too late for China to pullout, and then allow North Korea to rebuild their nation and nuclear toys for themselves. Then China will sit back and watch as North Korea attacks Japan as she once planned to, and then we shall see who'll come to your aid, once Japan becomes a nuclear wasteland. I have a word of warning to offer for the United Kingdom as well in this conversation.

"If the English dare to board any Chinese submarine without our permission first. Then China will regard this as an open act of war aimed against her mainland, and China's military might well react accordingly to this most unwarranted show of aggression against her interests. This we understand, and this we shall do. I have nothing else to add for anyone attending this meeting, sir." Ambassador Chow retook his seat and sat quietly, all the while continuing to stare at the Japanese Delegate, knowing he was making Ambassador Lang extremely nervous.

The great meeting room remained deathly quiet as all members of the Council quickly digested what was said by the upset Chinese Delegate. Ambassador Bartlett was deep in thought, as he stared at the painting on the east wall. He knew what he had to do, but he was dreading announcing it to the other members of the Council, and what the possible outcome of his words might be. He diverted his eyes down to the surface of the table for a moment as he picked up a pencil, and then began to twirl it between his fingers and then he offered in a low voice.

"Ladies and gentlemen, I have given this problem much thought of late. This is not a matter of who is right, and who is wrong. It's mainly a matter of understanding and patience." He turned to Chow and offered him calmly. "Ambassador Chow, I've known you for a number of years and have come to the conclusion you're a very understanding and just man. I trust you'll understand why I have to ask you this conclusion. This Council requests your government allow two appointed inspectors from this Council to board the Chinese submarines in question, sir."

Ambassador Chow instantly tensed up and shot to his feet and made a motion to be heard. But he was immediately held off by Ambassador Bartlett, who raised his hand and begged him to allow him to finish speaking first, before he was interrupted by any other member of the meeting.

"As I was saying Ambassador Chow. I have to request China remove her brave military troops from the South Korean city of Masan as soon as they're prepared to depart that city, sir. I made this request solely in the name of peace being maintained between the two nations involved in this situation, Ambassador Chow Sir." Ambassador Bartlett let out his breath, and then he waited for the explosion to happen. The Chinese Delegate calmly looked at each of the other Delegates attending the meeting, and then he spoke to them at the same time.

"I'm deeply appalled and greatly saddened at what I'm hearing being aimed against my country at this meeting today. China instead of being treated as an Ally to all nations represented here, she's being treated as if the enemy of this entire situation." Ambassador Chow then turned his attention back to Ambassador Alexander and aimed the rest of his words directly at her. "Exactly what is it the United Kingdom is accusing China of doing?"

Ambassador Alexander felt she had been waltzed around for too long by the smug acting Chinese representative, and her patience was wearing thin and she was having much trouble keeping her temper under control. She decided to put it all on the table and settle this situation once and for all as she offered the Chinese Representative. "Ambassador Chow Sir, we feel one of your submarines is the submarine responsible for firing on and sinking our ship, sir."

"On purpose Ambassador Alexandra?" The Delegate from Sweden suddenly cried out from his chair, stunned by the outright forwardness of the United Kingdom Representative.

Ambassador Alexander paused for a brief moment before she answered the Swedish Delegate. "Yes, we feel the Captain of one of these two Chinese submarines, fired on and is responsible for the sinking of the United Kingdom warship Invincible. And until we're free to examine these two Chinese submarines, we'll never know this for certain if what we believe is true, sir."

Ambassador Chow again jumped to his feet while screaming directly at the female United Kingdom Delegate.

"How dare this English sow accuse China of sinking her worthless Aircraft Carrier on purpose. I shall not stand here for a moment longer and allow my country to be accused of such foul treachery played out against what China was under the impression, was one of our true Allies. I shall not come back to this meeting as long as this woman is allowed to say these terrible things to a Chinese Representative only interested in world peace and ending a nuclear threat in the region." Ambassador Chow suddenly stormed out of the meeting.

Ambassador Bartlett called out his name, and just before he left the room, Ambassador Chow turned around and then he openly glared harshly at the French Ambassador as he waited a moment to hear what the other Ambassador had to add to him.

"Ambassador Chow please return to your seat so we can continue to try and workout an agreeable solution for both nations involved in this situation? Sir, please, we'll not be able to work out this problem, if you choose to leave this meeting before both nations are satisfied over the solution we have worked out, Ambassador." President Bartlett called out from his seat.

"As long as this foul woman is allowed to say such terrible things and aim these horrible accusations at a Chinese Representative, I shall never return to this meeting, sir. If my country does not receive a full apology by tomorrow afternoon before all the other members of this Council by the United Kingdom Representative. Then China will no longer be a member of this Security Council, and my nation will no longer be an active member of the Allies as well, sir. As far as I and my country will be concerned if these attacks are allowed to continue unchecked against my country, you can all go to the dreaded Dragon's lair, and then be eaten alive by the hateful creature." Ambassador Chow then left the room to the sound of murmurs behind him.

Ambassador Lang cried out from his seat a second time in an excited voice. "Now what do we do about China and her military troops, and what's going on in North Korea? I shall inform my government to prepare for a possible war with China, particularly if China doesn't remove her soldiers out of the South Korean city of Masan as quickly as humanly possible, sir. Japan cannot wait until the last possible moment before preparing herself for a war with China, if that nation continues to build up her military presence in South Korea so near to our country sir."

"Ambassador Lang please sir." Ambassador Bartlett said in sheer exhaustion to him.

The Delegate from India suddenly yelled out from his chair while not bothering to stand before addressing the other members of the meeting. "I already warned the members of this Council China could not to be trusted, and that country will do whatever it wishes without regard to anyone or the consequences of their foolish actions during this military response."

"Please Ambassador Dutrow not now sir." Ambassador Bartlett warned him.

Ambassador Walters, the American Representative attending the meeting, stood up in order to get the other members of the Council's attention, and then he spoke in a controlled manner and politely to the other members of the council. "Gentlemen, ladies, we have an extremely serious situation on our hands, and I'm afraid it'll not be solved today. So I suggest we call this meeting to a close, and report back to our Presidents and Prime Ministers and inform them of what transpired here today. I think we should resume this meeting tomorrow morning, when we had a chance to cool off and speak to our nation's Representatives. I'll send a message out to the Chinese Delegate, and I'm quite certain he'll return tomorrow morning to the meeting, and then he'll listen to reason at that time."

The French Ambassador Bartlett nodded in agreement to the American Ambassador's wise words, and then he announced to the other members of the Security Council. "I happen to agree with Ambassador Walters's decision, and I too shall send a message to Ambassador Chow, requesting he return and attend the meeting being called for tomorrow morning. It's late, and we have much paperwork to catch up on, before we can call it a day for ourselves, sir."

French Ambassador and Security Council President Bartlett banged his gavel down twice on his desk, and then added as was his usual way to conclude a meeting of the Security Council. "I shall call this meeting of the Five Hundred and Thirty Fifth Security Council concluded for this day, ladies and gentlemen. I trust we shall all meet here again tomorrow morning at ten o'clock sharp in the morning. I thank all Representatives of the nations you represent for attending this latest Council meeting, and I thank you for your time and patience over the many matters we discussed today, ladies and gentlemen. Good night everyone and please have a safe trip home, and I expect to see everyone back here tomorrow morning please." President Bartlett suddenly stood, and then he watched as many of the other members of the meeting rose, and they quickly started to file out of the massive meeting hall.

CHAPTER 30

The extremely pleased Chinese Ambassador Chow had no intention whatsoever of returning to any meetings called for on the next day, he went directly to his office and sent out a specially coded message to Chairman Mao Cheng-yu, the leader of China. Ambassador Chow informed him he walked out of the meeting as was planned when the United Kingdom Representative began demanding permission to board one of their submarines. He also reported all was proceeding as was expected, and he was awaiting further orders from the Chinese Leader.

Ambassador Chow was ordered to visit the Chinese Embassy in Mexico, and stay there until further notice. The wise Chinese Chairman wanted his United Nations Delegate well out of the way, but not to far to be useless if things did not go the way China planned.

BEIJING, CHINA,
THE CHAIRMAN'S PRIVATE MEETING CHAMBER.
3 A.M. MARCH 2nd, 1997

The Chinese Chairman was all smiles as he read the report describing how Ambassador Chow disrupted the entire Council meeting, and then he handed the paper proudly over to his Vice Chairman to read, and he asked at the same time, "Minister Chung, what is our next step?"

"Mr. Chairman, I have the 11th and 9th Group Army beginning their opening attack on Hong Kong at precisely six o'clock this morning, sir." The Minister quickly informed the Chairman.

"Ahhh... this is good news for me to hear, what Divisions are going to be involved in the opening attack against that so troublesome place, and these constantly troublemaking foolish kids who think they can force change in our government by their constant rioting against us, sir?"

"The 11th Group Army consists of one complete tank, and two full Motorized, and one fully Mechanized Divisions, and the 9th Group Army has three full Infantry Divisions backed by mechanized equipment, to support the 11th Group that'll lead the assault against Hong Kong, sir."

"Is this sufficient enough of our troops and military equipment to properly get the job done for us, Minister Chung?" the Vice Chairman asked him with concern.

"This is believed more than adequate for our purposes sir, you have to remember how the local population will react once they see our proud soldiers attacking the English crawling all over Hong Kong. Good Chinese people hates the pompous assed United Kingdom fools, and we cannot wait until they can help us drive the foul mongrels out into the sea, sir."

"How long do you believe it'll take for our troops to accomplish this feat, once we have stated our attack on the foolish English, Minister Chung?" the Minister of Justice Yu-wei asked.

"We plan on three full days of rapid military actions, four at the most to drive the English out of every nook and cranny they'll chose to try and hide in Hong Kong, sir. Remember, the English had many years to find every place in which to hide in Hong Kong, sir."

"Good, very good then you're free to commence your operation against the hated English squatting on Chinese soil," the Chairman ordered and then questioned. "Where are we in Korea? Have our troops been successful with destroying that foul nation of lowly dog eaters?"

The Minister of Naval Affairs spoke up and announced proudly the capital city of North Korea, Pyongyang had fallen, and all Chinese troops were pushing the remaining North Korean troops and civilians towards central North Korea for complete annihilation."

"Good, what about the worthless remaining English Aircraft Carriers? Do they pose much of a problem against our Naval ships, once we attack the fools living in Hong Kong sir?"

"No not at all Chairman Cheng-yu, we have three submarines well within striking distance of the remaining two United Kingdom Aircraft Carriers, plus one of our submarines is shadowing each of their worthless English Destroyers assigned to assist us as we continue to destroy all of North Korea. We're prepared for any contingencies that might surface against us, sir."

11TH GROUP ARMY, GENERAL DENG JIYUN IN COMMAND. 0345 HOURS

The phone in the Commanding Chinese General's headquarters rang, the Minister of National Defense wanted to speak with him immediately, and he responded, "yes Minister Chung Sir, yes I understand completely my orders sir. Yes, at six o'clock sharp I'm to commence hostilities against the English in Hong Kong, sir. I shall be well prepared by this time to jump off and attack sir, everything is at the ready as it stands, sir. Yes, I'll keep you well informed of our progress in Hong Kong against the British fools, sir. Thank you, and good day sir." With this, General Deng Jiyun hung up the phone, and then he turned to his Sergeant and ordered.

"You better wake them up, we'll move out today for our mission into Hong Kong."

The Chinese Sergeant instantly snapped to attention as he proudly saluted his powerful General, he was extremely proud to be part of the Army who would drive the hated English from all of China's soil. He waited for this order to be issued for all his life.

"Before you leave Sergeant, I want all my tank Commanders in my briefing room immediately, Sergeant." General Deng Jiyun added, as he went to get dressed in his class A military uniform.

At exactly Zero, Four, Fifteen Hours, seventeen Tank Commanders and officers met in the Commanding Chinese

General's briefing room. Ten minutes later, General Jiyun walked to the podium and began instruction his troops as what was expected of them in this opening attack in Hong Kong. "Loyal soldiers of China, we're going to drive the hated British off our entire continent. Tank Commanders, station two tanks at every bank spread throughout all Hong Kong. You have permission to shoot anyone who disobeys any of your orders. I don't want anyone to react too harshly against the evil English civilians, unless it's well deserved. A few dead fools will set a good example for the other foolish English civilians for our purposes here.

"The loathsome British are not allowed to remove any luggage or other belongings with them as they're forced out of Hong Kong. Your soldiers will check their pockets and their bodies for any hidden valuables. The women are known to stuff valuables down the front of their dresses, or in their underwear, or in that certain special place on their filthy bodies. You shall search every one of them, even if you have to strip them naked in order to do so. I don't want them to get out of Hong Kong with anything valuable, do you understand my orders Commanders?"

A chorus of yes' quickly followed his last question as all eyes stared back at their Commander.

"See you follow my orders faithfully as instructed. I don't want any of your men to get too rough with the British women, I cannot have our soldiers branded as rapists or animals. I need not remind you if anyone is caught taking an item of worth and not turning it in. He'll be punished with death." The angry General glared at his Commanders and then continued.

"I want our tanks stationed at each hotel, and a tank or armored vehicle at each restaurant, all foreigners are to be driven down to the docks, where cargo ships will wait to transfer them out to the British warships gathering in the South China Sea, a hundred miles from our shores. Be on guard, these loathsome British fools are a sneaky bunch to be forced to deal with. Now for the Infantry, I want you to line the streets on both sides. Your job is to control the masses, we estimate seven hundred and fifty thousand English devils live throughout Hong Kong, with maybe two hundred and twenty five thousand more spread out in the surrounding area. Again, your soldiers have permission to shoot, but shoot over their worthless heads first, before you shoot to kill any of the foul fools. I want you to remember these people we'll be forced to deal with are unarmed civilians, and all we want from them is their foul valuables and our land back.

"We don't have any air support for this entire mission, and we're allowed only three days for the completion of our operation from start to its conclusion. The British will have very limited communications with the outside world, and I don't want the world to believe we're slaughtering any of these worthless civilians. So be easy with your weapons. We shall have help from the Chinese Navy. There shall be four of our Destroyers stationed at the mouth of Hong Kong Bay. All my Tank Commanders, get your Squad Officers and move out, all other Officers stay until I'm finished with you." The General waited until the tankers left before he gave other orders.

"Infantry Officers you'll keep your troops under strict control at all times, until this operation is completed in Hong Kong. I shall not hesitate to shoot any foolish soldier being unnecessarily cruel to any of these people. Mind you, I'll be looking for someone to make an example of at the beginning of this operation. Your troops will be under a microscope by the outside world. Colonel Xeqian, 1st Infantry Division, 9th

Group Army. Your soldiers will be handed the task of destroying all the English communication centers on the opening attack against the fools.

"I understand there's going to be some communication left intact, no matter how hard we try to destroy all these foul systems. But I want it kept down to an absolute minimum. We shall be hard pressed to kill all E-mail and computer communications, but your soldiers will do their best and confiscate all computers and diskettes, and immediately destroy them. Your troops will also confiscate all Cellular phones, and any and all other types of communications the hated British civilians might employ, to inform the rest of the world what's happening to them in Hong Kong.

"Rip out all car phones, order your troops to use their heads, you know what you would do to reach the outside world, if you were under attack by outside troops. All news reporters, cameras and any other taping equipment either the newspapers or TV stations employ, are to be shut down or destroyed completely. Your troops are free to kill any reporters or cameramen taping what is going on in our country, if the fools don't obey any orders from your soldiers. Think ahead and destroy any equipment you can think of that can be used for communications. The Chairman will be watching our every action during this entire operation. So be smart about yourselves, good luck, go to your companies and start your troops moving. I want everyone in place by Zero, Five Thirty Hours. You're dismissed, so attend your troops Commanders."

The Chinese Commanding General stood on the platform with his hands resting threateningly on his hips, and he watched his Commanders moved out to order their soldiers to station. He smiled to himself at the knowledge that soon, all the foreigners would be driven out of China, as had been done on one other occasions in China's ancient past. The only thing different with this purge, was China was going to become a vastly richer nation from this action. He always believed the foolish British were taking advantage of his country with regards to Hong Kong.

The Chinese Commander went over to his communications center, and there he ordered the operator to transmit a coded message out to the Defense Minister he was aware was awaiting word on his operation, he was to state. "The mail has been sent out, sir."

A second message came across his desk, while the Defense Minister was yawning, reporting. "The government of China is expelling the Philippine Ambassador, and all his staff from China for spying against the nation of China." End of message.

The Minister of Defense immediately tore the sheet of paper from the machine and moaned to himself, "here it starts." He twisted the paper into a tight knob, and then placed it into a small incinerator and he hit the igniter and the paper instantly erupted into a small fireball. Once the paper was destroyed, the Minister mumbled again, "no paper trails left to us." He added to himself as he was just about to leave when the typewriter printed out a new report.

"The People's Republic of China has just expelled the Ambassador from Vietnam also for spying against the nation of China. China will send Navy warships off the coast of Vietnam for a series of special war games. End of Message." The Defense Minister shook his head over the speed at with which his government was moving along with their world conquest plans.

The Minister of Propaganda proudly announced even more of the Chinese ground troops will take their rest in

Masan. He left out where the government had threatened South Korea with an all out invasion, if they did not allow the Chinese troops to use Masan for their rest area.

Japan again screamed to the United States once she heard the Chinese Command was planning to increased the amount of troop strength being stationed in the South Korean city of Masan. Pressure from Japan caused the American President to order the Nuclear Powered Aircraft Carrier Stennis, from its standoff position off the coast of Korea and move over to a new position stationed directly off the coast of Japan, just near the Japanese city of Izumo. Japan was relieved with another American Aircraft Carrier Strike Group sitting off her coast between Japan and the Korean peninsula. The Carrier Stennis joined the Carrier Roosevelt.

When Vietnam and the Philippines heard the United States Command was moving a second Aircraft Carrier Group closer to protect Japan, both of these two countries cried they needed more protection from the new Chinese threat being aimed against their countries.

President Cole had to bite his lip as he decided to help the Philippines, he ordered the Carrier Group Eisenhower to leave her present position off the coast of Taiwan. To move to a position stationed between the Philippines and Vietnam, he then ordered the Carrier Carl Vinson to linkup with the Carrier Eisenhower, and station herself off the coast of the Philippines. While the Eisenhower Carrier Group moved over to Vietnam, in order to take up their position there. These orders were placed before the opening Chinese attack on the Colony of Hong Kong.

General Edward Campanelli, the Supreme Command of all United States military operations taking place in Asia, was steaming over the latest situation, and he quickly placed a call out to General Weidenbacher and bitched at his Commanding Officer over losing his Carriers protect.

General Weidenbacher cut his rather upset General off, and told him he ordered the Carrier Group headed by the Aircraft Carrier Lincoln to position off the south coast of Taiwan.

"Jesus H. Christ General Weidenbacher Sir, that'll leave me without any active Carrier Strike Groups between us and that damn nation of Taiwan, sir. This wil..."

"General Campanelli Sir, you have to remember you're in Command of aircraft power of four full Carriers Strike Forces sir. Plus you also have the capability of landing the large cargo aircraft on your decks, so calm down a little will you please, General. I have more important things breaking at the present moment than your problem with the Carriers, sir. So I'm going to be forced to cut this communication short on you, sir. Keep me informed of any new events taking place in your area of responsibility as they crop us, General Campanelli. I'll be back to you when I get more information on what the fuck the damn Chinese is up to in your region, sir."

CHINESE COMMAND HEADQUARTERS OF GENERAL JIYUN

The information on the American Aircraft Carriers being moved from surrounding the Island of Taiwan was immediately relayed to the Commanding Chinese General. A sort of smile slowly crossed over his lips as he told his Second in Command their plan to separate the American Aircraft Carriers away from the coastline of Taiwan, had worked out perfectly as was expected. He then handed his concerned Second in Command Colonel Xeqian the report, and then turned to a radio communications presently coming into his Command Center. His troops and military equipment were set in position and ready to attack Hong Kong. The General looked at his watch, it was Zero, Five, Forty Three hours. Seventeen minutes, and they will be in action.

ON BOARD THE VINEGAR JOE PLATFORM

Inside the CIC Chamber of the Vinegar Joe Platform, a Flash message came in from the satellite recon platform marked MR 141, informing General Campanelli it was picking up an unusual amount of heavy Chinese troop and tank movement in and around Hong Kong.

General Campanelli sat down hard as he read the information, and then he mumbled out loud at no one in particular, "shit, shit, shit, the Chinese are going to attack Hong Kong, that's what all this shit's been about all along, dammit. The stinking Chinese are going to attack Hong Kong. Boatswain, go to GQ, and then get General Weidenbacher on the horn for me STAT."

The sirens wailed throughout the massive Platform, as the monotone voice of the Boatswain Mate screamed over the intercom system, "General Quarters, General Quarters. All hands man your battle stations. Fire watch and damage control personal report to your assigned duty stations, this is not a drill..." The message repeated itself when General Campanelli growled.

"Will someone shut off that fucking racket for me, dammit. I can't hear myself thing."

"General Campanelli Sir, General Weidenbacher's on the horn, and he ain't happy, sir."

General Campanelli picked up the phone and he placed it up against his ear and then waited.

General Weidenbacher growled at Campanelli the moment he was certain he was on the phone with him. "What the fuck do you want now from my ass, mister? God dammit, I just told you I had my own crap to attend to, sir. I can't be holding your damn hand every second of the..."

General Campanelli cut General Weidenbacher off in mid-sentence as he reported. "General, I have information the damn Chinese are preparing to attack Hong Kong, sir."

"What the fuck are you talking about man? How the hell can you make such a damn warning to me, mister. Where did you get this information?" Weidenbacher growled as he took a breath.

"I just received a report from one of our recon satellites, and it clearly shows massive Chinese troop and tank movement going on throughout the area surrounding Hong Kong at this time, sir. I'm waiting for more pictures to come in, and then I can get a better picture of what we are..."

General Weidenbacher interrupted his General's report as he ordered him hotly, "Go to video secure line three, General Campanelli Sir. I want to see this shit for myself, mister."

A Sergeant handed the General a number of eight by twelve photos as he turned on the screens. General Campanelli quickly scanned the new batch of photos first, and then he reported to his Commander. "General Weidenbacher Sir, it's true as I stated sir, I see a number of column of Chinese tanks currently roaring down the main streets in Hong Kong, sir."

"Sonofabitch, it looks like we're going to be eating some shit over this one I'm afraid, General Campanelli Sir. Fax those damn photos over to my fucking office the moment we're done with this damn communication, sir. I need to see them first hand for myself, sir."

"What about those damn Aircraft Carriers you ordered moved away from my oversight, sir? Can I get them back in a quick hurry before I need them, General Weidenbacher Sir?"

"Christ Almighty General Campanelli, I need the fucking Carriers where I sent them, to help keep the damn Chinese from threatening these other nations in this fucking mess, sir. Go to Alert Status One with a hold, sir. Have you alerted the British about this mess, General?"

"I'll get on it the moment we're done speaking, General Weidenbacher Sir. I thought it was more important for me to inform you about this new situation cropping up on us first, sir."

"You're damn right on both counts General Campanelli. The Chinese are moving in tanks, looks like they're dissecting Hong Kong into a number of small and easier to control sections. Get the damn British, offer them any help you can just short of having any of your damn forces engaging any Chinese forces, I have to inform the President about this new situation. He's being such a damn shit when this kind of crap happens, and he wasn't expecting it, sir. If anyone needs me, I'll be at the White House giving the President fucking oxygen, General Campanelli Sir."

"Good luck with the President, General Weidenbacher Sir." General Campanelli laughed over the General last remark as the large center screen of the CIC went dead, he looked at his watch, it was Zero, Five, Fifty Six and he ordered, "Sergeant Cruz what the hell are the damn call numbers of the stinking British Destroyer Bristol, I need them mister?"

"One second sir and I'll get the information for you, here we go sir. It's Spider One, Skipper."

"Fine Spider One." His conversation was interrupted when a second satellite communicated, the word Flash screamed in the mike, and the screen instantly displayed the word Flash. A flow of paper came flying out of the machine and stacked up inside his lock box. General Campanelli unlocked the box and then pulled out the pages and began to read them.

:::Flash::: Flash::: Flash:::
:::Chinese troops are attacking communication centers throughout
all Hong Kong as of this time:::
:::Numerous Chinese main battle tanks have taken up positions in front
of all banks, hotels, restaurants and living quarters:::
:::Large groups of Chinese ground troops are also forcing numerous
civilian residents out into streets of Hong Kong at gun point:::
:::Many Civilians have been clearly shot, bodies lay scattered in the streets:::
:::Hot spots have been picked up: Tanks firing within city the limits:::

:::END OF REPORT:::

HONG KONG, CHINA

Chinese Commander General Jiyun's ground troops fired in the street at random to wake up the civilians. Jiyun laughed as he told his Sergeant he would give a months pay, to see the faces of the British mongrels when they woke to see our tanks sitting in the streets of Hong Kong. Chinese soldiers stormed into the Hong Kong Hilton, and ordered the manager to opening all room doors. The soldiers quickly moved in and drove the civilians out into the freezing air with just the clothes they had on their backs. Hundreds of civilians, soon thousands, stood in long lines while angry Chinese soldiers checked them for any possible hidden valuables, before the civilians were marched towards the docks of Hong Kong. Where they were forced to sit on the ground exposed to the elements as the civilian ranks increased by hundreds each passing second.

The Chinese soldiers were acting extremely harshly against the women, ripping clothes and underwear from them. If an English gentleman protested these attacks, he was severely beaten down senseless, and sometimes even shot and left for dead while lying in the street. Some Chinese soldiers selected certain women they found interesting, and they dragged them off into buildings. Never to be return to the ranks of the now homeless foreign civilians. Screams were heard throughout the city, as Chinese soldiers performed cruelties before killing them.

Some of the mostly United Kingdom foreigners quickly made their way for the banks to remove their life savings. But they were met by Chinese tanks and hordes of Chinese ground troops, only to be shot or taken as prisoner, and have what they were carrying confiscated by the soldiers. Hundreds of bodies littered the streets of Hong Kong. Chinese troops took to looting the banks, taking cash, and any valuables and stocks from the vaults of the banks, and loading them in armored vehicles, to be taken back to the Commanding General's Headquarters. Where they were placed in roll on roll off ship containers under heavy Chinese armed guard.

The electric had been cut off to all banks, stock market and oversea transfer centers, stopping money transfers, and computer transmissions. The Chinese soldiers moved quickly, all papers from the banks and stock market, were removed and placed in the empty vaults under heavy guard. Hong Kong was completely cut off from the watching eyes and ears of the outside world.

General Edward Campanelli stared at the extremely upsetting video report from the third recon satellite in stunned disbelief. He watched completely helplessly as countless Chinese troops shot at hordes of unarmed civilians whose ranks were being expanded by masses of young Chinese youths, as they started rioting against the Chinese troops attacking the foreigners of Hong Kong. The Chinese kids were receiving the same terrible treatment as the foreigners. They were being shot and killed in great numbers. The American General hit the ceiling when a Chinese tank lit his cannon and fire on, and then destroyed a speeding civilian car fleeing from it.

General Campanelli also picked up a good number of Chinese soldiers setting homes on the outskirts of Hong Kong ablaze. An unbelievable scene was quickly unfolding right before his eyes. General John White came up behind General Campanelli, and lightly rested his hand on his shoulder. General Campanelli looked up at him, and then moaned, "I guess you were fucking right about the damn Chinese going after Hong Kong after all, dammit. It looks like they ain't allowing any civilians to take their damn valuables with them as they're forced to leave their homes. This fucking soldier just ripped the shirt off that one woman's back. I think this is going to make the war in the Middle East look like a damn troop exercise on us, sir."

"Eddy, I hate to remind you, but weren't you supposed to get hold of the British Admiral, sir?"

"Shit, I forgot all about him, dammit!" he turned to Sergeant Cruz and then he ordered the young man. "Get me the damn Bristol Command Center, mister."

The light went on, instantly informing the angry General his call was ready, and he heard in his mike. "Spider One this is Homeplate. General Campanelli wishes to speak with Admiral Middleton immediately please. Over."

"Roger that Homeplate, please hold the line, and I'll inform the Admiral you want to speak to him immediately, sir. Over." The English Officer replied to the Sergeant.

Seconds later. "General Campanelli Sir, Admiral Middleton here, sir. What can I do for you General Campanelli Sir? I can't believe all the shit that has gone down since the last time we spoke together, sir. I'm so worried of this thing getting out of hand on us, sir."

"Admiral Middleton Sir, have you been in contact with any of your people from Hong Kong in the past twenty four hours, sir? I believe you nation has a new problem on their hands, sir."

"General Campanelli Sir, I have my own problems to deal with at this time sir. I can't be wasting my damn time with a bunch of crybaby civilians right now, sir." Admiral Middleton complained at the American Commander, upset he was actually bothering at this time.

"Admiral Middleton Sir, I just received a transmission from one of my recon satellites, and it clearly shows the civilians, mostly your people I believe, are under attack from many Chinese troops and armor who have just invaded the Colony of Hong Kong, sir."

Silence on the other end of the receiver was all General Campanelli heard.

"Middleton, Admiral Middleton Sir, are you still there sir?" General Campanelli asked.

"Yes General Campanelli Sir, I'm still here sir. Are you quite certain about this last report you have just briefed me on, General Campanelli Sir?"

"Positive Admiral Middleton Sir, sorry to say sir," the General offered in a sad tone.

"Gawddamn bloody hell the lousy wankers. I have to get my damn ships over to the coast of Hong Kong, and help out those poor souls. Those bloody Chinese bastards, can I depend on you if I need any assistance with this new situation, General Campanelli Sir?"

"Without asking for it Admiral Middleton Sir. I'll have the Missile Cruisers Virginia, Anzio and the Biddle, along with the Destroyers Sellers, Waddel and Merrill at your disposal at all times until we find out where this mess is going, sir. I'll also dispatch the Frigates Clark, and the Thach peel off from the Eisenhower Task Force, and has take up position twenty miles off the coast of Hong Kong. If you need any help, call on these ships, Admiral Middleton Sir."

"Thank you for your assistance General Campanelli Sir, I'll move the Ark Royal down, and order the Illustrious to come around from the North Korean coast, along with her support ships and suppliers, sir. I'll have these ships join up with the Ark Royal, and station themselves off the damn coast of Hong Kong. I don't know what the devil the damn Chinese troops are doing with our civilians. But I hope they'll just deport them if it comes down to that decision. I want to have my support for them set in place just in case I'm forced to pick the civilians up from the Hong Kong port where you reported the Chinese troops were herding them to, or elsewhere."

"Good call on your part Admiral Middleton Sir, I'll clear it with the Philippine government, for you to drop the civilians off there, if they have to be removed from Hong Kong, sir. I have pictures of the civilians being herded together at the docks. So I guess you're right about them being deported, sir. I also see a number of mixed cargo ships being moved to the docks, so you hafta be awful careful, Admiral. I picked up a good number of Chinese warships moving towards Hong Kong Harbor, and you can rest assure there are some submarines there also, sir."

"I'm well aware of that possibility at all times I assure you General Campanelli Sir. I'll call a number of submarine interceptors in to get over here on the double fast, sir. I find myself thanking you once again I see over this bloody situation, General Campanelli Sir."

"Do you have any idea how your country's going to respond to this terrible attack on your civilians?" General Campanelli asked the English Officer with concern lacing his voice.

"I'd go to a declaration of war, but the bloody politicians will try and work it out somehow."

"One thing else I have to inform you of at this time, Admiral Middleton Sir. Through some satellite pictures it looks like the Chinese soldiers are starting to loot the banks on you guys, sir. We picked up a number of instances of Chinese soldiers even shooting at the civilians showing up anywhere near the damn banks of Hong Kong, sir. The Chinese troops are also checking the civilians as well. I suspect they're looking for any valuables hidden on their person, sir. It looks like the soldiers are being extremely through about searching the civilians for any valuables, sir."

"Bloody Christ, how the hell are the little yellow devils treating our people trapped in Hong Kong, General Campanelli Sir? I have no information of this subject at this time, sir."

"Not very well I'm afraid sir, we've noticed some Chinese soldiers stripping a woman, and in other cases, the Chinese troops taking them away, Admiral. We filmed at least three civilian men being shot because they reacted to the harsh treatment of the women by the soldiers."

"The dirty devil bilkers, I'll get even with them for this insult I assure you, sir. I'll get my forces on the move, General Campanelli Sir. I'll speak to my Command after I get my forces going, sir. I'll be back to you once I get a handle of this mess, and let you know what we're doing, sir. I'll stop all military action in North Korea as of this moment, General Campanelli."

COMMANDING CHINESE GENERAL JIYUN'S HEADQUARTERS

The Chinese General read the latest report from his Commander assigned with taking over Hong Kong. He reported his soldiers had every bank under their complete control, and the vaults were being emptied, and all the worth of the foreigners on Hong Kong soil, was now on its way to his headquarters. His fourteen roll on containers was filled to capacity with everything, from gold bars to earrings stolen from the British civilians. The Chinese General's accountants placed the worth of the stolen items at well over one trillion and five hundred billion dollars, but the exact numbers were going in all directions. One report stated the real worth of Hong Kong was placed at over four trillion dollars, while another report placed the exact amount somewhere between two and three trillion dollars of cash worth for Hong Kong.

Yet the General had another convoy of military trucks heading in loaded down with more stolen loot from the British. The General smiled as he realized he accomplished exactly what he had set out to do with the worth of Hong Kong. He would bring to China's vaults, a worth of between one and three trillion, and eight billion dollars.

The General's rampaging soldiers had successfully looted over seventy percent of the worth of Hong Kong, and there were hundreds of thousands of mostly British civilians still being forced gathered along the docks, and up the roads stretching all the way back to Hong Kong proper. Riots were breaking out in many different areas of Hong Kong, and the Chinese troops were shooting or beating and getting more and more heavy handed on the rioters.

The first cargo ship scheduled to transport the civilians out to the waiting British warships, was moored at the Hong Kong Port and the Chinese soldiers, began to beat a group of frightened English civilians forward and up the loading ramp of the commandeered large Indian cargo ship. The cargo ship took over three hours to fill with nearly fifteen thousand civilians, mostly of English heritage. There was barely a place for each to even stand properly.

Chinese General Jiyun contacted the Commander of the British ships heading for Hong Kong, and ordered them to move thirty miles off the coast of Hong Kong, or the Chinese Navy would engage them. The British were informed that China was deporting all non-citizens of China from Hong Kong. General Jiyun spoke to Admiral Middleton personally, and he informed him the cargo ships would bring the civilians out to the thirty mile limit, and if his ships were not there to take the civilians on. The cargo ships would be sunk, and the civilians drowned.

On the Hong Kong docks was sheer madness with more shootings took place, and at one point it almost got out of hand, as the civilians stopped moving towards the second waiting cargo ship. The Chinese soldiers took long thick stalks of bamboo, and then they began to beat the screaming and frightened civilians forward, separating the men from women and children. When the angry male civilians saw the Chinese soldiers aiming their weapons at a group of women and children, they immediately backed off with giving the angry Chinese soldiers any further trouble, and they boarded the ship without further delay.

General Jiyun read this report, and then he decided to separate the men from the women and ship the English civilian males out first, giving his soldiers easier control over the remaining masses. Then they would also have more time to check the women for more hidden valuables.

At exactly ten, ten p.m. China time, the first of the commandeered cargo ships reached the assigned position, and it found three Naval Destroyers waiting for it. Two ships were English, while the third was an American warship. The transfer took over two hours to complete, with over twenty civilians lost overboard, before anyone could get to them. Two hundred more died on the commandeered ship from beating, or from being trampled underfoot by the masses.

Some civilians fainted, and they had to be carried off the cargo ship. Soon, all three warships were packed tight with the displaced civilians from Hong Kong. The United States received permission to bring the civilians over to the Philippines, but they had to resort to some heavy threatening of removing the carrier protection, before permission was finally given to them. The Aircraft Carrier

Lincoln shifted the civilians to the other ships in the support group, and launched aircraft, letting the Chinese Captains know they were being taped, and could also be attacked easily. Knowing this, the Chinese crews started to treat the displaced civilians more decently.

Both British and American recon flights were constantly being flown over Hong Kong Harbor, some aircraft came under fire by the Chinese military, but the aircraft continued filming the harsh treatment of the civilians, and the terrible conditions the civilians were forced to endure, while waiting for the cargo ships to return. The women, as usual, were treated to the worst assaults.

Admiral Middleton begged his Commander, the Prime Minister for permission to attack the Chinese forces attacking their civilians still trapped in Hong Kong. Offering to sail the Bristol right into the harbor, but permission was withheld from him. Admiral Middleton was beside himself with anger, especially when he watched the recon tapes General Campanelli sent over to him. After viewing the tapes, he ordered the Ark Royal to steam to the Bristol's side. He was going to board the Ark Royal, and use this ship as his new command ship.

ON BOARD THE VINEGAR JOE PLATFORM

General Edward Campanelli was overwhelmed with the many reports now constantly flooding into his CIC Chamber one after the other with blinding speed. One report was from Ambassador Walters in New York, who assured him this latest Chinese action would be brought up before the Security Council meeting planned for later on this day.

General John White was by his Commanding Officer's side and he spat angrily at the General. "This should do a lot of fucking good for us, sir. Scream and things happen huh, sir."

"If it was only that easy for the damn politicians to accomplish, John. How the hell's the Carrier Lincoln doing out there, sir?" General Campanelli asked his Second in Command.

"She reached her assigned position at about the same time as the Chinese cargo ship arrived. Her Commander reported the Chinese Captain was a pretty decent man to work with, sir."

"Don't believe that shit for a fucking second, John." Edward snapped at his friend.

"Christ sake Eddy, what the hell got in your damn drawers lately for cripe sake, sir? You sound like you hate everyone, and you're not getting any better as the days go by, man. I know this shit sucks the big one, but you can't let it get to you or it'll drive you absolutely nuts, sir."

"I hate anyone causing me to order our soldiers into the fucking battle lines, John."

"As I said in the past Eddy. War's hell." John tried a smile on the General, but it did not work.

"Fuck you and the stinking horse you rode in on John. I don't have the fricking time for this kinda shit my friend." General Campanelli snarled back at the grinning General.

John laughed, trying to get Edward to relax a little and start thinking clearly again.

General Campanelli came to the end of his patience, he wanted to act and he wanted to act at this very moment. But his orders were to sit tight and see what happened next. He was not the type of man to sit on his Laurels, and wait until the enemy was knocking on his front door step. He classified the Chinese as the enemy, he always had. He understood he was taking a helluva chance using his military warships as transport ships for the displaced civilians of Hong Kong. The Chinese command could easily take exception to this action, and attack his warships. At least then he would have a clear course of action open to him that he could react to correctly.

PEKING CHINA.
THE SPECIAL CHAMBERS OF THE CHAIRMAN
OF THE PEOPLE'S REPUBLIC OF CHINA

The powerful but well aged Chinese Leader Chairman Mao Cheng-yu, listened attentively as the aide read the latest report coming in from General Jiyun, who was in Command of the troops invading Hong Kong. He smiled as the aide told of the vast success of the lightening fast operation taking place in Hong Kong. Chairman Cheng-yu took a drag of his cigar, and then he announced proudly to the others he was meeting with, "as you foolish weak willed men can plainly see now, our plans are working out just as we have expected them to take place. The last report on the wealth we have successfully removed from the cursed banks of Hong Kong, is placed at well over one trillion and sixty billion American dollars, and the tally is constantly going up rapidly with every passing second of the day.

"One report sent by our Commander in Hong Kong has the wealth topping off at over two trillion dollars in short order and still climbing. This will easily replace the seventy billion dollars the cursed bankers have stolen from our country and her people. I'll have their loathsome heads brought back to China on a stick if it's the last thing I do in life. This I promise you all here today. How dare these lowly mongrels steal money from the People's Republic of China. I want to be briefed on our preparedness to invade Taiwan right now."

The Chinese Defense Minister dared to speak up next in a controlled voice, "Mr. Chairman, should we not wait for a few weeks and see how the rest of the world will react against our invasion of Hong Kong, before we open our attack against the loathsome Island of Taiwan, sir?"

The old man instantly became red in the face as he suddenly screamed with surprising strength in his voice and his movements. "How can China possibly invade a land that already belongs to her and her people? I don't understand your foolish way of thinking, you fool. All land of Hong Kong belongs to China, therefore, anything in Hong Kong, belongs to China and her people. I'll not listen to this foolishness or this proposed two govern system over Hong Kong any further. The next man who dares to display a weak spine before me, will be removed from here and have a steel rod placed in its stead, so he can stand like a true man on his two feet."

No one attending the meeting dared risk the well known and feared wrath of the old Chinese Chairman. There had been many other meetings held before where the powerful Chairman had disagreed with what was being offered to him, and the Minister who would not agree with the Chairman's wants and demands was taken outside and shot dead.

"I demand the preparations for the invasion of Taiwan to go ahead as I have ordered them. I want to know when we'll begin our attack, and what we're doing about this believed to be super carrier of the foolish Americans. Is there any truth in this most unbelievable rumor? A super Aircraft Carrier of the hated United States, bah. How much of a threat would this supposed super carrier possibly be against our military forces once we attack Taiwan, if this rumor has any truth to it? We have been successful with splitting the foolish American Aircraft Carriers up, but I don't want to be faced with a super carrier coming at us from out of the fog."

The Defense Minister fearing for his life, offered. "Chairman, our forces are massing in Zhao'an, Shantou, Xiamen, and Quanzhou. These cities are directly across from Taiwan, sir."

The Chairman interrupted, "Fool! The name of the Island is Formosa, not Taiwan."

"Yes Mr. Chairman, we're currently massing our ground troops at these four coastal cities in preparation for the all out invasion of Formosa in much the same way we did against Hong Kong. Our liberating troops are taking up their positions at night, using the darkness for cover of their movements. The tanks and armored vehicles are being hidden inside garages, and in building we took over by force in these four cities. We also took command of certain houses and open one side, and then hide up to three tanks inside the building. We have no reason to believe the evil American satellites are picking up our troop movements thus far, sir."

The Vice Chairman interrupted the reporting Minister this time as he requested harshly, "What troops do you have, and where are they located, sir?"

The Defense Minister was actually scared to death over the last question just put to him from the Chinese Vice Chairman. He quickly went over the five Army Groups he had stationed at the four cities that pleased the Chairman to all ends. At the end of his conversation he added, "I have no fear whatsoever over this supposed super carrier of the United States, not with the amount of military forces I have and will continue to assemble off the coast of the god cursed

Island of Formosa, sir. No country in the entire world will be able to stand up to our military might that'll be gathered and set to attack when commanded to do so. This I promise sir."

"It better be as you offered me Defense Minister Chung, because your very life depends on your words being correct." The old Chairman warned him in no uncertain terms.

"I feel you might be taking the hated American military forces a little too lightly at this time, Defense Minister Chung." The concerned Vice Chairman added in a warning tone directed solely at him this time, as he chose to get back into this conversation.

"Who cares what the devil the hated Americans do once our forces are set in place, and are ready to attack Formosa? From here and our preparations completed, we can strike at Vietnam, Japan, the Philippines, or even Russia if we have a mind to, and there'd be too much territory for the worthless American fools to try and protect with their precious Aircraft Carriers, and their inferior military forces and equipment. We'll have the great fools running around like a bunch of sprayed roaches not knowing where we might come at the fools next, yet they'll accomplish absolutely nothing with their foolishness and worthless threats and words. We shall come to an understanding with the hated Americans once we own all of Asia, and most of Russia."

The old man pulled his body out of the chair by grabbing the desk and using it for support. He stretched and then took his seat again, but he did not settle back. Instead, the Chairman sat down on the edge of his seat and leaned his bulk on the desk and said in an angry voice. "When will you have all your troops set in place and ready to attack that Island of lowly mongrels, Minister?"

The Defense Minister nodded politely at the angry looking Chairman, and then remarked, "my Armies will be ready to commence their opening attack on Formosa within three days time, sir."

"How can you possibly offer us this early a time to begin our assault on Formosa, if you're still involved with moving much of your troops around?" Minister Yu-wei asked.

"Most of my forces are already set in place, and the few remaining divisions needed for this operation will be in place by the time set I have just offered to the members of this meeting."

CHAPTER 31
ON BOARD THE VINEGAR JOE PLATFORM

The Supreme Commander of all American military forces stationed in the Asian region, General Edward Campanelli opened a direct communication to General Weidenbacher, and the General was busy informing Campanelli what took place at the recent White House briefing.

"Ed, the President ordered two shuttles prepared for immediate launch. The Discovery, and Star Search are being wheeled to their launch pads as we speak, there'll be a twelve hour launch separation between the two shuttles, enabling us to have an almost constant window of observation over the entire coast of China and the surrounding area in conflict, sir. As one craft leaves the reconnaissance window, the second shuttle will just be coming into the same area of responsibility. This mission's to be the longest in the shuttles history, it's scheduled to last at least eight weeks, longer if needed, sir. The President has also ordered the airforce to launch two new Eyehole spy satellites, I'm quite certain you know the satellites send back real time digital video tape images, so we can see any new Chinese troop movements being carried out in the region as they occur, sir. Hell, the President's sending so much crap up there, we're going to be forced to launch a fucking police force to try and control the space traffic over China, sir."

This made everyone stationed inside the CIC center to chuckle a bit, General Weidenbacher also laughed as he added to his orders, "Ed, all kidding aside sir, everyone thinks this attack on Hong Kong's just another damn step in the scheme of things to come from China. No one wants to speculate, but I'm betting the fucking bank Japan's next on their damn table, sir. I have the amphibious troop carriers taking on as many troops as they can possibly carry on board their damn ships safely, sir. I separated the troop ships from the Carrier Strike Groups in the immediate area, and they're steaming for your Platform as we speak, sir.

"I don't know what else to do to better defend our damn actions against China. There are more troops scheduled to land on your Platform, sir. Make them as comfortable as possible, I think it was a damn good call on your part to request the second latrine ship to be attached to the Platform, sir. It'll get a real workout when these extra troops show up. General Campanelli, remember this at all times during this fucking operation, you're in complete control here sir. If the Chinese forces get around you, and they land on Taiwan, we'll have one helluva fucking time with trying to root them out, sir. You have to stop the Chinese on their own land, sir."

"I'll stop them General Weidenbacher Sir." Instantly the wide screen went dead as General Campanelli turned to John and Colonel Locker standing behind him. He lowered his voice and asked his Second in Command. "Have you see the stinking Major hanging around anywhere?"

"Yeah Ed, she told me she was going to grab some sleep time over three hours ago." John leaned closer to his friend and smirked, "she told me she'd be sleeping in your bunk, and I was to tell you that she'd be waiting for your ass when you decided to take a little break, Eddy." John's face lit up as a huge grin crossed his lips.

"Yeah, some stinking rest I'll get around here I tell ya if she's waiting for me in my room, mister. Look John, say a little prayer for me will ya old pal? I'm going to bunk down for a few."

"Gees Ed, if you're trying to make me feel sorry for ya ass, it ain't gonna work this time around I can tell ya, old friend. I wish I had a problem like yours, sir. You know what they say, it's not just a job, it's an adventure, sir." The General smirked at his Commanding Officer.

The Commander left the CIC Chamber, but not before he called back at his General. "Fuck you John, what the hell are you all of a sudden, a damn commercial, mister?" General Campanelli left the CIC and got to his room, walking in the door he spotted Aleksandra laying in the bed. The sheet covering her right breast, running down the length of her body, covering half of her as it ran between her legs, with one leg resting on top of the sheet. She looked like a painting any artist would give his left ear to paint, a beautiful woman in a beautiful pose.

General Campanelli snuck into the room and quickly undressed. Then he slid in bed as quietly as he could. Aleksandra immediately wrapped him up in her arms, she was still half asleep, but she started to play with his dick. It got hard and she hummed, "I think I better do something with you little problem here, my lover."

She slid down his body and then she began to kiss his chest, and then his stomach as she went down his body until she found what she was looking for, and then she slid him in her mouth. At first she was just playing, but she felt his enjoyment and finished him off this way. In seconds she had him wiggling all over the bed as she nipped him with her teeth, licked him, and then blew her warm breath on him. Finally he came, some in her mouth, the rest on her face but she did not stop and for a second and the General thought he was going to get hard again. But she stopped before he came around. She sat up and then wiped her face on the towel by the side of the bed and then she asked him, "do enjoy what I do for me lover and soldier?"

"Are you shitting me young lady? Only a damn fool would say he didn't enjoy it, honey. It was just great, thanks a helluva lot there, I really need that Alex."

"I tell by way you seem enjoy what I do for you, big boy." They both laughed together.

Campanelli was so tired he fell off to sleep as they talked, so she snuggled in and quickly fell asleep herself. Not an hour later, Sergeant Cruz was tapping on his door.

"General Campanelli, are you up sir?" he said as he tapped on the door a second time. When no reply came, the Sergeant tried the unlocked door, he then entered the room cautiously. He saw the two on the bed, Aleksandra was almost completely out of the covers, and he took in the sight before calling out. "General Campanelli Sir, you're needed at the CIC unit STAT, sir."

There was still no response from the sound asleep General, so Sergeant Cruz walked up to the bed and he actually shook the General's arm slightly as he said just above a whisper. "General Campanelli Sir, you have to get up now sir, there's a problem at the CIC Chamber, sir."

Campanelli's eyes fluttered open, and he found himself looking into Cruz's scared eyes.

"Yeah, what the fuck's up Sarge?" The sleepy General then sat up and he leaned against the steel bulkhead of the ship's walls. The sheet fell off Aleksandra, waking her up she got up on one arm and she watched the two as they spoke.

Sergeant Cruz's eyes kept wandering over at Aleksandra and he was enjoying the view she was offering him. Finally, the General gave her a slight nudge, and she knew instantly what he wanted and she covered herself up, so the Sergeant could go on with his report. He grunted as he rubbed the sleep from his eyes as he grumbled at the Sergeant. "This better be real fucking important, or I'll have your damn ass in my desk, Sarge."

"General Campanelli Sir, a satellite just picked up some unusual Chinese troop movement where no Chinese ground troops should be located, and I was sent to get you General."

General Campanelli stretched and groaned like a wounded bear as he asked the Sergeant, "what the fuck are the damn Chinese up to now for the love of the good Christ child? Where the hell are these new Chinese troop movements occurring, mister?"

"I don't know for certain sir, I wasn't informed where this crap was taking place, General. I was just sent out to get you, sir. We drew straws and I won? If you want to call it that, sir."

"What the hell are you talking about Sergeant? You won, what the hell didja win with your stinking little straw game, mister?" he grunted with a sort of smile at him.

"General Campanelli Sir, everyone knew you were sleeping sir." Sergeant Cruz smiled as he threw a quick glance towards Aleksandra as he went on with what he was saying to his Commander. "So no one wanted to be the one to wake you up. So we all drew straws and I won."

"You got some balls there kid. I guess I better see what all the hubbub's about."

The Sergeant got the message and responded to his Commander. "I'll head back over to the CIC sir, and let them know you're on the way sir." He then turned to Aleksandra and took a good look as he bowed slightly to her before he left the Commander's private quarters.

General Campanelli turned to the Major and snapped at her angrily, "didja hafta leave your damn tits sticking out of the damn sheets like that for Pete's sake? You were driving the poor bastard crazy with them damn cannons of yours flopping around out in the stinking breeze. The damn fool was drooling all over himself, and he probably came in his stinking pants while he was at it, young lady. You gotta be a little more careful about those damn puppies of yours Alex. I don't want it getting around if anyone wants a cheap thrill, all they have to do is follow you around, and sooner or later your tits will be out and exposed for all to see, honey."

She smiled as she let the sheet fall completely away from her breasts again, and then she complained at him, "what matter you with all suddenly? You no like my tit no longer, mista? Men died see my tit, and you want me cover them all time up. I never see man want tit cover until this day. Is something all of sudden wrong you? You like men now maybe?"

"Very funny wiseass. One of these days sister. I'm telling ya, one of these days, it's gonna be pow, zoom straight to the moon, baby." He growled as he slid into his pants.

She reached out and played with him, he started to get hard as he pulled away from her, and bitched at her "No you don't, I'm not walking into the CIC with a hard on, cut the shit out."

"I give pleasure again if like me to?" she flipped her tongue in and out of her mouth.

"Don't tempt me honey, or I'll make you live up to that last offer of yours, Alex. I should make you take care of me in the damn CIC Chamber, and shock all those overstuffed shirts working in there some. Something has to get their blood moving again in there, dammit."

"Kiss ass, big shot General you sir. I no give anyone no more free show around here, sir."

"Any time, any place I'll kiss your lovely little ass for ya, baby." The General retorted as he slowly slide his tongue around his mouth while he grinned at the smiling female pilot.

"Now who tease who around here Mr. Big Shot leader you?" she cried as he left the room in a rush. She laid back down on the bed and then stretched with her arms over her head. Then she let out with a groan and decided to get out of bed and head for the CIC herself.

General Campanelli dragged himself into the CIC Chamber as if he was carrying a piano on his back, it smelled of stale air, body odor, old smoke, and the ever present but rather faint odor of diesel fuel that the massive oil tankers were once used to carry as a cargo.

"Say Eddy, we picked up some massive Chinese troop movement in and around the Chinese city of Shantou." John reported in an excited voice the moment he spotted his commander.

"Where the fuck's Shantou at dammit? Don't just give me a stinking name of some damn Chinese fucking city without giving me the damn location of the place in the same stinking report, mister." He demanded as he headed for his desk.

"Here you go General Campanelli Sir." General John White offered as he pointed out the location of the Chinese city on the wall map for his Commander.

"So what! What the hells around there we might have to worry about now, John."

John slowly moved the pointer across the large map, and General Campanelli followed it until it came to rest on the small Island of Taiwan.

Campanelli's heart instantly skipped a beat as he moaned and ran his hand through what was left of his hair at the same time. "Shit, you telling me China's preparing to attack Taiwan now, dammit? I hope you're drunk man. Where are these pictures you're talking about, John?"

John handed the photos over to General Campanelli just as Aleksandra strolled into the chamber, and she sat down by her man as she looked at the photos along with him. He quickly thumbed through the stack of pictures, and then he mumbled at his Second in Command.

"I don't see what pushed your stinking panic button here just yet, John. True, there's a lot of people moving around, but they look like ordinary civilians to my ass, maybe even some damn criminals. You know China has those damn Triad gangs all over the stinking place. No John, I think you might be wrong on this one, least wise, I sure as hell hope you're dead wrong with your concerns, man. When's the next satellite pass due over the same area, John?"

"Two hours Eddy." John reported back to his Commanding Officer with a snap in his tone.

"Good, keep your eye on this damn area for me, and report if you detect any other Chinese troop movements, sir. If the next Eyehole satellite picks up any further troop movement, we'll panic then I assure you. I don't see why the fucking Chinese would start anything against Taiwan now. Not with Hong Kong giving them all sorts of fits still, sir. How the hell many damn civilians do you think are fighting the lousy Chinese troops in Hong Kong now, John?"

"We figure maybe about three or four thousand civilians, and some Chinese police have taken to shooting at the Chinese troops as well, Eddy. Their actions are being taken out on the civilians though sir. We have films showing some civilians being pulled out of line and shot or beaten on the spot. Our Intel boys believe this action is to serve as a warning to the rest of them, not to make any further trouble for the Chinese troops or else, sir. The Chinese troops are still raping many English women, but they're letting them return to the lines of civilians to be evacuated though, sir. I guess they still don't care we're aware of what they're doing to the damn civilians. There's going to be some heads rolling after this mess is over with I assure you." John warned.

"I hear ya there John." General Campanelli grunted as he stared at the screen while waiting for the KH 17 Digital Videotape real time Eyehole satellite to transmit the latest pictures of the Shantou area in China. John took a seat and stared at the screen and mussed at the same time. "Sorta reminds you of a horror picture where the monster's hiding behind the door and you..."

General Campanelli laughed as he grumbled at the other General. "Christ sake John, will you cut the crap out and take this damn thing seriously for a change, man. A fucking monster hiding behind a damn door? Gees." He stared, resting his head on his hands, fighting to keep his eyes open. He jumped when the screen suddenly glared to life with the scream of static, he moved closer as did John and Aleksandra. He moved his finger across the screen, pointing out a number of civilians moving around the mostly deserted streets of Shantou.

At a few times the people spotted did resemble military troops moving about, but most of the times they looked like just a bunch of civilians up to no good, as the American Commander remarked to his Second in Command. "God dammit John, I still don't think any of these people are damn Chinese troops in any way, shape or form moving around in this one area, John. There's so few of them we're picking up here I'm almost positive of it, man."

All three of the concerned officers watched the screen, and the more they watched the less people they were able to locate. Some were even walking around with women on their arm. "Say Eddy, I'm beginning to believe you might be right, and I'm seeing ghosts behind every tree now, sir. They have to be civilian's the way they're just hanging around doing crap, man."

Campanelli smiled as he replied to his Second in Command, "look John, I'd much rather have you seeing ghosts hiding behind every tree than have you walking around blind, and have real ghosts come up behind and bite us on the damn ass, sir. Good work John, I want this damn film included in the package we're sending out to General Weidenbacher. Even though I feel they're a bunch of stinking civilians, I'm not going to ignore them either, sir. If there were enough to make you a little concerned, I'm concerned and we'll allow the General's staff sort it out."

John nodded in reply to his Commander's order, he was pleased the General thought enough of his opinion to take even this little bit of information important, as he replied, "I'll get this damn film out to the General as soon as the next pass has been completed, sir."

THE BRITISH DESTROYER GLAMORGAN

The HMS Destroyer Glamorgan was presently stationed directly on top of one of the Chinese submarines in concern, the Swaton, and she immediately detected it while trying to make a quick run on them. The British Captain instantly requested orders, and Admiral Middleton ordered the Captain to bring the Chinese submarine up to the surface, or sink it. The Destroyer instantly went into an anti-submarine warfare mode. She tried to drive the submarine to the surface by pounding it with powerful sonar pulses. When this failed, the Destroyer then fired off a number of depth charged missiles, setting the missiles off a thousand feet to either side of the submerged Chinese submarine, yet the submarine still continued to try and run on them.

This action from the submarine left no other alternative but to go in an all out attack against the fleeing Chinese submarine. The British Captain slowly walked the missiles right towards the submarine as a warning for it to surface. But the submarine ignored the warning and continued to run even though it was impossible for him to out run the much faster British Destroyer.

Admiral Middleton, keeping close tabs on the mission aimed at the Chinese submarine, and he informed the Captain to sink the submarine after all attempts to drive it to the surface, failed. The Captain ordered one depth charge fired directly at the submarine, it was a direct hit and the submarine broke apart in seven hundred feet of water. The Captain of the Chinese submarine did not try to surface until it was too late. The Captain of the Glamorgan, and Admiral Middleton on board the Ark Royal, listened to the death noises coming from the dying Chinese submarine.

ON BOARD THE VINEGAR JOE PLATFORM

General John White was instantly appraised about the British attacking the Chinese submarine in question the British Destroyer Glamorgan was trailing since first detecting it after the sinking of their Aircraft Carrier. John was just about to send for General Campanelli when he strolled in the CIC Chamber looking rather rested and refreshed after getting something to eat for himself. It was March 3, 1997, Zero, Six, Oh, Five, Hours.

"Morning John, whatdaya have for me today my friend?"

"Say Eddy, the British just sunk the Chinese submarine Swaton they were trailing, sir."

The General's smile immediately left his lips as he complained bitterly "shit, what the fuck's wrong with the damn English anyhow, dammit? I'm trying to keep a stinking lid on this damn mess, and they go off and attack the fricking Chinese submarine and sink the fucking thing. Get Admiral Middleton on the damn horn so I can practice some damage control around here, sir."

"Got him now for you General Campanelli Sir." John announced proudly.

"Yes Admiral Middleton, what the hell's this shit I just heard about you attacking the Chinese submarine, sir?" The American General growled at the British Commander.

"General Campanelli Sir, we didn't attack the damn thing, we sank the damn thing. I had the Destroyer Glamorgan stationed right on top of it, and she has a deep dive submersible over the side as we speak, sir. I'm checking this submarine out myself, and see if they're the ones who fired the damn torpedoes, and killed my flag ship the Invincible sir."

"Admiral Middleton Sir, why the fuck did you attack the damn thing for at this time, sir?"

"General Campanelli, the Chinese submarine tried to make a run for it on us, and I ordered the Destroyer to stop her from leaving the area at all cost, until we had a chance to inspect her torpedo stores, sir. I also ordered a second one of our Destroyers to take up position over the other Chinese submarine, Fuchou. I believe this is the devil bugger who really got the Invincible, and I'll not rest until I prove it to myself, and to the rest of the world as well they did it, sir."

There was a sudden commotion, and Admiral Middleton had to leave the phone for a second, and then he was back and reporting, "General Campanelli Sir, I have an emergency situation on my hands, sir. The Fuchou came up to periscope depth, and she's now taking a firing solution on the Bristol. I ordered the Destroyers to force the submarine to the surface, or sink it sir."

"Admiral Middleton, how the hell did you think the Chinese were going to react to this attack on their damn submarines, sir? You have to think about the damn civilians in Hong Kong."

"I'll worry about them later on, General Campanelli. If the Chinese soldiers take it out on our civilians then we'll attack the damn soldiers in Hong Kong. I have a number of troops sent to Thailand, and they're preparing for a fast attack operation against Hong Kong if necessary, sir."

"Admiral Middleton Sir, I warn you sir not to over react to this situation, or move too quickly against the damn Chinese forces in Hong Kong. You could start an all out shooting war, sir."

"In case you haven't noticed it by this time General Campanelli Sir, an all out shooting war has already started, sir. I'm only reacting to military actions taken against the United Kingdom, and her Subjects, sir. Err, excuse me for a few moments, sir." Admiral Middleton was gone again for a second, and then he was back and reporting to the American Commander again.

"General Campanelli the Fuchou just surfaced, and the Bristol has men boarding her as we speak, sir. They're reporting six of her torpedoes are missing from their racks. The Chinese Captain's trying to make us believe he was sailing light. Strange, the Invincible was hit by six torpedoes, sir. I have the evidence I was looking for, I'm suggesting to my people we declare war on China. If you'll excuse me General Campanelli Sir, I have certain duties I must attend to immediately, sir. I'll send you a complete report, and a copy of the videotape of the contents found in both Chinese submarines, sir. We're taking the Fuchou under tow, sir."

General Campanelli was absolutely furious as he ordered Cruz. "Sergeant, get me General Weidenbacher on the damn screen at once, mister. I have to inform him of this latest shit."

Once he was in communication with his Commander, Campanelli informed the General of the situation with the two Chinese submarines was done with. One had been sunk, and the other was under tow by the British warships, six torpedoes were missing from this submarine's racks.

"Shit, the British were right all along I guess, General Campanelli. The damn Chinese are the ones who sunk their

Aircraft Carrier after all. Okay, your ship or Platform, or whatever the hell you want to call the damn thing. Is now being given the code name of Iron Mountain. It has been determined we might be spreading some salt in the wounds of China if we maintained the Vinegar Joe name for the Platform at this time, sir. I want you to be prepared for an all out attack against any moving Chinese forces in the entire region of your responsibility, sir.

"I looked over the film you sent me Edward. We analyzed it in detail, and we think they might be troops moving around in the Chinese city of Shantou. The fact this is a possible Chinese troop movement almost directly across from the Island of Taiwan, has everyone's hair standing on edge over here, sir. I think China's going to start an all out war in this entire region, and I want to be well prepared for it when it happens, sir. I don't think the damn Chinese are going to attack Taiwan, I think this possible troop buildup at Shantou might just a ruse to draw our attention away from the real attack area, sir. I think the Chinese troops are still going after Japan, or maybe even South Korea. I don't know what the damn South Korean's are up to, but they're allowing the damn Chinese to build up their troops in Masan at will lately, sir.

"The President asked the South Koreans to stop allowing the Chinese troops to use this town as an R&R (Rest and Relaxation) station, sir. But his request fell on deaf ears I'm afraid, General Campanelli. I want you to keep a close eye on Shantou, in case the Chinese are up to something there. I wouldn't put anything pass them now. The shuttle's going to be launched at noon, and the second one's going off at midnight, sir. We're going to end up with a satellite or shuttle over China twenty four hours a day for your needs, General Campanelli. They won't be able to wipe their damn asses without us knowing about it as soon as they do it, I got to go sir."

When the General's image disappeared from the screen, General Campanelli sat back in his chair and then he took a deep breath and let it out slowly. He quickly gathered his thoughts for a few minutes before asking, "anyone here knows what the fuck's going on topside?"

Colonel Locker instantly answered his question, "General Campanelli Sir, we're launching and recovering aircraft every ten minutes now, sir. The Marines are working out and staying hot, they've taken over a certain section of the Platform deck, and the soldiers are staying sharp by staging a number or small war games, sir. They have quite an operation going on topside sir, and the Navy's playing a war game of their own, General Campanelli Sir."

 "Order that shit stopped as of this moment, no more playing around, we might be involved in the real thing in a few days, and we have to be damn ready if crunch times comes a knocking."

 "Aye aye sir, I'll order all war games being carried out between the Naval ships to stop immediately, General Campanelli Sir. And I'll also order the Marines to prepare for the real thing at the same time, sir." Colonel Locker offered as she pulled up the Navy Commander, and allowed him to listen in on the conversation going on between her and her Commander.

 "Good, continue with your report Colonel Locker." Campanelli ordered the female officer.

 "We're presently at ninety five percent capacity of aviation fuel, and all tanks and armored vehicles below deck are fueled and packed with ammo. All humvees are prepared and good to go as well, sir. The aircraft below deck are loaded with missiles and shells, and their fuel is topped off, sir. Their support aircraft are ready to refuel in flight at a moment's notice, sir. We have also increased the number of AWACS aircraft circling the area in concern from two to four, and we also have four Hawkeye's up to complete the radar coverage of the entire region of concern, sir. We have the Amphibious Assault ships packed to capacity with ground forces, and all warships are in the region, and could be off the coast of China in less than five hours sailing time, General Campanelli. We're well prepared, and we have a bomber wing from England on alert, and all aircraft stationed in Italy and Spain are fueled up, armed and ready for immediate action, sir. I feel if the shit hits the fan, we have enough forces in the region to clean it up, sir."

General Campanelli let out his breath as he replied to Colonel Locker's report. "Good, I like to be well prepared for anything coming at my stinking ass. By the way people, our new code name's Iron Mountain, this should help confuse the damn Chinese Command a might."

The rest of the day went by rather quickly for all concerned, there was little response from the Chinese over the sinking of their submarine, and the capture of the second one. The United Kingdom demanded a special security meeting be convened immediately, so China could explain her reasons for attacking and then sinking the Invincible.

General Campanelli went on deck twice, and he watched as countless aircraft were being constantly launched and recovered from the massive flight deck. The day was cold and drizzly, so he did not stay topside for long. Reports came flooding in to the CIC on the positions ships were taking, the Aircraft Carrier Strike Group Lincoln requested permission to leave the south coast of Taiwan in order to dock with Iron Mountain for replenishing of fuel and food supplies. Their refueler never showed up, and she was one of the only

Carrier Groups without a refueler or provisions ships in her flotilla. The situation in Hong Kong was bad, though most civilians were out of the city, it was estimated only one hundred thousand were still left in Hong Kong.

General Campanelli turned to General White and grumbled at the other officer, "I don't like this shit one fucking bit man. This shit reminds me of the damn calm before the stinking storm. I can't wait until the civilians are off Hong Kong. At least the lines will be more defined then."

It was late when General Campanelli finally looked at his watch, it was ten p.m. and he was dog ass tired. General Palmieri was picked to man the CIC Chamber while John left the chamber to get some sleep for himself. General Campanelli warned General Palmieri to pay close attention to any detected Chinese troop movement in and around the Chinese city of Shantou, and left further orders he was to be sent for if anything happened in this area of concern.

General Campanelli was a little hesitant to leave the CIC Chamber, but he left when General Palmieri threatened to have him forcibly removed from the chamber to get some needed sleep. The night dragged on, and General Palmieri did pick up some new Chinese troop movement in Shantou, but not enough to send for General Campanelli. He did not notice the tanks started up every night to charge their batteries, and check their sighting systems. Most Chinese tanks were well hidden in commandeered civilian buildings, while the rest of the war machines were hidden under cloth, straw or stacks of baskets. The satellites had no chance of spotting these tanks.

General Palmieri marveled at the pictures the shuttle sent to his CIC. They were clear enough to make out the clothes the Chinese men were wearing, he smiled until he picked up seven men dressed in obvious military uniforms. He watched as they ran into a building, and then he noticed a cloud of thick blue smoke coming from the same building and he roared out. "Shit, if I were a betting man, I'd swear to myself those soldiers just started up a hidden tank."

He sat riveted to the screen and tried to see what the soldiers he picked up were doing, when three other soldiers ran into the same building. He was happy because he had the foresight to have the tape machine running this time, as these Chinese troops were caught moving around.

General Palmieri turned to Sergeant Willis sleeping in his chair and growled at him, "Sergeant Willis, hey Sarge wake up, dammit!" He let out his breath in disgust as he picked up a pad, and threw it at the sleeping Sergeant, and it almost caused him to fall over backwards in the chair as it hit him on the side of his head. He blinked the sleep out of his eyes and then mumbled.

"Yeah, what's your problem?" he growled before realizing he was speaking to the General and immediately offered. "Sorry General Palmieri, I didn't mean anything by that sir."

"No problem there Sergeant. I want you to go and wake the General, tell him I want him at the Chamber to look at something I picked up on the video feed from the shuttle, Sarge."

Sergeant Willis stared at him as he swallowed and then he cried at the General. "C'mon General Palmieri Sir, you really want me to wake General Campanelli up, sir? Gees sir, can't I just volunteer to load bombs in an aircraft using a damn sledgehammer, sir? Christ sir, that order smells bad enuf to knock a stinking buzzard off the damn chuck wagon, sir."

General Palmieri laughed at the young man as he added to his order for the complaining Sergeant, "ah C'mon now, it can't be that bad an order Sarge."

"General Palmieri Sir, I'd much rather have my balls beaten flat with a wooden hammer sir. Then to go and wake the General up now, sir. Can't you do it yourself, General Palmieri Sir? General Campanelli won't have you strung up by your balls for disturbing him again, sir."

"Enough already Sergeant will ya please, and just go and get him for me Sarge. This is important and I want him back here on the double quick to see what I'm picking up here, mister."

"Yeah, yeah, I just hope the stinking government has my life insurance all paid up for my ass sir, that way at least my girl can get something out of this suicide mission you're sending me out on, General. Christ Almighty sir, I can read the headlines in the paper now sir. Another dumb ass soldier killed by friendly forces through no fault of his own, sir." Sergeant Willis moaned as he slowly left the chamber. He was still mumbling to himself when he turned the corner and almost bumped right into General Campanelli and he cried at him in an excited voice.

"Gees thank God, General Campanelli Sir, I was just coming to get you sir. General Palmieri wants you in the CIC center STAT, sir. He spotted something he didn't quite like, sir."

General Campanelli yawned as he mumbled at his excited acting NCO, "I guess it was a good thing I was already on my way to raid the stinking ice box, Sergeant. See if any cooks pulled some KP. If there are any cooks in the mess tell them I want something to eat, a sandwich will do me just fine for the time being, I'm starving for crap sake Sarge."

"Yes sir," the Sarge offered with great relief as he headed off for the mess and complained at himself. "Shit man, just what I fricking needed, another stinking suicide mission to go off on around here, dammit. The damn cooks might end up frying my ass over an open spittle."

General Campanelli laughed as he quick stepped and headed for the CIC Chamber, he never gave the female Major a second thought. He was unaware she was doing a night flight to keep up with her flight time. The still exhausted General burst in the CIC, and General Palmieri pushed the rewind button on the VCR the second he saw the General come in and he offered, "sorry for waking you up General Campanelli Sir, but I spotted something I think you should take a look at, sir. I picked up a number of obvious Chinese soldiers running into a building, and obviously starting up a vehicle that could very well be a tank, or another piece of armor, sir."

General Edward Campanelli watched as General Palmieri pointed out the Chinese soldiers he spotted running to the building in question. "Here you go sir." General Palmieri reported as he quickly pointed out the rather distinctive blue cloud coming from inside the building.

"Hmmm... from the height of the cloud, I'd offer that sucker's a T-95 tank, or maybe even a self-propelled Howitzer cannon, sir. Good eyes there sir, I'll have the shuttle aim its sights directly at this location, to see if we can pick up anything hidden in the woods, or by that old barn off to the side of the main building you're concerned with sir." General Campanelli pointed to a building so unstable, it looked like a slight breeze could collapse it in on itself.

The shuttle finally got in position and instantly started transmitting what she was detecting with her spy camera. The camera zoomed in close, and the General spotted a second tank hidden between a stand of trees, and he warned General Palmieri, "look at that lousy bastard there."

The two Generals found three more Chinese main battle tanks hidden in the surrounding area, and also a large number of Chinese troops hiding around the war machines.

"Damn, I think we have a major problem developing here on us, sir." General Campanelli moaned as the two military officers continued to watch the screen, and they found even more Chinese troops in the fields. Suddenly, the screen was covered with the word FLASH, FLASH.

"Shit," he hissed as he went over to the second screen and read the Flash message.

:::RIOTING BREAKING OUT IN THE CAPITAL OF CHINA, BEIJING, ALSO IN SHANGHAI, TIANJIN AND NANJING:::
:::CHINESE POLICE TRYING TO RESTORE ORDER:::
:::YOUTHS TAKEN TO STREETS THROWING FIRE BOMBS AND STONES AT RESPONDING POLICE:::
:::CHINESE POLICE RESPONDING AND ARE BEGINNING TO CRACKDOWN WITH HARSHER TREATMENT ON THE RIOTING YOUTH BY RELEASING TEAR GAS AND FIRING RUBBER BULLETS AND USING WATER CANNONS:::
:::SOME SHOOTING REPORTED:::
:::NO MILITARY TROOPS BEING EMPLOYED AT THIS TIME AGAINST ANY OF THE YOUNG RIOTERS:::
:::REPORTS STATE PROTESTERS ARE CALLING FOR A GENERAL STRIKE ACROSS ALL CHINA STATEING BEJING IS ERODING THE AUTONOMY HONG KONG MAINTAINS UNDER THE ONE COUNTRY, TWO GOVERNING SYSTEM'S MODE:::
:::CHINESE YOUTH PROTESTERS SURROUNDED CHINESE OFFICAL OFFICES IN HONG KONG AND BEIJING, HURLING EGGS AND SPRAYING

OBSCENITIES ON WALLS OF BUILDING AND CURSING
CHINA'S LEADER, PROTESTING THE TERRIBLE
TREATMENT OF ALL FOREIGNERS REMAINING IN
HONG KONG:::
:::CIVILIANS BELIEVED TO BE CHINESE TROOPS IN
DISGUISE ARE INDISCRIMINATELY ATTACKING
PROTESTERS WITH HEAVY CLUBS, PIPES AND STICKS,
KILLING MANY. NO CHINESE POLICE REPORTED
TRYING TO STOP THE PEOPLE ATTACKING AND
KILLING THE YOUNG CHINESE PROTESTERS:::

:::: END OF REPORT:::

General Palmieri read the report over a second time,
something sent a warning signal he was not picking up. He
read it a third time when it hit him like a truck. No Chinese
troops reported attacking the young Chinese protesters.
"General Campanelli Sir, look at this report will ya sir."

"Sure thing, whaddaya have sir?" General Campanelli
asked General Palmieri with concern.

"Since when do the damn Chinese use police to stop the
rioting by their youth, sir?"

"Since never. They always pull in the military for the
slightest infractions committed by their damn kids against
any of their government decisions. What's going on?"
Campanelli replied.

"I don't know yet, but I'm sure as hell am going to find out
what it is though, sir. I want a Keyhole satellite diverted over
to this area in question immediately, General Campanelli
Sir." General Palmieri pointed out one of the largest Army
Bases stationed inside China and he added, "I wanna see
why the stinking soldiers are staying in their damn barracks,
sir."

He checked on the satellite and then reported to his Commanding Officer in a kind of excited voice, "General Campanelli Sir, it'll take at least an hour to get the damn satellite over to that certain area of concern, she's just coming over the horizon as we speak, Sir."

MASAN, SOUTH KOREA

General Wang, the Commanding Officer of the Chinese troops currently stationed in South Korea, read the latest report from his Chairman. He was instructed to take practice rounds with his artillery into the sea. Aim, but not hit any land in Japan. He was further informed the Chairman wanted this area to become the next hot spot in the Asian region. General Wang smiled at the simplicity of his last orders, and the effect they would have in Japan, and the rest of the world for that matter. The Chinese General was informed to be expecting even more ships carrying Chinese troops to South Korea. He folded the report and then he ordered his artillery units to prepare for their practice fire. Within a few minutes, shells from the Chinese 122 mm cannons were landing in the water between Japan and South Korea.

Japan immediately responded to the shelling by sending a number of her surface warships to the area in order to repel any possible Chinese invaders to their Islands. The American Aircraft Carrier Roosevelt was ordered moved in the area. A Flash message went out to the Pentagon, and another to the Platform. General Weidenbacher's response was to divert the satellite and shuttle to this area, to see if they could detect any possible Chinese invasion forces heading for Japan. This diversion left the area between the Island of Taiwan and China with little if any intact recon network in place. General Campanelli was furious he lost his satellite coverage, as it was just entering its window to see if any Chinese troops stationed in Shantou, were moving in.

The Chinese Minister of Aeronautics, Chen Tongzhi reported to the Chairman Cheng-yu the American satellite heading for their city of Shantou, had been taken out of its flight path, and was now diverted to Japan as was expected. The old Chairman smiled to himself as he thought how predictable the foolish American Command was. He ordered his Chinese Armies stationed in the port cities of Zhao'un, Shantou, Xiamen and Quanzhou, to board the invasion ships that would transport them to the Island of Taiwan. There was no chance for the Americans to detect any of these troops moving before it was too late for them to react properly against his troops crossing the Straits of Formosa. Their plan has worked to perfection as far as he was concerned.

CHAPTER 32
ON BOARD THE VINEGAR JOE PLATFORM

General Campanelli and his Command Staff was delegated down to listening to radio reports as they came in, reports on the action between the waters of Japan and South Korea. Most action in North Korea was completed except for some minor mop up operations being carried out by the Chinese military forces. Chinese warships were putting to use the port facilities of North Korea. No one was interested in North Korea, the world's concern was for

Japan, the Philippines and now Island of Taiwan. It looked like China could have her way in the region if she chose to.

General Campanelli ordered all civilian bans to be constantly monitored at all times, in case someone from China broadcast what was happening in the interior of that country. He did not like not knowing what was happening in China, he believed this latest action to be a diversion to draw their attention away from the real point of the Chinese attack. The General tried to order up a quick flyover of China's coastline by the SR-91, but he was informed such a flight would take at least twenty four hours to order up, and he was positive that would be too late for his needs. He thought the Chinese forces were on the verge of attacking Taiwan today or tomorrow at the very latest. It seemed every twist and turn was blocked before him. Either the Chinese forces were smart, or the dice was bouncing the wrong way on his game board for him.

The rioting was still taking place by China's youth in Hong Kong, and the turmoil was still being controlled by Chinese police, and this scared him. Remembering the Tiananmen Square Democracy massacre, General Campanelli was certain this new wave of Chinese youth violence, would be stepped on by the military, more than by their police. Something was up, and he was going to find out what it was as he called out, "What's going on with the damn English? How are they making out with getting their remaining people the hell out of Hong Kong?"

"They're still working on the last boat loads of deported civilians that the Chinese troops are evicting as we speak, sir. This operation should be completed by three o'clock this afternoon, sir." Colonel Locker replied over her shoulder to her commanding officer.

"I want those civilians out of the area when the shooting starts!" General Campanelli roared while not pay attention to what he said, but his remark caused the CIC Chamber to grow as quiet as a tomb. He looked at the stunned faces, and then he bitched, "it's the way I feel, I think we're going to be fighting with China somewhere in Asia, and it's only a matter of a few damn days, or even a few hours before it finally happens. So you people better be prepared for this shit."

The faces continued to stare at him.

General Campanelli let out his breath and snapped. "Jesus, Mary and Joseph people, you better wake up to the fact a war's coming your way, and you people better be damn well prepared for it when it breaks out." He realized he had to break the trance everyone was in and asked, "what's the situation on the sinking of the damn Chinese submarine?"

Both Generals White and Palmieri called out at the same time, before Palmieri allowed John to have the ball and report to the Commander. "General Campanelli Sir, the Chinese are still being strangely quiet about it, sir. They haven't demanded the submarine under tow to be released yet from the British, sir. I don't know what the hell to make of this silence, General."

General Weidenbacher interrupted the conversation when the screen came to life before him.

There was no more pretense as the concerned General spoke in a rush, "General Campanelli Sir, what the fuck are you doing out there for the love of God, dammit! I sent your ass out there to try and keep a lid on things, and everything's coming apart at the seams on us, mister." He laughed and then went on with his report. "The President ordered the Chinese Delegate at the United Nations to get his ass over to the White House for a briefing. He has to wait until the

Chinese Ambassador gets a flight from Mexico, sir. The Boss is demanding to know what the hell China's up to, he's really pissed about their actions of late, sir. The last time I saw him, he was looking for some nails to chew on. I don't think he's going to stand for much more of this crap from the Chinese, sir."

General Campanelli cut his Commanding Officer off by offering up, "General Weidenbacher Sir, I need those damn satellites backs A-SAP, sir. Even one of the damn things would do me a helluva lot of good right about now, and maybe one of the shuttles too, sir."

"Yeah I understand this, but for right now the area between Japan and the Korea Peninsula is being classified as the upcoming hot spot sir, and I really need all the live Intel I can possibly gather in the damn area, mister. I'll cut you a satellite lose the first chance I get sir, but for right now, I need all of them and even a few more, General Campanelli Sir."

"General Weidenbacher Sir! I have my entire Command Staff preparing for an all out attack by an unknown number of screaming Chinese troops out here without any eyes, sir."

"You really think one's coming at ya, don't you sir?" General Weidenbacher asked his officer.

"I'm absolutely positive about it General Weidenbacher Sir. The damn Chinese forces are going to attack the Island of Taiwan, and then Japan I believe, sir. In that order, and then they'll go after the stinking Philippines and then stand pat to see what the rest of the world will do about their invasion of these few nations in the Asian region, sir."

"Shit, and you got it all worked out don't you sir? Why the hell would the damn Chinese take Taiwan first, for what reason, sir? What will it net them? Why not Japan first?"

"General Weidenbacher, Taiwan has an industrial region envied by all, so once China takes over Taiwan, and then Japan. They'll have a lock on the economy of many countries, even our own I'm afraid, sir. That'd hurt, but not kill us like it'd cripple the United Kingdom and most of Eastern Europe, sir. This move would wipe out the French economy, and force France into a state of emergency, and perhaps even a total collapse, sir. It'd also cause a shitload of South American nations to possibly go belly up as well, General Weidenbacher Sir."

"Look Ed, I heard all this bullshit before from you, and it didn't make very much sense then sir. And it still does and it's getting rather old at the same time, sir."

"Maybe so General Weidenbacher Sir, but you're gonna keep hearing about it till you realize this is what China has in mind, sir." General Campanelli complained again at the other General.

"General Campanelli, I'll do this much for you sir. I'll deliver your message to the Boss, and see what he wants to do about it, sir. Look sir, I have to get back and see how the President made out with the pain in the ass Ambassador from China. I believe the Boss sent out a special aircraft to pick his ass up from Mexico, he's that pissed off at the little fucker, sir."

When General Campanelli was through speaking with General Weidenbacher, John got his attention. "Say Eddy, I just received a message stating there are two more Chinese troop ships heading for Masan in South Korea, sir. What do you want to do about them, sir?"

The General growled angrily and then he roared at everyone stationed in the CIC. "I'll tell you what I'd like to do about this damn situation of the stinking new batch of Chinese troops ships heading for Masan, I'd like to sink the lot of the mother fucking things, but there's nothing we can do until something happens we can finally sink our damn teeth into, dammit." The General thought for a moment and then came up with an idea, he checked his list of warships under his command and picked out two ships, and then barked at his Second in Command.

"John, cut the Guided Missile Destroyers Cunningham and MacDonough, and order them to intercept these damn Chinese troop carrier ships. I don't want them to attack the damn things, I just want to see if their presence might cause the Chinese ships to turn back to China. If these damn troops ships get to Masan, there's going to shooting, and that means we'll be involved in the mess, and I'm not gonna like that one bit I tell ya, John. Order the Captains of those two ships to sorta zigzag in front of the Chinese troop ships. I'll clear it with the Joint Chiefs, you cut the damn orders. China's all over the damn place, and I don't know what she's up to."

Colonel Locker called out this time as she glanced at her Commander. "General Campanelli Sir, I just received a report a Chinese warship was spotted heading for the Philippines, sir."

"Christ Almighty, what the hell are these fucking people up to next around here, dammit? How many ships are reported heading for the god damn Philippines, Locker?"

"One so far sir, I'm still checking sir, trying to get a positive confirmation on the damn ship, and what kind she is, General Campanelli Sir. Nothing yet though, I just don't know if this reports true or not, sir." Colonel Locker replied with concern lacing her tone.

"Order the Aircraft Carrier Vinson to launch an information flight for that supposed Chinese ship heading for South Korea, Colonel. I want to know what type of

Chinese ship's steaming for the Philippines. Shit, I thought the damn Chinese were going to attack Taiwan, I might be wrong after all. God, I wish I had a damn satellite recon platform available to me."

"Maybe we can talk General Weidenbacher into giving us one of the damn satellites back, sir."

"Already tried that, no dice, sir. General Weidenbacher seems more concerned about a Chinese attack on Japan, than anywhere in the region. I don't blame him with his thoughts, if war breaks out in Japan, it'll explode in a World War with little trouble." He hissed as he scratched his head when he remembered about the rioting taking place in China and Hong Kong and asked, "what's the situation with the Chinese kids? Are they still fighting in the streets? I can't believe the youth of Hong Kong are actually going against the Chinese government, and the police over their harsh treatment of the foreigners China's driving out of Hong Kong."

"General Campanelli Sir, the last reports we received, stated they're still going at it sir. We picked up countless pleas for reinforcements and tanks to help deal with the masses of rioters suddenly rioting in the damn streets of Hong Kong and Beijing, and many other larger cities in China proper, sir. The kids are not wanting to calm down a bit with their actions, sir."

"Oh, the Chinese military's finally getting involved with the Chinese youth rioters, sir. That's more like it dammit. How heavy handed are they responding against the kids rioting?"

John gritted his teeth because he knew General Campanelli was going to explode when he went on with his report as he mumbled to him. "Well, not exactly sir."

The upset Commanding General glared angrily at General White, and then bellowed at his General. "What the fuck do you mean by not exactly, John? If they're calling for tanks and troops then all the military has to be involved in the ever expanding mess, sir?"

"Eddy, it's the police who are crying for the tanks and reinforcements in both extra police and military assistance, to help them deal with the hordes of kids rioting in these certain areas, sir. But as of this time sir, there's still no military units responding to the pleas of the overwhelmed police, sir. The military network's out, like they don't exist, sir. I don't know what the hell to make of their actions, sir. Usually, the Chinese military would be out stomping the kids into the damn ground under their boots because of their rioting, sir."

"God dammit, I was hoping some of the Chinese troops would've showed and started to get a handle on the riots, so the kids aren't beaten to death by the police. You know what I think, I don't think there are any more troops in all of China at this time, John. They're set to attack somewhere else, and it's bugging the living shit outta my ass that I don't know where the hell that attack's coming. John, contact the damn Taiwanese Command, and see if they have any new information as to where the Chinese troops might be stationed, sir. We know they're not up north, and we have to find them someplace out there, dammit."

General Edward Campanelli sat back in his chair and then placed his feet on top of his desk, and clasped his hands behind his head while opening and closing his burning eyes a few times rapidly to relieve some of the burning in them. Aleksandra snuck up by him as he had his eyes closed, she didn't want to disturb him, and when the general opened his eyes, she said to him.

"General Campanelli Sir, I have new report know you must read about quickly, sir."

Campanelli almost jumped out of his chair, because he did not know she was standing there.

Aleksandra laughed, and then she offered the startled General the report she held in her hand, as she tried a sexy smile on him. It did absolutely nothing to soften his rage and anger though, as the General nearly yanked the report from her hand, and then he let his breath out in a form of a hiss at her as he started reading the report.

"Funny, real funny sister," he growled as he sank back in his chair again, but as he read he took his feet off the desk forward. He placed the report down on the desk and reread it a second time as he sat forward in his chair now. It stated there was an unusual amount of shipping taking place between the four Chinese port cities of Zhao'an, Shantou, Xiamen and Quanzhou. General Campanelli looked at the wall map and found all four cities in question, and instantly drew in his breath as he suddenly realized where they lay. They sat directly across from the Island of Taiwan and he bellowed. "Sonofabitch, I think I found out where all the damn Chinese troops are hiding at, shit. Dammit, I should've seen this one coming at my ass."

The staffers working in the overcrowded CIC center, quickly gathered around the upset General's desk, and they stared at him as he carefully studied the huge wall map, and then he went back to the last report for a third time.

John asked the concerned military officer, "whatdaya have there, sir?"

"John, do you remember when I first told you that the damn Chinese weren't using their military troops to try and control the youth rioting in Hong Kong and Beijing, sir?"

"Yeah. What of it sir? You have some possible added information on the subject you might want to offer to the rest of us in here, General Campanelli Sir?" John replied to his Commander as he waited for him to finish with his words.

"Here's the reason why the Chinese Command aren't using their damn military forces to help their police control the kids rioting in their cities, John. I believe China has massed all her damn troops she could spare in and around these few port cities of theirs, dammit." He pointed them out on the map to the group and then he added, "this is why they can't use their troops to stop the kids from rioting. I'll bet the bank most of China's military are massed right here for an attack on Taiwan, sir."

John interrupted the kind of excited General Campanelli's words as he offered him. "Say Eddy, there's no problems anywhere near the fucking Island of Taiwan at this present time, sir. All the action seems to be shaping up near and around Japan, and now in the Philippines, sir. Besides, we were kind of worried about Hong Kong being attacked by the Chinese troops, sir."

"That's all bullshit and bad manners John. The Chinese Command want us to believe that they're gonna fucking attack Japan or the damn Philippines, when in reality they intend to attack Taiwan first, dammit. I guess when they have successfully destroyed Taiwan, they'll then hit Japan, and then the damn Philippines most likely in that order, John. Or maybe not in that exact order, but Taiwan's first on their list, as sure as Howdy Doody has wood balls, sir."

None of the members of his staff were completely convinced China was going to attack Taiwan in any case. Each member had their own idea on where China was going to strike next, after they finished off North Korea. But no one but the General believed the Chinese would attack Taiwan.

"Sergeant Cruz, patch me through to General Weidenbacher on the hookup as soon as possible mister. I need to speak with him immediately sir. I have to breach this concern with him A-SAP." General Campanelli barked at the young soldier as he waited for him to make the call.

"Are you certain you wanna approach Weidenbacher with this shit, Eddy? We have nothing positive he can hand his hat on that'll make him agree with your concerns." John asked with concern as he quickly added, "he didn't seem like he believed you the first time you tried to report your beliefs with him you know, Eddy. I think we should wait and see if we can get any more information on this crap, before we go off and start busting the General's horns with it, sir."

"For Christ sake John, how the fuck are we ever going to get any of this damn information we need, before it comes up and bites us on the damn ass, sir? Unless we have direct access to a satellite or one of the fricking shuttle systems, dammit sir. I need eyes over this damn section now, before all hell breaks out and then we're forced to do a catch up on this shit, sir. So I can make an intelligent summarization of what the hell's happening out there, and it looks like the only way that I'm going to get it done, is by busting General Weidenbacher's horns for it for Pete's sake." General Campanelli growled.

The center screen suddenly glared to life, and General Weidenbacher was standing behind his chair. The moment he saw Campanelli's face in his screen, he hissed, "for the love of God man. What the fuck is it now General? I'm busy around here, dammit! I'm standing dick deep in fucking reports, and the damn things keep flooding in my office every second of the day." He flicked his head, and Campanelli could see the President sitting in his chair looking upset as the General snarled. "What's your problem General Campanelli?"

"Sir, I have positive evidence China's preparing an attack against the Island of Taiwan, General Weidenbacher Sir." He offered.

The General cut him off as he moaned at his military officer. "Jesus Christ, not this bullshit again, mister. I just told you that I wasn't interested in any of this..."

He interrupted the General's anger. "General Weidenbacher, I have a report in hand that states a large number of Chinese ships are gathering at four major port cities on the Chinese coastline, sir. I want to report that I believe there's a strong chance that these damn troops are going..."

"So, it's their coast, they can do whatever they want on it, sir. Is this the proof you have, General? If it is, it's slim and it's not enough to get my attention."

General Campanelli ignored the sarcasm from the angry General as he continued on with his report. He went too far to back off now, "no General Weidenbacher Sir, will you listen to me for a second please, Sir."

"That's all you got, a second mister." The President snapped this time as he entered the conversation now.

"General Weidenbacher, Mr. President Sir. As you're aware, the youth of China have been rioting in China for the past two days now, sir. Why, I dunno for certain, but we believe it's over the way their military is treating the foreigners in Hong Kong. But I do know the Chinese police and only the police are trying to control them on the main land, sir. As far as we know, no military troops have been called up to try and help the police control the situation as yet, sir. Even though the police are actually begging for tanks and armored vehicles and troops to help support them to start controlling some of the kid's actions, sirs."

This got the General's attention, and he suddenly leaned closer to the screen, and intensely stared at his military officer, while waiting for him to continue with his report.

General Campanelli was pressing hard now because he did not want to be cut off by either the President or the General until he finished with his report for them, as he quickly went on with his concerns. "Mr. President, General, the serious lack of Chinese military troops getting involved in this action by their youth. Has lead me to believe the Chinese troops are no longer anywhere in the northern section of China, sir. I feel the Chinese troops were pulled from this area by the Chinese Command, and they are currently stacked up in these four port cities, and they're preparing for an all out attack against Taiwan, sir.

"We have a number of videotapes of a few Chinese troops running into a civilian building, and a tank or artillery piece being started inside that same building these soldiers ran into, sir. Add this to the mess of Chinese ships showing up in these four port cities, and you have an invasion force preparing to attack Taiwan as sure as the stinking sun is going to rise tomorrow morning, General, Mr. President Sir. All four of these Chinese cities lay directly across from the Island of Taiwan at its closest point to the Chinese coastline. General Weidenbacher, I need a fuc... excuse me Mr. President Sir.

"I need a satellite or shuttle flyover in this region in question as soon as possible. I need eyes so I can better determine if I'm correct, and then I can formulate my next moves to better defend against this possible invasion, sir." He took a deep breath, and then he waited for his commander officer's reply to his report. The General could easily see the President of the United States was sitting in his chair directly behind the standing General Weidenbacher. General Campanelli could also detect the President was obviously upset over his last words.

"Okay General Campanelli you aroused my attention, mister. You have to be clear on your next responses sir. Exactly when did you get these reports and pictures you're talking about, Edward?" General Weidenbacher asked him.

"Early this morning we picked up the pictures of the Chinese soldiers running into the building and starting up a definite piece of obvious military equipment, General Weidenbacher Sir. I was planning another flyover with the next satellite system, until you pulled it away from me, and you sent it off to cover the area between Japan and the coast of South Korea, sir. I now have no eyes over this section of China, General. Sir, I need a satellite dammit!" General Campanelli threw it all out on the table and actually outright demanded a satellite.

General Weidenbacher actually laughed at his demand, but inside he was burning up over his General's report, and it was being delivered in front of the upset President. He did not enjoy being showed in front of the President, or anyone else for that matter by a lesser officer under his command. If Campanelli was correct with his assumption, and the Chinese were planning to attack Taiwan, he was going to look like a first class asshole, even to himself. He ran a hand slowly through his hair and replied. "Err... okay you convinced me you might be onto something.

"The next pass by the satellites over Japan will be within the next two hours, sir. Once this flyover is completed, I'll have this satellite diverted over to your command to do flyover of this section of concern you wanted checked out, General Campanelli. This pass will occur at exactly Zero, Six

Hundred Hours tomorrow morning sir, by the time we make the necessary course corrections to the damn sat, (satellite) sir. You'll have your eyes back at that time General Campanelli. I also promise you from this time on sir, you'll have some kind of eyes overhead your area of responsibility at all times, sir. I certainly hope this move is going to finally sat..."

Campanelli went to interrupt, but was stopped dead in his tracks when the General held up his hand and then went on with what he wanted to offer to his General in the field, "will you allow me to finish with my words before you butt in on me, General Campanelli! This is the best I can do for you for the time being. Our computers have come up with the same solution the likely place for the Chinese to attack is Japan, and we're going to stick with the idea for now, sir."

"General Weidenbacher, I don't mean to argue with you over this matter, sir. But tomorrow morning's gonna be too fucking late for me and my needs, sir. I believe the shit's gonna hit the fan before that time, sir." Campanelli replied angrily, refusing to back down even though the President was listening to his words.

Now the Chairman was angry by the way he was embarrassing him before the President, as he snapped harshly. "Okay mister, we're going to throw away the computers on just your say so, General. We'll also dump the brain thrust working on this situation, and then we'll base all our future actions strictly on your prognostications, sir. While going against the people who studied the moves of China for their lives. We're going to throw all this crap in the shitter, and put you in place of it all. Are you that good General Campanelli? Because if you're not, I suggest you follow my orders to the letter." Weidenbacher glared harshly at his General over the screen.

Campanelli did not give up or back down for one second as he continued with his own heated words. "General Weidenbacher Sir, would you rather I keep my mouth shut and wait until the Chinese are flooding into Taiwan, sir. Because if you wanted this then you would've never picked me to run this operation, Sir." He glared at the image of the General on his screen.

"Don't try and blame that damn decision on my ass, mister. After all, I didn't pick your ass to command this project, General. It was your partner in crime sitting behind you, who dragged your ass up here from Florida for this mission, sir. Don't try and hide your puss mister, I see you hiding there General White. You can tell him for me to wait until I get my hands on his ass for his choice of leadership he offered us, mister. Okay look General, I value your opinion, but we have to stick to the rules of the game, and right now the rules say to protect Japan, and that's what I intend to do. If you can't get on with my orders. Then I'll have your ass replaced, immediately mister! It's that simple General." General Weidenbacher suddenly roared at his military officer. Stunning all listening to the angry General scream.

The civilian advisor sitting in the Oval Office along with the President, Manning piped up angrily to get his nose in the conversation between the two officers. "You see Mr. President, I told you he's nothing but a hothead, and he has no business being in Command of our military forces stationed in the Asian region, sir."

General Weidenbacher looked at the screen with the President sitting in the center of it, and snapped harshly before he even thought about his reply against the civilian. "For Christ sake, will you do the world a favor and shut the fuck up for once in your wasted life, Manning. I'm speaking with my Commander out in the field and you're fucking it up..."

Manning jumped up to his feet and stood straight from the shock of the General's harsh words he just aimed at him and he roared back at the powerful military officer. "How dare you speak to me in this manner General. I'm an advisor to the President and you'll respect me or I'll have you drummed out of the dame service..."

"Oh the hell shut up will you please Manning!" the President growled at him this time, and then added. "Allow General Weidenbacher to continue with this conversation, I believe General Campanelli's on to something here and I want it followed through. General Weidenbacher, I believe it's a good idea to send a satellite over the suspect area General Campanelli is so damn concerned over, but is there any way to do this before morning comes, sir?"

"With all due respect Mr. President, I wish there was, but with all the damn cut backs over the past years, along with the other pressures Congress was dumping on my shoulders..."

"Now is not the time to bring that crap up to my attention, General Weidenbacher. I wasn't in office when all that crap was ordered and went down, sir."

General Weidenbacher bowed slightly towards the President who then turned to Manning and ordered the civilian. "Will you please sit down already for Christ sake sir."

Manning plopped in his seat and glared harshly at the General as he waited for him to speak.

"Fucking Manning, he has no damn business sitting in on these military briefing. You couldn't find his damn IQ with a stinking flashlight for crying out loud." General Campanelli growled at John as the two Generals watched him drop in his seat like a discarded sack of potatoes.

General Weidenbacher quickly collected his thoughts for a moment, and then he replied to the President's last question, "with all due respect Mr. President, I can't possibly cut General Campanelli anything lose until tomorrow morning at the earliest, sir. But I'll do this for the pain in the ass though, I'll work all night, and if I can get you anything in the region earlier, I will. General Campanelli I want you to do a number of flyovers with your long range recon aircraft. Use the damn F-22 Raptors and YF-27s, let them work over the Formosa Strait. Have your damn air jockeys report anything unusual they might spot in the Strait. You're to use what's available to you, and get the damn Taiwanese Airforce on your side, and get them in the air, and allow them to earn their pay by running a number of their own recon flights in this region. They have two separate Wings of F-16 Falcons and a shitload of older crap, some F-5s, shit like that. That's all I have for now. Thank you for bringing this to my attention. Keep me informed sir."

No sooner did General Campanelli cut the connection, than John gave him another report that just came in, he was laughing as he handed the report to him, "shit man, you aren't making many friends over there in Washington, old buddy. The Taiwanese Airforce is scrambling as we speak, we really scared the living shit outta them time, when we informed them what we discovered taking place directly across from their stinking Island in China. They want any and all evidence, the Taiwanese have everything up, even a shitload of private and commercial aircraft. It'll be a helluva mess if we have to engage these assholes with this much crap airborne, sir. A Taiwanese General, named Shanhu Tan, I think you pronounce it, it means Coral Lake, sir. He's a real pain in the damn ass who won't take no for a fucking answer, sir. He wants to come out and review what we collected on the Chinese troop buildup along the coast of China, sir."

"Who the hell started this shit with these damn people anyhow for crap sake John? Who the hell shook the Taiwanese asses' outta their damn tree?" Campanelli growled at General White.

John snorted, "err... Eddy, if you remember correctly sir, you're the one who ordered me to inform the Taiwanese government what the damn Chinese were up to, sir."

"Shit, I remember now dammit, man do I have a big mouth sometimes, I'm telling ya John. Why the hell didn't you stop me from putting my stinking foot in my damn mouth, buster?"

"You won't get any argument from me on that one I'm afraid Ed. I know better that to try and stop you from making an ass outta yourself, sir." John smirked back at him.

"Thanks a lot there my friend. You're a real friend, not my friend, but you're a real friend John." General Campanelli complained with a smirk on his lips, and then turned to Locker and asked her, "anything new on the Chinese positions along their coastline, Colonel?"

"Nothing really new to report happening on the Chinese coast area, General Campanelli Sir."

"Okay, then let's start following General Weidenbacher's orders. Let's get a flight up. I want two sets of six aircraft each, inform the Taiwanese Command we're sending them in to cover the damn Formosa Straits. I want them to get close to China's coastline as they can fly, see if they can get any pictures that'll show us what the crap the Chinese military might be up to in the damn area, Colonel. Load them up for bear though, their orders are not to engage, but if they come under attack. Dammit they're cleared to defend themselves in any manner, Colonel.

"I'll not lose a single aircraft unless they killed their attacker on the way down. I want a ten minute separation between both flights, this way, if one Wing gets in trouble, the second flight can quickly move in and help the other flight out, if they come under possible attack. The first flight will consist of the F-22 Raptors, while the backup flights will consist of the slower YF-27 aircraft. I want a KC-135 tanker in flight for each flight of aircraft, order them out of Guam, Colonel Locker. By the way, how is the landing strip there coming along?"

General Palmieri spoke up now because this was his area of responsibility. "General, the civilians were removed and most of the Island's leveled, and the SeaBees have the landing strips about completed. The SeaBee's are making long runways, and we're moving in two Wings of B-52 H's from England, with a Wing of twenty five B-1D Bombers, and five B-2-R Stealth bombers, sir."

"Any fucking nukes mixed in with them damn long range aircraft this time around god dammit?" Campanelli asked hotly.

"Afraid so Eddy. Both the B-1 and B-2s bombers come equipped with a number of nukes stationed on board them at all times, it is SOP sir."

"Fuck it dammit. Okay, let's get those damn flights up then people. I want those specs on the B-1Ds. This will be the first time I'll be employing these air platforms in action, John."

General Campanelli quickly looked around the chamber, he then barked out, "where the hell's the damn Major at for cripe sake? Why the hell isn't she at her place working with the rest of us, we need everyone in the damn CIC if we end up going hot."

"General Campanelli Sir, she should be landing within the next few minutes, she's up and flying again, sir. The Major wanted to be in the flight patrolling the Formosa Straits, General." Colonel Locker said confidently to her concerned Commanding Officer.

"Damn women anyhow. Women are like frogs, no telling which way they're gonna jump until they do. I told all you people I didn't want her out there, dammit. I need her in this damn CIC, not flying all over the damn place for Christ sake!" General Campanelli snapped angrily.

"She'll never make it, the second flight took off fifteen minutes ago. You have nothing to worry about here, we don't have another flight scheduled for the rest of the day. She's down sir."

"Thanks, the damn Chinese have us running all over the stinking place, and there has been not one shot fired by the damn Chinese against any other nation but North Korea at this point. But it's coming and this is the reason I don't want her out there, in case I need her here."

Colonel Locker relayed an aide's message just delivered to her, and she reported. "General Campanelli Sir, she touched down a moment ago and is heading for something to eat, sir."

Hearing this report he was up in a flash and took off for the mess where he spotted Aleksandra sitting with two other pilots, and he sat down by her side and smirked nastily at her. The pilots picked up the Commander wanted to speak with the Major and they both quickly bugged out.

General Campanelli smiled now as she stuffed a leaf of lettuce in her mouth, and asked her. "Have you debriefed yet?"

"No yet debriefed, they more concern about flight to Straits to check on China actions there, General Sir. I debrief after eat something for me self and get called in to report, sir.”

“Good, because I want to speak to you, and this place is as good enuf as any Alex, for what I have to say to you. I don’t know what the next few days are going to bring us, but I was thinking. I hate living alone, never did, never will. I always had someone to share my life with, my divorce will be final by the end of the month, and I was planning to take a little time off after we know what the hell the damn Chinese are doing out there, I want to see Japan.”

She pointed the carrot she was eating at his chest and asked him with concern in her voice, “what you talk about me mista. If have something on you mind, you tell me now please.” She smiled, her Lithuanian accent rarely heard anymore because of being around so many Americans lately, leaked through again as she got excited at what she thought he was driving at.

He shifted his weight, showing he was extremely uncomfortable as he groused, “yeah, you’re right there sister. What I was trying to say to you is. Do you wanna marry me?”

She dropped the carrot as she stared at him, her eyes instantly filled with tears. She bit her lower lip as she cried out “I no more than Communist whore to you, American General you. Why want you marry for me for? You no got know what you ask for do you, mista?”

“Because I love you Alex and that’s why I just asked you to marry me. You’re the best thing that has ever happened to me young lady.”

She immediately jumped up and landed right in his lap as she began to kiss him all over his face and answered his question. “I love you, you bet’cha I marry you all time good, since ever first meet you, Popeye.”

She kissed him again, almost knocking him out of his chair as she put him in a breath robbing bear hug, kissing him again. Neither of the officers gave a thought as to where they were, until they heard the clapping, it was the grim covered Mess Sergeant.

She got off the General's lap and he whispered to her. "Whatdaya say we have a little private time together? I've been at it for over fifteen hours straight, and I think I'm kinda entitled to take a few hours off for myself, Alex."

Aleksandra was all for it and lead the way for him. They went back to the General's stateroom and made love, nice and slow this time. They took the time to get to know each other all over again. He wanted to do it now, because he was afraid what the future had in store.

CHECKER FLIGHT OF RAPTORS

The first flight of American warplanes did a quick flight through the Formosa Straits. The aircraft spotted a number of small Chinese boats and ships gathered in the Shantou harbor, and he reported this back to the Vinegar Joe Platform CIC center. Pictures were taken as the flight continued up the Straits towards Korea. The radio was suddenly jammed with chatter from the pilots off the Aircraft Carriers Roosevelt and Kelso, flying the ready air cap over the Carriers.

The two recon flights were up for nearly four hours straight, and the Flight Commanders were starting to make preparations to refuel for a second time while in flight. Even though the fighter planes were flying by light control, they still required constant monitoring, and minor corrections in flight. The pilots were now an hour and fifteen minutes from Iron Mountain, and each pilot knew every second they were in flight, was taking them a little further away from their home airbase. One of the pilots suddenly spotted a few Chinese fighter planes flying over China's coastline. He immediately identified them as outdated Sukhoi Su-24s, made by Russia and sold to China in the mid nineties.

The Chinese fighter planes kept their distance though, but they did let the American pilots know they were in the area by making a foolish charge at them, before breaking off and returning to their original course and altitude. The American fighter aircraft climbed up to thirty five thousand feet to hook up with KC-135 tankers to refuel in flight. Each American pilot was beat out, and their exhaustion showed in how sloppy they were with hooking up to the refueling aircraft. The Commander of the tanker aircraft got on the radio and made contact with the Commander of the Raptor flight, to give him final instructing for refueling in flight.

"Shooting Star Leader to Checker Flight Leader Sir. How do you read me now sir. Over."

"Checker Flight Leader to Shooting Star Leader. I copy you just fine sir, we're sucking up fumes and in danger of flame out if we don't take on some fuel, sir. Over."

"Checker Flight Leader. C'mon in, and I'll give you a little tail in the air, sir. Over."

"On my way in Shooting Star Leader. Over." Checker One cautiously guided his fighter aircraft under the belly of the massive KC-135 and then the pilot aligned himself with one of the tanker feed lines. "Checker One to Tiger, radio check. How you reading me sir? Over."

The boom operator nicknamed Tiger replied, "I'm reading you both loud and clear Major. You're now cleared to move in and get some fuel, careful, you're drifting laterally slightly, sir. Correct immediately Commander Sir. That's a little better sir, forward twenty, drifting again sir, correct to your portside sir. Careful, carefully sir. Back off, back off, you're going to take out our fucking wing, correct, correct, correct! Break off, break off, emergency break off, sir!"

When the pilot of the KC-135 heard the boom operator signal 'Break off', he knew the fighter aircraft was in trouble, and he followed his standing orders and he pulled back on his stick and his aircraft shot up and away from the fighter aircraft that followed his orders and dropped down away from the tanker. The pilot of the tanker hoped the fighter pilot remembered his standard instructions, and put his aircraft in a steep dive, or they were going to have a mid air collision.

"Boom operator. Where the hell's that sonofabitch at god dammit! I can't see hide or hair of him anywhere out there for the love of God! Where the hell did he turn off to? Are we in danger of a midair collision. Give me some input Boom Operator, or I'm going to continue my climb, sir." The pilot of the tanker roared into his radio.

"Tiger to Control. He's heading for the deck as instructed, sir. Man, we just cleared that asshole by mere just inches, sir. I don't want another miss like that one, Captain. Scared the living shit out of my ass, sir. It's a tuff day to refuel in flight, we're being pounded by strong headwinds from two separate directions, and throw in a few down drafts, and you'll understand why the damn fighter pilot was having such a hard time linking up with our feeder line, sir"

"I read you, it didn't do much for my ass either I can assure you, Sergeant. I'm heading for level flight at Angels Thirty Seven Thousand Feet now. Tell those other damn fly jockies if they want to take on some fuel, they have to come up to Angel's Thirty Seven Thousand and get it. Remind those flaming asses to be damn careful while they're at it, mister."

"Roger that last Captain, I'll surely inform the fighter pilots of the new position immediately sir. Checker One Flight Leader, Tiger. Our new position's currently stationed at Angel's Thirty Seven Thousand Feet, sir. Come on up and get some fuel and be damn careful about it while you're at it please. Over."

"Checker Flight Leader I copy that last Tiger. Sorry about what just happened sir. I'm afraid I'm really beat out and seeing double at the same time. I have to get some damn rest real soon. This is the fifth flight I was involved in the past seven days. Over."

It was rare to hear a fighter pilot complaining about being overtired while in flight. Colonel Locker knew she had to do something about it, or risk losing some of these fighter aircraft and their pilots, because they were being overworked lately. She called them.

"Iron Mountain to all Checker Flights. Refuel, and then you're ordered to return to base at once. I repeat, return to base immediately Checker Flight. Over."

"Checker Leader One. Copy that last order as received, sir. Over." The pilot replied.

"Checker Flight Two. Copy. Over." It's about time, Checker Two mumbled under his breath.

Colonel Mary Locker listened in carefully as Checker Leader One tried to line up for fuel for a second time. She was sweating for the fighter pilot to linkup successfully this time around.

"Checker One. You're aligned, forward twenty, easy, easy, forward fifteen, in the throat. Up ten, fine, drifting, correct. Better, five feet now, your pecker's out, contact. Hold it there. Over."

"Contact, coupling completed. Give me a thousand pounds. Over." Checker One ordered.

The boom operator and the Checker Flight Leader pilot heard the loud whine from the rushing fuel. Checker Leader felt the difference in his aircraft's handling almost instantly, as the fuel added weight to his aircraft. It took two minutes for the transfer of fuel to be completed.

The boom operator ordered Checker Leader to break off next. "Fuel transfer's complete sir. Disconnect sir." The boom operator watched as the smaller fighter aircraft pulled clear of the tail end of his plane, and then he announced to the Commander of his aircraft. "Completed. Pilot. Checker Two's moving into the slot for refueling at this time, sir."

Again, the worried boom operator carefully guided the second small fighter aircraft to the feeder line, his first words to the new incoming pilot were offered in a commanding tone of voice. "You're drifting slightly to portside, you are ordered to correct drift immediately sir. Careful, careful pilot. Correct, there that's better, C'mon in. Over."

Colonel Locker shook her head, because she understood these pilots were strung out, and they had another hour and a half left to their flight, before they got back to the Platform to deck down and rest some. Just as she sat back and rubbed her eyes, General Campanelli strolled into the CIC. He looked at her, and saw the strain and asked with a grin. "Didja miss me?"

"With every round I fired so far sir." Colonel Locker replied, making a quick joke of it.

"That was a good one. I didn't see that one coming at me. What's up Locker?"

"Man, didja ever have one of those type of days when you're holding a big stick, and everyone you meet looks like a damn Piñata, sir? Boy you seem to be in a great mood so far today General Campanelli Sir. By the way, I had to order

Checker Flight back to base General Campanelli." She said as she sat forward.

"How come you hadta do that, Locker? I need those damn aircraft up and keeping an eye on the fucking Strait for us, Colonel. They're the only eyes I have in the damn air at this time." He asked and then he growled, showing some concern in his expression and tone.

"These pussy hounds can't take any more of this crap, sir. One fighter almost crashed into the refueling tanker while in flight, General Campanelli. That's why I pulled their flight, sir."

"I trust you're ordering up another flight to cover for Checker Flight, Colonel Locker?"

Colonel Locker looked at her watch, and then offered to her Commanding Officer. "I don't want to, it's ten already sir. The satellite's going to be over the location in exactly eight hours sir, and I don't want another flight up the slot, sir. By the time we reclaim this flight, and send another out, it'll be less than five hours until the satellite shows up. I doubt even the damn Chinese could do much in that amount of time. I think we'll be safe until the next Sat flyover."

He slowly rubbed his chin as he thought for a moment, and then he responded, "all I know is after this fricking thing is over with, I'm gonna sleep for a fucking week straight."

"I believe I might join you there, sir." Colonel Locker whispered her reply to him.

"I guess Colonel Locker, that was a good call on your part to pull those two flights back in. But I want another flight sitting on deck and ready for an immediate launch, if we have need of more eyes in the air. Why don't you go and get yourself some damn shut eye. You look like you could sure use a little rest, Colonel."

"Thanks for the kind offer sir, but I was really hoping you'd tell me I look good today, General Campanelli. I don't mind tell you sir, I feel like a can of crushed assholes, sir." Colonel Locker said almost apologetically to her tall and good looking Commander.

General Campanelli smiled as Locker stood, and she gave him a slight kiss on the cheek, and then she headed off for her room to rest. He called out before she left the CIC.

"Any more damn trouble with the stinking Chinese while I was gone, Locker?"

"There's one complaint about our aircraft spotting a few Chinese aircraft flying along their own coast, sir. The Chinese flight came awfully close once to our boys, but our pilots gave them half a peace sign, and the Chinese pilots instantly backed off, and then they headed back a little deeper into their own country, sir."

General Campanelli laughed as he mumbled, "half a peace sign, huh Colonel." He had not even barely got comfortable in his chair when General Palmieri called out to him.

"General Campanelli Sir, it looks like the two Chinese troops ships heading for Masan in South Korea are stopping dead in the water, sir. Since the Carrier Roosevelt pulled up between the two countries, tensions seem to have eased up quite a bit there, sir. Maybe we might've over reacted a little to this whole mess after all from the looks of it, General Campanelli Sir."

"All I know is I'll be a whole lot more at ease when we get our damn eyes back over China." The Commanding General responded as he grunted back over the latest report.

"We have a few more hours left to struggle over the Intel we're gathering, and then you'll have your eyes in the sky back, Eddy." General Palmieri reported as he glanced at Campanelli to see if he was still paying attention to him.

General Campanelli let out his breath in a rush, and then he moaned back at the other two officer who was caught up in his vision at the moment. "General Palmieri, General White Sir. I'm not buying any of this shit for a fucking second I'm telling ya. I don't think this damn thing is over with by a long shot at this time you guys. I don't give a rat's ass what General Weidenbacher might think, I want a ready attack force standing ready on the damn deck and launched immediately.

"Once these aircraft are launched, they are to be instructed to reach the damn Straits at the same time the damn satellite reaches its window of transmission for us, sir. I want this fucking attack force to be backed up by a number of KC-135s and KC-10 Extender refueling tankers. Pull the tankers in from Guam, and clear this with the Taiwan Command for crap sake, because I want the damn tankers circling the damn Island for our aircraft needs, sir. I don't want any enemy aircraft knocking down our tankers, and putting our fighters out of the action for lack of refueling while in flight abilities, people."

CHAPTER 34
THE CHAIRMAN'S PRIVATE MEETING ROOM.
PEKING CHINA.
12:30 P.M. MARCH 5th, 1997

The well aged Chinese Chairman no longer wore his stuffy suit and tie. Lately, he took to wearing the soft silk, lose fitting pants and shirt fashioned in the old style of China's peasants working in the fields of the past times. He took his seat as if he had the weight of the world crashing down on his shoulders, and then he clasped his hands together as he mumbled at his gathered Ministers, "I demand to know what is the present situation happening with Formosa?"

"Mr. Chairman, we have the foolish American forces separated and spread out so thin their inferior forces won't be able to react quick enough to stop any of our plans as hoped for, and Hong Kong's now void of most of the devil foreigners, sir. We have reports stating some foreigners are still in hiding in Hong Kong. But we'll root out all the evil bastards before we're done with them, I assure you of this sir. We also have removed most of the worth from Hong Kong, and stored it in our city of Changsha, sir." The Minister reported proudly.

"What of our forces stationed along the Fujian coast and how are they doing? Are we prepared to begin our attack there? If so, when will we begin our opening assault?"

"Our forces stationed along the Fujian coast are well prepared and chomping at the bit to begin their opening attack against the god cursed Island of Formosa when ordered to do so. All our troops are stationed on board ships along with their military equipment. Our airforce is set to commence their opening attack on the Island at exactly five a.m. At six a.m., our ships will set sail to free our Island of Formosa from the hated traitors to China, Mr. Chairman."

"This is very good for my old ears to hear from you. Our honorable airforce, how are we going to keep our fighter aircraft fueled up for their ordered attack on Formosa?" The well aged Chairman growled while interrupting his Minister.

"Mr. Chairman, we have thirty five Soviet built lilyushin 76 long range fuel tankers with in flight refueling capabilities, ready for launching when our fighters are launched to attack Tai... err... Formosa, sir. These refueling aircraft will be stationed over the Formosa Straits when the attack on Taiwan... excuse me please, Formosa begins. Any of our fighter aircraft low on fuel, will have to find one of these tankers and refuel from them then fight on sir."

"Find one? How the devil do the pilots of our aircraft just find one of these refueling aircraft, fool?" the Chairman cried out with surprising strength as he glared at his Minister.

"Mr. Chairman, the fuel tankers will move alone with our fighters and bombers, as they conquer more of Formosa's airspace. The tankers will never be more than twenty minutes away from any of our fighters low on fuel. Another thirty of these in flight refueling tankers will be held in reserve, in case the American fighters find these few tankers and destroy them. The tankers will be priority targets for the enemy planes, just as theirs will be our prime targets when we begin our attack on Formosa. Without refueling tankers, the American aircraft will not be able to be involved in a prolong engagement with our aircraft. If we can keep the American fighter aircraft out of our war against Formosa for as long as possible, we can easily take over the entire worthless Island of lowly mongrels. Then the American military forces will never be able to root us off the foul Island once we command all of Formosa. Not with the limited resources the worthless American fools will have available for their needs in the area, Mr. Chairman."

"What about this Super Carrier the Americans are supposed to have somewhere near the god dom Island of Formosa as was reported to us?" The Vice Chairman asked with concern.

"Even if the worthless Americans have this supposed new Super Carrier anywhere near Formosa, who cares. How many aircraft could they possibly have stored on board it? One hundred? Two hundred? And how many weapons could they have for these aircraft? Enough for maybe two days worth of fighting? Three days, even a week at best? Then what will the foolish American forces do once they used up their full complete stores of weapons and aircraft stationed on this fictitious new super aircraft of theirs? Once we have the entire Island of Formosa in our possession, we can use it to the reverse of the American strategy. The Americans have referred to Formosa as a floating Aircraft Carrier they could operate from, to keep our nation of China in place. Well, we shall employ the lands of Formosa in the same exact way, but we'll use it to keep the hated Americans well out of Asia, Mr. Chairman."

The Chairman, looking like he aged ten years since the start of this invasion plan began, held aloft a boney and trembling hand and he snarled angrily at his Minister, "I order the start of the invasion of the cursed Island of Formosa to begin at the time set. Does General Jiyun have his targets picked out and set for slaughter, Minister?"

"Yes Mr. Chairman, the General reported he does have his troops set in place, and they're ready to begin the opening attack against Formosa as ordered, Mr. Chairman." The Defense Minister replied with confidence dripping in his voice.

"Then you'll allow him to begin this operation. I shall be in my state room until the fighting for Formosa has been completed, Mr. Defense Minister. If anyone has to speak with me, ask me any questions, or you want to voice any opinions or fears. Ask me now of them while I'm in your presence. Because now, I'd like to be left alone with my thoughts for a while."

None of the Ministers dared speak as they rose and quickly left the meeting room. When they were gone, the pleased Vice Chairman offered to the elderly Chinese Leader, "Mr.

Chairman, I'll keep you well informed of how the fighting goes for the Island of Formosa, sir."

The Chairman did not respond to his Vice Chairman's last words, he merely dismissed him with a simple wave of the hand as he rose on shaky legs, and fought with his body to carry his weight to his private quarters.

GENERAL JIYUN'S COMMAND HEADQUARTERS

General Ding Jiyun quickly assembled his pilots to hear their orders from their Chairman. "Soldiers of China, in your hands you hold the future of China. Don't allow the enemy to drive you from your assigned mission. Fighter pilots, your duty is to destroy all enemy Taiwanese aircraft trapped on the ground. Once you have accomplished this great feat then the bombers will move in next. Bomber pilots, your targets are all communication centers, military barracks and troop formations and military bases. Our first target in Formosa is Hsinchu, the Science Based Industrial Park. Don't destroy any buildings in this massive complex, just hit the airbase stationed in Chungli. Our ground troops will then march in and take over the buildings in this complex, and secure all experiments and projects these traitors were working on. Officers will see to it the enemy soldiers or complex workers will do no unnecessary damage to this area or buildings or project they had under construction in this complex when we hit the fools.

"Our second target on the Island of Formosa will be the huge Industrial region in Kaohsiung. Same orders will be in command here, as little damage will be created to the buildings as possible. The fighter planes will prowl the air over the rest of the Island, attacking any and all military installations or troop stations or resistance offered to our ground forces. You know where they are located in this country of mongrels, you have your maps and we have been over and over all the locations of concern to our ground forces, once we have invaded Formosa.

"You pilots can attack any military targets you happen across on the Island at will. The bombers will go after all assigned secondary targets, power plants, sanitation plants, radio and television stations, and all major transportation centers. Fighter pilots will attack all ports and shipping, once they have successfully destroyed all Taiwanese aircraft both in the air, or trapped on the ground. By the time my soldiers step foot on Formosan soil, I want the enemy Army completely destroyed, and their airforce helpless as discarded children's broken toys.

"When we finally take the cursed Island of Formosa away from the foul fools wasting their time defending the Island, I want our soldiers to quickly fortify the Island against any possible attack from the American forces operating in the area. The troops are to dig in and then prepare to repel any possible attack aimed against them, no matter who the fools are who are attacking. I want the port cities of Lukang and Kaohsiung kept in tact in order to accept our ships and military equipment and soldiers. Once Formosa is completely secure, I want an expedition sent out to Green Island to take over their small airbase.

"I also want our artillery pieces placed on the mountains aiming towards the Pacific waters. The Americans have their fleet of Aircraft Carriers stationed there we'll have to worry about, as soon as we begin our opening attack against Formosa. Soldiers go to your attack, our enemies are waiting your presence. Before any fighter pilots leave this room, I must inform you there'll be fuel tankers up, and they'll identify themselves and their positions to you over your radios. You'll not be forced to return to China for refueling. Remember Taiwan will be forever referred to as Formosa from now on, as has just been ordered by the Chairman of China."

The pilots clapped and then bowed to the General before leaving to follow their orders.

"I need not remind any of you once we have the foul Island of Formosa in our hands, you'll land at will on the cursed Island for refueling, rearming and needed rest. We have to take Formosa before the American military react to our attack against the Island of traitors to our country. Pilots, go to your aircraft, Army Officers, make certain your troops are on their assigned ships, and ready to go at the designated time ordered to begin our attack against the Island. Good luck soldiers of the Republic of China, we will claim what is China's to own."

ON BOARD THE VINEGAR JOE PLATFORM: 2440 HOURS, MARCH 5th, 1997

General Edward Campanelli stayed up to make certain his fighter aircraft took off from the Platform at the ordered time, to get them over the Formosa Straits as scheduled. The General was busy enjoying his fifth cup of coffee already, and running over in his mind the plans he would order if China did attack Taiwan. Colonel Mary Locker, who managed a quick catnap, came back to the CIC Chamber and she instantly bitched at the seated General.

"Man Edward, you look terrible this morning, I'm damn glad I'm not married to ya mister."

"Up yours too Colonel Locker." General Campanelli grunted no so pleasantly while not even bothering to look up at her to see how she looked, or what she was going to do in the CIC.

"I see you got your great sense of humor back today, General Campanelli Sir. Anything new happening in the Theater of War on us, sir? I'm pleased that most of the fighting has concluded in North Korea, sir." Colonel Locker asked as she took her seat before her computer.

The General exhaled and then he grumbled at the female military officer. "Locker, there's no Theater of War as yet, young lady. Most of the civilians from Hong Kong are now sitting safely at Subic Bay in the Philippines. A little beat up but at least they're safe. I hope we didn't move them right in the line of fire though, Colonel. I pray to God China doesn't attack the Philippines first, before we have a damn chance to get the civilians the hell out of the entire area. The Carrier Roosevelt has everything under control in the Sea of Japan at this time, Colonel. The Missile Cruiser Lake Champlain, and the Destroyer Chandler docked at the naval base stationed at Yokosuke in Japan, and there were no protesters to greet them this time, Ma'am. Strange, when someone needs you, no one wants to complain about your damn presence in their country. Damn whores they are. I okayed the ships to port, and get fresh drinking water, somehow, oil got in the Destroyer's reserve water system. I had a Cruiser tag along for support just in case."

Colonel Locker rested her hand on his shoulder and offered him in a calm voice, "I really don't think the Chinese are going to attack, sir. I believe they got what they wanted, sir."

The General looked up at her, his eyebrows arched and he was dead serious when he spoke again. "I do, and they're gonna go today or tomorrow at the latest, Colonel Locker.

The Chinese made too many preparations for war, not to engage in it when they're ready to attack."

"You're prepared for war just as well, sir." Colonel Locker replied sadly as she looked at him.

"I don't plan to lose nothing, you show me a good loser, and I'll show you a fucking loser every damn time, Colonel. If I lose, kids are gonna lose their damn lives in this mess. I've been trained not to show the enemy my big numbers, and not to allow the big numbers get dirty. I have no intention of paying for the same ground twice if and when hell comes a knocking. I don't plan to come in second place, because when you come in second place that only means you're the first to lose, Locker."

Colonel Locker understood full well what the General meant about the big numbers. The big numbers were always printed on the back of the football player's jersey, meaning not to end up lying on your back as she offered to her Commanding Officer. "Calm down a little will you General Campanelli Sir, you don't have to convince me what you believe is right, sir. If I didn't agree with you and your beliefs, I wouldn't be standing by your side like this sir."

"Colonel Locker, what's the fuel consumption of a tactical fighter wing per day, please?" General Campanelli asked, needing this information so he could work out how many days worth of fuel he had stored below deck for his fighter aircraft if war broke out against him.

"Hmmm... as near as I can figure General Campanelli Sir, I'd peg it at around three million pound a day per squadron, General Campanelli Sir."

"How much does one of those damn tankers below us hold in the way of fuel, Ma'am?" the concerned General asked of his lesser officer as he stared at the Colonel.

"Enough to keep seven squadrons of aircraft working four to five full weeks straight sir, depending on their work load of course, and if the pilots are forced to employ their afterburn systems during any flights, General. There are other reasons for the consumption of fuel that could either increase or decrease the days of supplies we have set aside for the aircraft, sir." The female officer reported to her Commander.

This meant he had enough reserves held in the three massive tankers to run an air war for up to nine to fifteen weeks, and he was promised by Command Central of his Platform being refueled every week, if not even twice a week if needed.

ON THE SHORELINE OF SHANTOU, XIAMEN, ZHAO'AN, AND QUANZHOU CHINA: 4 A.M. MARCH 5th, 1997

Under the veil of darkness, hundreds of thousands of excited and amped up Chinese troops quickly boarded anything that could float in water. The larger ships were saved solely for the tanks and artillery pieces and ammunition for the heavy weapons, that forced some Chinese troops to actually be forced to use Junks for the massive invasion force sailing against the Island of Taiwan. The only other time the world had ever witnessed such an overwhelming invasion force of troop and military transports and equipment, was during the invasion of France on D Day many years ago. General Deng Jiyun looked over his shoulder, just as a wing of twenty five fixed wing Shenyang F-12A fighter aircraft flew directly for Taiwan and his chest grew with great pride over his pilots heading off to destroy the Taiwanese military forces on the Island.

"Now it begins." The Chinese General moaned more at himself as he watched the heavy wave of his fighter aircraft quickly disappear. A second wave of aircraft roared overhead, the swing wing Shenyang F-12B tactical fighter aircraft. He smiled as he watched this Wing of Aircraft following the first Wing out. Soon, the sky was filled to overcrowded with aircraft ranging from the old F-7 and F-4 Mig fighters, to the B-7 and TU 16 Badger aircraft.

TAIWAN AIR BASE IN LUKANG

General Ho Yang was immediately informed that a large number of warplanes were presently taking off from the mainland of China, and the Chinese aircraft were heading directly for their Island. The worried Taiwanese General moved over to the radar scopes and he watched as the screens lit up with many air contacts displayed on the screen. His breathing was instantly labored as the Taiwanese General quickly realized what these blimps on the scope represented.

General Ho Yang mumbled at the radio operator, "maybe it's merely a Chinese training mission again. Nah, that can't be true, scramble all fighter aircraft, call in all pilots and have them man all standby aircraft, and then get them in the air and order the pilots to be ready to repel all enemy aircraft heading for our Island. Alert all military installations to go to full military alert, prepare our ground forces for an invasion from the Chinese forces. I'll contact the American Command stationed in the Philippine Sea immediately."

ON BOARD THE VINEGAR JOE PLATFORM:
4:35 A.M. MARCH 5th, 1997

General Edward Campanelli moved onto the massive flight deck of the Vinegar Joe Platform, to get himself some fresh air, and to also watch his aircraft taking off. He was launching twenty two F-22 Raptors, and twenty two YF-27s, along with twenty two F-18D Hornets, twenty refurbished F-16D/X Falcons, fourteen A-6E Intruders, and three EA-6B Prowlers for electronic warfare and jamming. The Guam Island was supposed to launch fifteen KC-135 tankers, and fifteen KC-10 Extender tankers, and two sets of five EF-111 for electronic jamming purposes. All American aircraft had orders to linkup over the Formosa Straits, at the same exact time the Eyehole reconnaissance satellite was to open its Formosa window. A Boeing E-3A Sentry AWACS aircraft code named Tinsel Town, was due over the area in fifteen minutes.

General Campanelli watched proudly as the aircraft took off from his flight deck, but that changed quickly. He was fit to be tied when the third F-22 Raptor stalled out after takeoff, and the stricken aircraft crashed in the sea. Anyone near him caught hell over it, one crew member thought the General was going to actually jump in to the sea to go after the pilot he was so angry.

Aleksandra walked in the CIC Chamber, awakened by the roar of aircraft engines and the fighter aircraft took off the flight deck. "Where General Campanelli? Why he no in CIC?"

"He's topside at the moment, but if I was you I wouldn't go anywhere near him today, he's angry enough to go bear hunting with a damn switch, honey."

"Why this is so Colonel Locker Ma'am?" she asked the other female officer calmly.

"We had another stall out, and the fighter aircraft crashed in the damn sea and this pissed him off real bad, Major Klevekaita."

"Why he so angry then? That happen anytime to pilot and aircraft, Colonel Locker."

"You tell him this and see what happens to ya pretty little ass, Ma'am." Locker warned her.

"I do this okay fine," she replied as he headed topside to Colonel Locker calling after her. "Good luck you young fool you. He's going to take a bit out of your little ass, Major."

She got up to the main flight deck of the massive Platform just as two more F-22 Raptors took off side by side. It was a beautiful sight to see, as the two sleek aircraft shot in the air with their afterburners blasting full power. The twin tails cut through the air like a hot knife through butter. The noise on the flight deck was deafening.

Aleksandra walked over to General Campanelli and then she said to him, "I hear had flame out aircraft. Is pilot okay sir? Lose aircraft okay, lose pilot no so good I afraid sir."

He turned to her and said in a pretty much calm tone of voice as he finally started to relax a little again. "Yes, thank God for that much, all four pilots are just fine Major."

The two officers stood in silence while watching the aircraft constantly taking off from the flight deck. An Airman ran over to the General and reported, "General Campanelli Sir, I have a message coming in from Taiwan Command for you sir. You can get it at the Control Tower sir."

The General jogged over to the Control Tower of the Platform with Aleksandra tagging along behind him. As the General climbed the stairs, an Air Traffic Controller saw him coming and he offered right off, "General Campanelli Sir, the radio's over there sir, you better hurry it up some General. Taiwan's under general attack across the entire Island from the Chinese, sir."

General Campanelli instantly froze in place as his mind registered what the controller just said to him as he mumbled, "Taiwan's under fucking attack? Shit! God dammit!" He grabbed the radio and barked in it. "General Campanelli here. Who the fuck am I speaking to, and whatdaya fucking mean that Taiwan's under general attack? From who? When did this shit go down?"

"General Campanelli, this is General Ho Yang of the Taiwanese Airforce Command. Sir, we detected a large force of aircraft taking off from mainland China heading directly for our Island, sir. We estimate the first wave of enemy aircraft to be moments away from our coast, sir. We don't know what their intention are, but we're picking up a mix of fighters and bomber aircraft. I ordered our country to full alert and... Wait, I hear engines..."

General Campanelli was able to hear the powerful blasts on the other end of the open line from countless numbers of bombs exploding. Then the terrible screams from the maimed and dying replaced the General's voice. He threw the mike away and yelled. "General Quarters!"

As the General ran from the Control Tower, his attention was drawn to a sudden movement as the ASROC anti-sub rocket and MK-15 CIWS Phalanx systems moved in response to the GQ order. In the stairwell leading back to the CIC Chamber, a voice screamed out in an excited voice, "General Quarters, General Quarters. All hands man you battle stations. General Quarters, General Quarters! This is not a drill, I repeat, this is not a drill. Man your battle stations. Fire control to your stations. General Quarters, Gener..."

General Campanelli almost had to place his hands over his ears, the noise from the speaker was so loud. He came crashing into the CIC center, just as General White and General Palmieri were taking their seats and preparing for work.

John turned to Campanelli and he asked, "what the fuck's up Ed? Why the GQ order, sir?"

"The Chinese are sending Wings of aircraft to attack the Island of Taiwan, dammit. They hit the airbase as I was speaking to some Taiwanese General. Christ, it's gonna hit the fan now for sure, sir." As the General was complaining, the three screens in the CIC Chamber suddenly went from black to a blaring white, and then to a test pattern.

General Campanelli just sat down in the chamber as the center screen came to life, and President Albert Cole's extremely upset face instantly appeared on it. Just as sudden, General William Weidenbacher's face appeared on the second screen. The third screen came in, and General Claiborne said as soon as he saw General Campanelli on his screen. "What the fuck have you done now mister? It seems no matter where the hell we place your damn ass, you start a shooting war on us, General Campanelli Sir."

No one laughed as the President took over the conversation and he bitched at the General angrily, "this shit better be important to wake me out of a dead sleep, mister." He aimed his complaint directly at General Weidenbacher as he turned to face the General on his screen.

General Campanelli interrupted him and offered, "Mr. President Sir, I just received word a large force of Chinese aircraft are presently attacking the Island of Taiwan, sir. They hit an airbase and we immediately lost all communications with the Island and their damn command structure, sir. We're trying to raise anyone on the Citizen's bands on the Island now, sir."

General Weidenbacher snapped angrily at General Campanelli this time, "are you quite certain the damn Chinese aircraft are attacking? Last word I had was, a large force of Chinese aircraft were taking off from mainland China, sir. But no direction was given to the flights or their destination or intended targets, General Campanelli Sir."

"Positive the Chinese aircraft are attacking Taiwan, sir. I have an Alpha Launch already in progress on the Platform, sir. The aircraft are heading for the Formosa Straits, and they're armed to the damn teeth with orders to defend themselves against any possible aggression aimed at them from any targets, General Weidenbacher Sir."

President Cole snapped out of his stupor and he barked at his General, "did you have advance word on this Chinese attack, General Campanelli Sir?"

"No sir, I was kinda playing it a little safe myself, Mr. President Sir. I felt the Chinese were gonna attack soon, and I wanted a ready force up in order to repel any attack from them sir."

"Are your aircraft prepared to attack? Excuse me that was a bad question. Surely they'd be if they're up and prepared to engage the enemy planes. Sorry sir." General Claiborne replied.

The CIA Director, John Raincloud asked this time as he got involved in the conversation while he was in General Weidenbacher's office at the Pentagon. "General Campanelli Sir, do you have any idea what type of Chinese aircraft are involved in this attack against Taiwan at this time sir?"

"No, not at this time I don't, but the Taiwanese General I was speaking with at the time they were attacked, reported to me a mix bag of Chinese fighters and bomber aircraft were in the process of attacking his base as we spoke, sir. He did report even the TU-16 Badger's are up and coming at the Island, sir."

"That's a Russian aircraft you just offered General Campanelli Sir. Please don't inform me the damn Russian's are assisting the Chinese attack on Taiwan, sir?" the Secretary of the Air Force, General Michael Schramm replied in an excited voice.

"Sorry sir, but this one's Chinese, I don't know the name and number for the Chinese version of the Russian Badger, sir. It's made in the Shenyang factories though I'm certain, sir."

"Enough of this horseshit General Campanelli Sir." The President suddenly growled, and then he went on with his angry words, "I don't give a rat's ass what the damn Chinese are sending up to attack Taiwan. I'm only concerned if we can stop them or not sir. You can rest assure if the planes are attacking, the ground forces can't be too far behind them. General Campanelli Sir, what's your next move to counter the attacks from the Chinese forces against Taiwan, sir? I must commend you on having those fighter planes up, and ready to respond to this attack though, sir. What a stroke of luck for us you were on the ball, General Campanelli Sir."

"Yes sir, you can bet lady luck will never spread her legs this wide again... Err... excuse me Mr. President Sir, I'm a little excited sir." Campanelli offered as an apology for his crude words.

"I see by your last statement General," the President replied with a hint of a smile.

"Mr. President Sir, I plan to allow the fighter aircraft we launched to engage any Chinese aircraft they happen across, sir. I'm also giving the Chinese bombers and fuel tankers top priority to be attack, sir. Some of our fighter aircraft will hit any Chinese ships they pick up in the Strait. If you give me permission to carry out these attacks that is, Mr. President Sir?"

President Cole was shaken to his soul as a crease of concentration showed on his forehead as he replied to his military officer, "Yes General Campanelli Sir, I'll give you permission when I'm certain the Chinese are truly attacking the Island of Taiwan, sir. How soon will that damn satellite be over the area in question for us, sir?"

"I'll know any second if what's being reported to us is true, Mr. President. I ordered an E-3A Sentry to the area of contention. They'll pick up any Chinese aircraft if they're in the air, sir."

"You get in touch with that damn AWACS plane immediately, General Campanelli Sir."

"Right away Mr. President Sir." He picked up the radio receiver and he snapped into, "Iron Mountain to Tinsel Town. Report! Over."

"Iron Mountain, this is Tinsel Town on call, General Sir. Go with your traffic sir. Over."

"Tinsel Town. Are you picking up any possible aircraft contacts over the Island of Taiwan yet, sir. Over." General Campanelli asked the radio operator stationed on board the radar plane.

"Iron Mountain, am picking up over two hundred contacts in the air at this time, sir. I have so many overlapping signals, I'm having trouble getting an exact count on the inbounds, sir. Over."

"Tinsel Town. Can you tell me where the damn aircraft are coming from sir? Over."

"Iron Mountain, yes, easy sir. Most of the inbound aircraft are coming from mainland China, sir. There's a good many of aircraft coming from Taiwan the other way as well. Looks like the aircraft from Taiwan's engaging contacts coming from China, sir. Am picking up many missile launches and mid air explosions, am also picking up a lotta scrambled communications, sir. I'd say there's a major air engagement happening over the Formosa Straits. Iron Mountain."

"Tinsel Town. Are you picking up any hits on the damn Island yet sir? Over."

"Yes, am picking up many smoke plumes, and am also picking up many aircraft attacking certain ground sections of Taiwan at this time, sir. It looks like the invaders are going after the entire Island on these opening hostilities, Iron Mountain. Over."

"Tinsel Town this is Iron Mountain responding. Are you picking up any of our guys coming in yet on your damn radar system, sir? I have four different Wings of aircraft that should be in the area just about at this time, sir. Over."

"Roger that, am tracking a large group of our aircraft since takeoff from Iron Mountain, sir. They're holding a good formation and coming in strong from the south, sir. Over."

"Who gives a shit about their fucking formation Tinsel Town. How soon before they make contact with the fucking inbounds from mainland China, mister? Over."

"Fifteen minutes to first contact, most aircraft attacking the Island I make out to be bomber aircraft, with a few Chinese fighter aircraft mixed in for protection of the bombers, sir."

"Copy that as received Tinsel Town. Keep me appraised over situation. Iron Mountain Out."

General Campanelli turned to the President's face still being displayed on the larger center screen of the CIC Chamber and reported. "The Chinese are positively attacking Taiwan at this time, sir. I hate to be the one to put pressure on you sir. But my aircraft are fifteen minutes from engagement of the aircraft attacking the Island, and I need an answer on their orders to attack, sir." He let out his breath, he did not want to make any demands of the President.

President Cole shook his head as he removed his glasses, and then he pinched the bridge of his nose and held it for a brief moment. He blinked his eyes to try and clear his mind, and then he moaned. "I know you need an answer to your request, dammit." He turned to the others of his command and asked them, "I need a yea or nay from all of you. Do we attack the Chinese aircraft, or move off and take a wait and see stance. General Tomasello, I'll start with you sir."

"No question about it Mr. President Sir. We attack, and we attack right now sir."

Secretary of State Hernandez replied next with a simply, "attack Mr. President Sir."

National Security Director Griffin looked at the President for a long moment, then he drew in a deep breath and responded with one word, "attack!"

Secretary of Defense Levenhagen answered next to the President's question. "Attack sir."

Secretary of the Air Force, General Schramm replied, "yes of course, attack immediately sir."

Manning even agreed.   "Mr. President Sir, we have to attack the Chinese aircraft if our presence is going to mean anything again in this region of the world, sir."

All eyes instantly went over to Manning, if anyone was going to vote against the attack, it would surely have been him.

General Weidenbacher growled angrily, "we must attack at once Mr. President Sir."

Claiborne agreed to the attack. Along with the Senior Military Officer, Marianne Matteoni.

General Weidenbacher then informed the President he had his Generals stationed on the Platform, and he would have to ask them for their opinion, before the vote was unanimous.

President Cole was irritated and he growled angrily, "let me put it to you this way people, is there anyone who doesn't go alone with the attack against the invading aircraft? Speak up now."

When no one spoke up, the President of the United States turned to General Campanelli and he added. "It looks like you were right all along here, General Campanelli Sir. I order you to attack any Chinese plane that attacks any of your aircraft, or is flying into Taiwan airspace, sir. We have an agreement to protect the Island Taiwan from any such attach from mainland China."

General Campanelli was furious as he barked angrily, "Mr. President, with all due respect sir. I'm afraid that's not good enough, sir. I have to know if my aircraft can engage the Chinese aircraft crossing the Straits, sir. I can't tie my pilots hands behind their backs, and force them to wait until they're attacked first, before responding to this latest threat sir."

"You do have some set of balls hanging between your legs there Mr. Campanelli. Yes, you're right in this case though, sir. I give you permission and orders to have your aircraft attack any Chinese plane not flying over mainland China at this time, sir. Is this good enough for your needs, General Campanelli?" the President growled hotly as he glared at the image of General Campanelli on the screen.

General Campanelli snapped to attention as he responded to the last orders he received from his Commander in Chief. "It's very good sir, I'll carry out your orders as received sir."

"Then I suggest you attend to your fighter pilots, General." The President said while turning to Manning he said something General Campanelli could not make out clearly. Suddenly, the President's screen went dead. The General was about to turn off his screen as General Weidenbacher put up his hand and ordered, "I want further words with you mister."

Campanelli sat back down in his chair and then he waited for the general to address him again.

"When I sent you out there, I was hoping we wouldn't engage in another war, mister. I like you for Command for this mess, I thought you'd surely stir things up a might over there, sir. But I never thought for a damn second you'd go so far as to demand an answer from the Boss Man, Keerist. That took some balls there General, it only serves to strengthen my feelings and belief. You're a good pick to Command my forces over there, sir. Edward, if you need anything, get hold of me, and I'll make sure you get it, sir. This is going to be one helluva mess for us to solve. Good luck man, you better get going, you have aircraft in the air, sir."

The General nodded and picked up the mike, "Tinsel Town, this is Iron Mountain. Over."

"Iron Mountain, this is Tinsel Town. Go with your traffic sir. Over."

"Tinsel Town, you're Command for this situation, you'll direct all aircraft involved in this new Theater of War developing over the Island of Taiwan. I want top priority given to the enemy bomber aircraft, and then the refueling tanker aircraft. Any ships coming from China towards the Island of Taiwan, and then their fighter aircraft. If our fighter aircraft come in contact with Chinese fighter planes, they're to engage immediately, no questions asked, sir. Mister, take care of my damn aircraft and pilots. I'm ordering the E-3 Magic Island aircraft to your location for cross references, and help you run your damn attack scenario against the Chinese enemy, sir.

"I'm going to a second launch of aircraft and ordering up more in flight refueling tanker aircraft as well, sir. I'm also pulling back some of my damn Aircraft Carrier Strike Groups for a little added aircraft support for this mess. I guess I'm gonna strip the Aircraft Carriers from the Sea of Japan. I'll use the aircraft from these Carriers for any secondary launches needed, and also have an operating platform nearby enough to recover any possible damaged aircraft, before the pilots are forced into a Blue Water Divert, and crash into the damn sea, sir. You make the calls and inform me of any aircraft you need. Out."

"Roger that last Iron Mountain. I'll control all aerial contacts and engagements, sure you'll be plotting your own attack scenarios as well, Command. Feel free to countermand any of my calls sir. I can sure use all the help I can get on this one, sir. Over."

"Will do as you suggested Tinsel Town. Good luck with your orders and protect my damn pilots and aircraft the best you can, sir. Iron Mountain Out."

Once he was off the radio with Tinsel Town, General Campanelli immediately issued orders for a second wave of fighter aircraft to be launch from the Platform. He also ordered a few of the Destroyers to break away from the

Carrier Strike Forces, and take up position between his Platform and the Island of Taiwan. Just in case the Chinese bombers jumped over the Island, and they made an attack against the Platform. He was worried about his ship being attacked, and ordered his anti-submarine warfare systems in action. The divers were in the water, and three mini submarines were quickly launched. He ordered the three Sea Wolf attack submarines to position between him and the Island of Taiwan. The SSN-21 Sea Wolf, SSN-22 Sea Lion and the SSN-23 Sea Snake steamed for their newly ordered positions.

"I want the two Aircraft Carriers, The Stennis and United States, to go into an all out Alpha launch immediately. Inform them the refueling tankers are set in position, or will be so by the time their aircraft engage any possible Chinese contacts. They don't have to worry about running out of fuel and ditching in the damn sea. Colonel Locker, order the Captains of those two Carriers to move the damn things to a much better position, to enable them to launch and recover their aircraft easier, Ma'am. I leave their new positioning up to them, let them figure it out and then notify us where they're repositioned their damn Carriers. The fighters and bomber aircraft are to attack any Chinese bombers, fighters, or ships.

"For all concerned in his new mess we're suddenly involved in, as of this moment an Alert One Status is now in effect for all American forces throughout the world, especially for all assets in and around the Asian region. We'll hold the aircraft from the Carriers Vinson and Washington in reserve, until we see what the fuck's going down, and where the hell they'll be the most good for our fucking needs, dammit. Colonel Locker, are our aircraft stored below deck ready for an immediate launch, if they're needed for backup for our attacking aircraft?"

"General Campanelli Sir, the English Jump Jet Aircraft Carrier Ark Royal's reporting she's coming under attack from a good size number of Chinese fighter aircraft. She and her support ships are holding off the attacking fighters, but she further reporting she has sustaining some minor damage to the ship, sir." Sergeant Willis called out.

"Who the hell do we have in the fucking area of the Ark Royal, dammit? I wanna know exactly what the hell's happening and help them out as much as we possibly can." General Campanelli yelled back at his Sergeant.

"General Campanelli Sir, all aircraft stored below deck are currently armed and fueled and are ready for immediate launch and engagement at a moment's notice, sir." Colonel Locker reported proudly to her Commanding Officer.

Campanelli ignored Colonel Locker's report as he listened to the Sergeant's reply.

"General Campanelli Sir, I can pull three Frigates from the Stennis Strike Force, and get them over to assist the Royal within the hour, sir."

"Will stripping these ships from the Battle Group put the Stennis Battle Group in any danger?" General Campanelli asked as he turned his attention to Locker and waited for her response.

"Not in the least General Campanelli Sir. The Aircraft Carrier United States and her full complement of support ships are close enough to lend any extra needed support to the Stennis Group, if she comes under attack from any Chinese forces, or any other enemy forces operating in the damn region for that matter, sir."

"Great then get it done for us, Colonel Locker. At least something is working out in our favor for the time being. I want to have all our god damn ships enjoying overlapping support in case they come under attack from any attacking Chinese forces." General Campanelli ordered the young female Colonel.

CHAPTER 35
OVER THE FORMOSA STRAITS:
THE CHINESE FORCES ATTACKING TAIWAN

Chinese General Jiyun listened to the latest reports flooding into his Command Center, about the great success his aircraft were enjoying during their opening attack against the Island of Taiwan. Most, if not all the Taiwanese aircraft were either already destroyed, or were damaged to the point they could no longer continue to engage any of the attacking Chinese aircraft. The Taiwanese Navy was also caught while still resting at port and pretty much destroyed at port. The

Chinese airforce ruled the sky, and the coast of Taiwan for now.

The American aircraft launched from the massive Vinegar Joe Platform, were rapidly closing in on the new war zone quickly developing over the Island of Taiwan. The first Wing of American warplanes already completed their refueling in flight on the back side of the Island of Taiwan, and they were now moving in for direct contact with the attacking Chinese aircraft. They were the twenty two F-22 Raptors. These American aircraft came in over the Niitaka mountains running right through the center of Taiwan. The AWACS aircraft transmitted the exact coordinates of the first Chinese targets to be hit by the incoming American aircraft, before they even saw any of the Chinese planes in the air.

"Tinsel Town to Blackjack Flight Leader. Come in sir. Over."

"Blackjack Leader to Tinsel Town. Go with your traffic sir. Over." The pilot of the small and sleek fighter aircraft offered to his Command Structure over the radio.

"Blackjack Leader. You have twenty Chinese heavy bombers working over sector three of the Island of Taiwan. Suggest you commence your attack against these aircraft from the southeast, heading south at Angels Twelve Thousand Feet, and then drop down on them from the sun, sir. This should give you a very good attack angle on the enemy aircraft, sir. Over." The Tinsel Town radio operator replied to the pilot of the American fighter aircraft.

"Copy that last as received sir. Blackjack Leader will comply with your orders as received, sir. Out." The young fighter pilot snapped right back at the radio operator from the aircraft known as Tinsel Town.

"Blackjack Flight Leader to all Blackjack followers. Get up to Angels Twelve, and come in on your enemy targets from the southeast. I'll lead the attack on the bastards, Cannon Ball and Skyjack, you two are my Wingmen for this opening attack, sirs. The rest of you people line up with your assigned Wingmen, and then follow me in. Let's go get some people. Over."

Blackjack Leader pulled back on the stick of his aircraft, and his aircraft immediately nosed up and climbed rapidly. He leveled off and headed directly for his assigned targets. His Wingmen matched his every move, no F-22 Raptors had their attack radar's operating, so the Chinese planes could not get a good fix on them. They were using the radar from the AWACS aircraft to operate with. When the American attackers were over the enemy bombers busy plastering the military base stationed at the city of Chiai in Taiwan, they attacked.

"Blackjack Flight Leader to all Blackjack followers. You're clear to attack any Tangos (Targets) of opportunity you come across from this point on, people. Over." The Flight Leader ordered the other fighter aircraft pilots in his Flight Wing.

Blackjack Leader's aircraft charged out of the sun, and the pilot took aim at the first of the YU-16 Chinese Badgers he picked up, while his Wingmen lined up for the kill on the Ilyushin-28 Beagles, a light bomber and fair fighter plane. Blackjack Leader armed his master arm switch, and then selected a pair of the Aim 90R AMRAAM Sidewinder missiles to attack with.

One missile dropped off the racks on each side of his attacking aircraft, and they instantly plowed through the air, and crashed into two different bombers, killing both enemy bombers in flight before they had a chance to even begin any of their evasive maneuvers.

Blackjack Leader called out in a booming voice into his radio. "Splash Two, Two Badgers Splashed." He did a quick roll over to his left, and pulled back on his stick and leveled off his aircraft, and then watched his Wingmen go after the Chinese Beagles. Both Wingmen killed their intended targets, these four planes were their easiest kills. The Chinese aircraft left, and took a new defensive stance to better protect themselves from any further attacks from the incoming American fighters. The Chinese bombers begged their fighters in the area to come to their aid.

The AWACS aircraft suddenly spotted twenty Chinese Shenyang F-6B Fantans turn as one, and then come their way, he immediately informed Blackjack. "Blackjack Flight Leader. Listen up Blackjack Leader, I have twenty what looks to be the F-6 Fantan Chinese fighter aircraft heading your way at this time, sir. They're coming right at you from One, One, Three, at Angels Twenty Thousand Feet, sir. You also have a second wave of our friendly fighter aircraft coming in just launched from Iron Mountain, entering into your area of responsibility, sir.

"Blackjack Flight Leader, these incoming friendlies are twenty two YF-27 fighters, sir. I suggest you place them at twenty five thousand feet, and use them to attack these new enemy fighter aircraft rapidly closing in on your position at the present time, sir. Your Wing of aircraft are ordered to continue to work over the enemy bombers hitting the Chiai region of Taiwan, they have the top priority target value for this attack, Blackjack Flight Leader. Over."

"Blackjack Flight Leader to Tinsel Town. Copy all as issued and received, and will follow all suggestions as received, sir. What's the fucking call name of the damn inbound YF Leader, sir? Blackjack Flight Leader Out."

"The YF Leader of this Flight is Ghostbuster, Blackjack Flight Leader. He knows what he's doing damn well in combat, sir. Over." The radio operator from Tinsel Town reported to the concerned sounding pilot of the American fighter aircraft.

"Copy that last as received Tinsel Town. Ghostbuster. Over." Blackjack Leader thumbed his radio until he found the correct frequency of the Ghostbuster Flight Leader, and then he grumbled in his radio. "Blackjack Flight Leader to Ghostbuster Flight Leader. Over."

"Yeah, Ghostbuster Leader here. Go ahead Blackjack Flight Leader. What do you have for me? Over." The Flight Leader from the second wing of American aircraft replied over his radio.

"We're continuing our attack on Chinese heavy bombers working over the Chiai area, but have at least twenty light enemy fighter aircraft rapidly coming to their aid. Get up to Angel's Twenty Five, we're bait and the Fantan's will ignore your presence and concentrate on our Wing and close in on us. You flight is instructed to come in from above, don't lag and let them hose us, we'll have hands full with these damn Chinese bombers who know we're coming for them, sir."

"Copy that last as received Blackjack Flight Leader. We'll do our best with our last orders, keep your eyes open for any bleeders though, sir. I don't think we'll get them all on them on our first attack against the bastards, sir. Over." The pilot of Ghostbuster replied in his radio.

"Roger that last as received, Ghostbuster Flight Leader. Will keep our eyes opened for any possible enemy bleeder aircraft, sir. Blackjack Leader. Out."

Blackjack and his Wing of fighter aircraft quickly lined up for another run over the inbound enemy bomber planes still trying to continue with their ordered bombing runs on their assigned targets over Taiwan. As the American attacking aircraft dove, the enemy Beagles suddenly flew in front of the Badgers, while the Badgers jettisoned their bomb loads, and then they tried to make a quick dash back for the safety of the mainland of China.

Blackjack's Wing of aircraft killed nine of the defending Beagles, and also crippled six more of the enemy planes, two of them went down after a short run from the engagement. The remaining Beagles instantly regrouped along with the surviving Badger Chinese aircraft, but the F-22 Raptors overtook the much slower moving Beagles, and the American planes easily killed all of them before they were able to regroup and form up for another attack again.

The Chinese fighters rapidly closed in on the attacking American aircraft from their Six (Rear). Blackjack Leader did not like leaving his tail feathers hanging out in the breeze like he was doing, but it was all part of suckering the enemy fighters in, so the incoming second Wing of American aircraft could then destroy them by hitting the enemy aircraft from the top.

"Ghostbuster to Blackjack Flight Leader. Enemy fighters fifteen miles off your tail feathers and they're closing in rapidly on your position, sir. Over."

"I know that for Christ sake man. What the hell are you going to do about it, dammit? I don't want them damn Zappers to get any closer to my ass then they are now, or I'll be forced to react against them instead of hitting my original targets. They know I have them pegged on my threat radar now, and I'm certain they're wondering why the hell we haven't turned and prepared for their attack against us, sir. You better do something real soon my friend."

"Blackjack Flight Leader, we're commencing our attack on the enemy aircraft now, sir. Out."

Ghostbuster and his flight charged into the Chinese formation of fighter aircraft at just over Mach Two from an attack angle of sixty five degrees, almost insuring a good kill for each of his attacking planes. None of the Chinese fighters could possibly leak out of this attack angle with his aircraft still intact. The enemy pilots never picked up the second wave of American aircraft coming directly at them. The attacking Chinese aircraft were more concerned with pursuit of the American fighter aircraft busy attacking their bomber aircraft.

Ghostbuster flight easily tore through the pursuing enemy fighter planes, killing eleven of them on their first pass through the enemy formation. But the Chinese pilots regrouped quickly, and then they charged after the YF-27s now below them, and the Chinese pilots tried the same tactic on the American pilots this time. The enemy planes attacked from above, killing six of the American fighters, and damaging another three of their aircraft. The dog fight was on.

General Edward Campanelli listened intensely in on all the communications going on between the American pilots as they engaged the Chinese aircraft.

"Ghostbuster Flight Leader to Doc. Calaway, get your ass the hell outta there man. You have a damn Zapper right on your tail feathers, sir. Rustler, get the fuck in there and help out the Doc before he's splashed by that damn Zapper closing in on him, sir."

"Tinsel Town to Ghostbuster. Come in sir. Listen up, a second Wing of enemy fighter aircraft are coming at you from the northwest in a tight formation. Prepare for their attack sir."

"How many fucking aircraft are you talking about here Tinsel Town? Over dammit!"

"I mark it as ten, maybe even twelve enemy inbounds on your present position, sir. Over."

"Tinsel Town. Can I get any extra help over here dammit? Over." The pilot asked.

"I'll try my best to get you some extra help out there, Ghostbuster Leader. Over."

"Bunker One Flight Commander to Tinsel Town Control. We're airborne and can help out Ghostbuster Flight in trouble, sir. Over."

"Roger that last Bunker Baby. Get your ass over to coordinates Six, Three, Zero, and then lend a hand to the Ghostbuster's endangered flight, sir. What the hell are you flying anyhow Bunker Flight Leader? I have nothing on your flight at this time, sir. Over."

"I'm controlling thirty six F-18D Hornets, all equipped with air to air, and air to mud missiles, sir. We're out hunting and it seems like you just found us some game to slaughter, sir. Over."

ON BOARD THE VINEGAR JOE PLATFORM

General Edward Campanelli's heart instantly jumped in his throat as he turned to General John White, and said in a concerned tone of voice. "I don't believe this shit man. I thought George Bunker was killed in the Middle East war, John? It's great to hear his voice again, my friend. Damn, I can't wait to see him again, he was one of my favorite turds you know sir. I'm gonna look him up after this mess is over with, and fall off the wagon with him for a few days, I tell ya John." Edward was ecstatic the pilot known as Bunker One was still alive.

General John White suddenly looked down at the floor as he offered in a sad tone, "Eddy, I'm afraid Bunker One didn't make it, he was killed in the nuclear blast over Libya, sir. What you're hearing now over the radio is George's son, sir. He adopted his father's code name, but the other pilots took to calling him Bunker's Baby, and the name really stuck with the poor kid, sir. The kid doesn't seem to mind the name in the least though sir. I can't believe the fighter aircraft stationed on the Carrier United States are already getting involved in the damn fracas, sir. The Captain from the Carrier United States has some really good reaction time in order to get his aircraft in the air so quickly, General Campanelli Sir. I think we might just be able to beat back this fucking attack yet from the damn Chinese planes, and start the damn talking over again, sir."

"I seriously doubt that'll ever happen on this one John. I think the Chinese troops will have to have the shit kicked outta them first sir. Before they'll even consider to start talking again and stop the shooting, sir. As for the aircraft from the United States. You're correct with that last comment John. The Captain did real good with getting his aircraft up as quickly as he did sir. How the hell are the work crews doing with the damn aircraft from below our decks John?"

"The aircraft stored below decks are already completely prepared for the attack, sir. They have been ever since we first went to the original Alert Two Status on the Platform, General Campanelli Sir." John reported to his Commanding Officer proudly.

ON THE BORDER BETWEEN CHINA AND RUSSIA

The American Rangers, along with a good number of Russian KGB security officers manning the border positions between China and Russia, quickly got involved in the war.

The decision was made rather easy for them, because the Russian soldiers were getting kind of tired of the constant probes being committed against them by the other Chinese forces stationed right on the Russian positions against them. The KGB Officer in Command of the Russian units, dressed in his worn out battle dress uniform of the KGB border guards, called for a surgical strike by a number of Russian fighter planes on the Chinese fortifications stationed right on the border line.

The Russian forces easily devastated the tightly packed and ill trained and ill prepared Chinese reserve forces. The American Rangers, along with the Russian troops immediately went in action employing Apache fast attack helicopters. They quickly wiped out the Chinese tanks and their armored vehicles parked in the open, because the Chinese troops did not fear any attack coming from the Russian troops stationed at the border area. This action completely cut off the Chinese troops still killing inside North Korea, from any further possible reinforcements, and their much needed military equipment and war supplies.

GHOSTBUSTER FLIGHT

The Chinese fighter aircraft quickly turned the tables on the Ghostbusters fighter planes, most of the Chinese fighters got behind the American warplanes, and they stayed right with them. This forced the American pilots to do a series of radical turns, hard banking and severe diving, in an effort to try and shake the Chinese fighter aircraft off their tail feathers. It was not soon enough when Bunker's Wing of aircraft suddenly entered the fighting arena next. Quickly forcing the Chinese fighter planes to break off their attack against Ghostbuster's aircraft, as Bunker's planes began to attack them from their rear this time around.

The constantly hovering AWACS radar and command aircraft kept a close check on the IFF markers on their scopes being transmitted from the three waves of American planes fighting the Chinese aircraft. It was maddening to have one hundred and fifty planes in such a tight area while shooting at each other. It was the AWACs Commander job to keep the American aircraft from firing at the wrong plane, and make certain no enemy aircraft get position on the attacking American planes under his control.

The radar officer kept a close eye on another wave of Chinese fighters he just picked up nearly fifteen miles from the present engagement. If these enemy aircraft entered the fighting, it was going to be totally impossible to try and control so many planes in the mess flying so close together. All the American planes were ordered to put their squawkers on Four, Zero, Zero, One so the AWACS Controller could easily identify them, and know where they were at all times, even the American in flight refueling tankers were ordered on the same squawking frequency.

The AWACS Aircraft Commander, along with General Campanelli, listened in on all the pilot's conversations and orders. The General was glued to the radio and bank of TV screens. This was a new addition to the AWACS control systems, a real time video long range camera system. He picked up some of the action happening in the sky over the Island of Taiwan, as it was taking place on live video feed.

An aide walked into the CIC Chamber, and he began to dish out some pills to everyone manning the equipment in the chamber, another young aide came up to the General, who paid little if any attention to him until he asked, "are you General Campanelli Sir?"

"I am unless you have a stinking subpoena on your ass, mister." He replied with a snap in is tone without looking at the young Seaman.

"Here you go sir, you have to take these pills please, General Campanelli Sir. They were ordered for you by Command Central, sir."

General Campanelli finally turned and looked at the aide with a scowl on his face speaking to him, and he quickly cast his eyes from the pills in his hand, back up to the Seaman's face as he grumbled at him, "what the fuck are these damn things you got here, buddy?"

"It's a caffeine pill in order to help keep you alert during this present situation, General Campanelli Sir. They're also laced with a heavy dose of amphetamines as well, sir. Command doesn't want any of their Commanders falling asleep at the switch, General Campanelli Sir. These things are speed balls with a little extra kick to them, sir."

"Yeah, now they're going to turn me into a fucking walking Zombie, right mister?" he grumbled at the sailor.

The Seaman placed the jar on General White's desk, and General White nodded and whispered to him. "Thanks, I'll make sure anyone who needs more, will have them mister."

General Campanelli listened to the radio chatter as the American warplanes continued their attack on the invading Chinese aircraft in the Formosa Straits and over the Island of Taiwan.

"Blackjack Leader to Bouncer. You better get out of there or the Geeks are going to get you."

"Workout Three to Blackjack Flight Leader. I have a fucking Geek on my damn ass right now, and he's going to hose me sir. I need some fucking help here in a fast hurry it up, or I'm gonna be a dea..."

Blackjack Leader looked to where he knew the pilot Workout was engaging and all he picked up was a black smudge in the air, and the remains of an aircraft as it spiraled out of control towards earth below. Flames and smoke came from the destroyed plane. Blackjack searched the sky until he spotted a chute. He thumbed his radio and announced to the rest of his Flight Wing. "Workout's aircraft has been destroyed, the pilot's out and is drifting to the sea. Over."

"Thank Christ for that much Blackjack Leader Sir." A second but unidentified American pilot mumbled back in the radio.

The dog fight raging between Ghostbuster and Bunker One's Wing of aircraft, and the Chinese fighter planes went on unchecked. Bunker's F-18 Hornets were rapidly getting the upper hand on the slower Chinese fighter planes. Out of the twenty Chinese fighters, five were left, and these planes had no missiles left, and they were now trying to hold off the attacking American aircraft with just their cannon fire. They were staying in close to any American aircraft, in an attempt to try and avoid their missiles. A tactic which was working for now.

The AWACS aircraft noticed a second wave of enemy aircraft staying high over the fighting, and continued on. The AWACS Commander instantly realized they were trying a new tactic against his aircraft. These Chinese fighters were ignoring the dog fight, and they were heading for the American refueling tankers circling east of the Island of Taiwan. He sent a priority call out for all American fighter aircraft to disengage the enemy aircraft, and then head for the protection of the refueling tankers. He knew full well if the Chinese killed these aircraft off, the American fighter warplanes would be forced to break off and get back to their prospective aircraft carriers, or back to Iron Mountain for their fuel needs. The Chinese tactic was perfect.

Bunker One heard the call, and he immediately ordered his Wing of aircraft to disengage with the Chinese planes. The remaining Chinese Fantan's turned and went right after Blackjack's wing ordered to continue their attack on the enemy bomber groups.

By the time Bunker's flight, along with the remaining aircraft from Ghostbuster's flight, got to the refueling tankers, all the action was over. The Chinese attacking aircraft tried a kill on the fuel tankers by launching their long range equivalent to the American Sparrow radar controlled missiles, in hopes of a fast and high kill ratio. So they could turn and get out of the area before the American supporting aircraft caught up with them. The missiles were launched at the fuel tankers from a range of just under twenty miles out.

The American tanker aircraft took immediate action, and the pilots filled the air with chaff, a radar absorbing material, and then the pilots dove their aircraft for the hard deck. They split up and kept popping off chaff at certain intervals. The evasive maneuver was a success, with only one tanker aircraft picked up and killed by the enemy missiles. The rest of the remaining aircraft were scattered all over the area and were one by one calling in, get the regrouping position. The American fighter planes picked up the scattered tankers, lined up on them and escorted them up to the forty five thousand foot position, and then refueled in flight.

A few of Bunker's aircraft requested permission to head back to their Carrier to rearm, they were given permission, but were directed to the Stennis, which was positioned much closer to the fighters than the United States Carrier. It was going to be a quick deck refit and topping off of fuel. Bunker watched as six of his fighter planes headed for the

Stennis. He did not think two of his birds would be back, because he noticed damage to their airframes while refueling.

Blackjack picked up the Chinese fighter aircraft coming at him before the AWACS Controller announced it. "Blackjack Leader to all Blackjacks followers, trouble sneaking in our back door. Prepare to repel the enemy fighters. Iron Hat, take Starburst and Flanker, and stay after them fucking bombers, we'll stop the enemy fighter planes trying to sneak in on our Six, sir. Over."

A monotone voice replied, "copy all as received sir. Will comply as ordered sir. Out."

Bunker and his remaining Wing of aircraft went after the Chinese fighters who attacked the refueling tankers. He was out numbered, and many of his warplanes were out of weapons, but the ones with no weapons was prepared to run interference for the aircraft that did.

"Err... Bunker One to Tinsel Town. It looks like I'm caught with my damn pants down, sir. My ammo minus zero on many of my damn fighters, so I'm now forced to use them as bait or interference, Commander. I could sure use some extra help down here sir. Over."

"Tinsel Town to Bunker One. I'll see what I can do for you sir. I'm quite certain I must have a Wing or two of aircraft in the area that are capable of coming to your aide, sir. Over." The Tinsel Town Commander checked his plot board, and detected he had another flight of fighter aircraft just coming in the area in conflict from the American Carrier United States. He placed a call to their Flight Commander. "Tinsel Town to American flight coming in from the north. Patch in priority request sir. Over."

"Ah yes Tinsel Town. This is Shoshone Flight Leader. I have twelve YF-23s in my Flight Wing, sir. What can I do for you sir? Over."

"Tinsel Town to Shoshone Flight Leader, Bunker One's fighters are in trouble, his coordinates are at, Zero, Three at Angels Twelve. He's being attacked by fifteen Chinese Fantan fighters, and a number of his aircraft are weapons light, sir. Can you handle this one, or should I try and find another American Fighter Wing that can help this flight out, sir? Over."

"Shoshone Flight Leader to Tinsel Town. We're on our way to assist Bunker One's fighters, sir. This is Chief to Shoshone followers, let's help the paleface out, follow me. Over." The radio filled with Native American calls, as the twelve fighters headed for Bunker's position.

The Wing of full blooded Native American pilots came at the Chinese fighters from below, because the Chinese aircraft were forced to climb in altitude to attack Bunker One's aircraft. The Chief quickly aligned himself up with the enemy lead fighter, and opened fire at the same instant he fired on a F-22 Raptor aircraft. The American plane exploded in a fireball, with large chunks of the destroyed aircraft tumbled towards the earth. No chute was spotted.

The Chinese pilot did not even have a chance to celebrate his kill, he did not even have the privilege to see his kill, before he himself exploded in his own fireball. Upon being attacked by this new Wing of American fighter aircraft, the enemy aircraft instantly split up, and some of their aircraft tried a series of barrel rolls to get underneath the new attacking American planes. But the Native American pilots were that good, and they were able to cut them off at the pass, many of the American aircraft got on top, slotted up and killed the enemy aircraft attacking Bunker's Wing of aircraft.

The Native American pilots yelled out over the radio as they attacked the Chinese fighter planes in the formation. The Shoshone Flight Leader pilot Chief, was controlling the attack of his followers as they engaged the Chinese aircraft. "Waterdance, help out Pathfinder will you. White Wolf, you have a sneaky little bastard trying to get behind you, check your six, sir. Move your ass out of there man, or we'll be singing your name at the next gathering, you fool. That's much better there White Wolf. Scalphunter, I need you by that smoking F-22 Raptor, he has a Cowboy on his damn tail feathers, and he can't shake the enemy plane off for himself, sir."

As the Chief issued out orders to the rest of the fighters in his Wing, he failed to notice an enemy fighter had snuck up on him, and only reacted when he heard the warning coming from his threat receiver, as the enemy plane's targeting radar locked onto his aircraft. The Chief immediately banked his plane hard to the left, and then sent out a stream of chaff flying from both sides of his plane, as ten hot bags also popped off his wingtips. He took to bouncing his plane up and then down and then to his right, as he dropped like a rock towards the earth, and then he bounced up from his left. He stopped his jinking when he noticed two missiles fly passed his twin tails, and go off in the distance and fade off.

Scalphunter picked up his leader was in some serious trouble, and he immediately went after his attacker. He got position on the enemy aircraft, and killed the Chinese attacker before he had a chance to try some jinking of his own.

The pilots hooked up and reformed their formation, and then headed back to the fighting side by side. The Chief was besides himself for allowing the enemy aircraft to get the upper hand on him, and he struck out at Scalphunter, "why the hell did you interfere with my attack against that Zapper? I knew what I was doing at all times Scalphunter, I had him just where I wanted him." The Chief lied and he was well aware of the lie.

Scalphunter laughed as he replied to his Flight Commander, "don't go off and have one of your visions on me, Chief. I don't think the Tribe's ready to sing praises to you over the camp fires at night, you old sonofa rattlesnake you."

Both pilots laughed as they went after the now fleeing enemy planes.

Bunker Baby and his remaining fighters charged after the fleeing Chinese fighter aircraft. He laughed as he listened in on the conversation going down between the Native American pilots. Then he butted in and offered, "hey Chief, Bunker Baby here, sir. What the hell's wrong with you Chief, don't you know who the hell the bad guys are in this mess, sir?"

Blackjack Flight Leader's remaining Wing of aircraft beat up on the Chinese bombers, and once he either destroyed all the enemy aircraft, or what remained left the area in a hurry. He ordered his fighters to regroup around him, and then they head back to Iron Mountain for rearmament and some much needed fuel and maybe a quick rest and some food.

General Campanelli quickly studied the horde of pictures almost constantly coming in from the satellite allotted to him to cover the area of fighting around the Island of Taiwan. The fuming General counted over four hundred Chinese ships shoving off for Taiwan from the mainland of China. He immediately ordered a new flight of F-18 Hornets to be loaded with bombs and air to ground missiles, rather than air to air missiles. Then he ordered the Hornets to attack the Chinese ships trying to cross the Formosa Straits. He wanted to stop as many of the what he believed were troop ships as he could. He also ordered many of his Guided Missile Destroyers to attack the Chinese flotilla at the same time.

His orders were being severely hampered because of the many Chinese fighter aircraft still harassing the American warships. The Chinese ships carrying the invasion forces, slowly moved towards Taiwan when Bunker's Baby and his flight, came in from the northeast on them. The Chinese warships instantly sent up smoke screens, as hundreds of cannons and machine guns fired at Bunker's incoming planes. Bunker was not the real threat against the Chinese ships.

Bunker One was ordered to run interference with his aircraft, while the Wing of thirty six F-18 Hornets came in low, skimming just above the wave tops. At the last possible moment, the Wing of Hornets suddenly shot up to Angels Six, and shot directly over the Chinese ships. The guns moved off Bunker's attackers, and they tried to lock onto this new threat against them. Too late, a quarter of their bombs fell short or missed the ships, but the ones that hit, did the desired damage. The Hornets were ordered to go after the larger targets, hoping these enemy ships would be carrying most of the Chinese war machines and supplies. As the American Hornets flew over the Chinese ships, and shot off in the distance, a recon F-111 was ordered to observe, and issue an immediate bomb assessment on the amount of damage done to the Chinese ships.

Campanelli was the first one to review the latest photos of the area in question, and he counted nineteen of the larger Chinese transports lay dead in the water, and he also spotted five places where he was certain a ship had sunk. Another five Chinese invasion ships were slowly limping towards Taiwan. It was a tough mission, he lost nine Hornets, with another seven sustaining some damage to their airframe. He was unaware two of his Hornets were forced to ditch in the sea before they made it back to their Platform. He decided he would leave the remaining Chinese ships to the heavy bombers who could stay well out of the range of most of the Chinese guns.

ON THE RUSSIAN, CHINESE BORDER

A number of elite Russian soldiers were causing all sorts of fits for the Chinese troops still remaining in North Korea. When the remaining North Korean troops realized the Russian troops were attacking the Chinese forces from their rear. They quickly reorganized, and made an all out frontal attack against them. The Chinese troops were suddenly caught a little off guard, and the remaining North Korean fighters drove a wedge right into the Chinese frontlines.

South Korea was suddenly getting cold feet as she realized the Chinese forces were being attack by American and British forces, and she asked China to remove her troops from their soil, the South Korean news agency Yonhap reported.

The Chinese Command's answer was their troops would stay where they are.

Japan offered to help South Korea rid her country of these Chinese troops and soon, the Chinese forces stationed in South Korea were being probed by a large number of South Korean soldiers, who took exception to having these Chinese soldiers on their soil.

Japan flooded the North and South Korean soldiers with money, hoping to cause the attacks on the Chinese troops to escalate against them. She would rather have the fighting take place in the two Korea's, and Japan was more than pleased to pay to have it stay there. China was now being attacked from Russia, Taiwan, and South and North Korea.

ON BOARD THE VINEGAR JOE PLATFORM

General Palmieri spoke to General Campanelli with concern, mainly because he wanted to start the Marines landing on the east coast side of the Island of Taiwan. General Campanelli gave this idea some extra thought. He was a little worried it would be too soon for a landing of the American Marines on the Island, because at this time he did not have enough support forces set in position yet, to protect the Marines once they were on the Island. He did not want to have the Marines caught out in the open without enough support units behind them.

General Palmieri quickly pointed out to his Commander there were not many Chinese forces on the Island of Taiwan yet, and he wanted to get a jump on the Chinese by getting his forces set in place, before the main body of Chinese forces finally landed on the Island.

He finally relented and gave General Palmieri the okay to invade Taiwan with the Marines stationed on board the Platform. General Palmieri ran over to his desk, and then made a connection with the Marine Commanding Officer, Colonel Rich Morgan. He advised Morgan to prepare his troops to invade Taiwan from the east.

Colonel Morgan was to pick out the landing zones, and organize what forces he needed for his own invasion of the under attack Island. Morgan ordered all Amphibious ships to pull free of their escort ships, and then make way to a gathering position twenty miles off the east coast of Taiwan. The American Amphibious landing ships Essex, Kearsage, Nassau, Wasp, Pelelieu, Belleau Woods, Iwo Jima and Saipan, along with the landing ships Newport, Schenectady, San Bernardino and Fairfax County, were ordered to dock up with the Platform, and then pick up their full complement of tanks, armored vehicles and ground troops.

The Dock Landing ships Anchorage, the Mount Vernon, Pensacola, Plymouth Rock, Point Defiance, Monticello and also the Tortuga, were ordered to linkup with the Amphibs. The Amphibious Transport Docks Vancouver, Trenton, Nashville and Cleveland, were ordered to linkup with the Amphibs also. Any American warships not loaded to capacity with ground troops or military equipment and supplies, were ordered to dock up with the Platform and top off their needs before heading for Taiwan.

General Palmieri ordered an airborne drop of Marines over the Island as well. He had a full Battalion of Naval Construction SeaBee's out of Gulfport Mississippi, ready to be flown to Taiwan at a moment's notice. Armed with orders to enlarge the airbases they were going to need and use to accept the larger, and new C-2-12, and the larger C-23 transport aircraft. General Palmieri showed General Campanelli what he had assembled so far, and the Commanding General gave General Palmieri his approval.

General Campanelli decided he was going to allow Aleksandra to fly cover for some of the ground forces, this move would keep her free of most of the heavier fighting soon to be taking place on the Island of Taiwan. When his ground forces engaged the Chinese troops once they made a beachhead on the Island. At least she would not be so apt to get involved in a dog fight with these orders she would be operating under. She would be used for support mostly, and some attacks on any dug in Chinese troops discovered operating on the Island.

While the American fighter aircraft were involved in refueling and regrouping their forces. Chinese troops and supplies landed at the two main targets on the Island of Taiwan almost unmolested. The Chinese troops quickly dispersed, killing any Taiwanese soldiers and civilians they came across. Many civilians were killed, as the Chinese forces quickly took command of the Hsinchu Science base, and the massive Industrial Park in the north section of Taiwan. While the second Chinese invasion force landed, and took over the Industrial section at Kaohsiung, in the south section of Taiwan with little if any real resistance offered from the Taiwanese troops. The Chinese troops then quickly dug in and setup their anti aircraft batteries.

The Chinese troops rapidly setup fifteen Russian made ZSU-23-4 Shilka's in the science facility area. The ZSU's armed with four 23 mm cannons mounted in a turret type structure, could traverse three hundred and sixty degrees, and elevate from four degrees to ninety degrees so the machine became an extremely efficient anti-aircraft system. This tank type machine could move at twenty eight mph, with a range of three hundred miles. Its rate of fire was between eight hundred to a thousand rounds per minute, and the cannons could also be used for air combat, or ground engagements, with its most effective range at two thousand yards out. In addition, the Chinese troops had the older and outdated version of this same weapon, the ZSU-57-2 and the newer version, the ZSU 30-2 system.

The Chinese troops setup the ZIL-137 missile launch vehicles. These weapons had a forty round 122 mm rocket, capable of anti-aircraft defense or ground troop support, and the ZIL-133 system, which fired proximity exploding warheads on a thirty five missile launch platform.

General Campanelli received a number of new reports on the Chinese defenses rapidly being setup in and around the Science Complex on the Island of Taiwan, via satellite and shuttle and recon aircraft reports. He knew time was of the utmost, the longer the Chinese troops had to setup their defenses, the harder it would be for his forces to root the enemy troops out, as he bellowed at anyone who would answer him in the CIC.

"Where the fuck's my damn aircraft at for crap sake? They should be pounding the living shit outta these lousy bastards, and here they are, setting up their damn defenses right under my stinking nose for fuck sake."

"General Campanelli Sir, most of the fighter aircraft have been refueled and rearmed, and they are going out to hunt down any enemy aircraft they come across, General."

"I don't give a flying shit about the enemy aircraft at this time, Colonel Locker. I have a horde of fucking enemy troops digging in on Taiwan soil, and setting up their damn defenses aimed at stopping our forces, and I want it stopped right now, dammit. How are we coming along with our troop landing on the fricking Island?" he snapped angrily at his Colonel as he suddenly glared at her.

General Palmieri answered for Locker, "General Campanelli Sir, we have a second wave of fighter aircraft moving in for us, but I'm afraid they're set to attack aircraft only, sir. There's few of our fighter aircraft prepared for any ground attack and support, and the few we have are being used to attack the Chinese ships trying to cross the Strait to invade Taiwan, sir."

"That didn't answer my question in the slightest, General Palmieri. I have a three step war erupting on my hands, land, sea and air, and I have to be able to attack all three of these damn threats at the same fucking time, sir. I can't eliminate one at a time, or things are going to get away from us. We shoulda been pounding the Chinese foot soldiers when they stepped foot on the damn Island. Jesus Christ, how long before we can get at the enemy ground troops?"

"I could have the aircraft from the Carriers we're holding in reserve rearmed, and then go to an Alpha ground attack situation, sir. This way we could then hit the enemy troops within the next hour, General Campanelli Sir. I know the aircraft from the Carrier Washington are armed for air to air engagement, it'd take the aircraft crews an hour to change them over to air to ground support capability, sir. I was informed the aircraft from the Carrier Lincoln are fueled, and the weapons are waiting to be loaded, so we caught a break there, General Campanelli."

"Do it then sir. Use the damn planes from the Lincoln to attack the Chinese ground forces already setting up their damn defenses on stinking Island of Taiwan, General Palmieri Sir." General Edward Campanelli growled at General Palmieri this time.

Aleksandra stormed into the CIC Chamber and she was as angry as a wet cat, and she immediately growled at her lover and Commander. "General Campanelli Sir, what shit no fly any air mission against enemy aircraft, sir? I have know you I train pilot good, and out fight most male pilot you have in you Command, sir. I demand right go combat like you male pilots do all time, or transfer me out Carrier where Captain use my fight skill right correctly, sir. I think you hold me back, you no think me good fighter pilot I believe, mista? I come to United States to be trained in you aircraft and learn you combat tactic, I no here to babysit ground troop, sir."

General Campanelli let out his breath angrily, he was in no mood for a confrontation with the pretty young Lithuanian pilot as he barked at her, "Who the hell are you to make any fucking demands from my stinking ass, sister? I'm in Command of this here god damn operation, and if you don't like it. You can always swim your lovely little ass back to your own fucking country, you got that, sister. I don't give a damn if you're a bitch or not, I'll explain even though I don't hafta explain jack shit to you. I'm going to use you, and the other female pilots for ground support. Period! And there's only two things you can do about, live with it, and nothing sister."

She suddenly threw her hands angrily in the air and then she complained again at the seated General. "I no you sister, mista. I better air to air combat fight pilot than air to ground pilot. I want fight in air as train, sir. I kill many enemy planes for you General Campanelli Sir."

"Dammit! I don't give a rat's ass what you think and want from me. And don't go and throw your damn hands up in the air like that again in front of my puss. Or I'll have them nailed down to the fricking deck on you, sister. Who the fuck do you think you're talking to here Major? I'm the fucking Commander of this here god damn operation, Missy. You'll fly air to ground, or you'll never fly again as long as I'm in fucking Command of this damn operation, Major. Do I make my orders perfectly clear to your purdy little ass, Major?"

She was still furious as she snapped at her Commander angrily. "Who call you Missy? I fighter pilot if you do no think so, General Commander of this fooking operation."

"You're pushing it beyond wise thought here Major, I suggest you get out of my sight before you have a real problem with taking a stinking dump for yourself, with my damn foot sticking outta your lovely little ass. Get the hell out of here and check your plane before you need it. I have ground troops about to land on Taiwan, and they're gonna need pilots to support them when they engaged the enemy troops on the damn Island. Get the hell outta here before I throw your ass in a fricking row boat, and make you paddle your lovely little ass back to Mother Russia." Campanelli went back to reading his reports, his back to her was her dismissal.

She let out her breath in a hiss and then stormed out of the CIC Chamber and into the hallway. She stopped walking and lean up against the cool metal bulkhead in order to catch her breath for a moment. She was suddenly feeling slightly dizzy, and she was getting an upset stomach as well. She was getting concerned because she never got sick before, so she blamed it on her being so upset at her commander. She understood the General was correct about checking her aircraft frame out, and using her as ground support also. She also understood her anger, there was little glory in most air to ground combat operations, unless you kill tanks.

She let her breath out and headed for the hangers below deck, and as she walked she continued to feel slightly ill. Then it hit her and she suddenly had to run for a bathroom to upchuck. Her stomach burned and gurgled as she wrenched out her guts in the stainless steel bowl. When she finished feeling sick, she sat down on the floor and rested her head against the cold metal divider for a few seconds. She was really becoming worried now, afraid she might have hurt herself getting so angry at the General in the CIC Chamber moments ago. It was the second time in her life she had gotten so angry that she actually made herself throw up and feel so ill.

CHAPTER 36
THE CHAIRMAN'S PRIVATE LIVING QUARTERS IN BEIJING, CHINA

The old leader of China was angry as he paced his living room in a rage, while waiting for the Minister of Defense and Vice Chairman to arrive. The Vice Chairman was the first one to enter his private quarters, and he bowed towards the upset old man, and then took his seat without speaking. He knew why he was sent for. Seconds later, the Minister rushed in and took his seat in silence. No one spoke, a trio of females appeared without being sent for with tea. After serving the men, they disappeared as quickly as they appeared before them.

The old man took a sip of his tea and then he glared at the Minister and barked at him at the same time, "Minister, where are all these god dom American warplanes coming from? They have devastated my invasion forces against us. These hated American devils have sank twenty of my warships, most of them carrying my tanks and other military equipment for the invasion troops. They have destroyed forty of our heavy bomber aircraft, and as many of our fighter aircraft at the same time, Minister. I was ill prepared to lose so much of our military equipment so quickly, while I still have my ground troops spreading out in Formosa. I thank the gods that be for the good roads on that miserable rebel controlled Island of mongrels.

"It's making it extremely easy for our ground troops to get around it and support each other's engagements. Bah I believe I'm getting away from the subject at hand here, and why I demanded you two to appear before me. I asked you where are all these god cursed American warplanes coming from Minister Chung, and you have failed to respond to my question? We know at least four of their worthless Aircraft Carriers are not engaging their planes, these ships seem to be holding their aircraft in reserve for some reason I don't understand. I want answers from you, or I'll have you dispatched and then find another Minister who can answer the question I asked of you, fool!" The elderly Chairman stopped speaking and glared harshly at the shaking Minister.

The Minister of Defense sat forward and replied briskly to the highly upset Chinese Leader. "Mr. Chairman, we have proof the American devils have some kind of a Super Carrier stationed somewhere behind the Island of Formosa. We have no idea how many aircraft this supposed Super Carrier has on board it. But I assure you Mr. Chairman, it's not enough to be overly concerned with. These planes are only a minor inconvenience to us at this time, sir."

The old man shot up to his feet and roared at his stunned Minister, "A minor inconvenience you have the audacity to offer to me, fool? These American planes are destroying my invasion forces before any of my troops even get on the miserable Island of Formosa, Minister Chung! Our troops are being massacred before they even have a chance to defend themselves. A minor inconvenience you say to me, you worthless fool? I'll have your cursed head on a stick if you cannot come up with something better than that to offer me, Minister."

The Chinese Minister of Defense wished the old Chairman would keel over and die before him. He was the one who started this war in the first place, and now it was going sour against their military forces. The Chairman was looking for someone to blame it on, as the Minister replied in haste, "Mr. Chairman, we're slowly getting the upper hand against the inferior American forces daring to engage our forces involved in invading the Island of Formosa. The American aircraft are equipped with air to air defenses, and we make our fighters and bomber aircraft scarce, until the American fools have to disengage our forces to refuel their cursed aircraft. Then we'll commence our attack on Formosa again, sir."

The wise Chinese Vice Chairman interrupted the Minister's words as he grumbled at Chung, "are you daring to hide our aircraft from engaging the god dom worthless American warplanes, Minister? If so then how soon before they realize what we're doing, and then the American warplanes start coming in waves after your hiding planes, sir? If the American pilots resort to this tactic against us, I guess you'll next tell me we no longer have any fighter planes in the air, because the American fighters are all over the worthless Island. I cannot, nor will I accept this weak response from you and your foolish and insulting tactics. I order you to send up enough of our warplanes to beat these tit sucking American animals back to where they have come from." Now, it was the Vice Chairman who was glaring angrily at the Defense Minister.

"Mr. Vice Chairman Sir. I don't think we have enough aircraft held in reserve to turn back the numbers of warplanes the Americans engaged us with in the Theater of War, sir."

The old man jumped back up to his feet and snarled again at the Minister of Defense as he held him locked up in his harsh glare, "fool of fools you dare want me to believe all is already lost to us so quickly with our war being waged against the traitors to take back our Island of Formosa that truly belongs to us, Minister? I'll have you sent out into the Strait with my fighting troops, and have a weapon stuffed in your worthless arms so you can suffer the same fate you're forcing on my troops, you fool. If you cannot do any better than this."

The Minister let out his breath in a rush and then replied to the fuming Chinese Leader as if his life depended on his words. "Mr. Chairman, I'm ordering two Wings of our fighter aircraft we have stationed to our north. To come down and help our invasion forces assigned to be ready to act if the situation in North Korea, and also at the Russian border got out of hand against us, sir. I'm taking them from the border guards up north. This is the only area in which I can remove the aircraft from that I'll need to help defend our plans against the American disrupters, sir. I always fear the loathsome American's and what they could do to stop our aims."

"My dear Minister, are you now telling me you're giving up the border with Russia to the worthless Russian defenders of the border against us? I read a report about the fighting taking place there. Are you giving China land away to these lowly dog eaters?" the Chairman asked.

The Minister of Defense grew angry over the way the two Chairmen were ganging up on him at the meeting, and trying to blame everything going wrong with their military plans on him as he spat back at the both of them. "I'm not giving away any part of China's soil to no other nation. I'm merely taking fighter aircraft from where they're presently stationed, and have desperately need of, and simply moving them to where I need them the most. I ordered other aircraft from the interior to replace the ones I'm moving from the border region, Mr. Chairman.

"I need these cursed planes in the Formosa Strait, and these were the closest aircraft I have available for my current needs. I'm not the least bit concerned about what the worthless Russian fools are doing. They're a defeated nation, and we'll prove this fact to the great fools, after I have destroyed this miserable Island of Formosa, and then turn my military forces in their direction. Mr. Vice Chairman, if you don't like the way I'm running this war, you have the ability to have me replaced, sir. I'm doing my best in this god dom war, sir." The Minister openly glared at the Vice Chairman.

The Chinese Vice Chairman stared at the slightly smaller Defense Minister as he slowly rubbed his chin, and thought over the words he just aimed at him. Then he turned his attention towards the Chairman, and saw he was smiling and he understood the reason why. The Minister just delivered an ultimatum, and he was waiting for the Vice Chairman to respond against it so he could truly judge his mettle. The Defense Minister understood his decision was going to be closely scrutinized by the elderly Chairman. The Minister then leaned back and waited.

"So far Defense Minister Chung, I'm rather satisfied with your actions in this conflict. But I don't want our pilots running away from the American aircraft any longer. I don't want to be involved in a war where we're fighting by running away from the war, or our hated enemy. I demand you order our pilots to stand and fight the American fools wherever they engage them. If they go down then they're to take an American aircraft with them, no matter how they have to accomplish this feat. Even if they have to crash their planes into the attacking American aircraft. Tell the foolish pilots to remember how the cursed Japanese reacted to the American planes and warships during their war with the worthless Americans, and they'll know exactly what is expected of them when their time comes. You are dismissed.

"Get back to your Command and see to your troops, I want victories from our pilots not excuses, Minister. I'll not have the Americans embarrassing China like they have done to their enemies during the Desert Storm and the Middle East wars. I'll not stand for this foolishness for one moment longer I warn you, Minister Chung." The Vice Chairman warned as he turned to the old man and announced he was going to take a much more active role in the war now. He informed the upset Chairman he was going to order China's submarines out, and have them hunt down and destroy this supposed Super Carrier of the hated Americans as he offered angrily. "I shall commit our whole submarine fleet of the task to the sinking of this supposed great Carrier if it truly does exist," he stood and then quickly left the meeting room in a huff.

The Chairman watched as the Vice Chairman rapidly left the room, and then he leaned forward and lit up a cigar. He wasn't very worried about the out come of this war yet. He felt he could always bring this war to a quick finish by threatening nuclear weapons to be employed. He was positive the Americans, and the rest of the world for that matter would not want to risk another nuclear exchange in this century. He leaned back deeply in his chair, and then he watched as the smoke from his cigar slowly drifted up towards the ceiling and smiled.

ON BOARD THE VINEGAR JOE PLATFORM

It was late as the American fighter aircraft prepared to regroup, and then make a second attack against the Chinese forces now hitting the Island of Taiwan. Two more skirmishes took place in the air, one between the Chinese bombers and American fighters, the second was between the fighter aircraft from both forces. General Campanelli received a communication from the Japanese Prime Minister, offering the American forces complete access to Okinawa, and the landing strip on the Island. Okinawa was to be employed in any fashion that would better serve the American forces in their rapidly developing war with China. Japan was more than willing to pay any amount of money to stop the Chinese possible conquest of their country. But she was still unwilling to commit any of her own troops to the war effort though.

General Campanelli was pleased to get access back to the Island of Okinawa, now he would get his heavy bombers much closer to the war zone.

John pointed out a small Island just east of Taiwan. It was a tiny speck on the map, but he informed the General there was a runway that could be used by their fighter aircraft in an emergency situation. It was just minutes from Taiwan as his Second in Command reported, "General Campanelli, we just received pleas from the defenders stationed on Lan Yu, or Green Island. The Chinese sent a small invasion force against the tiny Island, and the Taiwanese defenders are holding out, but they're crying for our help. Sir, I suggest we help them out, and then use the damn Island's air strip for our fighter aircraft needs." John glanced at the map for a second time, and then he pointed to a position ten miles from Green Island and announced.

"The Aircraft Carrier Lincoln could be set in position here within twenty minutes or so, sir. Although her attack aircraft are just minutes away from the Island, sir."

"Good John, order the Lincoln to use their Intruders to aide the Taiwanese defenders of Green Island. Inform the Captain of the Lincoln I want the Island taken while still intact. Tell the Commander we need the damn Island's airstrip and to be careful with his efforts with the Island, and inform him he has the option to use any of his aircraft he deems necessary to accomplish this action successfully, sir. Once the Island's secured, I want our troops and military equipment poured in there with haste. We can use this Island to help support, and also supply our troops soon to be landing on Taiwan, John. This will be our closest dry land to the Island of Taiwan in the region. Good call on your part so let's get it done, John." The General smiled as he went back to his desk to place a call to the Captain of the Lincoln.

General Campanelli listened in as his fighter pilots complained they were unable to locate any enemy planes to attack, they were keyed up and looking for action. Every once in a while, a fighter would come across a lost Chinese plane, and kill it. He thought, 'yeah, thank your lucky stars you don't find any enemy, you asses will stay alive a while longer in this damn mess'.

Colonel Locker called out over her shoulder, informing the General her forces were coming together, and the assault ships were linking up as ordered.

He ignored her report, as he continued to listen to the fighter pilot's constant chatter. Most American pilots were completing their refueling stage. It was just by dumb luck he had a number of his fighters in position when the Chinese began their main attack against Taiwan. His fighter aircraft were not prepared to engage in combat, and never organized for an attack. Nevertheless, they had a devastating effect on the Chinese invaders, and their war making equipment and abilities. The original flight of American fighters were sent out on a purely recon mission, when the aircraft got locked into a shooting war with a good many Chinese aircraft. But the Americans recovered quickly, and after the initial air fight, both American and Chinese aircraft pulled back and tried to reorganize.

The Chinese fighters and bomber aircraft were taken by surprise when they came across the flight of American warplanes coming down the Formosa Straits along the west coast of Taiwan.

Now the American fighter aircraft were refueled, they marshaled behind the refueling tankers, and they were going to make an organized effort against the Chinese warplanes this time. They flew back for the fight, but this time the American pilots were disappointed. In an hour of flying, they only come across a few Chinese straggler aircraft. The planes assigned to work over the enemy ships over in the Strait were also disappointed. Most of the Chinese invasions ships had either turned back for the mainland of China, and made their way safely into Chinese territorial waters. It did not take the Chinese Command long to realize the American warplanes were not attacking any of their ships or aircraft in their own waters or their sky.

The American aircraft patrols were coming extremely close to Chinese airspace, but they never once entered it. The fighters flew close to China's coast, and then watched helplessly as the enemy ships regrouped. Every pilot knew the ships were going to use the cover of darkness to try and sneak across the Formosa Strait to invade Taiwan.

The good size number of Chinese ships and troops able to make it to Taiwan, made strategic moves to guard themselves against any American fighter plane's attacks against their ground forces. They quickly mingled in with the Taiwanese civilians. The Chinese invaders forced the local population to help them, and more or less, used them for human shields.

A number of times an American attacking aircraft would set himself up for a strafing run over the enemy troops, only to be forced to break off his attack, when realizing they were Taiwanese civilians being forced to unload the Chinese military trucks he was setup and preparing to attack. The American pilots were forced to fly back and forth over the length and width of the Island of Taiwan, looking for any possible targets of opportunity. They killed three ZSU-23-4 Shilka anti-aircraft guns, the instant the weapon systems locked onto the American warplanes with their attacking radar. The fixed wing planes fired anti-radar missiles, AGM-65B Mavericks, and killed the guns. This was the days highlight for the American pilots.

Night was setting in fast, and most American warplanes were ordered to return to their home bases and ships for refueling, rearming and the pilots to rest until needed again. General Campanelli ordered a flight of twenty seven F-117 Blackhawk Stealth fighters flown in that were stationed on Guam from the 4450th Tactical Fighter Wing, their home base was in Tonopah Airforce Base at Tonopah, Nevada. The Wobbly Goblin as the F-117 Blackhawks had come to be know, were armed with two GUB-10 E/B MK84, two thousand pound laser guided smart bombs, with orders to attack any large Chinese ships trying to sneak across the Straits from China towards Taiwan. The American Command quickly realized the larger Chinese ships were the ones carrying military equipment, and they were give target priority for the kill.

The Chinese troops were not the only forces using the cover of night to get troops and supplies onto the Island of Taiwan. Seven CV-22 Ospreys carrying twenty two combat fully equipped Marines, were heading for the Hsuehshan, or Snow Mountain top, while a second wave of Rangers headed for the mountain top city of Lishan on the Island of Taiwan. The American soldiers were armed with orders to secure the crossroads of Central Cross Island Highway. This way, the American troops could attack any part of the Island from this vantage point. They were going to be backed by the force of Rangers now following the Marines in UH-60 Blackhawk troop transport helicopters, backed by AH-64 Apache fast attack helicopters. Marine CV-22s were to be escorted in by the Bell AH-15 Super Cobra helicopters, and the supersonic AV-9C Harrier 111 Jump Jets for added protection for the American troops.

A Wing of Marine CV-22s were coming to Taiwan from Guam, while their support helicopters came from the Wasp, Amphibious Assault ship. The Rangers helicopters were coming from the re-commissioned CV-59 Forrestal Aircraft

Carrier, now being used for training and landing purposes. The Forrestal had no fighter aircraft on board her. Instead, General Weidenbacher and Admiral Standlund ordered the Forrestal to carry only helicopters. Apache and Blackhawks were packed on and below her deck. The Forrestal carried seventy of both helicopters, and four full Divisions of Army and Marine troops. The Forrestal was pulled out of the war games in the Pacific, and made the jump to the fighting arena in seven hours. She was quickly refitted with helicopters, their weapons and troops while steaming towards Taiwan.

The eight American Assault ships grouped together, and they made their opening assault on Taiwan. The ships sent troops in between the Taiwan port cities of Hualien, Shihtiping and Shanyuan beach. Each Assault ship held a thousand Marines, forty two Sea Knight CH-46 helicopters, three Amphibious air cushion vehicles, called LCAC to get their troops and military equipment to shore. The Amphibious transport docks hooked up with the Assault ships, they each carried two LCACs, and stored twenty tanks, or fighting machines along with up to fifteen armored vehicles. The American forces were in place.

AT PRECISELY 2440 HOURS ON MARCH 6th, 1997, THE FIRST CV-22 LANDED ON THE MOUNTAIN RANGE KNOWN AS HSUEHSHAN, TAIWAN

There was no resistance against the American landing of troops on Taiwan. The Chinese invaders were too busy setting up their own fortifications, to worry about what the American forces might be doing for the time being. The Chinese Command had no idea there were so many

American troops stationed or moved into the Asian region. They believed they had at least three full days or more before the Americans could possibly get enough military troops in the region to make a good defense, or even a counter offensive offered against the Chinese troops. By that time, the Chinese Commanders would have enough of their own troops and equipment on Taiwan that it would take an act of the hated American's God to drive them off the Island.

The Marines and Ranger Units that were airlifted to the Island, rapidly dug in for the upcoming battle of their lives. Their job was to secure all the main roads of the Island. The CV-22s took off to pick up even more Marines troops and equipment, a flight of twenty Blackhawk helicopters sweep in low, and up the side of the mountain, in order to linkup with the Marine troops already stationed on top of the mountain. The Apache fast attack helicopters were at home in the darkness as they also moved in to support the ground troops. As their old saying goes, 'The enemy may own the day, but the night belongs to the us.'

The Marines and Ranger troops kept a close eye on the Marine landing taking place on the east coast of Taiwan. They were forced to dive for cover as a Chinese fighter aircraft suddenly roared over the mountain tops while looking for any possible Taiwanese resistance fighters. The enemy fighter came up the west side of the mountain, but never made it to the top before two Marine Harrier jump jets came up the east side, out flanked the enemy aircraft and killed it with little trouble. The Marines called in the Harriers assigned air cap duty over the Marine positions. From positions in the mountains, the American Units watched as a steady flow of large LCACs headed for the

Taiwanese shore, and dropped off tanks and more supporting troops.

The new Marine troops and tanks from the LCACs quickly disappeared in the heavy underbrush of this section of the Island. The second wave of landing crafts containing bulldozers and other construction equipment, was being unloaded quickly. Marine engineers along with two Navy SeaBee Construction Battalions went right to work clearing the brush, making a rough landing strip for the hardy C-17 transport aircraft.

It was amazing how fast the troops and military equipment was massing on shore. No sooner did a LACA leave then another one instantly replaced it. For three hours, the Marines stationed on the mountain watched this procedure repeat itself. The Gunnery Sergeant, known as Road Kill, Robert Walker was the first soldier to see the Ocean Going Tug pushing a floating dock towards the Island of Taiwan, a second dock followed. Both were loaded down with tanks and fighting machines, the first dock was pushed forward until it was grounded on shore.

A horde of engineers and divers rapidly moved in next to secure the dock to the ocean floor and unload the dock. Once completed, the second dock was pushed against the first. In less than an hour, the two docks were linked together and completely unloaded. The Navy divers were busy mooring the two platforms to the sea bottom. When connected, the two docks reached three hundred feet in the sea, and was ready for ships to more up to the docks and unload their military equipment and more troops.

As the young Gunnery Sergeant watched the operation below him unfold. He suddenly spotted the first American ship coming out of the heavy fog bank towards the docks. It was the LPD-2 Vancouver, an amphibious transport ship.

The Sergeant tore open an MRE, meals ready to eat pack, a packet of dehydrated chicken, and picked at the pieces with grime covered hands. Most military equipment was parked on the deck of the ship. A second American ship, the Nashville docked on the other side of the dock. The Nashville's cranes picked up massive tanks before the ship came to a complete stop. Here too, the tanks and military equipment were rapidly unloaded and then driven down the length of the dock, and onto shore. A horde of troops were busy setting up tents, command and communication posts.

Officers screamed angrily at their excited and overtaxed Sergeants, and the Sergeants in turn screamed at their troops, and the troops ignored the yelling and carried out their assigned duties. The ground pounders knew what was expected of them, and they did their jobs as trained. Navy SeaBee construction workers toiled on creating makeshift heliports, as a stream of heavy humvees carried troops into the heavy brush, making their way up the mountain to the Marine fast attack troops and Rangers stationed in the jungle of the mountain. Shooting broke out on the mountain top as a large Chinese patrol with the same idea, a quest to control the high ground, stumbled across the well dug in American forces.

The vehicles heading for the Marine positions pulled off the narrow road, as the tanks moved up to the head of the convoy, and then prepared to engage any enemy troops they came across. Apache and Super Cobra helicopters popped up from the undergrowth, and immediately opened fire on the now trapped enemy soldiers. The enemy had no air support with them, but they had a few tanks, armored vehicles and RPGs (Rocket Propelled Grenades)as support. The Chinese were not expecting any trouble from the American forces, and they were taken by complete surprise when they came under heavy fire from the waiting American troops.

The Chinese soldiers regrouped quickly though, and they fired RPGs (Rocket Propelled Grenades) at the helicopters, killing one Apache, and damaging another before the enemy patrol was completely overwhelmed by the American forces, even before reinforcements reached the Marine and Ranger Units.

The first American ships were unloaded and then quickly set sail, as two other LPD ships docked with the makeshift landing dock from the Island. The sky began brightening as the sun prepared to rise. Remaining Chinese troops from the attacked patrol tried to get close to the American forces in an effort to try and neutralize the devastating effectiveness of the helicopter attacks on their troops, as they ran towards the dug in GIs. The soldiers on shore heard the fire fight erupting, and easily picked up countless muzzle flashes being traded by both sides, but they could do nothing about it. Their job was to unload the support and supply ships.

The leading elements of the Marine convoy reached Highways Nine and Eleven, and they traveled at thirty five mph heading for Highway Eight, that would take them to the top of the mountain chain considered the spine of the Island. From there, the troops could look down the west coast, and observe what the Chinese were up to, and where their main forces were located or preparing to attack. A second force of Marines making their way down Highway Nine heading towards the Taiwanese Military Base above the city of Hengchun. From there, the Americans were to stage an attack on the industrial center and international airport at Kaohsiung.

The first of the tanks from the 4th Marine Expeditionary Brigade, Camp Lejeune, North Carolina, reached the Marine Advance Units securing the mountain tops. There were sixteen thousand Marines on the Island now. The 7th Expeditionary Brigade was scheduled to land on the Island within the day, March 6th, 1997. The second day of the fighting taking place on the Island of Taiwan. The 7th Infantry Division out of Fort Ord Cal., along with the 25th Infantry Division from Schofield Army Barracks stationed in Hawaii, reinforced the Army Rangers stationed at the crossroads at the Taiwanese city of Lishan.

The Marine Units stationed on Hsuehshan mountain spotted a large Chinese Unit on the road heading from the Science Based Industrial Park in Hsincha, towards the Freeway heading for Taipei, the capital city of Taiwan. Other Chinese forces landed at the CKS International Airport and quickly dug in. From the Marine position, they could easily see the Chinese fighter and transport aircraft parked on the runways of the airport. The Marines sent a Flash message out to Iron Mountain, informing the Command Center of the enemy's movement and strengths.

General Campanelli jumped and almost slipped out of his chair as the scrambled message came in, he had been taking a quick catnap at his desk. After reading the report he turned to General White and bitched at him in an angry tone. "Hey John, where the hell's Colonel Salsiccia hiding at, dammit? I haven't heard shit form him since showing up on the Platform."

John looked through his notes quickly and then he reported to his Commanding Officer, "he went ashore with the 4th MEB."

"What the fuck's he doing on the stinking land, dammit? I don't want him there for Christ sake. Get him on the box for me please so I can order him off the damn Island, John."

Seconds later, John snapped, "say Ed, pick up will ya."

He grabbed the radio and immediately barked into it. "Colonel Salsicca, what the fuck are you doing on land? You shoulda waited until the Island was secured first sir. I don't need any fucking cowboys working for me, mister."

"I went where I felt I was needed the most on this damn thing, General Campanelli Sir. I'm no REMF, (Rear Echelon Mother fucker) and neither were you, sir. Who are you to bust my horns about being where my troops are anyway, sir? I remember a young Captain in the Middle East conflict, who ran off with his men when they came under fire, sir."

"Touché Colonel," he gave in and then he went on with his gripe at the Colonel. "I want you to watch your stinking ass out there, mister. I need you alive sir. I have a report stating a number of Chinese ground units are heading directly for the capital of Taiwan at this time. You want me to make a hit on them, sir?"

"I'd rather you make a raid on the Chinese aircraft decked down at the Taiwan International Airport, sir. I don't need any of the damn Chinese fighter planes coming after my troops when we're ordered to move out against them, General Campanelli Sir."

"I'll order one up right away for you sir. How soon do you want it hit, Colonel?"

"I'm not going to move an damn inch for quite a while yet, General Campanelli Sir. I'm still involved with reinforcing the troops securing the mountain tops, sir. It'll take me at least the rest of the day for this operation to be completed." Colonel Salsiccia took a second and checked his watch, and then he added to his report for his Commanding Officer, "it's Zero, Seven, Ten, General Campanelli, so I want the raid to be put off until Ten Hundred Hours. Let the Chinese forces believe they have the upper hand for the time being, sir."

"Good thinking on your part, Colonel. I'll be back to you before the time of attack arrives, sir. You keep safe out there mister." The exhausted Commanding General stretched, and then he left orders with his Second in Command he was to be awakened if anything happened on the Island he should be made aware of. General Campanelli left the CIC and headed for his room. He immediately noticed the door was slightly ajar and realized Aleksandra must be waiting for him inside. "Oh brother." He mumbled to himself as he slowly entered his room, fearing what might be waiting for him inside.

She was curled up on his bunk like some exotic cat ready to make love, or pounce deadly on her prey. He swallowed as he wondered which he really was to her. She wore a nightgown covering most of her national assets with a thin film of black nylon, concealing, but not hiding her body very well. The effect was perfect, he felt all his strength quickly draining from his body. Her pose made the fabric spread apart to her crotch, which was clean shaven. She was pulling out all the stops this time around, and he knew she wanted something from him. She smiled, a smile that would have melted butter.

He drew in air as he moaned back at her while enjoying what she was showing him. "Whatdaya want from me now Alex?"

Her seductive smile instantly vanished from her lips, and a stone cold, murderous glare quickly replaced it as she barked at him angrily, "I want go on fighter mission with other pilots

I train with all time since come to you country, Mista General Campanelli Sir.”

"Ahhh... gees, not that stinking shit again from you for Pete's sake. I already told you once that's completely out of the fucking question, dammit! I wanna save you until the last possible moment before I use your flying abilities, Alex. I know what I'm doing so be patient with me will ya, and you'll see why I'm holding you back for the time being, young lady. I promise you when I finally use you, you'll like what I have in mind for you, Major.”

She sprang off the bed, the nightgown falling open as she placed her hands on her hips as she snapped at her Commanding Officer angrily. "Nosense, you no want me fly against Chinese forces some reason for. What it is? You no think me good pilot? You no want me to get involved if dog fight with enemy troops? I no fraid, no enemy pilot can kill me, General.”

"No, it's not that at all I assure you Alex. Trust me will you please and be patient and you'll get what you want from me, I promise honey." He said as he turned to leave the room.

"What then where you think you go?" she cried as she took hold of his arm, physically stopping him from leaving his room, and actually forcing him to look back at her. Her pleading eyes questioned why he was not allowing her to fly against the enemy forces. He had to look away from her harsh glare.

She pulled his face back to hers with her hands so they were looking at each other, and then she asked with concern in her voice. "Why you no let me fight like train to do all time, mista? I handle well in fighter of America, Edward.”

"C'mon, don't you think I know that for Christ sake Alex." He said as he sat down on the edge of the bed, giving into his body's need to relax, and then he offered to the female

Major. "I fucking know damn well you can fly stinking rings around many of my male flyers, dammit. I guess I'm kinda being a little selfish, because I don't want you flying because I'm scared to death you might get killed, that's all. I couldn't live if I lost you. I went through that pain once in my life, and I have no intention of going through it for a second time, Alex."

She pulled his head forward until it rested between her breasts and she said to him, "I love you dearly for that, mista. I no let anything happen to I. I come back you all time you see, but first I must do what sent here to do by my government, fight against my country's enemies. Right now, China country enemy to you country so China enemy me, sir."

General Campanelli smiled at the foreign Major as he offered her, "I didn't know Lithuania was at war with China now Alex?"

"I no remember say Lithuania my country. You no remember you told once married, I become instant American citizen, sir. I think America my country now, and I want fight for her Edward."

He pull away from her so he could breath and see her eyes at the same time as he remarked, "Aleksandra, give me this fucking raid and I promise you, I'll use you on the next ground support operation when it's needed."

She smiled as she let her gown fall free from her shoulders, and she unbuckled his belt. She pulled him to his feet and dropped his pants as she purred at him sexily, "I know beat, sit back enjoy what I do for you please."

She pushed him back on the bed and then she knelt between his legs and took him in her mouth. It took a few seconds, but she had him squirming all over the bed. A few times he tried to pull her off of him, so they could make love but she would not let him. Finally, he came then she joined him on the bed.

"That was real great Alex, thanks, I really need that honey." He announced in a weak voice as he smiled at her pleasantly.

"I glad you enjoy the pleasure I being for you my lover and soldier. I hold you word fly next support operation. I careful be plenty General," she purred.

General Campanelli pulled her close to him as he replied, "you betta be damn careful out there when I send you up, I don't want anything happening to you."

SITUATION ROOM IN THE WHITE HOUSE:
2300 HOURS, MARCH 5th, 1997

General William Weidenbacher was being questioned by the President at the Oval Office. "Mr. President Sir, the last report I received over the action taking place on the Island of Taiwan. Stated the Marines successfully landed on the Hsuehshan mountain range on the Island, sir. The report further stated the Marines are back by Units from the Army Rangers, have successfully secured a vital crossroads, and the troops are currently holding it, sir. The way I figure it, we should be in complete control of the Island in less than three days time, sir."

"That's an awful powerful statement you just made General Weidenbacher Sir." Manning snapped at the military officer, and then he added, "and what are the Chinese forces going to be doing while we're marching through the Island so quickly against them, sir?"

General Weidenbacher turned and glared harshly at Manning as he snapped back at the man, "they're going to be fighting for their damn lives and dying in the mud, mister. We'll have air superiority by tomorrow, and our ground forces will be better equipped, and we'll enjoy the luxury of the Taiwanese civilians and remaining military who'll aide us. But don't think for a second the damn Chinese troops are going to lay down and die though, they're going to fight to their death I believe. But there's not one Chinese General on that damn Island who doesn't understand he's already defeated. If not, I assure you they'll understand this at the end of tomorrow when we attack their positions in force. Look Manning…"

"Mr. Manning to you General Weidenbacher Sir!" the civilian snapped back at the General as he shot a nasty glare at the powerful military officer.

"Yeah, whatever buddy, look Manning, this is a military operation here, and I'd really appreciate it if you'd keep your fricking nose the hell out of it for a damn change, buster." The fuming General returned Manning's nasty glare with one of his own.

Manning stood, so did the President as he growled as he aimed a nasty glare at the military officer. "General Weidenbacher, I see you've been hanging around General Campanelli for too long lately, sir. I want you to treat Mr. Manning with the respect do him sir. I can't have the both of you at each other's throats all the time, dammit."

"With all due respect, I'll respect him when he earns my respect and not before, Mr. President Sir. One cannot command respect without first respecting the person he wants that respect from, Mr. President." General Weidenbacher interrupted as he refused to back down and be forced to be friendly with someone he wanted to hit in the head with brick.

The President glared and snarled at the same time at his General. "I have pressing matters to deal with at the moment General Weidenbacher Sir. I'll settle up with your insolence later on, proceed with your report, sir. Mr. Manning, will you please sit down."

Manning plopped down in his seat as the General continued on with his report.

"Mr. President Sir, the Stealth fighters are pounding the crap out of the Chinese ships trying to get their reinforcing troops and military equipment on the Island of Taiwan throughout the night. Iron Mountain and the Aircraft Carriers involved in this operation, are in the process of launching an all out Alpha Strike order. The Marines on Taiwan are being heavily reinforced and are on the verge of breaking out, and then carrying the fight to the Chinese troops. A second Marine Brigade's marching on the Taiwanese military base, they're also hitting the airport at Kaohsiung. Once we have a major airport under our command, it'll be far easier for us to supply our troops in the field, sir. Have you been in contact with the Chinese Chairman, sir?"

"I placed two calls to the Chinese Chairman, and neither one has been returned to me as yet, sir. General Weidenbacher, I want a possible nuclear workup of what I have available to me if one is needed. I know the Chinese are going to threaten our troops with this possibility, and I want to know what I'm talking about when I respond to this possible threat, sir."

"I'll have a complete list of what I have available in the area on your desk within the hour, Mr. President Sir. I know the full complement of three Seawolf Submarines are well within striking distance of all major cities on the mainland of China, sir. I also have nine Ballistic missile submarine platforms on position beneath the Aircraft Carriers involved in this I believe, sir. I'll know for certain once I review the positions of the nuclear end of this operation."

President Cole interrupted the General's report as he remarked with a snap in his voice, "General Weidenbacher, I don't want to be involved in any suppositions here, sit. I want to know, correct that, I demand to know exactly what I have available if and when I hear from the Chinese Chairman, and I understand how to respond if he tries to threaten me with his nukes, sir. I want to be able to negotiate with Beijing properly and go toe to toe with him, General. I really don't want to be forced to invade the mainland of China under any circumstances, sir. Do you understand me sir? Not under any circumstances General Weidenbacher."

General Weidenbacher smiled as he replied to his Commander in Chief. "I understand this very well and I agree with that order, Mr. President Sir."

"Good, now, what are the English up to in this damn mess, General Weidenbacher Sir?"

CHAPTER 37
ON THE VINEGAR JOE PLATFORM
CODE NAMED IRON MOUNTAIN

Sergeant Willis was sent out to wake the General, and he quickly informed him it was nearing the time to attack the enemy aircraft sitting on the deck at the Taiwanese airport.

Campanelli, Aleksandra and the Sergeant entered the CIC Chamber together. John spoke the moment he noticed his Commander. "General Campanelli Sir, I have thirty six F/A-18 Hornets rapidly closing in on the Taiwanese airport from the Aircraft Carrier United States, stationed north of

Taiwan. Twenty six of the Hornets are armed with air to ground and laser guided ordnance. The other ten Hornets are armed with air to air to fly cover and support for the strike force, in case they come under attack by any Chinese fighter aircraft in the region.

"Intel puts the Chinese forces stationed at the airport at twenty F-12B swing wing fighter bombers, and another ten F-6bs. We detected five ZSUs, and two BM-21 anti-aircraft systems protecting the airport for the Chinese forces. They're targeted and I have two EF-111 Raven electronic jammers there to eliminate these threats by disrupting their radar guidance systems, so they can't possibly vector in on our attacking aircraft, until we can get at and destroy them on the ground also, sir. The aircraft are fifteen minutes from final target engagement, General."

"Good call on your part John, who do we have as the damn Flight Leader of this attack group, John?" General Campanelli demanded from his second in command.

"We have a young Lieutenant Bill Walker, his call name's Speed Bump for this operation, General Campanelli Sir." John replied.

The Commander laughed over the name of the pilot as he remarked. "Who the fuck thinks up these damn names for these damn pilots, sir?"

John ignored his comment as he went on with his report, "say Eddy, you can listen in on Freak (Frequency) Zero, Three Zero if you want to hear what's going on in real life action, sir."

General Campanelli reached out and turned his radio over to the fighter aircraft frequency, and then he listened in on their conversations.

"Speed Bump to Three and Four, take out the damn Shilka to the left of the main runway. Blue Nine Leader, take all

Blues with you and get the Chinese fighters we caught in the open on the deck, don't allow the damn Chinese pilots to get anywhere near their damn aircraft. Red Flight Leader, you're responsible for the bombers and BM-21s we have trapped on the deck. I want a fast in and out here sir. Blue Leader, attack flight path is ordered for you to come in from the east and go west over the airport at Angels Ten Thousand Feet and drop down to the deck for controlled attack on the complex. My group will come in from the north and head south at Angels Seven Thousand Feet and down to the deck for the attack. Red Flight Leader, you're ordered to come in from the south and go west over the damn airport at Angels Five Thousand feet, dropping down to the deck for controlled attack first. All Chinese ground crews and troops are a free Tangos (targets). Out."

The American fighter aircraft in Speed Bumps group went after the three targeted Shilkas, while Hammer One, the EF-111 Ravens played sheer havoc with the radar aiming systems on the Shilka tank type machines. The guns could not lock onto the quick running and attacking Wing of F-18 Hornets. Once the Shilkas were knocked out of the equation, Speed Bump and his fighters went after the Chinese fighter aircraft resting on the deck, machine gunning them until they exploded or burst into flames. Then he went after the Chinese pilots running for their planes or cover. A fighter plane could be replaced, but the pilots were a different matter. The attack went off perfectly, when one flight left, a second American flight replaced them and attacked.

All this action took only ten minutes to complete, with just one F-18 Hornet receiving some slight damage to his airframe from the enemy defenders. The American fighter aircraft were on their way back out to their assigned Carrier for refueling and rearming, and did not notice the flight of Chinese F-12 fighters rapidly closing in on them from their east. Most American fighters were ammo light when the enemy planes attacked their flight from their six.

The Flight Commander grabbed his mike and cried out "Speed Bump to any American fighter aircraft in the area of C, One, Oh, One. We're being jumped by a flight of enemy fighters, we have no weapons available for our defense, and we're also low on fuel to allow us to engage in any evasion efforts for a protracted period of time. We need some help out here double quick, or we're going to be history. Over."

Many American pilots responded to the request for assistance, but none were in position to help before the engagement would be over with. The Carrier United States immediately went in another launch after hearing the request for help from his pilots, sending twelve F-14 refurbished Tomcats out to help. The F-18 Hornets dropped to just a few feet above the water, trying to outmaneuver the enemy attackers. It was hell, on their first pass, the enemy aircraft killed six Hornets, while damaging another three. On their second pass, two more F-18s went down as the Hornets assigned to protect them, did their best to fend off the Chinese attackers. As suddenly as they appeared, the enemy planes pulled off and fled the area of engagement.

Speed Bump, his Hornet used as a bomber for this attack, was smoking from his damaged portside engine, saw the reason why the enemy aircraft broke off their attack against them. The F-14s were bearing down on them fast from the north. Speed Bump watched helplessly as another smoking Hornet lost altitude, and then splashed into the sea below him.

"Speed Bump to all trailing fighter planes. Check in and give me your present status. Over."

"Three, I lost one aircraft to that last sneak attack from the damn enemy, sir. Over."

"Blue Flight Leader. I lost seven aircraft to the damn Chinese fighters, sir. Over."

"Hang in Blue Flight Leader, it's not your fault for the loses, man. I lost nine Chicks myself, with five damaged including myself. What the fuck happened dammit. Where's my damn radar umbrella for crying out loud? Speed Bump to Reader One. Over."

No response, so he tried his call again, "Speed Bump to Reader One. Come in sir. Over."

"Speed Bump, this is Tinsel Town. The Zappers killed Reader One before they engaged your flight. That's why they were able to sneak up on you flight so effectively, sir. I was committed and unable to help you out at the time of their attack against your flight, sir. Over."

"Roger that last, copy all as received Tinsel Town. Out."

General Campanelli was fuming as he roared at no one in the CIC in particular, "what the fuck's this shit, dammit? I only had one damn AWACS radar platform protecting that flight of Hornets. Tinsel Town couldn't help out the other damn fighters, John?"

John interrupted the General's latest tirade by offering to him in a calm tone of voice, "Eddy, Tinsel Town was on the wrong side of the mountain and Island to be of any real help to Speed Bump's flight. Who would have expected the Chinese aircraft to go after Reader One? How the hell did they get her without her sending out a Mayday call, sir?"

Colonel Locker added to the conversation, "we were just out flanked on this one sir."

"No fucking shit Colonel Locker! Even Stevie Wonder could see that one coming." General Campanelli suddenly bellowed as he turned his attention on her and continued his anger, "yes, we were outflanked on this one, but I'm warning everyone in this damn place it better be the last time we're ever outflanked by the damn enemy! It looks like the damn Chinese aircraft have our Carriers blanketed now. They knew damn well when we launched, and they set us up on this one flight good and proper. This will never happen to us again, this I promise you, from now on, I want any launch protected by fighter aircraft. As far as I can tell, the Chinese still have no idea we're out here. They're unable to set up our fighters. No more fucking around with these sonsofbitches on this one, I want..."

Alarms suddenly sounded inside the CIC as a booming voice called out over the intercom system. "General Quarters, General Quarters."

John jumped up alongside the General as they both put on their helmets and life belts and sidearm, and he groused at his Commanding Officer, "what the hell was that you were just saying about the fricking enemy not knowing we're out here, General Campanelli Sir? I believe we might be under attack my old friend."

"Funny. Real funny wiseguy." General Campanelli snapped at his Second in Command as he hit John with an open hand in the guts, making him grunt. The General then looked for General Palmieri, and yelled as the red lights came on in the CIC. "Palmieri, whatdaya have?"

"A coupla Chink submarines are trying to find out what we are, General Campanelli Sir."

"Shit! What the hell are we doing about the damn enemy submarines for crap sake, sir?" General Campanelli demanded to know from his officer.

"The enemy submarines were easily picked up by Sea Dragon towing a sonar sled, sir. We launched five S-3A Viking submarine killers, and there are twelve Lamp anti-submarine helicopters working six enemy contacts over with three LRAACA (Long Range Air ASW Capability Aircraft) Starfishers. I don't think the Chinese submarines will get through our defenses, sir. I also have a number of Frigates and two Destroyers moving between us and the contacts. They're launching helicopters to aide in killing the subs, sir."

At that very moment, the massive Platform was suddenly shaken by a heavy underwater explosion. Edward looked at John and then barked at him, "I don't know what the hell that was John, but I can only guess at it though, sir. I think we were just hit by a fucking enemy torpedo John. We hafta check on the damage..."

"No way in hell sir. It wasn't strong enough to be a torpedo hit on us, Eddy." John retorted, at least I hope it wasn't, he said under his breath as he took the radio and barked into it, "Central Command to Submarine Warfare Station."

"SWS here sir, go ahead with your traffic sir. We're kinda busy at the moment, General Campanelli," the operator replied to the incoming call.

"Yeah, this is General White not General Campanelli, sir. What the fuck was that last explosion we just experienced, mister?"

"General White Sir that was the death of a Chinese submarine that came a little too damn close to our Platform, sir. We're still tracking nine other enemy targets in the surrounding area of the Platform, sir. Strangest thing though General White Sir, all enemy targets are staying real close together sir. This is sheer nuts on their part sir, it's just making our job all that much easier for us to kill them all, sir."

Another deep underwater rumble was felt throughout the massive Platform again.

"Before you ask me General White, that was another enemy submarine just destroyed, sir. Oh shit, I have to go, they're trying to sneak a pair of submarines in from the south, sneaky little bastards they are, sir. Now I know why the subs were staying so close together, sir."

John turned to General Campanelli and offered in an excited voice, "Eddy, it's just our guys killing two enemy subs, and holding contacts on another eight targets, sir. They picked up two more subs coming in from the south. Looks like the Chinese are getting serious too, sir."

All the while this was going on, Iron Mountain and the Carriers were still launching their aircraft at Taiwan. The Americans were having trouble finding any enemy planes in the air. When they came across one, the enemy would immediately hightail to a city, and stay over the civilian population to avoid being killed by the American aircraft. Every enemy pilot knew the American pilots were reluctant to engage them while over these heavily populated civilian areas.

The American fighter aircraft assigned to work over the Chinese ground troops on Taiwan, were having much the same sort of problems. Because the Chinese troops had the Taiwanese civilians with them whenever they moved their military equipment around on the Island. It was frustrating, the American pilots had to gear themselves up for the kill, only to stop the attack when the plane or tank they were targeting, made it safely to a civilian area.

The day dragged by at a snail's pace, and General Campanelli was really pissed off. Because he found his troops were being forced to hold their fire because of the tactics being adopted by the Chinese troops and aircraft. He complained to General Weidenbacher, and though he was sympathetic, he ordered Edward to make his troops continue to hold their fire, if they were going to endanger any large numbers of civilian lives. The only America forces having any luck with the Chinese fighters and bomber planes, were the ones assigned to attacking the Chinese ships still trying to make it from mainland China to Taiwan. The American bombers got seven ships, and our fighter planes strafed a few more. Some American bombers caught the enemy ships moored to docks in Taiwan. These planes were cleared to attack, even if civilians were being forced to unload the enemy ships at this point.

There was a diplomatic move affront as well, to bring China to the United Nations to explain her aggressive moves in Asia, and to see if there was a way the fighting could come to an end with words. China refused to attend any of the ordered meetings, but the Chinese leadership sent a letter demanding the American forces in Asia stop shooting, and leave the Asia region immediately. Then and only then would China even think about sitting down at the United Nations, to discuss her problems with the world.

It was near mid-day and no major encounters had taken place. It was hard to fight an enemy who took to hiding in the midst of civilians. The war against the submarines was still taking place with five confirmed sinking, yet the enemy submarines would not pull back. An American attack submarine killed another enemy submarine.

The Marines stationed on the Island of Taiwan were rapidly being reinforced, and a force of Marines were gathering on the mountain top near the city of Lishan, preparing for a breakout. Attack helicopters landed on the empty highway, and waited until they were needed. The Americans had successfully driven the Chinese invaders from Green Island, and had already put the small airport there to use. The Marines confiscated fuel reserves stored on the tiny Island, and the Navy SeaBee's had a runway carved out on the beach, and the Mud Hog C-17 aircraft were making good use of them now.

Military information and failures were being withheld from the Chinese forces, and also the elderly Chinese Chairman. No Minister wanted to be the one who had to inform the old fool the Americans landed, and successfully carved out a strong foothold on the Island, and the American troops were in the process of preparing for a major breakout from their positions on the Island. The Ministers resorted to ordering more soldiers to the coast to be sent to Taiwan. The biggest commodity China had were her troops, and she was willing to waste them in an all out war effort with the Americans. The problem facing China was she was massing troops along the coast. But when she put her soldiers on ships, they were instantly being attacked by the ever present Americans aircraft constantly patrolling the Formosa Straits. The Chinese relief troops were not making it to Taiwan, this information was also being withheld from the Chairman.

By four thirty in the afternoon of the second day of the war, most of the fighting had stopped. Both American and Chinese forces took to hunkering down for the long night ahead. On this night, China was going to send in a large flotilla of ships to the Formosa Straits. Many would not make it, but others would.

The Marines stationed on Hsuehshan mountain were prepared for any attack. The Marine called Road Kill, had LP and OPs set up. (Listening and Observation Post). The only sign of any life on the mountain top was from the occasional bird chirping and flipping through the branches of the trees. The soldiers under Sergeant Robert Walker's Command, spent the entire night making certain that was what the enemy soldiers would see. Nothing.

The young Sergeant's troops were hard to spot, but he knew where all of them were hiding. Their faces were well camouflaged, any spot that might reflect light, was covered, down to their teeth. Each man had a black mouth piece covering their upper and lower teeth. The Marines wore night glasses called wasp eyes, so their eyes would not shine in the darkness of night. Road Kill remembered the warning he issued to his people before they went out in the bush. "Listen up you jungle green pussy hounds, remember, the bush is a world of its own, there's nuthin' like it in the real world. Get useta it people, and don't get lost, and watch out for any possible man traps. No telling what the enemy mighta setup against us out there. If anyone gets lost, you hafta stay where you are, and someone will find you sooner or later.

"Don't go wandering around by yourselves, because you could get killed by one of your own men, and I'll kill any asshole that gets capped by friendly fire." The Sergeant remembered the men's laughter at his remark as he went on with is orders to his troops, "another thing you people gotta remember at all times. Throw your damn hand grenades as hard as you can pitch them, make sure the fucking things bounce too. So the bastards can't pick the damn things up and chuck them back at your ass before they go off. Another thing you gotta remember, the rule is to hold onto the arm of any wounded soldier, don't allow him get holda your hand. You birds don't wanna be holding his hand if he dies 'cause of the possible death grip thing. You don't wanna hafta pry the dead man's hand from yours, many of you soldiers feel it marks you as the next to die. Be damn careful and keep your noggins down, dammit."

Each of the soldiers had to fight in an attempt to stay alert throughout the night, staying on the edge like they were for so long a time was nearly impossible. The long hours of the night, and having to stay absolutely motionless while they were at it, and staring out in the pitch darkness, served to make the soldiers more tired than they really were. The troops were on the one up, and one down watch. Each soldier had a partner sharing his foxhole, one slept while the other soldier stayed alert and ready to call out if he spotted any enemy coming at them. On top of everything else facing the American soldiers, it was a very humid and warm night, making the troops sweat, and the insects much more active and attacking them.

The soldier branded Road Kill lit up a cigarette between his cupped hands, his blood pounding behind his eyes, he snorted and scratched his balls while trying to get comfortable. His four day old beard looked like small, sharp spikes coming from his chin, and looked vicious, like he could actually kill with them. The Sergeant took a swig of almost hot water, and then he poured the rest of his canteen out. He was aware what it meant to have a half full canteen on his hip in combat. The enemy could actually hear the water slushing around in it, and it could get you killed. Many soldiers carried two canteens with them, one they drank from while hunkered down, and the second one they left until they really needed some water to drink.

The Marines were on their toes after a small Chinese patrol accidently stumbled over them the night before. The American camouflage uniforms were soaked with sweat, as a few troopers chowed down on their MRE packets. Road Kill, Gunny Sergeant Robert Walker checked his watch, it was Zero, One, Twenty Hours, he looked up towards the sky, it was pitch black out, just what he wanted. Walker smiled as he thought, even the stars were afraid to come out tonight.

It was only hours before the Marines were scheduled to charge down the side of the mountain range, in an attempt to drive the occupying Chinese troops out of Hsinchu. It was going to be a real mess though, with trying to pick out the Chinese enemy from the Taiwanese civilians. Road Kill swatted at a fly who just took a small chunk of meat from his neck, and he cursed because he missed it. The Gunnery Sergeant ran through his orders in his mind quickly, if his men were to attack on foot then there was going to be a flare fired. If his troops were going to be picked up by the APCs. The APCs were scheduled to pull up to them, and the troopers were to jump on board the armored machines and be driven down the hill.

Road Kill personally checked on his troops hiding deep in the bush, he knew flights American fighter aircraft were scheduled to come in and soften up the enemy positions below them, before they were to attack the complex. A twenty minute preparatory bombardment was scheduled commence at exactly Zero, Five Thirty Hours, artillery and key enemy positions would be hit in the opening bombardment. The artillery rounds would cover the Marines attacking the enemy troops. The artillery would then shift to more selected targets at Zero, Six Hundred Hours. Smoke rounds would cover his troopers movements.

Many MRLs would be held back in case of a counter bombardment coming from the Chinese forces occurred, and the MRL's electronics would instantly zero in on the enemy Command Posts directing the enemy fire. The Sergeant thought himself rather lucky. His company was one of few who had any battle tested soldiers attached to it.

He had fifteen troopers who saw action in the Middle East war last year, including himself.

Sergeant Walker's troops stayed motionless, even though they were being tortured from many outside forces around them. In their haste to conceal themselves, the soldiers toil made them sweat heavily, and it ran in their eyes and burned them. The smell of soldier's body odor brought in every biting insect for miles around them as well. Other bugs came after them too, the ones that did not bite, but they wanted the salt from their sweat. They were just as bad as the biting ones, if not worse, getting into the soldier's noses, mouths, eyes and even their ears, and driving them plain nuts while they were at it.

The heavy camouflage Bush Blanket or Guilly Suit the soldiers hid under also added to the heat on the soldiers. Their weapons were wet by sweat soaked glove hands, with the fingers cut off to make it a little easier for the soldiers to fire, and stop the weapon from actually turning in their hands. Some Marines laid down flat on the ground, and had sticks and stones jabbing them from underneath their bodies. The air surrounding the troops quickly turned bad, making them even more tired and attacked by the hordes of insects. It turned bad from body odor, while many soldiers had to take a dump or piss, but they would not move for fear the movement might give their hiding places away. Soon, body gas added to the many other odors hanging heavy in the night air around the dug in troops. Some troops wanted a cigarette in the worse way, but they were under a total blackout, including smoking at this time.

Soldier's legs cramped up on the dug in American troops. Backs ached, elbows hurt, and necks got stiff, as the soldiers eyes grew heavy from fatigue, and the constant staring into the darkness of the night in search of any attacking enemy troops. Yet the Marines continued to man their posts, ready to pounce on any enemy troops at the sound of a whistle. Weeks before, most of these children now turned men and soldiers, were going to school, or working in a nice, safe and comfortable job, or making love to their ladies.

Their biggest problem facing them at that time, was if their favorite baseball team was going to be ready for the opening day. Now, they found themselves hiding in the jungles, much like the ones in Vietnam, while being eaten alive by swarms of angry bugs, and preparing to kill or be killed. Many of these scared young children prayed to their own God to keep them safe, and alive for another day. While other soldiers wanted to get bloody. Some soldiers would break under the terrible strain of combat and the fog of war, but most of them were going to do as they were ordered, and die in the effort.

The mixed units of Marines and Rangers stayed in constant contact with each other by radio units built in their heavy Kevlar helmets. The Sergeant liked to see who he was talking to, so he started out for the foxholes in order to speak easily to many of his people in their foxholes personally. Road Kill moved out until he ended up in the last foxhole occupied by two young privates, Scorelli and Brown. The slicksleeve Brown smiled at the Sergeant as he slid into the shallow pit along with them. Both soldiers felt a little better now Road Kill was with them. All troopers in the outfit felt the wise and well trained Sergeant was lucky to be around, especially in a combat situation.

The Marine Sergeant looked at the two other soldiers, and then he bitched at the privates. "Lotta fucking shit still coming in on the stinking beach. How the hell are you two birds doing out here anyhow?"

"Getting kinda useta it slowly but surely, you know somethin' Sarge. The first thing I'm gonna do when I get down there and the complex is secured, is get me some of this slanted eyed poontang I've been hearing so much shit about from the other guys from the Unit, man. I hear they screw like crazy, Sarge. I can't wait until I can check out the local scenery, and see for myself how these Chinks make love, man."

The Gunnery Sergeant laughed, and then he added as a warning to the two young kids who were as green as their uniforms were. "You two birds betta take damn good care of that damn Elephant gun of yours, buddy. Then watch out for the Hurdy Gurdy Bitches walking the streets down there, they be some tough shit to tangle with you now."

The Elephant gun was slang for the M-79 single round grenade launcher.

"How the hell did the chicks ever get tagged with that kinda name, Sergeant?" Private Brown asked the NCO as he checked out the M-79 weapon.

"Cause them ladies have grounded down many a good grunt's organ, till it finally fell offa the dumb asshole on him, and it left him with a permanent case of the damn drips as well, asshole. Besides, what the hell makes you think any of these stinking Chink bitches are gonna let your stinking black ass anywhere near between their legs, dopey? You'll be lucky just to get a stinking mercy fuck outta one of them damn chicks down there, before they cut your fucking throat for your ass, man."

"Hey Gunny, I think this thing's gonna blow over without another stinking shot being fired by either side, man. I think the damn Chinese troops are spent and all they want is to go home." Brown offered to the Sergeant as he shot him a quick smile.

Road Kill's stubble covered face screwed up in a quizzical look, bitterness was etched deeply in his words as he shifted his weight under his knees, and then he snapped at the scared looking soldier staring at him. "Look mosquito bait, you're like a bowl of condoms at a lesbian bar, useless. You don't know jack shit about what's gonna happen in the next few hours, so give it up and pay attention to the soldier in front of you, man. Besides buddy, your stinking head was made for a steel pot, not for thinking in this man's service. So can all the fricking shit about what you might think is gonna happen around here, asshole. Besides, if you think for one second the Chinese troops are finished then I have a bridge in Brooklyn for sale real cheep, asshole."

Sergeant Robert Walker looked at his watch, it was Zero, Four, Twenty Hours. Then he warned the two young troopers, "you betta get ready, I gotta get back to the rest of the troops before we jump off. Keep your ears and eyes opened." Walker jumped out and headed back.

The Sergeant's troopers did everything they could possibly do to help avoid their dulling senses, and slowing reactions, by stretching their arms, legs and necks around every few seconds. Then shifting their positions and weight to avoid detection and changing their breathing habits. Nevertheless, the strength robbing fatigue and boredom set in on the troops, as the soldiers thought of everything not important to them at this moment. Like sex, football and baseball, and taking their minds off the many problems at hand, war and death. Road Kill was visiting all the foxholes in his group, in order to try and make certain all his soldiers were well prepared to jump off at the scheduled time. He was fast becoming rather concerned over many of his people, they were all suffering from sheer exhaustion, and they have not even engaged any enemy as yet.

Road Kill, Gunny Sergeant Robert Walker wanted to get his troopers some much needed rest, but he also knew this was totally impossible at the present moment. Not until after they had attacked the well dug in defending Chinese enemy troops waiting for them at the bottom of the mountain they were using for their cover. The fighting could not happen soon enough to suit the angry young Marine Sergeant as he now headed back to his own foxhole. Sergeant Walker hated with a passion the so called waiting game, and the overwhelming boredom it brought along with it as well. He was a fighting man, and not the type of soldier who enjoyed just sitting on his laurels while waiting for the fighting to finally begin. Sergeant Walker wanted to get bloody.

No sooner did Sergeant Robert Walker get back to his foxhole than the first LAV-25 8x8 light armored vehicle pull up in front of his position and parked. A First Louie instantly poked his head out of the rear scuttle of the idling machine, and he snapped at the scruffy looking grime covered Sergeant. "Hey Sarge, you better get your bunch on the vehicles moving and follow me." He slammed the scuttle shut and his machine roared off.

A long mixed column of LAVs, M-75 APCs, LVTP7s Hummvies and the Bradley Fighting Machines pulled up alongside the filthy and already exhausted bunch of Marines and Rangers.

Road Kill followed his orders and bellowed at the rest of his troopers. "Okay you pack of pussy hounds, saddle up, let's get a move on it. Get outta them woods on the double quick and get moving, we have enemy who need a visit from our asses." The excited Sergeant kept a close eye on his troops as they jumped up and climbed into the waiting war machines amidst countless grunts and groans and complaints. He scanned the area and noticed the heavy M-109 155 mm howitzers taking position where his troops evacuated from the tree line. He counted twenty seven pieces of armor setting up. Five M-110A2 eight inch howitzers from A Battery 6/37th Field Artillery pulled up alongside the M-109s. To Walker's left, three hundred tanks gathered up for the fast trip down the side of the mountain. He couldn't remember the last time he seen so much military equipment stacked up in one place and ready to open fire on their enemy units.

Other Marine or Ranger Sergeants screamed at their troops also, and a flood of curses were sent back at the angry Sergeants by the grunt soldiers. The artillery pieces were quickly setup and then loaded and prepared to open fire on the Taiwan complex. Road Kill heard the roar from Wing of American aircraft roaring overhead, and then heading down the mountain towards the dug in Chinese enemy troops stationed in Hsinchu.

The Marine Sergeant checked his troops again, and then bitched at them. "For Christ sake, First Squad, get in them frigging iron wagons before I hop the lot of ya in the asses. Mount up people, let's get going. There ain't no one coming this way. We hafta go get the muthafuckers where they hide, people. First Squad move your purdy asses before I bite them off on ya. Move it people. Remember pussy snifters, keep a close eye out for any tracers, dammit." Each M-18 had the last three rounds set as tracers, this was to inform the shooter he was out of ammo in the heat of battle.

The column of elite soldiers quickly moved out under their Sergeant's orders and watchful eye, with Sergeant Walker sitting on top of the idling M-113 armor vehicle while watching the troops move out like they were carrying pianos on their backs. Walker stayed on the top of the APC so he could keep a better eye on his troops. Weapon fire could be heard coming from below and off in the distance. The Sarge looked down the valley and saw the brightening sky light up from tracers being fired by the enemy at the attacking American warplanes.

The artillery opened up next with the sound of thunder. It was mesmerizing to see countless anti-aircraft shells exploded in the air, and the tracers criss crossed the explosions. Road Kill saw a fighter aircraft suddenly explode in mid flight, flaming fuel and burning wreckage landing on the Chinese troops below. The Shilka's were having a devastating effect on his attacking planes. The Hammer F-111 Raven radar jamming aircraft were out and jamming away already, but the Chinese soldiers firing the Shilka's were firing by eye, and effectively while they were at it. A Shilka suddenly turned their guns on the first American troops to attack their positions and opened fire and chewed them up badly.

A second American fighter plane came in real low, and it blew that Shilka apart with a Hellfire missile, that aircraft was followed in by four A-10 Warthogs, and they hit the rest of the Shilka's firing on the American aircraft. Rocket propelled artillery was used to reached the well entrenched Chinese troops, which rained down on them from the mountain top area. Most of the shells stayed well away from the heavier concentrations of Chinese troops and buildings, and possible civilians trapped inside the complex. A second wave of American fighter planes came charging in from the south. The Chinese troops were caught in the middle of a vice, a vice blocked from closing because of the civilians still trapped inside the complex along with the Chinese troops under attack.

Many reports getting back to Campanelli at the CIC on board Iron Mountain, complained about not being able to hit the enemy because of the hordes of Taiwanese civilians mixed in with the enemy troops. An aide stuck another report in front of his face. He did not look up as he growled at the Seaman. "Get that god damn thing outta my fucking face immediately, or I'll shove them in a place where only a team of surgeons will find them on your body, mister."

"Sir?" The aide questioned the angry General with some confusion etching his tone.

"Get those fucking papers outta my damn face mister." He demanded again as he placed a call to General Weidenbacher, inform him of the many problem caused by the Taiwan civilians giving his attacking forces.

General William Weidenbacher smiled through the screen as he told General Campanelli about the latest meeting with the President. He informed Campanelli the meeting did not go as well as planned, because Manning was able to get his two cents in, and he fucked it up again.

Campanelli growled as he thought of the civilian always getting in the way of many military conversations, "he stinks up a room like bad gas, General Weidenbacher Sir."

General Weidenbacher laughed at his crude remark. But his smile quickly disappeared as his General informed him of the many problems he was now having with getting at the enemy who seemed to be using the Taiwan civilians as sort of human shields.

"What do you want to do about the situation General Campanelli Sir? Shot down the damn civilians if they're in your way, mister?"

"Exactly what I was thinking General Weidenbacher Sir. I want permission to go after the enemy regardless of the damn civilians. I can't run a war with my hands tied behind my stinking back like this, sir. I have to protect my troops more than my trying to protect the Taiwan civilians. How the hell can I commit my troops if they have to hold their fire, and the Chinese troops are pouring lead at my soldiers, all because the Taiwanese civilians are getting in our way, and the Chinese troops are mowing them down to get at my soldiers, sir."

"Let me get this straight General Campanelli Sir. You're requesting permission to open fire on the Chinese troops, even if there's innocent civilians in the way of your getting at the enemy soldiers, sir? Even if the damn Chinese troops are using the civilians as human shields, sir?" General Weidenbacher asked with surprise in his tone of voice.

"That's exactly what I wanna do, General Weidenbacher. If I can't get at the enemy where they are then I'm gonna be throwing my soldier's lives away needlessly, sir. I have to get at the enemy where they are, or who they're hiding behind, or this is gonna be a wasted effort sir."

General William Weidenbacher thought for a moment and then was forced to agree with his lesser General's latest request as he replied to his request, "Ed, if you can live with it sir. You do whatever you have to do to protect your troops, and get those damn Chinese troops the hell out of that complex before they destroy everything inside the place, sir. I'll clear it with the President, he's not going to like it though, I can assure you that General Campanelli."

Campanelli broke the communication off, and then ordered John to patch him through to Colonel Salsiccia in Command of the American troops stationed on the Island of Taiwan.

Once he had him in the line, the General ordered, "Colonel Salsiccia, I want you to drive in, and get those damn Chinese troops now, sir."

The Colonel tried to interrupt the General's angry words, but Campanelli would not allow him to as he went on with his orders, "I know the Chinese troops are sort of hiding behind a wall of civilians. But I'm giving you orders to do what you have to, to get the enemy out of the damn complex. Try to avoid as many of the civilians as you possibly can. Get it done, I'll inform the fighter aircraft there's no longer any restricted targets inside the complex, sir."

Colonel Joseph Salsiccia decided this was going to be his last war, he was going to retire after this mess was concluded. The Colonel did not like he was going to put the lives of civilians in danger during their attack on the enemy soldiers. He reluctantly got in touch with his officers, and then he ordered them to move in, and disregard all previously restricted targets. This was a polite way of informing his officers the civilians were no longer considered to be a problem in the field of war. Most of his officers were rather upset over the new orders as well.

Road Kill's column of elite troops got down to the flatland, and then his soldiers instantly dismounted from the armored machines and fanned out to secure their places to fight from. A hundred American tanks opened fire on the Science complex. The artillery became much more intense also behind the tanks fire. A second American warplane exploded while in flight as it tried to attack a Chinese position. The Sergeant stared in stunned disbelief, finding it hard to believe the artillery was still trying to avoid most of the buildings in the Taiwanese complex. It was at this moment he received his change of orders, lifting the ban on some of the enemy targets. The orders carried the name of General Campanelli on them. The orders warned if any civilians were in the way, they were to continue with the attack no matter what. He was further warned, the faster the fighting came to a conclusion, the more civilian lives would be saved.

The combined tanks and artillery fire skillfully worked over the Chinese positions in this new order. Fighter aircraft came in at just above ground level now, while firing at the enemy soldiers. In the first three hours of fighting, all the Shilka tanks were destroyed. Enemy tanks and artillery pieces lay scattered about as twisted wreaks on the campus grounds. Hundreds, maybe even thousands of enemy troops covered the ground, dead or dying. The remaining enemy troops return fire was dropping down to mainly small arms fire.

Occasionally, a heavy machine gun would suddenly open fire on the attacking American troops, but it would be immediately attacked by the artillery, or now by the constantly hovering attack aircraft. War, and everything that made war the hell it is, was now taking place on the battlefield, with human bodies being ripped asunder by heavy explosions and attacking warplanes and artillery.

Twice, the American command asked the Chinese soldiers in the complex, to lay down their arms and surrender. The answer was a no, so the American command decided the only way to get the Chinese troops out of the complex before it was totally destroyed, was to go in after them.

Road Kill, Sergeant Robert Walker's outfit was ordered to attack the dug in enemy troops first. American troops were massed on three sides of the complex area, and they were ready to begin their attack on the Chinese troops. Road Kill split up his troops as he ordered some soldiers. "Hey Mutt, (Marine Sergeant Frank Hall) take two of the FnGs with ya and try ta keep them alive this time around will you, buster. Once you have them, head for that damn brick pillar over there by that light stand, and set up a machine gun nest there, man."

The two troopers swallowed as they stared at Road Kill, hoping he was only kidding about the Mutt keeping them alive. The Mutt got his tag name because he had a white mother and a black father. The FnGs were the Fucking new Guys to the company.

"Private Smith, you and Weston get over to that uther damn pillar and do the same thing and setup a cross fire machine nest. You guys are gonna protect the bulk of my troops when we jump off against the enemy." As Road Kill deployed his soldiers in the best possible places to attack the enemy from. The once trapped civilians began to run all over the compound as they ran away from the Chinese forces. The hostages were trying desperately to make it outside the fence area, and run for cover behind the rapidly developing American lines. Some Chinese troops changed into civilian clothes, and then they joined the civilians fleeing for their lives, so they could escape the oncoming massacre of their fellow soldiers now trapped inside the complex area. Not all Chinese troops wanted to fight to their deaths.

It was estimated there were well over ten thousand enemy troops still active and stationed inside the complex area. The American fighter aircraft were constantly moving in and strafing the ground, in an effort to try and kill as many enemy troops as possible, before the American ground forces were finally forced to move in after them. One section of the massive complex, with almost five thousand enemy troops supporting this certain section, quickly surrendered with no further fighting to the rapidly advancing and overwhelming American soldiers. They were about out of ammunition and exhausted with no reinforcements coming to their aide.

Three different sections of the massive Scientific complex of higher learning were now burning out of control, and many secondary explosions were also going off inside the complex, as it continued to burn out of control. The artillery stationed on the mountain top had already stopped firing at random. The artillery was now only responding to requests for rounds being fired off from ground forces, to help root out the enemy soldiers cut off from any further food supplies, ammunition or reinforcement soldiers from their fortifications.

Road Kill's troops followed tanks into the complex. One tank suddenly erupted into a shower of sparks and roaring flames when it was hit by an RPG round. His troops tried to get the tankers out of the burning hulk, but it was useless so they were forced to watch as the tankers burned to death. The flames and exploding ammo drove back the would be rescuers.

Sergeant Robert Walker was fired at from behind a pile of wooden crates and other debris. His troops instantly dropped down and returned fire at the hidden enemy soldiers. The Marines instantly moved to the rear of one of the badly destroyed buildings to regroup. There they were shocked when they came across the bodies of about a thousand Chinese soldiers and civilians. Heavy gun fire suddenly broke out off to his right, and Walker and his troops dove for cover, as three supporting tanks erupted into boiling flames right behind where he was just standing. There was strong resistance from a number of Chinese defenders.

The fighting was extremely heavy now, and Road Kill was keeping a close eye on his troops and where they were moving around as they cautiously entered the complex proper. He saw a kid go down, and he quickly moved over to the wounded soldier. The kid's eyes stared the stare of death, as steam rose from a gaping wound ripped in his chest, and his intestines slowly oozed out from the large hole. The Sergeant checked out the downed soldier's neck for any sign of a pulse, and then he growled out one word. "Shit."

Walker then pulled the dog tags free of the dead soldier, and placed one in the dead soldier's mouth, and then kicked his jaw shut. Breaking the jaw, and clamping the jaw around the small tin ID, so the Body Sweepers could ID the kid later on when they finally found his body. It was the only way to make certain the body would be properly identified.

A Chinese T-69 II tank suddenly rumbled up behind the dug in Chinese soldiers, and it had Road Kill's outfit pinned down and successfully cut off from any ground support. Road Kill plopped down and ended up sitting on a spent mortar fin, and cursed as he threw it like a grenade towards the enemy tank. He took the Prick 25 radio and quickly adjusted the frequency for ground to aircraft communications.

"Err... This is Alfa, Bravo, Bravo, Golf, Lima Two, Two, Seven. Listen up, I'm smack fucking dab trapped in the middle of an active enemy counterattack, I gotta lotta unfriendlies coming at me like a bunch of screaming banshees. I need a stinking hit at coordinates Quebec, Yankee, Zulu, Seven, Three, Rikky, Tik. Respond Tree Chipper support. Over."

"Yeah, Alfa, Bravo, Bravo, Golf, Lima Two, Two, Seven, I read you loud and clear. This is Tree Chipper Leader. Commencing my opening run at Quebec, Yankee, Zulu Seven, Three with three birds in support. What do you have in your way? I want the most important targets first, then we'll turn our attention on the enemy ground forces. Over."

The pilot in Command of the ground support aircraft responded to Walker's request for assistance.

"Tree Chipper Leader, I have a tank visible, and numerous ground forces and fire coming at me. Popping off green smoke to mark friendly positions. Anything outta the green's fair game."

"Copy that, anything outside the green smoke belongs to me and my Chicks. Starting my opening run now. Order your troopers to keep their heads down, I'm hitting the area with 30 mm cannon and air to ground missiles. Out."

Road Kill ordered his troops to take cover and keep low until the support aircraft completed their attack on the enemy troops, and then he watched as the attacking aircraft instantly lined up for their attack, and then started their run. The enemy tank picked up the attacking American aircraft and tried to make a run for cover, by slamming itself into the side of a building, and then entering it through the hole it just forced into the building, but it was to no avail. Tree Chipper picked up what the tank was up to, and fired two AGM-65 IIR infrared Maverick missiles at it.

The missiles chased the enemy tank in the building and then exploded, bringing a large section of the building down on top of the dead tank. A second and third attacking aircraft dropped a number of CBU-52B/B cluster bombs on the enemy positions. The ground turned instantly into a sea of bouncing sparks as small chunks of white hot steel ripped into the bodies of the enemy soldiers. The first aircraft, an F-18 Hornet came around again, and hit any enemy soldiers still on their feet with cannon fire.

In less than five minutes, the enemy tank and a large number of enemy troops were destroyed, the few survivors stood dazed, moving around in shocked with their hands up. The fighting for the Science Complex at Hsinchu was drawing to a quick end. The American soldiers moved in and took fifteen thousand enemy prisoners, and the engineers started to clean up the debris and bodies, and looking for any civilians or wounded soldiers that could be saved. Booby traps went off, so the engineers pulled double duty. In seven hours of heavy fighting, the American forces were in complete control of the major Taiwanese complex. The headquarters was setup, and Colonel Salsiccia and his command began to setup housekeeping.

When the American Armies left the mountain top to get involved in the action taking place below their positions, the troops split up, as half the troops went down the North Cross Island Highway, and then quickly worked their way over to the Taiwanese CKS International Airport. While the second part of the joint Army and Marine force went down the Central Cross Island Highway, heading directly towards the major Freeway of the Island.

The fast moving American ground forces took the Freeway over to the Taiwanese city of Hsinchu, where it got involved in countless small skirmishes with three different enemy Chinese patrols, which were easily overwhelmed and then completely destroyed. Once set in position, the American troops began their attack on Hsinchu with the large portion of the American force from the south. The Chinese defenders thought the Army coming down the North Cross Island Highway, was the force going to attack them, and they never imagined the major thrust was coming right at them from the south section of the city.

The American Command decided to leave the Capital city of Taipai for the time being. It was hoped once the American forces attacked the Chinese defenders of Hsinchu, the Chinese forces sent to take over Taipai, would turn and come to the aide of the Hsinchu defenders. It did not happen the way they had hoped it would work out.

The American Command went after the civilian airport in hopes of drawing the Chinese troops out of their defensive positions. The American troops wiped out the enemy defending at the Science complex, and they were now preparing to move out and start attacking any other enemy forces they came across on the Island. The Americans were going to take the freeway to the North Cross Island Highway. Once there, they were going to linkup with the second American force sent out to attack the Taiwanese International Airport. The soldiers were ordered to hit the heavily defended airport in force. The second force of troops was already set in place, and waiting for the first force to linkup with them so they could open a combined attack.

The first American troops made good time driving on the three lane highway free of any other civilian or military traffic but theirs. The second group of soldiers dug in, and was directing artillery fire on the airport to try and save as much of the airport as they could from total destruction. By three p.m., the second day of fighting for the Island of Taiwan, the two American forces finally linked up together. The shelling of the airport immediately intensified as the American troops moved out after it in force.

The Chinese defenders had a slight chance to quickly organize a reasonable defense with their remaining tanks and aircraft. There were seventy Chinese Shenjang J-8 attack aircraft resting on the tarmac of the base, and when the American shelling began, the Chinese planes took off and attacked the artillery firing on the airport. American F-15 Eagles and 18 Hornets responded and they attacked the enemy fighter planes. Spent shells, burning pieces of aircraft and exploding missiles, fell on the foot soldiers stationed below. Hundreds of the enemy soldiers were injured by the falling debris. When a damaged Chinese plane crashed into a squad of Marines, the rest of the soldiers pulled out of the area, moving much closer to the airport. Nine of the seventy seven American artillery pieces were destroyed by the attacking enemy planes.

The American Aircraft Carriers stationed off the north coast of Taiwan went into a major launch of their fighter and bomber aircraft, but they ran into and were being attacked by enemy fighters coming out of mainland China and or North Korea. Each Wing of aircraft basically neutralized the other, and the fight for the Taiwanese airport was boiling down to an outright ground war. The Americans held the upper hand though they were outnumbered three to one by the enemy aircraft. The ground fighting for the airport became more intense, with a large number of Apache and Super Cobra helicopters pressing the action.

The Third Marine Battalion was bogged down by a strong Chinese military presence, and they were receiving extremely heavy weapon fire. Three Apache fast attack helicopters came in low and strafed the enemy with 30 mm cannon fire. No sooner did the helicopters disappear to be refueled and rearmed, than a Wing of Chinese fighter aircraft came in from the mainland, and they began to attack the American troops attacking their soldiers.

The Chinese fighter aircraft caught the American 5th Infantry Mechanized units out in the open. Tanks and fighting machines were parked alongside the highway, and the enemy fighter planes attacked and came in and heavily chewed the American forces up. Nineteen Abrams tanks, twenty Bradley fighting machines, and thirty LAV-25s lay scattered about along the road, their crews lying where they fell in battle, charred black from the fires consuming their once mighty war machines. A grim testimony to what happens when any army's caught out in the open, and they are attacked by the enemy planes.

The Apache helicopters returned to the fight, but the enemy fighter aircraft attacked and picked them off rather easily. The fighting became a seesaw operation by both opposing forces. No sooner did the American troops take the upper hand in the action, than the Chinese fighters mounted a counter offensive, and they turned back the American gains. Then the Chinese forces were beaten back by an American counterattack. Most the fighting was now taking place in the northern section of the Island of Taiwan. The third American force ordered to attack the Chinese troops hitting the Taiwanese military base on the southern end of the Island. Was pulled back and then they were ordered to be held in reserve in case the enemy got the upper hand in the fighting for the Taiwanese main airport. The fighting was to be hard, nevertheless, the Americans did not expect it to be as bad as it was shaping up to being.

The Chinese forces stationed on the southern end of the Island were informed the American Army once heading directly their way, was pulled back. General Jiyun, ordered his troops in the south to mount up, and they headed for the north to help reinforce his other troops there. Twelve massive Ilyushin 11-76M transport planes, with fifty combat ready troops held inside them. Took off from the Kaohsiung International Airport, heading for the besieged CKS International Airport in northern Taiwan.

At the same moment the enemy transport planes took off from the southern tip of Taiwan in an attempt to split up the attacking American forces. They also launched a flotilla of troop ships from mainland China, armed with orders to head for the airbase stationed in northern Taiwan. These Chinese ships were loaded down with tanks and troops and military supplies, but half of the ships were also empty decoys. The largest ships were mostly empty, and they were to draw the overwhelming fire power of the American airforce when they attacked the convoys. A convoy of a thousand Chinese tanks and armored vehicles started out from Kaohsiung.

CHAPTER 38
ABOARD THE VINEGAR JOE PLATFORM; CODE NAMED IRON MOUNTAIN

General John White was hovering over General Edward Campanelli's shoulder, reading all the reports over his back as they poured into the CIC and mumbled. "It looks like the Chinese are going to use the CKS International Airport as their main battlefield. If we can destroy them here then there's a damn good chance the Chinese Command will be forced to sue for peace. They must know they're out gunned, and outflanked by now on the Island. I've been looking over the recent recon photos of China, and everything I seen, makes me believe the Chinese Command wouldn't be committing any further troops to the fighting for Taiwan, sir."

"You really think the Chinese would be willing to stop the fighting if you believe what takes place, happens sir?" General Campanelli complained.

"Look at the overall picture Eddy, if the Chinese command and their troops were going to continue fighting, they'd be moving a helluva lot more troops and equipment to the east coast for easier shipment to the fighting arena and their troops. I know that's what I'd be doing at least."

"You gave me something else to think about, John. If I commit my forces here, I know we can drive the Chinese troops back to the sea. But, if I stacked my forces up here, and the bastards attack my flank, I'd be forced to fight a two front war. You know what happens when an Army get trapped into fighting a two front war, they always lose. Remember John, China can reinforce their troops much easier than we can at the moment, sir. They're much closer to their main supply lines than we are. You sure you're not overlooking something here, buddy?"

"Eddy, I see no further Chinese troops being shipped out from the mainland to the coast for transit to the Island of Taiwan. Besides Eddy, there's many other problems facing China right now. Their youth are still rioting in Hong Kong and Beijing, and other major Chinese cities throughout their country, and the government's being forced to use more of their troops they have finally committed to try and stop some of the damn rioting. I saw some pictures, tanks are openly traveling the streets of both Peking and Beijing, and they're actually firing on the kids running wild on the streets. The Chinese police can't keep control over them, there's too many kids running around rioting. I think China's going to be pulled down from within if you ask me." General White offered and then stared at General Campanelli as if to enforce his thoughts.

General Campanelli stared back at his friend for a few moments before he replied, "John, you convinced me sir, and I'm gonna commit everything I have in order to crush the enemy troops we currently have trapped at the damn Taiwanese airport. I'm committing my reserves to action sir. I pray to Heaven you're right with your thoughts though, sir. I hate to commit these troops and they are unable to break the backs of the Chinese Troops, sir."

"I certainly am my friend," John replied in a flat tone to his Commanding Officer as he stared at him, and then offered a slight smile.

"Okay then John, I want you to order an attack flight up, use everything you need. Get those damn assault ships back here on the double quick and reloaded them. Use those flat barges we have and load the rest of the troops on them, and get them over to the Island of Okinawa, so they can be airlifted to Taiwan as needed. Use the big transports, what were they sir?"

"You mean employ the damn C-23s and C2-12 cargo aircraft, that's a good idea there sir." John offered to his Commander.

"We have to beat these bastards into the ground to get our point across to their asses, dammit. The more I think about it, the more I think you're right with these plans, sir. The Chinese are gonna use this fight as a test ground for our troops John, and if we beat them here, I think they'll want to stop the fighting across the board. I don't see them continuing the fighting if we're in a position to invade mainland China."

"Shit, you think we're going to have to invade the damn mainland of China, Eddy? I never entertained that thought, sir." John asked and offered with some concern.

"No way in hell, I don't have enough fricking troops or equipment in the region to successfully do that here, dammit. Think of the massive insult to the damn Chinese Command if we did pause to attack their stinking country. Even the die hard Communists will yell for the fighting in the region to stop, John."

The Vinegar Joe Platform suddenly shook violently under their feet.

"What the fuck was that shit?" John growled as he spun his head around towards the door.

"I'll tell you what that was, we were just hit by a fucking torpedo John." Campanelli said as both General's looked as if they could see through the wall.

Both men then made a mad dash out of the CIC Chamber and rushed topside to examine the damage to the Platform. General Campanelli ran in front of men trying to get out from below deck. Once on deck he quickly scanned the vast Platform surface, until he spotted smoke coming from the east side of the deck, and then ran in that direction. Before he got to the damaged area, he spotted Chief Kirby and he barked at him, "hey Kirby, how bad is it?"

Chief Kirby turned to see who was yelling at him now, spotting General Campanelli yelling at him, he replied in an angry voice, "they just hit the fucking latrine tanker, General. I'd be damn careful walking on the deck, sir. You might slip on the shit covering some of the deck and go down sir. The monkeys hit an Ocean Going Tug moored next to the shitter tanker. It was the extra one you called for. The Platform integrity's still intact, and I'm having the disabled latrine cut free so she can sink and not disturb the rest of the Platform operations, General."

General Campanelli stopped running and said while trying to catch his breath, "any chance of saving the damn thing, Chief?"

"No way in hell sir. The right side of the tanker's blown wide open, sir. Looks like the shit helped the force of the explosion some, General Campanelli."

"What the hell's going on with the dam sub that just hit us, Chief?" General Campanelli growled as he walked up to the weathered old man.

Chief Kirby pointed out to the sea to where a number of American warships was gathering.

General Campanelli looked in the direction the Chief pointed in, and he easily picked up three helicopters rapidly converging on a certain location. The helicopters hovered in the air for a few seconds as they dropped their sonar buoys in the water. Then, all three helicopters dropped torpedoes and then rapidly pulled back. Almost instantly there were three large explosions below the surface of the water, and then the bow of the destroyed Chinese submarine suddenly broke the surface for a brief second, before she slowly slid below the sea for the last time as smoke poured out of the water where the submarine just sank.

A voice on the ships intercom yelled out in a booming voice, "confirmed kill. One dead enemy submarine out there."

General Edward Campanelli was busy enjoying the fresh air until the breeze turned on him, and then he got a good whiff of the sewage from the destroyed latrine tanker. "Holy shit," he cried as he pinched his nose closed, and then asked. "How the hell are you ever going to clean up that mess, Chief?"

"Unholy shit you mean General Campanelli." Chief Kirby pointed to the fire control men busy spraying the deck down with salt water, "they'll get the stink off the deck quick enough sir."

"Any damage to the rest of the Platform, Kirby?" General Campanelli demanded to know.

"Dunno for sure quite yet General Campanelli Sir. I sent some divers over the side. If the Chinese submarine fired another torp, those poor bastards wouldn't have stood much of a chance to survive it, sir. Brave people we got us here sir."

Sergeant Willis came top side looking for the General, spotting him speaking with the Chief, he rushed over and announced, "sir, you have some reports coming in sir."

General Campanelli followed the young Sergeant below deck, and then he sat down and snapped, "give me the damn reports in the order they came in, Sergeant."

"This is the most important report that came through General Campanelli Sir. I'm afraid the Aircraft Carrier United States was just hit by a missile, sir."

"God dammit, what's the damage to her mister? How many casualties Sergeant?"

"We believe she was hit by a Chinese Silkworm missile, General Campanelli. The Carrier's out of business for now. She's in no danger of sinking, the missile hit the fantail, and the arresting wires are down. Thirty dead reported, three hundred hurt, the wounds run from broken arms, to minor burns to scratches. The Captain reports she'll be out of commission for at least nine hours. The Carrier Stennis is moving up alongside the States to intercept her returning aircraft, and lend a hand with her damage control at the same time, sir. There's a fire sir."

"Christ Almighty, where the hell did the missile come from, dammit Sergeant?"

"At first we thought the missile mighta come out from the mainland of China, sir. But the Destroyer John King detected a submarine signature off the east side of the Carrier before the hit, she's been working the contact ever since, sir. She'll get the damn thing if it's still out there General." The Sergeant reported with a slight smile.

"Phew, for a minute I thought I was going to be forced to attack the mainland. Next report."

"Sir, the LHD-4 Boxer's four miles from the coast of Taiwan, General Campanelli Sir."

"What's so fricking important about this one ship, Sergeant? I have many of my warships approaching the coast of Taiwan at this time, mister." General Campanelli asked him.

"The Boxer's a Wasp Class Assault ship, and she's carrying thirty five of the VMAO crafts."

"What the hell are they, mister? Do you have any specs on these new aircraft, Sergeant?"

"Yes Sir I certainly do General Campanelli Sir, I have the run up on them right here for you information, General. These aircraft's are supposed to replace the helicopter in our future plans. You were briefed on them before we came out to the Platform, sir."

General Campanelli rubbed his chin as he thought back and then responded, "yeah, yeah, I remember something about some kind of new aircraft that was going to replace our helicopters, refresh my memory for me Sergeant."

"Yes Sir General Campanelli Sir, the VMAO stand for Fixed Wing, Marine Attacked and Observation aircraft, sir. It's a smaller version of the tilt rotor craft much like the CV-22 Osprey you're currently employing as your personal transportation, sir. Armament reads out as one 30 mike mike Huges chain gun, a HPFC, helmet pointing fire control system. She's also equipped with tow, and side aim radar seeking, and Sidewinder air to air missiles, sir.

The aircraft has the new laser guided version of the Maverick missile, NTS, night targeting systems, with FLIR. That's the Forward Looking Infrared Sensors, sir. Laser designator/range finder with target auto tracking and video camera capabilities, sir. The laser designator gives the aircraft autonomous operation of the Hellfire missile system, General Campanelli Sir. This damn thing has everything on it, no wonder they expect this aircraft to replace the attack helicopters in our future, sir. How could it not sir." The Sergeant exclaimed in an excited tone.

General Campanelli took in the information without comment, and then he said, "is that all there is for me to be concerned with at this time, Sergeant?"

"No sir there's a little more sir, TAKs ship Corporal Louis J. Hauge Jr., the First Lieutenant Alexander Bonnyman Jr., Private First Class Eugene A. Obergon, the Private First Class Dewayne T. Williams, and the Staff Sergeant William R. Button, have also docked at the harbor in Haulien on the east coast of Taiwan, General. This makes our job much easier to accomplish sir, these five ships have equipment and a thirty day supplies for a full Marine Amphibious Brigade. We're currently unloading these ships on a hard harbor surface, which enables us to unload much faster than on the floating docks, General Campanelli Sir. This is the first squadron of the three, which are known as the Midnight Squadron. The report also states the second squadron of four other TAK ships were presently preparing to dock in the same region as the other ships are being unloaded, and once this is accomplished.

"We'll have enough military equipment and troops stationed on the Island of Taiwan to overpower the enemy forces there, and it'll give us one hell of a head start if we have to invade the mainland of China in the coming days, General Campanelli Sir. The third squadron of TAK ships are presently waiting one hundred miles off the east coast of Taiwan, sir. Once the first squadron's completely unloaded, the third squadron will move in and unload, sir. We're about ready for anything we might come across, we're better equipped than we were for the entire Middle East war, General Campanelli Sir."

"I hope to hell we can come to some kind of conclusion before and if we're forced to attack the damn mainland of China, mister. I hate to have to think about the number of troops we're gonna lose if we go into China to try and settle this mess, mister." General Campanelli mumbled just loud enough to be heard by the Sergeant.

"I hear you sir. Any word on how the meeting between our people, and the Chinks are going?" The Sergeant asked his Commanding Officer

"Dunno for sure, the last I heard there were no further talks scheduled to go on at all. I guess not enough kids on either side have lost their lives so far, for the asses in Command to sue for peace. It's the kids who pick up the stinking tab for the assholes who can't get along as always, Sergeant. When is it gonna ever end, dammit?" General Campanelli asked no one in particular in the CIC as he let out his breath in a disgusted sigh.

On the Island of Taiwan, a full Marine Company was cut off from the main support troops, and the Marines were forced to dig in and wait for reinforcements to arrive. The cut off troops were from the 2nd battalion, the 27th Marines. Echo Company was bogged down for over an hour, and the Captain in Command knew he had to do something about it, or his men were going to be slaughtered needlessly if all hell broke out before them. They were pinned down by horrendous enemy counter fire. Captain Ross sneaked a quick peak over the stone wall separating the Marines from the enemy troops, trying to get a good fix on them. He was careful, moments before his Sergeant had his head blown off doing the same thing.

The Marine Captain's eyes burned from the fear caused sweat, and his uniform stained red with his First Sergeant's blood and brains matter. Captain Ross wiped at the sweat running in his eyes as he stared over the stone wall. He saw a large group of enemy troops rapidly massing just two hundred yards away from his current position. The loud crackle of small arms fire, and the echo of exploding hand grenades filled the air. The Captain turned to the M-60 machine gun setup, it was hammering away at the cautiously advancing enemy soldiers.

Many attacking enemy soldiers fell dead in a vain attempt to try and carry out their last orders. The upset Captain looked at the dead piling up quickly. The eyes bothered him the most, the eyes of the dead never closed peacefully like in the movies. They stared out dumbly, or with a fright you could never forget for the rest of your life. The pained expressions on the bodies were to terrible to put to words.

The Marine Captain looked over the so called no man's land commonly referred to as the Buddha Zone, separating the two enemy forces. The frontal assaults by both sides had been beaten back, until neither side held the upper hand in the battle. The troops on both sides were locked in a stalemate situation. A grotesque pile of twisted bodies and torn limbs, spotted the ground between the two opposing Armies. It reminded the Marine Captain of the pictures he witnessed of the Jewish bodies piled up in the Nazi concentration camps of World War Two. He pulled back behind the stone wall and took time to light up a cigarette.

Every once in a while, a loud, eerie, nerve wracking horrifying wail, would rise up from within the broken large pile of the interwoven mass of humanity lying on the ground slowly bleeding to death. Informing the surviving fighting men and women from both sides that there were soldiers still alive in the masses, and they were suffering terribly from a slow and very agonizing death before their eyes.

The heavy machine guns opened up again, with long streaks of tracers crisscrossing the open area of no man's land. Flakes of hot gun powder landed on the Corporal's finger, and it burned him as he continued to fired his weapon. The spent shells were landing all around his feet. The Captain checked the area a second time with his night vision glasses, and was unable to pick up any enemy troop positions and he growled at his machine gunners, "What the fuck are you damn birds shooting at, cease fire for the love of God."

It took a second, but they finally stopped firing at what the Captain believed was nothing.

Captain Ross quickly made his way over to the gun and said to the operator of the weapon. "Corporal, whaddaya got going on out there mister?"

"I just saw something move and thought it might be some enemy shits trying to infiltrate our lines, Captain Ross Sir." The Corporal then pointed fifty yards ahead of him, as he adjusted his gloves with the missing fingers. The Captain quickly scanned the area with his night vision field glasses again, and saw nothing out of the ordinary moving, and then he replied in a snap at the young soldier. "Okay Corporal, you did well this time."

He was just humoring the scared Corporal as he added, "I want you to move your gun a hundred feet down to the left, I got the other gun moving fifty feet up to his right side, Corporal."

"Why is that Captain?" the Corporal asked as he stared at the captain with questioning eyes.

"Just do as I say, the move could save you your damn ass for ya, you just marked the weapon position out for the enemy gunners, mister." The Captain grumbled at the Corporal.

On the other side of no man's land, a Chinese Lieutenant smiled as he lowered his night vision glasses, happy as he made a mental note where the two enemy machine gun nests were positioned on the enemy lines. The Lieutenant knew it was a good idea to allow the Private to chuck a rock out into the death zone. He wanted to see if it would draw any enemy fire, and it worked out as he thought it would. He began to devise a plan on where and how to send his troops out, so the bulk of them would be out of range of the heavy machine guns setups. The Chinese Lieutenant mumbled at himself, 'stupid Americans to give your position away like this'. The Chinese Officer had no way of knowing his American counterpart had the two weapons already moved to different position, just for the reason he devised.

An American soldier from the ranks suddenly fired at the pile of bodies, attempting to silence the screams, and take the wounded soldier out of his misery. Soldiers accepted they might die on the battlefield, they could only hope the death that stalked them, would be quick and merciful. No soldier wanted to die slowly with out dignity. A wounded soldier would much rather be killed by a buddy then left to die in the mud created by his own blood. Soft moaning and the occasional agonized scream soon replace some of the weapon fire. A cry for a medic rose from a voice being choked by his own blood.

The Captain decided he would put an end to this checkmate, and reached for his radio. He felt too many of his soldiers were dying while they waited for a breakout attack to be ordered. He suppressed the button and then ordered, "Oak Tree, Ready, Ready, Zero, Zero, Three to air cap. Brass Monkey, I repeat, Brass Monkey. I need a Ground Pounder down here on the double quick, sir. Over."

Brass Monkey was a priority communication call for help, mostly used by the pilots. It usually got an immediate response from any aircraft patrolling the area. It was SOP for assistance.

Tinsel Town immediately responded to the emergency call. "Roger Brass Monkey request, Oak Tree. Do you wish emergency extraction, sir?" The Commander of the AWACS asked.

"Negative on that extraction request, too many of us down here to be extracted safely by air, sir." The ground Commander replied.

"I copy that Oak Tree, I already diverted a number of birds, and they're on the way to your present position, sir. You're ordered to switch over to the second net and pop off some green smoke when you spot the incoming birds, Captain." The Tinsel Town Commander broke off the communication with the Ground Commander and then he offered.

"Tinsel Town to Ramble Flight Leader. You and the birds with you are needed for a fast run for bogged down ground troops, switch over to second net sir, and respond to Oak Tree's Brass Monkey call on the double quick, sir. Over."

Aleksandra was in Command of Ramble Flight, and she immediately switched over to her second radio net and then responded in the mike. "Air Cap Ramble Flight. This is Twin

Peak Leader, with three Trailers. I hear good Brass Monkey call sir."

She checked the call name to make certain it was some of their troops calling for help. Once she checked her paperwork she knew it was Captain Ross, and he was in charge of a Company of Marines whose job was to clear out the southern end of the compound. "All Ground Pounder (A-6 Intruders) engaged. Twin Peak and Trailers respond. Give attack coordinate sir. Over."

"Who is this, a fucking bitch pilot? Over." The Captain growled angrily before he thought about what he was saying, and then he added to his bitch at the female pilot, "mine and my troop's lives are going to depend on a bitch pilot, dammit!"

"I female pilot if that what you mean by you remark, Oak Tree Commander. I need you attack coordinate immediately Oak Tree. Over sir."

"Jesus H. Christ, if this don't beat it all to hell and back again, dammit. A fucking bitch pilot now offering to come to my troop's damn assistance. Are you any good, lady pilot? I have ground troops down here, and I don't want any of them KFF (Killed by Friendly Fire) if you don't know what the hell you're doing up there, sister." The upset Captain hissed in the mike with as much venom as he could possible muster in his voice.

"Twin Peak, this is Mastercard. Let's leave this stupid asshole down there in his own shit and see how he makes out. He needs no help from us, honey. He has his man troops to help him get out of his trouble with the enemy soldiers. It must have been a mistake for him to bother to call us for help, Twin Peaks. Hell, all of a sudden I believe I'm having some radio trouble, and I can't communicate with the troops in question operating on the damn ground. Leave his damn ass down there so he can suck air and chew on enemy rounds."

"Enough shit from you Mastercard. Get off net so I communicate with ground troop again." Aleksandra snapped at her and then she went back to the Captain on the ground. "Twin Peak to Oak Tree Command. Here what I want you do big mouth man soldier you. Drop you pants, bend over and spread cheek wide as can possible. Then let know when ready, and I will find you sir. Then I place my missile right up you damn ass for you, you narrow minded Neanderthal bastard you. Will this prove you how good I am to you foolish mind? Over."

The Marine Captain snarled right back into the radio in an extremely angry tone of voice at the female pilot busting his horns, "you better watch your fucking step with me, Missy. I happen to be a fucking Captain in the Marine Corps, and I could have your ass for god damn supper if I decide to come after it on you..."

"And I Captain am Major, need you attack coordinate right now, Oak Tree Command. If want run to support you troops, we oblige you request sir. If no, get off air, I sure someone else need us help, and I sure they no care we female pilots at all, SIR. It you men die down there, not my pilot fault, Oak Tree Command. Over sir."

"Yeah, okay, right, you win this fucking round I guess, lady pilot. Here's your attack coordinates, get it right the first time around, Ma'am. The target grid's Delta, Delta, Yankee One, Seven, Foxtrot. I repeat, your target area's Delta, Delta, Yankee Seven, One, Foxtrot. It's a tight area down here, so watch out for my men on the damn ground, Ramble Flight. I'm marking out the area to be attacked by your aircraft with green smoke. I repeat, anything marked by your attack computer out of the green smoke area is to be destroyed.

Over." The Captain roared in his radio as he looked up to try and locate the aircraft, before they began their run on the enemy troops pinning his soldiers down.

Aleksandra totally ignored the Captain's insolence aimed at her as she replied to the ground Captain. "Target area as follow, Delta, Delta, Yankee, One, Seven Foxtrot, Oak Tree. Anything locate out of green smoke area is to be destroyed. Is right as repeat to you sir. Over sir."

"Correct as read back Ramble Flight Leader. Good luck and keep in mind I have troops skin close to the fucking enemy targets down here. Over." The Captain replied in haste to her.

"Tell you man babies keep head down low, we commence attack run now sir. By way for you information, my Wing all female pilots, sir. Out."

"Great! That's just fucking dandy. That's all I needed to make my damn day, a bunch of bitch pilots. Out." The Captain moaned into the radio as he shook his head angry at the female pilot.

Aleksandra was the lead attacking aircraft, she lowered the nose of her YF-27 as set her attack with Hellfire missiles for use against the enemy tanks her attack computer picked up on the ground. She spotted a lone Russian made T-69 tank, as it made its way for the safety of a building. She lit the tank up with her laser designator, and then fired at it. She was lining up a second tank when the first one exploded in death. On her first pass, she successfully killed four enemy tanks inside the compound, and then she cleared the hilltop as she climbed into the sky with Nightlife starting her pass at the enemy equipment and soldiers.

As her aircraft climbed, she suddenly belched in her oxygen mask. Marking the first time in her life she ever done this, and she smiled as she leveled off, and then prepared for a cannon pass against the enemy troops on the ground.

Nightlife was done with her pass now, and Voyeur started her attack, with Flasher lining up directly behind her to wait for her chance to attack the enemy troops. Now, it was Sleeper's turn to attack. Sleeper lowered the nose of her aircraft, and headed for the enemy troops. She was firing her 30 mm when her aircraft suddenly exploded in a ball of fire, and it somersaulted out of control towards the earth. She did not get out of the dead plane.

Aleksandra's stomach turned as she watched the remains of the damaged aircraft quickly disintegrate while in flight, and then tumble and crash into the ground. The dead plane was obviously hit by a ground to air missile, and she cursed as her hand tightened on the self centering control stick of her aircraft. The female Major intensely searched the ground for the possible shooter, while keeping her eyes open for any other enemy targets of opportunity. The American fighter planes made a number of passes over the enemy positions, and in less than ten minutes, killed nineteen tanks and armored vehicles, and strafed the foot soldiers. The heavier fire from the enemy side had all but stopped, and only some sporadic small arms fire continued.

The Wing of American fighter planes then moved to a standoff position and watched as the Marines moved out, only moving in when the Marines came across a machine gun nest and they requested help from the pilots. Most ground fighting was drawing to a quick conclusion, as the Chinese forces finally gave up fighting. Some, chose to disappear into the landscape to start a guerrilla war on their own against the American soldiers, or to wait until they could finally sneak safely back to China. The American soldiers were enjoying complete air superiority because most Chinese aircraft allotted to the invasion of Taiwan. Was either destroyed, or the pilots removed their aircraft from the fighting arena in an attempt of trying to save their aircraft for future engagement of the American aircraft or ground soldiers.

The Marines and fighter pilots had no idea of what was happening in the middle of the Island of Taiwan though and were not that concerned either. All they knew was their reinforcements had not made it to the airbase as yet.

ON THE FREEWAY BETWEEN
CHANGHUA AND HSINYING

The Chinese Commander General Deng Jiyun, was stationed with his tanks and armored vehicles heading north to relieve his forces under attack by the American forces at the Taiwanese CKS International Airport. In his column of troops and vehicles, the General had two thousand troops, and three hundred and fifty tanks and armored vehicles. He was proud to be in Command of such an overpowering force of soldiers and war machines.

The Chinese General looked off to his left side as the flight of Ilyushin transport planes airlifted more of his troops up to the besieged airport in the north. He smiled proudly as the massive aircraft lumbered in the sky. Soon, they were out of sight, and he settled down for the long drive over the Freeway to the airport. He was in a Chinese armored command vehicle YW-701A. It was a surprisingly smooth ride, at speeds of nearly fifty mph.

General Jiyun thought of the tankers being pounded around inside their tanks at this high rate of speed. His thoughts were suddenly turned towards the sky when his Second in Command suddenly pointed to a thick black column of smoke raising to the heavens just ahead of them, in the direction the transport planes had just disappeared in.

THE FLIGHT OF ILYUSHIN 11-76 M
CANDIDS HEADING NORTH

The massive Russian built transport aircraft the Chinese troops were employing for their needs, made their way towards the Taiwan International Airport at five hundred mph. Each aircraft contained over two hundred and fifty troops. They traveled at a height of forty five thousand feet to conserve fuel, and also be out of the attack zone for the American fighter aircraft. The pilots had no fear of being attacked on this side of the Island of Taiwan.

The American fighter planes sent in from the Aircraft Carrier Carl Vinson, hooked up with fighter aircraft launched from the Carrier Lincoln, and then they grouped up and went after the enemy transport planes. The American fighter aircraft were informed of the location, height and exact speed of the enemy transport planes by the AWACS aircraft known as Tinsel Town. The American aircraft flew over the mountain range running right up the center of the Island, so they could attack the enemy transports without being detected by them until it was too late for them to evade their attack. The fighter planes paralleled the transports then quickly closed in for the kill.

Space Invader was lead American fighter aircraft, he controlled the rest of the twenty four F/A 18 D Hornet American fighter planes that made up his Flight Wing. He ordered twelve of his aircraft up to attack the enemy aircraft from the sun, while the second wave of aircraft were going to attack from below the enemy transport craft. The Ilyushin's were being accompanied by eight Chinese fighter planes, the American aircraft from above were ordered to target the enemy fighters. The Wing of aircraft flying below the enemy aircraft started their attack, firing at the engines of the massive enemy transport warplanes, in an effort to put the enemy aircraft out of commission.

When the Chinese aircraft realized they were being attack by a Wing of American fighters. The Chinese fighter aircraft moved around to try and defend the huge troop transport planes, and they were caught by the American aircraft attacking the enemy aircraft from above, when the enemy fighter planes committed to their defense. The enemy fighters were easily killed off or quickly disabled on the first pass, and then the American aircraft turned their attention against the large aircraft and easily picked off the unarmed transport planes at will.

All the air action was taking place right over the Formosa Straits, and instead of going down in the water. The damaged transport planes tried to limp back to mainland China. Some transports did not get the message, and four of them went down in the water, and one exploded while in flight, leaving a large, black smudge in the sky.

THE SCIENTIFIC COMPOUND IN HSINCHU

Captain Ross intensely watched as the American support fighter aircraft quickly disappeared in the morning sky, and then they held position in their assigned standoff points. The Marine Captain had to admit he was thoroughly impressed by the flying capabilities of the female pilots who just came to his and his troop's aide, but he knew he would never tell them so. His Marines were cautiously climbing out of their hiding places, and then slowly moving out and checking the status of the enemy troops, and summing up the effects of the attack runs by the American fighters. Everywhere the soldiers looked, they discovered the bodies of the enemy soldiers killed by the attacking aircraft.

A flight of the new VMAO hovercraft came in low, and they immediately took position over the Marine Units. The planes were so agile and light they were easily able to pick out a single enemy ground soldier and take him out. The Marines walked through all the carnage, the large T-69 main battle tanks weighing over fifty four tons, were spewed about like a child's discarded toys, massive turrets were decapitated from the steal bodies of their tanks and lay on their sides. Some tanks were actually split open almost in half, as if they were hit by some enormous ax, wheeled by an unseen giant on the battlefield.

The Chinese armored vehicles fared no better on the battlefield as they laid about, ripped wide open like a can of sardines. Bodies, no longer recognized as human beings, were flung about like abandoned cord wood, burned black by burning fuel. Enemy foot soldiers were obviously cut down right in mid stride, and they now lay about on the ground like old rag dolls thrown around in a sudden windstorm. Surviving Chinese troops dragged their feet on the ground in a stunned stupor, no longer looking like the proud soldiers they once were. Oblivious to the Marine's presence as they searched the bodies of the dead for their missing brothers and friends who might still be alive in all the carnage.

The enemy soldiers uniforms hung from their shoulders in tatters, some were actually burned onto their skin. Arms hung broken on their bodies, with gaping bullet wounds bleeding freely, as the once proud enemy soldiers walked around the once battlefield. The will to fight was burned and blasted out of their bodies and minds. The enemy were in such a state of shock and confusion they did not even raise their hands when ordered to do so by the Marines, and they offered no resistance when the Marines stripped and then searched the daze soldiers for any possible concealed weapons. They merely walked in the direction the Marines pushed them in. The Captain mumbled aloud, "Christ, now I know what the gates of hell must look like."

Some American Marines killed the badly wounded enemy soldiers, who were beyond any possible medical help, and they were merely suffering until death slowly wrapped its icy fingers around their souls. The fighting was intense as artillery, mortars and aircraft continued to tear apart the enemy forces controlling the Taiwanese civilian airport. The eyes of the soldiers from both sides, burned from the cordite hanging heavy in the air, and adding to this was the blinding smoke of burning rubber, metal and wire from the tanks and human flesh. Hundreds of columns of smoke rose many feet in the air, each marking the death of a tank, or an armored vehicle.

Tank rounds and heavy machine gun shells cooked off inside the massive burning war machines. Sending shrapnel and lead flying through the air at twice the speed of sound. It was a terrible sight to witness for the American soldiers, forming lasting scars that would haunt these children for the rest of their lives.

The Marines had no idea of the absolute destruction of the enemy forces occurring on the Sunyat Sen Freeway between the two Taiwan cities of Changhua and Hsinying. The Aircraft Carriers, Lincoln and Vinson launched again, sending a hundred fighter planes of different kinds after this column of enemy soldiers still intact. The Vinegar Joe Platform launched seventy F/A 18 Hornets and YF-27 Vultures to join the attack on the enemy soldiers.

The first thing the Chinese troops saw was the black smudge of smoke in the sky where the American planes killed the massive Chinese troop transport aircraft. General Jiyun yelled at his troops to prepare for an air attack, because he quickly realized this black smoke marring the air was one of his transport planes exploding while in flight, obviously the attackers of the transport aircraft would be quickly coming after them next.

The Chinese foot soldiers did not fare as well as the transport aircraft did, they were caught completely out in the open with not much cover available for them to hide behind. The first flight of attacking American fighter aircraft closed in and attacked the leading elements of the column of enemy troops, tanks and trucks trapped on the open road. These pilots knew what they were doing, and they hit the lead tanks, and then the tanks and trucks in the rear of the column, effectively bringing all movement of the enemy column to a complete standstill, and enabling the fighter aircraft to pick and choose their targets at will.

Very few American pilots decided to use their cannons on the running troops, the war for these soldiers was effectively over with, and any further slaughter of these Chinese troops would only serve to add resolve to the surviving enemy soldiers. However, the tanks and other military equipment were still fair game, and they were attacked without mercy.

Another Highway of Death was rapidly being created, much like the one that occurred in Kuwait during the Operation Desert Storm War with Iraq on their Highway 8. Rockets, cluster bombs along with hundreds of five hundred pounders and laser guided two thousand pound smart bombs, ripped into the stalled Chinese column of steel trapped on the Freeway at a horrendous rate. The Chinese Army had nowhere to go to try and save themselves from this fierce attack being aimed against them by the American aircraft.

Chinese Commanders were forced to watch in stone silence as their tanks exploded like a thunderstorm into burning, flying metal, tearing into the trapped soldiers bodies. Parts of bodies were hurtled high in the air, as the American warplanes made pass after murderous pass over their stalled columns of enemy troops and military equipment.

The deafening roar coming from the passing American aircraft, and the manmade thunder from the countless exploding bombs and missiles, combined with the shattering enemy tanks. Were quickly replaced by another high pitched sound of war. The sound of the dying soldiers, screaming out in terrible pain, and with fear as the once proud Chinese soldiers slowly burned to death inside their iron and now steel flaming coffins.

The Supreme Commander of Chinese Forces was in one of the armored cars stalled near the front of the column. He was out of his vehicle watching the rapid death of his once proud and mighty Army and their war machines. A tank not thirty feet from him, suddenly exploded in a crackling ball of sparks and flames, as the T-69 war machine was instantly turned into a heap of scrap iron right before his eyes. The stunned Chinese General received some minor cuts and burns from the flying shrapnel, but he never flinched an inch as he glared at the death and destruction being leveled on his soldiers. His stomach actually turned as he realized he was hit by a spray of blood, bone and brain manner, he looked to where the tank once stood, and through all the flames and smoke, he could see a red mist staining the air, and he immediately understood this was once one of his men just killed in this attack against his tank.

The extremely angry Chinese General had enough and then turned his eyes up towards the sky as six American fighter planes sliced through the smoke filled air, and he cursed them to hell with a roar. His curses were not only aimed at the American warplanes flying off in the distance after they unloaded their bomb loads of his trapped soldiers. The General cursed his Chairman and government, for allowing his troops to be slaughtered on this miserable road in such masses.

His eyes quickly searched the sky until he spotted a second wave of fix winged enemy planes as they began their attack on his trapped troops and equipment. He tried to mentally will them away, but they still came right at his troops. He was completely helpless to stop any of this terrible slaughter, because his anti-aircraft weapons lay twisted and burnt beyond any use to his troops. He cursed the Americans because they knew what to go after first. He watched the wing of aircraft approaching, his mouth dropped open when the second wave of American aircraft suddenly stopped their devastating attack on his column, and they suddenly pulled back to a standoff position, and then the aircraft began to orbit the area.

The Chinese General quickly realized what this meant to him and his soldiers. He reached inside his APC (Armored Personnel Carrier) for the radio. He ordered his soldiers not to fire on the approaching American warplanes. The General decided to try and save at least some of his troops from the terrible slaughter being delivered by the attacking American warplanes.

It was good the American pilots grew tired of the horrible killing, and they requested permission to back off their attack on the trapped Chinese troops and military equipment from their Command. It was immediately given by General Campanelli, and the American warplanes took to orbiting a certain area of the enemy column. The American aircraft took out any surviving anti-aircraft guns during this low in the heavy fighting, by flooding the area with targets. The fighter planes crisscrossed right in front of the stalled ZSU-23-4 Shilka's.

The Shilka's radar became confused when it tried to lock onto one target, as a second target entered its range, and the gun would then try to go after this newer and more threatening target, considering it a more immediate threat to the tank. Then a third fix wing aircraft would come in and kill the Shilka. The American pilots did this time and time again, when they came across another surviving Shilka or active missile attack systems.

After three hours of attacking the enemy column, the fighting started to wind down, an occasional fighter aircraft would fire off a missile and hit a tank or truck trying to climb over the corpse of another destroyed enemy vehicle. In an attempt to try and escape the guarded ring surrounding the once great Chinese column of war machines and soldiers.

There was little if any return fire now coming from the surviving trapped Chinese troops. Because they fully understood any further firing at the marshalling American aircraft, would bring an immediate retaliation response from the fighter planes constantly circling over their heads. The Chinese troops chose not to fire on the American warplanes, and they realized they would be allowed to live. Three American planes flew over the full length of the stalled column of enemy tanks and war equipment, some of the once war machines had been turned on their sides. While others rested lying on their turrets, destroyed, and no longer looked threatening. The once massive harbingers of death and destruction, were now reduced to nothing more than piles of twisted and blackened steel.

Most American pilots grew sad over the terrible amount of death covering the road below their orbiting aircraft. Any human being with a conscious had to be affected by the horrible sight they witnessed. Secondary explosions continued to dot the broken column of Chinese troops and armor, as smoke made it dangerous for the fighter aircraft to get any closer to the trapped column. Suddenly, a pilot noticed the advance Units of Marines and Army personnel coming down the South Cross Island Highway, and onto the Sunyat-Sun Freeway. The second American Army came down the Freeway from the Central Cross Island Highway.

The lead pilot of the flight 'Why Me' notified the advancing American Armies the fighting was finished. The planes stayed in the air, and circled over the American troops to provide air cover and ground support for their advancing troops. The pilots watched as the two American Armies quickly converged on the all but destroyed Chinese column.

Two M-60 Blackhawk helicopters suddenly showed up from out of nowhere, they were from the Psy Ops section of the Army, and they were screaming in loud speakers in Chinese. For the defeated Chinese soldiers to lay down their weapons, and they would be well treated by their captors. It was ear piercing to say the least, and the American Colonel had to actually cover his ears with his hands to avoid the screaming coming from the hovering helicopter.

Colonel Richard Morgan was in the lead American personnel carrier, and upon viewing all the appalling carnage created by the American warplanes. He reached for his radio and called. "Medics to the front of the line, STAT." He then replaced the radio and poked his head outside the APC.

He looked around until he spotted a Chinese officer standing by a few of his stunned men. He knew right off he was an officer by the sword he had hanging from his hip.

Colonel Morgan climbed the rest of the way out of his APC and then jumped down to the crushed shell road surface. Six other American Officers quickly joined him, along with a few armed guards. Colonel Morgan walked towards the Chinese Officer.

The Chinese General spotted the American land forces coming at his troops from down the Sunyat-Sun Freeway, and knew all was lost to him and his troops. He moved to the front of his destroyed column to await his American counterpart to reach him. The exhausted General was relieved the fighting was over as far as he was concerned. He had enough killing to last him a life time. His Second in Command ordered his troops not to shoot at the American soldiers approaching their position on the highway.

As the General waited for the American Officers to come up to him, he could not help but think if things would have been different. If he was supplied with enough reinforcements of troops and the replacement of his destroyed war machines from the mainland of China. He then shrugged over this thought as he mumbled to himself angrily, "such is the fate of all wars and soldiers."

General Jiyun watched patiently as a sharp looking American Officer dismounted from the LAC-25 armored vehicle, and then he walked towards him as if he owned the world. Both officers took a second to view the destruction of the Chinese troops and war machines, which were reduced to mere rubble and leaving over one thousand troops, and fifteen tanks still alive and in working order.

Colonel Morgan stopped walking and snapped to attention and then saluted the Chinese Officer and offered to the Chinese Commander. "Sir, my name is Colonel Richard Morgan, would my medics be of any service to you and your troops, sir?" Somehow, Colonel Morgan knew this Chinese Officer could speak English just by the way he was standing and waiting for him, he could just see it written in his face as he waited for the officer's reply.

As the General lowered his hand, he bowed slightly towards the American Colonel as he replied. "Greatly Colonel Morgan, and my name is General Deng Jiyun Sir, and as you can see, I have many wounded soldiers here sir. I gave the order, and there'll be no further trouble or fighting from my troops, sir. I thank you for your concern Colonel Sir." Again the Chinese General bowed as he clicked his heels together and he offered the American Colonel his sword.

The American Officer pulled out his canteen, and then he offered the once enemy General a drink. But General Jiyun refused the offer as he said, "I have plenty of water, I just worry about my wounded men, sir."

"General Jiyun Sir, my medics are good, damn good in their craft as a matter of fact, sir. I also have two mobile field hospitals in my column, sir. I assure you General Jiyun Sir, your troops will be well cared for, sir." Again, the American Colonel offered the Chinese General his canteen as he offered to the other military officer. "Here you go General, you sure look like you could use something a little stronger than just plain water, sir."

The wise Colonel Morgan knew exactly what he was doing. He was trying to gain the Chinese Officer's trust. He also knew if the once enemy officer trusted him then he would be all the more ready to talk, and inform him of the General's Command Structure and strength.

The Chinese Officer smiled as he took the offered canteen and then took a good pull from it. The two officers then settled down and watched the American soldiers quickly set up the mobile field hospitals right in the middle of the Freeway. Some Chinese soldiers watching the American soldiers struggle with the inflatable tents, instantly moved forward and they pitched in and helped them set up the makeshift hospitals. At that instant, it seemed like all the hostilities left the bodies of the soldiers from both sides.

Both officers relaxed a bit as they watched the once enemies pitch in to help the wounded soldiers from both sides. After a while, Colonel Morgan turned to General Jiyun and offered, "General Jiyun Sir, I'm afraid you'll have to accompany me back to my headquarters, sir. There's many questions that needed to be answered, sir."

General Jiyun did not reply, he merely gave a last quick look at his troops, and how they were being treated by the American doctors and victors and then he remarked, "Yes Colonel Morgan Sir, I shall accompany you back to your headquarters, sir. I must thank you kindly for the way you and your soldiers are helping with my wounded soldiers, sir." General Jiyun then saluted the once enemy Colonel, and they walked towards the Colonel's waiting APC. Seconds later, they were both heading north, with an escort of two tanks and four fighter planes.

CHAPTER 39
COLONEL JOSEPH SALSICCIA'S FIELD HEADQUARTERS STATIONED IN THE TAIWANESE SCIENTIFIC COMPOUND AT HSINCHU

The fast moving APC carrying the Chinese Military Officer finally arrived at the American Command Headquarters within two hours traveling time. Once the Chinese General was introduced to Colonel Joseph Salsiccia, the Colonel realized who he had in his custody. The General in Command of all Chinese Ground Forces in Taiwan. Colonel Salsiccia shook his hand as he said to him. "General Deng

Jiyun, I'm pleased to meet you sir. General Jiyun, I thank you for choosing to end the fighting, and the useless dying of soldiers from both sides, sir."

The Chinese Commanding Officer bowed again towards the American Colonel, he did not expect to be treated so well by the American Officer. General Jiyun began his conversation off with the Colonel, by offering to call a truce on the entire Island of Taiwan, and then he added to his words, "but I shall make this offer to a General I have heard so much about during this confrontation between our troops, sir. Your General Edward Campanelli, sir."

Colonel Joseph Salsiccia instantly excused himself from the Chinese General's presence, and he immediately notified General Campanelli of the truce offering, and of his prisoner he had in custody. The deal was struck over the radio, and General Campanelli informed General Jiyun himself that he was on his way to Taiwan to meet with him. General Jiyun was lead over to a field radio, where he ordered his soldiers to lay down their arms immediately, and to wait until American soldiers directed them as to what to do next.

The Chinese Commander further ordered all Chinese tanks and armored vehicles were to open their hatches. The tanks were ordered to aim their cannons in the air, and warned any tanks found with their hatches closed, or its gun held level, would be considered still hostile and instantly fired upon. All Chinese artillery pieces were to have their breaches removed, and their guns leveled and broken down. All Chinese troops were ordered to assemble on open roads, and to wait until American forces came across them. They were to stack their weapons in the open, and were to be unarmed when the American forces approached them. Any Chinese soldier found with a weapon on his person, would be considered breach of truce, and he could be fired on.

Once these orders were transmitted to the Chinese troops still operational in the field, Colonel Salsiccia offered the Chinese Officer a cup of tea.

General Jiyun understood this was the American Officer who stopped his troops from firing on his beaten and trapped soldiers, and he thanked him for sparing the lives of his soldiers.

Colonel Salsiccia smiled at the Chinese General as he replied to his thanks, "what the hell purpose would it have served to annihilate all your troops needlessly, General Jiyun? I know if the tables were turned, and my troops were ready to be slaughtered, you surely would've shown the same compassion, and held your men in check and didn't slaughter my soldiers to the last, sir. After all General Jiyun, we're soldiers, not murderers."

The two once enemy military officers settled back to await General Edward Campanelli's arrival at their field headquarters. The tea General Jiyun was sipping on, was laced with a diluted solution of sodium pentothal. The Chinese General would be much more talkative when General Campanelli finally showed up, and he began questioning him. In a slight stupor, General Jiyun might not understand he was being questioned about his war making abilities.

IN THE FIGHTER PLANE FLOWN BY TWIN PEAKS

Aleksandra's aircraft quickly climbed up to forty two thousand feet, while heading for her Exxon station hovering in the sky. As she carefully approached the massive in flight refueling tanker, she notified the pilot her weapons were set on safety. She was immediately given permission to approach and then linkup to the tanker and refuel her warplane. While she was refueling, she was hit by a sudden wave of gas, she could not help herself and she farted and then belched at the same time. She also began to fell a little light headed. She checked her oxygen reserves and level, she had over forty percent oxygen left and that was plenty for her until she returned to the Platform. She blew into the mask to make certain the valve was opening and closing properly. It was working fine. She still could not understand why she was suddenly having this trouble.

Once her aircraft was refueled, she disconnected for the feed then dropped down, not waiting for the rest of her Flight Wing to finish with their refueling. She convinced herself she was heading down to protect the mud walkers on the ground, but she wanted to get lower to see if this would help her feel any better. She felt slightly better below thirty five thousand feet.

Her stomach started to settle down some, and her light headedness lessened. She could not help but wonder if there was something suddenly wrong with her oxygen system on board her aircraft. She made a mental note to include this in her gripe list to the flight crew for checking when she landed on the Platform. She was on level flight at twenty three thousand feet heading for the northern end of the Island of Taiwan. When she suddenly got severely sick to her stomach again, but far worse than the first time.

She had to actually pull her oxygen mask off as she threw up on her lap, and all over the lower instrument panel of her warplane. She heaved and then spat the terrible aftertaste out of her mouth. She snapped her oxygen mask back on and took three quick, deep breaths in an attempt to get the oxygen level back up in her body. She was getting really concerned now, and she was worried she might have had been attacked with some kind of chemical or biological agent.   There was a red warning flashed about possible Chemical Warfare waged against the American forces in the Chinese troops started to lose the war. She searched the sky for her Wing Person, she spotted her off to her portside of the aircraft and cried in her radio to her.

"Twin Peaks to Nightlife. Come in. I have slight problem here please. Over."

The tone in her voice instantly informed the second female pilot something was seriously wrong with her Wing Leader as she replied to her call, "yeah, this is Nightlife, Twin Peaks. Go ahead with your traffic Twin Peaks. What do you have on your mind honey?   What's your problem sweetheart?   Are you having some trouble with your aircraft? Are you losing fuel or suffering a flame out of one of your engines, talk to me girl. I have to know what your situation is before I can be of any help to you, honey. Over."

"Nightlife, have emergency on hand please." Her voice was near hysterical now as she got hit with another wave of gas and she cried out. "I sick, I get sick all over myself and me plane. Have to get back base before crash. I no know what wrong with me, hope I no attack with chemical or biological weapon from Chinese fighters. Over."

Now Nightlife was extremely concerned over Twin Peaks condition as she asked her fellow pilot with concern. "Twin Peaks. Is your oxygen level in your aircraft okay honey? Nothing's wrong with your mask or system, is there sister. Over."

"I check already, oxygen and oxygen system fine as far as can tell me self. I at forty percent left. Valve work fine in mask also. It no suffer oxygen problem. Over."

"Okay Twin Peaks. I'm going to order Manhunter and Flasher to escort you back to base, honey. I want someone with you in case your problem gets any worse, sister. Out."

"Nightlife, you in Command of Wing of plane now. Take Mastercard, Voyeur, Medusa and Spanish Fly, and protect mud walker on ground please. Cool Blue and Mermaid commit so they out of you flight wing for moment. I go back to the base now please. Over." She said as she belched again in the radio, she had to remove her oxygen mask again as she threw up all over her aircraft a second time, and she was becoming weak and extremely worried she might really be sick, or if this was a reaction to all the flying she was doing lately.

She banked her aircraft hard to the portside, and then she headed back for her home base on the massive floating Platform at three quarters speed. Her two escort aircraft copying her every move following her on her tail. Manhunter and Flasher talked to Twin Peaks all the way, to make sure she was okay, and not drifting off on them while heading for home base. Neither pilot could imagine what could possibly be wrong with her.

ON BOARD THE VINEGAR JOE PLATFORM

After General Edward Campanelli spoke to Colonel Joseph Salsiccia stationed on Taiwan. He placed a call to General William Weidenbacher manning his position in the Pentagon back in the States. General Campanelli explained to his Commanding Officer the Chinese Commander was looking for a special meeting with him one on one. General Campanelli requested permission to speak with the Chinese General Jiyun himself.

President Albert Cole, also listening in on the conversation, but he was out of camera sight, interrupted their conversation in a testy voice. "General Campanelli Sir, it's I who'll give you permission to meet with this Chinese

General, not General Weidenbacher, sir. I think it's time you people remember who the hell you're working for around here, god dammit."

General Campanelli waited until he was sure the President was done with his griping and then he replied simply, "sorry sir."

"Damn right you're sorry General Campanelli." The President barked angrily at him, and then he added at his military officer in an angry tone. "General Campanelli Sir, I'm giving you permission to meet with this Chinese General. One thing I want cleared up, is this General speaking for the entire Theater of War, and all Chinese troops stationed on Taiwan, sir?"

General Edward Campanelli let out his breath in a rush as he replied to the American President's angry words just aimed at him, "Mr. President Sir, I won't know that for certain until I get a chance to speak with him personally, sir. I certainly hope to hell and back he's speaking for the entire Chinese government and all the damn troops under his Command, Mr. President."

President Cole bitched, "who are you going to take with you on this meeting, General?"

"I was thinking of taking General White, and Colonel Locker with me, sir. I'm leaving General Palmieri behind to run the show from here. What's left of it that is Mr. President Sir."

"I approve of your decision sir, when are you planning to leave for this damn meeting with the Chinese General on Taiwan, General Campanelli Sir?" The still angry sounding American Leader snapped at his military officer over the radio linkup.

"I'd like to get going as soon as I'm finished speaking with you and General Weidenbacher if you don't mind, Mr. President Sir?"

"Very good then you're done with me General, and soon as you're done with General Weidenbacher, I'm certain you'll be on your way for this meeting, sir." President Cole snapped.

"Yes Sir Mr. President Sir and by your leave, sir." General Campanelli replied and the President then signed off with him so the General turned his attention to his Commanding Officer and asked. "General Weidenbacher Sir, are we done sir? Or do you have any further orders concerning this Chinese General and what you might want me to cover with him, sir?"

"You know what you're doing with this mess General, Ed. Good luck with him. You'll report back to me the moment you're done speaking with this character, right General Campanelli?"

"Absolutely General Weidenbacher Sir."

"Then get on with it General Campanelli Sir. And I want you to get back to me the very moment this Chinese General is marched away from your presence, sir." With that said, General Weidenbacher broke off his communication with his Second in Command, so General Campanelli can get a move on his orders to met with the Chinese Commander.

General Campanelli actually ran from the CIC room yelling at his people. "John, Locker. You two are with me so let's get going, dammit. General Palmieri, you watch the store for us till we get back to you, sir." The three officers then quickly ran out of the CIC Chamber for top side and the flight deck of the Platform.

Sergeant Willis was already topside, and had a CV-22 heated up and ready to go for the General and the rest of his group.

The General ran up the tail ramp of the spooling aircraft and took his seat. He looked to his left and saw Locker was strapped in her chair and he remarked, "shit girl, you're quick."

Locker smiled at her Commander as she replied, "you should know that General Campanelli."

The CV-22 moved out of her standby box on the flight deck for takeoff, but the aircraft was held up for a few moments as a YF-27 came in for an emergency landing on the Platform. General Campanelli watched the plane land, it was acting like it might have been damaged, though he could not see. Two more YF 27s overflew the massive flight deck of the Platform and then split in two different directions once they passed the flight deck. An ambulance was already chasing after the still rolling sleek fighter plane as it slowed down to a stop.

While the three military officers were waiting for their aircraft to be allowed to launch, the pilot piped in some music, the song "The Living Years'. It made General Campanelli remember his father. The CV-22 was finally cleared for takeoff as the fighter plane rolled pass the CV 22. In seconds, the Osprey was up and General Campanelli did not mind the way this plane flew.

The YF-27 fighter aircraft rolled to a complete stop, and a swam of flight deck crew members descended on the plane that requested, and received an emergency landing order. A rusty old flight deck crew Chief, pushed the rolling ladder up to the side of the plane. It fell short of the cockpit by just inches, with a small platform on the top end of the ladder for the Chief to stand on. The old man was up the ladder in a flash even before the cockpit was popped opened by the ill pilot, and the Chief actually pulled the canopy the rest of the way open by hand. Then he stuck his hand inside the pilot's compartment, and pulled the quick release for Aleksandra's harness that held her pinned in her seat.

The concerned Chief then quickly replaced the four safety pins in the ejection seat, disarming it in order to remove any accidental firing of the chair, and then he checked on his female pilot. She was a real mess, she was covered from head to toe with vomit, and she drawn and white as a ghost. Her hair was soaked with sweat, and it hung limply in strands as she removed her helmet and handed it over to the concerned Chief.

"Man, you look like hell, are you alright Major? I have an ambulance standing by if you have need of it, Ma'am." The Chief offered the female pilot with much concern lacing his tone, as he stared at her and waited for her to reply to his question.

"I no need god dom ambulance, Chief. I alright now I think, thank you sir. I got sick when fly plane, it must be something I ate, Chief. I sorry I mess up you plane like this, sir." She said as she tried to stand up inside the cockpit. She suddenly gagged and threw up all over the Chief standing on the end of the ladder staring at her.

The Chief had to catch and steady her in the cockpit as she almost passed out and tumbled into him. He made her sit down in the mess of the cockpit as he growled at the other deck crew members who gathered near the plane. "Get that damn man lift contraption in here on the fucking double quick, I got me one helluva sick pilot on my hands, Sergeant."

The flight deck man lift was quickly wheeled in place, and Aleksandra was lifted out of the plane, and then laid down on the machine. She was carefully lowered to the deck, and then placed on top of a stretcher.

A medic from the ambulance crew started an IV of Ringers in Aleksandra's arm to replenish her exhausted body fluids. Aleksandra was then placed in the ambulance, and was driven to the main flight deck elevator where it quickly disappeared below deck. She laid on a bed in sickbay, her uniform was cut from her body, and a sheet was covering her exhausted body. She was weak and worried about her condition.

A nurse drew blood from her, and took it to the lab for a quick workup, to make sure the enemy had not resorted to the use of chemical weapon attacks on the battlefield of Taiwan. That was the assumption the medical team was drawing on. The foreign pilot was hit by chemical weapons employed on the battlefield by the enemy, when they realized they were losing the war.

A doctor came in the room and checked her out carefully. After a lot of bitching, she was allowed to shower, with the help of a nurse. The doctor checked her eyes, neck and blood pressure. He checked out her fingers for their color, and behind her ears, she checked out perfectly. The doctor smiled as he offered. "Young lady, I can't find a thing wrong with you. What the hell did you eat this morning Major? That might be the reason for your sickness, I assure you it's not form any chemical weapons released on the battlefield."

Just as she began to answer the doctor's question. The nurse who drew the blood, came back in the room with the results of the test. She handed the doctor the report, and he mumbled to himself before looking at the report, "ahhh... now we'll find out what's bugging ya, Major."

A smile quickly spread across the elderly doctor's lips as he looked from the report then up at the Major sitting on the edge of the bed, with only a sheet wrapped tightly around her body and he announced, "hummmm..., I take it you didn't know you were pregnant, or you wouldn't have been flying young lady. Am I right Major?"

She blinked her eyes rapidly as she stared at the doctor, tears built in her eyes as she asked the doctor in a stunned tone. "Are sure I pregnant Doctor? I no believe I am pregnant."

"I'm positive you're pregnant young lady, congratulations might I add Ma'am. I'll have the nurse help you, I have wounded to attend to Major." The doc left the room humming.

The nurse got the Major a change of clothes and handed her a deck crew jump suit, and the happy sounding nurse offered to the stunned female pilot. "This will have to do for the time being Major, until you can get back to your room and change into your proper uniform, Ma'am. I'm sorry, but your old uniform was kind of trashed Ma'am, and we had to discard it."

"I know that, thank you." She said as she reached for the glass of orange juice she was just given while they were examining her, she was terribly thirsty and she was still very weak.

The nurse then informed her in a polite tone of voice. "You do understand it's not wise to be flying a fighter aircraft when you're pregnant, Major. With all that pushing and pulling from the G forces you suffer in the plane, you're lucky you didn't miscarriage, or hurt your baby or yourself, Ma'am." The nurse then asked her if this was her first baby, and when the Major answered yes. The nurse began to give her advice as to being pregnant for the first time in her life, and what to do and not do while she was carrying her new baby.

The Major cut the excited nurse off and she asked if she could send for General Campanelli for her. she was surprised and a little disappointed the General wasn't in sickbay with her. She was certain he would have heard about her emergency landing on the Platform even before she landed. And if not, the mere fact she threw up while in flight, would have been all over the ship by now. She was a little hurt he did not come down to check on her condition.

Before even the excited nurse could leave the room, General Palmieri strolled in the room smiling at her as he asked the pretty female pilot. "Major Klevekaita Ma'am, how the hell are you feeling young lady? I heard about your emergency landing on the Platform. What the hell happened up there Ma'am? Was your aircraft damaged and that force you to declare an emergency landing on the deck, Ma'am? I don't mind tell you, when the call for your emergency landing request came in at the CIC Chamber, you shook up all the personnel on the Platform, Ma'am. Seems like you have an awful lot of friends around here all of a sudden, Major."

She had the fear of God locked in her eyes, as she stared at the General talking to her the way he was doing. When she first saw him come in her room, she thought something bad had happened to General Campanelli.

General Palmieri, noticed the concerned look locked in her eyes, and easily read her mind and laughed to relieve her fears, "oh no Major Klevekaita Ma'am, nothing happened to that old war dog of yours, he couldn't come down himself because he's no longer on board the Platform, Ma'am. Right now he's on his way to Taiwan, Ma'am. Major Klevekaita, the fighting in the Asian region is over with. At this moment a Chinese General Deng Jiyun has called a cease fire for all his troops currently stationed on the Island of Taiwan, Ma'am. We did our jobs well this time around, Major."

Aleksandra was crying, yet she was laughing at the same time as she thought. The fighting's over on Taiwan, her soldier loves me and I am pregnant, and I can become an American citizen and have his last name. Life truly is beautiful.

The worried General brought her back to reality by offering with concern to her. "Major Klevekaita Ma'am, what the hell happened up there anyhow? Were you wounded, Ma'am? Was your aircraft hit by enemy fire? Did you flame out Ma'am?"

She stopped laughing and announced as proudly as she could speak, "General Palmieri, I pregnant, is no beautiful thing sir?"

The General took a step back as he removed his cap and stuck it under his arm, and ran his hand over his hair and moaned at her, "oh brother, I can't believe it, congratulations Major. Does General Campanelli know about this news, Ma'am?"

"No, and I no want anyone else tell him before I do, General Palmieri Sir. Please General. No allow anyone on Platform inform General I be pregnant and I carry his child in me body, sir." She said as she flashed one of her best smiles at the concerned looking military officer.

"Ha, you can take this to the bank young lady, I can certainly promise you one thing. You have my absolute word on that request Major Klevekaita Ma'am. I surely don't want to be the one to break the news to that old fart that he's starting a new family all over again, Ma'am. Damn, I can't wait to see his old puss when you drop this bombshell down on his ass, honey." General Palmieri laughed as he suddenly turned and then he walked quickly out of the medical room. She heard him saying as he left the room.

"Holy shit, fucking General Campanelli raising a damn baby again, holy shit and the Heavens too."

She smiled as the nurse came back in her room and she helped her get dressed in the borrowed jump suit.

General Edward Campanelli's aircraft slowly circled the civilian airfield on Taiwan once, before finally receiving permission to land and then coming in for a hover. The pilot pointed out the two THAAD Theater High Altitude Air Defense missile systems that replaced the old and outdated Patriot Missile system to the concerned looking General protecting the airbase now.

General Campanelli was not interested in the defensive missile system, as he and his entourage were quickly lead over to an undamaged building inside the Scientific compound area. As the General entered it, he immediately noticed Colonel Joseph Salsiccia sitting at a table with a second military officer. Colonel Salsiccia immediately stood, followed by the Chinese Officer. He and Colonel Salsiccia shook hands first, as General Campanelli congratulated him for the job he accomplished for the battle for Taiwan. Then both military officers turned to the Chinese General Deng Jiyun, and Colonel Salsiccia introduced the General to the once enemy officer. General Jiyun bowed slightly as he offered his hand to the American General.

General Campanelli took the offered hand as he quickly replied politely to the Chinese Commanding Officer. "General Jiyun Sir, I'm damn pleased you put an end to the fighting for the Island, sir. Before any more of our brave children from both sides died needlessly for our politician's wants. I thank you on behalf of both America and China's youth, sir. May the next generation of politicians and soldiers be smarter than the both of us, and avoid any future fricking wars, General Jiyun Sir."

General Jiyun smiled pleasantly as he replied equally as polite to the American General. "I knew you were a gentleman when I first saw you, General Campanelli Sir. Especially when you had your soldiers and aircraft refrained from slaughtering of my troops trapped on the Sunyat Sun Freeway, sir. Yes, by all means sir, let's hope our youth coming of age are much smarter than our generation is, General Campanelli Sir."

"General Jiyun Sir, one thing I have to ask you sir. Does this truce you're offering include your Command Leaders in China, sir? I hope there'll be no further attacks on Taiwan from the mainland of China, on my warships currently stationed in the Formosa Straits, General Jiyun Sir." General Campanelli asked as he stared back at the Chinese Commanding Officer.

General Jiyun lowered his head and shook it slightly as he mumbled back to the American soldier. "General Campanelli Sir, I can only speak for my ground forces stationed on Taiwan soil at this time, sir. I shall be most pleased to speak with my Command Leaders, and inform them all is lost, and offer to seek negotiations for a quick solution to the present situation, sir. I have to ask you sir. Where did all the fighters and bomber planes come from, sir? We realized you had eight of your Aircraft Carriers stationed in and around the Asian region, sir. We were able to force at least four of them out of the area for fear of being sunk. I must say sir, I was a little taken by surprise by the strength of your air power, General. It kept me off balance and unable to keep my forces ahead of your attacking aircraft, sir. We were unaware you had so many attack aircraft at your disposal during this war against Taiwan, sir."

General Edward Campanelli slowly rubbed his lips with his index finger before answering the concerned Chinese Commander. "General Jiyun Sir, I can understand your dilemma, sir. You see sir, we kept a secret from your Intel people, General. We have a sort of Super Carrier out there, and that's where the extra aircraft came from, that you shall soon see once we have finished speaking together. Even our transport aircraft were taking off from this special Carrier system, sir." The General opened his hands and he hunched his shoulders up as he smiled.

General Jiyun sat down in his chain and he grumbled at the American General, "ahhh, we have heard what we felt were foolish rumors of this supposed Super Carrier of yours, General Campanelli Sir. I see those rumors were true sir. As you can clearly see, our Intelligence was quickly catching up to you, General Campanelli. It was only a matter of time before we located this super ship, and then cause you the serious problems this great ship has caused my troops and military plans, sir." A strained silence arose between the two former combatant commanders as they both continued to size each other up. It was General Jiyun who chose to break the silence by asking, "are my troops being treated well, General Campanelli Sir?"

"Yes, by all means General Jiyun Sir. I assure you sir, your troops are being well cared for and fed sir. Are you being treated well sir?" General Campanelli asked him.

"I am being treated very well, thank you General Campanelli for your concern for my soldiers and myself, sir."

"Good." General Campanelli suddenly turned his attention back to Colonel Salsiccia, and ordered him, "Colonel Salsiccia Sir, I'd like to visit some of my troops out in the field before I leave with General Jiyun for the Platform, sir." General Campanelli then turned back to the Chinese

General Jiyun and added. "General, you're going to see this so call Super Aircraft Carrier first hand in a very short period of time sir. I'm going to allow you to speak with your people from the ship, so you can see it for yourself, and to place a stop to all fighting in the Asian region at the same time as well, sir."

"I'd truly like to see this great ship of yours if you do not mind, General Campanelli Sir. I'd like to see the ship that has turned the tide of this war for Taiwan in the American forces favor, General Campanelli Sir."

"Good, you'll see it General Jiyun." Campanelli bowed slightly towards the Chinese Officer.

Colonel Salsiccia interrupted the two Generals as he replied to his Commander's last request. "Very well General Campanelli Sir, but you must remember sir, there are still some bad guys out there who didn't hear General Jiyun's message, and they are still shooting at my troops, sir."

General Campanelli grunted at the concerned sounding Colonel Salsiccia. "Understood Colonel, but I still wanna go out in the field and visit some of these soldiers, sir." General Campanelli turned back to General Jiyun and said to him in a calm tone of voice, "I'll have you sent out to the ship while I stay behind for a few hours and visit with some of my troops in the field, and hand out some medals, sir." The General rose, Jiyun also stood and they shook hands again as two MPs instantly moved to each side of the Chinese General to securely lead him out of the room, respectfully.

General Campanelli turned to Colonel Salsiccia for a second time and he grumbled at him, "Colonel Salsiccia, I'd like an open Hummvee for my use, sir."

Colonel Salsiccia almost jumped off the ground as he bitched at his Commander, "you want to drive around a damn war zone in a open Humvee, sir? You have got to be shitting me General Campanelli. I'd rather pour your ass into one of the damn A-1 Abrams tanks for your visit to our troops out in the field, sir."

"An open Humvee is what I'll use to visit my troops in the field, Colonel Salsiccia Sir! I know what the fuck I'm doing around here sir."

"Christ Almighty General, talking to you is like talking to a foreigner, sir. Opened Humvee General Campanelli Sir?" Colonel Salsiccia asked his Commanding Officer for a second time to make certain he understood what he was requesting.

"Right, an opened Humvee I said, Colonel Salsiccia Sir." General Campanelli repeated and then laughed as he quickly headed out of the makeshift headquarters.

A heavy humvee vehicle pulled in front of him. It was open with a young Army Sergeant at the wheel. He hopped out and instantly saluted the number of officers waiting to mount the jeep. Colonel Salsiccia stayed behind and handle the transport of General Jiyun out to the Platform. General Campanelli, General White and Colonel Locker climbed in to the waiting humvee with the Sergeant asking where they were going.

"I want to go out to the soldiers at the east end of the Science complex, Sergeant." General Campanelli ordered the young Sergeant driver

The Sergeant forgot who he was speaking to when he griped, "you wanna what? Christ sake. That fucking zone's still hot as the hinges on the gates of hell, sir. They're still fighting over there sir. If you wanna go in that area sir, let me get a damn Bradley, at least she has some armor under her belt to better protect us, sir. You're going to get your ass fragged (Shot) in that area if you go poking around over there, sir. I can have a Bradley here in..."

General Campanelli immediately cut the Sergeant's bitch off as he snapped angrily at him. "I been doing this shit before you stopped drawing hairs on your fucking chest with a damn pencil, Sergeant. Now get your ass in gear, or I'll have you replaced immediately, mister." He glared at the kid, this was enough and the Sergeant started the motor, and then he slammed the machine in gear. Then he popped the clutch, making the humvee lunge forward. The angry Sergeant gave the officers one helluva ride, he made certain he hit every bump, and he took every back road to get out to the requested position.

General Campanelli smiled as the jeep bounced down the road. As they got closer to where he wanted to see, they started to pass a number of well dug in young and exhausted looking American soldiers. General Campanelli was amused as the Marines pointed in amazement at the jeep, and its occupants.

One Marine actually cried out in a booming voice. "Will ya look at this shit man. That fucking Vee has more brass in it, than a brass fucking horn, people." The Marines broke out in laughter as they saluted the officers.

The humvee stopped in front of the makeshift Command Post as the officers poured out, and saluted the General as he got out of the machine and snapped at them. "Will you assholes stop saluting my damn ass, dammit! You're gonna draw fire at me you asses. Didn't you birds pay any attention in class, dammit?"

A Colonel took the lead and remarked to the Commander as he walked the officers to the group of soldiers he wanted to visit. "General Campanelli Sir, I'm Colonel Keating, this is Captains Kenell and Garmise, and behind them are Lieutenants Ports and Crandell, Sir. May I ask the General, what the hell are you doing all the way out here sir? We're still taking heavy enemy fire out here every now and then, General."

General Campanelli completely ignored the warning from the Colonel as he introduced his officers to the other officers, and then he turned back to Colonel Keating and said, "I have a number of medals to give out to the troops, sir. I read a report on one of your Sergeants, a Sergeant Robert Walker, Road Kill I believe the other soldiers call him, sir. He's earned himself a Silver Star, can you get his ass over here for me, sir?"

Colonel Keating turned to Lieutenant Crandell and ordered him in no uncertain terms. "Go and get that lousy bastard, and drag his stinking butt over here double quick, Lieutenant."

The butter bar Lieutenant ran off on his mission, glad to be away from the General's crew.

AT THE CHAIRMAN'S SPECIAL
MEETING ROOM IN BEIJING CHINA

Chairman Mao Cheng-yu sat slumped over in his chair looking like he aged fifty years in so short a time, his cigar missing as he sat warily in his chair, and listened to the devastating reports coming in from the Island of Formosa. Realizing his Armies were smashed and surrendering to the American forces. He sought other means in which to win this war, or to stop it with the best possible outcome for China, and its people. He was fuming because his Ministers, his Army, Navy and Airforce has let him down, and they lost this war to the Americans in so short a time.

The Minister of Ordnance, Shi Zhang reported to the Chairman he was unable to get any more shells or tanks out to the Island of Formosa. He further informed the Chairman any Chinese ship headed for the Island, was immediately being set upon by so many of the enemy fighter planes, it was insane to try any more shipments.

Silence fell on the meeting room when the Minister finished with his latest report for the exhausted Chairman. The Chairman turned to the Minister of nuclear industry without uttering a word to Zhang. The Minister spoke as soon as the Chairman looked at him. "Mr. Chairman, we can hit the Americans with a nuclear strike, and destroy most of their forces in the Asian region, before they have a chance to reply with any of their nuclear weapons. But I know they have many nuclear weapons stored on board their warships and submarines. I fear these weapons would completely devastate our coastline, thus plunging most of China into utter chaos and complete economic despair. As the Chairman knows, most of China's income comes from the coastal areas of our land, and to lose this entire section of China, would most likely destroy much of China's economy for the years to come. Sir, the Americ..."

The old man suddenly snarled with surprising strength in his voice at the speaking Minister, "then what do you think we should do Minister Chi-mao?"

The outburst shocked the other Ministers gathered at the meeting and they looked to the Minister of Nuclear Industry. He swallowed before speaking further, knowing his next words might well cost him his head. He let out his breath in a sigh and replied. "Mr. Chairman, I think it'd be in the best interest of China to sue for peace. As we speak, even more American soldiers and military equipment are landing on the foul Island of Formosa, and incoming intelligence informs us the Americans are mopping up our Army, and they're also massing many troops on the west coast of Formosa for a possible invasion of our country."

Many Ministers were shocked by this new information as one stood and asked. "Mr. Chi-mao, do you believe the Americans would be so foolish as to dare invade the mainland of China?"

"Yes, they'll attack us here soon enough I believe by reading the reports coming back to us from our Commanders on Formosa, sir." The words echoed in the room like a gunshot.

The room was filled with much rapid discussion and hectically voices nearly shouting to be heard over the others speaking. The old man standing, suddenly raised his boney hands over his head as he hissed at his Minister, "let me understand what is being offered to me correctly, you are telling me we have two courses of action left opened to our military forces on the Island of Formosa. We can either attack the Americans now taking over the entire Island of Formosa with nuclear weapons, and risking a nuclear response from the American forces in the region. Or we can beg for peace, and allow the lowly Americans tell us what they're going to do with us. I find both solutions highly unacceptable."

"Mr. Chairman, there is one other course of action still open to us if we chose to adopt this course of military action. We could just pound the Island with missiles, we have a number of them that could easily reach the entire Island."

"And what type of warheads do you suggest we use on this attack of the Island. Chemicals? conventional? We'd need hundreds, maybe even thousands of missiles to make a difference in the outcome of this war. No sir, I think your first offering was the correct course of action for us to employ against the hated American forces. We either attack them with nuclear weapons, or we sue for peace, but on our terms mind you Minister. I shall dictate the terms in which

I'll accept for any cease fire, and place an end to all hostilities in the Asian region. Once I'm finished with my peace terms, you shall relay them to our Foreign Minister in Washington, and he'll offer them to the American government. You'll warn the great fool I'll not accept any other terms for peace but mine offered to him." The Chairman retook his seat and then he spoke his terms to be offered to the American Leader.

GENERAL CAMPANELLI VISITING
HIS TROOPS ON TAIWAN

The Second Lieutenant pulled Road Kill, Marine Gunny Sergeant Robert Walker out of the local watering hole. The other members from the LRRP, (Long Range Recon Patrol) had setup when the area was finally secured. The second louie walked up to Road Kill and informed him he had to come along with him to headquarters immediately.

"Hey man, I'm gonna talk to my fucking joint first, sir. Once I had me a good piss then I'll see if I'll go wit your stinking ass, buster." Sergeant Walker growled at the military officer, he was not very impressed by the man in the least.

The Lieutenant made a terrible mistake, he suddenly and foolishly grabbed Road Kill by the arm and barked at him angrily, as he tried to turn the Sergeant around by his arm, "you have to come with me right now, you motherfucker you."

Road Kill smiled at the Lieutenant as the watering hole quieted down to a morgue, as at least ten of Road Kill's soldiers immediately locked and loaded their weapons, and then they aimed them directly at the suddenly scared Lieutenant, who just kind of stared back at the other angry looking soldiers and not knowing what to do next.

Sergeant Walker looked for the Mutt, Sergeant Frank Hall, he had his weapon leveled right at the Lieutenant's chest. Road Kill nodded no and Mutt lowered the M-18. He seemed kind of disappointed he was not going to get to use it on the stupid officer.

"A big mistake muthafucker, in case you don't understand it yet Mac, I just saved your fucking ass, man. Don't ever touch me again Butter Bar. Stateside you're the damn man, but out here you're just shit on a shingle like the rest of us damn shitters are sir." Road Kill warned the Lieutenant as he pulled his arm free from the shaking Lieutenant's grasp, and then he called out. "Hey Mutt, you come with me and this Numba Ten Prick here. This must be awful important for this little sucka to risk his stinking life like this. I'll piss later on afta I find out what brass land wants from my damn ass, man."

Sergeant Robert Walker found himself standing with a number of other troops, while waiting for this hot shot visiting General to appear before him. The Mutt, Walker's lifelong friend, was crouched down next to him, and Walker said with a smirk, "hey buddy, you're my favorite fucking hard-on you know, and when this little frackis is over with and we get back to the real world. You stick close wit me man. I'm sorta having a wet one about this pretty sperm gargler I know back in the States. I wanna intro you to a hot looking cherry with a taut tit for a man in fucking uniform, even one that's half white like you man. You can take her for a good slide on that old skin bus of yours, all the way down to tuna town man."

The Mutt feigned great pride at being designated as Walker's favorite hard-on as he replied with a smirk on his lips "Fuck you man. Damn, I put on clean underwear for this shit? Jesus, will ya look at this chicken shit sonofabitch coming at us now man. He's got more fucking salad dressing on his stinking chest, than I leave on the floor after I upchuck from an all nighter at the stinking bar, Homes. Who the hell is the little sonofabitch anyway, and what the hell is he doing up here where he just might get a cap shot in his ass?"

"Yeah, a fucking big Three Oh Lifer in for the big payout from the damn Gov. I see." Road Kill referred to all Brass as Lifers.

"You want I should pop a stinking cap in his purdy little ass fur him, man? We can watch him dance around a bit if I place one in his can, man." The Mutt offered Walker as he slid his weapon around in his hands until it ended up in a much better firing position, and then Mutt stared at the General walking proudly towards them.

"Mutt sit down and shut the fuck up will ya man! We hafta see what the hell this stinking prick wants with me first, man. If he's here to fuck me over then put a cap in his ass and we'll burry him here and say we never seen the lousy little dude." Walker warned his friend as he turned to better see the military officer coming at him.

The General came into the clearing and he walked over to the men. The Mutt made no attempt to stand at attention as the General approached them. He offered a half assed salute to the General that Campanelli immediately waved off, and he nodded back at the dark skinned man with straight hair and eyes trying to burn a hole in his chest.

Road Kill gave the General the thumbs up signal as he shot a hawker out of the side of his nose while employing what was called as the farmer's hankie. That's when you place a finger on the side of your nose and close off one nostril and blow out the other, clearing your nose.

General Campanelli walked up to Sergeant Walker and he immediately realized how he got his tag name. His face was the same color as his Jungle Greens, and his face was covered with what the soldiers commonly referred to as their war paint. The Sergeant's uniform was filthy, torn everywhere, and dirt encrusted and he stunk like a four day old Road Kill. His body armor hung off his shoulder, what was left of it that was.

The General shook the painted hand of this derelict looking soldier, and he quickly realized his breath smelled as bad as his body did. Three bandoleers of machine gun ammunition crisscrossed his chest, and they looked as if they were actually growing from his body. Many rounds missing from the straps of rounds.

Sergeant Walker had shit hanging everywhere on and from his body. His steel pot hung off his ass by the chin strap, secured to his web belt by a shoelace. He had three hand grenades tied to his ruck pack also with shoelaces, extra clips to his pistol hung out of his half torn right breast pocket. A crumbled up MRE (Meals Ready to Eat) pack was stuffed in his back pants pocket, and a second canteen hung loosely from his right side, by another knotted shoelace. His K-bar sheath was empty and the General could only picture it being left in the chest of an enemy soldier on the field of battle. He noticed the dried blood splattered all over this soldier's uniform, mixed in with his body paint, sweat and dirt, and knew this soldier standing before him was in the shit during the fighting for the Island.

The General pinned the Silver Star on Sergeant Walker's chest, it was the only clean thing on his person. Then the General shook his hand again, and thanked Walker for protecting the younger troops in his charge. He saluted the Sergeant, and then the well respected General handed out fifteen other medals before he shared an MRE lunch with the ground forces, and he listened to the kids brag about the action they were part of in the Taiwan Theater of War. It was quite a picture for Stars and Stripes, two Generals and a female Colonel sitting in the mud, choking down the same field rats with the mud covered privates and corporals and upper strips.

Someone snapped a picture destined to show up on the front cover of all major newspapers of the free world. The General's uniform was soon covered with mud and grime, as he moved along with the mud stompers. Security guards were making real pests of themselves, trying to protect the Generals lives while nearly standing right on the still active frontline.

Every once in a while a shot would ring out, bringing an instant response from many tanks parked and surrounding the Generals, and the troops gathered to meet them. General Campanelli made certain he shook as many of the ground soldiers hands as he could get to. Then he climbed back in a few of the tanks and armored vehicles, looked around and shared some water from the soldier's canteens. It was good for both the soldiers and officers alike for this visit and rubbing shoulders with the ground pounders.

General John White finally got General Campanelli's attention and pointed at his watch to inform him of the time. The General realized he had been with the ground troops for over five hours now, and he nodded back to John. The officers quickly ended their visit with a flurry of hand shakes, along with some slaps on the back and off color jokes. Then the officers mounted their jeep for the twenty minute ride back to the field headquarters.

CHAPTER 40
AMERICAN FIELD HEADQUARTERS

Colonel Joseph Salsiccia escorted the Chinese General onto the spooling CV-22, and then he watched the once enemy General as he took in all aspects of the remarkable plane. It must have scared the shit out of him to mount such a radically changed aircraft. Colonel Salsiccia stayed with the Chinese General until the once enemy General was finally strapped in and comfortable. The American Colonel saluted General Jiyun one last time before he left the plane.

General Jiyun put his head down as he thought of his plight. He now knew he had made a terrible blunder, by not securing the east coast of the Island first. Because if he had, these American soldiers would not have been able to get as many of their troops and military equipment on the Island, and he would have won this war, or at least fought the American forces to a standstill. He shook his head as the plane's engines started, and then the aircraft slowly moved out. He decided right there to request political asylum in the United States when he got to this Super Carrier. He decided he would never again step foot on the mainland of China, because if he did, he knew it would cost him his life.

General Edward Campanelli, Colonel Mary Locker and General John White entered the makeshift Command Post on the Island of Taiwan. Colonel Salsiccia was seated at his desk, writing out requests for needed supplies and extra troops. The Colonel stood as the other officers came in the building they commandeered as their headquarters on the complex. A Sergeant was able to secure a bottle of American Rye, and it was resting on his desk. The Colonel poured four glasses, and then he offered them a drink before the officers left to return to the Platform.

General Campanelli refused the offered drink and Colonel Salsiccia stared at him, because he saw the General drunk on a few occasions during the Middle East war. General Campanelli saw the look and he smiled as he offered to the other officer, "put your eyes back in your head Colonel. I stopped drinking, and smoking too might I add, quite a while ago Colonel Salsiccia Sir. There's nothing wrong with me, I promise you sir. I'm still the same man you knew back when I was drinking my life away."

"Balls, then I guess I better sell off my damn stock in Seagrams, sir. Surely they'll go out of business without you drinking any longer General Campanelli Sir." Colonel Salsiccia offered with a smirk.

General Edward Campanelli asked for a soda after the laughter finally ended.

"I have some Cokes hanging around here some place I'm certain General." Colonel Salsiccia said as he shook his head.

"Coke, never mind that crap, I think I'll pass on it then. I'm kinda stuck on Pepsi and never got to liking Coke." General Campanelli grumbled and let out a breath.

Colonel Salsiccia put his arms in the air as if to ask a question, but John cut him off by saying. "All the pain in the ass drinks any longer is this stinking Pepsi crap. I suggest you buy some stock in that company, Colonel."

General Campanelli spoke up as he offered, "Colonel Salsiccia, you and your men did well, real well in fact with this one sir. When I get back to base, I'm gonna put you in for a full bird Colonel, sir. You'll get your damn Eagles, you truly earned them this time around, Colonel Salsiccia. I gotta go, is the jeep waiting outside for me sir?"

"General Campanelli Sir, how about you make me feel a little better and take one of the damn closed armored Humvees please. The covered Humvees are heavily armored and it might save your life if you come under attack on your way to the airport, sir. You driving around here in that open running is just begging to be fired upon, sir."

General Campanelli thought for a second and then replied, "you know something Colonel, I believe you're right, no sense in tempting fate around here sir."

The officers left the Command Post for the humvee to take them out to the CV-22. Colonel Salsiccia informed General Campanelli that General Jiyun was on his way out to the Platform and might already be on it.

THE WHITE HOUSE, WASHINGTON D.C.

An aide suddenly burst into the Oval Office, actually startling the President and his other people in the room meeting, momentarily. The President yelled at the young man until he heard what the aide had to offer him.

"Mr. President Sir, the Chinese Foreign Minister, Lao Shan-chung's waiting outside for a private audience with you, sir. He seems rather upset and even nervous, Mr. President Sir." The aide offered him.

President Albert Cole sat down and he thought for a second, and then he looked to the aide and grumbled at him, "it's good thing you interrupted me at this point young man. I'll see the Chinese Minister immediately, but first I want you to wait until I hit the button, and then escort him in to the Oval Office. You're dismissed for the time being, mister." The President turned back to his people and announced to them.

"Gentlemen, General Weidenbacher, you, Director Griffin, Secretary Levenhagen and Director Raincloud will remain until we see what this guy has on his mind, you'll stay as well General Claiborne Sir. You too Secretary Hernandez. The rest of you can go, I'll be back to you when I find out what the hell on the Minister's mind, people."

The group ordered to remain with the President for this meeting with the Chinese Minister sat in silence, Manning, Clifton, Schramm, Tomasello and Admiral Standlund left the office as they were directed to. They almost smacked right into the Secretary of State, Maria Hernandez. The President hit the button, letting her know she was wanted in the Oval Office.

President Cole waited until his Secretary of State to be seated before he informed her why he had sent for her.

"I feel it has to be some sort of peace offering the Chinese Minister wants to work out with you, I'd imagine Albert. I'm certain by know the Chinese leadership must understand they lost this war, sir." Secretary of State Hernandez offered to the President.

"We better see what he has to offer then," the President hit the unseen button, and seconds later, the Chinese Foreign Minister was escorted into the room, and he was seated in front of him.

President Cole nodded to the still upset looking Chinese Minister, and then asked the Chinese politician, "and to what do we owe to this visit, Minister Sir.

"Mr. President Sir, I was sent here to meet with you to seek a peaceful settlement in Asia, sir. I have come here with an offer from my government, offering a solution to end the fighting in and around Asia, sir."

President Cole interrupted the Chinese Minister by offering to him with a snap in his voice, "the easiest solution to this terrible situation is for China to put down her weapons and surrender, Minister Loa Shan-chung Sir."

The Chinese Minister stared back at the President in stunned disbelief for a moment. He was suddenly at a last of words by the American President's last words.

"Minister Shan-chung Sir. Exactly what is it your government is offering in the way of peace returning to the Asian region, sir?" President Cole asked.

"Mr. President Sir, my government is offering an immediate cease fire, and an end to all hostilities currently taking place in Asia, sir. If the American forces advance no further than the line they now stand upon, sir."

General Weidenbacher cut in and he snapped at the Chinese Minister, "you mean, if we don't invade mainland China, right sir?"

The Minister nodded yes to the General's last remark that was directed at him.

General Weidenbacher was really ticked off by the Chinese Minister's offer. Because he had all his troops set in place and ready to invade mainland China, and now the Chinese wanted to stop the fighting because they received a bloody nose in Taiwan, and did not want to have any fighting on their mainland as he asked the Minister, "and why should we do this?"

The Minister took a deep breath in, and then let it out slowly. He knew of this angry and powerful American General well, but he was more afraid of the black General known as General Claiborne. The Minister addressed his answer to the American President as he announced. "I've been ordered by my Leaders to sue for peace, but they have also issued this warning to the United States and her Allies, sir. If any nation's troops dare to set foot on mainland China's soil, China will react to this invasion with nuclear weapons to repel all such troops, Mr. President Sir."

President Albert Cole was thunder struck as he reared and growled at the Minister, "hasn't China learned anything from the Middle East war, sir? Mr. Minister, look at what's taking place to this day over there, sir. People, civilians, are still dying even today, for a damn war that took place over a year ago, and they'll still be dying for many years to come as well, sir. Is China's Leaders insane to dare threaten to unleash her own nuclear weapons again upon the civilians of the earth, and the fighting soldiers of this world Mr. Minister?"

The worried Minister allowed the American Leader to continue with his words uninterrupted. Because he understood he had him right where his government wanted him. He was aware the war in Asia was over with, and no foreign troops were going to step foot on Chinese soil. He smirked at the President as he continued to speak.

President Cole saw the smirk and he stared back at the Minister, and barked at him, "is there something funny about your youth dying in the mud of a foreign land, Mr. Minister?"

"No, not in the least Mr. President Sir, I'm truly sorry but I was just thinking sir. We're talking, why not stop the dying, and continue to talk to save the lives of our youth, sir. All your troops have to do is stop their advancing, and we shall stop the fighting, sir. Then we can set forth to work out the particulars of a true and lasting cease fire later on for the entire Asian region, Mr. President Sir."

"Perhaps you're right at that sir, our first concern should be to stop the fighting, Minister. The rest of this mess will work itself out later. There's one problem I have, I can only speak for America, you'll have to work out other arrangements with England, Mr. Minister Sir. After all, the way the British civilians were treated in Hong Kong by your soldiers, and the thief of their money has to be worked out between the United Kingdom and China, sir."

"Mr. President Sir, my government has given me the powers here too, sir. I can offer the United Kingdom the same deal we first offered them before the fighting started, sir. My country is ready to offer the United Kingdom the Colony of Hong Kong, it'll be owned by them outright sir. My government is also planning to return all the monies we can find that was mistakenly removed from Hong Kong, sir. We come up with a solution any monies not recovered, will be regarded as monies England had to pay for the Colony, sir. The lawyers can work out the rest of the situation, if this is acceptable to the English.

"If not, China will have to continue her war with the United Kingdom, and any other country who would be so fool hearted as to follow the United Kingdom to her own destruction, sir. Mr. President Sir, I hope we can come to an agreement between ourselves, and to show the rest of the world China is more than willing to take the first step towards restoring peace in this situation, sir. As of twelve o'clock midnight, Washington time, all Chinese forces will stop fighting and hunker down where their forces are stationed at this time, sir. This includes North Korea, and we shall begin removing our troops stationed in Masan to seal the truce, sir."

President Cole glanced at General Weidenbacher, who in return moved his head ever so slowly no. The President moved his finger to his neck, and then he drew it across it slowly, in a warning for the General to back off some. The motion was so covered the Chinese Minister did not notice the move.

General Weidenbacher sat back in his chair as a resignation to the warning from the President.

The American President looked back to the Chinese Minister, and then stated. "Mr. Minister, I'll offer you this much, sir. If I see the fighting stop from your troops at midnight, I'll then order my troops to stop where they are, and advance no further and cease all hostilities, sir. This will give your government the time for them needed to get in touch with me, and we can then setup a summit meeting, and begin talking peace between our two nations, sir. I promise you this much sir, if your troops put down their arms, none of my troops will enter your country unrequested. Will this do for you Mr. Minister?"

The Chinese Minister bowed towards the American Leader as he replied calmly, "Mr. President Sir, on behalf of my government, I can say this will do fine sir. We have all Chinese troops stand down and give peace a chance to take hold once again, sir. I have to get back to my Embassy, and inform my Leaders know of the terms we have worked out between us here today, sir. I thank you Mr. President for bringing this war to an end, sir." The now smiling Minister put out his hand and shook hands with the American President.

No one in the room spoke until the Chinese Minister was lead out of the room, and then all hell broke out in the Oval Office. The President sat back in his chair and smiled, as the Generals screamed at him for making this deal with the Chinese Representative. The President continued to smile at the angry military officers, until they were all screamed out. All he knew was, he had stopped the killing, and he was happy as hell with that accomplishment. He waited until his staff was finally silenced, and then spoke to his people in a calm tone of voice. "Gentlemen, Lady, all I know is the war in the Asian region is over as far as I understand, and no nuclear weapons were fired off by either side this time. We did well in this war as it was people."

AMERICAN FIELD HEADQUARTERS IN TAIWAN

Colonel Joseph Salsiccia watched as the humvee took off carrying the other officers to the airport for transit out to the Platform. He heard the buzzing from the Flash message receiver, and ran inside to receive it. It was being transmitted from General William Weidenbacher, informing the Colonel all fighting and troop movement in the Asian region was coming to a halt at exactly midnight tonight, Washington time. "The war is over." Were the last words the General spoke to the grinning Colonel in the field.

The Colonel was upset the humvee with General Campanelli, did not have a radio installed in it. He called the airbase, and informed the Sergeant there to make known to the General once he arrived at the makeshift airport. That according to Command in the United States, the war was to officially end at exactly midnight tonight Washington time. The Sergeant let out with a yell.

As General Edward Campanelli, General John White and Colonel Mary Locker rode together in the cramped armored humvee, along with two security guards and driver. They had no idea the war was declared over. The fifteen minute ride to the airbase was over rubble covered and bomb cratered roads. The heavy humvee was forced to stop a few times, and then it slowly climb over some debris, or was forced to go around a number of bomb craters. But the entire road was secured and free of any enemy troops.

The machine had to stop again, this time to allow an American tank and a number of foot soldiers following the tank to go by them. Suddenly, the massive A1 Abrams tank exploded, as machine gunfire erupted from the side of the road that scattered the American troops following the war machine.

The humvee driver cried out in an excited voice, "holy shit sir, anti-tank missile, it's a fucking ambush sirs." Just as the side of the humvee was heavily strafed by the gunfire, bullets easily ripped through the reinforced skin and bounced around the inside of the large jeep.

John leaned back and kicked the back door opened with the power in his feet, and it ripped from the machine from the force in General White's legs. Once he was out of the machine, he reached inside and pulled Colonel Locker over the back seat and out of the machine. Then he pushed her towards the woods and safety. Then he ran back to help

General Campanelli get out of the smoking and disabled machine. He grabbed Ed by the back of the collar of his uniform, and pulled him over the rear seat. At the same time, a second and third tank came up and took positions, and they returned fire, helping the ground troops fighting this small pocket of enemy soldiers, killing the hidden Chinese attackers.

The big man pulled on the General until he actually dragged him out of the now burning jeep by the power in his arms. The two officers suddenly tumbled back and landed hard on the ground. It was then John noticed the three gaping holes ripped into General Campanelli's right side and chest.

"Jesus Christ, Ed, oh God no man." Was all he could say as he saw the gaping wounds and he actually tried to stop the bleeding with his bare hands. Nothing he tried would stop the heavy bleeding from his close friend and fellow officer.

General Campanelli eyes suddenly fluttered opened, and then he winced in terrible pain as he looked in the eyes of his lifelong friend. He painfully reached a blood covered hand up and rested it lightly on John's face. "Locker?" He mumbled at him.

"She's fucking fine man, she's right here at my side General Campanelli Sir. See her here man? She's good Eddy." John cried as he watched his friend die slowly right before his eyes, and he could not do a thing to help him.

General Campanelli smiled lamely at her, and then he looked up to the sky and spoke to the clouds overhead, "Mendoza, Mendoza baby, I'm coming home for you baby. Renee' I'll find you again I promise you baby. Renee', Rene..."

General Edward Campanelli died while John and Locker cried for him.   The driver got out of the jeep okay, and he was there as the General died. He asked Locker who Mendoza was.

"A wife he had never lived with." Colonel Locker then turned to John and she cried, "Oh God, what about Aleksandra, John? How is she going to take the General's death, sir?"

John returned her stare and then he replied, "she's a soldier, she'll get by alright Colonel."

General John White crossed General Campanelli's arms across his chest and then he closed his eyes for him. Tears streamed down his face unashamed, as he pulled the General's dog tags free, and placed them in his pocket. A keep sake as he rocked his dead friend back and forth in his powerful arms, as other soldiers gathered around the injured soldiers and dead officer.

One of the tankers came over with a body bag, and he laid it on the ground and unzipped it.

John glared harshly at the tanker as he hissed at him savagely, "no fucking way man. No fucking way are you placing him in that fucking thing, buster. Go and get me a fucking blanket before I shove that damn thing down your damn throat, asshole." John glared at the tanker.

When the soldier moved off to locate a blanket, John leaned forward and he kissed the cheek of General Edward Campanelli as he whispered softly to him, "good bye old buddy, I'll never forget you for as long as I live, my friend. You died as what you were, a true soldier." One tear landed on General Campanelli's face, and he wiped it with a finger, and then he stared at it for some unknown reason.

This was too much for Locker, and she collapsed on John's back as she cried for her two friends, hugging John's massive back to her as she cried, "Oh John, why did he have to die like this?"

"Because he was a soldier, and that was the way he lived his damn life, that's why Locker."

General Campanelli was dead, and now the politicians moved in to take up his fight for him.

::: FLASH::: FLASH::: FLASH:::

::: TO ALL AMERICAN AND ALLIED FORCES :::
::: YOU ARE INSTRUCTED TO CEASE ALL HOSTILITIES
IMMEDIATELY :::
::: ALL ALLIED FORCES ARE ORDERED TO STAY
WHERE THEY ARE AND
ADVANCE NO FURTHER ON ANY FRONT :::
::: ALL ALLIED FORCES ARE TO PROTECT
THEMSELVES FROM ATTACK
FROM ENEMY FORCES AT ALL TIMES, REPEL, BUT DO
NOT PURSUE :::
::: CHINA HAS DECLARED A CEASE-FIRE., IT'S TIME TO
HEAL OUR WOUNDS
AND MOURN FOR OUR DEAD :::
::: ROBERT COLE ::: PRESIDENT OF THE UNITED
STATES OF AMERICA :::

9 781970 301120